STELLA GALE: A RARE BREED

STELLA GALE: A RARE BREED

Book I
"Only the animals is innocent"

a novel by
Nancy Kyle Kent

Dungeness Communications, Inc.

To my amazing partner in life, Mary Aubrey,
and to Milne Ongley, my inspiration for how to live it.

Acknowledgments

First and foremost, I want to thank Tano-rose Tembo, Simba-rose Tembo, Mister Niki Tembo, Popo-rose Tembo, Bibi-rose Tembo, and Delilah-rose Tembo—the six Dogues de Bordeaux who each shared his or her entire life with me. And I want to acknowledge all dogs for their die-hard loyalty to humans despite our often-insurmountable shortcomings.

I want to thank my partner of thirty-three years, Mary Aubrey, for enduring the grit and the chaos that came from the journey of putting this story to the page. If not for her, it may well have hung in limbo for eternity.

Also, I send a huge thanks to my dear Southern friend, Sally Johnson, for lending her ear and her laughter every step of the way. She has been a role model for navigating the good, the bad, the ugly, and the hilarious.

Then there are the two Jans—Janet Nichols and Janis Wolkenbreit—the only two people who read the excruciatingly raw first draft of this book, eight hundred plus pages. If not for them, I might well have called it quits—wasn't it enough that I had gotten the damn thing down on paper? Their encouragement was invaluable.

And there are those who read the second, or third, or fourth drafts—Ellen Skroski, Mary Ellen Salvini, Susan Stanley, Judy Karren, Leah Gans, Paula Olson, Bob Ryan, Brian Adams, Sally Johnson, Janet Nichols (again), Janis Wolkenbreit (again), Mary Aubrey, Candace Cassin, Ron Freshley, Ginny Mayer, and Kay Saakvitne. Thank you all. If I have overlooked anyone, which is more than likely, forgive me, and thank you!

Hall Stuart-Lovell, my copy-editor and new friend, has been an ace at guiding me through what I consider the most tedious aspect of reaching publication. Thank you, Hall, you handled my grunts and grumbles with great panache.

Sally Johnson did the watercolor on the cover of this book. Her talent is undeniable.

Joey Skroski photographed the painting and put the photo in the correct dimensions. Leah Gans designed the layout of the cover. Many thanks to you both.

And in the end, and from the very beginning, it was my muses who woke me each morning and kept me up each night, month after month. They pushed me, used me, and occasionally wrung me dry. They made me laugh, and they made me cry. I thank them whole-heartedly for giving me this story. They have more plans for me, and I look forward to whatever they may be.

I love you all.

Nancy Kent

Contents

If a story is in you, it has to come out.
—William Faulkner

Prologue

So, now you know even more about the infamous Stella Gale, probably more than you wanted to know. I warned you, and I may live to regret this, but what's done is done. When you first came here, you said you were seeking revenge and I can understand why. Well, this could be your opportunity. However, before you jump on it—and you'll need my cooperation if you do—I suggest you put together as many pieces of this complicated story as you can by whatever means necessary, and once you've put them all together, see how you feel then. Frankly, I doubt revenge will be foremost in your mind, or maybe it will. After all, what do I know? Not much. I mean look at me—you can't say "crazy" hasn't crossed your mind a few times during these two years you've known me, and understandably so. Here I am, in a cabin far away from all of it, desperate for glimpses of who I am, who I was meant to be—wondering if they are one and the same and trusting only my three dogs—and now you. Obviously, I don't care about appearances—I don't even own a mirror. I shoot cans from the same tree branch every day at the same time, run half naked through the woods with my dogs when it's warm enough, play "Reveille" in the morning, "Taps" at night, listen to music, read books, and write letters I never send to a little girl I once met. Oh, there are more than a few moments I'd like to cut Stella from my heart as quickly and easily as a paper doll from a flat page, and toss her away, but it's just not that simple, not by a long shot.

By the way, you once asked me why I only ever wear overalls and T-shirts, even in the cold, underneath the layers. I told you it was strictly for comfort and you accepted that. Truthfully, it's my "wrestlin' with the devil outfit," something Bobby taught me about. You just might want to think about getting the same for yourself.

Annie Evans

The Prelude: Stella's Piece

Note to reader regarding the Prelude:

The Prelude rolled through me fast and furiously. It was the steamroller that leveled the jagged edges of my resistance, making it possible for the story to emerge. I had to write it first, I had no choice. But you, dear reader, have the luxury of choice. Of those who have read this book, some wanted to be in the story immediately, so they skipped the Prelude and started with Part I. Others greatly appreciated reading the Prelude first, as it was written. Then there are those who enjoyed reading it in the beginning, and then again at the end. You can skim it, refer to it, pick it up, or put it down. Do with it as you will. Godspeed.

My So-Called Beginnin'

Stella Gale was not born yesterday. Fact is, the only day she could think she WAS born yesterday was the day after she was born, 48 years and 262 days ago. Even on that day it was just plain wrong to consider her born yesterday. She was always two steps ahead, always on the closing end of figuring things out, while everybody else was at the beginning or didn't have a damn clue and never would. Either way she had the God-given advantage and that's what mattered.

She snorted as she sipped her coffee, sucked on her joint, and scanned her black-and-white linoleum floor. Today was not a mopping day, thanks to the fact of Bobby being away. He was one of those men, like most, who was always dragging in dirt for her to deal with, both the for-real kind that came off his boots and the kind that rolled in on account of his big mouth or lack of knowing the way things worked. She didn't mind the mopping kind, but the other kind caused her nothing but grief, day after day, month after month. The fact of her staying with him all these years was one of God's great mysteries and she wasn't about to ask God about it because it just wasn't that important, all things considered. There were plenty of more important things she needed God for and the Bobby question wasn't even close to the top of that list.

She snorted again and thought about herself at two days old smelling the bullshit and already planning her way out. *Maybe my plannin' wasn't in words back then, seein' as I couldn't speak, but I was on it like white on rice and will be till the day I die.*

She glanced across the kitchen to her study, squelched what was left of the joint into the ashtray, and reached for the scrunched up pack of Pall Malls. *Speakin' of dirt, I just might have to spend this day goin' through my files and diggin' up a bunch on a few people.*

As she pulled a cigarette from the pack, the all too familiar distant roar of dogs suddenly burst through the pleasant fog that had settled in her brain. "Damn dogs! I'm gettin' too damn old for this shit." She coughed hard a few times and, as the fog lifted, the phone call from Margaret Appleman at 5 a.m. came back to her. *Who the hell does Margaret think I am? Born-yesterday-Stella?* She already knew about this latest attack on her and her kennel. A thousand people had called her—all damn night—acting like they cared. *How stupid do they think I am?* She was, after all, the biggest somebody in the business and had her hand on the pulse of damn near everything, anywhere in the world. The fact that this 'newsflash' from everybody else's point of view put her in deep shit was their stupidity. NO, she was NOT born yesterday and NOBODY was ever going to pull one over on her, not ever. Somebody's life was about to get real miserable and it wasn't going be hers!

The last time she recalled being this angry, which was a thirty on that itty bitty scale of ten, was when that ungrateful Annie Evans up and left with three of her best dogs.

Amen, you got that right. I was NOT born yesterday and that's the damn truth. But I'm tellin' you, before you get to thinkin' you got it ALL right, you can't be usin' dumbass words like "squelched" in my book 'cause A) it's one of those words that you people who think you're so educated use, B) it's got nothin' to do with a joint, and C) it's not a word it's a sound, as in that's exactly what it would sound like if one of my dogs stepped on a frog down by the stream I got runnin' through my land—and I say "if" 'cause they ain't never done it, thank God. As for me, I don't squelch anythin'—never have, never will. I don't believe in killin' animals, period.

And speakin' of my dogs, why the hell you think Annie takin' my dogs is even worth mentionin' is beyond me. She ain't nothin' 'cept ungrateful, just like you wrote. That little incident is like one of them stories on the last page of some big fat newspaper, way down in the corner in itty bitty writin', and here you are makin' like it was the 'quivalent to what I'm dealin' with in the present moment.

Now I'm real sorry we can't have a relaxin' conversation regardin' my book, like you probly want, but this is real life and real life don't allow for much relaxation. I wake up on a daily basis and the next thing I know, I got bullshit sittin' right in front of me, tellin' me I got to deal with it before I can do what I was plannin' to do. Fact is, bullshit interrupts everythin' I got to do before I get around to doin' it and the next thing you know, I'm mad as hell all damn day. Welcome to MY world! Now, I like what you wrote, don't get me wrong, but you got some learnin' to do regardin' me and real life, which means I just might have to tell my own story till you get it straight, which may be never. So you need to listen and listen close 'cause I'm only gonna say all I got to say just the once.

First off, we need to explain to the readin' public just how it is this all started and why I have to take attacks on a regular basis. I'll tell you why, 'cause I've worked my ass off and they all want a piece of me. Bein' the best in this business, or any damn business for that matter, brings shit on like you'll never know, which brings me back to thinkin' why I really DO need to tell this story.

How 'bout we do like they do in all those biographies, or whatever you call 'em, and we start at the beginnin', meanin' my so-called beginnin'—and I say "so-called" 'cause I don't really think of it as a beginnin'. Bein' born and knowin' you're shit-outta-luck before you can walk ain't any kind of beginnin' in my book. It's called bein' born in the middle of shit, not all innocent and fresh, waitin' on the world to lift my ass up and send me down that shinin' brick road where there's a pot of gold waitin' for me. Nope, nuh uh, that is NOT the way it works and anybody who says that is flat out lyin'.

In thinkin' about it, no person on the whole earth begins all innocent, pure and all. Well, maybe for a couple seconds. But I'm tellin' you there's bullshit waitin' within one minute, or less, after you exit your mama's belly—bein' slapped around by some doctor bein' part of it. I'm tellin' you, if you come into this world and are given some cockamamie (bet you didn't think I knew that word, did you?) fairy tale about life bein' a bed of tulips, or a lilac garden, or some crap like that, you are gonna land in a big ass amount of trouble and have no way of gettin' yourself out of it!

I have seen people come and go. I seen all kinds from all walks of life—and I say it ain't never a walk. And I'll tell you right now, it's the ones with stayin' power that keep their ass above the rest, those are the winners. Fact is, I'm thinkin' even if you did know about my "beginnin'," you wouldn't know how to explain it 'cause you'd be puttin' up roadblocks like "squelched" all over the place. We got enough bullshit in this world, I don't want you addin' to it. My life, meanin' my book, is about livin' in the REAL world, not in one of them IVORY or GOLD buildin's, or whatever you call 'em. Hell, I've got a ton of people, includin' myself, tellin' me if I'd gone to college I'd be the damn president by now. All them fancy words on top of what I know, it would be a cake walk. Most people are so stupid it's a cryin' shame—well, not really, 'cause that's why I'm on top and exactly why no one will ever bring me down.

And speakin' of college, you tell me what's so damn smart about them college kids lyin' around, by the hundreds, in the road protestin' us goin' in and killin' them sand-bastards who attacked our innocent people—well, not all that innocent. Some of those people in them towers were rich SOBs. God knows how many people they screwed to get where they were—and that's the way of the world. That's the way it is—end of story. You either get with the program or not. I'd rather be a rich SOB than a sorry-ass who's spendin' their life tryin' not to screw anybody over or piss 'em off. Isn't that just the way it works? You tell me. 'Course, let's not forget them people who go door to door beggin' you to see God and give up everythin' you worked your ass off for. I'll have you know, I have talked to God and God wants me to go after exactly what I want—case closed. Just don't hurt no animals, that's the only rule.

Did you see that bit on the news? It musta made a big impression on me 'cause I can't get it out of my head! All

*them so-called intelligent college types lyin' in the middle
of the damn highway. All I got to say is they better not try
that shit down here 'cause all they would be is speed bumps,
plain and simple. All that book learnin' and they end up
"squelched."*

*Anyway, you're right about one thing, I AM too damn old
for this shit! I got nothin' left of my arms from draggin' one
hundred 'n' fifty pound dogs all over hell and back. Back
in the olden days, which wasn't that long ago, it wasn't so
bad—then the change of life hit me, and a hell of a lot earlier
than it hits most people I might add, 'cause my life has
been longer than most peoples, as in one of my years is the
'quivalent of two of everybody else's, which makes me almost
a hundred years old!*

*I swear, every mornin' I pray I can get my ass outta bed.
I mean, I may be small from most people's perspective, but
I used to haul a hundred pounds at a time of food, gravel,
and what not back and forth to my kennel. That's only ten
pounds less than what I've weighed my whole life 'cept when
I was a kid. Not a whole lotta folks can carry the 'quivalent
of their selves back and forth all damn day, year after year.
And now look where it's got me! I got the arthritis and a crap
load of pain all up in my arms and neck and, some days,
I got no feelin' in my hands and I drop things. Oh, I got a
doctor who gives me pills that are s'pose to help, but they
don't. I'm thinkin' I need morphine or some shit like that, but
no, they won't give it to me 'cause it's a "regulated substance,"
so I stick to the unregulated stuff that I can smoke. And,
speakin' of that, it ain't no "pleasant fog that settles around
my brain" as you put it—it ain't no fog, period. That's called
gettin' my God-given right to a few moments of peace before
facin' the bullshit.*

*Now listen to me. Let's start back at the middle of shit,
you know, little me growin' up with "trauma" as you might
like to call it, though I see it a whole lot different—as in the
way it is—life. My granddaddy came over here from Ireland,
settled his ass somewhere in New England, and worked his
way up to ownin' his own cigar company. He was a lot like
me—a tough bastard. He didn't take no crap, unless it was*

absolutely necessary to get him where he wanted to go AND he knew EXACTLY where that was, and he got there. He was a millionaire, in olden days' standards, by the time he was thirty.

The sad fact is, people was so jealous of him they drove him to drink and the drinkin' drove him to screwin' every woman in sight, which drove my grandma to the psychiatric ward and to an early grave—well, she was kinda crazy anyway. Personally, I think she shoulda shot him and lived high on his hog for the rest of her short life. Anyway, he wound up dyin' of a beat-to-shit liver at forty-five years old.

The even sadder fact is, there wasn't no money left by the time he died—well, just enough for my daddy to pick up and move to Biloxi, Mississippi, to try to start his own business. He was only seventeen. He'd already run away with his younger sister a couple times when his mama, my grandma, was losin' her marbles and put in and out of the psychiatric ward—'cause bein' at home with a pissed-off-losin'-all-his-money drunk was not a "ride in the park" as you might say.

I tell Bobby every damn day, if he even gets close to bein' like that he is gone—end of story. I found out once that he was doin' that amphetamine shit to stay awake on the job after them nights when we was either up fightin' or screwin', or both. I was so hoppin' mad, I made him sleep in his pickup till he promised to stop and he did—three days later.

Anyway, back to my daddy—he took his sister with him to Mississippi 'cause he was the only one that gave a damn about her. Now, here's where you need to listen real close, LOYALTY is top of the list in my family, always has been. There's not a day goes by I don't talk to or think about my now dead aunt, my nephew, or my two boys. That's right, I got two kids—well had three. One of 'em had a lotta problems—kinda like my grandma. She was my oldest. Greta was her name. She killed herself when she was twelve years old—too damn young is what I got to say about that!

Now, my grandma, she overdosed on pills, but my girl, she took a gun and shot herself in the head. The Doc said it wasn't nothin' to do with anythin' me or Bobby did (hell, it wasn't even his gun and he isn't her for-real daddy). It was just that nuts gene that got passed down. Most females don't do that, you know, kill themselves in such a violent manner. But Greta, she got my genes, strong as shit. Given different circumstances, minus the nuts gene, she'da been just like me—born knowin' not to take no crap from nobody, man or woman.

Anyway, I don't like to talk about my kids too much, 'specially bein' in the high profile world that I'm in and 'specially 'cause I am real well known in this high profile world. 'Course, you already know that, which is why you're writin' my book—case closed. I just don't want people to start thinkin' they can breathe down my boys' necks. Nothin' makes me madder than that—nothin'. My family comes first, always.

I know, I know, I talk about my boys sometimes, but that's only to show people that I did SOMETHIN' right for chrissake! I mean, after all I been through, some days I think I got the wrong babies from the hospital, or maybe I did all the bad shit and the only choice they got was to be on the straight and narrow. Neither one of 'em ever got in trouble at school—they went right through and got their diplomas, with no help from me I might add. They're good business men. They got nice cars—BMWs and what not—and wives that are drop dead gorgeous and smart as shit. I got lots of pictures to prove it. I'll show you later 'cause maybe you'll be wantin' to put a few in my book. 'Course, I told 'em to go for bein' a doctor or lawyer, but business seems like a magnet in my family. I WAS and still am the businessman in my marriages—I AM the magnet.

I say marriages with an S 'cause I been through more than a couple, not all of 'em official, as in "I do." The first one was when I was sixteen. We got married in Vegas. That man was my ticket out of a bad situation, which maybe you'll want to know more about later, but I don't feel like talkin' about it right now. To tell you the truth, I got no interest in discussin' any of the men in my life 'cept Bobby, 'cause he's the only one worth discussin'. How many men do you know that would take on a woman like me with three kids, one of 'em nuts?

Now, don't get me wrong, Bobby had his problems when I met him—couldn't keep his ass out of prison bein' one of 'em. He'd been in and out for eight years, mostly robbery and mostly 'cause he needed to do what he needed to do to survive. I was the one that showed him he could do all that without landin' his ass behind bars. The ONE time I went to prison was my own fault, God knows. It was one of the biggest mistakes of my life. I was on my way to makin' more money than you'll ever see—even after you sell my book.

Now, I know people will eat up what I got to tell 'em, but like I said, you'll never see the kind of money I was on my way to makin' when I had my high-end escort service—and that weren't even what put me in prison—it was the money I wasn't givin' Uncle Sam. Do you think the Government gives a rat's ass about what you do to make money? HELL NO! All they care about is that they get their cut.

Oh yeah, they keep arrestin' the little dope sniffers and potheads who, by the way, I sympathize with 'cause I would be in some psychiatric ward somewhere if I didn't have my weed. It's a whole lot better for you than all them LEGALIZED drugs they like to push on TV. Things like Prozac—good Christ! Have you seen some of them ads? I mean they got some little rain drop actin' all down and shit, walkin' around, slouchin', frownin', can't hardly move. Then that rain drop takes Prozac and the sun comes out and dries up all the rain and he's all smilin'. It's just like that little itsy bitsy spider song, which is EXACTLY why they did it the way they did—it's all about the unconscious. Every one of us grows up knowin' all about that itsy bitsy spider. It's way deep in there somewhere and to some folks, not me, it's about wantin' some kinda rosy little childhood that didn't never happen in most cases. It's psychology, plain and simple—makes the average person want to run to the doctor and get their hands on them pills so they can have that imaginary, cozy little feelin' back—a feelin' they ain't never had in the first place.

I'll tell you, right now, I'd rather bank on my weed. I have been with people who take Prozac and they are addicted. They got to take it every day and they ain't never the same once they go down that road. They got no fire left in 'em, not even a glowin' amber or two. So, I say, stay away from the pharmaceuticals 'cause for the most part, 'cept for my pain pills and my occasional Valium, which I now happen to love 'cause they help me haul my big ass dogs around—for the most part, it's all about makin' big money off ignorant and stupid people.

Well, I ain't one of 'em and I ain't never gonna be.

I mean, how stupid are people? You know that bullshit about a four hour erection as a "harmful" side effect? That is exactly why men are racin' to the drugstore. I mean, what man do you know wouldn't die for a four hour erection? And what woman do you know that wouldn't die for a man with a four hour erection? Hell, it's the damn women drivin' their man to the drugstore to buy them pills. That is some smart as shit marketing is all I got to say about that—but I'm smarter and can see right through it. Fact is, them pills ain't nothin'—just more feedin' into the dreamin' end of life. I know all about that. Every business I been in, includin' this dog business, is all about knowin' the dreamin' end of life—settin' people up to think they got exactly what they want—end of story.

Anyway, gettin' back to MY story—I'm thinkin' maybe this book you seem so dead set on writin' will be the first one that, God forbid, tells people exactly what it's all about, thanks to me. But right now, I gotta deal with this recent uproar and those traitors who are about to have their lives made real miserable. I gave 'em warnin' shots and they went down for a while, but it looks like they're kickin' again, so I gotta bring out the big guns, which brings to mind another of my life's little lessons, you can't trust anyone and that's the God's honest truth—'cept the animals. God knew that from the get-go. Why do you think he put hundreds of animals on that boat and only two people? 'Cause people ain't all that important, that's why. Animals is where the goodness in the world is. No one seems to understand that but me and I didn't need no bible to tell me that, no sirree, jack.

Now, you might be wantin' to know a little somethin' about Bobby 'fore you go off and maybe write things that just ain't true. I first met him when I was twenty-six and my escort service was in the works—as in the groundwork *was bein' laid. I had the opportunity to be with some of the richest men alive and make connections while doin' so, without givin' up a damn bit, meanin' they got nothin' but my fine company. Any sex was by MY choosin', not theirs. I was not only beautiful but, most importantly, I knew exactly what I wanted and that's one helluva aphrodisiac for a lotta men. My point bein', I coulda picked from a whole litter of rich men to spend my life with, but I picked Bobby. Why? Well, it may be a good aphrodisiac, but bein' a woman of independent means and strong as shit is not who most of 'em want you to end up bein' if you marry 'em—that's the part where they start tryin' to work you into stupid, so you're nothin' more than a stupid beautiful woman. Anyway, I always made it clear from the get-go I wasn't interested in marryin' any of 'em, but still, stupid as most men are, they threw money at me, gave me damn near anythin' I wanted, always thinkin' in the back of their minds they'd make me theirs.*

Well, that's where understandin' the dreamin' end of life comes in real handy. I would get everythin' I wanted from them and more—then move on. They'd be left hangin' their jaws open and I'd tell 'em, "I told you from the get-go I wasn't interested in marryin' you." What could they say? Nothin'—case closed. I got what I wanted because of their dreamin' on me. Oh, they had a blast, but it just didn't end up the way they wanted it, which was gettin' me, havin' me, and makin' me theirs to do with as they please.

Bobby, now he was different. A) he wasn't rich, B) he liked my kids, unlike most men, C) he loved the animals and he was willin' to learn from me. When I met him, he was just outta prison for the hundredth time. And when I asked where he came from besides prison, he didn't know—and I'll tell you right now, that perked my ears right up!

The story, the way he tells it, is he arrived in Atlanta one day, at the age of ten, outta nowhere. Everythin' that happened to him before that was just a big fat nothin'—still is—and he chose to keep it that way just so he could sleep at night. You probably don't understand that kind of thinkin', but trust me, it's the best thing to do sometimes. I mean, the shit that can happen to a person! It's a great thing if you can just blow it out of your mind and never know.

Anyway, Bobby lived in a foster home in Atlanta for 'bout two years. He got damn tired of it, never told me the details, but I got my theories on it. So, one day he just walked out and never went back. That's when he got to doin' whatever he needed to do to survive. What he needed from me was to take that drive to survive and turn it into more than survivin' and prison time, survivin' and prison time. It was like takin' a potload of raw talent and turnin' it into somethin' useful and successful. I knew exactly what he needed and I needed him because he cared about me, for real, and for my kids AND, most of all, he loved the animals—a sure sign about anyone's character.

Anyway, the one thing he remembers from them two years in the foster home was sittin' on the couch watchin' the Wizard of Oz on one of those little black-and-white TVs. Well, he just loved that idea of a big ole tornado pickin' up a person and carryin' them off to another world. He liked it so much, that from that day on, he told people, includin' me, he was from Kansas and one of the biggest tornados you could ever imagine had ripped him from his home and dropped him right down in the center of Atlanta. From then on he was known as Bobby Kansas or Bobby K.

'Course, by the time he met me he was of the age where he knew his story was bullshit, plain and simple, but that didn't stop him. He just liked it and never changed it. You go on ahead and ask him. He'll tell you that exact same story, word for word. It just don't change and that's the way it is. Hell, sometimes I wish I had some little fairy tale to grab onto and that's the truth and exactly what everybody wishes, which is what you need to know to be successful in this world. He ain't no fairy tale though. I mean I love him and all, but I ain't stupid.

The biggest problem Bobby has is booze. I have told him a thousand times that I know exactly who at least one of his parents was and that's American Indian, as in one hundred percent squaw mama or arrow slingin' papa. I know it ain't both 'cause he don't look Indian, he's too damn white for that, but I'm tellin' you, you give that man a few drinks and he goes all crazy—as in a hundred percent madman. You mess with him when he's drinkin' and he'll kill you—not me 'cause it don't work that way. Hell, you mess with me when he's drinkin' and you are dead ten times over.

I had to stop takin' him to dog shows a long time ago, unless of course I want someone dead—which half the time I do—'cause I worry he'll get to drinkin' and, before you know it, we'll be behind bars because he took some punk ass, who's jealous as hell of me and my kennel, to the cleaners. I have told him a thousand times, "Don't touch that shit, Bobby, 'cause it's gonna be the death of you, or more importantly, when it comes right down to it, the death of me." Hell, his doin' those amphetamines was better than booze. It's somethin' in his blood and I just know it's Indian.

I know he appreciates me tellin' him about bein' part Indian, 'cause sometimes I hear him tell people that his Daddy was a full blooded Cherokee. His face gets all I'm-cool-as-shit when he says it. 'Course then he has to go on and tell 'em that same daddy ended up dead for beatin' the livin' shit out of one of them reservation cops—you know, the ones who keep the Indians hostage on those for-shit pieces of land that nobody wants. I think he says that 'cause he wants to beat the shit out of a lotta people. Well, not so much anymore, he's gettin' too damn old—but he used to walk around thinkin' EVERYBODY was keepin' him hostage, 'specially when he'd been drinkin' and 'specially if it was the hard stuff, as in Jack Daniels. It's like the jackal and hide thing. So, I don't allow the hard stuff in my house. He can drink beers, but nothin' else. I've told him a thousand times if he does that shit here, he's gone. That was especially when my kids was young. He'd get mean—not physical and not with the kids or nothin', just stompin' around sayin' who he was gonna tear apart next.

And speakin' of dog shows and me wantin' people dead, you're gonna need to tell the readin' public all about what breed it is we're talkin' about. Don't leave 'em in the dark, it's the quickest way to lose 'em. I mean, at least don't let 'em think they're in the dark. You can keep 'em in the dark and not let 'em know, but that, right there, takes a special kind of skill I'm thinkin' you ain't got. You need to start this whole book by tellin' people, right off the bat, that it's the Bordeaux we're talkin' about—and show 'em pictures. That way they have somethin' they can look at while they read about all the bullcrap that I gotta deal with. I'm tellin' you, it'll keep the readin' public right where you want' 'em, thinkin' they know somethin'.

Now, I first got into this breed—and you got to write down the whole name, all three words—Dogue de Bordeaux— 'cause it's important. You don't take shortcuts when it comes to tellin' people information such as that. Anyway, I first got into the breed shortly after I got released from prison, which as you now know was due to my not paying Uncle Sam his share of my earnin's—MY being the "operative word," and I bet you didn't know I knew that little phrase, did you?

Oh, I know how you book learnin' types think—like that I ain't smart 'cause I didn't get a proper education. Well, think again, 'cause I could open a whole institution of knowledge and call it Stella's School of Real Knowledge and I can tell you one thing for sure, no one in my School would end up lyin' around in the middle of some damn highway thinkin' they're gonna save some poor bastards half way around the world who, by the way, don't give a rat's ass about them. That, right there, is some backwards thinkin', now ain't it?

By the way, Bobby wasn't arrested with me, miracles of miracles, 'cause he weren't officially connected to my business and we didn't share the same name, we still don't. We figure it's best that way—kind of an insurance policy for each other. It's always good to have someone you trust—'bout as much as you can trust anybody—to put your belongin's in their name, just in case.

Goddamn, I gotta tell you though, I got no clue how Bobby did all them times in prison without goin' nuts. I mean, that was the longest twelve months of my life. Do you know I knitted two hundred and seven scarves while I was in there? Can you believe it?! ME knittin'?!! I never woulda thought in a million years I'd do that shit, but it's damned amazing the things you'll do when you got nothin' better to do—yes sirree.

See, there was this girl, Lucy was her name, she was in there for some kind of petty thievin' ring in the D.C. area, nothin' as big or successful as what I was doin'. She was smart, I'll give her that, and worked hard at what she did, I could tell—but like Bobby she was wastin' raw talent on just survivin'. I told her if I still had my business I woulda hired her in a New York minute. Maybe not to be one of my girls 'cause she just wasn't pretty enough—but there was plenty of other things she coulda done for me. She liked that I said that. I knew she would. Anyway, every damn day for six weeks that girl tried to convince me to start knittin' prior to my breakin' down and actually doin' it. She kept sayin', "Do it, 'cause if you don't, you'll go crazy."

I told her, "Honey, I don't knit. I'll be damned if I'm gonna take up knittin' needles after devotin' a lifetime to not bein' caught dead doin' shit like that."

Well, the time went by and I started thinkin' about things that didn't appeal to me. I mean, I thought about my third husband—one of the unofficial ones. The bastard just up and left one day. I thought about how if I didn't have two little kids I mighta just taken my gun—the very same one that my Greta shot herself with—hunted him down and blown his goddamn head off. And then I got to thinkin' about how I was raped a month after he left—right in my own house, on the couch, with my kids asleep in the next room! Do you know that bastard bit me so hard on my neck durin' the rape that I developed a nasty-ass infection and had to go the doctor and get antibiotics? I swear to God, I was scared to death I mighta caught the rabies.

Turns out it was some kid, only eighteen or so. He worked for a delivery company and had been rapin' women on a regular basis. That same night he already raped two other women at gun point in my same neighborhood. He didn't have no gun when he was rapin' me, just teeth. He musta left his gun at the previous woman's house.

Anyways, while I was bein' raped, there was cop cars and sirens everywhere. To this day, I can't hear sirens or see them flashin' lights without some part of me shittin' myself. 'Course there's a lot of other reasons for that reaction in me, like me breakin' the law on a regular basis and endin' up in prison. I don't like to attach that feelin' to the rape 'cause that gives that little bastard a kind of power he just don't deserve.

My whole point bein', it was durin' them six weeks I got to thinkin' about disturbin' shit like that. Then all I could do to help myself feel better was think about every girl that had worked for me and how lost they was when I found 'em and gave 'em a better life—Annie bein' one of 'em, by the way. Fact is, that girl got more than all of 'em put together and she ends up bein' the one who betrays me the worst. She up and left me one too many times, which is twice. Oh, she came crawlin' back the first time, but the second time she up and left and took three of my best dogs with her!! I gave her a second chance and that's the thanks I got! That girl is a whole other story. Come to think of it, you just might want to track her ass down and write a whole other book. And if you find her, which I highly doubt you will, tell her she ain't nothin' to me anymore, nothin' at all.

Now, where was I? Oh yeah, there I was in Club Fed thinkin' about shit I hadn't thought about for most of my life, includin' the time my mama boarded me in my bedroom when I was in high school. She thought she was savin' me from the "bad boys" I was hangin' out with and swore she wasn't lettin' me out till I changed my ways, meanin' became just like her, which wasn't gonna happen.

See, my daddy had picked a nut, just like his daddy before him—'course my granddaddy's drinkin' didn't help the situation much. I mean, in my grandma's case she mighta just been driven nuts by my granddaddy. In my case, it was my mama who was nuts and ran off when I was little, leavin' me and my brother with my daddy.

What kinda mama does that?!

Well, the last thing I wanted to be thinkin' about was ancient history!

So I started knittin' and knittin' and knittin'. We had a goddamn knittin' contest and that was how I got through those twelve long months. Think about it. Sometimes bein' a woman in this man's world is just like bein' in prison—well, not in my case 'cause I never allowed myself to be in that position, 'cept the once—but that's exactly why women love knittin' and sewin' and washin'—'cause if they didn't, they'd end up either blowin' their husband's head off or pullin' that crazy Andrea Yeager shit and killin' their whole family.

Hell, maybe if my mama did more knittin' she never woulda done all the shit she did.

As for my rape and all, that had a good side to it, as in I never woulda gotten into the big dogs if not for that. I started with havin' a couple Rottis and all these years later, I'm sittin' here with a whole herd of Bordeaux all around me. Nope, no one will ever mess with me, not in a physical way. I got plenty of people tryin' to bring me down in other ways, but I can handle that—trust me.

So, now that you got some of what you'll be needin' to write my book, you go on ahead and do what you do. I'll be right here doin' what I do, which is livin' my life, as in doin' what needs to be done, not readin' or writin' about somebody else's life.

From Gaille to Gale

It was late afternoon as Stella Gaille strolled through the front gate of Club Fed and out into the world at large. All two hundred and seven scarves slipped from her mind about as fast as one of those rats she'd seen on occasion could drop a turd from a heating pipe and scurry on. She'd been told every one of those scarves had gone to the city's homeless which meant a lot of poor bastards in D.C. were going to have warm necks that next winter. Of course, she knew that little story wasn't true, and to prove it, she vowed once she got out she'd take her own little trip through D.C. to see if any of those scarves were walking the streets. She figured during the year she'd been there, a couple thousand scarves were knitted, so it would be impossible for her not to see at least a few. If she didn't see any, she would sue the government for lying and making a profit off her and the other women in the prison—A CLASS ACTION SUIT! They may have been serving time, but making money for some fat cat was not part of the deal. As far as she was concerned, it was slave labor, plain and simple.

The fact of the matter was, the only charity she really cared about was her own—the Stella Gaille Fund—and, speaking of funds, one of her first plans of action regarding her next business venture was to change her last name from Gaille to Gale. She never much liked the spelling PLUS, according to her brother, it was pronounced GAY if one was to go by the "true olden days pronunciation." If her brother said it was so, it was so. She didn't have anything against being gay, she just didn't want to have it be connected to her name. It wasn't a good business move. She had no clue what her grandfather was thinking, using what might as well have read "Gay and Son Cigars." And why he had to throw "Son" in, she never understood, because his son was in diapers when the cigars came to be. She guessed he thought it sounded more established, which it did.

What she wanted was for her last name to have more meaning to it, strong meaning. How many times while watching the weather channel on prison TV had she heard "There'll be gale force winds"—hundreds, thousands? As far as she was concerned, when she blew into a room, a bar, or any damn place, she was a force to be reckoned with, or admired, depending on who was in the particular place at that particular time. One thing was for certain, she was never ignored. Heads turned, she made sure of that. *Gale ain't no different than Gaille as far as how most everybody says it—it just has a better meanin' is all.*

She'd hung onto Gaille through two official marriages because of family loyalty AND it was something she could count on never changing. *God knows, everythin' else does.* Besides, she felt there was a lot of good luck in the name, and some bad, but she counted on the good to outweigh the bad in the long run. It had worked for her granddaddy, for the most part—the money part—and it had worked for her so far, for the most part—for the money part. Something just needed a little tweaking was all.

She turned to face the place she'd been in the past twelve months and suddenly, in her mind, was in a scene from one of the thousand movies she'd watched while inside. This one was the last look by the star that'd made one small mistake and ended up in prison, the last look before she stepped back into real life. In the actual movie, the star was a man, but who the hell cared? She was just sorry there weren't any cameras around.

As she turned from the prison and crossed the street, a warm wind blew across her face and sent her thick red hair flying straight out behind her. She was sure it was a sign, as in God was sending her a mini-message about her name change, letting her know Stella Gale was on the right track.

She climbed into the taxi that had been patiently waiting for her. She was going home, AMEN. However, much to her annoyance, the first thing she faced once she closed the car door behind her was an I-know-you-done-wrong glare from the driver. That's when her good luck feeling came to a screeching halt. "What the hell are you lookin' at?"

She sat back and collected herself as the cab driver pulled out onto the road, still glaring silently at her in the rearview mirror. She was in no mood for him. She glared back and spoke again, keeping her voice low and steady, "For all you know, I own the company you work for, and for your information, most of the people behind them walls have more money and power than you'll ever see. I mean, show some respect, for chrissake! Most of us in there have worked our way up from the bottom, which was doin' things like scrubbin' floors and DRIVIN' TAXIS. It's not easy, not always pretty, but nothin' to glare at, that's for sure."

The driver shrugged. "Lady, if you're trying to tell me you didn't commit a crime, save your breath. I have heard it all while driving people like you around this city."

He chuckled.

His chuckle hit her like five inch nails on a blackboard. He was a man with a little beard and a mop of hair that said, *I don't have to do what I'm doin' if I don't want to 'cause I'm smart as shit.*

"Well," she retorted, "if you have heard it all, sir, then shut your ears because I'm going to talk for a minute, which will be of great benefit to me."

She leaned slightly forward to let him know she was not backing off for a second. "I'll tell you why I'm not, as you say, 'savin' my breath,' because" (she was careful not to use her usual language—words like "cause" just weren't going to cut it) "you know, deep in your heart" (she loved using that phrase) "that I'm talkin' to you as someone who has seen, heard, and smelled it all. I have seen the likes of you come and go and end up nowhere because you think you are better than the hundreds of people you drive around everyday. I'm guessin' you started this job as a college undergraduate, have now graduated, and now think without liftin' a finger, the world is going to hand you a life like I have."

Stella was in her groove. She sat back, fully aware the driver was switching his attention from the road to watching her in the rear view mirror. She pulled a brush from her purse and brushed back her hair. "No," she continued, "prison was not in my plan, but as you may have learned in your so-called classes, white collar crimes are, in most cases, crimes committed in the name of success. Some of the most powerful people in the world have done what I've done which, by the way, isn't any of your business, and some get caught and some don't. If they do, more often than not they come right back out into the world and continue with their success."

She put down the brush and placed her hand on the back of the seat behind the man's right shoulder. "In fact, how would you like to drive me all the way to the Atlanta Hilton? I'll pay you double and pay for your lunch and dinner, seein' as it's goin' to be a long ride."

Stella pulled her hand from the seat and sat back again, and waited. The driver's eyes had stopped looking at her. She could tell he was thinking. She'd already figured out that she would stop at some point, call her best girl, and have her meet them at the Hilton, dressed real fine and ready to hand him a stack of fresh one hundred dollar bills. The Feds may have taken a huge chunk of her money, but not all of it. She and Bobby were not stupid. They had stashed plenty away—enough so they could easily afford a little adventure like this. Besides, this would give her just the boost she needed. She could see her old buddies at the Hilton, have a few drinks, and be home by 9 or 10 p.m.

"Ma'am?"

Stella jumped. In her mind she was already settled in at the very hotel where her whole business had started, eating, drinking, being treated like a queen—the way it should be. "What?!" She was annoyed by his intrusion.

"You are a truly disturbed woman. No, I do not want the privilege of driving you to some swank hotel in Atlanta, so you can try to peddle your bill of goods to me. You think you've seen my type come and go? Well, sweetheart, I have seen your type come and go, in politics and business, in every facet of life, and what you represent is the bully end of life, the power and control at all costs end of life."

His hands were relaxed on the steering wheel as he spoke. "I am not as young as I look. In fact, I would guess we're about the same age, only the stress of your insidious lifestyle is drying you up faster than me—and you know what else?" He took his eyes off the road and turned around to look Stella square in the face. "I can tell by what you're wearing and the way you're trying to talk that you are nothing but trash, trash that's trying hard to not look or talk like trash—but you are. Imagine that? A little taxi driver seeing right through your act!" He smiled and turned back around, just in time to stay on the road.

Stella felt something snap deep inside. "YOU ARE NOTHIN' BUT A PUNK ASS NOBODY WHO IS JUST PLAIN JEALOUS OF PEOPLE LIKE ME! HELL, IF YOU ARE MY AGE, YOU HAVE NOTHIN' TO SHOW FOR IT BUT YOUR SORRY-ASS LITTLE TAXI AND A TRASHY LITTLE APARTMENT TO GO BACK TO AT THE END OF A LONG DAY OF DRIVIN' THE LIKES OF ME AROUND. I'M THINKIN' YOU'RE PROBABLY SOME PSYCHO WANNA BE LIKE ROBERT DINERO IN THAT TAXI MOVIE, WALKIN' AROUND ALL FULL OF HISSELF THINKIN' HE WAS ALL THAT, WINDIN' UP DEADER THAN SHIT—A WASTE OF A LIFE, IS ALL I CAN SAY."

As she was yelling, the cab pulled into a gas station and the driver got out. He walked to her door and opened it. "Right here, Ma'am, is where you get out."

Stella knew now, for certain, he was just another jealous bastard. She'd met so many she'd stopped counting a long time ago. She eased herself out of the cab and stood facing him. "You just got busted, didn't you?"

She walked away before he had a chance to respond. It was perfect. There was no better feeling than hitting the nail on the head and walking away, leaving a person to drown in their own crap.

And that is exactly what I woulda said to that cab drivin' rat IF, and I say IF, it had happened. However, I can't say that I woulda yelled, like you wrote, 'cause he just plain didn't deserve that kind of attention. He wasn't even worth a whisper, far as I can tell.

Why the hell would I "snap," as you say, over some little cab driver dribblin' bullshit?

And when, might I ask, have you ever seen a cabbie pull that crap on anyone? I mean, they know they can lose their jobs over shit like that. They is in public service and when you are doin' that kinda work you have to be 'nice' to your customers. Trust me, some of the assholes I had to be nice to in my business, I wanted to kill 'em half the time, but I didn't.

I'll tell you right now, what I woulda done. First I woulda turned on my itty-bitty hidden tape recorder, somethin' I rarely go anywhere without—but seein' as I was just in prison I wouldn'na had one—so, I woulda calmly got out my pen and paper which I woulda had with me, just for occasions like that, and wrote down his name and ID number. And I woulda made damn sure he saw me writin' it down. Then I would thank him for his opinion with a big ole smile on my face and when I got to where I was goin', if I was still pissed off, which just ain't possible because who was he? Nobody— case closed—but if I was, I woulda called his company, asked for the manager, and told 'em the man was doin' drugs, right there in front of my eyes, drivin' recklessly and, on top of that, he was insultin' me and I had the proof on tape. I'd tell them if nothin' was done about him, I would be contactin' my lawyer who would be in touch by the end of the week.

And just so you know, I had some BIG ass connections back then, from my business. Hell, I got big connections from my Bordeaux business now. I got people from Hollywood who own my dogs. I got doctors, lawyers, surgeons, and damn diplomats buyin' my dogs, and for good money I might add. And trust me, they are sweet on me and I make sure it stays that way.

Anyway, back then I dealt with some higher ups from D.C.—meanin' politicians—people I can't say nothin' about 'cause they'd be in deep shit if I did. They hired my services, well, my girls' services, and it ain't exactly what they want on their records, now is it? Truth is, I burned all my records

*just days before I got busted. I could smell trouble was comin'
and I wanted to protect my girls and the good folks who'd
been so kind to me all them years. Trust me, any number of
'em woulda been happy to make a phone call or two to some
punk-ass cab company.*

*To this day, they don't know that I burned my records and
I let it stay that way, which is called "keepin' my cards close
to my chest."*

*Hell, I probably shouldn'na told you I burned 'em, but
who's gonna believe you? Who they gonna believe, you or
me?—case closed. Anyway, bottom line is, I got connections,
whether from back then or now, and people know it and don't
fuck with me because of it.*

*Now, let's get back to that "snappin'" thing you wrote
about. What you need to know, up front, is "snappin'" is what
I do when I need the BIG GUNS—and that, right there, was
not a situation where I needed 'em. You gotta be real careful
with the readin' public 'cause they're trustin' you to tell them
the damn truth, not mix 'em up. Lettin' 'em think I needed to
bring out the big guns in a BB gun situation just ain't right,
it's downright misleadin' is what it is.*

*And while we're on the subject of misleadin' the readin'
public, there weren't no rats where I was. You need to rewrite
that little bit. I wouldn't be caught, dead or alive, in the same
place with ugly-ass rats. You was mixin' up some blue-collar,
no-collar, prison-from-hell—which is somethin' Bobby knows
all about—with the white collar Club Fed, as I like to call it.*

*We white collar criminals, we eat well and share a room,
not a punk-ass cell with psycho-gonna-rape-your-ass people
sleepin' above you or below you. We got our own beds, on the
floor, not piled on top of each other.*

*And while we're on the subject, I know I told you I knitted
two hundred and seven scarves, but it coulda been two
thousand—the mind ain't clear in those situations—but I
do know, for a fact, those scarves didn't go to no homeless
people. They went to some children's home and I don't mess
with anythin' that has to do with children, so you can forget
about a "class action suit." I'm just glad to know my hard
knittin' went to a good cause.*

And to set the record straight, AGAIN, it wasn't no "slave labor," it was a goddamn godsend 'cause, as I already told you—and I don't like repeatin' myself—in a white collar prison, life gets pretty borin' cause you don't got to worry about somebody tryin' to beat you up or steal your shit—and borin' means too much thinkin' about all the wrong stuff—which is where knittin' them scarves came in handy. And, I'll have you know, as soon as I started knittin' I started thinkin' on what my next business was gonna be. It was like the minute my hands got busy doin' somethin' constructive and all, my mind got busy doin' somethin' constructive and all too.

What you got to remember is this was one of them places like Martha Stewart was in. Do you think she spent her days protectin' her ass from psychos and punk-ass guards, or lookin' at rats droppin' turds from heatin' pipes? Hell no! She spent her time like me, probably baked or knitted her butt off to keep from thinkin' too much. And if you think Martha don't got stuff she don't want to think about, I can guaran-damn-tee-you she does, everybody does.

See, if I was in prison now, instead of back then, I coulda been one of her roommates. Do you get my meanin'? This was no life threatin' rat infested place, that's for damn sure—'cept that it was borin' as all hell, which coulda been life threatenin' if not for that knittin'.

OK, now that we got that straight, right here's the part where you got to explain my kennel business and the people I have to deal with regardin' the Dogue de Bordeaux, like I been tellin' you to do. I'll give you some photos of my dogs to put in there. Only thing is you got to put my phone number on every one of 'em—just in itty bitty print up in the corner will do fine. That's the least you can do for me givin' you all this free information, information that if you didn't have, you wouldn't have a damn book—end of story.

So this is how it worked. While I was in "Camp Cupcake" like they called that place Martha went to—hell, why don't you just use that name from now on, seein' as it's public property. It's been on damn CNN and if that don't make it public, nothin' does. Besides as an author and all, don't you have some kinda license to do that?

Anyway, while I was in there I got to thinkin', while my fingers was busy with the knittin', why don't I give up the people business? I mean, I know I helped a lotta girls get back on their feet and I feel good about that, and I helped a lot of important people have a good time, but I was damn tired of doin' so much for people. People will suck you dry, I'm tellin' you that right now.

So, I got to thinkin' how much I love animals, dogs in particular and, like I told you, I always had dogs, especially big dogs, ever since my rape. I had Rottis and Bulldogs and Boxers—not all at once, but here and there—a couple at a time. So I thought to myself, why not make a business outta somethin' I love? I don't love people and I made a potload of money off them. I love dogs so, God-damn, how much money will that make for me? I mean if my equatin' things was right, I stood to make a ton of money doin' somethin' with somethin' I loved!

I thought about it some more and realized my previous business was dealin' with the breedin' end of humans. So now, I was gonna be dealin' with the breedin' end of dogs, only this time the whole point was to take it all the way to the producin' end. How hard would that be?

And I didn't want just any kennel, I wanted the BEST and that was the part where my God-given business gene kicked in. I knew that Rottis, Boxers, Retrievers, none of them was gonna cut it. Those were popular breeds, meanin' there was already a ton of established kennels. Why go into a business that already had all that established competition? I had to deal with that in my escort service, the competition and all. I figured why not make my next business about being one of the first?

See, I had this burnin' desire to be the establisher of somethin', like my granddaddy with the cigars. So I said to myself, why not be at the establishin' end of the dog breed business?

I was damned excited! I knew I was on to somethin' and all I needed to do was find me a breed that was real rare, at least in this country. So, I called Bobby and told him to send me every dog magazine he could find, ASAP, I didn't care how big or small they was, and I told him I wanted the new issues of every one of them soon as they came out.

Anyway, as soon as they started arrivin' I went through 'em one by one, page by page. I looked at all the pictures, read all the ads—even read some of the articles. You gotta put in the work if you're gonna be successful.

Well, it wasn't long before I saw a particular pattern with a certain breed—the Bordeaux. There was, over and over, only two main breeders, the same two—big ass ads with photos and all—one in Kansas and one in Pennsylvania. I deducted they was probably the only two breeders in the whole country—at least the only two worth a damn. There was a few other tiny ads, but the way I look at it—tiny is tiny, end of story.

I never even bothered to look at the small rare breeds 'cause I was only interested in the big dogs—and, as you know, these are BIG, that's for damn sure—or can be. I mean, as far as I'm concerned, no matter what anyone says, the bigger the better in my book, especially when it comes to the head in this breed, 'cause this breed is a "head breed." 'Course, you ain't even thought about introducin' the breed to the readin' public yet, which is just plain stupid—but, oh well, live and learn. Come to think of it, I should do the introducin' when the time comes, 'cause I don't want any misinformation out there and remember, I got the photos for you to use.

Anyway, my next step was to call one of them two main breeders, so I picked the one in Kansas, Charlene Peets— now ain't that funny? I mean with Bobby blowin' in from Kansas and all. AND, I'll have you know somethin' I ain't never told anybody—'cept Bobby and Annie—Charlene was the number one reason I followed through on the whole idea of dog breedin'.

Yup, I did all that research and all, but if that bitch hadn't behaved the way she did when I contacted her, well it just ain't clear as to whether I woulda gone through with it or whether it woulda just been the beginnin' of a long line of ideas. Maybe if I'da called the other breeder, Pete Strate in Pennsylvania, I'd be in a whole other business, a business without all the damn stress!

All I can say is look at where Charlene is now—nowhere! I accomplished that mission and many more, includin' Pete Strate, who also ended up nowhere. The truth is the truth—and it's a damn good weapon, Amen.

Anyway, before I get into the story of my original contact with Charlene, the ground-zero bitch of the Bordeaux world—it makes my blood boil just thinkin' on how she treated me from day one and every goddamn week, month and year after that. 'Course, in reality, I should send her some flowers and a thank you note. "Thank you, Charlene for givin' me the opportunity to kick your ass to kingdom come. Much love, Stella."

Where was I? I'm gettin too damn old to keep my thoughts straight. These Bordeaux people have been like livin' in hell and, most times now, I wonder if it was ever all worth it. 'Course, I know this means that I'm goin' to heaven when I die 'cause I have been in hell with a capital H. There ain't nothin' worse than bein' around so many, crazy, downright mean people. I figure they was probably put here by God to test us well meanin' people. If you can survive bein' with them, then you go to heaven, if not, you get to be with 'em for eternity.

Can you imagine a whole eternity with Charlene, Margaret, Tara, Molly, Biff, Tiffany, or, God forbid, Mabel, who, by the way, still thinks she's my closest and dearest friend. Sad fact is, I gotta keep a couple of 'em close to me—'specially during these stressful times.

Now, seein' as you ain't even introduced the readin' public to any of them yet, we got to get back to the day I left Camp Cupcake (we're usin' that name from now on, like I told you) 'cause there's no point in me talkin' about people that don't exist to the readin' public. It's a sure way to lose 'em as customers. Then where does that leave you?

You need to listen to me and start introducin' these people, along with the breed, or you ain't gonna have but one person pick up your damn book and that will only be 'cause they need something to write on, or worse yet, wipe their ass with.

Now, to get back to what I was sayin' before my blood started boilin' regardin' Charlene, there is no way I woulda walked outta Camp Cupcake and called a cab, or vice versa. Who do you think you're talkin' to, I mean writin' about? I was SOMEBODY, not some nobody who walked her lonely little ass out onto the street and got into a cab after twelve months of bein' shut out from the world. No sir, I was not gonna let the Cupcake guards, or anyone else, even begin thinkin' I was a sorry-ass loser who pulled the cotton over all their eyes. I worked hard in there to keep my image alive—well, not that hard, I mean, they all knew I was somethin' special. Anyway, it woulda damn near killed 'em if they saw me leavin' like you wrote.

Now, what I DID do was call my beautiful Greta aka Annie-who-stole-my-dogs-the-second-time-she-left-me, the first time bein' after twelve years of livin' with me. Anyway, I got her to hire a stretch limo and pick me up at the front gate. You were right about one thing, Bobby and I HAD stashed away a chunk of cash and, as for the clothes I was wearin', the ones that cabbie of yours thought was trash pretendin' not to be trash—what was he thinkin'?

You need to make sure that bastard knows all about my five hundred pairs of shoes, my dresses, my pant suits, and the fact each one cost more than he makes in six months! It has damn near wore me out havin' to deal with the likes of him—and he wasn't nothin' next to some of the others, which if you ever get off your ass to tellin' the readin' public about, they will see exactly what I have had to put up with all these years—case closed.

Now, where was I? I MEAN, WHO THE HELL DOES HE THINK HE'S TALKIN' ABOUT SOME "INSIDIOUS LIFESTYLE"? WHAT ABOUT HIS "INSIDIOUS" LIFESTYLE? DOES HE EVER LOOK IN THE MIRROR AND ASK HISSELF WHY GOD EVEN PUT HIM HERE? NO, AND YOU KNOW WHY? 'CAUSE HE KNOWS WHAT THE ANSWER TO THAT QUESTION IS—FOR NO DAMN REASON OTHER THAN TO DRIVE ALL THE SMARTER THAN HIS ASS PEOPLE AROUND IN SOME STINKIN' CAB.

Goddamn, I need to take one of my Valium right now 'fore I have a damn stroke!

So, now that we got that out of the way, as I was sayin', Greta was one classy lookin' woman. Greta, of course, was my dead daughter's name—the one who I already told you about—but I gave the name to Annie because after the hell I'd pulled her out of she needed a new name to go along with the new life I gave her. She liked it so much she said she didn't want no last name. She was just Greta, like Cher is just Cher.

But don't get me going on her again, 'cause after all I did for her—whew! All I can say is nobody does that to me. In fact, I'm speechless over it. It's like some damn nightmare, somethin' you wish you'd wake up from—but oh well, I will get a lot more than the last word on this, don't you worry 'bout that.

Anyway, back before she STABBED me in the back which, by the way, I must still be in shock about, which don't seem possible considerin' more than two years have past—'cause if it ain't shock that's keepin' me this calm, I don't know what the hell it is. Back when I could DO NO WRONG in her eyes— the good ole days—she was FINE with a capital F and that afternoon when she arrived at Camp Fed—or whatever the hell we decided to call it—it's your damn job to remember that shit—she stepped out of that long black limo, tinted glass and all, dressed to the nines and greeted me with so much class, it musta made them guards stop breathin'. I taught that girl everythin' she knows. It was just too bad I didn't have the business anymore 'cause they woulda been crawlin' all over themselves to get one of my cards and get a damn date with her. 'Course none of them could've afforded her.

Anyway, she walked with me, her arm tucked under mine, opened the door to that limo, allowed me to step in first and we drove away—and that's the damn truth.

So, you need to put that down, right where that dumb-ass cabbie can read it, in black and white.

The Bottom of the Bucket

Charlene Peets had no idea who was on the other end of the line when she picked up the receiver...

Of course she had no idea, there weren't no caller ID back then! You are messin' with the readin' public, yet once again. Nobody wants to be treated like they know nothin', even if they don't. You got to let 'em in on things that ain't so obvious, like when I called her that day it was 2:30 in the afternoon on a Monday— her time—and there wasn't nothin' but silence all around her. She said she was just finishin' cookin' lunch for her kids and could she get my number and call me back in fifteen minutes? I thought about it for a second 'cause I knew somethin' just wasn't right. I don't know too many people who are "just finishin' up cookin' lunch for the kids" at 2:30 on a Monday, or any damn day. On top of that, I didn't hear no kid noises and why the hell didn't she just have me call the same number back?

I smelled a rat from the first moment I heard that bitch open her mouth. Even so, I had to give her the benefit of me bein' polite 'cause it was just her and the breeder in Pennsylvania—blowin' one outta two shots ain't a good idea when you got your future ridin' on it. So, I gave her my full name and my home phone number. Of course, seein' as I was in prison, I told her I was on vacation and was talkin' to her on a phone the waiter had brought me by the pool, which meant I would have to be the one to call HER back.

She told me to hold on a second, which I did, which I don't usually like to do, but I did. Then she gave me a number to call in fifteen minutes.

Fifteen minutes later, EXACTLY, I called her. I said, "Hello, this is Stella Gale callin' you back regardin' your Dogue de..." She didn't even let me finish introducin' myself. She started right in with this holier-than-me voice. "Well," she said—and I remember it like it was yesterday 'cause I got a memory for the important stuff, as in every damn detail remains in my brain, permanent. "Well," she said, "if you're callin' about my dogs, I have to tell you, up front, if I don't know you, you can't get a show or breedin' quality dog from me. If you're interested in a pet, we can talk."

First off, she didn't sound like no Kansasonian. That was a north or northeastern accent. I knew that 'cause I have been everywhere in this country and I got the ears like a damn hawk. As it turned out, she was from Detroit—figures, huh? I mean, knowin' what we know now.

Anyway, I stopped listenin' for a couple seconds when she said "we can talk," 'cause I was aware of the sounds of a bar in the background—glasses clankin', people squawkin'. Plus, I heard the sound them pool balls make when they hit each other—even the sound them pool sticks make when they're bein' chalked, I swear. Like I said, I got the ears like a hawk. Well, that's when I knew she'd gone to a whole different place from where she was before, and who knows where that was—probably somewhere with rats, which is exactly what you need to write in my book seein' as you're so dead set on puttin' rats in there somewhere.

So, that's when I said to myself, this woman has been in a heap load of trouble with the law, or is tryin' to avoid bein' in a heap load of trouble with the law—either way she's up to her forehead in some kinda shit, that's for sure. Well, as far as I was concerned she was in kindygarden compared to me. That bit she said about me only deservin' pet quality blah, blah, blah—well, that's exactly what put it in cement that I was going ahead full steam with this Bordeaux idea. That bitch was gonna be sorry she ever talked to me like I was nobody. The first thing on my list of things to do once I got my new business up and goin', was to kick her ass to kingdom come—there ain't no motivator as good as that when it comes to me. I interrupted her blah, blah, blah and said, "I just want you to remember my name 'cause I garran-damn-tee-you it's gonna come back to haunt you, bitch!"

That is EXACTLY what I said to her, and then I hung up. I was pumped. Nothin' was gonna stop me now. I called Bobby and told him to start buildin' the kennel and fencin' in a chunk of land 'cause we was gonna be enterin' the world of the Bordeaux and we was gonna be THE BEST in the business if it was the last thing we did!

Bobby was kinda surprised and all, but the second he heard my voice in that particular tone he knew this wasn't no flash on the grill idea—it was time for him to get to work. Him and Annie and my boys built the whole thing from the ground up.

Annie, she learned everythin' there is to know regardin' buildin' anythin'—and all because of Bobby. That girl, when I went off to prison, was lean and sexy, drop dead gorgeous. When I got out, she looked like a whole different person. She had muscles where she never had 'em before and it seemed like dirt was ground into her face permanent and her hands was all hard and her nails was pretty much gone, but what's truly amazin' is she was still drop dead gorgeous!

I'm tellin' you, as much as I hate that girl, there was nothin' she could do to look ugly. She was born with the I'm-so-gorgeous-I-don't-got-to-do-shit-to-stay-that-way gene and she could speak all them languages on top of it, along with bein' able to build damn near anythin'. She had it all, then had to steal my dogs and run off to China, a place where they speak a language I know she don't know—so what's she gonna do? Nothin'—case closed.

You've seen the size of my kennel with all them fine details and all them fields! Well, Annie's hands is in there, whether I like it or not. It's a fact of my life.

Anyway, gettin' back to Charlene—that bitch had no idea what she had lit that day over the phone. I was about to be the damn H-bomb of the Bordeaux world! As soon as I hung up, I said "Fuck it, I'm going to the source."

I knew, right then and there, I would go to France or damn Africa, if I had to, and was gonna get me the best damn Dogue de Bordeauxs I could find and become the kiss-my-ass Bordeaux breeder of America.

See, Charlene thought she blew me over, bein' all rejectin' and all. Well, she had no idea what would be comin' her way as soon as I got outta Cupcake. All I needed was a little more information, so I called that other main breeder, my now ex-buddy Pete Strate, who was in Pennsylvania. When I talked to him, I didn't make my motives known. I just asked him simple, polite questions and praised the photos I'd seen of his dogs till it damn near made me sick. I asked him about the parents of his dogs, where they was from and all, what a great job I heard he was doin' and blah, blah, blah. He was your typical man—once you start to stroke his dick, he gets a hard-on and just can't help hisself.

Anyway, I got kennel names, breeders, countries, all of it, in about ten minutes flat. He never knew my name and, to this day, has no idea that I'm the one who was on the other end of the line all them years ago. If I was to tell him he was the one that got me started on the right track, he would shit hisself, sure as I'm sittin' here. He's the man who got left scratchin' his head after a good blow job, not realizin' that the woman, whose name he never bothered to get, had taken his wallet and was about to go on a big ass shoppin' spree at his expense.

Actually, in thinkin' on it, he probably does remember talkin' to me 'cause, like Bobby has told me over and over, nobody forgets my voice. He says, it sounds like if one of them lions could talk while strollin' across one them prairies—that would be my regular everyday voice, not my big guns voice—Bobby ain't come up with nothin' to describe that, not yet. Still, men is men and they don't got the memory for that kind of stuff, so he probly don't have a clue, like I said.

Anyway, one thing Pete did say to me after I told him I had talked to Charlene—as in I wanted to find out what he might think about her—he said he never met her and she had only been in the breed for a year, but he did know some "things" that "suggested" to him Charlene would be "the breed's worst nightmare." He didn't say what things and I didn't ask him because I was busy thinkin', in that moment, how I was gonna be him and Charlene's worst nightmare.

There's a particular humor, or as Annie probly woulda said "a certain irony," to the fact of Charlene's last name bein' the same as his first, don't you think? Those two hated each other and that was just fine with me. 'Course now I know what them "things" were that he was talkin' about, which we'll get into when we do our official introducin' of that bitch, which it looks like we're already doin'.

Alls I got to say is poor Pete, he really was nothin' far as competition. Turned out he was one of those obsessive types. You know, just couldn't produce exactly what he wanted, which is exactly where he went wrong. It ain't about that. What you gotta do is produce what the customers want, or make damn sure that they think you are producin' exactly what they want. He musta spent fifty thousand dollars just on the travelin' part of goin' back and forth from Europe to here, back and forth, importin' tons of dogs and ended up spayin' and neuterin' damn near all of 'em.

By the time he left the breed, he musta had a garage full of x-rays and vet bills up the ass! He was spendin' a thousand times more than what he was makin', which was nothin'. It's no wonder his wife left him, which was the final straw that broke him. He was obsessed. He was a damn fool is all I can say.

By the end, he was known as the "pet quality breeder," thanks to yours truly. My point bein' that the world had to know the truth about him, didn't they? That's all I was doin', tellin' the damn truth. A garage full of bad hip x-rays and importin' new dogs every damn year! All I did was warn the public about his obsessin' self.

Now, I will admit Pete did produce a few good movin' Bordeaux, but they just didn't have nothin' else going for 'em—no head at all, he never cared about that. If he'd been a little nicer to me, I coulda helped him out, but he was stuck on some twisted idea that I was no better than Charlene. Hell, I even used a stud from him once. He was real surprised about that. My thinkin' was, I'll see what happens if I add a little of his good movin' dogs to my stock, but it was nothin' to shout about. I lost all my heads in the one litter I got from that dog. I didn't make no stink about it till he started tellin' people that he never got his money for that stud service. That's when I just turned up the volume on that bastard. It was all too damn easy, really. Poor bastard was already half down—alls I had to do was blow him over with a little of his own medicine, only my medicine was the damn truth.

And just so you know, this is a "head breed" and that's what people want and what matters the most. By head, I mean big and intimidatin'. And don't even start with tellin' me "head" means more than size. I am so damn tired of hearin' that!

I was no slouch when I got into this breed, just like I was no slouch back in the day with my escort service. Within the 'quivalent of the first five minutes I was in this breed— meanin' within the first six months—I had memorized damn near every line, all the ones worth memorizin'. Hell, people's jaws dropped open when I spit that stuff out, it's like I was God or somethin'. I ain't God, I just did my homework, the kind that was worth doin' if you want to sell somethin'. Impressin' people with what you know is exactly how you run a business. People want to know you know what you're talkin' about and I got the cash profits and the numbers to prove that's just the way it is.

Fact is, I feel sorry for this poor breed with all the stupid people that are breedin' 'em. So, when you FINALLY get around to introducin' the readin' public to 'em—which it seems like is gonna be when hell freezes over—you need to listen to me 'cause there ain't no book out there that will ever tell you the truth about 'em. I got the truth right here in my back yard and I got hundreds of people, all over the world, wantin' to kill me 'cause of it. What does that tell you? It tells you I'm doin' somethin' right, don't it?

I don't care what people say about me. The more people talk, it's all the better for me. A lot of folks they just crumble— all pitiful and all—when the bad talkin' goes their way. I just get stronger, plus I use it to my benefit. I have produced the best in this country and done exactly what anyone with any brains would do. Goddamn, just look at the history of hits on my website, best website ever made. I had a couple Bill Gates types help me put that thing together. I have had thousands and thousands of hits from all over the world, people wantin' my dogs from as far away as damn India and

Australia, even countries I ain't ever heard of. I have sold dogs to people who have so much money you could swim in it—that's success now, ain't it? I have made mistakes, sure as shit, but I learned from 'em and that's exactly what Pete did wrong.

Now where was I? Guess I got a little ahead of myself, didn't I? We ain't even got to discussin' my very first Bordeaux and we're already talkin' about the end of Charlene and Pete!

We'll get back to that, but right now I'm realizin' I forgot to tell you my boys was fourteen and sixteen when I went into Cupcake. And my little girl, the original Greta of my family, she was dead—like I already told you. That girl sure was hard to live with, but she was family and I loved her. She woulda liked livin' the high life with us, even though it ended up with me goin' to Cupcake. And now, here we was in the middle of startin' a whole new life, one I think she woulda liked real well, even better then the other life, 'cause she loved the animals, just like me. Hell, maybe havin' all these dogs woulda kept her from killin' herself. I mean animals, as I already explained to you, are God's true grace and if all my Greta did all day was tend to the dogs, help with the birthin', play with the pups, it just mighta kept her wantin' to stay here.

'Course, I woulda had to keep a close eye on her 'cause she just wasn't like us normal people. She mighta squashed a pup, thinkin' she was huggin' it, if you know what I mean. Sometimes she just took little things an' made 'em bigger by mistake. I think her shootin' herself was one of those things. Pickin' up a gun and pointin' it at her own head—it was nothin' but a little thing in her mind, wasn't nothin' at all. The fact that it blew her brains out, well, I think it woulda shocked her as much as anybody. That's my opinion. I know, that might be just my way of believin' it just wasn't for real— who wants to think shit like that is for real? Truth is, I still don't believe it most days.

In thinkin' on it, I got a touch of that gene too 'cause I sure as hell have thought about endin' it all some days, but it ain't never about suicide, it's plain old homicide that would help me feel a whole lot better. It's just too damn bad Greta didn't see it that way. Homicide beats suicide in my book any day.

For one thing, you ain't dead in the end, and for another, it means a few less nasty-ass people.

Anyway, to get back to what I was sayin', when I went into Cupcake, Annie, aka Greta number two, took care of my boys and Bobby, 'cause God knows he needed as much takin' care of as them when I wasn't around. Do you know how tirin' it gets pickin' up underwear right where they come off? Or comin' into the house to put my raw pie in the oven and findin' it half eaten with a fork stuck in the center of it, then being told "Stella, darlin' that pie was real good"? It's an amazin' thing, ain't it? It didn't never occur to him that raw dough meant it ain't cooked yet. I mean, why do women bother to cook? Apparently, it don't make any damn difference.

That man who wrote that book about women bein' from Earth and men being from Jupiter, well, he got that right. 'Course most of us already know all about it, deep down. He was smart is all—made his million writin' down things that everyone wanted to hear, so they don't feel so damn miserable and like they was the only one that was that way. People will pay a lot of money to feel like they got company in the hell they're livin' in.

And while I'm on the subject of men and women, I'm rememberin' that you mentioned something about "gay" back there somewhere regardin' my name. Truth is, some days I wish I WAS gay. It sure would take care of some of the bullshit I gotta put up with. 'Course, I'd miss the man part of sex, IF I HAD ANY, which I don't anymore, so who gives a shit?

Anyway, what you wrote about my granddaddy and "Gay and Son Cigars"? You got that dead wrong—and you're the one who's s'pose to be so educated! What you seem to not know is, even if the true pronunciation of Gaille was gay—like I told you my brother once said, but I ain't never verified 'cause nobody but him seems to know that fact—it didn't mean nothin' like that back then. When you have me, Stella, thinkin' about my granddaddy usin' "Gay and Son" and wonderin' what he was thinkin', well, you're makin' me look just plain stupid. The fact of the matter is, there WAS gay people back then, but it weren't called gay, like it is now. It was called somethin' else, I don't know what—you need to talk to somebody from back then. Being gay then was a no deal situation, as in nobody talked about it—they just did it and kept their mouth shut. It wasn't like now where you have neon signs everywhere and nobody 'cept the stupid folks really give a shit. Hell, you got gay t-shirts, whole gay cities, gay bars, gay hotels, gay datin' services. God damn, in thinkin' about it Gay Cigars might be a billion dollar business in the here and now.

Hell, I had a couple gay boys who worked for me back in the day, but they didn't last long 'cause they was harder to manage than my girls—besides, Bobby didn't like dealin' with 'em. Straight men get all screwed up if they have to deal with gay ones. Alls that tells me is they is scared they got some of that in 'em and want to stay 'bout as far away from it as a pig from one of them bacon factories. Hell, I don't know any woman who gets so bent up as a man does about that stuff.

Anyway, gettin' back to the subject at hand, there wasn't nobody looked at my granddaddy's cigars and thought "Gay and Son cigars"—so, you ain't so smart as you think you are, and I sure as hell don't want you makin' me look stupid! If you want to be stupid, you go right ahead, just don't do it usin' my name. Now, the reasons I changed my name was because of the wind, just like I told you and just like you wrote, PLUS I wanted it to be spelled less complicated, as in exactly how it sounds, which is good for business.

Now, where was I before I got interrupted by rememberin' you screwin' with things regardin' my name and my person? Oh, yeah, me leavin' Bobby and the boys while I was at Cupcake. Fact is, Annie was the stabilizin' factor. I mean she kept an eye on the whole bunch of 'em. I trusted her with my family, which she did a damn good job of, by the way, and still she ends up betrayin' me—and Bobby. It don't make sense no matter how you look at it.

And, when we went off to Europe, it was her who stayed home with the boys. 'Course they weren't hard to take care of or nothin' 'cause they got my independent gene, thank God. She was just there to remind 'em mama may not be there, but she was watchin' from a couple thousand miles away.

Fact is, soon as they was done with high school they was gone, as in they went off to make good lives for themselves—so good I hardly see 'em anymore. I did somethin' right, that's for sure. That kind of independentness is a rare thing.

Anyway, Annie was family back then. She lived with us for a lotta years before Cupcake and for a couple years after Cupcake. She was part of my kennel business till she ran out on me that first time. Hell, she was even a part of it for that bit of time after she came crawlin' back and before she ran off AGAIN—and now ain't the time to get me goin' on that subject 'cause that's gettin' away from the subject we're talkin' about, somethin' I've done too many times already—especially considerin' the fact of you slackin' off on your part of the work on this book. Here I am tryin' to explain a few things about Charlene, who was about as low as you can go regardin' dogs or anythin' else, includin' rocks, and we ain't even officially introduced her yet, which I guess we ain't gotta do, 'cause there ain't a whole lot more to say about her except that the first time I actually laid eyes on her was at a Rarebreed Show in Kansas, about three months after I got back from Europe.

Now, that was a hell of a trip, I gotta tell you—but I won't right now, 'cause that would mean havin' to drag a bunch of other countries PLUS all them Europeans into my book at a time when we ain't even covered what goes on right here in our own country.

Anyway, I didn't tell no one at that Kansas show who I was. 'Course a lot of people had heard of me from them Europeans who had put the word out about a Stella Gale who was spendin' a fortune on pickin' up some fine dogues, one of 'em bein' my Oz, who was about to be the envy of the whole U.S.A.

I even had Annie make a few calls from here and there to people around the country, sayin' she'd seen the kennels I built and the dogs I bought and they was jaw droppin'— you know stir things up a little, as in remain a fig in their imagination for a while, growin' and growin' till the time was right.

So, there I was there at that little show in Kansas—in the background—collectin' information with my hawk ears like a good business person does. I even dressed down for the occasion, as in made myself damn near invisible. Trust me, it was hard to do, but I did it. By that time, there was five main Bordeaux breeders, already up from the original two, Charlene and Pete, and there was a growin' bunch of itty bitty ones.

See, I was gettin' into it just in time, 'cause as it turns out there was this movie with a Bordeaux that had come out the year before I went to prison—talk about God-given coincidences! Turns out, that movie was the beginnin' of the 'I wanna breed Bordeauxs' virus. Charlene was the first one to catch that little virus. Pete was already in the breed—God only knows why 'cause nobody gave a shit about 'em till after that movie came out. He brought the first pair into this country back in the ANCIENT DAYS.

Anyway, it took about five to six years for that virus to hit full force, meanin' after that you couldn't keep track of 'em anymore 'cause there was gettin' to be so many. So, when I turned up at that show in Kansas it was near the beginnin' of that period of time and I was well on my way to establishin' my mission.

The unfortunate part is, durin' that time, Charlene brought in a ton of scumbags 'cause all she did from the beginnin' was sell to white trash, spics, and niggers. Now, I ain't prejudice 'cause what I'm talkin' about is the snake-side (no offense to the snakes) of decent white, black, and Mexican people, if you get my meanin'. Every race of people got their snake-side—and what I'm sayin' is the Bordeaux got a big-ass chunk of it. It's a damn shame.

Anyway, somewhere in them five to six years, that's when Margaret Appleman, Ms.-my-Mama-kicked-ass-in-AKC-but-I-can't-do-shit, decided to try startin' a national Bordeaux club. Up to that point she'd been a little peewee who would show up at the Rare Breed shows with her ONE Bordeaux and blab on and on about her dead mama's Boxers, tryin' to impress us Bordeaux folks into wantin' her company or some shit like that. I guess she got to thinkin' the way she was goin' wasn't workin', so she took it upon herself to start a club. That's when she stopped talkin' about Boxers and AKC and started talkin' about the breed we owned—don't take a rocket scientist to know that might be the better subject with Bordeaux breeders, but apparently it took her damn near a year to figure it out.

She started going to every pissant little Rare Breed show she could find, took notes and actually interviewed people, just like she was somebody. And she wore a name tag and carried a clipboard, all official and all. She even started takin' addresses and phone numbers, lettin' people think she was the one who was gonna "save the breed."

When it comes right down to it, she was just a wanna-be-me. She followed me around at the shows like a damn puppy, beggin' me to help her support the damn club she was dead set on gettin' up and runnin'.

See, up to that point there wasn't no national club, no nothin' regardin' this breed, it was just too damn rare and in thinkin' about it, the few people who was in the breed just wasn't the types to be holdin' hands and makin' rules and settin' up meetin's with each other. Hell, I didn't want to. I didn't want anyone to have any piece of what I had and as far as I was concerned, unless I could run the whole thing, as in keep people in the dark who I wanted to keep in the dark, I wasn't interested. I mean it's like someone with a lot of talent agreein' to hook-up with a group of people with no talent! What was in it for me? Nothin'—case closed. I had MY club all set up. I had my circle of people who had kennels full of my dogs, most of which I co-owned for obvious reasons—and they was never gonna cross me. Now you tell me if that ain't a high functionin' club?

Margaret couldn't do shit on her own. She just didn't have it. What she wanted was a club where she could be the queen. Oh, I know, they all say they's in it for the "love of the breed."

The problem with the National Club, thank you Margaret, is they don't love the breed—a bunch of goddamn hypocrites is what they is. If they did love 'em, they wouldn't sell most of the shit they're producin', let alone breed it. Just look at most of them dogues, then look at mine. SOMEBODY'S GOT IT WRONG and it ain't me. My dogs are a breath of fresh air in a room fulla stink and I don't give a rat's ass about *the standard they is always yappin' about, because none of them know any more about it than I do—and that's the God's honest truth. I got the eyes for a FINE Bordeaux and I'd rather fly by the ass end of my pants and produce what I got, than fly by any part of any of their pants—case closed.*

The funny part is, Charlene wouldn't join no club either, neither would Pete. What Margaret did was talk the new peewee breeders into joinin' the club. They all wanted to get to where me, Pete, and Charlene had gotten to in a heartbeat. That's what Margaret promised 'em, I mean, not in those words, but it's how it came out. And, just for the record, Pete wasn't as successful as me and Charlene, but he was as well known—I'll give him that. He just didn't do the amount of producin' and sellin' that me and Charlene did.

I know, I hate admittin' Charlene was successful, but she was in her own scumbag way. She'd be in a state of shock if she heard me say this about her—well, she can KISS MY ASS, and you need to put that in there for when she reads this, just in case she gets to thinkin' things she's got no right to.

Notice I said she WAS successful 'cause, as you know, I blew her to the side just like I did Pete. All her drinkin' and druggin' and lyin' caught up with her, with my help. 'Course, I had to be careful of her husband, now ex-husband, Gabe. He was, and still is, far as I know, one nasty motherfucker—and if you ain't noticed I don't generally use that particular word, but in this case, I got no choice. He's the reason not a few of Charlene's dogues ended up in fightin' rings. And he was the main reason if she screwed someone over, no one would hold her legs—or any part of her—to the burnin' flame. Just thinkin' about that man makes the hair on the back of my neck stand up and that ain't easy.

Bobby even told me, after the first time we met Gabe, "Stella," he said, "that ain't a man we ever want to push too hard—I'm tellin' you now." BOBBY said that! And the second he said it, all them hairs that was already standin' up on my neck, damn near fell off! Bobby ain't afraid of nobody, nobody at all. I mean, it weren't for real fear in his case, it was more like self preservation. My point bein', there are some things you just don't mess with and Gabe was one of 'em. He was into breedin' and fightin' Pit Bulls, that was one of his obsessions. I seen some of his Pits one time when Bobby and I decided to do a little spyin' on Charlene—and I will tell you those dogs was built like bricks!

Gabe did not fuck around, no sir.

The scariest part about him is he was squeaky clean on the outside—looked like a clean-cut regular business man type. I mean, you know how they say Hitler didn't drink, or sleep around, didn't eat meat, all those things that mighta made you think he was an upstandin' citizen? Well, you know how that turned out. Gabe, now he didn't touch alcohol or drugs neither, it was like a religion to him and when he talked, well, it was like someone on the inside was makin' damn sure he didn't blow his cover—it's hard to explain, but I saw it clear as day—Bobby did too. He may have acted real high functionin' and all, but the truth was, he was one itty bitty screw away from bein' a total psycho, and Bobby and I wasn't interested in loosenin' that screw.

His other obsession, outside of fightin' Pits, was plannin' the NEW AMERICA—as in a country full of the likes of him. And I'll have you know it wasn't easy diggin' up this bit of information 'cause it was top secret, as in Charlene didn't even know about it. I got my ways though—and God help us is all I got to say!

Now, I got my prejudices, as in I'm prejudice against anybody who tries to screw me over. And, in my way of thinkin', the best way to take care of them people is by bein' smarter and richer—you know, smile at 'em as you drive by in a Mercedes and laugh all the way to the bank.

Take that cab driver for instance—'educated' trash like him ain't worth thinkin' twice about. There's no way I woulda wasted my time yellin' at him and that's the part you need to understand, otherwise you'll screw up my book.

But, Gabe, he spends his life thinkin' about trash and plottin' to kill trash. 'Course his idea of trash just ain't right. I know the difference between trash and dignified human bein's—he don't. All he sees is red just thinkin' about anybody who ain't the same as him. He's a white boy with a giant stick up his ass that's got nothin' to do with anythin' but *what a sorry ass he is—ain't nobody's fault but his own, is all I got to say. I mean, the only way he can live with hisself is to think about riddin' the world of so-called garbage. The funny thing is, some of that same garbage is exactly what Charlene sold a lotta her dogs to, which has created a big problem for this breed. That particular garbage is garbage, I'm in agreement with him on that.*

Well, I got a newsflash for him. He needs to bring his mission back to maybe shootin' his own self in the head and riddin' hisself and the world of his miserable self. Now, I'm not sayin' I want him dead 'cause that's not the way I am. There's not a lot I won't do to people who screw with me, but for real death? Well, that just ain't my job now, is it? I can't say I don't have days where I feel like takin' a gun and shootin' a whole lotta people, but that's a feelin' that I ain't never gonna do for real, 'cause I don't want to end up in a place a million times worse than Cupcake. My whole point with Gabe is I think he'd just feel better if he shot hisself. I mean look at the hell he's livin' in. He's so twisted he can't turn around without seein' someone he'd like to kill. And look what he does with them Pit Bulls of his!

Do you have any idea what those fightin' rings sound like?—dogs fightin' and dyin' while people is cheerin' and booin.' Now, that I think about it, people who do that are right up there at the top of that list of WORST PEOPLE ALIVE. Leave the animals out of it. That's God's number one rule and I agree with it. People killin' each other ain't nothin' next to screwin' with the animals. That line, right there, should never be crossed over, NEVER. And just so you know, I don't care if his mama made him eat turkey shit—rules is rules— and God put that one in place a long, long time ago. Now, I know he just might kill me if he reads all about hisself in my book, and I can't think of a worse way to go than by his hands, but oh well, the truth is the truth—somebody's got to speak up for the animals.

Now, the reason I brought that bit about me not carin' if his mama made him eat turkey shit is 'cause you mentioned somewhere, that you heard Charlene was beat-up real bad by her mama. And between you mentionin' that AND the tone of your voice, I knew right then and there you was one of them 'bleedin' heart' types.

In fact, now that I'm thinkin' on it that may be one of the reasons I decided to go on ahead and be the one to introduce her. All them details about Charlene, includin' the ones that ain't been mentioned yet, have to be up to me to tell the readin' public 'cause if you was to go on and talk to her, then write it down, you would be misrepresentin' her in my book.

The point bein' that you'd get all messed up with your bleedin' heart and say things that ain't true, meanin' believe everythin' she tells you. And just so you know there are people, and Charlene's at the top of that list, who will get your bleedin' heart number and say things just to yank your collar into their way of seein' things.

Fact is, I'm thinkin' you been yanked around like that for a whole lotta your life and the really sad fact is you ain't alone, not by a long shot. I'll never get it, but I know it's true.

Charlene will smell out your bleedin' heart and do what's necessary. Now, you can't blame her for that 'cause that's what life is all about, playin' the game, and she's damned good at it—or WAS for a little bitty while. Then she blew it and now everybody knows her true colors.

See, the only reason she put that information out about her mama beatin' the crap outta her when she was little—oh my heart bleeds—was 'cause she knew she would suck in people like you, in a New York second. And why do you think she never bothered to tell me that? 'Cause I don't give a rat's ass. People like yourself will suck it up and before you know it, you ain't seein' her true nature, which is a lyin', manipulatin' bitch. Oh well, God made you that way for some damn reason—he ain't never explained that one to me, probly 'cause he knows I ain't never gonna see eye to eye with him on that.

Now, I don't expect you to believe me, but Charlene don't care what her mama did to her, it's over and done far as she's concerned, but she sure-as-shit knows you do.

Let's just stop here for one second—why do you care what her mama did to her? It don't change who she is in the present moment. I mean, if she pulled a knife on you and told you all *about her mama beatin' her while she was cuttin' you, would you just lie there and shed a tear for her? Don't answer that 'cause I ain't interested in hearin' the WRONG answer.*

Take them speed bump people for instance, their hearts is bleedin' for the well bein' of people who are laughin' all the way to the suicide bomb department store—those bastards are laughin' as they cut the heads off innocent people! Why aren't those speed bump people mad about that? I'll tell you why, because they have been sucked into a 'Bleedin' Heart Scam.' Those speed bumps are weepin' for the likes of people who would hold a damn party if they was blown up or even worse, tortured to death. It ain't pretty out here in the real world. Bottom line is, people will do whatever is necessary to get what they want—and that goes for every walk of life— and like I said, it ain't never a walk.

Now, where was I? Oh, yeah, Charlene and her lyin' self!

Did you know back when I was in Cupcake, she didn't have one Bordeaux, not one?! They was all figs of her imagination. I know that for a fact. When I went to Europe to pick up my first Bordeaux, it was durin' the same time she was there, and it was her first trip! Almost every breeder I talked to over there, and I talked to most of 'em, had seen her within a couple of days or weeks of seein' me, and a few of the crap breeders had seen her and sold her some dogs. Now, what does that tell you about her? She'd been advertisin', big time, for almost a year and didn't even have no dogs yet—and the ones she did finally get were all from crap kennels. She was usin' pictures of dogs that got sent to her from God-knows- where, and she was usin' pictures of somebody else's property pretendin' all them fields and fences was hers. God knows, I shoulda known somethin' was wrong when I didn't see any Dogues in them fields! And she didn't once show a actual picture of her "air conditioned kennel" which, as it turned out, was a big sloppy barn that had no heat or air conditionin'.

What she did was take deposits from people wantin' pet quality dogs 'cause they're the ones who will sit on their ass and wait without askin' questions. She took them deposits and when she had enough of 'em went off to Europe, bought some pregnant bitches, some pups, and some dogs—ones none of them Europeans gave a damn about—and started sellin' and producin'. And I will tell you right now, she ain't the only one pullin' that kind of crap. Just like I told you, it ain't pretty out here in the REAL world.

One difference between me and Charlene—one of a billion—was at least I was willin' to spend a whole lot for the dogs I bought. I went over to Europe with ten times more money than her 'cause I knew Europeans aren't no different from us, as in they want exactly what we want if we is gonna let go of anythin' worth while—which is BIG BUCKS! I also went over there with a hell of a motivator walkin' right next to me the whole time, that bein' to put everybody over here under me, startin' with Charlene. She started the fight, like I told you, and I was gonna finish it.

Now, since we don't got a photograph of Charlene to show the readin' public and because I don't want one in my book, I will just go on and tell 'em to imagine the ugliest bull-doggy lookin' face a woman can have, put her flappy, lumpy I-ain't-been-doin'-shit-but-gettin'-drunk ass in a pair of them three-quarter length spandex tight-as-all-hell pants and cover 'em with so much dog hair it looks like she's got a 100% mohair wrapped around her legs till you get up real close and see the truth. Then put one of them polyester sweaters on her, one that's one of them colors from a circus and make it real tight, as in too small. Throw a bunch of bleach in her dried out hair—make sure the roots is loud and clear—and that's her—and you know that's the truth seein' as you've met her.

Like I said, God knows why anyone would believe anythin' she says when talkin' to her in person. She ain't like her ads was, you know, havin' you believin' she had a hell of a thing goin' on. No sir, she is hard to look at from the get-go. Now, I ain't prejudice against ugly unless the inside matches the outside—and hers does, end of story.

So, that's my introduction of Charlene Peets and I hope you got every word 'cause I ain't doin' it again. And just so she don't think she's important or anythin', I'm gonna tell her right here, that I'm just usin' her as an example of how to introduce people to the readin' public. I figure why not start with her—and Gabe—since they is one of the nastiest examples of humans on this earth, meanin' the bottom of the bucket.

You ain't never gonna have the inclination to describe those kinds of people 'cause you don't got the stomach for it, but it's real important that the readin' public know the likes of them are livin' out here in the REAL world.

Now, I ain't gonna be introducin' anybody else. That's your job. So, here's where I'm actually gonna suggest you DO track down Annie—and when and if you find her A) tell me where she is, B) tell her I sent you 'cause that'll keep her honest, if you know what I mean.

Fact is, she met a couple of these dogue people, or maybe it was only Margaret, I can't remember. Annie never went to any shows 'cause she wasn't interested in that end of things. But Margaret, she visited us 'bout a thousand times while Annie was still livin' here with me—damn near drove us both nuts. Sometimes I left the two of them talkin' right here in this kitchen when I'd had enough of Margaret hangin' on my every word.

Goddamn, where the hell is that joint I just rolled?

See, just thinkin' about them two blabbing at this table, all them years ago, makes me drop things I don't usually drop. The good ole days is what I woulda called 'em if things had turned out different with Annie.

Anyway, she was a lot different than me, as in she'd sit here and blah, blah, blah with Margaret for hours. She didn't like her anymore than I did, but she said Margaret was "interesting." Fact is, Annie could find a ROCK interestin'. My whole point bein', I'm sure she could help you in introducin' Margaret and herself—'cause in thinkin' on it, seein' as Annie was a part of my life, I guess she'll have to be in my book somewhere.

Oh, yeah, and she also met Tiffany once durin' that time she was here after she came crawlin' back and before she ran off with my dogs. She never met any of the others, but I'm tellin' you, if there's one thing she's good at, it's readin' and writin'. After she ran off that first time, she musta wrote me a thousand letters durin' the eighteen months she was gone.

Yessiree, that girl can write some fine letters, but you ain't seein' any of 'em, cause they's private—case closed.

As much as I hate her for betrayin' me, I gotta say she could help you with a bunch of stuff regardin' my book. Hell, she could turn around and write it in a bunch of different languages, make it international. She could sit here at this table and talk to three people, each of 'em from a different country. It never happened, but it coulda 'cause she knew three different languages—hell, it coulda been six, only that was just too amazin' to me so I only remember the three. You'll have to ask Bobby about that. Yup, she was the educated one in this family and I was the smart one—I mean ex-family—end of that little story.

Anyway, no sense in talkin' about it 'cause you ain't gonna find her. I'm guessin' she's gone a long ways away, like she did the first time she ran off. That time it was Greece. This time, like I already told you, it's probly China or Africa—so good luck!

Margaret Appleman
(Founder and Secretary of the American Bordeaux Club)

Margaret Appleman leaned forward and gripped the steering wheel of her lime green Gremlin. A victorious sneer slipped from her lips as she shifted her large frame and settled back into the seat. It had been a good day, even quite possibly a great day. She'd met twelve new people at the Rare Breed show and ten were ready and willing to join her National Bordeaux club. All of them were innocents who'd never been to a Bordeaux specialty before and all had purchased Bordeaux pups within the last year. Incredibly, she'd even gotten a few familiar though resistant faces to concede to join.

She hiccupped as her victory sneer grew broader. The parade in her head was going full tilt, drums rolling, trumpets tooting, people cheering. It was all so perfect until the stark images of Stella and Charlene smacked her from within her rearview mirror.

Stella spoke. "I ain't interested in any damn club, Margaret. I got me all I need and I'm already at the head of it. What would your club have to offer me? Nothin'. What do I got to offer you? Everythin'. Case closed, but thanks anyways."

Before Charlene could speak, Margaret's mind leapt further back in time.

"If we can't hit Margaret, we couldn't hit the broadside of a barn! HAHAHHA."

"You're just a nosey nerd, Margie. You may be smart, but you're not intelligent and never will be."

"Margaret can't produce half the caliber her mother could produce."

As the laughter and voices screeched through her head, her grip on the wheel increased ten fold and her once pink, fleshy knuckles were depleted of all color.

She reached up and smacked the mirror to the side. She would show them all what Margaret Appleman was about! It was just a matter of time before she'd reel in Stella, Charlene, and anyone else who posed a threat to her plan. The key was in the numbers. The more people she got on board, the more pressure it would put on the 'big bananas' to join. It was as simple as that. She snickered at the private nickname she'd given them as she reached up and adjusted the mirror back to its correct position.

She glanced at the clock on her dashboard. It was 6 p.m. She wanted to be home by 10. If she drove straight through, she could do it. That would give her time to get started on her newsletter which would detail the show and its winners. No one had ever done this for the Bordeaux in the U.S. She was the first. She was fast, efficient, and willing to put in the effort. Now she was headed to where she wanted to be, at the helm of the Bordeaux Information Network. It was all so similar to when she was in high school and made her way to the position of chief editor of the school newspaper. Once she got there, she was mistreated no more. It was a wonderful feeling, a feeling she'd been wanting back for fifteen years. This time, however, it was not self-defense that motivated her. This time she simply craved it.

She reached up, pulled the thick hairpin from her dark brown bun, and let her hair fall freely down over her shoulders. As she put the hairpin on the passenger seat, she eyed the pile of yellow notepads. Not only had she taken details of the winning dogues and their owners as she'd done at every show over the past year and a half, but she'd also taken voluminous notes on each of the new people she met. This had been the missing piece. She needed to make each person feel important by asking them a slew of questions, jotting things down, all the while complimenting their dogs, their clothes, their vehicles, whatever worked to get them to open up and step up to her plate. It wasn't easy, as the importance of other people was not high on her list of things to think about, but she did what she now knew she had to do. She then, of course, gave each of them her address and phone number, and told them she was the person to contact for the latest national and worldwide information on the Bordeaux.

Margaret pressed harder on the gas pedal feeling momentarily overwhelmed by all she had to do. Aside from the newsletter and recruiting potential members, she had to get to work on her communications with the European breeders and judges. It was a huge task!

She took a deep breath and slowly managed to turn the feeling of being overwhelmed into one of excitement and anticipation. She eased up on the gas, released the wheel with her right hand, and patted the yellow notepads. This was her chance to get it all back, and then some.

Her thoughts turned to Frank. He was at home, probably cooking up a tasty meal that he would heat and serve to her when she got there. Or else he was diligently working on setting up the new computer he'd bought her. Oh, how glad she was to have met him. As it turned out—thank God—he was exactly what she had been looking for in a man. He owned two new car dealerships and soon would own another, making more than enough money for her to pursue her dreams, unfettered by financial distress. She never wanted kids and he was fine with that. All that mattered to him was to be with her and that was music to her ears! There would be no road blocks put up by him. He was perfect and she couldn't wait to get home to him.

She settled into a steady 65 mph as her excitement leveled out to the status of calm conviction. Her thoughts traveled back to the show. They were probably having their dinner now and listening to the judge, Monsieur Pierre Lemont, talk about the breed standard and the breed's future. He had picked one of Pete Strate's dogs for Best of Breed which, she just knew, had sent both Stella and Charlene around the bend—something she took great pleasure in thinking about. However, Pete, who under normal circumstances would be seated next to the judge at the table, wouldn't be there because he'd left the show as soon as it was over, visibly shaken.

She, of course, had followed Pete and managed to snag him as he was loading his dogs into his van. No one else seemed to have noticed or cared, which was typical of these people as they were all so self-involved. He was clearly relieved to see that someone actually gave a damn and so laid it all right out to her. He said Charlene had gotten one of her "low life buddies" to try to poison his dogs while he was in the bathroom. He didn't bother to explain how he knew this or any of the details—he didn't want to take the time. Then he said, heatedly, that this was "possibly the last straw." He went on to say he was sorry this breed was starting out in this country in the hands of such "unscrupulous people." He said he could see the writing on the wall and was fully prepared to leave the breed for good. Then he was gone.

Her foot pressed the pedal a little harder. Now this was just the kind of thing that set Margaret's blood all ablaze—in a good way. She was learning all the 'dirt' and, oh, how the dirt was piling up! She considered it fertilizer, grist for the mill, the grit that would become the concrete that would pave her way to exactly where she wanted to be.

Her foot eased again as her thoughts turned to Charlene and Stella. They were a big concern. Neither one liked the other, which was a good thing, but neither one liked her either. They never said anything outright to her, but she could tell from the tone they took with her, plus they barely gave her the time of day at a show, except to ask her questions about any new people on the scene or any 'gossip' she'd heard. She always obliged them in hopes to get an in, but somehow it never worked that way. They always got what they wanted and she came up empty handed. There were not a few people who had said to her, "For some reason Stella and Charlene just don't like you, Margaret. Why is that?"

Margaret would simply shrug her shoulders and smile like it made no difference to her. But inside, well, that was another story. Margaret had what one could call inner tantrums at moments like that. Those tantrums could last minutes, or even days, but rarely, if ever, were they visible to the unaccustomed eye, which turned out to be most people.

The art of covering them up was something she had taught herself years ago.

As the Green Gremlin scurried along the pike, Margaret thought back to the horrible days with her mother at the AKC dog shows. Those Boxers were everything, while she, Margaret, was merely the water girl, the food girl, the "stay out of the way and respect your elders" girl. When she was ten she wanted desperately to show one of their prize dogs, My Best Boy, in the ring at Westminster. She'd been practicing with each of the dogs in their yard since she was five and with My Best Boy, in particular, for several months. However, her mother declared her unfit for the job. She told Margaret there would never come a day when she would be pretty enough or graceful enough to be in that ring with her dogs.

As it turned out My Best Boy won Best in Group and, when he did, her mother snatched Margaret into her arms, cheering, tears streaming down her face and declared, "You see? If you had been in there with him, it would have been a disaster!"

Looking back on it, all her mother had to say was she was too young to show at Westminster. It would have been the kinder thing to do. But no, not her mother—mother? The word had no meaning to Margaret.

Her head started to throb so, once again, she pushed the rearview mirror away. The headlights were only adding insult to injury. Her usual cure for this kind of headache was a soothing hot shower, followed by a very milky cup of tea, but clearly that wasn't going to happen for at least a couple of hours.

She flipped on the radio to her favorite "pillow talk soft rock" station. She was tone deaf, something her mother never let her forget, but she didn't care. She bellowed out every word of every song, her large frame heaving back and forth, but the Gremlin stayed steady.

———

Margaret's mother died suddenly when Margaret was a senior in high school. She simply dropped dead one morning while taking a shower. Many claimed her death was due to a broken heart because My Best Boy, who had lived to be fifteen, had died just a month earlier. The two of them had been nearly inseparable. Whenever possible, Boy was at her side. He even slept in her bed most nights, ultimately forcing Margaret's dad to sleep elsewhere. Like clockwork, Margaret would be awakened by her father's voice as it echoed down the marble floored hallway. It was always the same: "Why do we have to sleep with that dog, he always manages to either crush my legs or force me into a fetal position!" Then, there would be a brief silence followed by "Why can't he sleep in that kennel that we spent one hundred thousand dollars on? Christ, it's better than most peoples' houses!" Her mother would say something that was never quite audible to Margaret. Then her father would announce "I have had enough!" The next thing Margaret would hear was her father moving down the hallway and slamming the door to one of the many, rarely used guest rooms.

Oh, how Margaret had grown to hate those Boxers, and Boy in particular. After he'd taken the Best in Group at Westminster, whenever he was left in her care, she would 'forget' to feed him and 'forget' to exercise him, except to drag him around the circumference of their kennel allowing him to smell all the bitches. Once he got riled up, she'd yank on his leash and yell and scream at him.

Then there was one afternoon when she tied him to a tree with his choke collar on, right across from May-Belle, who was in standing heat. Margaret was eleven at the time, and all the while Boy was struggling to break free and get to May-Belle, she sat comfortably in a wicker lounge chair, sucking a lollipop, and reading *All About Reptiles*. The cover of the book had a photo of a pale green chameleon crawling across a branch of pale green leaves, one eye looking forward and the other keeping watch behind. Oh, how she wished she could do that, and how magical it would be to be able to change one's colors to blend with one's surroundings!

It was only when the furious barking and gagging fell suddenly silent that she looked up from her book and saw Boy lying lifeless on the ground. She panicked, fully aware of the wrath that would befall her if he were dead. She dropped *All About Reptiles* and rushed to Boy's side. She quickly untied the leash from the tree.

At that precise moment, over and above the loud clanging of her desperation, she heard the familiar soft, low rumble of her mother's Mercedes as it pulled into the driveway. Nothing would ever block that out, ever.

She quickly unhooked the long lead from Boy's taut and lifeless neck, shoved it into the back of her pants, and reattached the short lead. She then knelt down beside him and began to shake him, all the while allowing agonizing shrieks to escape from her lungs.

Her mother, upon hearing the horrifying shrieks when she stepped from her car, kicked off her precious florescent blue heels and sprinted across the yard towards them. Margaret had never seen her move like that. By the time she reached them, Boy was gagging. His breath had returned.

Margaret turned to her mother who had dropped to her knees beside her. She was in so much distress she couldn't utter a sound. She threw her arms around her mother's neck. "Oh Mother, it was awful. I was playing ball with Boy, like we always do, and suddenly he just fell down and stopped breathing." She gripped her mother's neck ever tighter. "I was so scared, Mother, so scared."

"Margaret, will you let go of me before you strangle me! I have to get Boy to the vet immediately!" She sharply unhooked her daughter's arms and helped Boy to his feet. "Now, run and get his purple collar and meet me at the car!" She pushed Margaret towards the house, never once allowing her attention to leave her Boy.

Thousands of dollars and dozens of diagnostic tests later, Boy was pronounced healthy and the incident was left unexplained.

Her mother's death had a dreadful effect on Margaret. After all, she was the one who found the crumpled body on the bathroom floor, the blonde hair streaked with blood from the gash in her head. She was the one who sat in silence beside the body, unable to utter a word, riveted to what seemed almost like a grin on her mother's face. It was their maid, Christina, who found them there and it was Christina's screams that broke the silence.

———

The Green Gremlin left the pike and headed down Route 20 towards home.

———

That had been a very cold day for Margaret. And it was an even colder day when she found out she'd inherited her mother's entire kennel operation. Her father, however, was thrilled. It never occurred to him that perhaps she would rather have gone to college. All he cared about was that the kennel wasn't his problem to deal with. He'd never been interested in the dogs. He'd never gone to any shows and barely lifted an eyebrow at the dog's successes. In fact, he barely lifted an eyebrow at Margaret's successes. Her straight A's all through school, the prize science project in sixth grade, her achievement as chief editor of the school paper in high school, none of it raised his brow. The most she got was a pat on the shoulder while his head was buried in the *Wall Street Journal* or other work related reading.

For the next eight years after her mother's death, Margaret stayed in her parents' home. Her father's business had begun to crumble, which took him away for long stints in search of a way to rectify things. So, faced with what seemed like no choice at all, she plunged headlong into the work her mother had left her and, like anything she put her mind to, she became fiercely determined to succeed at it. She not only wanted to produce more 'Boys' but wanted to eventually have a kennel full of better-than-Boys Boxers, thus making a name for herself in the AKC world.

She kept up with her mother's circle of friends which meant sacrificing the few she had made on her own. She tried to blend in and get from them what she could to make her "plan" happen but, somehow, despite how efficient and knowledge-able she became, she was never considered on the same level as her mother had been. And no matter how hard she tried, she could never breed the right combination of Boxers to produce even close to what her mother had produced.

It was at what would turn out to be her final Westminster Show that Margaret met Frank. He was a curious onlooker perusing the breeds behind the scenes, in search of a good guard dog. He'd been drawn from the Rottweiller area of the hall to Margaret and her Boxers because one of her young males was raising an enormous stink over a man wearing sunglasses and carrying an umbrella. The man was vehemently expressing his distaste for her dog's behavior as Margaret frantically tried to explain to him that the dog was young and in need of more socialization. She couldn't calm him down and the unspoken disgust of the breeders around her was palpable.

Frank walked over and calmly explained to the man that the only reason she had the dog there at all, was because he'd asked her to bring him and that, in fact, he was buying the dog for twenty thousand dollars. At which point, he pulled his checkbook from his pocket and asked that the man to please excuse them while he completed the transaction.

Margaret was dumbstruck. No one had ever given her that kind of attention, not ever. That was the warmest moment of her life, thus far. She basked victoriously in the commotion and mutterings that spread throughout the hall when Frank handed her a check for twenty thousand dollars. Her ten-month-old, unknown, unchampioned Boxer was being treated like royalty. Even more importantly, she was being treated like royalty. This man of average stature and unimpressive looks, who was dressed impeccably in a silky dark suit, white shirt, and pale yellow tie, then told her to hang onto the dog. He said he would be back at the end of the day to collect him.

The check was real and Frank did come back. No, he was not the handsome man she had hoped would one day come her way, but she quickly cast that illusive expectation to the wind and grabbed hold of the golden ring while it was right there in front of her. Her father's business had gone belly up, unknown to everyone, and they were on the edge of losing their house and everything that went with it. Frank was her opportunity to get out and move on.

Within a month they were married and all the Boxers were sold, including the young male that Frank had bought from her. She was finally free from all the people who had never appreciated her and all the work she had put into something she had never wanted to do in the first place.

She moved with Frank from Englewood, New Jersey, to New Bedford, Massachusetts, where Frank had recently become the owner of his first car dealership, something that had been his goal since he was fourteen years old and lying on his back beneath car after car after car in his father's auto shop. He had even agreed to sell his current modest home and buy one that was to her liking.

And she did, indeed, find the perfect house. It was not a sprawling New England Tudor mansion like the one she had grown up in. She didn't want that, which was fortunate for Frank because he had not yet achieved the success that could have afforded it. What she wanted, and what she got, was a mid-sized contemporary redwood house that jutted out from the side of a mountain and overlooked a major highway. She loved seeing the traffic and, at the same time, being far above it, so far above it that the sound was nothing more than a soft rumble. Frank said he would have preferred a lake or river, but after she explained to him the marvelous feeling it gave her, he understood completely. And so, Margaret began the job of decorating her new home, fully convinced this was all that stood between her and complete and utter contentment.

First, she got rid of all the furnishings Frank had moved from his old house. Of course, he was horrified, but when she explained to him that the furnishings were sad reminders to her of his years of working so hard and having so little, he immediately and happily conceded. Then, she began the work of replacing them with what she wanted. It was during this process that she discovered how much she had hated the house she had grown up in. All that marble and leather, just thinking of it made her feel cold and empty.

She frantically, though meticulously, filled her living room with voluptuous sage upholstered chairs, matching sofa, glass-topped coffee table, brass-on-wood grandfather clock, and set it all on a plush cream carpet. Her bedroom was similarly plush with a king-size Victorian bed, oak drawers, a lounging chair with ottoman, and all of it done in the same color scheme. There were no mirrors, except for the one in the master bath. She wanted it that way. Mirrors had never done anything other than create tension within her.

She busied herself, that whole year, trying to create a world that was entirely hers. She literally broke into a cold sweat over every decision for fear it would be the wrong one and, as a result, her world would fall away from her. On the rare occasions that Frank was with her, he would try to ease her tension by saying, "Honey, we can always bring it back." But that didn't help her at all. She didn't want to make one single mistake because, if she did, the time between the mistake and when she was able to right it was unbearable. She couldn't sleep, she could barely think, she was caught in a continual inner tremor that would not leave her alone. Those were the times when she was unhappy with Frank. She hated the way he ate, the way he talked, his friends, his work, etc. But the moment things were 'right' again, those things didn't bother her anymore and she could let him hold her and adore her.

Margaret's life took an unexpected turn the day after her home was completed. It was a Sunday morning and she was sprawled comfortably across one of the upholstered chairs. Her stocky legs were crossed and dangling off one of the thick soft arms, her back leaning up against the other, her brown hair neatly bound and stabbed upon her head. She was reading an article in *People Magazine* on Princess Diana. As she read, she became increasingly upset, even enraged at how the princess and the whole royal family, for that matter, had done nothing to get where they were except be born with the right blood or marry the right blood. They had done nothing and there they were, especially Diana, in every magazine, week after week after week!

She turned the page, smacked the open magazine down on her lap and put her full attention on her surroundings, all the while taking deep breaths to calm herself. She had put so much effort into this house, so much effort into everything she had ever done and no one, absolutely no one, noticed or cared.

She glanced down at the freshly turned page of *People.* There, right in front of her, was a full half page photo of Diana, dressed from head to toe in red—even a red purse. On her head was a crown of jewels. On her face was her usual shy and innocent expression, an expression that served only to reinforce the voice that was screaming through Margaret's head, *"The bitch has done nothing and look at her! Just look at her!"*

Margaret took a deep, trembling breath and glanced down at the caption beneath the photo. It read, "The queen of the people's hearts." As she read it, the wind was suddenly knocked from her chest and she gasped in the silence of her plush living room. She was utterly alone, no one could see her and everything she had done this past year was for naught. In fact, everything she had done, thus far in her life, was for naught.

Her hands leapt from their resting place on her lap and dealt a fast and crushing blow to the photo before her. *THE QUEEN OF THE PEOPLE'S HEARTS, THE QUEEN OF THE PEOPLE'S HEARTS, THE QUEEN OF THE PEOPLE'S HEARTS!*

Margaret was on her belly gagging and coughing into the soft carpet. The coughs soon turned to a hollow cry that repeated itself over and over. "I never asked for this, I never asked for this, I never asked for this, I never asked for this."

The neat bun had moved precariously over to the side of her head and the hairpin was fast losing its grip. When the cry finally died, a new one moved in and, as it did, her open hands curled into fists. "I AM THE GODDAMN QUEEN, I AM THE QUEEN, I AM THE QUEEN."

Her chubby fists pounded the thick carpet, which was when the hairpin finally lost its grip and fell from her head, leaving her hair completely undone.

Margaret Appleman ceased and lay rigid, face down on the floor. The seconds that followed were seconds that dragged on for an eternity. Her mind had spun into chaos and the sweat poured from her armpits. A decision had to be made and, in this case, a mistake would definitely bring on her worst fear.

The soft low rumble of the car engines below made its way up across her balcony, through the open glass doors to where she lay on the floor. The familiar sound brought with it a flash of her mother emerging from the Mercedes, the precious blue heels flying through the air as she ran fast and furiously towards her Best Boy.

Margaret rolled fiercely from her belly onto her knees and picked up the Red Princess who lay crumpled on the floor beside her. A long low gurgling sound came from her throat as she gathered what was necessary to annihilate the pretentious Queen of Hearts. "I am the Queen of Hearts, you bitch!" As soon as she said it, the massive wad of saliva flew from her mouth and landed square on the crown of jewels.

She watched, riveted, as the saliva, her saliva, dripped down across the shy and innocent face. The tremors in her body had stopped. She was finally breathing freely.

Right at that moment the front door opened and Frank's passive lean body walked in. He put his briefcase down. "Hon, I got off early—thought we could do something fun to celebrate your birthday."

Margaret looked up at Frank, who still hadn't seen her, probably because she was on her knees. She had completely forgotten it was her birthday. How odd, she thought. She quickly picked up the crumpled, moist picture of the princess, stuffed it in the pocket of her housedress and stood up. "Frank, honey, that is so sweet of you to have remembered." She brushed her hair back behind her shoulders and smoothed her dress.

Frank had heard the crumpling of paper and turned just as she was getting up from the floor. "Pumpkin, what are you doing?" He approached her and saw that she'd been crying. "My God, what's wrong? Did you think I had forgotten?"

Margaret wiped her eyes with the skirt of her house dress and stepped towards Frank. "Well, I had hoped you hadn't forgotten."

Frank moved in and put his arms around her. "Oh, honey, I would never forget such an important day!"

Margaret rested her chin on Frank's bony shoulder; one hand was in the pocket of her house dress clenching the crumpled paper that was the princess. "It's just so hard. I haven't heard from my father since we married, I have no brothers or sisters, I've only made a few inconsequential friends through you, and I've been so caught up in making the house just right that I've lost track of everything."

Frank patted her on the back. He never dreamed he'd be married. It was something that he had assumed just wouldn't happen. He was the fourth of four boys and he was the least attractive, by far. The scars on his face leftover from terrible acne as a teenager plus his inability to fill out, despite the fact he was plenty strong, had forced him early on to the conclusion that a wife was just not in his future. Margaret was a miracle to him. She had accepted him completely, from the start. Yes, she got irritable with him, even angry at times, but he could always make it 'right' and he was proud and grateful to her for that. He did wish she would change her mind about kids, but it wouldn't be the end of the world if they never had them. He hugged her tightly. "I have something for you but you have to come outside to see it." He released her and smiled triumphantly.

Margaret looked at Frank. She released the crumpled princess from her grip, spread both hands out on either side of his face, leaned in, and kissed him. He was wonderful. She had forgotten her own birthday and here he was to remind her and make it right. "Frank, you are a doll. Let me get out of this robe and I'll come outside with you." She gave his face a quick squeeze, released him and walked swiftly to the bedroom.

Once in her favorite blue and white cotton dress, Margaret stepped into the master bath and looked into the mirror. As she studied her face, something she rarely did, it became clear to her that things had to change. She twisted her fallen brown hair back up into a tight bun, stabbed it with a fresh hairpin and splashed cold water on her face. As the water dripped down her cheeks, she vowed tears would not fall from her face again—at least not any time soon.

———

Margaret left Route 20 and headed up the mountain to her house. That was her thirty-third birthday and one she would never forget. When she walked out the door that day with Frank, his gift was sitting in the driveway wrapped in a large red ribbon. It was her lovely green Gremlin—the very one she was driving. Though the Gremlin had long been off the market, Frank had managed to find one and refurbish it to near brand new.

It had been during one of their more intimate moments, the first year they were together, that Margaret told him she was taken with the Gremlin as a young girl. It was unlike any car she had ever seen. Its shape was simple and funny and the colors—orange, bright blue, and particularly the lime green, or chameleon as she liked to call it—were simply magical to her. They still were.

She was so shocked when she saw it that her recent bloodless battle with the princess retreated rapidly into the recesses of her mind. She rushed to touch the shiny green.

As she did this, Frank marched triumphantly to the hood of the car and raised it. Inside, he pointed out, was the spanking new engine of a Porsche.

It was perfect. He really did understand her and knowing that made her delirious with joy. She threw her arms around his neck and squeezed him so tightly that he nearly lost his breath.

But that was not all.

Frank unhooked her arms from around his neck and opened the driver's side door.

Margaret took a sudden step back.

On the seat sat a wrinkled, amber colored, blue-eyed pup. She was speechless. Her mind was reeling. Was this some kind of a joke? How could he possibly think she would want a puppy? "Frank, not a puppy! I can't possibly take this on after all I've been through with dogs!"

Frank stepped in beside her. "I knew you might feel this way, but think about it! This is the perfect dog for you. It's not a part of the world you were once involved in, it's not an AKC breed, plus you will have a wonderful companion who will protect you."

The pup and Margaret locked eyes. The pup didn't jump up or bark the way a Boxer pup might have. They stared at each other until the pup finally gave in and lowered itself into a lying position, then planted its head between its front paws and released a long, low sigh. A Boxer pup would never have done that. It felt disturbingly unfamiliar to her. She was intrigued. "Well, what kind of dog is it, Frank?"

Frank struggled a bit with the correct French pronunciation. "Dog de Bordeaux."

"Well, I've never heard of that breed, or maybe I have in passing, and I'll bet my mother never knew of it either." Now that was a thought that appealed to her.

She turned back to the blue eyes that were peering up at her from beneath raised brows. She reached in and lifted the pup off the seat. "It's a girl," she declared.

The pup was still focused on Margaret's face and its chunky little body remained completely relaxed despite the tension emanating from Margaret's hands. The dissonance between them threatened to cause Margaret to drop the dangling pup, so she quickly placed it back onto the seat. "I don't know, Frank. What am I going to do with her?"

"You're going to take care of her, and when she grows up, she will protect you and take care of you. You know how I've always wanted a guard dog. Remember, honey? That's how we first met."

Frank did not want to plead with her, but he couldn't contain himself. "We're not going to have kids, so why not? You know everything there is to know about dogs, maybe not this breed in particular, but you'll learn, I know you will. Your whole life, except this past year, has been about dogs."

The pup hunkered back down into the seat and sighed yet again.

Margaret took a few steps back, to the edge of the driveway, and took in the whole picture—the green Gremlin with the Porsche engine and a pup of a pure breed that her mother had probably never heard of lying right there in the driver's seat. Could it be that Frank had given her the perfect gift? "Are there any books on this breed?" she blurted. "Where did you get her? I would hope it was not a pet store! I need details, Frank."

This was how Margaret got her girl, Better Than Boy, aka Betty, who as it turned out, had come straight out of Stella Gale's kennel. She was not a bitch to write home about in terms of quality, even though Frank had bought her as a 'show quality,' which Stella had claimed she was.

Now, a year and a half later, she knew otherwise. She had brought this up with Stella and was promised another pup, a pup out of Oz, something she looked forward to with great enthusiasm. She hadn't gotten a specific time as to when this would happen, but she knew not to pressure Stella. However, it had been over a year since their discussion and Oz had sired quite a few litters, but still no pup was offered to her.

Stella was a force to be reckoned with in the Bordeaux world and the last thing Margaret wanted was to irritate her this early on in the game. She knew how Stella treated people who pushed her and was unwilling to go through that, not at this point in time. She would simply wait.

As Margaret drove upwards, towards her jutting hillside house, she was thrilled by the thought that her plan to found a breed club was only months away from being realized.

Greta… Greta… Greta…

Well, nobody can accuse you of havin' no wind. I thought you was just gonna describe how she looked, which is chunky with a bun on top, and tell everybody what a pain in the ass wanna-be-at-the-center-of-everythin' gossip she is. See, that didn't take long. Two sentences to be exact, which is all she's worth. 'Course you could add that all these years later, she's still the same old same old. She never bred anything worth a damn, never bought anything worth a damn, and she's still married to Frank. That's a short but sad story, now ain't it?

But what do you do? You go on and on about stuff nobody but you gives a rat's ass about. Who cares what she was readin' when she was TEN YEARS OLD?!! What does that got to do with anythin'? And the stranglin' of the dog part?— well, I gotta tell you, I stopped breathin' when I read that part. It took me damn near five minutes to recover myself and there ain't a lot that stops me for that long. If that right there is true, then she shoulda been locked up in a psycho ward a long time ago.

Did she tell you she did that?! Did she tell you she was readin' some damn book about reptiles—somethin' I ain't never been interested in, by the way—while she let that poor dog strangle itself? That speaks volumes, don't it?

I'll tell you, right now, if she told me she did that I woulda said, "Margaret, you don't deserve to be in my book." Then I woulda walked away and left her to cryin' and spittin' all over a picture of MY face. 'Course, stranglin' animals makes spittin' all over anybody's face while cryin' and crawlin' look like she just smoked some bad pot is all. But she don't smoke, so I don't know what the hell is wrong with her. It sure does explain a lot though. And, just to set the record straight, Margaret never did get a pup back from me and I'll tell you exactly why. There was nothin' wrong with that bitch I sold Frank and I am sick and tired of people usin' that particular "it don't look right" excuse to try to get more of my pups.

Also, we "big bananas," like you said she called us, had an unofficial understandin' with each other, meanin' we already had a club. She just wasn't a member is all. None of us BIG BANANAS liked each other. The fact of the matter is, a few of us hated each other's guts, but somehow without killin' each other—God only knows why that didn't happen—we managed to take turns footin' the bill for a judge to come over from Europe now and then. Whoever paid the bill got to pick the judge, that's the way it was and it worked just fine, 'cept there was no way in hell Pete's dog shoulda beat my Oz at that show, no way.

Hell, I was the one who got that judge. Why would I pay for a judge to come all the way over here if I thought he wasn't gonna pick my dog? No reason. That's the way it was supposed to work—end of story. How's that for tellin' the truth? Now that ain't somethin' you're gonna get out of too many other people in this breed, but that's exactly what you need to stick to in writin' this book—the truth.

And speakin' of the truth, if her mama produced a Boxer that got Best in Group at Westminster, then my mama was Greta Garbo! Now, I know her mama did win a Best in Breed at Westminster, I will give her that, 'cause I looked it up waay back when Margaret first started braggin' on it. Apparently, she's clean forgot we all know the truth about that little lie.

As for all that other stuff you went on and on about—which was a million more things than I wanted to know—it took me all damn day to read it, which means I won't be readin' but itty bitty bits of my book on occasion while you're writin' it. Mostly, I want to see the whole thing when you're done, right before you publish it. And at that point, just so you know, it'll be my lawyer readin' it right along with me, with a fine-tooth comb.

Anyway, back to what I was sayin' about the good ole days and our unofficial club. We had a good understandin' and Margaret, well she just had to come on in and start messin' with it. She wanted to have official this and official that, rules and more rules.

Hold on, I got to get me another joint if I'm gonna keep givin' you all this free information, 'course nothin' is free 'cept the air you breathe and some day somebody's gonna figure out how to charge for that.

OK, now where was I? Where am I? Goddamn my mind just plain stops sometimes—and let me tell you, it ain't a bad thing. It's like God comes down and says, "Stella, stop thinkin', stop talkin', and for once just enjoy yourself and all the good things you got." *Then He goes away and I come back from that little God-given moment, back to the real world where it just ain't that way. I mean, what does God know? He ain't never had to live here and sweat his ass off to survive. If I stopped thinkin' and stopped talkin' for more than the few moments God gives me, I would be dead—as in stone-cold-in-the-ground dead—or else I'd be just another nobody drivin' a Gremlin, which in my mind is worse than bein' dead.*

Anyway, Margaret runnin' around collectin' people for her club was real irritatin' and the whole idea was just plain wrong, but I wasn't no fool. When I saw she was actually gonna pull it off, I donated a bunch of money and rushed right in and joined. Anything they needed, any info, any advice about judges and breeders in Europe, I was right there givin' them my precious time. There was a lot of educatin' that needed doin' and I was gonna make damn sure I was the one that got it done.

Charlene, Pete, and the other "big bananas" took longer before they joined, which was a whole lotta not thinkin' on their parts. See, I got the ability to see the writin' on the wall and make my plans accordin'ly, they didn't have that.

And, by the way, like you wrote in that long ass bit on Margaret, Pete DID leave the breed a year after that, but it wasn't due to no attempted poisonin'—'course Charlene would do that shit in a New York minute, and maybe she did, but the point is, he saw the writin' on the wall and it said, "Pete, your time is runnin' out, so quit now. Love, Stella."

Now, I gotta get back to Margaret and her cryin' and kickin' on her livin' room floor and spittin' on Diana's photograph. There is no way in hell if I'd done that I woulda told anyone! I mean, if you did that would you tell anybody? No. So why are you writin' it? 'Course, if she did do that, it explains a lot about her. Still, it beats the crap outta me how that could be true, as in amen-true—and just so you know, don't be writin' stuff like that about me, 'cause that will be irritatin' and everybody knows exactly how I treat people who irritate me—just like Margaret said. It ain't no secret and it ain't s'pose to be a secret. I don't let nobody screw with me. I will do whatever it takes to make 'em crawl back into the hole they came out of. I will stop at nothin'—and you can write that in my book. Put it before chapter one and on the back of the book, right where my picture is gonna be.

I want the readin' public to understand exactly what I'm about from the beginnin' right on through to when they is done and turn that sucker over to take a good look at me. I ain't as good to look at as I used to be, that's for damn sure, but they won't forget me—I can guarandamntee you that. And there's somethin' else I wanna do when my book gets published, and that is find out where that punk-ass cab driver lives and send him a complimentary copy. That'll shut his ass right up.

Now, speakin' of Greta Garbo, that name has been stuck on me like glue for my whole life, at least the Greta part. Aren't you wonderin' why I said that about my mama bein' Greta Garbo—you know, when I was makin' my point about Margaret's mama and the lie regardin' her breedin' a Best in Group at Westminster—and why I named my daughter after her, then gave Annie that name? Well, maybe you're not, but I sure as hell think the readin' public might be. I mean, every other page is Greta this, Greta that.

Well, there's a reason for me obsessin' over that name. It all goes back to my mama who decided to disappear and reappear five years later—two years after my daddy died of a heart attack. Remember how I told you my mama left when I was a kid? Well, my daddy explained to me and my brother that Mama didn't "abandon" us, she was just needin' to "find herself."

Well, bein' eight years old I didn't have a goddamn clue what my daddy was talkin' about. I mean, as far as I was concerned she wasn't lost, and I said that to him as I sat on the floor cryin' my little eyes out wonderin' why it was that when she was here she was lost, and now that she was gone she was gonna be found. It made no damn sense at all.

I remember my mind spinnin' so fast I couldn't see straight. My daddy, he sat there on that big ole stuffed chair, looking about as pitiful as I'd ever seen him, which made me feel sick in my stomach. He said it was somethin' I would understand when I got older and it had to do with how much she wanted to be like Greta Garbo and be in the movies and that should make me proud.

Well, he didn't look proud. Fact was, he didn't even look like my daddy anymore—sittin' there all pasty and puffy lookin', like a damn sick hog—he scared the shit outta me. It seemed to me, I was losin' both my mama and my daddy that day.

See, Mama was obsessed with Greta Garbo from as long back as I can think. I mean, she dragged my little ass to Garbo movies so many times I lost count. 'Course I couldn't count some of that time—which is one reason I lost count. See, she took me even before I could walk which is generally a time nobody, not even me, can keep track of anything.

Anyway, apparently I kept my mouth shut for most every time we was in that theater. She said it was because I was stuck on Greta Garbo, just like her, that it was in my genes. All I remember when I was real young, as in four and five, was eatin' popcorn, pickin' at the gum on the underside of my seat, and watchin' Mama mouth the words I was sometimes hearin'. By the time I was eight and she abandoned me to go "find herself," I was actually watchin' the movies and even tryin' to memorize 'em as best I could.

I started to think of it as some kinda secret club that Mama and her friends let me in on. See, there was lots of times when a couple of her friends would come with us. They didn't bring their kids, which told me that I was somethin' special—that right there is somethin' my mama gave me.

Then when we was at home, she was always puttin' on little Greta performances for me and my brother who, by the way, never got to go to the Greta movies because she claimed it was "girls only time." Come to think of it, I believe that taught me a lot. I mean knowin' that girls had a right to their own time was not a normal state of knowin' back then and that could be exactly why I kept my mouth shut durin' the movies. She was teachin' me a lot that there was no words for—I just didn't appreciate it back then.

Do you know she had damn near memorized every Greta Garbo part from every movie? Hell, I practically know all of that shit by osmosis (it's damned amazin' that I know words like that, ain't it?).

Well, in her thinkin', becomin' a star was a far better proposition than raisin' a family. I can't blame her for thinkin' that 'cause it is a better proposition, but then she shoulda never started a family in the first place if that's what she wanted. 'Course, I wouldn't be here if she'd made that decision so I guess it wasn't all bad.

Anyway, when I was twelve, almost thirteen, she contacted my uncle who I was livin' with at the time—right here in Georgia. Well, you can imagine what I did when I heard my mama had decided to find me. I guess she got tired of findin' herself and went for a sure thing. I was mad as shit. I didn't want nothin' to do with her. First off, she never became no famous actress and that was frustratin' as all hell. I had been braggin' on her for years, as in "My mama is gonna be rich and famous—you all just got mamas who is lost." And they was jealous, which is exactly what I wanted them to be. I swear to you, there musta been a hundred girls in Atlanta who went home to their mamas every damn day and begged 'em to go find themselves.

Well, it made for a tough situation when my mama wanted me back and had nothin' but bein' poor to offer me. My uncle didn't put up any stink, which was disappointin', but I believe he was tired of me 'cause I was a hot-headed-

way-ahead-of-my-time girl, thanks to my mama. Now ain't that funny? Unlike Margaret who I know wasn't no president of her class or whatever the hell you wrote. She was one of them kids who was always tryin'—tryin' bein' the operative word—and never gettin' anywhere. ME? I had everybody at the school wishin' they was me and it didn't take no effort on my part.

Hell, I coulda been president of the whole damn school, but I didn't want it 'cause I had bigger ideas, like how I was just waitin' for that magic age of sixteen so I could take off and find the life I wanted which was gonna be a whole lot more than a school president or editor of some damn school paper. Margaret just didn't have the 'bility to look at the big picture, which was the world. I wanted the world, she wanted her schoolmates to like her. That is like comparin' a potato to a damn Arabian stallion—me bein' the stallion.

My school mates were nothin' to me, but they all admired me. There was always somebody hangin' on me askin' me what I would do in any given situation. There wasn't no situation I didn't have an answer to. That was my God-given talent and it was bein' wasted in school. I knew when I was sixteen I was gonna be on my way to a better life than what I had.

Now, it wasn't like my uncle wasn't good to me. He just didn't think very big is all. He never saw past fightin' me to do my homework, which I already knew had nothin' to do with the life I was gonna have. His idea of accomplishin' was me gettin' through school, findin' a nice boy, and settlin' down. He sure as hell didn't have what his daddy, or my daddy, or my mama had, which was the desire to go after the 'big life.' See, the way I see it is you got one shot on this earth, so far as I know, and I think I'm right on that one—and shootin' low was not my idea of a good shot.

Anyway, I figured I had four more years of battlin' it out with my uncle, then I'd be on my way. Well, my mama comin back' into the picture threw a big ole hammer into that particular plan. My mind was spinnin'.

I swear, I remember the exact moment he told me my mama wanted me back. It's just like it was yesterday. Now, that was a situation that I couldn't wrap my mind around.

There I was, lyin' on my bed dreamin' 'bout the 'big life,' just like I always did, when he walked into my room and interrupted me. I was prepared, as usual, for him to ride me about doin' my homework—which was as predictable as my havin' to pee every mornin'. Well, he came in and sat down on my bed, which was somethin' he never did. Usually, he just stood in the doorway and talked to me from there. That's when I knew somethin' real big was up.

Now, my uncle was a good man, he did the best he could with a hell raiser like me—he just wasn't the nurturin' type is all. If he was alive today, I'd apologize for all the shit I put him through. I mean I wouldn't take it back or anythin'. There's not a thing I woulda changed far as my life plan at that point—but an apology woulda been a nice gesture.

Anyway, he put his hand on my shoulder—I'll be damned if I can't feel it right now—and he went for my heartstrings. This was his opportunity to get some peace in this life, I know that now. He convinced me that I belonged with my mama, who needed me because she had nothin' else. One thing I never got was why she didn't need my brother. He got to stay with my uncle for no reason, other than my mama just didn't need him like she did me. I guess her "all girls" club was still up and runnin'.

She needed me alright, and she wasn't no fool. She knew all about my plan, probably 'cause she had the hawk ears and nose, just like me. So, when I turned sixteen in that dinky ass trailer park outside of New Orleans, she said happy birthday and proceeded to board me up in my bedroom, windows and all. She said I wasn't goin' to go nowhere.

Somewhere between spendin' all those hours in the movies together, her leavin', and then her comin' back, she had become nothin' but a hateful woman. I was all she had alright, my uncle got that right—but the problem was, she crapped all over me for stuff I had nothin' to do with, like her bein' a miserable failure, which I knew for damn sure wasn't gonna happen to me.

See, she knew I had the same drive as her, which is exactly why she locked me up. Think about it. She had lost herself in tryin' to find herself and re-findin' me was all she had left. Once I was gone she had no reason not to shoot herself.

Well, I knew my drive wasn't gonna turn to stink and I knew there was but so long she could keep me in that bedroom—besides, I was already prepared for that type of situation. See, the moment my mama tore me from my life in Atlanta, I didn't look back, there wasn't no point. I shut it all away, kinda like Bobby did, but not so dramatic. I mean he don't remember anythin', probably because if he could remember he'd be nothin' but a puddle right here on the floor. My point bein', the only thing I took with me was my plan—and I stuck to it.

So, when I arrived in New Orleans, I went right to work creatin' the kinda environment I needed, just like I did in Atlanta. I mean, what I had to work with was different—like I had a mama who was white trash instead of a movie star— but I got creative, you might say, and four years later when she locked me in my room—well, that's when the Danny part of my plan kicked. He pulled me out of my window and we ran off to Las Vegas together.

Danny, he was my knight with shinin' arms—meanin' he complied with my plan to save my ass from a bad situation. He was also the father to my Greta, who I never shoulda named that. I think it was like puttin' a damn curse on her. Don't get me wrong, I loved my mama, and I still do—I am just sorry as shit it didn't work out for her and sorrier that she tried to suck my God-given drive right outta me. She shoulda appreciated it, is all I got to say—like I appreciate seein' that drive in my kids.

'Course, then I went on to give Annie the name Greta, which I never shoulda done. That right there is probably the whole reason things turned out the way they did with her— case closed.

Part I: Annie and Bobby

1

The First Time Annie Left Georgia

The shotgun blast, not fifteen feet from her bed, followed by the screeching litany of abuse from Stella's mouth, sent Greta, aka Annie Evans, scrambling from a dead sleep to speeding out of the winding driveway in Bobby's pickup, nearly crashing into trees as she went. In a matter of minutes, her twelve years with Stella and Bobby had come to an end. She couldn't have predicted it in a million years and, yet, knew instinctively to get as far away as she could. All she had were the clothes on her back, her purse, and a few thousand dollars in the bank.

She pressed the gas pedal to the floor. She knew Stella would be fast on the track of making her withdrawal of funds impossible. Just how she would do that was a complete mystery, seeing as it was Annie's personal account. However, Stella could make things happen, or not, using means that were beyond what most people would think of.

Annie could barely see the road. What happened? Everything had been going so well—better than ever. She had seen Stella cruel—absolutely, and often—but not like that, not ever. It made no sense. The kennel was going well, the boys were about to go off on their own—there was no reason she could think of...

She was visibly shaking as she gripped the steering wheel and sped up the ramp onto the highway. What now? She had nowhere to go. The only family she'd known for the past twelve years was ten miles back and had just run her off with a shotgun.

She looked around wildly as cars honked and swerved to her left and right. The rage she'd seen in Stella's eyes was nothing she'd ever seen in her before.

Yes, I was wildly confused, to say the least. I had been living and working with her for half my life. I was the "best girl" in our business, meaning, as she would say in a variety of ways, "You are the official billboard, as in the best damn advertisement we have! Hell, we can stroll you damn near anywhere on this earth, then come home and I'd have to get me a hundred Bobbys to beat the dreamin' and droolin' men off our doorstep."

See that? I speak Stella fluently. She's a part of me and always will be. How that will look next year, ten years from now, I don't know. How it's been is intense and complicated.

Anyway, unlike the other girls, the most I had to do was ride on an arm for a night. I never had to trick, except when I felt like it, which was for reasons that had nothing to do with the business. And, unlike the others, I lived with Stella.

The truth of the matter is, within my first months with her we were partners. She had the real world smarts, as she liked to point out constantly, and I had the book smarts, plus, as she would also say, "You have exactly what we need to pull in all them rich foreigners"—meaning my language skills.

I was crazy about her—I was.

You know, she was my mother and my big sister—AND we needed each other, truly we did. Even knowing what I know now, I still know that to be true. I can only imagine how that sounds to you or anybody who wasn't in my shoes, or hers. But I'm not concerned about that, not anymore. If I were I wouldn't be able to speak the truth—something I've already not been able to do more than once in my life, not without painful consequences—nuff said. You may learn more than you care to learn and want to shove it away. I did. I tried like crazy to make everything that was me disappear when I got here to Wisconsin. I managed, day to day, not without tremendous difficulty—but I did it.

Then the day came when I couldn't do it anymore,
something I'll tell you more about later.
So, Stella, Bobby, and the boys were my family. It was that
simple. When Stella went off to prison, I stayed on. Not as
a favor to her, not because I was told to, but because I loved
them—and we needed each other.

And, by the way, I could have gone to prison with her, but
she didn't allow that to happen. What she told the authorities,
so she says, was, "The Greta you is lookin' for is gone. That
Greta ran like the chickenshit she is and, no, I never did
know her for-real name or where she came from. I don't give
a rat's ass. But I will tell you Annie Evans ain't that person.
Now, I know they look a lot alike, which is what you might
call an amazin' coincidence. Truth is, they is nothin' alike,
'cept on the outside. 'Course, if you're lookin' for the official
Greta that was my daughter, you already know how that
story ended."

Do I believe she said that? No, not really, because I was
never in danger of being arrested. Stella was always careful
that my name stayed far away from anything related to the
money she was laundering. And I know you probably think it
was for selfish reasons, which is what most people will think,
but that wasn't the case. It's far more complicated than that.
So, even though she most likely never said any of that to the
authorities—still, she protected me.

So, let me continue.

For the two years after she got out of prison, I helped get
Galestorm Kennels off the ground. It was an exciting time
and, frankly, one of the least chaotic times we'd ever had
together, which is what made that day she burst into my
room such a shock. It wasn't until much later that I came to
understand why that happened.

But I think I should back up a bit and tell you how Stella
and I met. I was seventeen and she was thirty-one when she
found me. I say "found" because that's what it felt like. No one
had ever known the truth of me, until I met Stella. At times
I actually believe I was meant to meet her—you know, my
destiny, my raison d'être. It's funny, I know, but I wouldn't

even think such a thing if there wasn't some truth to it—do you understand what I mean? Well, maybe you don't.

And, just as an aside, you know how people can be completely uninteresting to one person and fascinating to another? Well, Stella is rarely uninteresting to anybody—but I think you already know that.

Anyway, at the time she found me, I was already a third of the way through college. I'd skipped a year in elementary school, another year in high school, and entered college at barely sixteen—one of the top colleges in the country. The point being, I was painfully smart, which according to educators meant I could handle "this kind of advancement." Painful is what I called it, "ahead of your peers" is what they called it. Well, they didn't know me at all, nobody did, as I have already said—but Stella did. And so, needless to say, when she found me I dropped everything to be at her side.

It was during winter break and I had decided to drive fifteen hundred miles to New Orleans on my own. It was one of my personal dares. You see, I was always pushing myself to do things that seemed as though they might be unbearable, as in unbearably lonely, unbearably scary, unbearably sad—anything, it just had to be unbearable, that was the only criteria. It was how I kept myself intact, strong and special, or so I thought! I also didn't have any friends, because it was unbearable to not have friends. I know it sounds nuts, but it wasn't, not to me.

So, there I was, sitting in one of the thousands of bars in the French quarter in New Orleans when two obnoxious smarmy men started hitting on me—yet another thing I had to deal with routinely, being hit on all the time. You see, unbearability was even in my genetic make-up, as in I was unbearably smart and unbearably attractive no matter what I wore or what time of day it was. I never said that to myself and I never felt it. I simply heard it all the time.

Well, suddenly a vibrant husky voice broke from behind those two men. "You boys need to step aside, unless of course you're holdin' five thousand apiece in cash, and that would be just to stand next to her, in which case we can talk."

Both the men turned, and there she was—small, strikingly beautiful, with a Herculean presence. Stella had something that when it was turned on it cleared a room, filled a room, destroyed a room—whatever her intention was, it simply happened. The men apologized and moved on.

She proceeded to sit down beside me with a familiarity I'd never experienced. She snapped her fingers at the waitress. "Two margaritas, please." She was utterly mesmerizing and not because she was beautiful, which she was, but we've all seen beautiful a thousand times. She was, in my completely non-intact mind, the Goliath I longed to be—the person who could make the unbearable go pale.

Annie Evans, soon to become Stella's Greta, was facing her nemesis and had no clue. And the irony is, Stella was also facing her nemesis and had no clue. It makes me shudder, even now.

Anyway, after she ordered our margaritas, she looked at me and said, "I can tell you're not from around here and that's just how you want it. I know the feelin', honey, trust me. When I was your age, which I'm guessin' is about seventeen or eighteen, I was already married, had me a kid and was livin' two thousand miles away from anybody and everybody who knew me. It was called survivin' a bad situation. You and me, we have a lot in common."

And she was right. We did have a lot in common, which was that neither one of us was intact and neither one of us knew it.

So that was it. I was hooked on Stella and was loyally at her side until that morning when she shot a hole in the wall beside my bed and started yelling.

I can't tell you what she said because I won't let those words come out of my mouth. That would be dangerous for me. Writing it down, like this, will keep it one step removed. I'm using all capitals because, well, Stella was all about capitals and, besides she was yelling. Also, it keeps it even more distant because I don't normally write in this way.

YOU'RE NOTHIN' BUT A GODDAMN WHORE! I SHOULDA
LEFT YOU WHERE I FOUND YOU. HOW FUCKIN' DARE YOU
FUCK BOBBY!!!! WHO THE HELL DO YOU THINK YOU ARE?
WAS DADDY THAT GOOD? HELL, BOBBY AIN'T EVEN OLD
ENOUGH TO BE YOUR DADDY. MAYBE YOU DID YOUR BIG
BROTHER TOO. IS THAT THE WAY THE STORY GOES YOU
DUMB BITCH? DO YOU THINK I EVER GAVE A SHIT ABOUT
YOUR DADDY HAD SEX WITH HIS LITTLE GIRL STORY! OH
MY HEART BLEEDS! IT HAPPENS ALL THE TIME ONLY IN
YOUR CASE, YOUR DADDY HAD NO CHOICE 'CAUSE YOU
WAS BORN A WHORE. GET THE HELL OUTTA MY HOUSE
BEFORE I DO WHAT NEEDED TO BE DONE WHEN YOU WAS
BORN. YOU IS TAINTED GENES IS WHAT YOU IS—ONE OF
GOD'S BIG ASS MISTAKES.

*I will say, though, those words have run through my head a
thousand times since she yelled them. There was more, but
I can't remember because I stopped hearing her after that.
A monster in her was on a rampage and it was unbearable.
See there it is again, unbearable. Are you starting to see the
pattern?*

*Stella had reached in, fluidly and flawlessly, grabbed the
place where I was hurt the most, and beat it silly. By the time
I jumped out of bed, pulled on my jeans, picked up my purse,
and ran out the door, the young woman who was Stella's
Greta was rapidly waning. I was becoming just Annie again.
I had finally found a situation as unbearable, possibly more
so, than the one my own father had put through when I was
his "little Annie."*

*So, within thirty-six hours of looking in the rear view
mirror and seeing the raging red haired Goliath running
down the long dirt driveway with that shotgun in her hands,
I was in the air and on my way to find another life.*

————

Once on the plane and settled in her seat, Annie didn't feel
relief. For nearly two days she had been filled with the kind
of terror a gazelle holds in its body as it flees from a hungry
lioness—and now here she was. How was it she'd stayed
ahead of Stella? Was it that she wasn't even in the chase

because she hadn't walked out, but rather had been thrown out? Had Stella simply put down the gun and washed her hands of her the moment she was gone?

As the plane sped down the runway, her throat tightened. After twelve years with Stella, had she been erased as if she'd never existed? She'd seen Stella do this with others, but had never imagined it could happen to her.

She clutched the luxurious leather bag Stella had given her on her twenty-sixth birthday. There was no relief.

As the plane lifted into the air, her mind was frantically searching for a place to land.

"Please remain in your seats, with the seats in an upright position, until we reach cruising altitude."

She took a deep breath and looked out of the thick round window. As she watched the Atlanta airport grow smaller and smaller, she imagined Stella at the ticket counter demanding Flight 112 be turned around due to the fact of there being a car thief on board. She could picture it perfectly—the larger-than-life red-head dialing 911 as she smacked the counter and demanded to speak to whoever was in charge, threatening a lawsuit if they didn't comply.

Annie eased her grip on the leather bag. Stella had not given up. She would hound her to the ends of the earth. What she needed to do was focus and stay ahead of the chase.

And that's how it was. I sat in that seat and clutched the leather bag as if it was all that stood between me and the lost world of little Annie Evans. At the same time, all the words that Stella had flung at me that previous day went round and round in my head, like a hamster running round and round on its wheel. I kept trying to make excuses for her because I needed to. I knew her mother had been brutal to her during her teenage years, both verbally and physically. I'm sure she's told you the story of how her mother, out of the blue, boarded her up in her room when she turned sixteen. She loves to tell that story, and the way she tells it makes it sound as though she was in control and had it all figured out.

I met her mother once, you know. In all my years with Stella, it was one of the rare times I saw her as other than the Herculean force the world knew her to be—the other times I may discuss later on, maybe not. They may not even be relevant. However, I will tell you that her mother was a woman from whose lips meanness dripped as easily as the slobber from a dogue's jowl after a hearty drink.

So, as I sat on that plane, I thought about her mother and dug out enough compassion for Stella to keep hold of a connection with her. I absolutely needed that.

By the time I reached Paris, Stella's Greta was just a memory, or so I thought at the time. I was Annie again. I bought a small rucksack, two pairs of light weight pants, two pairs of khaki shorts, a few light weight T's, underwear, a one piece bathing suit, and a rugged pair of hiking boots. That was it. My stay in Paris lasted only a matter of days because, in short, the men were awful—persistent and annoying with their smooth talk and slick manner. Perhaps it was that I was fed up with men in general, having been in the "business" for so long—and I was fed up with women too. In fact, I was fed up with the entire human race.

I was back at square one and I hated it.

So I took to the hills, literally, and after a few weeks of gypsy-like wandering I chose Greece as my final destination. I chose it partly because it wasn't anywhere that Stella would have thought to look. She knew I was fluent in German, French, and Spanish, so I figured in her mind any countries associated with those languages would be the countries I would go to. What she didn't know was that Greece was a common vacation spot for Germans—verstehen?—and I actually do know a fair amount of Greek, enough to get by anyway.

You see, for those first weeks, I was guided purely by the Stella factor. That was how I got through without falling into the abyss of my true circumstances. Every day I would think of what Stella would think or do and guide my actions and thoughts accordingly—sometimes I worked with her, sometimes against her.

For instance, while hitchhiking across Italy on my way to Greece, I was picked up by a man who, after a long period of

*silence and lewd staring—in between watching the road—
begin asking me, in broken English, if my nipples swelled
when I had sex.*

I asked myself, "What would Stella do?"

*Well, right there in the middle of nowhere, on some
winding country road, I turned to him and yelled. "STOP
THIS CAR YOU DUMB ASS!" My low-key demeanor was gone.
He went into such shock that he stopped the car immediately.
I grabbed my canvas shoulder bag, which contained a huge
guidebook to Greece, swung it at him and continued yelling,
"WHO THE HELL DO YOU THINK YOU'RE MESSIN' WITH,
MISTER ITALIAN WANNA BE STUD?!" The bag hit the side
of his face with a loud smack. He let go of the wheel and put
his hands to his face.*

*By that time, I was out of the car and still mad as hell.
I turned to face him. "YOU KEEP TREATIN' WOMEN THIS
WAY, ESPECIALLY WOMEN LIKE ME, YOU'RE GONNA WIND
UP DEAD OR WORSE!"*

*He was utterly confounded and extremely pale, except
for the giant red mark that glowed from the side of his
face. I had the power of Stella surging though me and
felt sorely tempted to continue, but somehow, God only
knows how, I resisted the temptation and marched down
the grassy bank and out across a pasture. I heard him get
out of his car and turned to see him, fist in the air, yelling,
trying hopelessly to get a grain of his machismo back.
I laughed and muttered a prayer of gratitude to Stella,
savior of young women in trouble.*

*Well, eventually I got to Brindisi on the East Coast of Italy,
which was where I would catch the overnight ferry to Petras
on the west coast of Greece. By then, I had wandered for weeks
through France, Spain, and Italy, fending off men, ignoring
everyone else. I walked for hours and hours a day, eating
yogurt and fruit, waiting for God or Stella, it didn't matter
which one, to guide me to somewhere other than where I was.
Talk about misguided thinking, that right there (do you hear
Stella?) was the root of the reason my hole just kept getting
deeper and deeper.*

At the end of every day, I would find a room and drink wine till I fell asleep. And as each day passed, I piled more and more onto my hope of finding some kind of reprieve in Greece. You see, Greece meant more to me than just a place where Stella couldn't find me—keep in mind, of course, that my imagining her furiously in search of me was both my greatest fear and my greatest hope.

Greece had been a huge part of my world as a child. My best friend and neighbor, Pano, was Greek. I learned to read the adventures of Puff and Spot in Greek class in the basement of his church, and by the time he and I reached the third grade, we had made our plans to marry, run off to Greece and become the proud owners of a herd of a thousand white horses.

By age thirteen, our plans had faded and so had the 'we' we thought we were. Boarding school, brilliance, and lonely bravado awaited me, while he went on to public school, found girlfriends, lost girlfriends, found a wife, opened his own Greek restaurant, and lived happily ever after—or so I want to believe.

I was also fascinated and comforted by Greek mythology. It was my father, bless his heart, who had introduced it to me and, I might add, with the same care and enthusiasm that he introduced me to sex. According to him, he was teaching me things that were important for my development as a person—a little girl.

Well, as Stella once said, "That right there was a sorry-ass man shovin' his sorry-ass life down your throat and walkin' away thinkin' he was some kind of Daddy with shinin' arms."

Of course, the mythology part wasn't the sorry-ass part. That was actually something that gave me respite from the agonizing reality that the world I lived in—essentially his world—pretty much sucked. You see, whenever my father pulled out that big blue volume of Greek myths my world expanded, which was the opposite of what happened when he pulled out his big pink penis.

The idea that thunder was an angry Zeus or that rain, night, seasons, wars, turbulent oceans, accidents, and plagues were all a part of the antics and interplays of many unseen gods and goddesses was magical to me—the rise and fall and antics of my father's penis was not.

During those prepubescent years I spent whatever time I could at Pano's house, eating glorious Greek food, listening to Greek conversations, going to Greek church, singing Greek songs, and reveling in the huge family celebrations that occurred on a fairly regular basis. He never came to my house—I never asked him to and he never asked. My parents rarely spoke to his parents, except to exchange information regarding where I was and what I was doing. There was no animosity or anything like that. I think it was that they had nothing in common except the friendship that Pano and I shared. However, in my child's heart of hearts I believed it was an invisible boundary that everybody understood would be catastrophic if it were crossed, or at least it would have been for me. A small miracle is all I can say.

2

When Annie Became Greta

"GRETA, YOU NEED TO SNAP OUT OF THIS HERE PROBLEM YOU SEEM TO KEEP RUNNIN' INTO ON A REGULAR BASIS. IT'S INTERFERIN' WITH OUR BUSINESS AND ITS GIVIN' ME A DAMN HEADACHE!"

Stella crossed the bedroom and threw open the shades. "WHAT YOU NEED TO DO IS GET UP, TAKE A LONG STROLL THROUGH THAT CLOSET YOU HAVE, THEN PUT YOUR ASS IN YOUR MG AND TAKE A DRIVE. IF THAT DON'T TAKE CARE OF WHAT AILS YOU, I DON'T KNOW WHAT WILL."

Annie cringed as the hot midday sunlight burst through her eyelids and forced her to turn her head away from the window. "Who the hell is Greta?"

She buried her head under the pillow. "Look, I just want to sleep for a while. I'll be fine. I'm just tired."

"HONEY, TIRED JUST DON'T EXPLAIN IT. YOU BEEN LYIN' HERE FOR ALMOST TWO DAYS AND I GOT NO CLUE HOW YOU DO IT. I MEAN, DO YOU SLEEP WALK TO THE BATHROOM OR DO YOU JUST PEE RIGHT HERE, GOD FORBID?"

Stella sat down on the bed, lit a cigarette, and lowered her voice. "Greta is your new name. It's the name of my now dead daughter, who I ain't never mentioned before 'cause I just don't talk about her. She killed herself when she was twelve, and that's all I got to say 'bout that, 'cept that I loved her even though she got the nuts gene from my grandma."

She pulled the pillow from Annie's head, then got up and paced back and forth between the window and the bed. "That girl was a blaze of fire, just like me—and looked the most like me of all my kids—just couldn't regulate the fire.

It was burnin' her up till one afternoon she decided to put the fire out. I think of her every time I look at one of my guns. Anyway, her name was Greta and that's my birthday present to you, which is now two days ago, somethin' you wouldn't know anythin' about seeing as all you been doin' is lyin' here in the dark. You don't got a blaze of fire in you, like my Greta did, at least not yet—but you got the glowin' ambers, and alls they need is some fresh oxygen, like a new name, to get you on your way."

She stopped at the window and looked out. "It ain't like everybody don't got somethin' eatin' away at 'em. You think I ain't noticed that on your birthday, Christmas, Thanksgivin', and some days in between, you end up face down, face up, whatever, in bed? It happened all last year and it's happenin' this year. It don't take a rocket scientist, honey."

She blew smoke into the sunlight and turned back towards Annie. "Look, here's what you gotta do—why do I always end up teachin' people stuff?—you gotta take that load of crap your daddy handed to you, and your mama too, 'cause she ain't no angel, and come to an understandin' that it's a gift. How many times do I got to tell you this?"

She sucked in hard, blew the smoke out of her mouth, up her nose, and back out of her mouth again. "All I know is, I will keep repeatin' it till it sinks into that brain you is supposed to have—and speakin' of that, how is it that you can know all them languages and don't understand what I'm tryin' to tell you?"

She walked over and shook her burning cigarette in Annie's face. "You wouldn't be makin' the money you're makin' if not for him. Do you think just bein' beautiful is what it takes to pull a man in? Hell no, what your daddy gave you is the tendency to pull on the strings of every man who is deep down fucked up—as in lonely and lost and needin' to find the company of someone who will make them shine. There's all types of men out there—and where you lucked out is that your daddy wasn't no violent type. Bein raped and gettin' nothin' but pain, now that right there is the worst kind of rape, or bein' beaten along with bein' raped. Now, you ain't never gonna draw that type of fish into your pond, it just don't work that way. You'll always get the ones who'll pay out the ass just to have you on their arm when they go out. And if you give 'em just a little somethin' extra, they'll be so grateful they'll throw money at you—us, I mean."

Annie opened her eyes and peered through the smoke at the face of the woman whose shadow she was lying in. "I'm sorry I ever told you about my father, and besides, he's not what I'm thinking about. I hardly ever think about him."

Stella didn't hesitate. "Annie—I mean Greta—you listen to me now. You wanted to tell me about him, A) 'cause I knew without you havin' to tell me, B) 'cause I asked and no one ever asked you before, and C) if there's one thing I know everyone wants, it's to tell someone about their dirty little secrets. It beats carryin' it around inside like some kinda cancer. There's a ton of stuff that'll kill you slowly, why let your daddy be one of 'em? And you sayin' you never think about it—that right there is your problem. You think because you ain't thinkin about him he ain't there? You need to rethink that!

"What you got to do is get up every mornin' and say to him, as you're strollin' through your closet lookin' for the right dress, 'Daddy, I thank you every day for givin' me the gift to milk every bastard like you dry—the gift to get me my own swimmin' pool that I want, the gift of my car, the opportunity to rub elbows with the rich and famous, travel, and one day, find me a fine man, nothin' like you—but not till I'm so goddamn rich I don't need anybody. Amen.'"

Annie suddenly burst out laughing. She didn't understand it, but Stella had managed to reach in and pull her out.

Stella's green eyes narrowed. "What? You think I ain't serious? I'm serious as shit. That right there, is the key to your well bein'. You need to stay on top of that shit or it will bring you down for good. You and me ain't so lucky as Bobby. He don't remember jack about the hell he's probly been through—I mean the hell back when he was a child, which is a different kinda hell than the stuff he puts hisself through now. Bein' an adult creatin' your own hell is a whole different ball of gum. The difference bein' that the child hell can take you down by the knees when you ain't lookin'—no warnin', nothin'—you can be all smilin' and laughin' and bam, you're down so low you can't figure your way out 'cept through drugs or guns or some shit like that.

"My boys, I tell 'em every day to think about the shit they ain't had to go through 'cause that right there will give 'em a better life than I ever dreamed of. I'm tellin' you this now, 'cause I know. You're nineteen as of two days ago. I got fourteen years on you, and it's a long fourteen years. I got a lot, don't get me wrong—but I intend to get more. Nobody is going to get in the way of what I got to do to get to where I intend to go. That's just the way it is—case closed. I am never..."

Annie could tell that Stella had stopped seeing her. She butted in. "You know what Hans wanted me to do once we got back to his hotel room?"

Stella watched as Annie sat up. Her job was done, but she was getting awful damn tired of trying to keep her on track. She figured this whole Greta idea was her last shot. She leaned over and put her cigarette out in the ashtray on the bedside table. "No, I don't know what Hans wanted you to do, why would I?"

"He wanted to lie across my lap and have me spank him with the back of my hand. Not the front or the side—but the back. He was very clear about that. And then he wanted me to tell him, in German, what a bad boy he was." Annie laughed. "He looked as though he would burst into tears if I didn't say OK."

Stella snorted. "I'm tellin' you, that is exactly what I'm talkin' about! Mister CEO of a damn bank is willin' to pay out the ass for a spankin'. Like I said, most of 'em ain't playin' with a full deck and the good news is that we're the ones holdin' all the cards."

And, I remember that day as clearly as the day I tried to confront my father for what he had done to me. Both were significant landmarks in my life.

I suppose you could say I might not have taken that long drive to New Orleans if that confrontation with my father hadn't happened. That was the day—Thanksgiving actually—that marked the end of any hope I had of ever getting close to him, or anyone in my family. Staying in college and working towards an academic future, or any future for that matter, became utterly meaningless after that. So, I took that long drive.

What did I hope would happen? Honestly, as misguided as it sounds, I believed—or wanted to believe—my family would pull together and celebrate the fact I'd finally come forward and laid the truth out on the table, just like that marvelous long awaited holiday meal that, once eaten, would make way for the first real sense of family—something I believed each one of them longed for. Surely, they must have noticed my having been gone from them most of my life.

And I imagined the prayer before the feast, right after I'd laid out the truth. "Annie, we are so sorry for what you had to go through, and have had to keep inside you for so long. We're so proud of how courageous you've been and, most of all, we are so very happy to have you back with us."

And then my father would solemnly add his bit. "Annie, my dear sweet Annie. I am so grateful to you for holding my feet to the fire after all these years, making me aware of how truly awful it was for you. I take full responsibility for what I have done. I had no idea, but I do now and you are truly special and I am so sorry that..."

He would be unable to finish, as the tears would begin to fall, first from him, then one by one from each of my brothers, then my mother. Round the table they would go, unstoppable tears of sadness that would slowly make that sweet transition to tears of joy, followed by hugs and laughter that no longer carried with them that dreaded "if only" that always left me cold.

Well, needless to say, once again little Annie had used her vivid imagination to gird herself to do the deed. In truth, what she faced was yet another worst day of her life.

So, sitting in that bar in New Orleans, feeling the firm and protective hand of Stella Gale fall upon my shoulder and hearing her speak on my behalf in the face of two people who wanted me for nothing other than their own pleasure—well, it was the miracle I'd been waiting for.

Then that day when Stella came into my bedroom and gave me the new name Greta—that was the day that marked the beginning of my newfound hope. Yes, I'd been with her over a year, I'd learned the ropes, could walk the walk, talk the talk, and help manage things. I was an invaluable part of a thriving business. The problem, which you've laid out quite well in that little piece, was that I suffered terrible depressions. Simply put, I hadn't completed the transition to my new life, and it was looking like I might never be able to. Stella knew this.

What she did that afternoon was sheer brilliance. I grabbed hold of that new-used name as if it were the only water in a world that each time I visited was becoming more stark and dry. That was the day I became Greta and joined, full throttle, a platoon of fifteen to forty other girls, each armed, I'm certain, with their own version of a Stella Prayer.

I did, indeed, feel a blaze begin to rise in my belly that day.

For the next eight to nine years I sucked a lot of men out of more than just their money—and it was most satisfying. They were putty in my hands as far as I knew—but then what did I know? I was being held together by the strong arms of the Stella perspective which made many things other than they really were.

You see, being given the name of Stella's first-born child felt endearing and special, as did her awareness of my depressions and effortless intrusions into my psyche. It's all so ironic and unmistakably tragic in the end.

Of course, that day she ran me off with her shotgun isn't the end I'm talking about. The fact that I would be back with her eighteen months later was the last thing I would have imagined at the time.

So, there I was on the ferry to Greece, sans Greta, sans Stella, sans family, back to square one—little Annie Evans doing her best by car, by rail, by air, by sea, to retrieve something she knew she had lost. She was tenfold stricken by the fact she didn't even know what that something was, but Greece seemed the best answer at the time.

3

Crossing to Greece

After a rather precarious all night ferry ride, Rosy Fingered Dawn plucked Annie from the deck and planted her solidly on the western shore of Greece. Exhausted, though invigorated by a renewed sense of hope, she stood and faced the sea.

She took in a last breath of the salty air, then turned and walked quickly past the small clumps of waiting family members, a handful of taxi drivers, and clusters of curious children, beyond the town and onto the open road.

She walked and walked and walked. She was seventeen again, only this time she was headed to Delphi rather than New Orleans. Her years of total immersion in "The Stella Rules of Etiquette" wafted out from beneath her hiking boots and into the Grecian earth in spits and spats—thump, thump, thump. Her Greta legs, once sleek and comfortable with the clickity clack of high heels and soft cover of silk stockings, were thickened with newfound muscle and, now relieved of their daily stripping, were covered with a thin coat of hair.

Bar the door Nelly! (Annie chuckles)

While I can appreciate your attempt to wax poetic, this is not the time or the place. I was not Ahab and it was not "the best of times and the worst of times." Yes, I told you what Greece meant to me before I got there, but you must remember I was a woman who'd had the rug pulled out from under her, utterly and completely, when she was too young to find a way to get back up, except by clinging to the 'treasures' a few screwed up adults handed her as her life unfolded.

In truth, I was hollow and scared. What I longed for and what I got were two different things. First of all, I had been duly muscled before that trip. Remember, I'd helped build and run a kennel. But more importantly, when I walked off that ferry I was powered by desperation, not hope. It was the very same desperation that had motivated me to get into that car and drive to New Orleans all those years earlier.

Also, the ferry ride was so much more than "precarious." I'd spent the entire night on the deck, lying under a light blanket, unable to sleep. It was the first time since I'd landed in Paris that I'd been still for so long, and fully awake, without being drunk. Usually at day's end, as I've said, I drank wine until sleep overcame me, but not that night. That was the night it hit me, full force, how alone I was. No one, absolutely no one, knew where I was and no one cared. It was one of those moments that dropped into my belly like a cold stone.

No, it wasn't self-pity—it wasn't like that. I couldn't have felt sorry for myself—I didn't have enough awareness of a self to have that luxury, and I say luxury because I would have welcomed it over what I was feeling.

So, as I lay there, I frantically tried to reclaim the notion that Stella was somewhere behind me, pursuing me. Even if her goal was to blow my head off, it seemed better than that cold stone in my belly—but I couldn't reclaim it.

I then tried on the Stella perspective that I knew so well, as in, "I'm in a bad situation, one I can't wrap my mind around. What the hell do I do now?"

I decided Stella would get up and start right in on an action that would enable her to feel in control. Something along the lines of lashing out, as in finding somebody to blame, someone to control, someone to piss off, or someone to adore her. Basically, damn near anything that would get her to where she no longer felt in a "bad situation."

So, I looked around. There were sleeping bodies scattered all across the deck—mostly young people. Surely there was someone I could pull in to turn my situation around. What in God's name would Stella do?

In her imagination, Annie watched Stella get up from her deck chair and stride over to a cluster of blanketed sleeping bodies. She leaned down and shook a few shoulders. "You all need to wake up now 'cause what you ain't thought about is why it is those people with all the money get to sleep inside, in beds, and you got to sleep out here in the wind, rockin' and rollin' like sausages in a fryin' pan—well, no, since it ain't hot, just warm, more like sausages on a plate being brought to you by some trashy waitress at one of them diners. Have you ever asked yourselves that? I mean, just 'cause you don't got the high payin' jobs or the right connections, that ain't no reason to be out here, now is it?"

Stella didn't wait for an answer. She didn't need one. "Listen, I got a plan as to exactly how you can get yourselves some decent sleepin' quarters, a least for future times—it's called a class-action suit!"

She pulled a cigarette from her pack and lit it.

A young man lifted his head and peered out from under the blanket that was tightly wrapped around his face and shoulders. He was bleary eyed and astonished at the sight of Stella leaning over him, her face barely visible through the cloud of cigarette smoke surrounding it. "I don't know what the bloody hell you're talking about. Who are you? We like it on the deck. We don't want a lawsuit! What is it about you Americans and lawsuits? You need a bloody barrister for everything! Why are you bothering us?"

Annie then imagined Stella's rush of anger.

"What the hell is the matter with you? If you think this is a fine way to spend a night then you need to come to terms with everythin' you ain't never learned—one of those things bein' what comfortable means. 'Course, now I'm thinkin' you is one of them high and mighty British people who's thinkin' you're John Wayne and all, rebellin' against either your daddy or the Queen, take your pick, tryin' to show them that you is different, as in dumber. You think sleepin' on a hard-as-rock deck is gonna show 'em who's got it right? You're funny, I'll give you that, but what you got to understand is that you got it ass backwards, darlin', which is exactly why I'm out here on the deck when I could be back in my suite sleepin' like a baby. What you need to understand is till you stop thinkin' this is any kinda way to influence people or make a man of yourself, you will be shit outta luck in about ten years.

Now I'm guessin' I'm about fifteen years older than you and the last time I slept on a hard-as-rock surface was when I was fourteen years old and ended up sharing a jail cell with eight hookers for drinkin' while smokin' two different substances, while drivin', while bein' under age—dws2wdwbu is what I call it—and while French kissin' my boyfriend, which wasn't a part of it because that ain't breakin' any law. Anyway, my white trash mama told the police to keep me for the night to teach me a lesson."

Stella glanced around. More people were waking and gravitating over to her. Satisfied, she lowered her voice and continued, "I learned a lesson alright, which was don't drink, drive or smoke while bein' fourteen, 'cause if you do you'll end up spendin' the night with a bunch of hookers who walk around in circles prayin' their sorry-ass pimp is gonna come and get their ass out of jail within the hour—case closed."

She paused to suck in some smoke while her words settled on eager ears. "The other thing I learned was I was never gonna be a woman who got beat up and pushed around, only to end up in jail prayin' the guy who beat me up and pushed me around would come and get my ass out. Now that right there was a lesson worth learnin'."

By this time, at least a dozen young travelers had crawled or walked to where Stella was standing and settled cross-legged at her feet. They were, if nothing else, intrigued. She kept count within the quiet of her mind, and as the numbers went up, so did her sense of being on top of her bad situation.

So there I was, under my blanket in the dark, in the middle of the night, in the middle of the sea, allowing this scenario to unfold in my imagination. Stella may not have been looking for me, but I'd found her and in doing so found relief from that stone cold in my belly. Ironically, and you have to admit it is the ultimate irony, it was only then that I was able to feel some comfort in the low rumble of the ferry as it plowed through the night and feel soothed by the warm smell of the sea air.

Frankly, in describing that night, I can't help but cringe at just how vulnerable and misguided I was. And yet, I've made it to where I am now which, despite how it may seem, is a much better place. That's a testament to some God-given something that was with me from the beginning, as in since I was born. (Gee, I sound just like Stella, don't I?)

By the way, that story about being left in a jail cell with eight hookers? Well, that was true—it really did happen to Stella. I heard her mother tell it during that one day we spent with her. It was at the top of her list of things to share about her daughter. She told it as if it were some marvelous prank she'd played on Stella and she expected me to laugh right along with her—I didn't, but Stella did. She laughed her gruff laugh and rolled her eyes. "Oh, yeah, that was a fine time I had in that cell—gave me a good long look at the trashy side of life—somethin' I was all too familiar with livin' here with you. Thank you, Mama."

Then Stella snorted and stepped out of the trailer to smoke a joint, leaving me to suffer her mother's sour anecdotes. I couldn't imagine that woman had ever been the mother Stella adored as a child. Stella's stories of going to the movies with her mom and "the girls club" were magical. She softened when she told them, in the same way she softened when she talked about meeting Bobby.

Now, speaking of Bobby, I'd like to talk about him for a moment and what Stella had accused me of that final day when she burst through my bedroom door with her shotgun. The truth is, I never slept with Bobby and if she truly believed that, she never would've taken me back in, period—and Bobby would be gone from her life.

Through all those years I lived with them, sleeping with Bobby never entered my mind, with the exception of that year she was in prison and he and I were home with the two boys. However, if we had slept together it would've been out of mutual comfort, not love or anything Stella would have had to be concerned about. Bobby was crazy about Stella and I was too. What neither of us could risk was the possibility of losing her and bringing on a type of loneliness far worse than the loneliness we would've been seeking to alleviate by sleeping together.

That said, there were moments, particularly after she'd been gone for a few months, when the possibility of life without her seemed real, almost desirable. Those moments were terrifying for me. I ran from them and I believe Bobby did the same, though maybe not. He was so damned steady in his love for her—it was, and is, an amazing thing. You'll understand that more as we go along.

However, during that year, I could tell Bobby was struggling with something that Stella's being gone had brought to the surface. There were moments when I felt he wanted to confide in me and he'd come right to the edge and suddenly pull back. I could see it in his face, and it made me uncomfortable. Actually, there were quite a few of those moments—after a long day of working on the kennel, after a night out to the movies or dinner with the boys, after one of us had visited with Stella. It was as though some inaudible, unconscious, lightning quick conversation flashed between us. I would say, silently, "Please don't tell me anything that will crack the world Stella has provided me with," and Bobby would reply, "If I tell you, your world will crack and so will mine. I will be alone again. I can't."

Then it was over, the moment would break, the TV would go on, and the beers would come out. Bobby was not a big talker, not by a long shot. I wasn't either, not then, because it was Bobby who set the tone. Mostly, what we shared as a family was the doing end of life, doing breakfast, doing dinner—both, by the way, things Stella bitched about him not doing when she was home. And for most of the twelve months Stella was gone, we were immersed in the immense project of building the kennel.

Bobby loved to build things, anything. He put his whole being into it. Just as a musician or a dancer puts their whole being into what they create, so does Bobby—and I say "does" because I know it's still true of him. It was in the building of the kennel that I learned everything I needed to know to do the work I've done on my cabin. He was a great teacher.

And now I'm feeling tired, but I don't want to stop before I say something about Stella and Bobby's relationship. They fought constantly, usually over small things like"Why'd you pick that up with your left hand? What the hell is the matter with you? Don't you know you're s'pose to use your right hand when you do that?"—"that" could've been anything at any given time. It was part of their dance and it worked for them, really. It wasn't unpleasant to be around, like it can be with some people. More often than not it was amusing and entertaining—to them as well.

Anyway, as I came to find out from Bobby, what happened the day Stella ran me off the property was the end game of one of the rare humongous fights they had, fights that normally had nothing to do with me and ended with a brief period of sulking—no grudges. However, the way that particular fight played out is what ultimately broke through to the something that Bobby had almost told me about, but couldn't, during the year she was in prison. That was the day that something cracked so wide open that, until I returned and he was finally able to tell me, he stopped talking to everyone, including Stella, and pulled in, drank beer, and built endless fences. He even stopped going to dog shows with Stella. In fact, he stopped going anywhere except to the kennel and out into those fields.

Stella announced, to all who cared to listen, that his not coming to shows was because he was just too dangerous, "and might get to drinkin' and killin' off all the people who is rotten and jealous of me."

Dangerous is not what Bobby is.

4

When Annie Left the First Time, Bobby
Never Got to Say Good-bye

Stella could have shot the rear tires out of the pickup and
Greta would still be in the driveway, or at least no more
than a mile down the road, but she didn't. She knew Greta
would be back because Greta needed her. It was as simple
as that. There was no point in destroying tires when it
wasn't necessary. And when Greta did come crawling back,
which she figured would be in a couple of hours, they could
get on with the work at hand, making Galestorm Bordeaux
the biggest damn name in the business. And if she didn't
come back, she'd go on ahead and file a stolen car charge—
end of story.

As she walked back to the house and up the front steps,
she heard Bobby's tractor in the distance. She'd planned
on telling him all about the nightmare she'd had regarding
Margaret and Charlene—the two of them raising hell in her
head all damn night—but of course, being the dumbass that
he was, he just had to go on and on about Greta this, Greta
that. Fact was, ever since she'd gotten out of prison, coming
up on two years ago, she'd had to put up with occasions of
his going on and on about Greta in ways he never did before.
Now, normally, she just let it pass, it wasn't no big deal, but
this time she didn't. Maybe it was due to the stress of her
needing him to concentrate on the kennel and all the shit
she had to deal with regarding these people, including them
appearing in her dreams. On the other hand, it was probably
as simple as the fact she and Bobby had some kick-ass sex,
and the next thing she knew they was at the kitchen table,

and he was going on and on about Greta. Men just never learn was how she saw it.

She opened her screen door and glanced down at a pair of Greta's work boots. She picked them up and tossed them out onto the porch. She listened for the thump-thump as she walked across the living room—the thump being the best part of throwing anything.

———

"Stella, I been thinkin' I might just start buildin' a separate house for Greta, you know out in the far fields or by the stream or wherever she pleases. Hell, livin' in that itty-bitty place attached to the kennel just don't do her right. I mean, look at what she's done for you and me and the boys. As you been sayin' all along, she's a part of the family and no family sleeps off a kennel. I mean, them dogs is the best thing in the world, but she's not of that species, now is she? Besides she could build it with me. It'd be kinda fun. I mean, we made a damn good team when we built the kennel." Bobby was putting his work boots on while trying to drink his coffee and smoke a cigarette at the same time.

Stella couldn't take it, not this morning. Why couldn't he just shut up? "Bobby, what the hell are you talkin' about? You and her already built her a place, as in the one she's livin' in right now and that's exactly how she wanted it. Besides, we got plenty of room right here in the house, but I'm thinkin' maybe we don't got any room for her anymore, not anywhere on this property! The only reason she's been stayin' here is she got nowhere else to go. Nobody wants her 'cept us and I'm thinkin' maybe it's time she haul her ass outta here!"

Bobby looked up from putting his second boot on. "What the hell are you talkin' 'bout, Stella? You ain't in your right mind, I can see that clear as I can see my boot sittin' here on the floor. She's been like a daughter or little sister to you and me. You're talkin' crazy right now and I just ain't got time to hear it. You have yourself another joint and get back to me when you is thinkin' like the Stella I used to know, as in this morning when we was in bed and yesterday when you was tellin' me what a find she was."

"The key word bein' 'find,' Bobby! I found her and I can make her lost again whenever I want." Stella suddenly felt a surge of rage she hadn't accounted for. She strode over to Bobby, cigarette in hand, and kicked the boot he didn't have on yet. As it sailed across the room and hit the far wall, she stood and faced him. "YOU KNOW WHAT I THINK BOBBY? I THINK YOU SLEPT WITH THAT WHORE WHILE I WAS AWAY. ISN'T THAT ALL YOU MEN THINK ABOUT WHEN THE ONE YOU DO FUCK IS IN PRISON—FUCKIN' SOMEBODY ELSE?—EVEN IF IT IS YOUR 'DAUGHTER' OR YOUR 'SISTER' AS YOU IS CALLIN' HER. THAT RIGHT THERE IS A SIGN YOU IS HIDIN' SOMETHIN' FROM ME AND I THINK IT'S JUST PLAIN DISGUSTIN'!"

She kicked his other boot, the one he had on. It stayed put.

Bobby jumped to his feet and started yelling back. "GODDAMN WOMAN, WHAT THE HELL IS WRONG WITH YOU? I AIN'T NEVER LAID A HAND ON HER, NEVER WANTED TO!! YOU IS SCREWED UP RIGHT NOW, AND IT AIN'T THE FIRST TIME, SO DON'T GET ALL CRAZY LIKE YOU DONE BEFORE." The moment he said it, Bobby felt scared and had no idea why. There was a buzzing in his head that had started the moment she'd accused him of screwing with Greta. It was like the buzzing of high-tension wires from twenty feet away. And once he'd yelled, the sound was only four feet away and dangerously close to running right through him and God only knew what that would be like. He sat back down in hopes the buzzing would stop.

Stella stormed into her study and reappeared with her shotgun. She walked past Bobby and yanked open the front door. She stopped and looked back at him. "BOBBY, I AIN'T CRAZY AND THAT NO GOOD BITCH AIN'T WELCOME IN MY FAMILY ANYMORE. HELL, SHE FUCKED HER PAPA, AND THAT ABOUT SAYS IT ALL RIGHT THERE, DON'T IT?—SHE GOT NO RIGHT TO BE HERE, OR ANYWHERE FOR THAT MATTER 'CAUSE THAT SHIT IS LIKE SOME KINDA NASTY ASS POISON THAT WILL KILL YOU IF YOU DON'T GET RID OF IT. AND NOW YOU SLEEPIN' WITH HER? WELL, THAT IS

THE NAIL IN HER COFFIN IS ALL I GOT TO SAY 'CAUSE I'M DONE TALKIN' AND I'M GONNA TO DO WHAT I SHOULDA DONE A LONG TIME AGO!" Stella walked out and slammed the door behind her.

Bobby sat in his rocker for about fifteen seconds. He couldn't think past the buzzing, but thinking wasn't what he needed in this situation. He had to stop Stella no matter what it would take. He got up and rushed out the door, nearly stumbling down the front steps. Having only the one boot made his balance precarious, at best.

Stella lifted the shotgun off her shoulder as she strode through the kennel door.

Lopsided as he was, Bobby ran as fast as he could, only to stumble on the stone step he'd so carefully built to mark the entrance to the kennel—a touch that had been unnecessary according to Stella, but he'd wanted to do it. On it he'd engraved "Galestorm Bordeaux, above the rest."

He fell through the open kennel door and landed on the cement floor. That's when he heard a gunshot followed by Stella's yelling at Greta about how she was "nothin' but tainted genes," and that's when the buzzing in his head was no longer near him but upon him, inside him. He pulled himself up and started walking back towards the house. It was over.

A couple of minutes later Greta ran past him and jumped into his truck. Then Stella ran by, nearly knocking him over, shotgun in hand.

Bobby heard a loud snap inside his head as he watched his truck speed silently out of the driveway with Greta at the wheel. The snap had been so loud it took away his hearing. He could see Stella standing there, shooting the shotgun in the air, yelling and yelling and yelling, but he heard nothing. Her mouth was simply flapping and flapping and flapping. And all he could think to do was turn and walk back to the kennel—get on with feeding the dogs.

The next thing he knew Stella was in front of him with her hand on his chest, her mouth still flapping. He pushed her aside and kept walking and she kept appearing in front of him, pushing his chest, and he kept pushing her aside until, finally, she was gone.

If he could've, he would've jumped in his truck and done the same thing as Greta, as in drove right on out the driveway and down the road, but he didn't have his truck—Greta did. So, he was just going to go on and feed the dogs, and then fix the section of fence that needed fixing.

———

Bobby was not a man who cared to do a whole lot of thinking. He'd been that way for as long as he could remember which went back to the day he woke up in a foster home at age ten. He didn't know if he'd done much thinking before then, but he assumed he probably hadn't. From day one in that foster home, everything he did was based on getting through each day, one foot in front of the other.

Being in school back then was nothing more to him than trying to do what the people around him wanted him to do and keeping his mouth shut in between. The problem was that the reading and writing skills he had, which he didn't know how he got in the first place, were not up to par. This caused a whole lot of trouble inside himself and with the people he was trying to please. His refusal to "apply" himself was interpreted as "sullen" and "uncooperative" rather than he just couldn't think.

There was one thing he was good at and that was Shop. He could build or fix anything he was asked to build or fix. It was easy because it didn't involve much thinking, at least not the kind that he couldn't do. He liked Shop more than just about anything—he even looked forward to it. It wasn't enough, however, to keep him out of the constant trouble he was in. And he didn't have any friends because, from day one, he hated being asked where he was from, where he lived, what he liked or didn't like. It just didn't seem like it was anybody's business.

At his foster home, all he did was watch TV, eat, and play with the two German Shepherds that lived there. He'd named them Do-this and Do-that and they were the only living beings that gave him comfort. When he was with them, he didn't feel a constant pull to be anything other than who he was in the moment, which was the only place he wanted to be.

His foster parents never bothered him much, which was fine. They never told him when to eat or even when to go to bed. He made himself sandwiches when he was hungry and stayed up most nights and watched whatever was on TV until he fell asleep, either on the floor with the dogs or up on the raggedy old green couch that sagged in the middle.

Occasionally, he would overhear his foster mother on the phone saying they were doing everything they could to get him to do his homework and behave, which was a lie, but not one that he cared to correct. All it meant to him was they were going to continue to leave him alone. He knew, in truth, all they were interested in was the check they got each month. Just because he didn't read or write well didn't mean he was stupid. In fact, knowing what people were all about, as in what their intentions were, was as easy to him as Shop was. That bit of knowing was how he got by and precisely why, after a year of school and foster care, he decided to go missing. He knew a time was fast approaching when someone was going to do something drastic to him and he didn't want to be around to find out what that something was.

The saddest thing about his decision to go missing was leaving Do-this and Do-that behind. He wanted them with him, more than anything, but knew it wouldn't work out because going missing meant he had to be completely alone. His last hours in that apartment were spent sitting on the floor watching TV in front of the raggedy green couch with an arm around each of those dogs. It was the first time, in the only year he could remember, that he came close to what he figured to be the feeling that comes right before tears. He'd seen tears at school and on TV but never had them. He was glad, though, as he sat there with Do-this and Do-that, that the tears never came because, from what he'd seen, he might not have been able to do what he needed to do if they had.

He left in the middle of the night—right out the front door. The dogs barked frantically as he walked down the front steps and out onto the street. His walk turned into a run. The dogs had no one now, but he couldn't think about that, he just couldn't.

The next seven years were years he valiantly survived without detection by the authorities, only to end up in prison at the age of eighteen for armed robbery.

There wasn't nothin' valiant about it—nothin' at all. I did what had to be done. Alls I knew was "Bobby get food whatever way you can and don't never get caught by the police or anybody that even smells like someone wantin' to put you anywhere but where you want to be."

It wasn't nothin' to be hungry or cold next to bein' in a situation where I had no say about anythin' particurly anythin' pertainin' to me. The point bein', I went missin' and there wasn't nobody lookin' for me and that's the part where a lot of folks go all stupid, as in "How can a kid be walkin' the streets and got nobody lookin' for him or at least givin' a shit?"

Well, if nobody was thinkin' on me, then it just weren't that hard to be missin' and not be found. And remember now, I was in the middle of a big-ass city. This wasn't no small town, everybody-all-cozy-and-all, America. So long as I didn't do nothin' real stupid, it just weren't all that hard to stay out of people's minds who never had me there in the first place.

There weren't no posters, no parents on CNN cryin' for me, and no rewards for findin' me. The most dangerous kinda person durin' them seven years were the do-gooder types who mighta thought they was doin' me a favor by turnin' me over to the authorities—but they was rare, let me tell you. So rare it woulda had to be me searchin' for them if I wanted 'em to find me. Come to think of it, I don't think I ever met one of them durin' that whole seven years.

Now, you might be wonderin' how I even knew people like that existed if I ain't never met one. I'll tell you how. I watched a potload of TV when I was in that foster home. I learned most of what I knew from that TV. It was all right there in black and white. And the good news is there wasn't no CNN 24-hour news back then. If there was, I never woulda gone missin'. That, right there, is enough to scare the livin' shit outta any kid who is even considerin' goin' missin'.

I mean the world didn't look so bad to me on that little black-and-white screen thirty-some years ago. In fact, it looked a whole lot easier than the situation I was in, I'll tell you that. The difference bein', without CNN and all them other stations, I had no clue there was pedophiles, people pickin' up missin' kids and sellin' 'em, puttin' 'em in cages or closets, screwin' the shit out of 'em, then killin' 'em. Hell, all I was worried about was the people I knew who was tryin' to control my situation.

So, goin' missin' was my way to be free of that worry. It wasn't "valiant," not one bit. Far as I was concerned I was free—hungry and cold a lot—but that ain't no big price to pay for people to stop botherin' me, now is it?

I will tell you, though, when I wound up in prison is when I started havin' to worry about people I didn't know squat about messin' with me, as in tryin' to control my life.

Like I said, I didn't mind them years I was missin', it was my little corner of freedom 'fore I wound up in prison. After that I could never be missin' again 'cause I had a record which meant somethin' or someone was always breathin' down my back, and knowin' that made me madder and madder. So I'd do shit, like break into places. I just kept doin' stuff that if I weren't so damn mad I never woulda done—and next thing I knew I was back in prison and the situation just got worse. I never shoulda done that first big robbery with them other kids, I shoulda just kept to myself and stayed alone and missin'—under the radar. Them seven years are the only ones I can look back at and see a person beholdin' to no one.

Like I said, I didn't know where I came from back then. When I had to, I just used my story that Stella already told you about, the tornado and all. The way I saw it, it was true as anythin' else, plus I'd seen it on the TV. Fact is, from the day me and Stella met, there was no end to what she could tell me about me. Every time she told me somethin' new 'bout myself, I said, "Fuck it, sounds good and it's better than what I got"—so I took it. I never had anybody so interested in who I was and it wasn't like she was bein' nosey or nothin'—like most people. I don't know how to explain it. She was crazy about my tornado story, told me not to change a thing about it. And she didn't give a crap about the other stuff I told her about me, meanin' it didn't make no difference to her that it don't add up to much. I mean ten years of nothin', seven years of bein' free and hungry, then more years of bein' in and out of prison learnin' how to be tougher than the next guy to stay alive— what did that add up to? A big fat nothin'. But she cared a whole lot about what she had to say about me and I liked the feelin' of her thinkin' so hard on me.

She came up with things like me havin' an Indian papa who was beat to death on a reservation by the reservation cops, or that I can beat the crap outta anyone any size, and me havin' somethin' real special with dogs—somethin' nobody else had. She said that was somethin' that God gave me. Like I said, no one ever did that. Everythin', includin' me, was just plain old black and white till I met her, which was in a bar in Atlanta.

There she was, surrounded by a ton of people, like she always was in them days—'course I didn't know that on that particular night. Anyway, I was high on bein' out of prison and I was nobody in particular, she was somebody—that was clear as day. She was like a shinin' light in that crowd a' people. She was the only one talkin' most the time. Everybody else was listenin' and laughin' and grinnin'. Now that right there was somethin' to me. I knew she was somebody special and I wanted to be next to that somebody.

I don't believe she was lookin' to be with me, except like she said, she never met a man who didn't want somethin' from her and she liked that a whole lot. I did want somethin', she was wrong about that; it just wasn't the somethin' that most men wanted. See, she didn't want no one to own her. I told her, "Why would I want to own you, darlin'? I ain't never owned nobody and that's the way I want to keep it 'cause ownin' somebody means you ain't free."

Well, she said she never heard that before and maybe we could spend some time together.

Now, I weren't ugly, which was a good thing 'cause I knew that was important to her. Like I said, I know people and what they want and nobody in my whole life ever told me I was ugly, so I knew I wasn't. I heard a lot of other things said about me, but not that.

When she got around to tellin' me she had three kids and couple of dogs, we were sittin' alone. She was drinkin' a margarita and I was drinkin' a beer. I never drank anythin' but beer—'cept on that trip we took to Europe back when we first started the Bordeaux business. I drank a bunch of them tiny bottles of Jack Daniels on the plane. And that's when I learned exactly why I never drank that stuff. God had told me never to touch hard liquor from as far back as I could remember, but I just never knew why that was till then.

And besides God tellin' me in his own way—which I'll tell you about when I get around to it—it was real important for me to keep my head straight when I was just about anywhere. I ain't a big man, meanin' there a' ton bigger than me and I didn't want to lose the only advantage I had which is knowin' what people's intentions are and makin' sure I'm ready if their intentions is bad. From what I could see being drunk is losin' that advantage.

I mean, I wasn't no tee-totter, or whatever the hell you call it. Don't get me wrong. I liked my beer, but never more than gettin' a buzz. 'Course after Annie got run off the property I didn't give a shit anymore about what I lost and I sure as hell didn't want no part of what my clear mind saw on that day.

Anyway, when this beautiful, shinin' light of a woman told me about havin' three kids and them dogs, I swear that brought tears to my eyes, somethin' that just never happened before—hell, up to then I didn't even know my eyes could do that. It was some damn miracle. That was about it, right there. Between my brand new tears and not wantin' to own anybody and her bein' somebody and her kids and them dogs—well, we each had us somethin' the other one wanted real bad.

How'd I get to be alone with her in that bar? Well, like I said, I was flyin' so high from bein' outta prison, I just wasn't being my usual under-the-radar kinda person, so from the way I was actin' when I walked right up to her in front of all them people and asked her to have a drink with me, I do believe she thought I was a big somebody, somebody worth knowin'.

She got right up and said, "Why not? I like meetin' a new man, 'specially a new man who don't think twice about walkin' up to a woman like me, in front of a bunch of good lookin' men who I already know."

She turned and looked at all them people and they laughed and cleared out, just like that. 'Course, when they all left I went back to being nobody in particular and couldn't say much, but bein' tongue tied around Stella don't last long. She don't skip a beat, she had me talkin' like I was somebody.

When we went back to her house that night, I helped her to bed 'cause she was pretty drunk. Some girl who was watchin' her kids, she left and I fell asleep on the couch. The next mornin' I met the kids. Greta was ten at the time, Jonathan was eight and Darren was six. They cozied right up to me like I'd been there forever. And them Rottis and that Bulldog she had? Well, we were crazy about each other. I hadn't been with dogs like that since Do-this and Do-that.

I swear it felt like I was home for the first time in my whole entire life. Now, don't get me wrong, it weren't easy—none of it. We started fightin' almost from day one. There weren't no big ole honeymoon section for us. We got that in little pieces over the next couple years and if you was to put all them pieces together you got what most couples got at the beginnin', probly more.

I was twenty-seven and she was twenty-eight when we met—I think. I don't keep track of that kinda of thing. Anyway, it wasn't but a year later that we, meanin' mostly she, started thinkin' on the business she wanted to start—the escort service. Well, I didn't care much, one way or the other. I told her I wanted her to do whatever she wanted to. I had everythin' I wanted already.

So, while she was thinkin' on it and figurin' out the details, I got me a job with a buildin' contractor who was willin' to hire me under the table. He didn't give a damn about me bein' an ex-con. I made good money, meanin' Stella could take the time she needed to set things straight so she would, like she said, "Never have to kiss any motherfucker's ass, ever again."

Now, Stella ain't no homebody like a lotta women, but she is a damn fine cook and she keeps a clean house. And when we had the kids livin' with us, she could do all the stuff that women with kids do, and still run a business. I will tell you though, she weren't one bit happy with my cleanin' skills when we first moved in together. I mean accordin' to her, I had NO skills regardin' that.

Well, I didn't believe her and said far as I could tell I did just fine. I never shoulda said that 'cause startin' that same day, she took it upon herself to prove her side of things. She said she wasn't gonna pick up one more thing of mine that was lyin' where it shouldn't be. I said "fine." So, then everythin' of mine that she picked up, she started puttin' in a big pile by the front door and left it there, right where anybody could see it. My underwear, my jeans, my lighters, my boots, my socks, it was all right there, piling up every damn day. She even put a damn sign on it, "Bobby's shit—don't nobody mess with it but Bobby."

She told the kids that anythin' they found lyin' around that was mine, just toss it in that pile—and they did. I swear they started huntin' for my stuff just to make that pile bigger. They teased me on it, almost every day.

I would tell her, "Damn, woman, why not just leave that shit where you found it? Why take the time to pick up my shit and build that damn pile when you could be usin' that time to get on with whatever you're gettin' on with?"

She'd tell me it was her damn business what she did with her time and she happened to like lookin' at a pile of my shit every time she walked through the door. She said it reminded her of how useless a man was and it was just the motivator she needed to make damn sure she was never in a position to have to count on me for nothin'.

Truth is, she did count on me. She just never considered the alternatives to her idea of countin' on somebody.

Anyway, that pile kept growin' and I just let it grow. Then one day I come home and there's a new sign on it—"This shit is goin' up in flames by 11 p.m. if it ain't gone."

She loved makin' signs that's for damn sure. Well, that sign pissed me off enough to make me swear I wasn't gonna do nothin' at all about that pile. "I don't give a rat's ass what you do, Stella!" That's what I said.

Well, wouldn't you know, at 11 p.m. she was out in the front yard throwin' gasoline on top of my stuff, not sayin' a word. Our bedroom window was right there and I smelt the gasoline, it was strong. Before I could get up and look out the window I heard the blaze. I swear Stella had no clue how fast that stuff would burn. 'Fore I knew it she was screamin' that the fire was gonna spread to the front porch and yellin' for me to call the fire department, which I didn't need to do due to the fact that one of our far neighbors had already did that—and I say "far" 'cause there weren't nobody for a half a mile.

That blaze and all its smoke filled the sky and made a helluva stink. I mean there was all kinds of stuff in that pile—leather, rubber boots, hats, plastic cups, dirty socks— she even threw in my favorite rockin' chair and my favorite foot stool along with a bunch of stuff I ain't never seen, just to make her point!

When the fire department arrived, I was out there tryin' to save my chair and my footstool. I heard Stella tell 'em it was my fire and that she had done what she could to stop me by tellin' me it wasn't junk and I coulda given that stuff to the Salvation Army and she didn't know why I had a need to burn it!

Well, I tucked that away in my memory and waited for the day I could get back at her—and that's how it was between us. There weren't never a moment where neither one of us was bored, that's for damn sure.

The kids? They saw it as entertainin' mostly. It wasn't like we ever hurt each other when we had one of them kinda fights— they learned that early on. Once things was settled down and we got back to laughin'—it was all OK. It wasn't nothin' for them. It's partly how they is survivin' so well now—well, not Greta.

The boys, well, nothin' bothers them. Hell, when we was raided by the FBI, they were cool as cucumbers. I was mad as shit they were put in the papers and all, but it didn't bother them. They grew up and left home more prepared to deal with damn near anythin' than anybody. Yup, I got pissed off a lot, so did Stella, but most the time it wasn't about them—I mean they was real straight next to us. From their way of lookin' at things, we was damn near crazy half the time and they took it for what it was—and don't that beat all? They knew the difference between the crazy part and the good part. They left home with mostly the good part.

Anyway, that day Stella shot a hole through Annie's bedroom wall and sent her packin'? Well, that fight we had was a different kinda fight. That was when the color drained right outta me. It was like I was walkin' backwards out that bar door, the one where I met Stella, and there I was, back on the street, alone, just like all that color never happened.

After the last time Stella had appeared in front of him flapping her mouth and pushing on his chest, Bobby just kept walking—nothing was going to distract him. And once he got to the kennel, he pulled a case of beer out of the fridge, hiked it up under his arm, and went out to fix the section of fence that had been busted for over a week. When he was done fixing that, he decided to build another fence for no reason other than he needed to do it. So, he got on his John-Deere-does-everything little tractor and started digging the fence postholes.

He sweated and pounded and drank one beer after the other. It wasn't just a buzz he was after this time. Slow beers while he was working, sweating, and drinking water, never gave him more than a buzz, but this time he was hungering for a lot more than that.

As he drank and dug and pounded, the one other time he'd gotten real drunk came back to him. It was on the plane on their trip to Europe. Greta, aka Annie, had stayed home to be with the boys. It was the first time he and Stella had a stretch of time alone together since she got out of prison and it was his first time on a plane.

Being alone with Stella wasn't the part that drove him to drinking that hard liquor. A couple beers was always enough to cut the sharp edges with her and, besides, she didn't have any edges that day. She was excited about the new business they were about to launch and she was crazy about traveling. She loved meeting people and talking and talking and talking, so long as most everybody else was willing to listen and listen and listen, which they were most of the time.

He wasn't much for traveling or meeting new people. He only did those things to get something done that needed doing, and he'd never done either of those things anywhere but on the ground, as in both feet on the earth, preferably the red earth of Georgia, and if not there then at least somewhere in America. Bobby Kansas had never been off the ground before and had never willingly put his life in the hands of anybody, especially not anybody in a uniform.

As he sat there in that seat and felt the plane lift off the ground, it was as if a huge invisible octopus had grabbed him and was squeezing the breath out of him. All he could think to do was suck down some hard liquor real fast. He'd never had it before, not once in his entire life. He hated the smell of it and the sound of it. The smell part some people understood, but it was the sound part that was confusing to most everyone. He'd just say he was born being able to hear the sound of liquor and it was an awful sound. Most people would laugh like it was some kind of joke, but it wasn't, not to Bobby. The strange part was he could tolerate people drinking hard liquor in bars. That's when the sound was far away, like a whisper—but just about anywhere else, it was a sound that got so bad sometimes he couldn't think. When it got that way, he'd have to sit a ways off, go for a walk, or go to another room to get relief. Stella had stopped taking him to social occasions early on, except for bars, because she said it was embarrassing to have to explain to people why he behaved the way he did.

"What am I s'pose to tell people, Bobby? That you can't stand the sound of the hard liquor in the room?! Now that right there will lose me any connections I'm tryin' to make. Everybody's gonna think you is just plain nuts. I can't have people thinkin' that whether it's true or not. I ain't never heard no sound, so as far as I'm concerned you ARE nuts, but unlike the rest of the world I know that it's all just a matter of what kinda nuts you can handle and hearin' hard liquor ain't half bad compared to the shit I seen."

Bobby could never explain to anyone exactly what the sound was. All he could say, when pushed, was the only thing that even came close to it was the sound they played in the movie "Jaws" when the shark was approaching, but even that didn't really do it justice.

One particular night, he tried real hard to explain it to Stella, who he knew wasn't really interested, but since she was busy smoking joints and doing paperwork, the room was quiet enough for to him to voice his explanation with the chance she might hear a piece of it.

"Imagine if you was sittin' in the quiet, I mean the real quiet—not like what you're doin' now, which is suckin' on a joint and cussin' real soft under your breath and hearin' the sound of your pen on them papers. I mean no sound at all— and it's all black at the same time. Quiet as shit and blacker than any night you ever been in. Well, that right there has a sound if you got the ears for it. It's deep, real deep. Take the deepest sound you ever heard and put it at the bottom of a mile deep well, it's even deeper 'n that—and it's creepin' up on you, like some kinda doom, slow at first and then it's closin' in and you can't see nothin'. You got no goddamn idea what it is and why that sound is fillin' up your whole body. See, it ain't just a ears sound, it's a sound that your hands and feet and belly can hear. Fact is, it makes your belly curl in on itself like one of them puddin's you keep tryin' to make that fills that little dish and a half a minute later it's sucked flat on the bottom. I'm tellin' you it's there, it's loud and it's clear as day to us people who can hear it."

Stella looked up from her paperwork. "Bobby, can't you see I'm workin' here? And why the hell are you draggin' my puddin's into somethin' that just don't make sense. No, I ain't never heard no sound like that and I'm thinkin' it's a damn good thing that I ain't, 'cause from the way you're talkin' it's a goddamn miracle you ain't spendin' most of your time hidin' under that rockin' chair of yours, which I'm thinkin' you need to go out on the porch and sit in till you get yourself straight. Why the hell would anyone want to hear that shit? You say, 'us people who can hear it' like it's some kinda special power. You got that all wrong, buddy, far as I can tell. Like I said, don't be talkin' shit like that around any of my friends and I say MY 'cause they definitely ain't gonna be yours if you go on like that."

Bobby dropped the empty beer can, grabbed another beer from the back of the tractor and walked to the next fence post. He had no idea how many holes he'd dug, how many posts he'd laid or how many more he would do, but it didn't matter. He hesitated before he picked up the large mallet and felt his front pocket for his gold lighter. For some reason, he thought maybe it would be gone. It wasn't. He pulled it out and looked at it. It was the lighter Stella gave him during the first year the escort service took off. Money was falling from the sky as far as he could tell. The lighter was solid gold plated and had an inscription on it that read "To Bobby K. love Stella." Every pair of his jeans had a spot on the right front pocket that was worn deeper than anywhere else on his jeans, except the knees. He put it back in his pocket, picked up the mallet, and got back to thinking about that plane trip.

As soon as the plane was in the air, he waited for Stella to go to the bathroom to smoke a cigarette and ordered himself a bunch of those tiny bottles of Jack Daniels. He poured them all into his empty soda can and shoved the bottles in the pocket on the back of the seat in front of him. He had gulped most of it down by the time Stella returned to her seat.

Before long, a blonde hostess appeared and accused Stella of breaking the law by smoking in the bathroom.

Stella, being smarter than the hostess, and not the least bit intimidated, claimed she didn't know it was illegal to smoke in the bathroom. She said if people can screw in there she figured it was the one place on the plane she could smoke, and besides she thought the law only applied to the seating area of the plane.

That was when the man in the seat in front of them twisted his head around and faced Stella. He was a college looking type with little round glasses and a puff of a beard hanging off his chin. He said something to Stella about her being "ignorant."

He remembered it, like it happened yesterday. All he wanted to do was rip that man's little beard and glasses from his cocky little face. It made his blood boil. It was a rage that he'd tucked away inside himself and belted down with a hundred chains. It had peeked out on occasion before he'd met Stella, which is how he kept ending up in prison, but it had never come out since his life with her began, not until that moment on the plane and with a belly full of Jack Daniels.

What happened after he felt that burning desire to rip that man's face apart was lost from his memory. He'd put it away in the fuzzy part of his mind. However, Stella spent the rest of the flight apologizing for the foul language and threats that had spilled out of his mouth as he leaned across her and caused her to spill her soda all over her lap.

What he did remember was Stella pacing back and forth across that hotel room in Paris the morning they arrived. She talked as she paced.

"Bobby, that is the first and last time you will ever drink booze again 'cause I now got me a full understandin' of exactly why you can't be doin' that. And as far as the 'sound' you been tryin' so hard to explain to me, well, don't bother anymore, 'cause the way I see it, that sound is a big ole message from God tellin' you that shit will be the death of me. And on top of that, I now know for certain one of your parents, probly your papa, was one hundred percent Indian 'cause that's the only thing that explains what booze does to you!"

That was the very morning his identity as part Indian came to pass.

She kept pacing and smoking and pacing and smoking. He couldn't keep track of her, so he just looked at the wall in front of him.

"It was awful damn hard to get us outta the trouble you got us into. And as much as I hated kissin' that son of a bitch's ass, I had to. Do you know, I had to shove you back into your seat by smackin' you in the head with my plastic soda cup? I hit you so hard the cup broke, but that didn't even work! So I pushed the broke edges of that cup right into your face. The way I saw it, a few little cuts on your face was a small price to pay for us bein' picked up by French police when we got here, is all I got to say. And once I got your ugly ass face outta the way, I had to explain to that man that this was our first trip to Europe and you was extremely nervous and upset about leavin' our poor sick child back in a hospital in Atlanta!"

She stopped pacing and stood facing him as he just lay there looking at the wall and listening. He could see her, plain as day, he just couldn't look right at her.

She shook her head and continued to pace.

"I prayed to God, Bobby, right then and there, that he weren't no doctor 'cause if he was, I was about to dig myself a hole so deep it wouldn't have been worth my while to kiss his ass in the first place."

The pacing continued. "I TOLD THAT MAN AND MOST THE DAMN PEOPLE ON THAT AIRPLANE—MEANIN' EVERYBODY WHO HEARD THAT PSYCHO SHIT THAT CAME OUTTA YOUR MOUTH..."

She stopped suddenly and lowered her voice. "Damnit, Bobby, do you want me to wake up everybody in this hotel?"

He knew the right thing to do was just lie there and keep his mouth shut.

She sucked in on her cigarette and blew the smoke out her nose. "I told them, the whole bunch of 'em, that you and me were going to France to consult with a specialist regarding our daughter's 'condition.'"

She raised her arms and made quotation marks in the air above her head. "Which was some kind of condition I couldn't discuss because it was all so complicated and distressin', but I told them to imagine if their daughter was lyin' in a hospital bed with a kind of pain that no amount of drugs could stop, a kind of pain that made her vomit and have the diarrhea twenty-four seven. I told them you'd had too much to drink because of bein' so upset and well, you put your upsetness where it didn't belong and I was real sorry."

————

Bobby dropped one can after the other as he walked the line of posts. As far as he could tell, Stella was probably the only person that could've stopped him from beating the man to death. That was the only thing he remembered about the particular rage he felt just prior to Stella smacking him in the face—it was a killing rage. It had never before come out in the form of wanting to take a life, but it did in that moment and it most certainly had something to do with the liquor that God, and now Stella, never wanted him to touch—not ever again.

The sun was now high in the sky, and he only had a couple beers left and no water. He decided to climb on his tractor, go get the last case of beer out of the fridge, pick up a few more posts, a bunch of wire, and another couple of gallons of water. His clothes looked and felt like he'd been swimming in the creek out back, so he figured if he didn't drink a bunch more water he'd be nothing but skin and bones in a couple of hours.

As he bumped along, back towards the kennel, he wondered if he was drunk or not because he really couldn't tell. What he did know was he hadn't thought for one minute about what happened that morning or the loud snap that had shut down his hearing, and that was the main thing, meaning that was all that mattered, one foot in front of the other, nothing more, nothing less.

Before he knew it, he was headed back out in the pasture, shirt off, and fully prepared to continue doing what he did best.

————

That's real nice what you're writin' and those things did happen, just like I told you, but you got to understand I was out in them fields not thinkin' on anythin', period—'cept the particular job in front of me which was either diggin', poundin', or hammerin'. And I heard nothin' all day, not the engine of the tractor, not the hammerin' or poundin', nothin' at all till that evenin'. All I could do was feel the poundin'and hammerin' and that was all that was goin' on. My whole point bein', I didn't want no part in thinkin' on anythin' that day.

5

The Evening After Annie Left

The blue sky had gone pink and the sweat had ceased to drip from Bobby's forehead about the time he heard Stella's voice, way off in the distance. He didn't pay much attention to it, except to feel some annoyance at the intrusion on the contentment he had found. He had stopped thinking about everything—Greta running out the driveway, Stella blasting off her mouth and her shotgun—everything, including where the fence he was building was going. He just dug, hauled, and pounded, and it made no difference to him that the light was fading. It was all about the feel of the task at hand, something that was second nature to him.

"BOBBY KANSAS, WHERE THE HELL ARE YOU?" Stella stopped at the far side of the kennel and listened. Clear across the nearest field and into the woods, she heard the hammering. "Let's go, Oz, and see what Bobby's up to. I swear if I don't keep an eye on his ass, somethin' gets done or not done that shoulda not or shoulda been done."

She patted Oz on the head as he stood steadfastly beside her, ears forward, his sight focused on the woods, same as hers. She slowly followed the new fence line, studying it carefully as she walked. She knew the fence was at least four feet tall because it was just above her shoulder height, which was taller than she'd asked for, but acceptable. She just couldn't wrap her mind around why it was he'd gone so far, that part was not in the plan.

At about twenty-five yards, she nearly tripped over two empty green beer bottles. Then at hundred yards, she spotted two more. "OK, I get it," she snorted and rested her hand on Oz's head. "Mr. I'm-gonna-build-me-a-puppy-fence is having a fine old time while I've been on the phone dealin' with puppy buyers and inquirin' minds—meanin' spies tryin' to get a fix on my plans. On top of that, I been cleanin' up his shit from damn near every room in the house, along with tryin' to get the damn police to get his damn truck back from Greta who don't got the balls to stick around and face the music. Well, she's gonna pay big time. I swear, I get stuck with dealin' with all the bullshit while everybody else just goes about their business like it weren't never there."

She patted down her pockets for cigarettes—there were none—then stumbled upon a joint that was lying deep in her breast pocket, right next to the seam—squashed flat. She was damned grateful for joints that were lost and then found. She lit it and offered a hit to Oz who turned his head away to keep smoke from getting up his nose. "Someday, buddy, you'll understand why I smoke this stuff and that's exactly when you won't be gettin' any."

She took a second long hit and moved along the fence to where there were two more empty green bottles. She stopped and studied the fence again. Not only was it four feet tall, it was about as solid as a fence could be. She couldn't imagine even a truck being able to crash through it. "Hell, a pup will probly kill hisself if he runs into this thing. Bobby has gone overboard this time—wastin' his time, which is my time. Goddamn, I could put a herd of elephants behind this thing!"

She leaned over and picked up one of the now predictable, every-so-often pair of beer bottles. "This is startin' to have the appearance of that Hans and Gretel story, only Bobby ain't neither one of them and these ain't no bread crumbs!"

She and Oz walked on, following the fence line into the woods, away from the setting sun. As she walked, she calculated that Bobby had, thus far, put in about three to four hundred yards of fence and she hadn't run into any corners yet. "Oz, Bobby ain't hisself right now. He just ain't right and we gotta deal with it, 'cause I smell trouble if we don't. He ain't thinkin' on what he's buildin', as in the overall plan, and that ain't like him. If he thinks on anythin' right, it's what he's buildin', so we got us a little problem to clear up and I just know it's got somethin' to do with that damn Greta."

She dropped the burning roach to the ground and stomped on it. "Bobby, you and me got to talk about this fence you're buildin'—that among some other things!"

Bobby had stopped hammering. He was busy digging when Stella walked up behind him.

"Bobby!" She waited for him to turn and look at her, but he just kept on with his pole digger. "It's gettin' late, Bobby, so you need to stop this crazy-ass fence buildin' and get your head straight! This ain't no goddamn puppy fence! What you're buildin' here is a pasture big enough for a herd of elephants. Hell, you even got the damn thing runnin' into the woods so they can scratch their backs on them trees. If we let them pups loose in this thing, by the time we find 'em, if we ever do, they'll be starved to death. What the hell are you thinkin'?"

Bobby kept digging and the red dirt piled up by his feet. "I ain't thinkin'."

Stella walked around in front of him and grabbed the pole digger. Bobby wouldn't let go. He pulled back on it, and as he did so, Stella lost her footing and fell to her knees, still holding the pole. "LET IT GO, BOBBY! EVERY BIT OF IT! WE DON'T NEED GRETA NO MORE, DON'T YOU SEE THAT? WE GOT EVERYTHING WE NEED WITHOUT HER. SHE'S NOTHIN' BUT A WHORE!"

Bobby released the pole and Stella fell all the way forward catching herself with her hands sunk deep into a pile of red dirt. She grabbed a fist full of it and threw it at Bobby. "YOU AIN'T NOTHIN' EITHER, BOBBY, NOTHIN' WITHOUT ME. YOU DO REALIZE THAT DON'T YOU?"

Bobby brushed the red dirt off his bare chest and grabbed the digging pole again. His voice stayed steady. He wanted nothing more than to just be left alone. "Oh, so I'm nothin'? Well if I is nothin' than you is worse than nothin'. You coulda killed her, you know. You really coulda killed her! We both know that." He looked at her silhouette as the light from the setting sun shot straight through the trees and hit her in the back as she faced him.

"WHAT THE HELL ARE YOU TALKIN' ABOUT? YOU'RE THE ONE WITH THE VIOLENT PAST, REMEMBER?" She put her foot in the hole Bobby was digging. "GO ON, SHOVE THAT THING RIGHT THROUGH MY GODDAMN FOOT." She pulled her cell phone from her jeans pocket and opened it. "AND WHEN YOU'RE DONE, I WILL CALL THE POLICE SO FAST AND AFTER THAT YOU WON'T HAVE NO TOMORROWS, AT LEAST NONE OUT HERE UNDER THAT DAMN BLUE SKY YOU LOVE TO GO ON ABOUT, DAY AFTER DAY! AND IF YOU DON'T THINK THEY'D BELIEVE ME YOU BETTER THINK AGAIN! YOU GOT THE ARMED ROBBERY ON YOUR RECORD AND GUESS WHAT? YOU GOT SOMETHIN' ELSE THAT I AIN'T NEVER TOLD YOU."

Bobby stepped back and tried to see her face, but couldn't. All he saw was a thick mass of hair flaring out from on top of a lean dark shadow of a body. He looked away as the orange sun bore painfully into his eyes. "And what would that be?" he asked.

Stella stopped yelling. She had his full attention now and would make good use of it. "Well, Bobby, I did a lot of checking all them years ago and you might be real surprised to know that I found out who your parents was and what happened to 'em. I never told you 'cause I didn't think you should know, bein' as it's kinda deranged and all." She stepped in closer to him. "You got a cigarette? I'm clean out."

She watched him as he reached into the pocket of his open shirt. She scoffed, "I hate your damn Marlboros but it's better than no smokes at all."

He handed her the pack and she studied it as she pulled out a cigarette. "I swear, you are such a sucker for them advertisements. What I'm wonderin' is where's your damn horse and all 'em cows you should be herdin' while you is smokin'. Hell, you could throw a hundred of them Marlboro cows behind this big ass fence when you is done."

"I ain't interested in cows." Bobby retrieved his pack of Marlboros and looked at her. He still couldn't see her face.

Stella placed the cigarette between her lips. "The way I see it now's a good time to let you in on my little secret. This situation is just callin' for it—you get my meanin'?" As soon as the cigarette became still, she let loose the flame from her lighter.

Bobby watched her and waited. He had no idea where she was headed, but figured he'd find out soon enough. One thing he was sure of was that it was going to be real interesting.

Stella inhaled and closed her lighter. "You never lived in Kansas, Bobby. I always knew that, even before I found out the truth, but bein' the kind person that I am, I let you just go on with your little fairy tale about the tornado, the Indian papa who killed a cop on the reservation 'cause he was so mad about bein' held hostage on a for-shit piece of land, the whole ball of gum, all of it! I've let you have it and chew on it for all these years. Well, the sweetness has kinda wore off, in my book, so I think it's my duty to set you straight."

Bobby picked up the pole digger and started digging again right next to the hole that Stella had her foot in.

"Bobby, you can keep on diggin' that hole which, by the way, is now gonna be out of line, but I ain't gonna shut up, not no more, and you are gonna have to listen to every word 'cause it's what's gonna keep us together, and you will know exactly what I mean when I'm done." Stella sat down, keeping her one foot in the hole, and sucked in on her cigarette. She had all night to make things right.

Bobby turned for a moment and watched her as she began to blow smoke rings out into the air. She was at a different angle now. The sun was no longer directly behind her and her wild hair looked an even richer red than it actually was due to the red/orange light. Her skin, once as soft as the skin under the belly of a newborn pup, looked tougher now with all the outdoors work she had been doing, not ugly tough, but beautiful tough. He had always told her that what she needed was a good amount of sunshine and fresh air, and now that they were running a kennel she would get plenty. He had claimed it would bring the Italian part out in her face. "You is one expressive woman," he'd said one day. "Hell, ain't no one can match what comes outta your mouth, 'cept maybe an Italian, which is what your mama was—and what that means is you got the skin that can take the sun without a whole lotta burnin'. A little brownin' and toughin' up is a good thing. Puttin' all the stuff on to keep the sun off your skin just ain't the way it should be. Hell, beautiful as you think it is, it just don't match who you are, bein' pale and all. Don't get me wrong, you are gorgeous no matter what you do, but what I'm sayin' is you is tough and gorgeous, and you oughta look it, at least that's the way I see it."

Stella stopped blowing smoke rings and looked over at him. "Bobby, lookin' at me all bleary eyed ain't gonna change the facts of what I tell you, so you better put that pole digger down 'cause you just may wanna be sittin' down for this."

Stella could tell he was going to try to squirm his way out from under what she had to tell him, but she wasn't swayed one bit. What she had to do was for the necessity of all involved. She watched him put the pole digger down and pull a cigarette from his pack. She almost felt sorry for him, all that building, all day, on a fence that wasn't what it was supposed to be.

Bobby sat down and stuck the cigarette between his lips, but didn't light it. He just flicked the flame of his lighter on and off and on and off. "So, what you got to tell me?"

Stella formed another smoke ring and spoke as she watched it leave her mouth. "Well, I did a lot of searchin', Bobby, and what I found out ain't pretty, not by any stretch of the 'magination, meanin' there ain't no 'magination about it which makes it bad, as in real life bad, not movie bad. And, while I'm thinkin' on it, I got no doubt somebody has already told you this along the way—'cause it just ain't possible you went through prison and all without hearin' this stuff—'course maybe nobody cared, or maybe you just never heard it 'cause you got what we call selective hearin'. Hell, I seen that in you every damn day, but you sure as shit are gonna hear it now!"

She looked over at him as he continued to flick his lighter on and off. The game playing was over. "Look at me, Bobby!"

Bobby stopped flicking his lighter and looked at her. The way her eyes were burning into him, he knew what was coming next was going to be real hard.

Stella settled down, satisfied that she had his full attention. "See, when you was ten years old you saw your papa take a gun and shoot your mama, then he turned around and shot hisself—and that, right there, is the reason you don't remember or hear much of anything about anything. Your little boy mind, seein' all that blood and guts comin' outta your mama, her fallin' to the floor dead, then your papa shootin' hisself in the head, blood spurtin' out everywhere, well, your little boy mind said, "Fuck it, I ain't seen this and I ain't never gonna put this away in my memory album of life and I ain't never gonna let nobody put it there."

She looked at him long and hard. "It weren't no damn tornado that set your ass down in the middle of Atlanta like you say. No, just like you said, you weren't born in Atlanta, at least you got that part right. Where you was born was in some hick town way south of here, right outta a couple of crazy hick country parents, which is exactly why you talk like a hick boy. You ended up here 'cause this is where they found you some folks who would take you in."

Bobby felt a jolt sear through his head, and the unlit cigarette fell from his mouth onto his lap. His arms and legs were heavy, like cement, and he felt as if he were sinking slowly into the ground. Meanwhile, his mind ran faster than it ever had, so fast he couldn't keep track of where it was going—but he heard her, just like she wanted him to, every single word. His throat was so tight he could barely find a breath. He looked over at Stella and then past her. He remained silent because he had no choice.

Stella continued, "So what that means, Bobby, is you got the violent genes all through you and any court of law is gonna know that—they got all that information—so if you step one foot outta line here in my house, you are done for the rest of your life. See, I got none of that particular kinda shit in my past, so if you was to even suggest anythin' to anyone, well, you think about it. I got all the cards, darlin'. 'Gosh, officer, it wasn't me that shot that gun off, it was Bobby here. I tried to talk sense into him, but as we all know he got the genes—case closed.' So, when it comes to Greta or any other kinda lies you might try to tell regardin' me, well, you won't get one single person 'cept your own self to believe you—got it?"

Stella slowly and deliberately pushed her half smoked cigarette into the pile of red dirt beside her and stood up. "Now, I had me a long day dealin' with a lotta bullshit, includin' tryin' to get your truck back from that bitch who took off with it, so I'm gonna go get me some sleep. You come on home when you are done here with diggin' more holes than is necessary. You are wastin' your time, which means you are wastin' our time."

She turned and called out to Oz who had settled down beneath a nearby tree. "Come on, buddy, let's go and get us some dinner and some sleep—somethin' God may or may not give me tonight. Bobby here will be joinin' us soon as he sets hisself straight as to how things go 'round here."

Bobby said nothing. He still could barely breathe. He watched Stella walk away with Oz beside her and started to hum without realizing it. As he sat there in the woods at the end of his long sturdy line of fence and watched her disappear altogether, his hum grew louder. Then the words came, softly—"We're off to see the wizard, the wonderful wizard of Oz because, because, because, because, because, because of the wonderful things he does." Over and over he sang it to himself, steadily with his breath. He didn't know for how long, but when he finally stopped and got to his feet, it was the dark of night, there was no moon, and he had to use the top line of the fence to guide him back to the house.

Once inside, he went up to their bedroom. The light was still on, but Stella was asleep. He sat on the bed and watched her. Her wild red hair was perfectly still and her mouth, though open, was silent except for a whisper of a snore. He was stuck on her and would always be—it was the way it was. He lay down, fully clothed and still smelling of a full day's sweat. He hummed again for another minute or so, real slow and quiet, then curled up against her and fell asleep.

That's pretty good 'cept you skipped the part where Stella woke me up and started yellin' and accusin' me of stinkin' worse than a wet dog who'd been skunked and ordered me to take off my clothes, take a shower, and sleep somewhere else. And Stella weren't lyin' about any of it. I knew that the second it come outta her mouth.

Anyway, after that night, me and Stella slept in different rooms—my room was the couch where I watched TV till I fell asleep—and where most mornin's, when she had the opportunity, Stella would yell at me 'bout the 'lectricity I was wastin' by leavin' the TV on all night.

See, I didn't sleep much, plus I was in a daze, and I kept it that way for my own good. I just kept buildin' my fences, drinkin' my beers, all day every day, and at night the only thing that kept that daze goin' was the TV. The truth is, after that night I forgot it all, every damn word. All I knew when I woke up each day was that somethin' was real bad between me and Stella and I had no hankerin' to know what it was. It was sittin' in my head somewhere but I didn't want to know what it was—sounds crazy, don't it? But it just happened that way. Then everything changed again after Annie came back.

6

Annie Returns from Greece

Imagine my surprise when I found myself back in Atlanta in a police station being held with the charge of car theft! I got my one phone call—and, yes, it was to Stella. I had no choice and I don't think I wanted one.

Well, she wasn't home, but Bobby was. He said he was in the middle of building a fence and what not, but would come in and clear the situation up. I was a little taken aback at how flat he sounded, but I chalked it up to, I don't know what—I just let it go and waited.

When he walked into that police station, I was thrilled to see him! I mean, I had no idea how much I'd missed him until I saw his scruffy, tough as leather face. I threw my arms around his neck and kissed him on the cheek.

It wasn't until he stepped back and smiled, that I saw the change that I had heard. "He's broken" was my first thought. Bobby K., the free-spirited, gentle—for the most part— mustang was broken. It was as if all those muscles that create a smile didn't work right because they'd been unused for so long—it was like the failed smile of a crying infant.

I hugged him again and told him how much I had missed his ugly face. And it was in that moment I realized it was Bobby whom I'd missed the most. The only person who'd never tried to engulf me with what he wanted had been missing from my mind the entire time I was gone.

He quickly removed my arms from around his neck and told me, in a voice I barely recognized, dusty and shallow, that there was nothing for me at their house and it would be best, after he cleared up the stolen car mess, if I just move along.

I watched him as he explained to the police how the whole thing had been a misunderstanding. He told them Stella only thought Annie had stolen his truck, but what actually happened was that he'd told Annie she could have it to drive to the airport. He also explained that Stella was mad at Annie for reasons that were personal and so she flat out refused to withdraw the charges once the truck was found in the airport parking lot. He then said he meant to get around to withdrawing the charges, but forgot about it because of all the work he was doing. It was his truck and therefore his business whether it was stolen or not, and as far as he was concerned it was never stolen. Somewhere in there, he said he was sorry and would pay for any inconvenience he'd caused. The conversation was long and I only heard bits and pieces of it.

Anyway, it was during that exchange between Bobby and the police when I learned what his real last name was, as in the name of his family of origin, which I had never heard before. The name was Lancaster. His birth name was Bobby Lancaster.

When I heard the name spoken by one of the officers, I was taken aback because here I was standing with a man I had shared a life with for over twelve years, helped raise two young boys with—a man who seemed to have changed quite dramatically during the year of my absence and, now, I was hearing an unfamiliar name attached to him. It just wasn't a coincidence. Bobby Kansas was gone, literally.

So, there we were, Bobby Lancaster and Annie Evans, unaware of the new chapter that was about to unfold for each of us.

Annie walked with Bobby out of the police station and into the parking lot. Neither one spoke a word until they reached his truck.

Bobby spoke first as he unlocked the driver's door. "So, you got a car?" He didn't look at her. He couldn't.

"No, I don't. I'll have to rent one, but I was hoping to go with you back to the house to pick up a few things that I left there." Annie had nothing at the house that she needed or wanted—nothing material. What she wanted was to get in the truck with Bobby and go home.

Bobby looked at her. "I already told you there's nothin' there for you and nothin' you say will change that. It's done, Annie."

Annie's blues glimpsed his as she looked past him and across the parking lot. "What do you mean, 'it's done'? What's done?" She watched a cop car speed out onto the main road, lights flashing. "Are you telling me that Stella is still mad?" She laughed. "You're kidding, right? That whole thing was crazy. She has to know that AND gotten over it."

Bobby turned to watch the flashing lights as well. "No, she ain't mad. Fact is, she don't even think about it. She stopped thinkin' about you the day you was gone, as in once you went missin' you was gone from her mind."

The sirens and lights faded and he looked over at her. She went missing and didn't keep it that way—why? There was nothing here for her. She was as beautiful as ever, probably been places he'd never bother to go, met people in all them other languages, and yet here she was, aching to get back to nothing at all. "If you was to come back to the house, you'd be right back in it, up to your eyeballs, and you'd never know you was gone in the first place. I'm tellin' you, anythin' you did between when you was here before and here now would be gone like it never was. Now, do you want that? I mean, darlin', if you don't mind bein' up to your eyeballs in Stella then come on back, but don't tell me I didn't warn you."

Annie looked at Bobby, but barely saw him. *She washed her hands of me the moment I left!* Her worst fear as she sat on that plane clutching the luxurious leather bag was true, she just hadn't known it at the time. And now, it barreled into her stomach like the stone cold piece of information it was—and sucked the air out of her. "I'm sorry to hear that, Bobby," she said as she struggled to hold herself upright by placing her hand on the hood of his truck. "I guess I didn't know what to expect."

She forced a laugh. "You know I don't even know why I flew back here. I could've flown anywhere. I used the excuse that I'd left some important things at your house, but I didn't.

So here I am, looking at the one person I actually missed but didn't know it until now, and I find out the person I couldn't get out of my head, never gave me a thought. Well, that just plain sucks." Her eyes wandered around the lot again. "Now what the fuck do I do?"

She turned her back to Bobby and faced the police station, keeping her hand on the truck. She didn't want to let go.

Bobby watched Annie turn and suddenly remembered the shock on her face when she ran past him in the driveway that day. All he could think to do was get into his truck and go back to working on the fences. "Annie, I got to go, darlin'. I'm real sorry 'bout everythin.'" He climbed into his truck and shut the door.

Annie spun around. "Don't go, Bobby!" *God, where will I go now?* She calmed herself, afraid Bobby would speed up his exit if she lost control. "I mean don't go without letting me give you my parents' address."

She pulled a pen and pad from her pack, scribbled the name and address and handed it to him. She then quickly put her hand back on the hood of his truck, flat down. It felt warm and solid. "If you ever need to get in touch with me, contact them."

He took it, folded it, and tucked it into his shirt pocket as he backed the truck away from her.

As the truck moved, Annie realized her hand was stuck to the hood, literally. Whether it was the combination of sweat and dirt, or the sheer strength of her unwillingness to let go, she didn't know, but as he started to back out, she had to trot to keep up with her arm and hand. Then she panicked as it occurred to her Bobby might just drive away, tearing her arm from her body, but only after dragging her a couple hundred feet. He wasn't paying attention at all—he was driving backwards, his head turned for what seemed to be a very long time.

Once she pulled her hand free, while at a full run, she fell to the ground. She sat there in the parking lot, as the red truck drove off, and suddenly burst into wild laughter. All she could think about was the look on Stella's face if, in fact, Bobby did drive up to the house with Annie's arm dangling off the hood of his truck. She would know "exactly" whose it was because it bore the very ring Stella had given her on her twenty-seventh birthday, a few months prior to the FBI raid. It was a gold thumb ring that was embossed with an SG intertwined around a pearl. Stella had told her that the ring meant they were inseparable.

She laughed until her head and neck cramped, and then looked down at the ring. Apparently, they were separable, very separable. The laughter fell flat into the hot tarmac and she picked herself up and turned to face the police station. Clearly, her time in Georgia was over and the only option she felt she had was to travel back to the only other home she'd known.

As she stood there and thought about it, she also asked herself what it was that Stella had blown a hole through, besides her bedroom wall—because whatever it was, a year in Europe, most of it in Greece, had done nothing to heal it, nothing at all.

She held one arm for a moment, then the other, then glanced down at each of her legs and felt grateful that at least she still had all of her limbs and a neck that could still cramp from too much laughter.

She turned as another police cruiser whizzed by with its lights flashing, then another and another. As she watched them, one after the other, then heard the cacophony of sirens, it occurred to her that this could be a bad sign regarding her trip decision, but she decided to ignore it and caught the first train she could to The City of Brotherly Love.

She was exhausted and all it took, once she settled onto the 2 a.m. departure, was the rhythmic sound of the train to settle her into a deep sleep. She hadn't dreamed in weeks, but on this night as she chugged northward, dreams came. *First, she was running towards Stella who was walking away from her. The solid ground suddenly altered beneath her and became like quicksand, which made gaining any ground impossible. Stella turned and motioned for her to come quickly because she needed her. She couldn't do it. The ground was just too damn soggy. With every step, her frustration mounted. Stella stood and watched for a moment, then shrugged her shoulders and turned away. She watched Stella disappear into a cloud of cigarette smoke, then collapsed helplessly to the ground, her arms and legs now completely engulfed by the soft earth.*

She shifted restlessly and fell across the armrest into the seating space of the man next to her. Her head landed on his shoulder. He didn't wake her. *She was driving to her parents' house in Philadelphia. She hadn't been there in years and was anticipating the reunion. She parked at the end of the long driveway and walked down to the house. As she approached, she noticed water surrounding the house, up to the first floor windows. There were people in the water— two of her brothers and her father were floating happily, obliviously, on rafts and furniture. They glanced up at her as she approached and barely took notice. She was taken aback, took a deep breath, and passed by them and into the house. Her mother was in the kitchen busily preparing a meal. She walked up to her anticipating a face that would be delighted to see her, followed by a big hug, but her mother simply kept working. It was as though her mother knew who she was without having to look up. Her work at hand grew more frantic and intense as if to say, "Go away, can't you see I have things to do?"*

As this went on, storm clouds were gathering and the water was rising fast. The house began to tip and she realized this was a dangerous situation. Nobody else seemed to notice the danger except for one stranger, a man, who met her glance and nodded in agreement to her silent communication that they should get out and save themselves.

She grabbed his hand and together they struggled out of the house and back onto the driveway. As they walked away, the house was now on its side and afloat in the murky water. There was a loud screeching sound.

Annie opened her eyes. The train was pulling into Penn Station, and she was squeezing the hand of the man whose shoulder she had been leaning on. She let go and apologized profusely. He smiled and said it wasn't every day an attractive woman took his hand.

———

Yes, I don't know how long I had been squeezing his hand, but from the looks of it, maybe a while. There were red and white marks across his knuckles and into his fingers. All I can say is I was grateful we were at our destination because I really didn't want to have to explain anything to him. I left him and the train station as quickly as possible.

Once on the street, I took a cab to my parents' house in the suburbs which, unlike in my dream, has a short driveway and is made of sinkable stone rather than floatable wood. It's one of those beautiful old colonial houses that will last forever.

Anyway, from the moment I stepped out of the cab I sensed a change. It was nothing visual—the house looked exactly the same as it always had. It was simply a feeling which, at the time, I attributed to my having been gone for so many years.

It was noon when I arrived, though that really meant nothing to me as I was tired, jet lagged, and my head was spinning from all that had happened since my arrival back in the States. The front door was locked, which was unusual, and there were no cars in the driveway. I had to remind myself that over thirteen years had passed which meant my brothers were long gone. That left just my parents who were both probably either off teaching or involved in some Quakerly activity, which means more than I care to think about, but does include saving the world's poor and putting an end to all wars along with any and all acts of violence, period—end of story.

I am reminded of Stella and Bobby's reaction when I first told them about Quakers and Pacifism.

———

"Are you tellin' me you was raised surrounded by people who believed that you 'never,' like you said, raise your hand against another human bein' for any reason?"

Stella leaned over the kitchen counter, coughed six times, and took another hit of her joint. "Now, that right there is just plain nuts! That's enough to make any kid get to wonderin' who the hell was gonna look out for their ass.

I'll tell you right now, my kids knew from the beginnin', meanin' the minute they came out of my body, that I would take down anyone who even thought about hurtin' them. I showed 'em I had the means, includin' a gun, to do so and I would throw myself into any life threatenin' situation if it meant savin' their asses. That's called protectin' your young and lettin' 'em know that they is all that—case closed. What the hell kinda security is that, knowin' that your mama and papa wouldn't protect you if some freak, which the world is full of by the way, tried to take you down?"

She put the joint out in the ashtray and sat down at the table across from Annie. "The sad fact is, a freak did take you down and you know why? 'Cause he was a man, your father I might remind you, who had no goddamn spine—which is exactly what a pacivist or whatever the hell you call it is— just a spineless wimp feelin' his oats by screwin' his little girl!! That's exactly what that kind of thinkin' leads to—it just ain't natural to not be willin' to do anythin', includin' hittin' or killin' someone if that's what it takes to protect yours. It's exactly the kind of thinkin' that leads to screwin' with your own kin. I swear that is the sickest shit on this planet, besides hurtin' innocent animals. And speakin' of animals, I'll tell you right now, most animals will sacrifice themselves or take down another to keep their young safe— that's not includin' the occasional lion or hamster that eats its own young—God screwed up on that one, but he ain't perfect, now is he?"

She picked up her Pall Malls and pulled one out of the pack. "So, who made up this rule about not hurtin' no one for any reason? I mean what kind of crazy-ass thinkin' is that? God, woulda made us non-violent if he wanted us to be, so the way I see it is we is s'pose to work shit out in whatever way we choose, 'choose' bein' the operative word. Now, if I was bein' raped, would I just lie there and take it? No, I WAS raped and I'll tell you right now, if I coulda got to my gun that man would have no brains—case closed. And if you was bein' raped, I would get to my gun and he would have no brains again. Now, what would your papa or mama have done? Nothing—and they proved it and that's the end of that little sorry ass story. Which family would you rather be in, mine or yours? I know you only been here about a year, but honey, you got more here than you ever had your whole life. You got people now who would kill any rat bastard who tried to hurt you, or at least beat the crap outta him. It's called standin' up for your own, somethin' the likes of your kind don't have a goddamn clue about. BOBBY!"

Stella twisted around in her chair towards the open windows in the living room.

"THAT WOULD BE ME, DARLIN'!" Bobby was in the front yard stacking and sawing wood to begin a long morning of doing what he loved best, building—this time building a front porch to put his favorite rocking chair on.

"BOBBY, IF SOMEONE WAS RAPIN' ANNIE, WHAT WOULD YOU DO?" She waited.

"BEAT THE CRAP OUTTA HIM. MAYBE EVEN SAW HIS ARMS OFF!"

Stella looked back across the table at Annie who was taking it all in. "See? He didn't have to even think about it, not for one second. It just ain't no question in his mind and that's what you call normal and doin' God's work. See, God gives us the 'bility to choose and some people choose to kill and rape, some people choose to jump in and beat the crap outta the people who is killin' and rapin', 'specially when the people they is killin' and rapin' is friends and family. Accordin' to you, if you is one of them passafists, you is choosin' to sit and be all high and mighty talkin' 'bout how it's all wrong to be violent. Who do you think is doin' right? Doin' being the main word here—the person stoppin' the rapin' and murderin' or the person puttin' their tail between their legs and claimin' they is doin' nothin' cause it's wrong? I would take Bobby over your passafist any day. God says you gotta do somethin' about the evil that people do, if you don't, then you is evil too. It's his way of leavin' it up to you and me to decide whether you is going up or down after you die. He don't want to do all the thinkin' for us. So there's your choice; be a passavist or DO something—end of story. "BOBBY!"

"YUP, IT'S STILL ME, DARLIN'." Bobby stopped and rubbed his sleeve across his forehead to soak up the sweat.

"OUR ANNIE AIN'T NEVER HAD PEOPLE WHO'D BEAT THE CRAP OUTTA SOMEONE IF THEY TRIED TO HURT HER!"

Bobby put another piece of wood across the sawhorses and picked up the saw. "IS THAT RIGHT? WELL, THEM DAYS IS OVER, NOW AIN'T THEY!"

———

Annie assumed her parents wouldn't be home until 4 or 5 p.m. She was too tired to wait outside the house or seek an alternative, so she broke a small pane of glass in the back door and entered. As soon as she got in, she was standing in a kitchen that was almost unrecognizable. Only the copper sink was familiar and in the right place. She was so overwhelmed all she could do was make her way to the bedroom she'd slept in for her entire childhood and collapse onto the bed. She would deal with the changes later.

- 7-

Emily

"MMMMMMMMMMMMOOOOOOOOMMMMMMMMMMMM...
THERE'S SOMEBODY IN MY BED!!"

The scream blasted through Annie's head not unlike the sound of Stella's shotgun that final day. She sprang up from the bed, landing squarely on a large teddy bear, and looked into the deep brown eyes of a young girl standing about six feet from her, palms outstretched, mouth wide open. A woman appeared right behind her just as another scream was on its way. "MOMMMMMMMMMEEEEEEEEEEEEEE!!"

The woman dropped her hands onto the girl's shoulders. The young mouth closed as her mother's opened. "Henry, call the police!"

"Wait, there's been a misunderstanding!! My parents live here! Who are you?!" Annie felt as though she was playing a part in a child's fairy tale, the monster part.

Mom retorted, "I don't know who you are, or how you got in here, but this is our house and you're sleeping in my daughter's bed!!"

Annie glanced around at the toys that were scattered across the floor, then at the large, extremely soft teddy bear that lay, face down, squashed flat beneath her feet. She quickly stepped off it, which allowed both the bear and the little girl to breathe. She then glanced at the quilt imprinted with little yellow ducks walking across a blue sky dotted with white puffy clouds, and then back at the little girl whose screams had melted into a defiant glower. This was the point where she hoped to wake up before having to get into the complexities of who, what, and where.

She waited as the three of them stood in a taut silence, just long enough for Henry to appear. Henry was a robust bearded man wearing rimless glasses. She guessed he was approximately Bobby's age, age probably being the only thing they had in common. And here they were and here she was—Mama Bear, Papa Bear, Baby Bear, and the stranger who was sleeping in Baby Bear's bed, which had been just right.

Annie burst into laughter for the second time in twenty-four hours.

Henry spoke. "Miss, this is not the least bit funny. You've broken into our house and terrified my wife and child."

Annie couldn't stop herself. She laughed and laughed and laughed.

The little girl stepped forward. "Why are you laughing?"

Annie's laughter softened so she could speak. "Have you ever heard the story of the three bears?"

"Yes, I have." The girl was interested.

"Well, doesn't it seem like you could be the little bear who found someone sleeping in your bed? That's why I'm laughing. We're in that story right now!"

The child reflected and Annie continued. "You know, when I was your age I slept in this room and had a mommy and a daddy just like you do."

"Well, you can't have my room 'cause it's mine and so is this teddy bear." She bent over and picked up her squashed bear.

Annie looked at the little girl as she hugged her bear, then at Henry and his wife. Her laughter stopped. She remembered Bobby's truck pulling out of the parking lot and onto the highway. She was alone again. She spoke softly. "Look, I'm really sorry. My name is Annie Evans and I left this house thirteen years ago on bad terms with my family. I haven't been in touch with them since. I had assumed they still lived here. Obviously, I've made a mistake."

Henry stepped forward, his stern academic face softening. "You're Grant Evans' daughter?"

"Yes, I'm Grant's daughter. Did my parents move? I mean, obviously they did. Was this house too big for the two of them? Do you know anything about what happened?" The red pickup was long gone. The only option she'd had left was to go back home. Clearly this wasn't home any longer.

Henry nodded. "Yes, they moved." He then looked at the floor as an extremely awkward moment swept into the room.

Annie looked at the teddy bear in the girl's arms and realized she didn't really want to know the answers to her questions.

That's when the front doorbell rang and the police walked in.

Henry sent the police away. He told them a mistake had been made. Then, he and his wife, Claire, invited me to stay for dinner. I agreed. However, they wanted to have a private talk with me first. All was not well. My longtime pal, cold-stone-in-the-belly, had dropped in on me the moment Henry had nodded and looked at the floor. God, how I wished I had gotten in that truck with Bobby and taken on whatever it was that Stella had to offer.

What I learned from them was that my father had died of a heart attack about the same time Stella had gone to prison. Then, around the time I fled to Greece, my mother had married an old family friend and was presently living in Vermont where he was dean of a college.

Henry and Claire Hanson were so kind and, to this day, I feel bad for the situation I had unwittingly put them in. Honestly, if I were them, I don't know if I would've undertaken the task of delivering news of such weight to someone I didn't know. I might very well have let the police take care of it or at least made a call to my mother and had her tell me.

Anyway, before they broke that news to me, we talked a bit, and as it turned out, in the few years Henry had worked with my father, he'd heard him talk of his daughter who was off traveling the world finding all kinds of interesting work. It seems my father had remained proud of my linguistic abilities and "fierce independence"—even after that Thanksgiving meal. And from the expression on Henry's face, I may very well have accomplished things that I had no knowledge of. I found myself anticipating questions regarding my work with domestic violence in Ghana, or saving the orphaned children in the Sudan, or my role as a translator for "Doctors without Borders." However, those questions didn't come—but they certainly would have been preferable to what did follow once the reflection of my father's pride had waned from Henry's face.

When he did finally break the news of my father's death, I became so disoriented I nearly passed out. Claire sat beside me on their living room couch fully prepared to hold my hand or all of me if need be, which never happened. The huge dissonance between what they were expecting me to feel and what I actually felt, created such tension that I simply ceased—in medias res. It was more than I could bear. I couldn't cry, period, let alone in their presence, let alone in their arms. All I remember was an overwhelming desire to get away from what felt like their need to have me feel what they imagined I might feel.

They were in a terrible situation, as was I. What did reach me, though, was when little Emily suddenly appeared in the middle of the living room with her teddy bear in hand. She had been asked to play quietly in her room while "Mommy and Daddy talk to Annie." Well, clearly she was done playing on her own and had decided to join us. She stood there and demanded my attention by calling out my name quite loudly.

"ANNIE!" she said.

I looked over at her, on cue.

"Will you tell me the story of the three bears and maybe even do it again, like before?" she asked.

And that's when I burst into tears.

Emily walked quickly over to Annie and put her bear on Annie's lap. "It's OK if you don't want to play right now, but Bear would like to sit on your lap until you do, if that's OK with you?"

Annie took hold of the bear that she'd stood squarely on top of an hour earlier and immediately felt six years old herself. She dried her eyes on her sleeve and looked at Emily. She no longer wanted to be with the adults because she was feeling more overwhelmed as each second dragged by. Soon she would be crushed by the weight of all that she couldn't feel or say. She looked at Emily and took her first deep breath since 'the talk' had started. "I would love to tell you the story of Goldilocks and the three bears. In fact, I was just thinking, right before you came in, how wonderful it would be to do just that. You do remember, though, that it was Goldilocks who screamed for help when she woke to face the three bears, not the bears. However, when I think about it, it must have been pretty scary for the three bears to find a stranger in their house... mmmm... what do you think? Do we need to rewrite the story?"

"Of course, I know the bears didn't scream, but before I wasn't a bear, was I? I was just a little girl who found YOU in her bed! I don't know, you coulda been mean or scary, but you're not and you never even broke my chair or ate my porridge. I don't even like porridge, I like corn flakes." Emily offered up her palms. "I didn't know anything, did I? You useta live here when you was six too, but I didn't know that either, did I? Maybe we could write in the story that nobody was scared of anybody, it was just a fun adventure."

———

After two days and a dozen colorful rewrites of Goldilocks, each one chock full of outstanding adventures with no love ever lost, no fear ever found, and laughter around many a corner, Annie hit the wall.

On the third morning, she woke to such pain she wanted to blow her brains out. Her family name was screaming through her head, mercilessly assassinating all available words except a certain few that kept repeating themselves randomly: *this, will, now, die, time, is, your, to, not, begin, again, the, life.*

She crawled out of bed across the floor of the guest room to her pack, which was sitting by the desk. Aside from a gun, which she didn't have, she somehow understood that these words were another way to end her immediate agony. She pulled a pen and pad from her pack as EVANS continued to screech through her mind like a thousand two-inch fingernails on a chalkboard. The key was to grab each word as it squeaked through and write it down. The task was to make sense of them.

now die time is your the to not begin again life this will

Annie squinted through the pain and scanned the words. *What are they saying? What the hell is happening to me?*

———

Henry had invited Annie to stay in their guest house for a few days. She had accepted, grateful to be able to spend time with two very kind people and little Emily, who was pure joy. However, she had been somewhat apprehensive as she knew the guest house all too well. It was once her father's study and the very place where he would so often read to her and 'educate' her about sex—oral sex, digital penetration, orgasm and eventually, by age eleven, she was his "special girl" who could accommodate his penis, soft or hard. Orgasms brought on by her father's fingers or tongue were among her first real accomplishments, right along with being able to read Spot and Puff in Greek. Unlike reading Puff however, an orgasm brought on by her father was an overwhelming experience—one that at times brought tears to her father's eyes.

She learned from him that being "truly special" meant so much more than being able to read and write and play games on the playground or going on picnics. It meant being able to hold her breath, tremble, feel a vacuous terror, and hold on to nothing until it was over, and then her father would hold her tightly in his arms. At times she'd watch him cry and receive his whispered apologies, which meant she had the power to bring a big man to tears—her big man whom she needed more than anyone.

Little Annie Evans was "the most special girl in the world." She had skills other kids didn't have. She could writhe through the unbearable terror of losing total control of her little body, sometimes even pee in the middle of it, and survive it all. She would grow up to be the best at everything she did because her Dad told her so. She was his "shining star."

However, their "special times" together ended suddenly in the fall she entered junior high school. She was frantic. She didn't understand what had happened. What had she done wrong? Her father barely gave her the time of day anymore, so she worked even harder in school and at sports. If she could become a champion at whatever she did, maybe he would take notice again. But it didn't happen.

Then, when she was sent off to boarding school, her drive to achieve escalated even further. It became all she had, and by the time she went to college she started to lose her oomph, and no amount of attention for what she could accomplish could meet the undying, unmet need she had. Everything and everyone became ever more redundant and unbearable. The terror that her body remembered, the very terror her father could initiate and then rescue her from, began to haunt her and make unwanted appearances in the middle of the night or during the quiet times of every day, and there was no one to save her.

It was this unrequited terror and incalculable loneliness that became the Cold Stone in her Belly. Her attempt to bring it all to the table on that Thanksgiving had been an act of desperation.

Now here she was back at what had been her home, on the floor of that guest house. She'd talked to her mother by phone the previous night. "Your father's heart was broken when you left, Annie. He missed you terribly and felt so badly that you felt the way you did when you left. We all felt badly for you. I hope you've changed and found what you needed. I hope wherever you've been has been good for you."

Annie said nothing. She couldn't speak.

Her mother continued, "You know, he left you a large trust fund. It had nothing to do with me, so don't thank me. He really loved you, Annie, and your leaving was so hard on him. He became a different man." She sighed. "My only hope for you is that you find happiness. I know I have."

There was more her mother had said, but it was beyond Annie's reach as she sat there staring at the paper with the thirteen words. She'd responded in spits and spats, nothing ground breaking, and her mother had paid little attention.

Annie knew the only thing that might have gotten her mother's attention would've been a retraction of what she'd confronted her father with that Thanksgiving, followed by a plea for forgiveness. She'd let her family down and now her father was dead.

———

now this die time is your to the not begin again life will

Annie stared at the thirteen words—and struggled with their meaning—until a familiar voice came in, loud and clear.

Annie, what the hell is the matter with you?! You're thirty, almost thirty-one, years old and look at you, all crawlin' on the floor writin' words on paper, words that you is hearin' in your head. Don't be goin' all nuts on me 'cause I ain't got the time for that.

Your daddy is dead, thank God. Like I told you a thousand times, he shoulda been shot. Dyin' of natural causes when he is responsible for rapin' his own is just plain wrong. There weren't nothin' natural about him—end of story and end of him. I don't give a rat's ass if he was like you said 'a kind and gentle man, who done a lot of good.' Goddamn, he shoulda been tortured to death!

Annie, he was nothin' at all. I can't believe after what he done to you that you can still be thinkin' about how 'wonderful' he is, well was, 'cause honey he is dead, dead like that pile of bricks Bobby has out back, and you need to plug up your bleedin' heart 'fore you bleed to death.

What you need to do, right now, is get up off your ass and get you a gun and go after your mama. Killin' her ain't what we're talkin' about here. What you need to do is scare the piss outta her. Show that sorry ass example for a mama exactly what it's like to be so scared you piss yourself. She's sure as shit wearin' Depends by this time, so don't worry about her ruinin' any furniture or nothin'. Hell, I bet she pisses every time she sneezes, but that ain't the kind of pissin' I'm talkin' about. I'm talkin' about you hold that gun to her head and you tell her exactly what kind of a piss poor mama she's been and how you ain't never known what it's like to be normal, as in 'finding happiness' like she says she's found.

Hell, I don't believe her for a second. You can't marry a pervert, have his kids, and be happy and that's the damn truth and the end of her little story, now ain't it?

Somethin's real twisted in her head and it ain't nothin' to do with you. When my mama did all the shit she did to me, do you think I thought for one minute that I was the bad part? No—case closed.

You need to get your ass up off that floor, take all that money your rat bastard father left you, and get the hell away from your kin. As smart as you is s'pose to be, you are just plain dumb sometimes.

By the way, I can tell you exactly what them words is you s'pose to say. 'Now your life will begin again, this is not the time to die.' And I will tell you exactly what your kin wants you to write down on that piece of paper. 'Now, this is the time to die, your life will not begin again.' Now that, right there, shows you how sick they is.

Annie, they'd be happy as shit to see you blow your brains out, that's the part you just don't get. What you got to remember here is I got a direct line to God. I ain't never gone to church or read the bible, it's just too damn long and I ain't got the inclination to read it and maybe that's exactly why he talks to me, but I'm tellin' you, right now, them words, the way I told 'em to you, is God's words and I'm thinkin' you best be listenin' to him. Amen.

And another thing, if your family name is causin' your head to hurt so much that you want a gun instead of a aspirin or a Valium—well, hell, get rid of it. That's another little message from God. He's tellin' you it's a dumb name.

Now, I've already told you a hundred times what God is tellin' you right now. I even gave you a different name. Now, I ain't God or nothin' but it's lookin' to me like we is agreein' an awful lot, now don't it? I got a lot of stuff figured out, somethin' you ain't even begun to do.

Annie got up off the floor, went directly to her family's lawyers, and got the first and only thing her father had ever given her with no strings attached—access to a hefty sum of money.

Yes, I did get up off that floor and go to my lawyers, but it took a few days. I was exhausted. After I heard Stella's words, and I swear it was as if she were right there in the room with me, well, I laid there and cried until I could barely breathe or move. They weren't tears of sadness. They were tears of agony, the only kind of tears I'd ever known. That was another thing, one of many, that my father took from me—my sadness. It was mine to have, not his to take.

With that said, you've written intimately about my incest and in a way that is almost bearable. But then, I may be wrong as I'm the one who went through it and anything is more bearable than that.

I wonder if you do decide to keep those details in this book, will a considerable number of readers put the damn thing down and recommend it to no one? However, I would be ... mmm ... can't think of the word—happy? relieved?—to have you put it in, because there it would be, in black and white— and not residing as the isolated Cold Stone in my Belly or the belly of anyone else who has been through it.

Regardless of what you choose to do, I thank you for giving me the chance to speak about it. Stella and Bobby were the first people outside of my family to know about it—and, unlike my family, they believed me. And, despite all that has happened, I am grateful to Stella for helping me, in her own inimitable way, to break through my isolation and show me ways to survive.

Yes, she used the incest to pull me in and keep me close and she used it against me, in a most egregious way, on the day she ran me off her property. She may even try to use it against me again, but truth be known, she offered me words that before I met her had been unavailable, words you have put down in these chapters, words that have helped me tap into my anger and shrink my shame. And, ironically, it's Stella who has armed me with what I need to face any further attempts at humiliation from the likes of her or anyone else.

Anyway, my stay with "the Bears" lasted well beyond the few days that had been my intention. After that horrific morning on the guest house floor, Henry and Claire, without having witnessed it, sensed my fragility and simply and supportively let me be and let me stay for as long as I needed. They invited me to meals where we talked about everyday things, included me on family outings, and were delighted to have me spend time with Emily writing stories. I also, through Henry, picked up some work tutoring students from the college in French and German, something I once did, but didn't think I could do anymore. After having been through all those years in Georgia, how the hell would I pull it off?

Well, it turned out to be much like riding a bicycle—once you learn it you don't forget, at least that's how it was for me. I suppose that must also mean my life as a prostitute and fine 'business woman' is also ready and waiting in the wings, should I ever need to use it again. As Stella said to me on many occasions, "All things considered, you're a natural, honey, and you can thank your papa for that."

So, I ended up staying with "the Bears" for a few months, until the day came that I felt ready to move on and find my own life. It was hard to leave, but Henry and Claire made it manageable by offering me an open invitation to come back and stay with them whenever I needed to. I was certain I would, though I never did.

With Emily, my plan was to send her, once a week, a new story with new adventures involving places I'd been, people I'd met, etc. And, whenever I was in one place for long enough, her plan was to write to me. She had given me something I'd never had before, which was time with a healthy, open, and optimistic six year old! She was the primary source of my renewed sense of hope.

Unfortunately, it only took a month on the road for that hope to stagger and then fall. I had managed a couple letters to "the

Bears" and several lovely stories to Emily and that was it. I woke up one morning in a tent by a beautiful lake somewhere in the Adirondacks—birds were chirping, a breeze was softly slapping up against the sides of my tent, and I felt completely lost, yet again!

From there I drove several thousand of miles, from one state to the next. I camped and drove, camped and drove.

You see, each morning I would wake and write a letter/story for Emily. It was the only thing that got me out of my sleeping bag. But, by the time I made coffee and stepped out of my van to see the colors of the day, there were none. I felt stale and needed to move on. Each evening, I wrote more letters as it was the only thing that would calm me so I could sleep. Those letters are what got me from one day to the next. In the end, I had written hundreds of them, but never sent even one. My fear was if I let them go, as in dropped them in the mail, I would be more than lost, I would be gone.

Then, somewhere in there, I started to smoke, heavily, not something I'd ever done. I'd been an occasional smoker when I lived with Stella and Bobby, but I'd let it go completely when I went off to Greece.

And to this day, I swear it was the constant smell and taste of cigarette smoke that led me back to Georgia.

————

Goldilocks was gently wakened by Baby Bear, Mama Bear, and Papa Bear. They weren't frightened at all. There was nothing at all scary about finding a strange girl in Baby Bear's bed, not at all. And they knew the broken chair was just an accident and could be fixed. They also knew that she ate their food only because she was hungry. In fact, they were delighted to see her.

She was a brand new surprise to them. They didn't know anything about her except that when she woke up she was kind and smiled and could laugh—and that was all they needed to know.

Whether she had run away from home because she did something she thought was bad—like squeeze the toothpaste tube too hard and get toothpaste all over the sink—or something bad had happened to her, like having to eat all her vegetables, or she just wanted a fun adventure, or whether she just got lost—well, the truth was that whatever it was, if none of it had happened they never would have met her, which would have been very sad.

Of course, they would help her find her home if she was lost, or they would give her a home if she needed one, or she would just visit for awhile. If there was anything bad that had happened, they would all sit down and figure it out together because that's what families do.

Sometimes getting lost or wandering or running away or hiding means having the chance to be found and what a thrill that can be! And that is why, to this day, children and parents love to play hide and go seek and why there is a special box or place almost everywhere you go that reads 'lost and found'!

And Goldilocks was never scared of the Bears either, just as they weren't scared of her, not even when she opened her eyes and saw them there. She didn't jump out of bed or squash any of Baby Bear's toys by mistake, like some people might think she would. No, Goldilocks was not scared at all because Mama and Papa Bear were big and warm and kind and Baby Bear was small and warm and kind. And that's the end of this story for now.

And Goldilocks isn't always called Goldilocks; sometimes she has a name like Emily or Annie.

Emily and Annie

Part II: Wrestlin' With The Devil

8

Annie Lands Back in Georgia

As Annie turned down the very driveway she'd fled out of a year and a half earlier, all she knew was her father was dead, her mother had washed her hands of her, and the only thing that had kept her from falling into a thousand pieces on the guest house floor that day was Stella's voice in her head. The gunshot that had awakened her from a dead sleep, followed by the torrent of abusive language from Stella's mouth to her ears, and the resulting fear that had ripped her from her bed and landed her on a plane to Europe—none of it was present or accounted for. So, as she started down that long dirt driveway, it was with a heart full of gratitude and a longing for a place to call home.

As her van rocked slowly over the bumpy surface, she recalled how Stella had never wanted the driveway paved— "It's a hell of a lot harder to sneak down a dirt driveway than a paved one—case closed. Fact is, I keep as much of them little and big stones thrown on there as I can, makin' it real bumpy, as in makin' it a bitch to drive on—and all them stones rustlin' an' flyin' all over won't make it no quiet trip neither. Hell, I ain't got where I got to by makin' it easy for anybody."

She rounded the first curve and Stella's voice followed her faithfully. "I want as many of them curves as possible, PLUS a big ass tree right there across from each one of 'em, so if you is to come too fast down my driveway, you will be sayin' hello, up close and personal, to one of my trees."

Annie chuckled as she slowed down even more.

As she rounded curve after curve, memories and images continued to blow through her—among them was that first night in New Orleans when Stella planted her hand on her shoulder. Then there was Stella sitting across from her at the kitchen table, sucking on a joint, telling one of a multitude of fresh, colorful, and at times shocking stories, each of which had a variety of effects on her—admiration, amusement, and awe. Then there was the afternoon Stella woke her to tell her she'd slept right through her birthday and to give her a present. "Greta is your new name. It's the name of my now dead daughter who I ain't never mentioned before."

Annie loosened her grasp on the steering wheel as Stella reached in and made her feel special. "You don't have a blaze of fire in you, like my Greta did, at least not yet—but you got the glowin' ambers, and alls they need is fresh oxygen like a new name to get you on your way."

Suddenly, she could barely see the driveway and Stella's voice grew louder and clearer. She turned to see Stella in the passenger seat, puffing away on a cigarette as she laid out what Annie's father had given to her. Her words were no longer literal memories. She was right there. "You were a kid and you had him by the balls, honey. He showed you what dumb weak li'l bastards they all is inside. I mean, think about it! He showed you that you was everythin'—meanin' men got nothin' without us. Fact is, they is just like this burned out roach lyin' in this here ashtray you got in this dumbass van—case closed. And since when did you start smokin' pot?"

Annie watched Stella pick up the roach to see if it was worth lighting. Stella propped her cigarette in the ashtray and put the roach to her mouth. "How many girls learn that when they is young? You tell me. See, I got that lesson too. My daddy showed me the power of bein' a girl around men, the day he told me my mama had left us. He was nothin' after she left. I remember his pale-as-shit hound dog face just like he is sittin' right here, right now. Goddamn, I had to look at that face while he informed me my mama left and if that wasn't enough, he started cryin' like a baby—Hell, I just lost my mama and HE was cryin'!! I had to get up off my chair and hug his ass till he stopped. Did he do that when he told my brother??!! HELL NO—now that, right there, tells you volumes! In summation, 'cause I don't got the patience to lay it out like some kinda psychologist, who in my mind wastes a potload of time writin' and talkin' volumes—and besides, we ain't got a lot of time 'cause you is about to 'round the final curve in my kick ass driveway." Stella hesitated, lit the roach, sucked in a lungful of smoke, held it in for a moment, then spoke in her most gravelly voice as she slowly let the smoke back out. "Anyway, we can get whatever we need—end of story." She paused. "What the hell month are we in, anyway?"

"April, it's April, Stella, remember? It's my birthday today."

Annie lurched forward and her world went black.

———

Her father was done with his "responsibility" to her. It was the day after her twelfth birthday. He'd taught her everything about her body and now he would do the final act. He'd put his special semen inside her special vagina, just as he said he would when she turned twelve. "Now, sweet Annie, you'll go out into the world wiser, braver, more powerful, and more prepared than any other little girl out there."

———

"BOBBY, WHAT THE HELL ARE YOU DOIN'? YOU CAN'T PULL SOMEBODY OUTTA A CAR WHEN THEY IS UNCONSCIOUS— SHE COULD HAVE A BROKE NECK FOR CHRISSAKE! AND I'LL TELL YOU RIGHT NOW, I AIN'T TAKIN' CARE OF NO QUADROPEDIC IN MY HOUSE, SO YOU NEED TO PUT HER BACK IN THAT CAR, VAN, OR WHATEVER THE HELL IT IS, RIGHT NOW AND LET THE AMBULANCE DEAL WITH HER."

Bobby pulled Annie onto the grass. "Stella, alls you need to do is calm down. We don't need no ambulance. Hell, she couldn't of been doin' more than ten miles per hour! She just bumped her head is all!"

Stella lit a cigarette. "I'd say more like two miles per hour 'cause I got the eagle ears and didn't hear jack-shit.

I'm thinkin' I need to put more of them stones and gravel down—there's too many spots with just plain dirt—spots big enough to allow some creepin'—speakin' of which, why was she creepin'?"

Stella looked down at Annie as Bobby laid her head down and stood up. She walked over, stood next to Bobby, and sucked in on her cigarette. "After all I done for her, she up and leaves us and now she's creepin' down my driveway! How's that for gratitude?! Just look at her! She looks nasty don't she? I mean that girl is skinny as shit—looks to me like she been in one of them concentrated camps. I told her the world wasn't no bowl of apples, but she just had to go see for herself."

She walked over to the camper van. "Well, if she thinks she can walk back in here and have her place back, which don't exist anymore, she's got another thing comin'. She's gonna have to live in this dumb hippy camper van till she proves herself—as in apologizes for leavin' us high and dry."

"Stella, there weren't no 'high and dry' about it. Goddamn, she had no choice but to leave 'bout as fast as she could." Bobby was practically whispering. The days of Bobby yelling back at Stella were over. She had stamped the desire clean out of him. In fact, it was a miracle they were even within proximity of each other when Annie drove off the driveway avoiding Stella by a hair and hitting the tree. He'd been on his way to the house after a long day of fencing and she had started up the driveway to get the mail. Barely a word had been spoken between them all day—just like it had been every day since Annie had left.

"Shut up, Bobby." Stella's voice faded to a muffle as she leaned into Annie's van and looked around. "You got no say in this 'cause you got a memory that plays damn tricks on you—we have discussed that little topic on more than one occasion—Why don't you just go back to buildin' that fence and leavin' well enough alone?"

She pulled her head out of Annie's camper and turned to face him. "WHAT THE HELL ARE YOU DOIN' HERE ANYWAY? YOU AIN'T NEVER HERE FOR NOTHIN' ANYMORE AN' NOW HERE YOU COME APPEARIN' WHEN ANNIE IS CREEPIN'

DOWN MY DRIVEWAY! IS THERE SOMETHIN' YOU AIN'T TELLIN' ME?"

She stepped away from the van, brushed her clothes off, and lowered her voice. "It's a stinkin' mess in there. I'm tellin' you, she has been up to all kinds of shit. It smells like wet dogs and burnt perfume in there, only I don't see no dogs or flamin' bottles of perfume."

She walked over to Bobby, still brushing her clothes off, cigarette dangling between two fingers. "Why am I even talkin' to you anyway? This is like some kinda nightmare, I mean you and me and Greta, right here, passed out on the ground next to us. Fuck it. Why don't you just pick her up like a damn man with shinin' arms and bring her back to the house—that would just beat it all, wouldn't it? Only, like I said, I don't want any quadrophilic in my house, so you better make darn sure she can walk 'fore she sets foot in there."

Annie opened her eyes just as a massive cloud of smoke blew through the air above her. All she remembered prior to that moment was realizing it was April and then everything went black.

Stella leaned towards her. "Goddamn, Greta, I gotta tell you, you look nasty—and that ain't includin' the fact you just ran into a tree going at two miles per hour and knocked yourself out. Alls I can say is I hope to hell you can walk 'cause as I just said to Bobby, Mr. Man with the shinin' arms, I ain't takin' care of no quadopathic."

Stella dropped her burning cigarette butt and stomped on it. "What the hell have you been doing for the last God knows how long? First you up and leave me with a huge ass kennel to manage BY MYSELF I MIGHT ADD—meanin' no help from Bobby—and now here you are flat on your back expectin' me to give a rat's ass."

Annie sat up. "My head's fine. I don't know what happened, except that the last thing I remember was realizing it's April and today is my birthday."

"Oh, well, that explains everythin', don't it, Bobby?" Stella placed her hands defiantly on her hips. She said 'Bobby' as if it was simply a fixed part of a sentence—not the name of the person who was standing behind her. "It's your birthday so you decide to hit one of my trees while creepin' down my driveway... mm... mm..."

Stella pulled another cigarette from her pack and lit it. She inhaled and looked over at Annie's van. "Now, why should I believe anything you tell me? For alls I know you is creepin' down my driveway, hired by one of those jealous motherfuckers who would give both their legs to get their hands on my boy Oz—or else kill him 'cause he sure is one fine producer."

She looked back at Annie. "Then you saw me—not somethin' you anticipated 'cause you clean forgot about my eagle ears—and that's exactly when you decided to hit a tree and play the 'Poor me I'm ahurtin' all over and I wanna be your friend again cause I is sick and tired of the world that I run off to see.'"

Annie looked past Stella to Bobby. She watched him as he put his hands into his hip pockets. His shoulders were slumped forward like a man who'd been put in his place and had agreed to stay there until further notice. The change she'd seen in him at the police station all those months ago had stayed.

She got up and brushed the dirt and loose gravel off her jeans and leather jacket. "Stella, you came after me with a shotgun and I ran, wouldn't you have?" Annie tried to sound angry, but didn't and couldn't. "And, by the way, my name is Annie now."

Stella jumped in before Annie even took a breath. "Greta, I got somethin' I need you to do for me right now. Let's go to the house so we can get on the computer." She gave a quick tug on Annie's arm.

Annie stepped in beside her as if no time had passed and no shotgun had ever gone off. The sound of "we" coming out of Stella's mouth was pure comfort. She was back home and it was good—all of it. If Stella wanted to call her Greta, fine, she wouldn't fight her on it.

She turned quickly to find Bobby, but he was gone. In that moment, her comfort was disrupted, but she pushed his whereabouts aside as quickly as if she'd swiped a fly from her shoulder. The fly left a bite however, the kind that can only be ignored for a while before it starts to itch and burn.

Stella talked as they walked down toward the house. "See, you know those neighbors, the ones who lived about a quarter mile from the end of our driveway on the other side of the road? The ones who were livin' on the land we wanted to buy? You know, back before we was busted and we were plannin' to build our mansion and own every bit of this land for miles around—which will happen one day, mark my word, don't you worry 'bout that."

Annie didn't bother to respond. She knew the questions weren't ones waiting for answers. She simply walked with her and listened.

"Well, fact is, they moved out a year ago and sold out to some folks from up north, your neck of the woods, high falutin', highly educated—man runs his own sports attire business out of Atlanta—blah, blah, blah—which translates into dumb-as-shit in my book of Daily Livin', and what happened the other day proves my point!"

Stella led the way as they turned off the driveway and up the front path to the house. She continued her story, confident that Annie was right there behind her. "Anyway, they tore down that piece of shit house and built a brand new one. Hell, musta spent hundreds of thousands of dollars and it ain't really anythin' to write home about."

She started up the front steps. "So, about two weeks ago Bobby was takin' Oz, Alice, and Grace—two of Oz's girls who are eighteen months old now—in fact, they was born shortly after you left. Well, Bobby was walkin' 'em out to the mailbox, God only knows why. It's not like they don't got plenty of exercise in them BIG ASS fields we got, all fenced in by the way—which reminds me," she turned and grabbed Annie's arm midway up the steps, "you need to have a talk with Bobby 'bout his fence buildin' problem, it's one of them obsessin' things that I saw on TV, you know, crazy people gettin' carried away with this or that and drivin' the people they live with nuts—well, he's one of 'em now and we got to live with him."

Stella let go of Annie, but stayed put on the steps. "All I can say is thank God his obsessin' is takin' place out there," she gestured with her cigarette-free hand towards the fields, "and not in my house."

Annie glanced out over the fields, then up the driveway. She could see her van with its fender still up against the tree. She'd nearly forgotten the whole incident. She turned and followed Stella across the porch and through the open screen door.

Stella continued with her story as they walked into the livingroom. "So, Bobby was walkin' with Oz, Grace, and Alice to the mailbox and when they got there, Bobby, of course, took his mind off of everythin' 'cept the mail he was pullin' out the mail box and openin' and readin' ONE by ONE."

She stopped in front of the couch and turned to face Annie. "All of a sudden, Alice she takes off towards the neighbors, I mean haulin' ass as fast as she could. Now, I know this part 'cause I seen that bitch haul ass—Bobby didn't notice nothin', but I got a right to put that in there 'cause I know it to be a fact, that bitch never WANDERS off anywhere, she and most of my other Bordeaux if they go, they usually got a mission as to where they're goin' and why, and that bitch had a mission."

She paused to straighten the couch pillows. "Anyway, Oz and Grace took off after her 'cause they just didn't want to miss out on a little fun. Bobby, of course, just kept readin' the bills and lookin' through my magazines and God knows what else. He can't read, so I have no idea what exactly he was doin', 'cept probably lookin' at the pictures in my magazines."

Stella snorted and moved on. "Oh, he'd heard some screamin', so he says, but he just figured it was the neighbors goin' at it with each other. I told him I ain't never heard the neighbors go at it from a quarter mile away and, in fact, I ain't never heard 'em go at it period, so that right there shoulda told him there was a little bitty problem."

She entered the kitchen and walked over to the cupboard to get coffee mugs.

Annie had been looking around as she followed both Stella's steps and her words. Nothing had changed and it was spotless as usual. Stella was relentless about keeping things clean and orderly, she had been that way for as long as she could remember. "Must be a gene I got. One that Bobby's family probly never had for a hundred years back—same as you, Greta, 'cause you didn't know shit about keepin' a house up till you moved in here."

In the middle of the kitchen was the same yellow table sitting on the same black-and-white large checkered linoleum floor. "It woulda been solid marble if things hadn't got so messed up with the business." And there was the same wooden sign with red lettering hanging over the sink "Don't mess up my kitchen."

Annie took it all in, remembering the hundreds of hours sitting with Bobby and with Stella, separately and together, drinking coffee, smoking, and talking endlessly at all hours of the day and night.

Stella put two mugs down on the counter. "So, now listen to me. You can look at all the same stuff later. These new people, the Cranshaws—what the hell kinda name is that? Sounds like some kinda fruit, don't it?" She filled one of the mugs with coffee and handed it to Annie—lots of milk, two sugars, just like she'd always liked it.

Annie took the coffee, somewhat bewildered. Had she ever left?

Stella poured herself a cup, black. "Anyway, they got these two little dogs, a Toy Poodle and a Shitzu who probly weigh all of 'bout twelve pounds together and they yap all day long behind an invisible fence—invisible bein' the operative word here. Now, my dogs, every damn one of 'em have heard them dogs yappin' way off in the distance, day in and day out, yappin' like they is four hundred pounds and King of the land, which they honest to God believe they is 'cause little dog people don't have a goddamn clue about raisin' a dog with respect and all."

She sat down and placed her coffee on the table and lit up a joint. "I mean, have you ever been in a regular little dog person's house, regular meanin' not my house where my little dogs have been raised with the same rules of respect as my big dogs. Hell, your regular little dog person ain't even no dog person in my book. They let them dogs run all over the furniture, all over their laps, on the goddamn table, feedin' 'em off their plates and shit like that. Hell, they can't do no wrong and that right there is the BIG PROBLEM in the mind of a big dog and if you consider it long enough, it's a big problem for the little dog too, 'cause they is like children raised with no understandin' about jack shit—just the kinda kid that ends up on drugs or dead."

She paused to suck in on her joint and offered it to Annie, who turned it down. "I know you started smokin' this shit 'cause I smelled it in your van along with God knows what else. Anyway, as you well know 'cause you've known me a long time, I don't ever wish no harm on any dog, big or little or any of God's creatures. Fact is, the harm I wish is on the dumb asses who owns little dogs and got no understandin' of the rules of the dog kingdom. There should be some damn school you have to go to if you are gonna own a little dog where you have to get it crammed down your throat that your doggie ain't no itty bitty baby of yours who is 'cutesy wootsey' no matter what the fuck he does. I seen it a hundred times at shows—big dogs pickin' up those itty bitty 'babies' and tossin' 'em 'cause they've had enough of bein' given the finger every two seconds while their owner smiles and thinks nothin' of it."

She took a couple more tokes and dropped the remaining roach in the ashtray. "Anyway, to get back to what I was tellin' you, Bobby comes strollin' back down the driveway with Oz and them two bitches at his side lookin' like a pride of cats that just slaughtered a thousand mice—I know that look a mile away. I said, 'Bobby what the hell have these three been up to?'

"He said, 'I dunno, I guess they just ran off for a bit is all, but they is back now.'

"Well, that's when I laid into him and told him these dogs don't just 'run off for a bit'! They had a goddamn mission and I wanted to know what it was.

"He told me he did hear some screamin' at the Cranshaws' house, but didn't think it had anythin' to do with the dogs. Well, before he finished that sentence I was in my truck doin' ninety miles an hour up my driveway, damn near hittin' every tree at all fifteen turns—which, come to think of, is exactly why I didn't hear you comin'. I skidded so hard so many times I musta thrown a ton of rocks off the road leavin' a ton of smooth spots."

Annie chuckled.

Stella responded with satisfaction. "Anyway, I knew exactly what my dogs had been up to. You can't listen to a couple of punks tellin' you to go fuck yourself day after day, no matter how close or far away they live, and not want to do somethin' bout it the first chance you get—especially if you is a bitch like Alice."

She pulled a cigarette out of her pack and lit it. "I swear to you, I did take the time outta one of my days to stop and tell those people that an invisible fence was not gonna protect their dogs from anything wantin' to come in, includin' big dogs and coyotes. They looked at me like I was nuts. I'm thinkin' they were thinkin' their little babycakes could never be hurt 'cause who would want to hurt somethin' so cute—ain't nothing so evil as that in the world is how they were thinkin'. WHAT IS WRONG WITH YOU PEOPLE FROM THE NORTH!? You got no understandin' of how things work in life, far as I can tell."

Annie attempted a response. "May I remind you that 'The North,' as you like to call it, is a big..."

Stella snorted. "No need to finish that sentence. You can call it big, but size don't make a damn difference far as I'm concerned."

Annie rolled her eyes and lifted her coffee cup to her mouth.

"So, anyway, I tried to explain to 'em that it ain't about evil, just animals doin' what they do. As I am sittin' here right now havin' a joint with my best girl who left me and came back, I told 'em that only people do evil, not animals. I told 'em all I was doin' was wantin' their dogs to have a longer life than I expected they would."

She paused, released a few smoke rings, and carried on. "Greta, I swear to you, I stopped and had that conversation with them on the day I was drivin' by and saw that invisible fence van in their driveway—and I told that invisible fence man that he needed to stop sellin' shit that, as you would say in your educated way, 'wreaks havoc' with the dogs. Mind you, I wasn't thinkin' Alice had killed those dogs, but I was thinkin' she mighta given 'em a good ass whoopin' and knowin' those people I saw LAWSUIT written across the sky as far as the eye could see. I knew they couldn't win anythin', but I just didn't want to deal with the waste of my time it was gonna take. What I needed to do was damage control, plain and simple.

"So I pulled in their driveway and walked up to the house. As I was walkin', I noticed a table on the side deck that had stuff like tea cups and plates with half eaten food on them, chairs were lyin' on their sides—looked to me like a damn tea party that had been raided by the damn mob. Uh, oh, I think to myself this ain't gonna be good and I cursed at Bobby under my breath 'cause if he had been payin' attention to the dogs, he coulda kept them from completin' their mission.

"Anyway, I walked around and stepped up on the deck. I heard cryin' inside and said to myself, 'That damn Alice has gone and done it this time,' and pushed open the glass doors half expectin' to see twelve pounds of chewed up little doggie!"

She sat back in her chair and looked across at Annie. Annie was right there with her, just like she always was. Satisfied, she continued, "Well, what I did see was three women on their knees, pale as the white squares on this floor, each one holdin' a LIVE little dog. Each one of them women looked up at me with them glazed eyes like people get when they been raided by the cops or worse, had their kin killed by some whacko on the loose.

"Mind you, when I was raided, as you DON'T remember 'cause you weren't there that day and I don't snitch—case closed—otherwise you'd a been knittin' right along with me, I was just mad as hell—weren't nothin' glazed about my eyes. I was mad 'cause they came to my house in front of my kids scarin' the bejesus outta them."

Annie opened her mouth to add her two cents on that subject, but stopped. Stella had already soared on.

"So, there I was at the Cranshaws standin' surrounded by three pale, glazed eyes women on their knees. I said, 'What the hell happened? I know my dogs was here, but what I wanna know is where's the damage?'

"One of the women, who I didn't recognize and was holdin' the one little dog I never seen before, said her dog was hurt, but she couldn't figure out where. Her accent, by the way, wasn't from around here, which didn't surprise me 'cause usually you northerners stick together down here 'cause you can't find no friends—and we all know why that is." Stella rolled her eyes and pushed her thick red hair back over her shoulders where it belonged, but rarely stayed.

Annie laughed without comment. She was completely absorbed. Nothing mattered except what she was hearing in the moment, which was fine with her.

"Well, I walked over and took her dog from her—there was blood on her hands, so I knew Alice had done some damage. See, I knew she was the one who had the mission. I didn't need no verification on that. The other two went along for the ride, they didn't have nothin' to prove, but they'd be more than happy to back her up. Alice now, she is one of them uppity types, you know lookin' for the next rung on the ladder no matter what it takes. Well, sure enough, I found a puncture wound on the little dog's ass and told the woman to either take him to the vet and get it cleaned and stitched or I'd do it myself if she wanted 'cause it wasn't so hard and I had everything I needed to do it at my house. She said she didn't want to do that and would take her to her vet and, she added, in one of them quiet whispers, she knew there wasn't no bad intentions involved."

Stella picked up the roach out of the ashtray, lit it, and took the last big hit it had to offer. She continued to speak as the smoke billowed out of her mouth. "I said to her, 'Of course there weren't no bad intentions, only people got bad intentions. This was a bunch of dogs workin' some shit out and it just so happens that my dogs is a hundred and fifty pounds apiece and your dogs think they is four hundred pounds apiece, which is why we had this little pissin' match in the first place, which is all it was 'cause if it was anymore than that, well, put it this way—I have seen little dogs tore clean in half, not 'intentionally,' as you would say, but because of the facts of the size of them and the size and power of the big dog's jaws—and bein' tore in half because they were mistakin' themselves for the king of dog kingdom because the very fact that the people who owns 'em don't have the brains enough to teach them the proper etiquette of the dog world. Some little dogs are on top and earn it, through the proper channels—but most of 'em are so damn misled by the people who owns 'em that they think they is on top—Hell, no this had nothin' to do with me or 'bad intentions.'"

She got up and walked over to the coffee pot. It was empty, so she opened the can of Maxwell House and started another pot. "That is exactly what I said!"

She looked over at Annie and snorted. "Well, if looks could kill, I'd been dead and in a hundred pieces on that shiny brick floor. That bitch got up and left with her dog and a dozen or so corn cobs tryin' to squeeze up her ass.

"I sure wasn't sad when she left, I'll tell you that right now." She glanced at the percolating pot and leaned back against the kitchen counter facing Annie. "Anyway, then I went over and picked up each of Claudia Cranshaw's dogs—one of 'em, by the way, Ziti, the little poodle, he jumped up and down off of the couch 'bout a thousand times before I could grab hold of him. I figured he was fine, which he was, and I figured, in the privacy of my own thinkin', that he was probly the one Alice was after. Well, then Claudia she started in on how my three dogs came chargin' up onto their deck, led by the smallest one, and they was fully intent on killin' all the little dogs. She said when she saw them tearin' across the lawn, she picked Ziti up and ran for the door and somehow managed to shove all the little dogs through the glass door while her friends beat my dogs off with chairs—and oh, she said, by the way, the one in the lead jumped up and tried to grab Ziti from her, but got her arm instead—but, oh, there weren't any broken skin or nothin'.'"

Stella glanced at the still percolating pot and turned back to Annie. "Her friend, meanin' not the bitch that had already left, was dead quiet and just kept starin' at me the whole time Claudia was talkin', like I was some kind of criminal. I ain't no fool about people and I knew the minute I walked in that door that these three was potential trouble."

The percolator stopped and she poured herself a fresh mug of coffee, then walked back to the table and sat back down. "Well, I looked at Claudia and I looked at that bitch and I said, 'I think what you all need to realize is that if my dogs was 'intent,' as you say, on killin', the killin' would be done. There ain't no way you coulda stopped four hundred pounds of dog from killin' if they wanted to kill, chairs or no chairs, and by the way, how dumb are you pickin' up your dog when a pissin' match is on its way? That right there escalates the problem—as in you were givin' the message to my Alice—and I know for a fact she is the only one of my dogs that came up on your deck—you gave her the message that your dog was way up high on that ladder, which only drove her to want to knock his ass down even more—and that screamin', which Bobby heard all the way from my driveway—that along with beatin' my dogs with chairs? Well, you are damn lucky my dogs got the impulse control and know the difference between a human bein' and a dog—cause if they didn't you'd be in a crap load of trouble, as in all tore up—end of story. Now, I understand that this was real terrifyin' for y'all—otherwise you wouldn't be pale as my bed sheets and kneelin' on the floor like you are—and I'm sorry 'bout that—not sorry as in it's my fault and you all can feel free to sue my ass off 'cause you ain't got shit, ain't a lawyer in the county who would touch this, but sorry as in I'm sorry you had to learn this particular aspect of the dog kingdom by endin' up on your knees scared shitless. I told you over a year ago that fence was beggin' for trouble, and now you know.

"So, I left them there kneelin' on the floor with their mouths open so far you could see their tonsils—if they had any." She took a sip of coffee and looked past Annie, half expecting somebody else to walk in and have a seat. The more the merrier.

Annie was fully attentive and, at the same time, still in shock over how it seemed no time had passed. She looked carefully at Stella, who at that moment was looking past her, and tried to grab hold of that red-headed demon who had terrified her that day, but she couldn't.

"Hello?" Stella turned and leaned across the table towards Annie. "Don't tell me you're sittin' there feelin' sorry for them women 'cause I'm tellin' you right now it ain't worth your time. I know you well enough to know you was just now starin' at nothin' and imaginin' their way of lookin' at things. All I can say is that's my Greta, always tryin' to understand all sides of a thing."

She settled back in her chair. "Have you ever stopped to think that's exactly why you can't get anywhere in this world and exactly why you came back here and ran into my tree while tryin' to do so? You spend so much time wonderin' what everybody else is wonderin' that you wind up lost and drivin' into trees. Well, there ain't no wonderin' about this situation, so you can stop wonderin'. I am layin' it out just like it happened—speakin' of which, what the hell happened to you while you was gone? You look like shit, all skinny like you been doing crack and hangin' out with the scum of the earth, which ain't possible 'cause the scum of the earth are the people in this breed who I have to deal with on a daily basis. I'm tellin' you, you think we had to deal with shit back when our 'business' was up and runnin'—well, it wasn't nothin' next to what I'm seein' with these people. I don't know how these dogs stand it, lettin' people like this own 'em. I am shocked they ain't revolutionized and taken these people out. I wouldn't blame 'em one bit."

Stella snorted and reached for her pack of Pall Malls.

Annie took the moment to respond. "Actually I wasn't wondering about those women. I was wondering about..."

Stella interrupted Annie, satisfied that her point had been made. "But you WAS wonderin' and since you is so good at wonderin', how bout you try wonderin' how it felt to be Alice and be on a mission to knock a little bastard down the ladder a rung or two and wind up being beaten with chairs, hearin' three women screamin' like the gates of hell had opened—like some damn horror movie, when all it was, was you tryin' to make things right in the dog kingdom. If that was happenin' in the human kingdom, damn near anybody in that particular position woulda turned on those crazy people in a heartbeat to protect their ass—case closed."

Stella flicked open her lighter and lit up. "Now what I want to know is what the hell have you been up to? What happened to your now skinny as shit self?" She sat back, waving her hand across the front of her face to clear the smoke that rose between her and Annie.

Annie seized the moment. "Well, I went to Greece, wandered around, lived with a family for awhile—helped them run a restaurant, then lived with a gay German ex-film maker, now sheep herder, came back, found out my father died and then nearly had a complete breakdown in a guest room that used to be part of my home, but it wasn't my home anymore." Annie made it short as she knew full well Stella wasn't interested in the long version, at least not now.

Stella sat forward and tapped her cigarette over the ashtray. "Well HALLELUJAH AND AMEN—what you need to know about your father dyin' is that right there is a good reason for us to celebrate. That is what you call a good endin' for a man who screwed up his daughter for what is appearin' to be her whole life 'cause she's gettin' too damn old to not be gettin' a grip on shit. His bein' dead is the end of that little story, which unfortunately ain't the way it worked with this little story that I been tellin' you."

She sighed and looked past Annie towards the kitchen window. "It just don't ever seem to end when I get myself in these kind of situations. I don't know what it is about me, but I just seem to bring on every whacko situation on earth. I guess they'll be an end to it some day, as in when I'm dead and gone. And I'm wonderin' exactly what God is gonna do with all his whacko shit then, send it to you?—HA—or better yet send it all to mister-can't-stop-buildin'- fences-to-save-his-life, which is exactly why he's doing that. He ain't got nothin' to live for anymore, at least that's how I see it. And lookin' at you, I'm thinkin' you got a lot in common with Bobby right now, which ain't a good thing, so you need to get a grip and start lookin' at what's right in front of you, like this situation I'm tellin' you about."

Annie was perfectly satisfied to settle in and hear the rest of what she knew would be an intriguing tale.

Stella's voice dropped to a revved-up whisper as she leaned across the table toward Annie. "See, two whole weeks after this whole 'massacre' at the neighbors—which is what it was accordin' to them—I picked up the phone, like I usually do when it's ringin'.

"Well," she nudged Annie's arm and straightened up when she was sure she had Annie's one hundred percent attention, "I'll be damned if it wasn't Mr. Allen Cranshaw, talkin' about how 'traumatized' his wife was and he didn't want things to 'escalate' between us good neighbors to the point where he might find himself thinkin' about me and Bobby just like his friends do who have heard the 'story' and are referrin' to me and Bobby as 'my trashy neighbors and their dogs.'. And, you know, here's the funny part, he was talkin' all reasonable and all. I mean, his voice was as calm as the sun that shines on my fields every day, 'cept when it's rainin'—he mighta even sounded a little scared, I wasn't sure at the time—of course, I know all about it now. Anyway, I kept my voice real calm in return and I says, 'And what is it that you want Mr. Cranshaw?'

"See, I wasn't gonna bite on that little 'trashy neighbor' bait. His bein' calm and all and throwin' that little bit of misinformation out there in such a quiet manner, I knew the guy was mad as shit and just waitin' for me to go off on him, so he could sit back and think exactly what his 'friends' may or may not have been sayin'. 'Course, as I come to find out during our 'talk' that guy lives with a whackjob for a wife and I kinda feel sorry for the poor bastard.

"Anyway, I'm gettin' ahead of myself here." She lit up the last cigarette in her pack. "So, he says, we've been neighbors for almost two years and he has no problem with us. He just wants to make this right and the way to do that is to talk it out like decent people.

"I says, 'OK, I'm fine with talkin'—'course there ain't nothin' to talk about, but whatever makes your wheels spin—when do you want to talk?'—and he says, 'how 'bout now? It's just Claudia and me here, so come on over.'

"Well, I went collected a few things I might need, one of 'em bein' my shotgun, and drove over there by myself. I figured Bobby, well, he was a wild card before and even more of one now, so I left him at home—didn't even tell him I was going, partly 'cause I didn't want to spend a hundred hours lookin' for him.

"Anyway, to make a long story short, I got there and them Cranshaws were all smiles and sat me down, offered me a beer. I said, 'No thanks.'

"That's when Al started talking—the man of the house— 'course he didn't look like no man 'cause he was all huddled up in his big old couch holdin' a pillow like it was a damn teddy bear. He started talkin' about how his wife can't go outside anymore and she's got golf clubs all around the house to protect herself and she's not sleepin' and she's drivin' him crazy and then, don't it beat all, tears start comin' from his eyes.

"Well, that right there woulda done me in—as in he woulda had me in the palm of his hand—if he didn't say what he said next. He said he came racin' home from a hard day at work which, in my mind, meant he had a bad day at the golf course 'cause it was Sunday—and he found broken chairs, blood all over the curtains by the door and blood all over the carpet. He said he scrubbed and scrubbed but couldn't get it out. Then he said his wife, she laid on the couch in pain for two days and was too scared to go anywhere, 'cept to the doctors, which he'd insisted she do.

"That's when I knew I was gettin' sucked in to some crazy ass shit that had nothin' to do with Alice leavin' a single puncture wound on a five pound dog. I said, 'Hold up, buddy, from what you're tellin' me it sounds like Charlie Manson got outta prison and dropped by after I left 'cause that is so far from the truth it boggles the mind.'

"So, Claudia tapped Al on the arm and said, 'You've said enough Al, let me talk now.'

"Well, she looked at me with eyes as pitch black as them squares on this floor and she pointed her finger at me and said in a voice that sounded like that Darth Vader guy from them Star Wars movies, 'I need you to tell me your dogs are vicious killers!'

"I looked at her, thinkin' what the hell is wrong with this woman? She just didn't look normal, I mean her eyes was like some kinda psycho. I looked at her and said, 'Why would I tell you that when it ain't the truth?'

"That's when she leaped up from the couch and jumped all up and down talkin' about how the doctor said she had shredded muscles all over her body from Alice bitin' her while tryin' to get Ziti outta her arms and kill him. She said she had it documented by the doctor and that if she hadn't jumped in, them little dogs would be dead.

"I looked her in the eyes and I said, 'Claudia, honey, you need to calm your ass down and show me them "shredded" muscles and all that broke skin, 'cause if you got them "shredded" muscles that you say you have, then you got broke skin, PLUS if you got "shredded" muscles how is it that you're hoppin' around your livin' room like a teenager on cocaine? Where's your goddamn wheel chair? Where's the bandages?'

"She was hoppin' mad. 'I DON'T NEED TO SHOW YOU ANYTHING, MY MUSCLES WERE SHREDDED BENEATH THE SKIN. WHAT I NEED YOU TO TELL ME IS THAT YOU KNOW YOUR DOGS ARE VICIOUS KILLERS.'

"She didn't stop yellin' for quite some time—over and over, wantin' me to admit my dogs was vicious killers. Al was sinkin' back into his big stuffed up couch, pipin' in from the peanut galley that he knew my dogs had killed rabbits on occasion 'cause I had told him that when I stopped once for a chat. He was still speakin' real soft.

"Anyway, that's when I stood up and took my little container of valiums out from under my bra and said, calmly I might add, 'Claudia, you need to take one of these and then you need to tell me that you are a certified whack-job and need some help.'

"Then I turned to mister-all-scrunched-up on the couch and told him that as far as killin' rabbits, hell yes, that's what dogs do—it's called havin' a prey drive and goin' after prey—'so what y'all need to understand is that you are just plain nuts, end of story.'

"That's when I got up and told 'em I was gonna take my leave, meanin' get the hell outta there 'cause they had wore me out with their bullcrap. Darth Vader started up with the yellin' again, so I looked at them Darth Vader eyes and waited for her to shut up for one second and then told her my Alice may have over stepped her bounds a little by jumpin' up on her to try to get Ziti and give him an ass whoopin', but pickin' him up in the first place was somethin' she never shoulda done. Still in all, I said 'I gotta tell you she wasn't even close to how nuts you are right now.'

"That's when I looked at Al and it hit me like a lightnin' bolt. That man was scared of his wife. This yellin' and screamin' she was doin' was exactly what their marriage was all about, somethin' I know a lot about, only unlike Bobby and me, it wasn't a back and forth thing that fizzled out and ended in some kinda peace. He just took it, like the pussy whipped man that he is—poor bastard. I'd say I walked into what I'm thinkin' was the tip of the iceberg when it comes to all that went on in that house.

"Anyway, as I was walkin' out the door, I turned around and said, 'By the way, I ain't "white trash" mister and I know you were meanin' to throw the "white" in there before the "trash," but kept it to yourself 'cause you is so "civilized." The fact of the matter is you and me got a lot in common. I was once rich like yourself, probly richer, but Uncle Sam, well, he wasn't too happy 'bout not gettin' his share and, well, he made me a certified white collar criminal. Now, the only difference between me, my fellow inmates, and you is, you ain't been caught yet. There ain't a rich man alive that ain't done a lot of screwin'.'

"Then I looked right at Darth Vader and I said, 'I don't mean just the screwin' of Uncle Sam.'"

Stella looked across at Annie and shook her head. "And when I shut the door, I thought I was done, but I found myself turnin' right around and openin' it again. See, I was startin' to feel real pissed off and that's when I said real loud, not yellin' like I wanted to—I was bein' restrained like Alice was—'And another thing that y'all need some help with, them golf clubs ain't gonna do it! What you need is a couple of good ole fashion shotguns—that's what we call peace of mind down here!'"

Stella laughed. "I just know that put them over the top."

She pushed her red blaze of hair back over her shoulders and let out a long sigh. "Alls I gotta say is what happened over there with Alice is a testament that puts her high up on the scale of dogs that got a handle on things. There ain't a few dogs out there that probly woulda taken Claudia out just to help the human race. However, Alice had the good sense to know doin' that woulda made my life a livin' hell. That bitch is a good bitch, that's for damn sure."

Annie had put herself through the whole ordeal as Stella told it. "Jesus, aren't you worried that a woman like that will press charges based on her pack of lies and fuck with your life or Alice's?" She knew, absolutely, if she'd been in that situation she would've kept her mouth shut and probably felt guilty that Alice had been the cause of so much agony in one room.

"Hell no, and you know why? 'Cause all that crazy shit would come flyin' out in the court room, which is where I would make sure it got to, whatever it took. That shit was a load of dirty laundry that them two don't never want to hang out, rain or shine—and here's the good part, the part I been holdin' back on this whole time. 'Member I told you I got a couple of things that I needed before I got in my truck and went over there? Well, you know me, and you used to know exactly what I woulda brought besides my shotgun, which I left in my truck, by the way. Come on, you tell me what the other thing was. I raised you to be almost as smart as me, so tell me." Stella waited.

Annie scrambled through her mind and found it. "You're something else, Stella. You brought your tape recorder didn't you?" She didn't know how she could've momentarily forgotten that little lesson Stella had pounded into her at least a thousand times over the years. Stella never went anywhere without a tape recorder.

"Yessiree, I brought me my itty bitty tape recorder. I taped the damn thing to my belly and ran the mike out to my sleeve and recorded the whole damn thing, every goddamn word. So, if I hear so much as a peep outta them two, I'm gonna let them have a good listen. This here is a one party state—meanin' I can record them without them knowin' it and it's legal. You listen to that shit and you look at the facts of what happened and the discrepancies is loud and clear—that along with what a whack job that woman is. Ain't no lawyer gonna want to take this case on. And on top of that, the other lady, the one whose dog got the bite in its ass—well, she called me and left a message the day after the so called 'massacre.' She wanted to inform me that she called the Dog Officer.

"That was almost three weeks ago and I ain't heard nothin' and never will! And what does that tell you? He didn't see jack-shit wrong with what Alice did and he knew I ain't had no other incidents of this nature from ANY of my dogs. Nope, I was not born yesterday and I don't know why I have to keep provin' that over and over and over—which brings me around to why I started on this whole thing with you in the first place. I got a letter from that lady, her name is Margaret—a name I can't forget seein' as we got one hell of piece of work in the Bordeaux world named Margaret who I ain't got the energy to tell you about right now." She hesitated. "No, you did meet her! Fact is, she came down a bunch of times when you was here."

Annie chuckled. "Yes, I remember her."

"Anyway, this other Margaret was writin' about how she wanted me to pay for the emergency vet bill—meanin' the one stitch—along with any 'after care,' as she called it."

Stella got up from the table. "Hold on." She walked over to one of her kitchen drawers and rifled through it.

Annie watched Stella dig through the drawer, her red hair jerking back and forth as she did so, and fully realized what she admired about Stella. The woman never crumbled under any fire regardless of the nature of it, and if she were ever to crumble it would only be for a moment. Her bag of "savin' her own ass" tricks was infinite.

"Here it is, I knew I had it somewheres." Stella turned to face Annie as she opened what looked to be a single typewritten page. "This here letter tells you everything I already knew about this woman who I never met before in my life. Listen to this."

Stella walked out into the middle of her black-and-white kitchen floor and cleared her voice. Right as she did this the phone rang.

She scowled, walked over, and picked up the receiver. "Whoever you are, I ain't interested, call back later." As she put the receiver down, a voice was heard tryin' to get Stella's attention. "See, it is never endin' around here. I can tell you right now that was one of them whack jobs in the Bordeaux world wantin' somethin' from me. Anyway, listen to this."

Stella cleared her throat and began reading in a flat and deliberate manner. "Dear Stella, I am enclosing an itemized bill for Penny's visit to the emergency veterinary hospital. There will be a follow-up visit as well. Penny may have some nerve damage to her hind end. She holds her tail strangely and has fits of attacking her rump as if sensing something is biting her when nothing is. Also, one of her canine teeth loosened this week and fell out yesterday, and I can't think of any reason that would have happened except for the trauma of two Sundays ago."

She stopped and smacked the page with her free hand. "Can you believe this shit? I mean, the dog's tooth fell out and she's blamin' it on Alice bitin' her in the ass two weeks back. That right there is gonna turn into a thousand dollar dental bill from some quack tooth vet, I can guarandamn-tee you that!

"Now, where was I? ...oh, yeah—'I understand this event must have been very hard on you and that you would give anything for the attack not to have happened. But it did happen. As a health care professional, and maybe as just a plain old human being, I feel obligated to say I think your dogs are untrustworthy and need to be euthanized.'"

Stella stopped again and looked over at her once fine lookin' best girl who looked like hell. "Can you believe this shit? I mean, who the hell does she think she is? Who 'obligated' her to say jackshit about my dogs! I didn't, and I sure as hell know Bobby didn't. Mmmm... mmm... Some days it's just amazin' that I can even get outta bed in the mornin' considerin' the folks I got to deal with."

She put the letter on the table and searched her pockets for cigarettes. "Goddamnit, where the hell are my cigarettes?"

Annie picked up the empty pack from the table, "You finished them, but not to worry, I have a pack right here." She pulled a pack of Camel non-filters from the pocket of the brown leather jacket that she still hadn't taken off.

"Since when did you start smokin' for real, as in buyin' your own? Hell, last time I knew you, you was tellin' me I should quit this shit and save my life. I guess you decided on the long slow path of suicide right along with me." She laughed and picked up the pack from the table. "Ain't nothin' like smokin', it's like breathin', one of them necessary things in life for some of us."

She lit her cigarette and picked the letter up off the table. "Now, back to this fine piece of literature...mmm...okay, here it is. 'I think your dogs are untrustworthy and need to be euthanized.'"

Stella inhaled and blew smoke across the page. "Hell, she can't even spell euthanized. Ain't there s'pose to be an 'a' instead of an 'e' in there somewhere?"

She walked over to Annie and showed it to her. "Even I got a clue how to spell it 'cause I've had to do it so many times and, besides that, if she's a 'health care professional' how come she don't know how to spell it?"

Annie looked at the word. "You're right, she spelled it wrong, it's the 'e' after the 'th,' that should be an 'a'."

"I knew it! I may not got all that education you got, but I knew there was somethin' wrong with that word. It just didn't look like the way I seen it before. Anyway... ah hem..."

Annie jumped in. "Stella! Just give me the damn letter and let me read it, I can't keep it in my head with you interrupting at every single sentence."

"Okay, okay. Take it! Damn, no need to snap like that!" Stella put the letter down on the table.

Annie picked it up and began to read it to herself.

Stella sat back, blew a smoke ring from her mouth and watched it rise towards the ceiling. She looked over at Annie and felt calmer than she had in a long, long time. "You know," she said, "I knew the minute I read that thing that this woman was playin' in your particular field of life or whatever the hell you want to call it. I mean you wasn't even here and you were the first thing that popped up in my mind, as in the person who would know exactly what to say back to this woman."

She waited and watched Annie read some more. "Now, you know full well, I ain't made to deal with this kinda person, it's way out in some field I ain't never walked in and I have walked in a lot of 'em, as you well know. I can deal with Mrs. Darth Vader, but this?! This is way beyond my call to duty. This is right up your alley, made for you. In fact, as I was sittin' here watchin' you read that, I know exactly why you ended up in my driveway. I believe it was God who sent you. I mean, think about it. You been gone all this time and you show up now, when I'm in the middle of some crazy shit with this woman who don't believe in killin'—'cept when it's personal to her, which ain't a part of that rule from everything you told me. Anyway, I think all this happened to bring you back here where you belong."

Annie finished the letter and looked across the table, "And I think you've lost your mind, right along with this woman." She put the letter back down on the table. "And what this woman is doing is taking the moral high ground, thinking she has universal backing and every right to make all kinds of assumptions about you and your dogs. On top of that she's ignorant—I can't think of a more dangerous combination."

Stella snorted. "Well, whether I lost my mind or not, here you are, stale Camels and all, lookin' like hell and sittin' across from me readin' a letter that coulda come from somebody from another planet, as in your particular planet, meanin' you is the only one who can write the letter I need you to write. You tell me if that don't seem like God's been doin' his work."

9

Stella Discovers Emily

Despite the fact Annie had helped build Galestorm Kennel and helped run it for over a year before she left, she had much to learn and relearn. For one thing, the number of adult dogs had increased from five to eighteen, mostly bitches, which meant the workload had increased a hundred fold, and that didn't include the litter and puppy care that Stella told her came along on a regular basis.

As she walked the kennel with Stella and Oz the morning after she arrived, Stella was all business, which was just fine with her.

"Now, the way it is around here, people are wantin' pups like they was hamburgers comin' off the grill at McDonald's. I tell 'em this ain't no fast food restaurant and they have to wait longer than five minutes, but that don't seem to stop 'em from pressurin' me and, not only that, they all want one outta Oz.

"Now Oz here," Stella patted Oz on the head, "he's gettin' damn tired and I tell him I understand his pain. See, it just ain't possible for him to breed so damn much. I mean people don't understand the stress breedin' can cause a dog. Hell, I seen some dogs drop down to lookin' like they been in a concentrated camp." She looked over at Annie. "Just like you do right now, which ain't gonna be for long, mark my words. A ton of home cooked meals and what not, that'll do the trick."

Annie attempted a response to the brief blast of warmth. "Stella, I'm ..."

Stella interrupted. She'd left the moment behind her in a waft of cigarette smoke and continued on, "Anyway, sometimes we gotta do what we gotta do to keep the business alive."

For the next three days, Annie worked alongside Stella who didn't stop from morning till night. If they weren't hauling bags of dog food and buckets of water around, breeding bitches, or cleaning the house, Stella was on the phone or rifling through the mounds of paperwork that lay sprawled across her desk—a sharp contrast to the meticulous order of the rest of her house.

Annie would rest whenever Stella disappeared into her study to tend to paperwork, or during her animated and rather lengthy phone conversations. She found it hard to believe Stella had been doing all of this, day after day, particularly when it came to the physical labor part, i.e. the kennel work. Stella was tough, absolutely, but it just wasn't her style to be as hands-on as she was. When she asked about it, Stella set her straight.

"First off, Miss lyin'-on-the-couch-while-I'm-workin'-my-ass-off, I didn't do it all. I fired my help, Lisa-Lee, the night after you came back. I called her up and told her she was no longer needed to work for me 'cause my best girl was back. I'm just doin' it with you till you get the hang of it, which will be soon 'cause I got a ton of more important stuff to attend to, like all this communicatin' to people and doin' the damn paperwork, that bein' the biggest pain in my ass."

She picked her cell phone off the kitchen table, started to dial it, then hung up and looked back at Annie. "See, the paperwork is where people get real testy, 'specially when they're wantin' to buy my pups to breed or show. I tell 'em they'll get their paperwork eventually, but I ain't got the 'bility to hurry them people in Puerto Rico along, which is where I register my dogs—hell, they're slow as shit down there and we all know why that is—and when they is tired of being lazy down there, they move up here so they can collect welfare and be even lazier—case closed.

"So, everybody who wants their paperwork yesterday, meanin' pedigrees, is gonna have to wait till tomorrow, which means on my time. Besides I don't trust nobody, as you well know. See, there's a bunch of shit I gotta do to protect me and my dogs, meanin' I don't give a shit about whether people get what they want, but I do give a shit about my dogs and the fact that my kennel keeps the respect it deserves, and that's what I tell people and that shuts 'em up for long enough so's I can do what I need to do to get them off my back."

She poured herself a coffee, lit a cigarette, and sighed as the smoke blew across the room. "Some days I wish I was back in the business with you—the way it was, but oh well, this is what I got to deal with now so I deal with it. People is so damn dumb anyway, even the ones who thinks they ain't. So, between you and me, just like our old business, there are tricks of the trade to be learned and I'm teachin' 'em to my own self and learnin' 'em from my own self faster than any of the dumb asses in this breed and that, right there, is exactly why I am fast becomin' the most successful kennel in the country. Not a lot a' people can be a teacher and a student all in the one body—but that's what it takes 'cause if you is havin' to teach your own self, then you know you're onto somethin' that nobody ain't thought of yet—which means you is on top."

Her eyes narrowed as she picked up her phone again. "And I'll tell you right now, I ain't never givin' up any of the tricks in my bag. Everybody's gonna have to learn it the hard way, just like I had to—case closed. And if they ain't smart enough to do so, then they can suffer the consequences, which is gettin' nowhere fast and watchin' me zoom ahead of 'em so far they can't see me no more." She snorted and dialed, leaving Annie to think on everything she'd just said.

———

Annie took in from Stella's course on how to run the kennel only as much as she needed to know to do the job she was expected to do. She didn't care about the paperwork, the "tricks of the trade," or any other aspects of the "trade" for that matter. It didn't interest her in the least, not anymore. She simply shut that end of things out of her mind. Her job was to take over the feeding, watering, help with the whelping, the vet trips, cleaning the kennel, errands, and letting the dogs out in their "proper groupings" to run in the multiple fields that Bobby had meticulously fenced in.

———

"It's 'cause of Bobby they got more fields to run in than most dogs in the whole world will ever dream of. And if you didn't notice, he even put little carvin's of Bordeaux heads on top of some of them fence posts—and, trust me, he ain't done yet. Sure as I'm standin' here with you, he's gonna come up with a bunch of other shit like that, just to keep hisself busy. I'm tellin' you, he ain't right anymore.

"Anyway, you just be sure you put the right dogs in the right groups when you let them into them fields 'cause if you don't you will have a fight on your hands, meanin' a big fat vet bill due to havin' to stitch 'em back together—'cause unlike that Margaret's little Toto—or whatever the hell his name was—it won't be no single puncture wound we'll be dealin' with.

"So if you got to write it down—I don't have to because I know each of them dogs like they was my own children— then you write it down. Now, I'm trustin' you like I always did, Greta, which means I'm forgivin' you for runnin' off on me for all this time.

"Besides, you writin' that letter to Margaret, that right there proves you still got somethin' I need, which is somebody who understands me and knows how to help with all the bullshit, particularly the kind I got no desire to deal with. We make a good team, that's for damn sure."

———

So, for the first two weeks following her return, the learning curve was steep, the physical labor was hard, and the errands were many. At the end of each day, she was so tired she would fall into bed right after dinner and not wake up until the next morning. In truth, if it were up to her she would've been more than happy to have things go on that way for another two weeks, or even the rest of her life. She didn't want the extra time or energy to think about anything.

Stella, however, was not happy. Annie's sleeping while she continued to do the hard work of keeping an eye on the big picture was not sitting well with her.

So, on the fifteenth night, after eating one of the finest meals she'd ever made, and while she had Annie and Bobby sitting in the same place at the same time with their eyes open, Stella rose up and banged on her glass with her fork.

She had dressed up for the occasion. Rather than her usual jeans and flannel shirt, she wore one of her "drop-dead-gorgeous" dresses. This was something she rarely did anymore, which meant only at some shows—the important ones—or when she was meeting prospective rich puppy buyers, or at times like this, when she had a particular plan and needed maximum attention to set it in motion.

She put the fork down as Bobby and Annie looked up. "I got somethin' I need to say to the both of you—Annie in particular because, Bobby, we both know you is a lost cause right now and until you find a way to make yourself found, as in be more a part of this family rather than just the fixin' and fence buildin' and watchin' TV part, I got nothin' to say to you."

Bobby grunted and lifted his beer bottle to his mouth.

Stella snorted. "Now, I know you want to start a fence buildin' company, God knows you got the know how. Hell, I'm surprised the governor ain't called you yet and hired you to put a fence around Georgia to keep all them northerners from invadin' our territory. God knows, we don't need any more Cranshaws, that's for damn sure—and I'll be glad when you do start your business 'cause we need the money, but we both know the business ain't gonna start itself. So, instead of sittin' in front of that huge ass TV night after night, you need to start thinkin' on how to get your business goin'—end of story."

Bobby had no response.

Annie looked on with considerable amusement.

Stella banged the glass again, this time with her knife. She rolled her eyes and put the knife down. "Now I see why I never seen nobody use a knife, it just don't sound as good."

She picked up the fork, banged it on the glass, and grabbed the pack of cigarettes and the lighter that sat next to her dinner plate.

"Now, Annie." She looked over at Annie as she placed the cigarette in her mouth.

Annie burst out laughing. "You're not serious, are you? And, by the way, why ARE you so dressed up? I mean you look fabulous, of course, but I feel like I'm in a play."

Stella flicked her lighter, stuck the tip of her cigarette into the open flame, then sucked in and exhaled. "Took you over an hour to notice my dress, which don't surprise me one bit considerin' the state you're in day in and day out. And Bobby here, he probly don't notice a thing. Hell, I could be stark naked and he wouldn't notice. Fact is, I'm serious as shit and for your information this is NOT a play." She purposely didn't say 'ain't,' a choice she could make whenever she slowed herself down enough to consider the option.

She closed her lighter and placed it back on the table. "First off, how could it be a play, seein' as I ain't never read one, been in one or seen one—case closed—'cept *The Sound of Music*?"

Annie had stopped laughing, but was still amused.

Stella snorted. "Seems to me I recall a time when you was sleepin' all the time way back when, and you always had some excuse—and as it turned out you wasn't really all that tired, you were just 'runnin' away from yourself' as you sometimes put it, if that's possible, which I don't think it is 'cause I ain't never seen anyone succeed in doin' just that."

She took a few long hits on her cigarette and waited.

Annie had no response.

Satisfied, Stella continued, "Anyway, the way I see it is you are choosin' to sleep rather than let me and Bobby in on exactly what you were up to all that time you were gone. Now, I bring this up because, since you been either workin' or sleepin', I have had to take it upon myself to try to find some answers and all I found, so far, is more questions because what I have found don't make any sense. As for my dressin' up, I figured the occasion of celebratin' your return with the stipulation that you ain't been up to no bullshit, is reason enough to wear this dress."

"What are you talking about?" Annie recognized the look on Stella's face. The next thing out of Stella's mouth was going to require a lot of explaining on her part. She wasn't up for it—but she knew it was going to happen some time and, apparently, now was that time.

"As you well know…" Stella sat down and leaned back in her chair. She had both of their hundred percent attention for the first time since Annie had returned. She pushed her hair back over her shoulders where it belonged, but seldom stayed, and blew a few smoke rings out across the table. "…I don't like not havin' answers, especially when I have asked for them on not a few occasions."

Annie jumped in. "Stella, whenever you asked me anything about what I was up to all those months, you were in the middle of one story or another and barely took a breath or even hesitated for one second to hear my answers. The way I saw it, you weren't interested."

Annie picked up her plate and walked decisively toward the sink.

Stella watched Annie make her way across her kitchen. "Oh, I'm interested now, considerin' what I found—and I don't want you walkin' around my kitchen while I express my interest, so sit your ass down!"

She waited until Annie put her plate by the sink and returned to the table. "Now, I was out in the barn the other day and I walked by your van, which ain't been driven since you got here, so I know everythin' in there is a hundred percent yours—and I says to myself, maybe I ought to take a good look in there and see if there ain't somethin' that could give me some answers to my questions. So I opened the door and stepped in."

Annie looked sharply at Stella. She was somewhat taken aback, but then reminded herself of who she was with. Stella was doing what she did best—and she certainly looked her best as well. She was now in her forties and despite twenty-five years of residing within a cloud of smoke and a lifetime spent in battle, both voluntarily and by draft, she was still remarkable to look at when she chose to shine.

Annie looked across the table at Bobby who was already looking at her. It was the first time they'd fully acknowledged each other's existence since she'd come back. The bite on her shoulder began to burn and she looked away.

Stella didn't miss a thing. "Don't you two be gazin' at each other, somethin' you ain't done since Annie got back, which is only for the best in my book 'cause you two have too damn much in common at this particular point in time—and while that can be a good thing between people, it ain't in this case."

She waited as they each shifted their focus from each other to her, then leaned over and picked up a small zip-lock bag from the floor beside her chair. "First off we have these." She opened the bag and dumped the contents onto her plate next to the lamb chop bones. There were two roaches, a bunch of Camel butts, a partially burnt incense stick, a used tea bag, and a few wads of bubble gum coated in ashes.

She shoved the bones off the plate and pushed it out into the middle of the table. "Now, from this, we'll call it exhibit A since the ashtray was the first place I looked—from this, I concluded that our Greta is a pot smokin', gum chewin', tea drinkin' person, all of which are normal in my book—'cept for the incensed burnin'. That, right there, is some nasty shit that only serves the purpose of stinkin' up the air I breathe—and it ain't normal for Greta. Anyway, I think to myself after all them years of not smokin' anything, 'cept the occasional cigarette from me or Bobby, why would she start now? Which is why I decided to continue my search and, by the way, durin' my whole seach, I found no evidence of food—no wrappers, no crumbs, no half eaten donuts, nothin', which means Greta wasn't eatin', which explains why she is so damn skinny, which could mean she's bein' eaten up by somethin' real nasty."

Stella leaned down to the floor again. "Anyway, then I found this." She put a manila envelope on the table next to her dinner plate. "This is exhibit B. In this here envelope is all this lawyer writin', the contents of which explains why she ain't had to work and probly ain't never gonna have to work again." She looked at Bobby. "Our Greta is livin' off a big ass inheritance. 'Course there is nothin' wrong with that in my book, 'cept that it can release the devil in a person, because as you know hands that ain't busy is hands waitin' on trouble. So I start lookin' for the trouble and I found it."

Stella paused.

Annie was more fascinated than anything else and still had no clue where Stella was going with this. "I'm all ears, Stella."

Stella's green eyes narrowed. "Well, you should be all ears 'cause this is YOUR life we're talkin' about."

She got up and walked into the larder off the kitchen. Her voice was barely audible from within. "What I have to show you next is the part that raises all the BIG questions!" She walked out holding a fairly large cardboard box. She pushed the plate and the manila envelope towards Bobby's side of the table and plunked the box down.

Annie recognized the box and felt suddenly annoyed. "Stella, those are…"

Stella raised her hand. "Now, you hush. You may know what these are, but you got some big time explainin' to do regardin' them."

Stella looked over at Bobby and noted he was a hundred percent interested for the first time since she'd had her talk with him the day Greta left. "What we have here, Bobby, are a billion letters written to some girl named Emily, who can't be more than about eight years old, which I can tell because they is written in a manner that would be communicatin' to a eight year old. Remember, now, I was eight once."

She pulled out a handful of the letters and sat down. "Well, I started readin' 'em one by one and I have to tell you when I was eight, there wasn't a chance in hell somebody woulda wrote or read this stuff to me, seein' as I was all tied up with my mama walkin' out on me and my daddy countin' on me to keep HIM from fallin' into that 'I'm so lonely I could die' hole, which ain't what I wanted to do 'cause then where would I be—case closed, but that's life now ain't it? Hell, I surely would rather have been readin' this stuff!"

She put one letter at a time on the table in front of her. "I mean these letters, they talk about nature and all kinds of animals and campin' and lookin' at the stars and all the interestin' people in the world—only the good ones, I might add—and all the fine things on God's earth. Some of 'em are whole stories that are told in a bunch of letters at once, so you gotta read 'em in order. They is about everythin' from sittin' around a campfire with a family of bears or wolves or damn skunks—talkin' with 'em, learnin' all kinds of shit about their different way of livin' and the shit they got to do to get by every day. And then there's the story of runnin' with a bunch of wild pigs—who all have names, by the way—clear across the state of Georgia gettin' into all kinds of situations, situations that I imagine a lotta kids like to hear about so long as they don't got a mama who walked out on 'em and a daddy who might just disappear down a pity hole any damn second."

She ran her hands across the letters. "AND I might add, these here letters is written in the usual Greta style, real nice and easy on the ears. Now, there ain't nothin' wrong with any of this 'cept for a couple of things, A) Why ain't they sent or are they just waitin' to be sent? AND B) Have a billion already been sent and, if so, why? Now, that's just one 'why' and, trust me, I got a lot more whys where that came from. For instance, if you are sendin' this many letters off to some little girl somewhere then, in my book, you is stalkin' her. I mean there are as many as three written on the same day! That just ain't normal and if I was this Emily's parents, if she has any, which she may not—which would be exactly why you mighta chose to stalk her—I would be callin' nine-one-one to get you off my daughter's ass."

She pulled more letters out of the box. "Anyway, as I kept readin' I started tryin' to put shit together—pot, cigarettes—why? See, another 'why,' as in why would Greta start smokin' all that stuff now, after all them years, unless she is nervous as shit about somethin' and needin' to medicate herself—like I have had to do due to all the shit I've had to deal with in the world, 'cept I gotta tell you, this kind of shit, well, it crosses a line in terms of everythin'. I ain't never walked across this line or met anybody who has and if I did, it wouldn't be no pot I would be smokin'—it would be me gettin' a gun and holdin' it to my head 'bout as fast as possible."

Bobby abruptly pushed back in his chair and started to get up.

"Bobby, sit your ass back down!" Stella's eyes blazed for an instant that was meant to be strictly private—for Bobby only.

Annie took note of it.

Bobby sat back down and Stella continued, "See, the other possibility, is that Greta has an obsession—just like you do with the fence buildin'—and this girl ain't real, which means she's been writin' a billion letters to someone who don't exist, which means she's more crazy than you are."

"Stella, there is a third possibility here." Annie was caught between amusement and annoyance.

Stella turned. "And what is that possibility? I'm all ears 'cause I am NOT likin' the questions or the answers I been comin' up with—all of which leave me to thinkin' you just might need to leave this house for the second and last time."

Except for the instant when Stella's green eyes blazed at Bobby, Annie didn't feel particularly threatened. "Look, there is an Emily. She's the daughter of the people I stayed with before I drove all over the country and eventually landed back here. I'm very fond of her and did send her a couple letters, but I stopped sending her any after a few weeks. I don't know why, I just did. All those letters you have may say 'dear Emily,' but they're really to me—you've got that part right. Well, they were to her as well, but—shit, I can't explain it."

She sighed. "Look, I wrote them because it made me feel good and gave me a reason to get up every goddamn morning. You just said yourself that you would have rather been reading those letters than doing what you were actually doing at eight—the age is six, by the way. Emily is six."

Stella rolled her eyes. "Six? Well, that's a whole other story! I didn't have no time to read letters when I was six. I was busy watchin' Greta Garbo movies with my mama and pickin' gum off the bottom of them theatre seats—those were the good times I might add."

Annie ignored her and continued, "Look, it's a long story, but basically I wound up at the Hansons by mistake—Emily Hanson is her name. They now live in the house I grew up in. I thought my family still lived there so, when I arrived and found nobody home, I broke in because I was too damn tired to wait until someone came home. I fell asleep in the first bed I found. So, the Hansons came home to find me in their daughter's bed."

Stella burst out with a deep gruff laugh. "Now that right there is funny as shit, ain't it, Bobby? All I can say is you are lucky as shit they didn't call the cops and have your ass thrown in jail."

"Well, they did call the cops, but I managed to explain to them who I was, so by the time the cops arrived we were straight with each other. See, as it turned out, the Hansons knew my family. They were the people who broke the news to me that my father had died and my mother and brothers had moved on to other parts of the country."

Annie picked up Stella's pack of Pall Malls and pulled one out. "So, they were incredibly kind to me. They consoled me and offered me a place to stay until I pulled myself together."

Stella handed Annie her lighter and snorted. "Consoled you? Hell, that right there tells me they didn't know the truth of that little matter, which means they didn't know you near as well as I do. What they shoulda done was brought out the champagne and toasted to that man's death. The only consolin' necessary in that situation was that it didn't happen sooner, as in all them years ago—end of story."

"STELLA, I'M TRYIN' TO TELL YOU WHAT HAPPENED TO ME BECAUSE YOU ASKED!" A touch of Stella had crept into Annie's sudden unexpected anger. "NOW, IF YOU JUST LISTEN FOR TWO GODDAMN SECONDS YOU MIGHT LEARN SOMETHIN'!"

Stella reached into her bra. "Goddamn woman, you need to take one of my chill pills."

Annie snapped back, "I'm not interested in your damn pills! Just you listen!"

Stella pulled her hand back and glanced down at the

table. "OK, but hurry up and light your, I mean MY, damn cigarette! Where the hell are yours? Ain't you bought yourself any? Seems to me with all that money you got now, you could at least be smokin' your own damn cigarettes!"

Annie opened the lighter and flicked it. "You see, I called my mother—or she called me, I don't fucking remember— but I do remember that she was as distant as the moon to me on the phone and gave no hint of ever wanting to see me again—and you already know why that is." She lit her cigarette. "So, there I was in the guest house at the Hansons', where I nearly fell into a thousand pieces on the floor a few days after getting the news of my father's death. I thought I was going to die right there, if not literally then in every other way. As you so rightly have pointed out many times over the years, Stella, I was L-O-S-T with capital letters."

Annie looked straight at Stella. "You know, it was your voice that helped me get up off that floor—loud and clear as if you were right in the room with me."

Stella looked back defiantly. "Now, I don't mind hearin' your story like your tellin' it, but don't be pullin' me into this. I don't have jack shit to do with any of it, as in I never spoke a word to you till you was layin' in my driveway. Alls you need to do now is get back to the subject at hand which now seems to be narrowed down to why you got a box load of letters that ain't never been sent and never was intended to be sent."

Stella glanced over at Bobby who was taking it all in. "Bobby, what the hell do you have to say about all this, you're as crazy as her—why don't you try explainin' it mister-fence-builder-of-the-universe?"

Bobby barely flinched except to rest his own cigarette in the ashtray. "Alls I got to say is Annie here has been writin' letters to herself 'cause she didn't have no one else to talk to. Hell, I talk to myself all the time, so do you—hell, I seen you do it out loud on a daily basis. If you was to put that on paper instead of sayin' it or thinkin' it, you would have a Mack truck load of them boxes filled with paper, now wouldn't you?"

"Well, the difference being, Bobby, when I talk to myself I is just as old as when I'm talkin' to you, I ain't six or eight—

which, by the way, is somethin' you know nothin' about seein' as you don't even remember bein' those ages."

Bobby sat up a little straighter. "Hell, I may not remember bein' them ages, but I sure as hell remember bein' eleven and lovin' to build shit! Fact is, that's the only thing I remember lovin' about them days that was worth rememberin' and now look at me. I'm buildin' day in and day out. Seems to me Annie here is writin' letters 'cause it makes her feel better. Hell, that ain't complicated to understand." He settled back and picked up his cigarette from the ashtray.

"Bobby, what you're sayin' is you 'loved' buildin' when you was eleven so you is buildin' now 'cause it makes you feel good, like you did then. Greta here was gettin' titillated by her daddy at age six and likin' it I might add, as in it felt good—she told me that herself—so, if we was to go by your particular logic, she would now be titillatin' six year olds, which means we ain't just talkin' about stalkin' anymore. Fact is, from what you is sayin', what we may have is a pedophiliac sittin' here at our table."

Stella sat back and tapped her fingers on the table with dramatic flair as she looked decisively over at Annie. "Which I'm thinkin' ain't so because it just don't make sense, all things considered, your little piece of wisdom not bein' one of 'em by the way."

"Wow, now that's a relief! Are you two done yet?" Annie was visibly unnerved at the direction the conversation had taken. She got up and grabbed Stella's plate—bones, butts, roaches and all—then grabbed Bobby's and took them to the sink.

Stella's voice followed her. "Greta, you need to stop and think for one minute about all the evidence and ask yourself if you was me wouldn't you be a slight bit curious as to what you've been up to all this time you been gone?"

Annie kept her back to Stella. "Of course I'd be curious, and you've had plenty of opportunity, after the dozens of times you asked me what I was up to, to actually wait for an answer." She scraped the butts, roaches and bones from Stella's plate into the trash. "But no, you had to make it into some big secret that I was hiding from you, which led you to snooping around in my van."

She emptied Bobby's plate and turned to face both of them. "Did either of you take note that I wasn't the least bit unnerved that you were snooping in my van? Now, is that the behavior of a criminal? I know you well enough, Stella, that if I had anything I didn't want you to know, I sure as hell would not have kept it in my van or anywhere in this entire state for that matter!"

Stella swelled with pleasure at the compliment. "You got that right. I don't miss a trick AND you have made your point—a damn good one."

She got up and walked back into the larder. Her voice could still be heard. "So now that we got this whole thing over with, we can have us our little celebration. I mean, here we are the three of us havin' a real conversation, like we used to. On top of that, your daddy's dead."

She walked back into the room carrying a tray of cornbread with a baggie of pot on top of it. She set it down on the table. "Your daddy's dead—amen. And you're back here where you belong, just as crazy as Bobby is—there ain't no doubt about that—but somethin' I can live with. The only thing bein' you need to start writin' them letters to the you that is standin' right there at the sink, letters tellin' you to snap out of it, eat more, and get with the program—meanin' no more Emily. For one thing, you ain't six anymore and the real Emily, well, she's got real parents and a real life, so what the hell is she needin' from you? Nothing—case closed—and speakin' of that, I'm gonna keep them letters because I ain't done readin' 'em yet."

10

The Impending Silence

The night of Stella's inquiry was Annie's first without sleep since her return. They celebrated all night long. The next morning Annie brought up the fact they'd had no sleep and then, mistakenly, wondered aloud how any of them would get through the long day ahead.

———

"Greta, honey, it ain't no big deal. As I've told you a billion times over the years, you could use a lot less sleep and a whole lot more survivin', like the rest of us. Hell, Bobby here don't hardly ever sleep. Between bein' in that foster home and prison and livin' with me, he's probly slept the 'quivalent of one of your nights, ain't that right, Bobby?" Stella paused and picked up her mug of coffee.

"Yup, sleep ain't nothin' but a waste of time—it takes away the edge you got to have to survive." Bobby was typically already out fencing by this hour, but he just couldn't seem to get himself up from the table they'd all been sitting at for the past twelve hours.

Stella's mug landed back on the table. "That's right—and doin' shit like buildin' fences ain't all life's about either. There's the part where you're thinkin' about how to stay on top of everythin', there's the gossipin' part where you learn how everybody else is tryin' to stay on top and failin', and there's the bitchin' and plannin' part, somethin' you do only with the people you trust. And there's the part where you sit around all night and talk your ass off..." She hesitated. "...you know, without havin' to watch yourself—

that right there is somethin' worth doin' as opposed to sleepin'."

————

Regardless of Bobby and Stella's philosophy on sleep, Annie was physically exhausted, which made her kennel work harder than usual. However, her mind felt clearer than it had in months. She was glad she'd been pushed to talk about what had happened to her at the "Bears" and afterwards. Yes, she'd tried a few times before then but, in truth, she hadn't wanted to. So, Stella, in her own way—something Annie had counted on—managed to break through and bring her back home again.

Unfortunately, her relief and clarity of mind was short lived. As she swept the kennel floors and prepared the dishes of food for the dogs, the lingering question of what was wrong between Bobby and Stella, or just Bobby, began to nag at her. From the moment she'd awakened in their driveway, she knew something had changed. Bobby was always in the distance, just out of reach, or gone. Stella included him when speaking, but not as if he were a part of her life or even real. And Bobby showed no signs of wanting it any other way. Truthfully, she'd had no room for worrying about what was going on between them. She didn't want to know. So, she'd let it go.

However, during Stella's inquiry, Annie had taken note of a particular look Stella had shot at Bobby, one that had clearly been meant for his eyes only. It was a look that made Annie's belly go cold. Then, not minutes later, Bobby nearly got up from the table, only to be pulled back by Stella.

After that, any hint of dissonance had disappeared completely for the first time since she'd come back—and she wanted it to stay that way, but she knew it wouldn't. It was the bite on her arm that she would either tend to, or not.

She turned to feeding the dogs, which first included a private conversation with each of them, followed by letting them loose into the fields in their "proper groupings."

As she stood at the fence and watched them enjoy each other and their day, she came to the decision that her renewed sense of home was the most important thing. So, once again, she chose to ignore the itch and continue to avoid contact with Bobby, other than the most superficial of exchanges. This wasn't hard because they spent their days in completely different locations, with only occasional crossovers.

Annie was content to do her work, spend private time with Stella, time with Stella and Bobby together each night, go to sleep, wake up, and start over again.

———

Two months passed without a glitch. Stella walked about the house and property in a perpetual state of dramatic outrage over one thing or another regarding the dog world, which was no different to Annie than when she'd run her previous business, and Annie's role was no different now than it was then, except that Stella didn't want her to have any contact with the dog people.

"You don't got the thick skin and besides it's a different game than the old days and I ain't got the time or inclination to teach you what I know. Don't take it personal, it's just the way it is. Besides if you was to ever run off again, I wouldn't want you knowin' what I know—case closed."

Though Stella's expression of distrust irked Annie, as it had at times in their previous life together, this rule didn't bother her at all. It freed her up to enjoy Stella's dramatic and entertaining descriptions and perceptions of "these people" without experiencing any conflict in loyalties, not that she felt there would be any—not at this particular point in time. She was content to be what Stella referred to as "my silent partner," which meant to be of help when Stella needed her.

Her only other loyalty, besides to Stella, was her newly found loyalty to the dogs. When Stella had first ordered the building of the kennel to begin, it seemed like a cruel endeavor to Annie. She felt breeding dogs for profit crossed a line, and breeding pure breeds seemed "Hitleresque." She'd said this to Stella early on, in hopes of changing her mind.

———

"Greta, you go on and on about me bein' all 'dramatic' and all, and here you are comparin' dog breedin' to bein' like Hitler Esk. Now I'm not positive who you is talkin' about, but the only guy I know with that name is the Hitler who killed all them Jews and if I recall he didn't have no last name Esk, in fact he didn't have no last name, period—Hitler was like Cher, didn't have but the one name—but for the sake of our argument, I'm gonna assume we is talkin' about the same guy, which means I now know, for sure, you is from a different planet than anybody I ever met. That's about as crazy as you believin' in that pacifist crap! If I had your kinda thinkin' runnin' through my head all day long, my life woulda never got nowhere—first it's don't hurt no one for no reason, never mind that you might have to save your ass or mine someday by hurtin' somebody—and now it's 'don't breed dogs 'cause people might be mistakin' you for Hitler.'

"Well, for your information, there ain't nothin' about dog breedin' that comes close to killin' a billion Jews—that right there is a leap, honey, even for you. For your information, people who breed dogs is tryin' to breed fine animals, animals that has been mankind's best friend for a million years.

"The purebred dogs are somethin' I have had one or another of for most of my life as you well know—and you loved a number of 'em, by the way. Each of the breeds got special qualities that make 'em special to certain kinds of situations and people, meanin' people want a dog that appeals to the nature of their way of livin'—what's so bad about that? Nothin'.

"And another thing, I never seen you complainin' when we was puttin' beautiful but damaged goods—meanin' girls—out there to collect money from men who wants nothin' from 'em but sex and their own selfish good times—and you was one of 'em—so it seems to me that you would be chocked full a good feelins' about me gettin' out of that business and makin' some fine companions for people. Ain't nothin' wrong with it, nothin' at all, and speakin' of your friend Mister Esk—the Bordeaux, somethin' I've done a lot more studyin' on since you was last here—was almost wiped off the face of the earth 'cause of him. There weren't but a handful left by the time he was done tryin' to do the same to them Jews.

"Fact is, there was a lot more of them Jews left than these Bordeaux—so all we is doin' is the good work of bringin' 'em back into the world so people can enjoy havin' their company. And for your information, the Bordeaux is the oldest purebred on the earth, which makes 'em real special and real valuable, meanin' they're a good investment. Makin' money while bringin' 'em back from not bein' here at all? Hell, ain't nothin' wrong with that in God's book—and we both know His book is more to the point than yours—case closed."

———

The case WAS closed and the work of building the kennel, breeding dogs, and whelping puppies went forward, but it was only now that Annie was beginning to find an appreciation and affection for this breed. Her daily intimate contact with them was nothing short of wonderful. She'd caught "the Bordeaux virus" as Stella put it. "This breed will shake down your rock hardest of hearts to a puddle, and on top of that they will protect your ass. That's a combination that can't be beat."

Annie had begun to grow particularly fond of Alice and Grace, aka Amazing Grace, both of whom took turns sleeping with her most nights. She didn't know if it was due to the Cranshaw affair that her attention had gone to them first—or if it was based solely on who each of these bitches were. It was probably both.

Grace was smaller, darker, and in her opinion, the smarter of the two. She watched all that went on around her with great thirst and did everything in her power to manipulate her environment to her favor, which included Annie. And Grace's expression was undeniably the most magnetic of the entire kennel. Through expression alone, she had Annie allowing her freedoms such as spending most of her time outside her run where she could freely cavort with any and all of the other dogs. She was accepted by every one of them, either alone or within the various groupings—and that was what had gotten her the name Amazing Grace. "This bitch got no bones to pick and no rungs to climb—she ain't a threat and ain't threatin' to none of the others. Personally, I think she just plain gets under the radar, I don't know how."

Oz was the only other dog who enjoyed more freedom than Grace as he was allowed to spend all of his time outside the kennel, always at Stella's side or in the house.

Just Plain Crazy Alice, aka Alice, was given the name because she was a far cry from the breed standard and was intense and threatening to anyone who didn't know her, but unusually affectionate and gentle to those who did. "Hell, anyone would think that bitch is completely outta control—but she ain't. See, she'll never make it up that ladder 'cause none of them other dogs take her serious. The truth about Alice is she ain't real secure—huge as shit, but not secure and not all that good lookin', which makes her not good breedin' material, which means I'm gonna be findin' her another home when I get around to it."

Stella reminded Annie to keep a close eye on her if she was to take her anywhere outside the kennel or the fields because she was just the kind of bitch who would go back down to the Cranshaws. "I believe Alice has found a rung that she can climb up to and it's through those two little dogs down the road. She ain't gonna give up that opportunity, not in a million years. Besides I don't want her beat to death by Big Bertha, which for your information is a type of big ass golf club that's used to hit that ball further than the eye can see. Now, I didn't see one of them hangin' out by the house, just the puny ones, but you never know—all it would take is one Big Bertha comin' down on her head and it might just be good-bye, Alice."

———

By the end of the two months, Annie's fondness for Alice, whom she had renamed Big Bertha, and for Grace, now a mom to a litter of pups, had grown into a fierce and indisputable attachment. This pushed her, one morning, to broach the subject of Stella's plan to find Big Bertha a new home. She had just rolled out of bed and entered the kitchen. Stella was pacing between the kitchen, her study, and the living room, a cigarette burning in an ashtray in each room.

Annie let Stella pass as she walked to the coffee pot. As she poured herself a cup, she spoke up. "Stella, you can't give Bertha away because I'm crazy about her."

Stella disappeared into her study and reappeared as Annie sat down at the table. "Hell, you can have her. I don't got the time to find her a home 'cause I got me the national show to prepare for, meanin' I got to think who I'm takin' and who is gonna show 'em for me. And for your information, the show is clear up in New Jersey, which means you and Bobby will be runnin' things around here for what looks to be anywhere from five days to a week, dependin'. I'll be taking Lisa-Lee with me to help with the dogs that I do take, 'cause she knows my dogs and she keeps her mouth shut and does exactly what I need her to do." She picked her cell phone up from the kitchen table, then turned and faced Annie. "Bertha?"

Annie didn't respond. She couldn't. She had become instantly unnerved at the news of being left with Bobby to take care of things.

Stella walked over and waved her phone in front of Annie's face. "Hello? Who the hell is Bertha?" She waited for about one second. "Well, since you ain't speakin' I'm gonna assume that's Alice you're referin' to." She started to dial a number, then stopped abruptly, put the phone down, and rushed into her study where her hands frantically tore through piles of paper work as her voice sped back into the kitchen where Annie still sat motionless. "Hell, name her what you want, that bitch ain't worth a damn—insecure and ugly as shit! I'm just glad I don't have to waste my time tryin' to find a place for her. What I do got to find is that damn paperwork on that bitch I gave to that Mabel woman 'cause she's expectin' me to bring it to her at the show. I swear the things I do for people, it's a miracle I ain't moved up that ladder to the status of Jesus hisself!"

She picked up the papers she'd finally found and walked back into the kitchen. As she pulled a chair out from the table, she looked across at Annie and abruptly stood to attention, her mass of red hair surging forward. "What the hell is the wrong with you? Why is it you just keep starin' at nothin'? I said you can have the bitch and I don't give a shit what you call her—end of story." She put the papers on the table and sat down. "I gotta tell you, this Mabel woman, the only reason I gave her the damn pup is 'cause I feel sorry for her—and besides, between you and me, I got a feelin' about this one. Sometimes it's good to give shit away, because as we both know it's all in the who, what, and why part of givin'."

In her mind, Annie flung her hands over her ears and started screaming at Stella to SHUT UP, but what actually came from her mouth was controlled annoyance."Stella, don't start with me on your little philosophy about 'giving.' I've heard it a hundred times. Remember me? Or maybe you don't. I'm the woman who lived with you for a very long time and for equally as long I've never accepted what you have to say on this particular topic and, while I'm at it, a lot of other topics as well. What you're saying is everybody's deep-down selfish and only looking out for numero uno! I think it's sad you see it that way." She sighed in hopes of relieving the pressure that had damned up in her head—a week alone with Bobby.

"Don't you 'numero uno' me! And for your information, this little philosophy which you claim you have heard a hundred times is the damn truth and there ain't nothin' wrong with repeatin' the truth a hundred or a billion times—sad or not. It's the way it is. The big problem here is, even after all you been through PLUS all I taught you, you is still tryin' to find somethin' that don't exist. But none of that is what this little conversation is about, is it?"

She looked across the table at Annie who still looked too skinny, but more like the Greta she'd known before—too damn beautiful for her own good. She locked her sharp green eyes into Annie's deep blues and held them. "I know exactly what this is all about, you'd have to be a damn fool not to, which is somethin' I ain't, or have you forgot that too?"

She leaned back and picked up the almost burned out cigarette from the ashtray and sucked in on it. "Actually, it's one of two things, probly a little of both. First off, you is jealous of Lisa-Lee 'cause she's goin' with me, but I already explained why you can't go, so we don't need to talk about that. Secondly, and more to the truth of the point, this is all about Bobby, ain't it?"

Annie flinched ever so slightly and Stella caught it as instantaneously and skillfully as a spider feels the vibration on her web when the tiniest of insects hits it. She rushed in, "BINGO—guess I ain't lost my touch yet!" She snuffed out the cigarette and reached into her breast pocket for her morning joint. She hadn't had the time yet because of the call from Margaret Appleman regarding the upcoming show, something she did not need to be reminded of. Of course, she knew Margaret just wanted to know which dogs she was bringing so she could tell the world. She lit the joint and, as she sucked in, Margaret disappeared like magic.

She looked over at Annie as she held the sweet smoke in, then released it. "Honey, you don't think I haven't noticed how the two of you never talk 'cept when the three of us are together? I have watched that since DAY ONE of you comin' back here and I know exactly why that is. Bobby is a changed man, darlin', and you ain't been interested in just why that is. Don't tell me otherwise 'cause I know it's the damn truth. It's sad as shit his buildin' a hundred miles of useless fences for every one mile that has a use."

Stella's voice flattened. "Now, what you need to know is, he's been that way ever since you stole his truck and ran off on us. Oh, I tried to tell him, day after damn day, it wasn't nothin' and you'd be back, but he's not so smart as me. So…"

Annie interrupted her. "Stella, I didn't steal anything, and that can't possibly be the reason because…"

Stella leapt in. "Now, you listen to me!"

Annie sat back, bewildered. Stella's green eyes had gone black, her shoulders and neck were rigid with rage. Her voice was hard, low and guttural.

"What you got to get through that thick skull a' yours is it's all different than it was 'fore you run off. The Bobby you once knew is dead and gone. You up and left a mess here for me and Bobby to clean up and it didn't go so well from Bobby's way of lookin' at things. Family is everythin' to him and far as he was concerned you broke a big-ass family rule and that's exactly when somethin' snapped inside of him. You messed with somethin' you just don't mess with around here!"

The room went silent and Annie closed her eyes for what seemed an eternity. When she opened them and looked across the table, Stella was comfortably settled into her chair, her shoulders and neck were back to normal, her black eyes were green again, and she was sucking peacefully on her joint. Annie felt momentarily confused—what had just happened?

Stella handed the joint across the table. "Greta, you look about as uptight as a person looks shortly 'fore they pass out. I suggest you take a hit of this seein' as I know you ain't no virgin anymore. Ha."

Annie shook her head.

Stella put the joint back into her mouth. "Look, it ain't gonna be all that bad. Just accept Bobby for the man he is now, like I do. God knows I love the man and he'll be by my side till the day I die, ain't nothin' could change that. Alls you got to do is talk to him, like normal. He ain't no monster or nothin'—hell, you already know that 'cause the three of us, we talk every damn night, just like we used to. And when you need some help regardin' the dogs or the kennel while I'm gone, all you do is ask and he'll stop buildin' his fences for two seconds and help—that is, if he ain't in the middle of the next state wonderin' where his fence took a wrong turn. But that part's in God's hands, nothin' you can do about that—and I thank God I ain't God on account of just that kinda thing."

She took a double hit and sucked in, still talking. "I gotta tell you I'm sick and tired of watchin' the two of you, day in and day out, and not seein' a damn word spoke between you, not till I'm in the picture."

She emptied her lungs into the room. "Well, I ain't gonna be in the picture startin' on Friday, so you is on your own durin' them days, and the less you two talk, the fatter them days is gonna get, and the fatter them days get the bigger the chances that the two of you will be suffocated from the big fat silence around here by the time I get back."

She dropped the burned out roach in the ashtray. "Just think of my goin' away as God's way of tryin' to make things a little bit better than they been, as in you two are talkin' without needin' me around. I gotta tell you, it would make my life a whole lot easier."

She coughed and got up from the table. "Now I gotta go call Mabel and let her know I got the papers on that bitch, then I gotta call Margaret back and tell her to keep her nose outta my business, then I gotta call Lisa-Lee, who I know you ain't too fond of right about now—then I gotta get me a new outfit 'cause I just gotta look as fine as Oz when I'm in that ring."

She stopped and turned around just as Annie pulled a Pall Mall from the pack she'd left on the table. "Bobby'll forgive you—just like I done—and when you're done smokin' MY cigarettes, make sure you replace 'em, double."

Annie sat by herself at the table and finished off Stella's pack of Pall Malls, one by one. Aside from extreme confusion and disorientation, she felt as if a load of bricks had just pummeled her, two or three at a time, before coming to a collective rest onto her shoulders. She had no idea of how to get out from under them.

11

Keep an Eye on Gracey

Annie stood with Amazing Grace and Big Bertha as Stella roared out of the driveway in a cloud of grit and dust. She watched as the cloud rose above the trees long after the truck was out of sight and out of earshot. Between Georgia's ongoing drought and Stella's ongoing flare for the dramatic, Annie figured the cloud could possibly hover at around a thousand feet before settling back to earth.

She looked down at Grace and Bertha who had gone from standing to sitting to lying in the few moments she stood there. It had been a long, long morning, which was underscored by the tired beasts at her feet and the fact that the entire kennel had been as quiet as a Quaker Meeting when she'd approached it to feed the dogs breakfast—not even a whisper. Along with the dogs, it seemed unlikely that any living being for miles around could have slept beyond 2 a.m., which was when Stella had been awakened by her "wake-up call" from the infamous Margaret Appleman. It had been preplanned, of course. Margaret, as Annie so clearly remembered, was a woman who would jump into the Grand Canyon if Stella so requested. Her call was the first in an endless stream of calls to and from various parts of the country, each of which was chock full of exasperated exclamations and obscenities. And whatever slips of time there were between calls, Stella spent dashing between the bedroom closet and the den, desperately torn between her need for the "right" outfits and her need to find the correct paperwork on the dogs she was taking—Oz being one of them.

In the end, every single piece of Stella's clothing lay strewn about the bedroom, on the bed, over the chairs, the dressers, and some had even ended up on the floor. And the heaps of papers on Stella's desk—usually the only sign of disorder in the house—were now spread beyond the desk to the kitchen table, the coffee table, and the couch which Bobby had vacated by 2:30 a.m. He had decided to begin his next project in the far field in the pitch black of the night. From all of this, Annie concluded that last minute show preparations were a hellish affair at the Gale compound.

She turned as she heard the distant chugging of the tractor grow louder. Here they were, she and Bobby, sans Stella. She watched the tractor come through the tree line and head down the dirt track toward the barn. She waited for him to look up, and then waved in a first attempt to cross the enormous chasm that lay between them. He responded with a single limp gesture that may or may not have been a wave.

Right at that moment, Grace let out an impatient moan which diverted Annie's attention to the fact she and Grace needed to tend to Grace's six-week old litter. But first, she had to put Bertha in the house. "Don't lose track of that bitch 'cause she'll go back to the Cranshaws in a heartbeat, you can count on it!"

———

The seven blue-eyed pups were in the "Puppy Cottage" which was once Annie's apartment, a large living/bedroom area, tiny kitchen, and a bathroom. Bobby had overhauled it with everything necessary for whelping several bitches and their litters—including room dividers, tiling, heated whelping boxes, carpeted play areas, and then some. Hanging over the entrance where there had once been a wooden sign that read "Annie's Place," was a similar sign that read "Puppy Cottage, enter with care."

Annie smiled as she and Grace herded the pups down the grooved rubber ramp and out into one of the puppy yards. Unlike Stella, Bobby never talked much about his affection for the dogs or any animals, but it was evident throughout the kennel—his meticulous attention to the details of their comfort and his playful, loving touches such as the signs and carvings.

As she sat in the sun and supervised Grace and the pups, she went back in time to when she and the boys had helped Bobby build the core of this now vast kennel. It was what had helped them get through the months and months of waiting for Stella to be released from prison. Her sudden absence had been devastating to each of them, mostly for the same reason—she had been the center of their lives. Those first months without her were months spent in the chaos of loss. Bobby's beer drinking had increased to the level it was now and her sleeping had increased to the level it had been for her first two weeks back here—and the boys, well, it was a miracle they got off to school each day and came home most nights. Some nights they stayed with friends, and the nights they did come home, the first thing out of each of their mouths was, "When is Ma comin' home?" Stella was not the best listener in the world, never would be—but there was something about the way she didn't listen that was far more appealing to the boys than the way someone who was half asleep listened or the way someone who was in an alcohol induced haze listened.

The adjustment to life without the life of the party was unbearable, and just about the time it seemed all hope was utterly lost, along came Stella's call from prison with the order that Bobby begin the job of building the kennel. They all jumped in as if their lives depended on it, which they did. Stella had given them a way to bring her back into their lives. She was suddenly everywhere. The concrete they poured, every nail they pounded, every board they sawed and every conversation they shared: "What do you think Stella would think about the way I did that? What would Stella do? I think Stella would like it this big. Can't wait to tell Ma about how much we've done today. Do you think Ma will like it? How many dogs do you think she'll want?" Every other day, when Stella would call to hear of the progress that had been made, they would squabble over who got to talk to her first. Of course, no matter who talked to her first, unless it was Bobby, the conversation, or whatever the one minute exchange was, would be cut short with an abrupt "OK, now put Bobby on!" Then they would wait for Bobby's dozen or so drawn out "yuup, uh huhhhh, nooos, OK darlin's" to come to an end, after which they would literally gather round as if Bobby were about to deliver a message from above, which he was, and listen carefully as he repeated everything she had said—it was their sustenance. Bobby's drinking eased up, Annie stopped sleeping most of the time, and the boys were home and ready to work every day, with or without a friend or two.

Annie watched the pups romp around the yard, yank on each other's extra skin, bump into each other, trip over nothing, and growl at the nothing that was responsible. Then there were the occasional attacks on mama that resulted in getting shoved onto their backs by her gentle though forceful muzzle.

She sighed.

The truth was, as time rolled by, Stella began to lose her place in the kennel project. The first evidence of this was when they began making decisions without consideration given to her approval or disapproval and they no longer squabbled over who would get to give her an update on the project when she called. That job was Bobby's and they left him alone in the den to speak with her, sometimes with specific instructions to lie if necessary to keep her satisfied. What was even more significant was that Stella was no longer the sticky tape that held their conversations with each other together. At first, this change compelled one or the other of them to bring her into a conversation even when it made absolutely no sense, an attempt to put a square peg into a round hole—but it was shoved in anyway, a Mea Culpa of sorts, and often an awkward moment of silence would follow, a silent scrambling for solid footing on shaky ground, but it would pass, and soon the awkwardness disappeared completely.

It was a period of time that Annie had forgotten about until this moment as she sat on the ramp and watched the pups. A shift had taken place that was unsettling. It felt like a sin and yet it felt right. Maybe she was the only one who felt any of it. Perhaps she was remembering it all wrong. It was hard to know because none of it was ever talked about. When Stella did return home everything instantly shifted back to the way it had been, only to fall apart a year later with a shotgun blast and a stream of obscenities.

She turned and looked up at the driveway, half expecting to see Stella either coming back down it or still packing up the truck to go. The dust had settled. She was gone. That was when every brick Stella had thrown at her the previous night came in for a second landing. "You up and left a mess here for me and Bobby to clean up and it didn't go so well from Bobby's way of lookin' at things!"

Annie turned and hoisted up one little Amazing Grace pup into her arms, then another—two was all she could handle as they weighed in at around fourteen and eighteen pounds apiece. She then whistled for the others to follow and walked up the ramp into the cottage. The five remaining pups stopped mid-mayhem and romped joyfully up the ramp after her. Mama Grace took a few quiet moments to pee before following her brood.

Two days had passed and the chasm between Annie and Bobby remained solidly in place. The only times Annie ever saw Bobby was off in the distance driving his tractor to and from the barn. Aside from that, the only other signs of his presence were the sounds of hammering and sawing from the far field and the dirty work clothes and damp towels that hung over the shower rod in the bathroom of the Puppy Cottage. She did hear his truck head out the driveway just after sunset, on both days, within an hour or so after she and Bertha left the kennel for the night and entered the house to cook dinner.

On the first night, she had cooked for the both of them. Then when she heard his truck leaving, she'd felt a mix of relief and sadness. Relief because she didn't really want to talk with him, not without Stella in the room, and sadness because she felt even more lonely than if there were no Bobby at all.

On the second night she cooked only for herself.

On the third afternoon, when she returned from running errands in town, Annie found a note nailed to the kennel door. It read "keep an eye on gracey—bobby." She stuffed it in her pocket, and walked through the kennel to the Puppy Cottage. As she entered, Grace sat up on her bed in the far corner, then wagged her tail and trotted over to greet her. She was less enthusiastic than usual, but not so much that Annie felt alarmed. She knelt down beside Grace and stroked her, checked her nose, eyes, and ears. All seemed normal. She then stood up and walked over to the three-foot wall to the puppy room. The pups were already on their hind legs, up against the wall, screaming with their usual exuberance, their bright blue eyes riveted to the top of the wall as she peered over at them. They seemed fine. She put food down for Grace and went about the messier business of feeding the pups.

By the time the pups were done, Grace still had not touched her food. She sat next to the dish panting slightly and drooling a bit more than usual. It was fairly hot, but not the dead heat of summer, and she hadn't just been drinking water or playing vigorously with the pups. They had been separated for the last few hours. Annie decided she would go give all the other dogs their late in the day exercise, feed them, and check back on Grace when she was done.

As she walked the fields with the various groupings of dogs and watched them zigzag amongst themselves, chase one another, fence fight with members of other groups, and do their 'business,' she could hear the sound of Bobby's hammer in the distance along with Bertha's barks from the house. They sounded almost equal in their distance from her. Only she knew Bertha actually existed, Bobby she was not so sure of anymore.

She felt around for the note in her pocket and pulled it out. It had been a shock to see his words scribbled in blue on white and tacked to the door. He had used an actual hand that he put to paper to communicate something to her. It was a small miracle, to be sure. She crumpled it again, even tighter, and shoved the tiny wad back into her pocket. It seemed this game had gone on long enough, and yet she wasn't sure whether she should wave the white flag, throw down the gauntlet, scream 'I quit,' or call out 'ally ally in free'—or whether she could bring herself to do anything at all. One thing she did know for certain was that they shared an equally rock hard determination to hold the status quo, though she'd begun to wonder if Bobby was holding up his end without thought, in the same manner he drank beer, dug holes, and watched TV. If that were the case, it was one hundred percent on her shoulders as to whether the chasm between them would shrink at all.

When Annie returned to the cottage, Grace still had not eaten, so she took up the food, took her temperature, which was normal, and decided to chalk up her mild malaise to being a mom who was ready to be done with being a mom. She then took the pups out into the now near dark to play and do their business as she and Grace sat dutifully on the sidelines. Frankly, she was amazed at how well Grace had handled being a mom thus far, considering her unbridled, four sheets to the wind, joie de vivre. Stella had exclaimed with certainty, "This litter'll be a damn sight more work than it'll be worth, mark my words, 'cause this bitch will be takin' off half the time to play with her friends which is everybody in the whole damn kennel. I never seen a bitch in heat behave so not normal in my life. Hell she might even be a pup squisher if you don't keep a good eye on her—not like she'd do it on purpose or nothin', she just don't have that particular kind of thinkin' that a good mama needs. Alls I gotta say is good luck to you 'cause you is gonna be, what you would say, mama numero uno most of the time. It's gonna be hell I'm tellin' you, gettin' that bitch to lie still long enough to nurse—you got a lotta not sleepin' ahead of you." Stella was dead wrong, as Annie pointed out to her not infrequently. Grace had been handling it beautifully. It seemed she was just getting tired of it now.

————

That night Annie didn't hear the sound of Bobby's truck heading out the driveway, so when she did her last check at 10 p.m. on Grace and the pups she half expected she'd find him asleep on the cot in the cottage. But there was no sign of him. She was curious about where he was, but not so curious that she went looking for him. As for Grace, she was settled on her bed, not asleep, but settled enough that she felt able to put Bobby's scribbled concern to rest for the time being.

However, as she lay in bed an hour later with Bertha sprawled out on the floor next to her, she began to feel annoyed at his having stirred her concern in the first place—where was he? If he had a concern, why didn't he find her and discuss it with her or take charge of it himself? She only knew a fraction of what he knew about these dogs. He was well aware that she was learning by the seat of her pants and now with Stella gone, how dare he assume she knew what he meant by "keep an eye on gracey—bobby." *It's a miracle I could read his chicken scratch in the first place—and just who did he think I would think the note was from, one of the other dogs? Is that why he signed it?*

"Jesus!"

Bertha lifted her head and grunted.

Annie leaned over and scratched the large head between the ears. "It's okay, girl."

Bertha settled again.

Annie laid back and stared into the dark. *Here I am, completely alone, with no idea where he is, fully responsible for all these dogs. If anything happens to any one of them, not only will I feel terrible, I'll have to deal with Stella.*

Her annoyance shifted away from Bobby. How dare Stella accuse her of being responsible for Bobby's "crazy ass" behavior and then leave her with him, expecting her to fix it AND take care of all the dogs AND clean up the mess SHE had left strewn about the house. *It's as if a goddamn tornado went through here!*

She suddenly felt tempted to light a match to that pile of 'paperwork' that was so bloody important to Stella and, if it was so important, why was it always in a heap spread across her desk with a goddamn bong sitting on top of it? Stella had been fanatical when it came to the paperwork associated with the escort business—every bloody hour was accounted for every girl—every cent—every expense—every stinking rich John, Dick, Daryl, Charlie, Harry, Hans, Helmut, Gregor—names, addresses, phone numbers, birthdays, shirt, pant, and shoe size for gift purposes. She knew the names of their pets if they had any, their travel schedules, and where they each were any week of the year. She collected every bit of dirty laundry she could get on each of them, most of which came from confessionals to and from 'her girls,' which included herself. Stella had it all written down and neatly filed it away, alphabetized and put under lock and key—not piled in a heap under a bong. The FBI couldn't have kept better records. There was no reason she could think of that Stella wouldn't have impeccable paperwork related to her present business somewhere. Her angle never was about breeding wonderful, healthy companions with God's blessing—who was she kidding? What was it? What the hell was her angle?

Annie sat up so abruptly that Bertha leapt to all fours and started in with her most ferocious of barks, horrified that she may have missed the first signs of an intruder. She got out of bed and steadied herself enough to try to calm Bertha. "It's OK, girl, no one but me and my mind." She stepped around her, opened the bedroom door, and stepped out into the kitchen.

Bertha burst in behind her, nearly knocking her over. She was no fool, and she had a job to do.

Annie hit the light switch. "Bertha, that's enough, now settle down."

Fully in tune with Annie's energy and not her words, Bertha rushed from the kitchen to the front door, cocked her head, and listened. When she was satisfied she'd completed her job, she laid down facing the door.

Annie walked into Stella's study and flipped the switch. Whatever was going on she was going to get to the bottom of it. She first looked at the pile on the desk, and then scanned the room. "Where the hell is the real paperwork?" She scoured the two closets, every cabinet, even looked behind the large photos of Oz that hung on the wall in hopes of discovering a secret safe—of course that would mean she would have to know the combination, but at least she would know her intuition was right, that real paperwork did exist.

This was all new to Annie. Never before had she felt so in doubt, so angry, and so determined to get to the truth about anyone or anything. A cold sweat started on her brow and increased with every minute that passed. The Truth was not her friend, never had been, and the longer she searched the greater the chances that she may have to deal with it.

An hour later, she had nothing except an increasing sense that an injustice had been dealt her and she wanted to know what it was. That was when Big Bertha began to roar. Annie ignored her and dropped to her hands and knees to search the floor under and behind the furniture. She was under the large oak desk when Bertha ceased barking and she heard the loud squeak of the front door as it opened.

"ANNIE?"

Annie backed out from under the desk and looked up to see Bobby standing anxiously in the doorway. *It's about time, and you sure as shit should be scared!*

"Bobby, what the hell is going on around here?" She surged to her feet without skipping a beat. "What's the real fucking deal? What have you done to me, you bastard?!"

She stood uncharacteristically with her hands planted on her hips. "I lived with you how many years—and you can't talk to me in private? Why? I spent twelve years of my life with you and Stella and look where it's got me—just look at me!"

She stepped back and dropped her hands to her sides, her oversized soft white T drenched in cold sweat, her light brown curls stuck to the sides of her face. "I'm scared, Bobby. I don't know where I am or who I'm with—or what has happened to me. I can't take care of all these dogs. I can't even take care of me."

That's when the tears came.

Bobby spoke low and steady. "Annie, Gracey's got the bloat. I gotta get her to Doc Burns 'fore I can think on anythin' else and I need you to come with me."

He looked at Annie and suddenly felt the same mix of apprehension, curiosity, and sadness he'd felt the night Stella carried on about her and her letters. He put it aside and turned and walked back into the kitchen. "Now, get dressed and let's get this done."

Annie said nothing. Bloat? She'd heard it mentioned a few times over the past couple of months, but only in passing. What she did know was it meant Grace could die. So, without another thought, she rushed to the bedroom and threw on her jeans and a sweatshirt. When she returned to the kitchen Bobby had already gone out the door.

With her brown curls still stuck to her face and her oversized T falling from beneath her sweat shirt to just above her knees, Annie left Bertha to mind the house and ran down the front steps to Bobby's truck which was in the driveway and running.

He leaned out the drivers' window as she approached. "Get in back with Grace. She's droolin' like a damn spickett and her stomach's hard as a rock, but she ain't started throwin'up yet. If we hurry we might be able to get her to the Doc 'fore she twists completely. Jus' keep her calm and don't let her fall off that seat."

Annie climbed into the back. Grace was sitting up, with her head slumped downward. She was panting heavily and the blanket beneath her was soaked with saliva. She raised her eyebrows and her tail wagged ever so slightly as Annie sat beside her. "OK, go!"

They were on the highway within a miraculous fifteen minutes and that's when Bobby's foot got even heavier. Annie looked over his shoulder as they soared past a string of late night truckers. He was going well over 100 mph, but she didn't care. She just prayed that they got to the clinic before the police got to them, which could be a catastrophic loss of time for Grace.

————

When they arrived, the clinic was ready and waiting for them. Bobby had called ahead before he'd gone to the house to get

Annie. The good news was that Grace was still able to walk and there'd been no vomiting. The consensus as they let the vet tech and attendant lead her away was that she would be fine. Bobby insisted they just skip right through all the 'bullcrap' and get in and tack her stomach, twisted or not, ASAP.

"I'll sue your ass if you don't do exactly as I tell you." Those were his last words as they whisked Grace down the hall.

Once they got outside, Annie stopped abruptly and grabbed Bobby by the arm. "Bobby, that was completely unnecessary. How does threatening a lawsuit help Grace?"

Bobby pulled his arm from her grasp and glanced around the dimly lit parking lot. It was a fairly large lot and there were only about eight cars and no people within sight. "That was called makin' sure they do right by Grace. One thing the Doc knows 'bout us is we don't piss around and I was just remindin' them of that fact. Ain't nothin' wrong with it." He tried to look directly at Annie but couldn't, so he settled his attention on the cars that whizzed by on the highway over-pass that rose above her brown curls. "Grace'll be fine and if they go ahead and tack her stomach this ain't gonna ever happen to her again."

He looked very briefly into Annie's face, which was only partially visible, then looked over her shoulder at the entrance to the clinic. "Just so you know, darlin', it's the people who got the best lawyers who get the best care at the hospital and it ain't any different for the animals." He began searching his pockets for his cigarettes.

"Bobby, don't you darlin' me!" Annie stepped back from him, her hands wrapped into tight fists. The rage she had begun to tap into while searching Stella's study had resurfaced as he spoke. She barely heard any of what he'd said, except the darlin' part.

"Where the hell have you been every night? What if any of the other dogs got sick and God forbid died on my watch? What if those pregnant bitches have complications? Bobby, what are you thinking running off every night—they're too damn big for me to pick up, let alone get into a truck! I don't know shit except what Stella has taught me and nothing she's taught me so far prepared me for this or any other health crisis. All those dogs and me? It's completely crazy!"

She released her fists, dropped her arms to her sides, and turned away from him, facing the clinic. She thought of Grace lying under the knife and spun back around. "Who the fuck do you think you are, playing with Grace's life like this?! What is it? Some kind of sick little game between you and Stella called let's see how long it takes for Annie to crack while we're away? Who am I to you? Who the hell are you and why do you build goddamn fences all day—or whatever the hell you do out there!"

Bobby shrugged and kept his tone calm despite the fact his heart was beating fast and loud in his ears. "Annie, I been gone part of the nights, but I always been back and sleepin' right there with Gracey and them pups and keepin' an eye on every one of them dogs." He walked past her towards the clinic and mumbled as he did so. "You don't understand shit. This ain't nothin' you want to go messin' with is all I got to say."

Annie watched the smoke rise over his head as he walked away. "Funny thing, Bobby, Stella talked to me just the other day about my 'messin' with things.' She explained to me how I've gone and messed with way too much around here, mostly you. She says I broke your heart and you never recovered, that it's my fault you drink endless beer and build endless fences! According to her, I've already messed where I shouldn't be messin'.'"

Bobby just kept walking, unable to think about anything, but his chest was growing tighter and tighter and the beating was louder and louder as he walked. As he approached one of the two glass doors, Doc Burns was there to open it for him. They stopped and faced each other just inside the door.

Annie's anger slipped away, for the second time that night, as she watched the two men from where she was standing in the parking lot. Bobby's shoulders slumped forward as the man she assumed to be Doc Burns talked to him. He was a good five inches shorter than the doctor, which was not unusual. Bobby was shorter than most men—but for some reason it was a startling discrepancy in that moment.

Then the doctor walked away and Bobby stood there, shoulders still slumped, staring at the floor, his cigarette still burning in his hand. That's when Annie realized it had been the burning cigarette that had so rapidly silenced her anger and tipped her off to what she now knew for certain was bad news. Bobby hadn't been asked to put it out when he walked in the door, despite the huge no smoking signs on the front doors and in the waiting area. Amazing Grace was dead.

She watched him walk over and sit down in one of the waiting room chairs, smoke still streaming from his hand. She felt tears on her face, but not what was behind them, though the image of her at Grace's side watching the pups appeared fresh and clear in her mind.

She reached into her jeans pocket. The wad of paper was still there. She pulled it out and uncrumpled it as best she could, the chicken scratch barely visible under the dim lights.

"keep an eye on gracey—bobby." Had she let the chasm between them get in the way of saving Grace? She dropped the note onto the pavement, watched it drift slowly away with the breeze, and walked back to the truck.

She climbed into the driver's seat and searched for the key, but it was nowhere to be seen. If it had been, she might very well have driven away. It then occurred to her that this was the very same truck she had driven off in almost two years ago and now here she was, again. She looked into the rear view mirror where she could see the little man in the chair, smoking and waiting. What was he waiting for?

———

Bobby looked up as Doc Burns approached.

"You can take her now, Bobby."

Bobby said nothing. He got up, stomped out his cigarette, and followed Doc Burns down the hall and into the room where Gracey was laid out on the steel table, sewn up from her chest clear down to her mid-section. It was a sloppy stitch job because it was meant only for transporting purposes.

Bobby had agreed to it. He just wanted to take her home without her insides falling out. He walked over to her head and patted it. "Ain't nothin' we coulda done girl, it was your time is all. Now it's time to take you on home, so you can rest in peace."

He turned as Annie walked in behind him. He looked at her and answered the unspoken question he saw scrawled across her face. "Annie, it weren't the bloat that killed her. She'da been good 'cept on account of her heart. Doc here says she got a bad heart—it just gave out on her and he says we gotta get her pups checked 'cause they might've got the bad heart from her and she got it from either Oz's lines or her mama's. He says it's a miracle them pups even got born without her dyin' right then and there from the stress of it."

They carried Grace's body out to the truck, wrapped her up in the blanket, and laid her on the back seat. It was a long silent drive home. Bobby couldn't speak because the tightness in his chest had become unmerciful. He could barely breathe.

Annie had succumbed to exhaustion and fallen asleep.

One thing Bobby knew about Annie was when she fell asleep on account of things getting real stressful, nothing outside of Stella or a bullhorn right in her ear could wake her.

As he pulled his truck into the barn and got out, it occurred to him that might be the only thing he knew about her any more. During those twelve years she'd reminded him of earlier, he'd never seen her the way she was the last time she was awake and he didn't care to see any more—he'd had enough. His chest was still so tight he could barely breathe. One more string of words out of her and he just might find himself lying next to Gracey in the grave he was about to dig.

As far as he was concerned, for the time being, they were both better off with her sound asleep, sprawled across the front seat of the truck while he went about the business of burying a bitch who had more life loving spirit in her than anyone he had ever met. Her dying from a bad heart seemed like one of God's bad jokes, as in there was nothing the least bit humorous or justified about it, not one bit—dead and gone at barely two years old. She didn't even live long enough to see her first litter of pups go out into the world.

Bobby pulled two shovels off the wall, one narrow and sharp for breaking through the earth, the other broad and dull for scooping the earth out. He threw them into the wagon and started up the tractor. It was 3 a.m. and still dark, but the sky was clear and there was a half moon and a ton of stars. Between all of that and the headlight on his tractor, there would be plenty of light. As he headed out of the barn, he knew he would bury Gracey somewhere along the edge of the near fields so she could be with the dogs when they were out during the day and keep an eye on the kennel at night. There was no doubt she had a way with people that made them crazy about her and she liked that well enough, but her true heart and soul were with the other dogs. There wasn't a dog in the kennel that wouldn't notice her being gone and show it in some way—how they would do that he had no idea. What he did know was it meant a change was about to happen and it would become clear soon enough. You can't lose the one dog that seventeen dogs have in common and think everything will go on as usual.

12

First National ABC Show Preparations

It was Thursday, late afternoon, at the Holiday Inn in Ridgemont, New Jersey. After two days of show preparation with a few club board members and a handful of volunteers, Margaret Appleman was finally free to take her first long breather, though she hardly considered it that because she could barely breathe at all as she walked quickly and deliberately back to her room. In truth, she hadn't taken much of a breath since she'd said good-bye to Frank and climbed into her Gremlin three days earlier. The breadth and depth of her anticipatory anxiety and excitement regarding this show, was something she desperately needed to keep private. Were she to take a large or even medium breath, all could break loose in front of God knows who, and the consequences would be catastrophic. Four years of the grueling work of 'making nice' to anyone and everyone, which included bearing abuse the likes of which she had known her entire life—all of it could go up in smoke should anyone catch even a glimmer of what was going on inside her, or so she believed. This was the show that would make her national club "official" and put her on the map forever. She was not about to give anyone the opportunity to take it from her.

She picked up her pace as she suddenly felt an over-whelming desire to take a very deep breath. The room she had picked was perfect. It was on the third floor and overlooked the front entrance and parking area of the hotel. She glanced down at her watch—her timing was perfect as well. This was precisely when people from all over the country would begin to trickle in, one by one. And by tomorrow evening the hotel would be buzzing with activity—all because of her.

She entered her room and the moment the door closed, her lungs burst wide open and sucked in every inch of air. She collapsed onto the bed as the excitement sent spasms and quivers throughout her entire rather robust body. The sturdiness of the bed was sorely tested—and passed. As she laid there waiting for the final spasms to cease, she recalled Frank's recent suggestion that she put all this "dog stuff" aside and have a baby. He was a dear, but she didn't want a baby, she wanted this! She rolled to her side and sat up. THIS was her baby!

She walked to the dresser and pulled her binoculars and notepad from the top drawer. A chair had already been placed in front of the window in preparation. It was the first thing she'd done when she got out of bed that morning. She looked again at her watch as she sat down. She had two hours before she had to pick up the judge at the airport, which meant she had two hours to do what she loved best.

Not twenty minutes passed and the ever familiar GALESTORM BORDEAUX truck pulled up to the front entrance. It was a huge bright red Dodge Ram 2500 with a special customized shiny black cover over the truck bed where she kept the dogs. Margaret knew, of course, that Stella's precious Bobby had a hand in building that—both hands. She had to admit it was beautiful, all decked out with hand painted Bordeaux heads, wide windows with screens and retractable metal awnings to block out direct sunlight. It was truly a sight to behold.

Margaret ticked off the name that was at the top of her list, set her elbows on the window sill and focused the binoculars. She'd put Stella's name down as the first to arrive and she was right—of course. She was no fool!

The passenger door of the Galestorm truck opened and Lisa-Lee, Stella's young blonde sidekick, began to emerge. She put one foot on the pavement when the truck suddenly started to move forward. She yelled out something that Margaret couldn't quite hear, then fell forward catching herself with her hands. She struggled to her feet and the red truck came to a stop about twenty-five yards away. The passenger door then closed and the truck moved on. Lisa-Lee shook her head and walked into the hotel.

Margaret grinned. This was the arrival of the first big fish. And after she parked her truck Stella would head straight up to her room, which was just down the hall from Margaret's, though Stella didn't know that yet. Once in her room, she would make the calls to her brigade. Margaret turned and looked at her cell phone which lay on the table by her bed. And while Stella did this, Lisa-Lee, who had been Stella's sidekick for the past two years—loyally at her beck and call—would collect the crates and the dogs from the truck and bring them up to the room.

Margaret sighed. From what she had gathered—and she gathered well—Stella met Lisa-Lee at a diner in some God forsaken part of the country on the way back from one of many shows. Stella took to her like a fish to a tasty fly and offered her a better deal than what the diner could offer. Lisa-Lee quit her job on the spot and drove back to Georgia with Stella. She never looked back, but did spend a lot of time looking up and out for Stella. According to Lisa-Lee, Stella had rescued her from a life with a drunken father and an abusive boyfriend. And she had told not a few people that Stella would make her a partner someday.

Margaret felt a tinge of envy burst through her left temple causing her head to tilt slightly, which skewed her focus momentarily. She pulled away from the binoculars and glanced around the room for fear somebody might have seen it, but she was still alone, thank God. She breathed freely for the second time in four days and put her eyes back behind the binoculars. Sure enough, there was Stella, strolling casually across the parking lot. Her full head of blazing red hair had been the first thing that caught Margaret's roving eyes, then the outfit. She was dressed in a sage green pant suit and a soft cream blouse with a black silk scarf that flowed out from beneath her red hair, down either side of her open jacket. It gently swayed back and forth as she walked.

Margaret could hear, in her mind, the rhythmic click clack of Stella's high black boot heels as they moved across the pavement. She moved with such confidence that Margaret swore she could see splashes of white light all around her—as if a hundred cameras were flashing. Envy then crawled into her right temple and started to smolder.

Stella glanced up in the direction of Margaret's window and tossed her hair back over her shoulders.

Margaret ducked. There was no way she would let Stella catch her doing what she was doing. She was fully aware that Stella knew if anyone was at a window, their eyes would be on her. She calmed herself, waited a few seconds, then peered out again. Stella was nearing the front entrance to the hotel. Margaret considered the possibility she had driven all night long in that outfit, but it just didn't seem possible. Nobody's clothes looked that good after driving all night!

She put the binoculars down and wrote a brief note next to Stella's name: Do not spend much time with Stella or even look at her, and do not take her picture at any time this weekend, even if she insists—cross your heart and hope to die. She then put the pen down and went back behind the binoculars. Stella was gone, but Lisa-Lee had re-emerged and walked out to where the truck was parked. She took the dogs out one at a time—there were three. And one at a time she took them to the patch of grass that had been designated by Margaret and crew as the pooping area.

Margaret looked matter-of-factly at each dogue. She knew Oz, of course, but not the two young bitches. She'd written down somewhere who the bitches were, but she really didn't care. She lowered the binoculars and glanced quickly around the room again. That little tidbit about her not caring was not something anyone was to know. When she'd started the club, her interest in the dogs was there, somewhat, but now it had shrunk down to near nothing. Her first dogue was her birthday bitch from Frank, out of Galestorm Kennel. She was not only a poor quality dogue, but she keeled over from a heart attack at three years old while Margaret was walking her around the neighborhood. Her poor Betty, aka Better than Boy, just laid down and died, right there in front of her as the neighbors watched from their windows.

Margaret's cheeks went hot just thinking about the humiliation of it. She'd had to drag that poor dog a thousand yards up hill by her front paws, on the pavement. Now, each day she saw her neighbors out with their children or their dogs, she prayed for the same to happen to them so she could peer out her window and see them dragging their dead child or dog up the street.

She glanced over at her phone, thinking it might be on vibrate, which might be why she hadn't heard from Stella. It just sat there, pink, flat, and lifeless. She felt a touch of lifeless herself and walked over to the tiny fridge. It had been a few years now, and she still hadn't gotten a replacement pup from Stella, or even any sympathy. All she got were threats regarding what would be done to her if she told anyone anything other than it was a "car accident" that killed Betty.

Margaret pulled a Coke out of the fridge. Oh, she'd keep her mouth shut, but only for so long. In the meantime, the two dogues she had were plenty, more than plenty—and they were back at home in a boarding kennel, where they belonged. Dogs just weren't worth the trouble OR the humiliation. The only reason she had her hands on any at all was because she couldn't be secretary and founder of a breed club if she didn't—it was a must.

She put the Coke on the table and checked her list again. It suddenly occurred to her that some of the people on it, particularly the ones at the top, might have arrived while she was at the show site. She picked up the binoculars and scanned the parking lot, in search of familiar cars. She didn't see any, but at the far end of the lot she did see a tanned woman in short-shorts and a cotton blouse prancing in a circle with a dogue. Margaret's binoculars weren't strong enough to get intimate details, but it was a chilly spring day, which meant it had to be Molly with her dogue, Tank, which meant Biffer Bradford was around somewhere, which then meant Stella had not been the first to arrive!

Margaret reprimanded herself for having been wrong, put a check by the second names on her list—Molly and Biff Bradford—and went back to watching the prancing short-shorts. The Bradfords drove her to near insanity. Molly had been so thrilled when she first heard Margaret was trying to put a club together that she bombarded Margaret with offers to help whenever she got the chance, which was far too often. To her credit, she had pulled in quite a few people from the West Coast which was a boon for the club. However, there was a particular kind of desperation about Molly which Margaret found severely suffocating, so much so that inner tremors were not uncommon when she was in Molly's company. This, of course, pushed Margaret to go digging. And she surely did find the glaring red light in Molly's life résumé. She'd been a second string cheerleader throughout high school and college.

When Margaret saw that little piece of information, it cried out to her, "This is it!" It may have been years and years ago—and it may have been only the tip of a bigger iceberg, but this was the sum of who Molly was. And Biff, he'd been a bench warming quarterback. Thus, she had in her midst two very insecure, obnoxious second stringers, looking to get off that bench.

She watched the short-shorts trot around the swathe of grass. She knew Molly would be out there with that dog for at least another hour. She scanned the parking lot. Biff would be showing up at any moment donning his muscle shirt, despite the cool air. And there he would stand, flexing his biceps, cheering his second stringer wife on, and drinking beers, all at once. He was a brilliant multi-tasker.

Margaret scowled. She figured Molly probably spent six hours a day working with Tank—a dog not worth shouting about to anybody, in her opinion. She had to admit, though, that Molly's obsession was paying off. She'd won dozens of small rare breed shows out west and two of the four regional ABC shows in this first year of the club's existence, and she was fully expecting to take this National.

Molly had studied the art of dog handling as if her life depended on it, plus she knew every cheap trick in the book, which included covering her dog's faults and flirting with the judges both in and out of the ring. Molly's goal had nothing to do with breeding dogs, selling dogs, or making money. This woman was driven by the singular need to be seen and applauded, something which disgusted Margaret to the point where she longed to see her humiliated into mush in the middle of the ring, or anywhere, it didn't matter.

And that was where Stella came in. Stella had never met Molly and Biff, but she had heard all about them and seen photos of Tank. And, of course, Molly and Biff knew all about Stella—who didn't? Stella wasn't impressed or worried about them. She was never worried about anybody, but she WAS insatiably curious about anyone whose dog made any kind of splash in the Bordeaux pool which, of course, had forced her to pick up the phone and call on Margaret who was armed and ready with information to fuel the fire. Of course, Margaret never gave up all of her information on anyone, at least not unless she got something in return. Also, some things were best kept close to her rather large bosom.

Margaret glanced at her watch. The time had flown by and her list had only two checks on it. She made a note in her head to be sure she got at least three hours tomorrow afternoon to take up her position here at the window—even if it meant she had to claim she felt sick and needed to lie down.

———

Stella stood at her window, joint in hand, and watched Margaret walk out into the parking lot. She shifted her sights to the man in the muscle shirt and the woman wearing short-shorts who had been prancing in circles with her dogue. She knew exactly who they were.

Lisa-Lee walked into the room with the third dogue and put her in her crate.

Stella turned. "Lisa-Lee, you're gonna need to be out there runnin' in circles with Oz wearin' nothin' 'cause it looks to me like that's where the competition is gonna be—in the who's wearin' closest to nothin' category—so if you is wearin' nothin', you win."

She snorted a laugh. "What these people don't understand is what I been tellin' you for a long time. If you got everything ridin' on whether you win in the ring, then you will fail—case closed. The real winning takes place before, after, and in between the shows. Now you know me well enough by now to know winnin' in the ring ain't the real reason why I come to these damn things—it's all, shall we say, part of the dance." Stella was quite pleased with having come up with that.

Lisa-Lee lit a cigarette and sat down across from Stella. "Well, I'm glad to hear winning isn't all that important because I'll be lucky if I can even hold onto the dogs while I'm in the ring." Her wrist was swollen and throbbing from having to break her fall out of Stella's truck and, on top of that, having to use it to carry the crates up to the room AND manage the dogs while they did their business.

Stella looked over at her unsympathetically and sucked in on her cigarette. "Honey, don't worry, you just got the two dogs to show, I'm gonna show Oz. Anyway, by the time you is my partner in this business, there won't be any part of your body that don't hurt. I been dragged the 'quivalent from here to Texas by my dogues. I figure by the time I'm fifty, which ain't that long from now, I'll be in a wheelchair on account of these dogs. You is just in the breakin' in part."

Stella looked back out the window. "I'll be damned, Margaret has stopped her car and is talkin' to them Biffer people. Somethin' is up, I can smell it. Lisa-Lee, get over here. I need you as a witness!"

Lisa-Lee slowly got up and walked over to the window. "They're just talking, is all, and I might remind you that I've been the one taking care of these dogs and dragging them around for the past two years."

Stella didn't respond—she watched Molly hand the leash over to Biff and trot back to the hotel. Biff walked off with Tank towards the pooping area. Margaret's car stayed put.

Stella squashed her cigarette in the ashtray. "Lisa-Lee, you got to make a phone call right now and you got to say exactly what I tell you!"

She pulled her cell from her purse and handed it to Lisa-Lee. "OK, now when Margaret answers, I want you to tell her that I'm sound asleep from all that drivin' but wanted you to call her, just in case—and that it's real important I know where she is when I wake up 'cause I got a newsflash for her that will knock her socks off—don't worry about what that is,

I'll come up with somethin' later—got it?" Stella grabbed the phone, dialed the number, and handed it back to Lisa-Lee.

———

Margaret's cell sounded as she sat in her car waiting for Molly, still unsure of why she was doing so. Why did she opt to spend an hour alone with someone who did nothing but give her tremors most of the time?

She opened her phone. It was Stella. She straightened up and answered. "Hello." As she listened to what Lisa-Lee had to say, she thought for sure it must be Christmas. Stella was interested in her whereabouts! She responded with flawless confidence. "Tell her I'm on my way to the airport to pick up the judge and will be back by 6 p.m.—then I'm off to wine and dine him." She hung up and stuck her chin in the air. She had finally arrived!

———

Stella watched as Biff strolled back across the parking lot, Tank in hand. "That dogue's big, I'll give him that—and almost as deep red as my Grace, which ain't real common and half the reason I bred that bitch, aside from the fact that she's one of Oz's." She studied him as best she could, given the distance. "Fact is, I'm thinkin' he looks redder than I ever seen him in any picture. I do believe he's redder than any dogue I ever seen." It was the fact of Tank being from Charlene Peet's kennel that made Stella even pause to check him out. Charlene was the devil as far as she was concerned, and no dog of hers was going to be worth a damn, not if she could help it.

She watched Tank and Biff disappear into the hotel. Then a few minutes later Molly re-emerged, all decked out in a black suit. She crossed the parking lot and got into the car with Margaret. Stella snorted, "I knew it! That bitch is plannin' her win already." She settled back in the chair and finished off her joint. *No sir, it ain't about what happens in the ring, it's all about everythin' in between and that's the part I know more about than damn near anybody.*

Stella studied Margaret's green Gremlin as it left the parking lot. She thought to have Lisa-Lee call Margaret again to suggest she turn her ass around and get a different car because no European judge—no European period—in their right mind was going to step into that car and not think the worse for it. Porsche engine, brand spanking clean as could be, or not, it was still a piece of shit. There wasn't any getting around it. A Gremlin was not the way to make a good first impression—but, oh well, that was not her problem, not one bit. The fact of the matter was it could work in her favor.

13

The Gremlin Makes the Limelight

By the time the Gremlin had returned to the hotel, unloaded, and then reloaded to go out to dinner, Stella had alerted a number of incoming exhibitors of the situation at hand—the Biffers, which she had to explain was her new name for the Bradfords, had accompanied the show secretary to pick up the judges at the airport and had then gone off with them to dinner! And she added the very important tidbit that she had taken the photos necessary to prove it.

She settled in her chair with her cigarettes, ashtray, and cell phone within easy reach on the table next to her. She knew within minutes every Bordeaux phone in the country would be buzzing with this information and then some, so by the time they all got to the show, tensions would be running high and there could possibly be a World War III by the time it was all over, which was the part when things got real good—for her anyway.

And what Margaret didn't know yet was that her evening with the "Biffers" was the very 'newsflash' that Lisa-Lee had tantalized her with earlier—it just hadn't gone on or off the press yet.

Stella snorted. Three days ago Margaret had given HER a wake up call all the way down in Georgia and now SHE would be giving Margaret a 'wake up call' from right down the hall. The difference between the two said it all.

She lit a fresh cigarette and glanced at the clock. It was 10 p.m. She had sent Lisa-Lee down to the lobby fifteen minutes ago with the camera. Her instructions were to stake herself outside just in case the Biffers tried to make a quick exit from the car before reaching the hotel lobby.

Chances were they wouldn't want to be seen strolling into the lobby with the judges. However, they may also be just that stupid, or they figured nobody else was there yet, OR they actually thought it would work in their favor to be seen with the judge. They did seem to be that type—look at me, it don't matter what I'm doing, just look at me. Hell, a lot of these people probably never heard of not fraternizing with the judges, seeing as most of 'em were either so used to having no rules that they didn't think about it, or they were brand new to dog showing and had no clue. But an official National club was all about rules and whether this one was in the ABC book of rules yet, or not, it should be, seeing how the official world works, and she was going to be the one to bring it home.

The real bottom line was she just needed to find some shit to get the stink flying and this would work just fine. Lisa-Lee, naturally, was not happy about having to do this but, as Stella pointed out, this was part of her job. After all, she wasn't paying her to sit on her ass and do nothing. Besides, she'd told her, this was the learning part of becoming a partner in her business.

That's when Lisa-Lee had brought up the existence of Greta and wondered how it was that she got booted on the spot from her job at the kennel on account of her. Stella had to explain to her for the thousandth time that Greta was only temporary, that she'd run off on her before and would do it again, it was just a matter of time was all. She added that it was highly conceivable Greta could be gone, right then, while she was explaining to Lisa-Lee what she didn't need to explain to her in the first place, on account of there being a big fat silence between Greta and Bobby that was probably the size of Georgia by now. She told Lisa-Lee that Greta was not a woman who would tolerate mister-I-don't-want-to-do-nothin'-but-keep-my-mouth-shut-and-build-fences. She was too damn lonely for that, and there wasn't a chance in hell Bobby wouldn't just keep doing what he was doing.

Course, Bobby would be in a fix if Greta left, wouldn't he? He'd have to step up to the plate and do some real work for once, as in take care of everything. Now that right there would be a damn miracle! The fact of the matter was, in conclusion, she had a couple of nut jobs taking care of her dogs right now and she just hoped the big fat silence between them hadn't crushed both her house and kennel.

She also pointed out to Lisa-Lee that Greta wasn't here at the show, now was she? And how was it if she was planning on replacing her that she chose her, over Greta, to accompany her to first ABC national?—case closed.

"Stella, I don't understand most of what you're talking about, but I do know Bobby takes really good care of the dogs when I'm around. And he talks to me just fine." Lisa-Lee was pleased to hear this Greta person would be gone soon.

"Well, you ain't Greta, now are you? Which means you ain't lived around Bobby and me for a ton of years, which means it ain't really none of your business, now is it? And I am done talkin' 'bout somethin' that ain't worth talkin' about due to what's presentin' itself at this present moment. Now you need to get your ass downstairs and out that door before they come back! And try not to let them see what you're doin'—and if they do, just take the damn photos and get your ass back up here 'cause I'm thinkin' that Biffer fella got him a short fuse and if this pisses him off, he ain't gonna care one stick whether you is a girl, a guy, or some itty bitty child—he'll beat the crap out of you and take the damn camera. Now, go on!"

Lisa-Lee left, reluctantly, with strict instructions to not return until, and unless, she had photos of the "whole deal" from beginning to end, and if she didn't know exactly what that meant she sure as shit would not be replacing Greta back at the kennel, not ever.

As the door closed behind Lisa-Lee, Stella suddenly thought about those letters Greta had written to that Emily girl. She'd actually brought a handful of the damn things with her and had no clue why—but before she had time to figure that out, her cell rang. She picked it up off the table. This was it, the calls would come roaring in from now until she decided to turn the damn thing off and get some sleep, which was unlikely to happen. Everybody in the world would be wanting more details, which she was more than happy to supply—which included the extra red color of Tank's coat, which she suspected might be dyed.

The truth of the matter, something Stella knew all about, was that the Biffers weren't exactly on the top of the list of people to like. Nobody was whose dog won too much, meaning more than one show every once in a while. They were real stupid to think winning show after show was good for business—of course they didn't have a business which was lucky for them, but business or not, nobody but a few of their close friends, and Charlene, were rooting for them right now. Everybody else was all ears.

———

It was 11:15 p.m. Lisa-Lee had been crouched behind one of the huge round bushes by the front door for over an hour when a young hotel employee stepped out for a smoke and took note of her. He'd seen the bush shake as she changed positions to get more comfortable which, by this point, seemed impossible. When he leaned in behind the bush and asked her what she was doing, she told him she was waiting to take some surprise photos for a friend of some very important people—not important to him of course—just to her and her friend, so she would really appreciate it if he would ignore her.

He laughed and tried to flirt with her, but she begged him in her sweetest voice to leave, which he did, but not willingly. That's when she decided to move to the bush on the opposite side of the entrance, hoping that if he came out again he would assume she'd gone. But it didn't work out that way. He came out a second time, walked right over to the first bush—then behind it, then came out and looked around, by which point she assumed he would give up—but no, he just had to be what she was very used to, a guy with a hard on for her—kind of cute actually—and not the type to give up. He went back behind the first bush, just in case he had missed her and then walked directly over to the bush where she was.

"There you are!" he exclaimed. "I was thinking it was only twenty minutes ago that I saw you out here and nobody that looks anything close to being important has come in the front door since then, so I figured you were still out here somewhere." The young man, who looked to be about Lisa-Lee's age, was quite pleased with himself. He pulled his cigarettes out of his front shirt pocket. "Would you like one of these?"

"This is NOT the time for this! Would you please stop bothering me?" That was when Lisa-Lee spotted the neon green Gremlin turning in off the road under the far lights. "Shit, you need to move along, OK?"

The young man lit his cigarette and looked out to the entrance of the hotel parking lot. "Are you telling me that is the important person? In that green thing! What the hell is that?"

Lisa-Lee felt her face flush. "It's a refurbished Gremlin for chrissake, got a top of the line Porsche engine, along with a bunch of other expensive stuff. Worth sixty-five grand at least!" It was hard for her to believe she was even doing this ridiculous stunt.

"No shit! Do you think they'd let me see the engine?"

"Would you just go away? Pleeease. This is important." She ducked back behind the bush and checked the camera to be sure it was ready.

Just as the car pulled up, the young man leapt behind the bushes, grabbed Lisa-Lee's camera and handed her his burning cigarette. "I'll take care of this, just watch me!" He grinned ear to ear and rushed back out onto the pavement.

Lisa-Lee took his cigarette on reflex and waited. It was too late, there was no way she would allow herself to be seen coming out from behind this bush, especially not by Margaret Appleman or any of these fruit-loop dog people for that matter. She listened.

Margaret stepped out of her car and around to the passenger door. As she did this, a young man with a Holiday Inn suit coat and name tag came racing down the concrete walkway.

"MY GOD, IS THAT A GREMLIN? I haven't seen one of those in my whole life and it's so shiny. Is it refurbished? It can't possibly have the original engine, does it?"

He looked to be in shock from Margaret's perspective. His eyes were bulging and his cheeks were taut with all the screaming, like the skins on the African drums she'd bought for Frank. She glanced at his raised camera and froze just shy of the passenger door as it was opening. The door pushed on her a bit as a very tall, casually dressed, fair-haired man donning a wool beret emerged. He smiled cheerfully as the young man clicked away with his camera.

The young man smiled back. "I hope it's OK if I take photos, this is unbelievable, really!"

The back door swung open and out rushed Molly, anxious to be on camera, Biff right behind her, followed by another tall, casually dressed man. They all smiled, except for Margaret.

The young Holiday Inn employee was ecstatic. "Wow, look how many people there are in there!" The camera flashed away.

Margaret felt herself coming undone. She had never gotten this much attention regarding her Gremlin—raised eyebrows, yes—but not this. She glanced around the paved walkway, not really knowing what she was looking for, and just as she was about to chalk it up to her imagination gone particularly wild because of all the excitement—that was when she spotted a stream of smoke rising from behind the big round bush by the front doors. She knew cigarette smoke when she saw it. Maybe it had nothing to do with any of this, but maybe it did. "Excuse me, but..."

The young man spoke up. "Ma'am, could I please see the engine of this fabulous car? I would bet from the way that thing purred right up to this curb that it's a Porsche on the inside—am I right?"

Margaret snapped, "OK, THAT'S IT, EVERYBODY INSIDE— NOW!" Something wasn't right. There was no way any stranger would have Porsche even cross their mind when looking at a Gremlin. But what did this mean?

The smiling crew ceased smiling and looked at her, disbelief written all over their faces.

The camera stopped flashing and all was quiet.

Margaret went blank. The evening had been over-whelming. Molly and Biff chatted up the judges through the entire dinner, barely let her get a word in edgewise, and now here she was looking about as foolish as a person could look. She shook her head and looked at the ground as she spoke. "I'm so sorry, really. I'm just tired. It's been a long couple of days and I've worked so hard to make this show special. Please forgive me."

Lisa-Lee dropped the cigarette in the dirt and belly-crawled under the bush to where she could watch what was going on from a low inconspicuous vantage point. She was riveted.

The tall fair-haired man walked over to Margaret and placed his arm across her plump shoulders. His accent was soothing. "I certainly know how it must feel. This is all very much work and we are very pleased to be here and very grateful for your hard work. Don't worry, we understand this very well."

Margaret shuddered and let her body relax under the gentle weight of Claude Montfort's arm. "Yes," she said, "it's been a lot of work and there is so much more to do. Thank you for your understanding." She was recovering nicely.

Claude squeezed her gently. "And now, Pedro and I will leave you to your much deserved rest. Don't worry, it will be a wonderful show, I am sure." He lifted his arm from her shoulders and signaled to Pedro that they head into the hotel.

Molly hooked her arm around Pedro Alcrudo's elbow and smiled ear to ear. "Yes, you've done a terrific job. Thanks so much, Margaret."

Margaret's recovery came to a screaming halt. All she wanted to do in that moment was rip Molly's second stringer head from her neck. But she just smiled and turned away.

The young man persisted, even as the others walked through the lobby door, Molly still latched onto Judge Pedro Alcrudo's arm. He caught up to Margaret as she walked towards her Gremlin. "Ma'am, wait! Can I please see the engine?"

Lisa-Lee stuck her face into the dirt to keep from laughing out loud. She couldn't believe he was pushing it this far. He had no idea the kind of people he was dealing with.

Margaret simply scowled and crawled into her car.

As she drove slowly away her full attention was on the rearview mirror. She watched the young man turn and trot back up towards the bush that had had the stream of cigarette smoke rising up from behind it. He stopped. She stopped. He turned and glanced at her car, waved, leaned back against the wall and casually pulled his cigarettes from his breast pocket. Margaret moved on.

————

Not twenty minutes later as Margaret struggled down the hall to her room, her head near bursting, her stature significantly diminished, if not totally collapsed, she caught a glimpse of Lisa-Lee going into her room. She was covered with dirt from head to toe and had a camera in her hand.

14

Margaret is a Big Fat Jerk

As soon as Margaret opened her eyes, the bomb dropped. It didn't matter that she'd had a splendid dream about herself standing in the ring, Claude Montefort on her one side, Pedro Alcrudo on the other, cameras flashing, and people applauding and cheering. What mattered was that what was supposed to be the beginning of a grand day, the arrival of Bordeaux enthusiasts from all over the country, was quite possibly the beginning of the worst day of her life. She let out a long low whistling sound and closed her eyes, desperate to retrieve the dream, but it was gone.

She opened her eyes again. Her only consolation, the only thing that got her to even think about getting out of bed, was that her mother was dead and gone—thank God. She'd been on the phone until 2 a.m. with each of the five incoming board members, plus the two who were already there and fuming in the privacy of their rooms. "How could you have been so stupid?" they asked. "No, it doesn't matter that Lisa-Lee was lying in wait, in the dirt behind a bush and even coerced a hotel employee to snap the photos." "No, it doesn't matter that Stella is behind it." "Molly and Biff are exhibitors and shouldn't have been wining and dining with the judges," they said. "What were you thinking?" "No, it doesn't matter that Molly manipulated you into taking them and that she and Biff dominated the entire evening with the judges. They shouldn't have been there." "What does matter is we now have Stella Gale up our ass with legitimate fuel to throw at the club and it's all your fault," and on and on and on.

Margaret looked over at the clock and realized she had conveniently forgotten to set the alarm. It was 8:06 a.m. They would already be gathered in the conference room, waiting for her. The five incoming members had reluctantly driven all through the night to attend the emergency meeting.

Margaret felt a hideous sense of dread, rolled over, and tried to go back to sleep. Then her phone rang. She let it ring again and again. "Leave me in peace and have your stupid meeting without me!" she muttered into her pillow. "I am, after all, the whole reason this club exists!"

She finally picked up the phone. "No, of course I haven't forgotten. I spilled steaming hot coffee on my chest! I've been lying here with ice on it for the last twenty minutes! Well, no, that's not true anymore. I hate to admit this, but due to all the work I've had to do these last two days, I've taken to drinking coffee. I never would have made it through these last two days without it. It's been such a nightmare! Yes, yes, I'll be there. I'm on my way in five minutes. Why don't you do some brainstorming while you're waiting for me?" She hung up and glanced at her cell phone as she forced herself out from between the sickening polyester sheets. She hated the damn things, it made her skin crawl just to think about them, let alone sleep in them.

She thought to call Frank and ask him to be a dear and call down to the waiting board members via the front desk and tell them Margaret was found lying in her hotel room with a badly burned chest, unconscious, and an ambulance had just been called. Sadly, she would be unable to attend the board meeting. They would have to go on without her. She groaned and got to her feet. Maybe Frank was right. A baby might have been the wiser choice. At least she could do what she wanted with it and no one would give a damn.

She glanced out the window as she dressed. Unfortunately, she was not surprised to see that the steady stream of arrivals had begun hours earlier than expected. She knew full well the phone lines had been bursting with the news of what had happened and that those who might otherwise have stopped on the road to sleep for a few hours chose instead to keep going, fueled by the intrigue of what was going to happen next. Oh, how she loved all of it! She wished SHE could be flying down the highway towards the biggest

American Bordeaux show ever, gripping the wheel, raw with the excitement of the first big scuttlebutt to hit the airwaves! But why did SHE have to be the scuttlebutt? If only she had ripped Molly's head from her neck when she'd first approached her car!

Her cell phone rang just as she stabbed her bun into place and took a few final deep breaths. It was Stella! What amazed her was that she actually felt relieved. "Stella?"

Stella launched right into what she needed to say. "Margaret, you need to thank me for what I did last night and particularly that new friend of Lisa-Lee's. Goddamn, he got better shots than the ones I took when you was leavin' for dinner. Just so you know, the Biffers had no right to do that to you. Now I know exactly what you mean about them. I didn't believe you when you told me, but I sure as hell do now! They will stop at nothin' to win, includin' usin' you. I seen a thousand of that type. They represent the worst kind of show people and need to be taught a lesson 'fore they bring everythin' you worked for down the damn toilet. Now, I know full well that you know it just ain't right to allow exhibitors to have dinner with the judges before a show—you ain't dumb like most of these people are and I ain't either, so I will back you one hundred percent that they are the ones doin' this club wrong."

Margaret felt a bit lighter and glanced into the mirror that hung just over the low dresser. Her bun was a tad crooked. She made a mental note to straighten it as soon as she got off the phone. "I have to tell you, Molly was awful the way talked herself into my car. She really didn't give me a choice."

Stella snorted. "I know that, Margaret, and that's what you need to tell them when you get down to that meetin' that you're late for. Ain't nothin' wrong admittin' that you was victim to a couple of manipulatin' sons of bitches. Call me when it's over, OK?"

"How did you know there's a meeting?" Margaret felt stupid the moment it came out of her mouth. Of course Stella knew. She would be off her game if she didn't.

"Margaret, I wasn't born yesterday. I thought you'da known that by now—bye."

The phone line went dead.

Margaret shoved the phone into her purse and straightened her bun. Stella was absolutely right. This meeting was about Molly and Biff and what needed to be done about them, not her. She had done nothing wrong. She had simply made the mistake of falling prey to a couple of ruthless second stringers who attempted to use the club secretary, meaning the club, for their own selfish ends. The issue at hand was what to do about them. This could possibly be her chance to see that bitch brought down a few notches and gain some sympathy for herself. She sucked in a load of air and walked quickly out of her room and down to the elevator. She might not get any sympathy from the board members, but chances were good that most of the members would fall in on her side of the fence. This was, after all, a member driven club and Molly and Biff were not much liked by any of the other members.

She strode out of the elevator and down the hall, passing the dining room and stopping just outside the closed door of the conference room. A big fat 'DO NOT DISTURB' sign hung heavily from the doorknob. She tried to take another deep breath and nearly choked. It may as well have read 'MARGARET IS A BIG FAT JERK.'

———

Stella put her cell phone next to her plate and looked out the dinning room door to the hallway. It was 8:15. In about five to ten minutes, she expected Margaret to walk by. If she didn't, it meant her tactic had failed. Already this morning, Lisa-Lee had seen the hurried arrival of the five remaining board members and their subsequent gathering behind the closed door of the conference room. Lisa-Lee had even gotten herself a good laugh. She told Stella that as they rushed by her one would have thought the president was here and an assassination attempt had happened. Stella laughed with her. As young as she was, Lisa-Lee was no fool, nor should she be after all the time they'd spent together. These people were so dead serious about everything that it took very little on her part to get them tripping over themselves. She had called Margaret because she figured Margaret probably needed the help. Sure enough, she was hiding in her room like a damn coward. What Stella had to do was get her to that meeting, ASAP, which hopefully was exactly where Margaret was headed.

Lisa-Lee returned to the table with French toast from the breakfast bar.

Stella looked away from the doorway for a second. "Lisa-Lee, I don't want them board people commitin' some kinda coop and gettin' rid of Margaret 'cause that would be not so good for us."

Lisa-Lee just looked at her. She was so tired she could barely speak.

Stella pulled out a cigarette. "You know what I wish right about now? I wish you was Greta and could whip up one of them fine letters she's so good at and pass it into that board meetin'. She would know exactly what to tell those people and in a manner that would leave them mighty shook up. Not like you, who apparently don't even have the 'bility to talk right now."

Lisa-Lee shoved some French toast in her mouth and without looking up, she mumbled, "And you can't smoke right now. Can't you read?"

"I can read well enough. And for your information there ain't nobody workin' here in this room right now who looks a day older or any smarter than you and it's gonna take a whole lot more than that to stop me from doin' what I want, so until that happens, I will do exactly what I want. And just remember, a lot of people will be comin' through that door startin' in about an hour, so if you is gonna mouth off at me, you might as well get it outta your system right now 'cause I ain't gonna tolerate it once the people are here and needin' to hear from me. You got that?" She shoved the cigarette back in the pack. "God damn, what is wrong with you? I just lost my stomach for a cigarette on account of you and that just don't come along but once a decade, so you watch yourself."

Stella put the pack by her plate and picked up her coffee. "What time is it, Lisa-Lee? And where the hell is Mabel? I thought she was just goin' back to her room to change and that was over an hour ago. Speakin' of which, her leavin' that dog on the sidewalk back at her house? Alls I got to say is it'll be a freezin' cold day in Mexico 'fore I count on her for much." She drank down some of her lukewarm coffee and looked over at Lisa-Lee. "So? What time is it?"

Lisa-Lee looked at her now black and blue left wrist then remembered her watch was temporarily on the other hand. The strap had been unable to accommodate so much swollen tissue. "It's 8:30 and I have no clue where Mabel is."

Just then Stella caught a glimpse of Margaret's round figure rushing past the doorway. She settled back in her chair. "OK, well, I'm sure she'll be here soon. 'Course, anyone who leaves a dog on the sidewalk and drives a thousand miles without knowin' it, ain't runnin' on all cylinders." She watched as a few familiar faces began to trickle into the dinning room. "Now, it's just about time for people to start rollin' in here. So get ready, the real show is about to begin. You ain't gonna regret one minute of bein' here, I can guarantee you that."

Sure enough, not to Lisa-Lee's surprise, by ten o'clock Stella's table was filled and there were not a few people standing around or sitting at other tables anxiously waiting for the opportunity to jump into a vacated seat and hear all she had to say. The good news for Lisa-Lee was she was now free to go. She happily gave up her seat to go walk the dogs, do her duty as 'detective,' and then meet Billy, who'd turned out to be as sweet as he was cute.

As Stella watched her table fill with people who were anxious to be 'in the know' about damn near anything, she was well aware that the draw to be with her was always there, at every show, regardless of the circumstances. The Biffers' night out was just the cherry on top of a whole load of goodies she had to offer.

She looked up at the line of people waiting to enter the dinning room. This whole national club idea of Margaret's that she'd once been so dead set against, just might be her ticket to a new pile of goodies.

15

Lisa-Lee and Billy Go Undercover

When Mabel Dowd got the call from Stella ordering her to "get your ass down here as fast as you can, all hell's about to break loose," she packed her things as quickly as was humanly possible and leapt into her car. The awful part was she'd driven so fast, furiously, and faithfully towards her new found mentor, it wasn't until she arrived at the hotel around 5 a.m. that she realized she'd forgotten her beloved Angel. To make matters even worse, Angel was an Oz daughter that Stella had given her six months earlier.

As she rushed into the lobby of the hotel, she prayed she hadn't literally left Angel on the sidewalk in front of her house. Frantic, she picked up her room key and went immediately to Stella's room. The moment she walked in, she burst into tears. However, Stella's undeniably steady lack of concern gave her what she needed to calm down and take the steps necessary to check on Angel's whereabouts.

As it turned out, she had left Angel on the front walk, but thank goodness, her dear neighbor had spotted her and returned her to the house. Stella merely shrugged between important phone calls when Mabel delivered the good news. Somehow, she didn't know how, Stella had known all along that things would work out fine.

Unfortunately, when she left Stella's room with the promise to meet them at breakfast in an hour, she suddenly became completely immobilized by a migraine, something that was not uncommon for her to get under stressful circumstances—positive or negative. This one was rooted in the positive, at least she knew that. However, positive or not, all she could do was take her medication, lie down on her bed, and hope it would recede quickly.

As it turned out, she was an hour late. By the time she arrived, the dining room was packed and the volume of chatter was deafening. As she scanned the room, a loud voice boomed out above it all.

"MABEL, WHERE THE HELL HAVE YOU BEEN? WE BEEN WAITIN' ON YOU!"

Mabel turned and as Stella yelled and waved to her, it seemed every head in the dining room turned in Mabel's direction. She was mortified, but handled it in the best way she could. She simply nodded and smiled.

Stella continued, "COME ON OVER, I'M SURE EVERYONE HERE WOULD LIKE TO HEAR ABOUT HOW YOU FORGOT YOUR DOG." She glanced around the table, all eyes were on her. She laughed. "I MEAN IT AIN'T EVERY DAY SOMEONE COMES TO A DOG SHOW AND FORGETS THEIR DOG!"

Mabel was horrified, but walked quickly to the table anyway.

Stella waited until the faces turned back in her direction. "It's OK, Mabel, we all done crazy shit." She had lowered her voice, but spoke loudly enough that everyone at the table could hear. "Hell, once when I was in Europe for the billionth time picking up Oz and doin' a little sight seein', we were stayin' at the 'quivalent of the Atlanta Hilton in Amsterdam. They let me have Oz there because I paid them double and promised he wasn't gonna eat nobody.

"Anyway, one afternoon we was in the lobby—big ass, fancy as shit—and I had to go to the bathroom. Well, I didn't feel like goin' all the way back up to my room, so I decided to take him into their main bathroom with me 'cause there was no way I was gonna leave that boy outta my sight. So, once I got into the bathroom—huge by the way, with marble sinks, satin lounge chairs, even had one of them faintin' couches—anyway, big and luxurious as it was, I couldn't fit Oz and me in one of them stalls, so I decided to put him in the one next to me—which was empty at the time—and I shut the door, leavin' it open a crack. The point bein', I sure as hell wasn't gonna leave him out in the open—no sir, we came a long ways for that boy and I was not gonna take any chances.

"Bobby, by the way, was off somewhere lookin' at a couple of bitches and some pups. He had all kinds of deals goin' on—he's got the eye for fine animals, let me tell you.

"Anyway, he left me to fend for myself, which ain't hard considerin' it's what I do even when he is around. I mean ain't that just the way it is with most men? I swear, some days I wonder why I bother even havin' one—fact is, I'm thinkin' them Mormons got it right and it weren't no man who thought that whole deal up, hell no. It was one clever as shit woman. How to make a religion that looks like it's all about the man bein' king, but the truth of the matter is the man's got a life of being tired and lonely waitin' for him once he starts bringin' in the second and third wife, which is when life gets less tirin' and less lonely for the women—case closed."

Mabel had pulled up a chair and, thankfully, faded nicely into the lively and attentive audience. She was relieved Stella hadn't made her talk about poor Angel.

"Anyway, so there was Oz in the booth next to me and the next thing I hear is the click, clack of them real high heels. I knew, the minute I heard 'em, that wasn't no dog person who was wanderin' into a high falutin' bathroom lookin' to see herself a big dog. Well, before I could warn her she opens the door to where Oz is and starts screamin' like there was no tomorrow, which I'm thinkin' she thought was the truth of the situation, considerin' she was facin' a hundred and seventy pound Bordeaux about four feet from her!

"Now Oz, the last thing he wanted to do was stand there while this woman was screamin' her head off. So, first off, he lets out one of them deep roars which, of course, caused that woman to fall backwards towards them marble sinks—I couldn't see her, but I knew by the way her heels was scraping and not clacking that she was stumbling. And her screamin'—well, let's just say it was loud enough to crack them mirrors. That's when I could feel that Oz might be gettin' it into his head to charge towards her and roar some more—you know, to make her shut up. The big problem bein' that I had his leash looped around my ankle.

"Now, the good news is I'm real quick thinkin' when it comes to those kinds of situations, so before the words "*full charge ahead*" hit his brain, the words "*get on the floor and get over there*" hit mine. See, I knew there was no way I could get that leash off my ankle before he charged, so I dropped to the floor and slid into his stall head first and I did that so fast it was like I done it a thousand times. I swear to God— that's what that adrenaline shit does for you, makes you an Olympic bathroom floor slider in a New York second.

"Anyway, I didn't really need to grab his legs the way I did 'cause just my flyin' under the divider on my back with my pants still down, was enough to distract him from chargin'. He turned and looked at me like he couldn't decide who was crazier, me or that damn woman with the mink stole around her neck who was leanin' back against the sinks with her mouth so wide open you could see that thing that hangs off the back of your throat, you know, like them things that hang down from the ceilin' of caves. I swear Oz just froze from the shockin' sight of human behavior."

Laughter roared around the table as Stella continued, "Now the good news is, if Oz had been of a different breed I wouldn't of had the time. See, as many of you already know, the natural good tempered Bordeaux, which of course Oz is, takes a moment in a situation like that to think about things. Now, this wasn't no life threatenin' situation, he knew that from the get go, and so he took a moment to assess what the best thing to do would be. And that was the moment that saved me from gettin' my ankle tore off and the woman dyin' of a heart attack."

Mabel laughed along with everybody else. She was thrilled to be sitting with Stella. She was right where she wanted to be, a feeling she'd only experienced twice in her life. The first time was at her Communion, the second was when her ex-husband kissed her at the altar. Both times she felt she would now be secure and well taken care of. It was a wonderful feeling, albeit her ex had let her down horribly, but God hadn't yet, not really—and she was sure this new relationship with Stella would fill her to the brim with something extraordinary.

Stella continued rolling along. "The hotel wasn't real pleased about what happened. The woman wasn't either, but at least them Europeans don't jump to call the cops or a lawyer for every damn thing, not like here in America, that's for damn sure. That lady did have a couple of broke fingernails from hittin' up against them marble sinks, but that was it—and when she finally shut up and crumpled down to the floor, like tumblin' jello, Oz he walked right up between her legs, which was all stretched out on the floor, and sniffed her face which was just about as white as this table cloth. Then he turned around and damn near sat on her lap. He was so big compared to her that I couldn't see her—'course I was still on the floor tryin' to get up. Well, I guess she had plum run out of scared 'cause she reached out and stroked his back just like he was wantin' her to do."

The people howled and the questions and comments flew like confetti around the table. By the time she'd finished her story, most of the people in the dining room had dropped their own conversations to listen. Stella was truly in her groove.

———

Meanwhile, Lisa-Lee found Billy. He was waiting for her in the lobby just as he'd said he would be, smiling broadly beneath his puppy dog eyes as he ran his hand quickly through his freshly shorn hair. He was dressed in civilian clothes, i.e. jeans, sweater, and a light jacket. All things considered, upon seeing him Lisa-Lee really just wanted to take him back to her room and have a good screw. Maybe that would have happened if she'd mentioned it, but she didn't because he was so dead set on doing more of what he'd done the previous night, particularly after she'd explained it was her job to keep track of all that went on "behind closed doors." Then when she told him an emergency meeting had been called, he became ecstatic and informed her that he'd just seen the California guy and his girlfriend walking into the main conference room.

Lisa-Lee tried to rise to the occasion and feel the same thrill he did, but she couldn't. This was her job, after all, not a fun thing to do on a day off. So, it was her call to duty along with the consequences of not following through on a lead—which of course, Stella would flush out somehow from somewhere—that swayed her to go along with Billy's course of action.

He told her to wait, right there, in the lobby for fifteen minutes while he went to "get the ball rolling." When he returned he was accompanied by a fellow employee who was not in civilian clothes, but rather a neat little maroon skirt and white blouse with a nametag pinned to it that read "Jennifer Morales, Asst. manager, Hospitality team."

Billy explained to Lisa-Lee that Jennifer had access to the kitchenette that was off that main conference room. He grasped her arm with excitement as he further explained that there was an outside entrance to this kitchenette.

Lisa-Lee forced a smile and tossed her hopes of a good morning screw in the trash. She followed Billy and Jennifer out the main door and around to the side of the hotel. The promise to Jennifer was that if any trouble came of this, it was Billy who'd taken the key from Jennifer without her knowledge.

Once inside the kitchenette, Lisa-Lee and Billy could hear the muffled sound of voices. They walked quietly towards the sound and discovered a vent in the lower half of the door that separated the kitchenette from the conference room. They exchanged glances—Billy's being the one that cried 'Eureka!' Lisa-Lee simply sighed and settled in for the long haul.

They crouched down next to the vent and peered through it. The eight board members were seated on either side of a long rectangular table—Margaret sat at one end fiddling with her bun and taking notes, and Molly sat at the other. To Lisa-Lee's seasoned eye, Margaret looked tense and seemed ready at any moment to stick that barrette of hers right through somebody's heart. Molly was not looking as perky as she had the previous night. And where was Biff? Lisa-Lee pushed Billy to the side as she tried to see every part of the room through the vent. Billy nudged her as she did this and she looked over at him.

He giggled slightly, did his best strongman imitation by flexing his biceps through his jacket, and pointed to the lowest slot in the vent.

Lisa-Lee rolled her eyes at his antics and lowered her head. A laugh began to rise from her chest, but she cut it off before it reached her mouth. Every few seconds Biff's head came up within view, just to the side of Molly's chair, then popped back down. There he was! His mouth was closed tightly and his cheeks were bright red. Biff was doing sit ups!

Billy pulled a camera from his jacket pocket. Lisa-Lee signaled a big 'no.' It was a stupid risk to take, despite the fact it could bring home the gold in the most ridiculous thing she'd seen yet department. They waited.

"...and so, Molly, you claim that Margaret asked you to join her and she claims that you persuaded her to take you, but the way we look at it, it doesn't really matter in the end, does it? The point is, you went to the airport to pick up the judges, then you and Biff went out to dinner with them. How this happened is irrelevant. The only thing we can do now to put this whole thing to rest, is to deny you the right to show a dog tomorrow. Tank can be shown, but not by you or Biff." The club president, Mick Saber, looked straight at Biff and Molly and then glanced around the table.

Lisa-Lee looked carefully at Mick. He was the man Stella claimed blamed her for Pete Strate leaving the breed. "I'm tellin' you, he won't ever show it, but revenge is what that man is after." Lisa-Lee had never met Mick, but she had met Pete on a couple of occasions and she'd liked him despite the things Stella had said about him. The truth was—she didn't really care what the truth was—none of these people were important to her, except Stella. She watched Mick settle his gaze on his hands which were on table. From what she could see, through the slats in the door, he didn't look to be a man out to get anybody. However, if Stella said it was so, it was so, which meant she'd have to keep an eye on him. "The only thing I can figure as to the two of them bein' friends was they was probably in the army together and one of them saved the other from gettin' his brains shot out, the most likely scenario bein' Pete saved Mick's ass, so now Mick is so beholdin' to Pete that he won't leave him alone no matter what—case closed, and he'll believe everything Pete tells him. The bad part of that bein' that leaves Mick highly motivated to get my ass. Hell, them two got nothin' in common, but I will tell you right now that Mick is probly gonna be a whole lot more trouble to me than Pete could ever dream of bein'."

Lisa-Lee heard a sniffle and shifted her attention from Mick to the other side of the table.

Molly dropped her head and burst into tears. "You can't do this to me, you just can't. I've worked so hard."

Margaret stopped fiddling with her barrette and looked somberly at her notepad. She dropped her left hand to her thigh and took firm hold of a fold of her flesh and squeezed it until her eyes began to water from the pain. It was all she could do to contain her joy and on top of that the seven board members each visibly squirmed in their seats. What a coup!

Suddenly there was a scuffling sound followed by a loud crash, followed by the sound of Biff's voice, filled with rage. "WHAT ABOUT STELLA, HUH—WHO THE FUCK DO YOU THINK YOU BUNCH OF ASS KISSERS ARE ANYWAY? THAT BITCH IS THE ONE YOU SHOULD BE KICKING OUT OF THE SHOW! JESUS CHRIST WHAT IS THE MATTER WITH YOU PEOPLE!!?"

Lisa-Lee and Billy had seen the head pop up for the hundredth time, right as Molly burst into tears. Then they saw his legs for the first time—then the legs disappeared and that was when they heard the crash. They scanned the room as best they could, given the restriction of eleven slanted slots in the bottom of a door. They couldn't see anything except that the empty chair that had been sitting to Molly's right was gone. Biff had thrown it against the wall!

Mick's fist hit the table. "Stella, unfortunately, didn't break any rules you meathead!"

Margaret grabbed hold of the opportunity. "What Mick so poorly stated is..."

That's when Mick jumped out of his chair as Biff lunged towards him.

Lisa-Lee and Billy saw four legs crash together and the torsos of the two men fall to the floor. There was more shouting and half a dozen legs rushed to where the two men had gone down. The three male board members were trying to break up the fight.

That's when the outside door to the kitchenette suddenly opened and Jennifer rushed in. "Get out now!"

Margaret was the only one who remained calm enough to hear the voice coming from behind the door at the back of the conference room. As much as she was enjoying watching this fiasco unfold, she felt the need to check it out. After the previous night's events, nothing seemed impossible.

As the chubby skirted calves approached the door, Billy and Lisa-Lee scurried to the far side of the kitchenette and hid behind the coffee counter.

Margaret opened the door to see Jennifer Morales kicking at the door of the broom closet. She looked up. "I'm sorry, did I interrupt your meeting? It's a mouse, they try to come in when the weather is cooler." Jennifer smiled and pulled a stack of coffee filters from one of the shelves. "We have a very important business meeting in an hour that I must prepare for." She turned her back to Margaret and proceeded to make a pot of fresh coffee.

The thick Hispanic accent coupled with what Margaret felt was a slightly patronizing tone could have sent her around the bend at another moment in time, but she was too flooded with everything else that was going on. She shut the door and turned around just in time to see Biff and Molly leave the room, slamming the door behind them.

Mick was sitting up nursing a bloody nose. She seized on the opportunity. "Well, that was about as official a meeting as a mud wrestling match! Let's just hope word of this little fiasco doesn't get out—and if it does, Mick, we will be voting on a new president as soon as this show is over, I will see to that!" She took an appropriate moment of silence to let that sink in as she looked from the three men who were standing, straightening out their clothes, to the three women who were seated at the table. "You have to know that this behavior was completely and utterly unacceptable! If you want this club to have a modicum of respect then we must take the appropriate steps to make that happen! I know I made a mistake by allowing Molly and Biff to dine with the judge and I am more than willing to apologize in public for my mistake. In fact, I will do so at the awards dinner on Sunday night."

She scooped her notepad from the table. "And on that note, I am leaving this so called 'meeting' to get back to the hard work of making this first ABC National happen."

The two female board members who had been working alongside Margaret for the past two days got up and followed her out of the room.

———

Stella looked up from her table as the Biffers rushed by the doorway and noted that Molly's head hung about as low as a head can hang before it comes clean off. She was in the middle of fielding a discussion about pedigrees—something she knew a whole lot more about than anyone else because she had taken the time to memorize just about every Bordeaux that ever existed, and then some—and had the brain to retain that information and recall it at any time at the drop of a hat. "No... um... he was the offspring of Andros who was the sire to Frishe and the half brother to Roulette. See, what you got to understand is that it's real important to get this shit straight, otherwise you'll be doin' this breed no damn good. There are a lot of sloppy-ass people out there who don't give a rat's ass about who came from who way back when—well, that right there is a big problem when it comes to keepin' an eye on makin' good dogues."

She glanced towards the doorway again, fairly certain that she had seen the eye-catching fat splash of Margaret's brown and black dress soar by. It had to be Margaret, because in hot cozy pursuit were the two women members who had been here for the past day working with her. *Well, well—I be thinkin' she got through that meetin' just fine.*

Stella looked back to her table and picked up without hesitation. "No, now you ain't gonna breed good dogues if all you do is x-ray their hips and all—what you ain't never gonna be able to keep track of if you don't know the dogs behind the dogs behind the dog behind the dogs you is breedin' is TYPE and that right there is the most important thing when it comes to keepin' this breed alive—case closed. Now I gotta leave you fine people and get my ass up to my room to make sure Lisa-Lee has taken the dogs out—keepin' an eye out for their well-bein', as in fed, watered, and loved, is the only thing more important than what I been tellin' you. If you don't do that then you got nothin' and no right to breed any livin' thing 'cause that is flat out abuse in my book."

She got up and left the now only partially filled table. She had done her job and with what she had just seen pass by the doorway she didn't feel like sitting around with a half a dozen folks who wanted to pick her brain till she dropped dead from boredom. It had been a fine time and now it was over. She never did get around to telling her perspective on the Biffer affair, like she knew some had wanted. She never intended to. She'd just as soon let that simmer and cook on its own. It would all be clear soon enough and if it wasn't she would make it crystal clear at a later date. What was important was that she'd had a fine morning with a load of people who paid her the respect she deserved.

16

The Burning Hair

Morning had broken. Mick's nose had not. However, the news of what had happened to it had. Not only did every guest in the hotel seem to be in the know, but all of the employees as well. For the entire day after the incident, Mick had fielded knowing and intrusive glances along with chuckling and mutterings, peppered with "Meathead" from damn near everywhere. He'd even gotten a phone call, within hours of the meeting, from Pete Strate who lived over a thousand miles away! It seemed impossible. Pete didn't give a crap about any of this anymore.

As it turned out, Margaret had called Pete right after the meeting believing he might want to know about it since Mick was his close friend. She'd told him she had no idea Mick had that kind of temper—it was just awful and why hadn't he warned her about it before she asked him to be the first president of the new club? Pete had handled it well and told her whoever Mick had gotten into it with must have deserved it. He then told her to please lose his phone number, which was private and he'd never given it to her in the first place, and not to call him again. He explained to Mick that the only reason he'd bothered to call him was to advise him to get out now, while he could, that things would only get worse. He reminded Mick that he'd forewarned him about getting involved with Margaret and her club in the first place. "None of these people really care about anything other than their egos, spreading slander, and scamming innocent puppy buyers."

That's when Mick told Pete what Margaret had said regarding getting rid of him as president. Pete jumped on it, told him Margaret had handed him a 'get-out' ticket and he should take it or, even better, preempt her and walk out. He reiterated something else he'd told Mick a number of times before. "Life without those people is pretty damned terrific, it's like being born again." Mick didn't want to get into it with Pete as to exactly why he'd taken on the position as president or why he'd gotten involved with "those people" in the first place, so he just left it with Pete that he'd think about it, and that was the end of the conversation.

He climbed slowly out of bed feeling as though several things in his body must surely be broken, even if his nose was not. He just didn't want to go to the ER and have to explain himself. He limped over to the dresser where he leaned forward and looked in the mirror. His face was so swollen it squeezed his eyes to damn near shut, which gave him a most terrifying constant grimace. He thought about the ER again, thinking surely his face was cracked in a dozen places, but what would they do?

His thoughts turned back to Pete. Ironically, his position as president had been handed to him because of Pete. Margaret had approached him, thinking he would be perfect for the job because he had stayed under the radar and had no "reputation" to speak of in the Bordeaux community. All that was known about him was he was a highly respected Schutzhund trainer and architect who'd quietly taken over Pete's kennel and minded his own business. Even Stella had ceased her 'concern' regarding Pete's dogues once Pete exited.

Mick grimaced for real, then cringed from the pain it caused. It was Stella who'd, almost single handedly, brought his quiet, open, generous, and life loving friend to the point of near suicide, and all it took was one year. The day he found his friend passed out in a motel room with a gun by his side was a day he wished he could erase from his memory. Pete had managed to erase it, and he was glad he had, but Mick would never forget it.

He shook the image from his head and brought his mind back to the Bordeaux. It was Pete who had brought the very first one into this country—before Stella, before

Charlene—before all of them—and tried to apply his impeccable sense of responsibility to his breeding program, and he was slain for it. Every responsible action he took was spun to its polar opposite by Ms. Gale and her cohorts, then spread far and wide.

When Pete no longer had it in him to fight her lies and everything else she threw at him, he left—rather he fled. Pete now claimed he probably would have left the breed anyway, in due time, because he was so discouraged about the lack of soundness and general good health of the breed. As hard as he tried to find healthy, sound dogues, when he did, which was rare, too many of the offspring came up short which inevitably caused terrible heartbreak in the families they had gone to. By the time Mick took over Pete's kennel, Pete had nearly gone broke trying to do the right thing. Mick's reasons for taking over Pete's kennel, which was down to only four dogues, were pretty simple: he loved dogs, he'd grown up with a father who had bred German Shepherds for decades, and his fascination with the Bordeaux had been with him ever since he'd traveled to Europe with Pete to find his first ones. He was thrilled to have a shot at what Pete had tried to do. He took the responsibility seriously and promised Pete that he would let it all go if progress could not be made.

Mick left the mirror and walked over to the window. The parking lot was buzzing with activity. Exhibitors were out walking their dogs, letting them do their 'business' and hopefully cleaning up after them. He would hear all about it if they didn't. He drew in a deep breath and thought again about what Pete had advised. He could just walk out of the club—why not? This certainly was looking to be a headache that would only get worse with time. He knew Pete was right about that. Besides, he hated the dog show world, always had—ever since attending German Shepherd dog shows with his Dad—and a few with Pete early on in Pete's breeding career. Now, as president this past year, he'd had to attend a number of shows, mostly small ones, thank God, and he hated it; though he made a point never to express that to anyone. Now, of course, with this first National

Show there would be more and more of everything—bigger shows, more breeders, more buyers. Why not just sink back into the woodwork and quietly enjoy his dogs and do an occasional breeding?

He glimpsed Lisa-Lee walking across the parking lot with a young man and two of what he assumed to be Stella's dogues. His thoughts flew back to his best friend's destruction. There were photos sent to Pete's wife of Lisa-Lee flung around Pete's neck in a bar, placed there by Stella no doubt, and phone calls to his home from various strangers telling his wife she was crazy to stay with him, and calls to the hospital where his wife worked, accusing her of drug addiction and stealing drugs from patients, and calls to the school where Pete was principal, accusing him of having sex with frightened students who didn't dare speak up and on and on and on. It was unbelievable. Pete became, understandably, a whole different person. He began to drink and drink and drink—never had before—then lost everything. Pete's life, one that had once been pretty wonderful, and one Mick had found inspiring, had turned into a nightmare.

Mick's thoughts then landed, once again, on the day he found Pete with the gun, something which he would never have imagined, not ever, not Pete. Pete was not a man who'd had that kind of darkness in him anywhere. Mick had grown up with Pete. He knew him almost as well as he knew himself, maybe more so, because his own psyche was far more complicated and had plenty of dark corners—but not Pete's. No, the darkness that came out in Pete had been masterfully planted there. Mick had to hand it to Stella; she was really skilled at what she did.

Fortunately, Pete had managed to get back on his feet, but he was a changed man. The world was no longer the good place he'd tried his whole life to convince Mick that it was. Mick missed those lectures terribly. His good friend, thanks to Stella, had been battered to worse than nothing—bereft, without his wife and kids, and bankrupt. He got sober—thank God, AA, and others who cared—and now led a quiet existence in a small town in Wisconsin, doing another of his passions, which was building boats—beautiful wooden, hand crafted boats. His life was good, but still he was a changed man and that haunted Mick.

Mick walked back to the mirror and studied his swollen face again. Margaret's little reprimand came to his mind. Why was it he had agreed to this job as president of a dog club that was started and basically run by a woman who was perpetually sticking her nose where it shouldn't be— and reprimanding others for doing the same?

He leaned in closer to the mirror and noted that the extent of the bruising seemed to be increasing as each moment passed. Aside from having thought it could be interesting and fun to spend time with others who loved this breed, the bare bones truth of the matter was, deep down, he believed he just might be able to exact some kind revenge on Stella Gale if he were president of the national club. He never told Pete about this because Pete would never approve. In fact, he'd never told anyone and never would.

He turned from the mirror and decided to begin the agonizing process of getting dressed. *The good news is, my position as president is only temporary—hallelujah and amen.* As soon as the club was established enough to have elections, he would probably be gone, which didn't matter anymore as it was not looking as though his desire for revenge would be satisfied, not any time soon, especially after this whole fiasco. Good Christ, Stella was having a field day! As for Pete's warning about these people having absolutely nothing but ego, money, back stabbing, and slander on their minds, Mick had chalked that up as coming from a man who had been screwed over by one rotten apple, albeit a big one, and thus had lost all perspective.

Mick was not naïve, not by any stretch—he had not only experienced the German Shepherd Dog world, but the world in general had fallen out of his favor practically from birth. Still, it seemed impossible to him, at the time, that an entire community of people devoted to a particular breed of dog could be as crazy, selfish, or malevolent as Pete had portrayed them, but now he was beginning to wonder.

―――――

Margaret took Saturday afternoon off and felt quite sancti-monious about it. She had used the disgraceful behavior displayed during the board meeting as her justification. She'd sought out each board member and told them, quite frankly, that six of them ought to pick up all the work right through till the dinner Sunday night, but since she knew that would be impossible, she would settle for just the afternoon. They had each agreed, and so they should have with all the work she'd put in for the two days prior to when they so righteously rushed to the hotel to have an emergency meeting regarding her behavior—and look what happened!—complete idiots the whole bunch!

She settled in at her table by the window, binoculars and notepad out and ready, TV tuned in to the shopping channel—no sound. She needed the quiet to think and right now she was thinking it was a miracle the Club was functioning at all—no thanks to any of the board members. She suddenly had a moment of panic thinking of them over at the showgrounds handling things. Could they manage without her?

She reached up and released her barrette from her bun, which allowed her brown hair to fall down over her shoulders. She grabbed a handful of it, wishing it were thicker, then let it go. Of course they could handle things. All that was left was the Parade of Pets, the Costume contest, the 'longest drool competition' and the Auction for the rescue fund. God knows, a handful of eleven-year-olds could handle that.

She swung her hair over the back of the chair and spread her legs to allow air to flow up between her sweat laden thighs. She had four long hours to do with as she pleased. She let out a long low sigh and, as she did so, thought back to the morning's event—the weighing and measuring of each dogue that was to be shown the next day. She would not have skipped that for the world. There she stood, clipboard in hand, marking it all down, slowly and deliberately, bathing in the whole spectrum of emotions that little exercise had caused in the hearts and guts of each owner/breeder. It was spectacular! Just thinking about it made the hair on her arms stand up.

Of course, they had two ABC witnesses present at all times to be sure no cheating of any kind went on. That had been her stroke of brilliance, along with the addendum that she be one of the witnesses—the one who wrote it all down. The whole idea was to pre-empt any bitching and finger pointing that could emerge and, oh, there would have been plenty had it not been so structured. This was the first Bordeaux show in the U.S. where such measurements had been done and tensions ran very high because of it. She had spent from 5 a.m. to 7 a.m. fielding phone calls regarding the weighing and measuring. "Is it really necessary? Who will be doing it? What if my dog won't get on the scale? Can I get a signed fax from my vet regarding the weight if I think it's incorrect here? Who will be writing it down? Will this information be with the judge in the ring?" And the big question that popped up with every call was "Will these measurements be made public?" Every single person fell silent for a moment or two when she gave them a resounding "YES." They would be published for all to see in the first edition of the ABC's official *Bi-monthly Drool*, due out within the next few months.

The hair on her arms rose again. She was gaining more friends than she'd ever dreamed possible. It was glorious. Frank would be proud. She glanced over at her dresser where she'd placed the clipboard, now plump with the gathered information. Between now and the *Bi-monthly Drool* print date, there were sure to be many, many more calls regarding this—some might possibly beg her to either delete them or even change them, just a smidge!

She glanced out over the half empty parking lot. She had no doubt it would start filling up slowly as bored breeders trickled back in from the show site. The afternoon's events were primarily for pet owners. They needed their day. After all, they were the ones who were willing to take on a breeder's mistakes and even pay for the opportunity to do so. So, they get their pat on the back, are told how wonderful they are, and then the breeders are free to move on to the real business of showing breed-worthy dogs.

She scoffed and picked the binoculars up from the table. Pet owners were nothing more than stupid people who were particularly useful to breeders, particularly the bad breeders who pumped puppies out by the dozens without a care. Of course, then there were breeders like Stella who had the balls to sell her mistakes as "show quality" to stupid people like Frank, poor dear. He had walked right into it. Three thousand dollars for a pitiful example of the breed who dropped dead of a heart attack at three years old.

She gripped the binoculars and raised them to her face. That would never happen again. She felt a rush of heat. Once she'd realized how poor an example of the breed Betty was, she had changed her name to Cranberry and stopped bringing her anywhere near a showground.

She scowled, dropped the topic of Stella, and looked back out the window. "Rather than the Pet Parade," she mumbled, "it should be called 'The Parade of Pitiful Mistakes.'" She put her hand over her mouth and glanced quickly over her shoulder, then looked back out over the parking lot just in time to see Galestorm Bordeaux pulling in. Well, well, well, of course Stella would be the first bored breeder to return to the hotel. She had more important things to do, like spy on people and then squash them like flies.

She shook her head in disgust and banged the bridge of her nose on the binoculars as she did so. She dropped the binoculars from her face and stroked her nose as she continued to track Stella's truck with plain eyes. How predictable! Stella Gale felt no need to pat the backs of pet owners, why would she? Once she got her money, they were left blowing in the wind, ever grateful and still willing to kiss her ass—stupid, stupid people—and meanwhile, Stella laughed all the way to the bank and was still laughing to this day, every day. It was a surprise to Margaret that she'd even brought Oz to the show considering the number of someones who were probably waiting in line to use his semen. Surely she had a long list of lousy bitches to stud him to, and an equally long list of homes to sell more of her mistakes to.

Margaret's body twitched with rage. In the next instant, her mother appeared. She wasn't donning her usual satanic scowl or sardonic grin. She was smiling tenderly, dressed in her fur coat and blue heels—the very garments Margaret normally despised.

Margaret felt a surge of warmth until she realized Mother's smile was not directed at her, but rather at Best Boy who was sitting beside her. The warmth turned quickly to thick disgust as Best Boy looked up and Mother leaned forward and rested her hand gently on his head.

Margaret grimaced as her hatred of that coat and those shoes returned. Mother was a pillar of responsibility and affection when it came to these Boxers, and Margaret hated every one of them. Frankly, she hated all dogs! She quickly glanced at the door and around the room, then took a deep breath.

She sat calmly back in her chair and resettled her hair over her shoulders. Cranberry had simply been a stepping-stone to get where she was now. Stella may have sold her dear Frank a dud, but what she didn't realize at the time was she had sold a dud to the woman who would one day be running the American Bordeaux Club, and whose ass she would one day be kissing and the kissing may very well begin soon!

She looked over at the plump clipboard that sat next to the TV—right as a pearl necklace flashed up onto the screen. That clipboard contained the valuable information that Oz's head was not thirty inches around as Stella claimed in all her ads and on her website. It was, in fact, twenty-eight inches and he was twenty-seven inches at the withers—a head that was merely within the range of normal considering his height. Ms. Kennel of the "biggest heads out there" was only speaking of herself, not her dogs. She laughed as she looked out the window and watched the scrawny little woman climb out of her souped up truck onto the pavement.

As soon as Stella closed the door to her truck, she turned and looked directly up at Margaret's window.

That's when Margaret's laughter ceased and she fell like a rock. She'd had no time to think about how to fall—she just rolled off the chair and hit the floor, dead weight. By the time she'd gathered her senses enough to climb back onto her chair, Stella was gone and there was a loud knock on her door.

"Margaret, I know you're in there. Now, open up, I need to talk to you!"

Margaret straightened out her dress, walked reluctantly to the door, and opened it.

Stella strolled past Margaret into the room and took note of the binoculars on the table. She then looked at the TV. The pearls were gone and a set of gold bracelets stood in their stead. "They ain't real, Margaret."

Margaret was taken aback. "What isn't real?"

"Them bracelets. I know real gold when I see it and that ain't it—case closed."

She turned from the TV and looked at Margaret. She'd never seen her without her bun. "Damn, how long have you been growin' your hair? It looks like your whole life from where I'm standin. Have you ever considered cuttin' it? Hell, it just might suit you to have one of them bob cuts, you know, make you look lighter and younger. The way you look now, you could be my mama when the real facts is you could be my baby sister."

Margaret quickly grabbed her hair and rolled it up. "What is it you want to talk about, Stella?" She snatched her barrette off the table and stabbed her bun into place.

Stella took Margaret's chair by the window. "It's about Mick. I heard you're thinkin' on gettin' rid of him and that's good thinkin' on your part. It's the responsible thing to do." She pulled her cigarettes out of her vest pocket.

"Stella, please don't smoke in here!" Margaret was scrambling. How did Stella know what she'd said to Mick?

Stella pulled out a cigarette and lit it. "And don't ask me how I know about this little idea of yours 'cause it ain't none of your business. The fact is, I know and what I want to know now is if you're gonna have the balls to follow through on it?" She inhaled. "Don't worry, I ain't gonna tell anybody, unless it's necessary of course. Your little secret is safe with me."

Margaret walked over to the window and tried to open it.

"Them windows don't open, Margaret." Stella snorted a laugh. "Hell, a little secondhand smoke ain't gonna kill you. Don't believe everything you hear. Fact is, it's the first hand shit that does the killin' and I ain't afraid to die, so answer my question." Stella had been up the second half of the night—the part where she was supposed to be getting some sleep—rolling the words that Lisa-Lee had repeated to her over and over in her head. "Unfortunately, Stella didn't do anything wrong, meathead." It was the "unfortunately" part that both bothered her and verified her theory about Mick. He was out to get her, just as she'd thought. There were a lot of times when it was a pain in the ass to be right and this was one of them.

Margaret was still scrambling. She then remembered that oh-so-innocent little Hispanic girl in the kitchenette and made a quick note to herself to call the INS as soon as she got rid of Stella.

"I ain't got all day, Margaret. I got a lotta shit to attend to, unlike yourself who apparently has all the time in the world to sit up here with your binoculars and watch all them exotic New Jersey birds." She snorted a laugh, picked up the binoculars, and looked out the window. "I ain't seen nothin' more than pigeons around here. Not all that fascinatin' in my mind."

Margaret succumbed and sat on the end of her bed. "I can't get rid of him, at least not right away."

Stella stayed with the binoculars. *Damn, why didn't I think about bringin' a pair of these?* She scanned the parking lot and beyond. "Why not? You heard him. He has a deep down dislike regardin' me—you heard it in black and white—'Unfortunately, Stella didn't do no wrong!' That little statement right there makes it clear as day he's just waitin' on me to do some wrong—which he's too dumb to ever catch me at, but still the intention's there and that ain't s'pose to be the intentions of the president—not in my book and it shouldn't be in yours either!"

Stella turned from the window and tried to find Margaret with the binoculars. The blur of Margaret's blue dress filled her sight, followed by a blur of flesh that she hoped and prayed was just Margaret's face. She rested the binoculars on the table and looked over at Margaret, who was back to her normal fat self. "Do I have to spell it out for you? God damn, woman, intendin' to get rid of the biggest breeder in the country, well it seems to me that would run against the purpose of a new club which is tryin' to gain the respect it needs to make a name for itself, don't you think?"

Margaret wanted to cram her binoculars right down Stella's throat, but the sad fact was Stella had HER by the throat and there was nothing she could do about it. "I can't get rid of Mick without the approval of the other board members and I don't think that's going to happen."

"Well then, Margaret, put it to a vote by the members." Stella picked up the binoculars again and rechecked the parking lot. "It's just like you said at the meetin', when they hear about the fight, like they already have, thanks to me, most of 'em ain't gonna want a president who gets into a knock down drag out with anybody, and I ain't even talkin' about a club member."

She caught sight of a purple Chevy van pulling into the lot. "'Course Biff ain't just any club member, he's a meathead, just like Mick said. Goddamn, me and Mick do agree on somethin'! I'd a kicked his ass too, 'specially for yellin' about kickin' me out for no damn reason."

She watched the van pull up to the hotel entrance. "The funny part is Mick was standin' up for me if you was to look at it from a particular pair of glasses—but I ain't lookin' through that particular pair 'cause that pair is as fake as 'em bracelets you was lookin' to buy right before I walked in here."

Margaret got up and turned the TV off. "I wasn't looking to buy anything and we can't have a vote, the club isn't set up for that kind of action, not yet. Do you know how much work it has taken to get this far? No, you don't because you haven't walked in my shoes. For your information, I have sweated my ass off to get this club up and running and all I get back are complaints and demands!"

Stella held the binoculars steady as the door opened on the driver's side of the van. "No, I ain't walked in your shoes, Margaret, thank God 'cause A) they is probly way too big for me and I don't mean too long and B) I would never sweat my ass off for a bunch of people who don't really give a shit." She immediately recognized the spandex pants as soon as the feet hit the pavement below the door. The face was hidden behind the tinted glass, but there was no need to see it. "Well, I'll be damned if the wicked witch of the West hasn't decided to show her sorry face. Margaret, get over here and check this out!"

Margaret sprang up from the bed. She was desperate for a change of subject and, moreover, thrilled to feel the sudden heat of burning curiosity surge from her thighs to the top of her head. She pulled the curtain all the way back and looked down to where Stella was aiming the binoculars. Charlene Peets had made it. The last time she'd talked to Charlene was right after the board meeting 'fight.' Charlene was at a gas station in Lexington, Kentucky, extremely drunk and trying to decide if it was worth her driving the rest of the way. She was tired, which meant she was probably too drunk to drive anymore, and wondering if she shouldn't just turn around and go back home because she'd left Gabe's Pit Bulls in the hands of her fifteen year old nephew for five days and Gabe would kill her if anything happened to his Pits.

That's when Margaret told Charlene about the fight and how it was decided by the board (something she had no control over) that Molly could not show Tank. She waited. The slurred obscenities that came screaming through the phone were exactly what Margaret had hoped for. Nothing would stop Charlene now! Prior to this conversation, Margaret had alerted Charlene about the photos Lisa-Lee and Stella had taken. She was guessing that that 'tidbit' had motivated Charlene to get in the car in the first place, even though she'd already claimed she was coming to the show before hearing this news.

This second round of news was the carrot needed to get Charlene all the way to the show. There had been more than a few shows where Charlene never showed up due to some horrific "accident" of one kind or another, i.e., her best bitch jumped out of the car window and died, a train hit her and dragged her and her dogs two hundred yards, she was stuck in a snow drift all night in the middle of nowhere and nearly froze to death with her dogs, and on and on! No one was ever clear what really happened any of these times. Stella said she was just a lying coward who never had any dogs she could show without totally humiliating herself and so thought up every excuse in the book to not to show up.

Well, this time Charlene did have a dog at the show, but was hundreds of miles away and so drunk that the chances of her safe arrival were down around zero in Margaret's mind. Now, here she was! "Let me have a look, Stella!"

Stella handed her the binoculars, which shocked Margaret. "Go ahead. I can't stomach lookin' at that bitch for more than about one second. I swear the likes of her makes me stop to think what the hell I'm doin' in the same country as her, let alone the same damn state, let alone the same damn hotel. Goddamn, I'm gonna have to be walkin' around the same damn showgrounds with her tomorrow! I mean look at her—hell, she makes you look like some kinda queen. She wears them black spandex pants to every damn show—which ain't been that many lately and I wonder why that is? Hell, she's either got fifty pairs of them or just the one pair—it don't matter either way. I mean those things, when she's walkin' make her butt look like she got two hogs in there fightin' it out for dear life 'cause there ain't breathin' room enough for the two of 'em! I wouldn't be caught dead in them things, not if I had me a body like that. Hell, I wouldn't wear them things anytime 'cept if I was one of them ballet dancers—which I ain't never gonna be, you know with all them muscles—they ain't like most of us who got nothin' but fat back there."

Margaret pulled her face away from the binoculars for a moment and looked at Stella.

"I know, Margaret, it's sad as shit, but even I got me a fat ass, trust me. I mean I ain't used my butt for nothin' for years. Bobby's so busy buildin' stuff for my kennel, I think he's forgot what sex is."

Margaret laughed. "I know all about it—Frank is so busy with opening his second new car dealership—I haven't seen him in clothes, let alone naked!"

Stella pointed out the window. "Now, don't lose sight of her, Margaret. Tell me what she's doin'." She wasn't interested in where this conversation was going. She settled back in the chair, lit up a joint, and looked at Margaret who was looking at Charlene who was doing God knows what, and it occurred to her that somewhere she might've crossed over that line into crazy, just like Bobby, and never saw it coming. She was real positive that talking about sex with Margaret was a part of that line, there was no arguing with that.

"I think she's gone to check in and get her room key and there might be somebody sitting in the passenger seat, I can't quite tell because of the tinted glass, but it did look as though she was talking to somebody." Margaret squinted into the binoculars thinking it might help her see through the tinted windshield, but it didn't. What she was most enthralled with, at the moment, was not Charlene, but the fact that she and Stella were in cahoots.

"And when she comes back out, Margaret, check out that stack of bleached hay stickin' every which way from her head. I swear it looks to me like she never takes her head off that pillow in the mornin'. It's like there's an invisible pillow, two of 'em that follow her everywhere she goes, on both sides of her head, day in and day out. Hell, it sucks the air clean outta my lungs just lookin' at her and let me tell you, I have seen a ton of ugly and, what's worse, hers ain't just skin deep. She's got the insides to match!"

Stella took in a long slow hit off her joint.

"Stella, she's back and she's getting something out of the back of her van. Maybe she actually brought some dogs!" Margaret watched the spandex pants walk away from her and disappear around the back of the van. Stella was right, those pants were hideous, and everyone thought so, but no one said anything. God help them if they did!

"Hell no, she didn't bring no dogs. The only thing that bitch is diggin' out of the back of her van are brown paper bags, or possibly even a box—containin' more booze than you seen in your lifetime—end of story. You just watch and learn darlin'."

Sure enough, Charlene emerged from the back of her deep purple Chevy van hugging two large paper bags. Margaret was impressed by Stella's accuracy—though why would she be? She had seen it over and over and it was precisely this side of Stella that unnerved her. She just might have to find a way to get Mick to walk away from the club.

"Margaret! Is that Mick comin' in from the far end of the lot?" Stella took multiple hits on her joint, and then grabbed the binoculars from Margaret. "Yup, sure is! You need to get on your cell right now and call Charlene and tell her Mick is comin' her way!"

Margaret was horrified. "Stella I can't do that! I'm the club secretary. If they knew I was up here with a pair of binoculars spying on people, they would crucify me!"

"Margaret, it ain't no newsflash to anybody who's got any brains, which ain't that many come to think of it. Hell, even those with half a brain know you're always tryin' to put your nose where it don't belong—binoculars or no binoculars. Why the hell do you think you got to be where you are?" Stella put her joint in the ashtray. "Give me your phone."

"You can't call her, you hate each other!"

Stella chuckled. "Oh yeah, watch me." Stella leaned over and picked the pink phone off the table. "What's the number?"

Margaret was flabbergasted. Stella and Charlene having a conversation was not a good thing, not for her anyway. She felt her whole body tighten as the numbers squeezed out from between her taut lips. "1-202-451..."

"Never mind, I found it. I figured you musta called her sometime in the last twenty-four hours." She looked up at Margaret. "Calm down, woman. You don't think I know you call her on a regular basis and say shit to her that ain't true, just for the sake of creatin' more of a pissin' match between us? 'Course you do. I'd be dumb as shit to think anythin' else. Now hush up!"

Charlene opened her phone. "Yeah?"

Stella had watched Charlene put the bags gently down on the pavement beside her van before she opened her phone. She chuckled—*wouldn't want to break them bottles now would we?*

"Charlene, its Stella. Now before you hang up on me, consider this—we both got a enemy in common right now and that enemy is about to pull up in the parkin' lot right in front of you. It's Mick who got Biff and Molly yanked from showing your Tank tomorrow. Now, you can still show him—but he ain't worth shit without Molly and we both know that. Anyway, I'm just calling to tell you he's the scruffy lookin' guy in the worn out army jacket who is drivin' that fine lookin' Land Rover that's pullin' into the parkin' lot right now, to your left. I know you probly know what he looks like, but I'm tellin' you just in case all that drivin' you been doin' cleaned out your brains... bye."

Stella hung up and watched Charlene jerk her head in a million different directions, mad as shit. One thing that was so predictable about Charlene, with the added benefit of her being drunk most of the time, was she was impulsive, just like Bobby used to be when he came to a show tanked. It wouldn't have mattered if Godzilla had called her, her mind couldn't take in but so much—the immediate moment being the "so much." Stella closed her phone and handed the binoculars back to Margaret. "OK, now just watch—this could be real good."

———

Meanwhile, Jennifer Morales of the Hotel Hospitality Team had gotten a whiff of the pot coming out of one of the rooms. Normally, she did nothing about a little pot wafting through the hallway of the Holiday Inn. It happened fairly frequently. However, on this occasion, she recognized one of the voices coming from that particular room and felt compelled to look into it further. She then put two and two together with the help of a call to Billy who was with Lisa-Lee who hadn't considered that Stella would be in Margaret's room, with Margaret, both of them spying on Charlene.

Of course, if Lisa-Lee had thought about it with a clearer head rather than off the cuff, while trying to measure the length of drool in a ring full of dogues who were barely drooling (it just wasn't all that hot), well, she would have put two and two together and known exactly who was in that room with Margaret and told Billy to tell Jennifer to leave it alone. However, Lisa-Lee wasn't thinking very clearly and once it was verified to Jennifer that it was Margaret's room, Jennifer didn't leave it alone. She recalled

Margaret's patronizing 'better-than-you-you-stupid-little-Spanish-woman' expression quite clearly. It was the kind of expression she had to put up with every day, but it wasn't every day she had the opportunity to get some revenge, however small it might be. That's when she put in a call to the hotel manager.

———

Mick pulled into a parking space—he was worn to the bone and his face hurt so much he finally had to excuse himself from the festivities and get a much needed break, along with some aspirin and ice. Surprisingly, talk of the fight had faded completely in the light of the morning's weighing and measuring exercise. In fact, it was such a total turn around from the previous twenty-four hours, he'd walked back to his car twice and looked in the mirror to see if his face was still as bad as it felt, or if by some miracle it had healed. People were talking to him as if nothing had happened, nothing at all. It was a relief on the one hand, but on the other it was a depressing piece of evidence that backed Pete's theory on just how self-centered these people really were.

As he pushed open the door of his Land Rover and stepped out onto the pavement, he mumbled to himself, "Who cares about the guy with his face so swollen he can barely see, or maybe he can't see at all? My only concern is about my having to get my dog measured today. What if his head's too small? His girth too small? His nuts too tiny? What if they make a mistake? Good God, it's all going to be in public! I can't be bothered to show a wink of concern for the guy with the swollen face—what swollen face? I'm so caught up in how much my dog weighs I wouldn't notice if there was an arrow stuck straight through the middle of his face." He chuckled, which brought great pain to his face, then closed the door.

"WHO THE HELL DO YOU THINK YOU ARE, BIG BOY?"

Mick turned towards the screeching sound and faced a woman, about forty-something, blood-shot eyes, head full of ragged, partially bleached hair, and an expression that was far more terrifying than his own. He had the excuse of an injury, she didn't. She stood with her fists on her paunchy hips, which were barely covered by black tights that were both too short and too small, and her hot pink sweater looked to be something she had quite possibly worn since about age six. He was so mortified he couldn't speak.

"WHAT'S THE MATTER? CAT GOT YOUR TONGUE? YOU ARMY BOYS ARE ALL ALIKE—TINY DICKED CHICKENSHITS!"

Before he could think, the woman marched forward, smacked him across his swollen face, yelled something else that he didn't quite catch, and marched away.

———

Margaret watched in horror while Stella nearly fell off her chair she was laughing so hard—until she started to cough so violently she had to calm herself. That's when there came a loud knock on the door followed by an official and demanding voice.

"This is the management. We've had reports of the smell of marijuana coming from this room! Ms. Appleman, please open this door immediately!"

Margaret felt a sudden wave of weakness flood her entire body. Dear God, due to all the excitement she had totally ignored the fact that Stella had been smoking a joint in her room! She looked to Stella as she melted onto the bed.

Stella watched Margaret collapse and rolled her eyes. "HOLD ON A SEC, I'M COMIN'." She calmly popped what was left of the joint into her mouth, swallowed, then picked up her lighter and walked over to Margaret who was now lying flaccid on the bed. She grabbed a handfull of Margaret's hair, flipped open her lighter and lit it. When the stink filled the room, which it did immediately, she snuffed out the small blaze on the bedspread, strolled over to the door, and opened it. "I'm sorry, sir, I believe you are mistaken, but feel free to come on in!"

A medium-sized man in a maroon shirt, flanked by two women wearing skirts of the same color—each holding clean towels—looked briefly at Stella, then walked past her and into the room. He stopped and wrinkled his nose in disgust. "What is that?" He looked quickly into the bathroom and then at Margaret who was nursing a severely singed hunk of hair. She was weeping.

Stella stepped in beside the man and looked at the label on his shirt—Scott Jenkins-Hotel Manager. "Well, Scott, as you can see, my friend here burned her hair on one of your dryers that got a whole lot hotter than it should have—which will be at the top of my list of complaints once I leave here. That and the fact you are intrudin' on somebody who just found out her husband was in a car accident just north of here. He was on his way to see the opening of her first show. So we'd appreciate it if you would just move along so we can have a little privacy."

17

The Night Before the Show

It was finally the night before the big show and Stella, along with most everybody else, was considerably pumped. The hallways of the Holiday Inn were filled with the loud laughter and high-pitched chatter of at least a hundred and fifty excited dogue enthusiasts—a very big turnout for a very rare breed. Doors opened and closed as people scurried from one room to the next, anxious to be in the know as to how it might all turn out.

Stella, of course, made a point to leave her door wide open for the entire evening—for any and all to stop in at one point or another—which most people did. And, despite the constant comings and goings along with the thick cloud of smoke generated by her and quite a number of others, she was easily able to keep close track of who stopped in and when. The WHY part she would discuss later with Lisa-Lee. When an occasional unknown enthusiast showed up, she simply clicked a photo in her head and put it aside to check out later. She was so practiced in this skill she barely had to think to do it, which left most of her free to pour out story after story and breathe in the laughter and admiration as if it were the source of life itself—which it was for her.

This night was a gift from God and, somewhere in the midst of it, she told Lisa-Lee to remind her to send Margaret some flowers and a thank you card along with a renewed promise to give her a pick pup out of Oz.

The final act of Stella's night was when Charlene showed up. It was around midnight. Charlene suddenly appeared in the open doorway and burst forth with a loud greeting, "HELLO, ALL! IT'S A FUCKING MIRACLE BUT I MADE IT

ALL THE WAY FROM KANSAS, ALMOST WRECKED MY CAR IN KENTUCKY, ALMOST GOT ARRESTED IN VIRGINA, AND IT WAS WORTH IT BECAUSE I SLAPPED THAT PRICK MICK IN THE FACE SO HARD HE DAMN NEAR WET HIS PANTS!" She howled with laughter, almost spilling the contents of her paper cup.

A whisper-filled silence fell across the room as she stumbled through the doorway.

Stella grabbed Lisa-Lee's arm, knowing that Lisa-Lee would try to kick Charlene out. She whispered, "Leave her be."

The black spandex and weathered calves moved unsteadily through the anxious crowd. Legs and arms moved out of her way as she passed. She stopped just short of the table where Stella was seated. "I scared the shit out of that motherfucker and I told him I would beat him to a pulp if he ever fucked with one of my dogs again—son of a bitch! For such a big strong guy, he sure shrunk right up when he turned around and saw me standing there." She bellowed out a second laugh that sent a shiver of shame and embarrassment through the twenty or more bodies in the room. "Then I just slapped his sloppy face. And it's all thanks to my new buddy, Stella, for givin' me the head's up." Charlene lifted her paper cup towards Stella. Nobody responded except to turn to Stella—helpless sheep in need of their leader.

This was a golden moment for Stella. She looked at her herd, then straight at Charlene. "You're drunk, Charlene, plain and simple."

Stella pulled a fresh cigarette out of her pack, flicked on her lighter, and lit it. She already had one burning in the ashtray, but since there were at least four other people sharing that same ashtray she figured nobody would notice. She sucked in the fresh smoke and blew it across the table right into Charlene's baby pink sweater. "Now, I ain't heard nothin' about you slappin' Mick in his face, not that I don't believe you did it 'cause I'm sure you is capable of that kind of thing. I just hope that ain't true 'cause that poor man can hardly see due to his face bein' all swoll' up on account of

Biff. And besides that, slappin' a swollen blind man ain't no kind of achievement, not in my book."

She paused and sucked in long and slow on her cigarette, sending the smoke out into the baby pink once again.

Charlene was visibly taken aback. She wobbled significantly and grabbed the side of the table.

Stella continued calmly, "Now, I don't mind a little squabblin' here and there or the takin'of a few photos when it's necessary to keep a show on the up and up, but slappin' somebody just because you got some kinda bug in your tights that you ain't happy about? Whew, ain't nothin' more to say on that topic—end of story." She shook her head, let out a few "mmmm, mmmm, mmmms," and continued, "And as far as my bein' your buddy—ain't a person in here that don't know what I think of you, as in you are the lowest form of dog breeder on the planet—and if there is a person in the room that don't know my feelin' regardin' that, they know it for sure startin' right now."

Charlene steadied herself and drank down what was left in her cup. "You two faced bitch! I will see you and everybody else in here in that ring tomorrow and then we'll see who gets the last laugh!" As she spoke her saliva flew across the table.

Stella picked up the end of her green scarf and dramatically wiped her brow. "I'm glad it ain't a spittin' match we're havin' tomorrow 'cause you got that all locked up, Charlene."

A soft rumble of chuckles squeezed out across the room.

Charlene turned and scowled at all the faces that were watching her. "If Gabe were with me, she wouldn't be the lyin' bitch she is!" She swaggered back through the crowded room to the open door and turned around. "You're all just a bunch of ass kissin' nobodies. I smelled CUNT the first time she called me beggin' for a dogue and I refused to give her one because of the stink."

Charlene snorted a laugh and disappeared down the hall.

That was when a dead silence came in for a heavy landing—not a whisper, not even a breath, smoke laden or otherwise, could be heard.

Stella looked around the room. The new faces were in shock—the others were stuck in the thick of disgust. She waited for the moment to pass, then chuckled. "Well, I do believe that calls for a bar of the ivory soap—ninty-nine percent pure and all that. My papa woulda grabbed my ear, nose or whatever part of my face he could grab a hold of, and shoved that whole bar right down my throat if I let them words come outta my mouth. Now, I ain't sayin' I'm an angel when it comes to my speakin' my mind, but that right there went into the toilet and right on through them pipes to wherever all the real crap ends up—case closed."

A handful of people let out a loud breath. Some even laughed.

Stella continued, "We got all kinds and that right there is a kind this breed don't need. As some of you know, for years that woman has been cryin' about how I been tryin' to get rid of her and the fact is I have been. Now just maybe you all can see the reason for it! However, from what I seen tonight, in actual truth she don't need any help bein' got rid of. I'm thinkin' she's doin' a fine job all by herself, now ain't she? And on that fine note, I'm gonna kick you all right on outta here so I can get my beauty sleep—'cause even if my dogue don't win, there's nothin' wrong with lookin' fine while tryin'." She laughed and stood up. It was time to bow out and close the curtains.

———

There were three doors that had been closed all evening. Two of the three had been closed all afternoon as well—dinner was ordered in. The first of the two, the one that had allowed absolutely no one to enter at any time, was on the first floor at the far end of the hall, next to the Exit door. It was the Bradfords' room, or the "Biffers" as Stella and now most everyone referred to them. Within these four walls, Molly and Biff were neck deep in a bitter brew.

Molly sat on the end of her bed staring at the TV screen. She was playing and replaying the video of her and Tank's last win, the very one she hoped to show a crowd of cheering onlookers after her anticipated win at this first National. Her jaw was locked tight and her eyelids were puffy from crying. Biff paced around the broken pieces of a chair and a table muttering obscenities.

That morning Molly had pulled herself together for long enough to get Tank's measurements done, just in case they decided to let someone else show him—something she was vehemently opposed to, but Biff was not. She then came back to the room where Biff was holed up in a dark sulk with a couple of six packs of beer. She reluctantly reported to him that they'd measured Tank's chest as being a full inch and a half smaller, and his head a full inch smaller, than what they knew them to be. That's when Biff broke his second chair in two days and his first table—and the mirror he had thrown the chair against was cracked to the point where it was barely hanging on to the wall. Molly spent most of the day trying to convince him that the best thing to do would be to pay for the damages to the room and quietly head back across the country. She didn't feel she could bear sitting ringside at the show. It would be all too reminiscent of sitting on that bench throughout high school and college, while everyone else got all the glory.

Biff, however, felt differently. The news of the mis-measurement had given him a surge of energy that, besides being responsible for the broken chair, table, and mirror, had helped him clear his head. He was not going to walk away from this like a baby with his tail between his legs because that was just how it would look if they left. No, Tank would be shown and he didn't need Molly to do it because he was the finest dogue there and when he won, without her, the taste of victory would be even sweeter.

That's when Molly burst into tears once again.

Biff walked over and patted the top of Molly's head. "Don't worry, Mol, I'll take care of the assholes who mis-measured his head later. They will correct that mistake, or else."

Molly wiped her eyes with the sleeve of her blouse and pushed his arm away. "Biff, you just don't get it! If I don't show him, it means nothing—can't you see that? His stupid measurements don't matter, none of it matters, not if I were showing him! I don't care about that stuff, it's not why I'm here!"

She stood up and looked into the cracked mirror. This was about the worst day of her life! Everything was falling apart. All of her hours and days and weeks of hard work were for nothing! She looked over at the video and watched herself moving with perfection. She was unbeatable and proud of it! There just had to be a way to get herself in that ring, there had to be.

———

The second of the rooms that had been closed all afternoon and evening, but did allow for some entry, was Mick Saber's. After he'd recovered his senses in the parking lot, he came to the hard and fast conclusion that someone had slipped him some kind of hallucinogen and he needed the time to ease off it. He had absolutely no idea who that woman was or why she had slapped him. She certainly didn't look to be an aging anti-war activist from the sixties who was triggered by his father's worn out army jacket, nor did she come across as a concerned Mom who was disturbed by the tattoo of the German Shepherd on the back of his neck, or a member of MADD who saw his swelled up face and confused him for a drunk who'd just crawled out of his car.

Mick hated stereotypes and tended to stay away from them, but this woman had given him no choice. She was exactly what he imagined one would call "white trash." Such a thing did indeed exist, and he had just come face to face with it in the parking lot of the Holiday Inn in New Jersey. What he was confused about was why White Trash had smacked him across his already painfully swollen face. Did he look like "white trash" himself? Which was within the realm of possibility since his ugly swollen grimace matched hers quite well—and, if so, was this how White Trash flirted with White Trash? Was this possibly the beginning of the White Trash Mating Dance and, if so, what would happen next if he ran into her again or, God forbid, she sought him out? And that was the second reason he chose to go directly to his room and shut the door for at least the next twelve to eighteen hours.

Once in his room, he went straight to the mirror, still somewhat concerned that what had happened to him in the parking lot was indeed a flirtatious gesture. Nothing else made sense. He leaned into the mirror. Sure enough, he now looked even more hellish than he had that morning. The exquisite pain that had seared across his face when she struck him, and was continuing to do so, was neither here nor there. What horrified him was just how much he truly did look like a male version of that stocky, bloodshot eyed, sloppy mouthed, polyester pink end of a long line of inbreeds from Hades.

He walked slowly to the ice machine down the hall, shaking his head the entire way. When he returned and was finally able to lie down on his bed with the ice to his face, he suddenly burst out laughing. What WAS that? And he laughed and laughed and he laughed some more.

Then came a knock on his door and he froze—My God, she had found him!

"Mick, it's Margaret, we need to talk."

To Mick's ears, because of the shock he was in, the sound of Margaret's voice was actually a relief.

He got up and opened the door. "Hello there, Margaret!"

Margaret stepped tentatively into his room, peering at his face from behind a barrel of shame—and the barrel grew even bigger when she saw the fresh red mark on a now more swollen left cheek. He looked awful, barely recognizable, and what's more she had heard him laughing out loud when she knocked on the door, a laugh that hadn't sounded like him at all. She peered around the room. "Are you alone?"

"Yes, I'm alone, Margaret." Margaret's glaring paranoia killed his moment of jolly relief. "And if I weren't alone and someone was actually hiding, as you seem to be thinking, why would I tell you? Obviously, if they were hiding, it would be from you!" He looked at her and saw shame written all over her face. "Margaret, I'm kidding. I've not had a good couple of days here, no thanks to you in part—but I certainly don't hold you responsible for the whole deal."

He pulled out a chair for her from the table. "I haven't been to ten thousand AA meetings for no reason, at least I hope not—we'll see by the time this weekend is over." He chuckled and motioned for her to sit.

Margaret felt so awful in that moment that she wanted to throw up. "Mick, that woman who slapped you in the parking lot a little while ago, that was Charlene. I saw the whole thing and so did Stella." She was frantic. "And I didn't know she was going to do that, otherwise I would have warned you, honestly!"

Mick looked at Margaret, who he thought might just tumble to the floor and start crawling towards him. "Margaret, you need to get a grip here. The sky did not fall on me. Some woman who I have never met before slapped me. It's not a huge deal. I mean good God, I was attacked and socked in the face just yesterday, full force, by a muscle bound beach boy and was ..." Mick stopped suddenly. "Come to think of it, not only didn't that incident concern you regarding my injuries, you threatened to impeach me by whatever means necessary, simply for keeping that bastard from breaking every bone in my face. I mean, you saw what he did to that chair for chrissake—and there but for the grace of God, and my ability to defend myself, went my body!"

Mick crossed himself sarcastically. "So, I ask, why are you tripping all over yourself over some....some...some THING that slapped me in the face? And why am I even bothering with you? I hardly know you, I mean not really—thank God. And I don't want to know you or any of these other crazy people. How so many crazy people can gather in this one hotel is beyond me—AND all for the 'love of the breed'! Poor breed is all I have to say!"

He walked over to the window, looked across at his Land Rover, thought about the beautiful buildings he poured his heart into designing, all the wonderful dogs he had trained to protect and save lives, and then he thought about Pete and the elegant boats he put together while putting himself back together. "I have a life for chrissake! I don't need this, not any of it. This is possibly the most ridiculous series of events I have ever witnessed and, God help me, participated in."

He looked back at Margaret, who was literally bending forward holding her belly as if she were preparing for a huge bowel movement. She was staring at a fixed point on the floor. The only thing missing was the toilet. He laughed. "Margaret, you are ridiculous, this whole thing is ridiculous, and I am ridiculous for staying here for even one more second!" He walked over and dropped down to sitting at the foot of one of the two beds. He looked across at the mirror. "And on top of it all, I look ridiculous!"

He laughed and shook his head.

Margaret kept her eyes fixed to the floor. "Mick, I don't want you to go. I'm sorry Charlene slapped you. Stella knew that was going to happen, but I didn't, really I didn't, and I'm not ridiculous, please don't say that!" It was all Stella's fault. She had put Margaret in this hideously uncomfortable position, literally. Her stomach was in knots. Mick was beating her mercilessly for no reason. Stella should be the one sitting there, not her!

Mick looked over at Margaret and actually felt sorry for her. "Why am I not surprised to hear the name Stella invoked? That woman is truly ubiquitous. It boggles the mind." He shook his head. "Now, what may I ask would she have to do with Charlene slapping me? From what I've heard Stella has dedicated herself to bringing that woman to her knees—just as she did Pete. The irony of that being, as of right now, I am all with her on that little mission and that's a miracle! I've never had the pleasure of meeting Charlene until today. I even felt sorry for her because I was certain she was just another victim to Stella's merciless slander—but, no, Stella is dead on. No breed, dog, human, or otherwise deserves that in their midst."

Margaret hesitated. Mick's sudden alliance with Stella was confusing to her. Why should she give Stella any credit for this? She spoke up. "What I meant is the reason Charlene slapped you is because of Stella pulling that ridiculous photo stunt that got Molly pulled from showing Tank. Tank is her first real shot at getting some revenge on Stella and you ruined it, I mean in Charlene's mind. I know it wasn't your decision, but that's how Charlene saw it."

Margaret bit her tongue, literally, and cringed. That hadn't come out right, not at all. She braced herself.

Mick laughed. "If I hadn't heard it all before, I have now. You're right, it wasn't my decision. As you well know I was against it. The vote was five to two. Now, just how is it that that woman got it in her head it was me that evicted Molly from the ring? Was it a little birdie perhaps?"

He looked at her. She was clearly suffering from real anguish and he decided to let her off the hook. "I do not suffer fools gladly, Margaret." All he wanted in that moment was to get her out of his room. He continued, "What Charlene did in the parking lot was not anybody's fault, but her own." He picked up the plastic bag that was now filled with cold water and leaking all over the bed. "Now, if you'll excuse me, I have to get some fresh ice and, hopefully, get some sleep. We have a circus to put on tomorrow."

Margaret got slowly to her feet as Mick walked into the bathroom. She was not happy with how this little tête-à-tête had gone. She couldn't put her finger on it, but something was very wrong. She was certain Mick would have taken the Stella bait, and then they would've had a huddle, made a plan, and all would be zooming along nicely. But he didn't. He dropped the whole thing and had now left her hanging.

She straightened up and faced the bathroom. "OK, Mick, I was just trying to help you understand how things worked. You may be president, but that's only because we picked you, and we picked you because you were respected, meaning you haven't been involved in all the infighting and gossip over the years. However, that's all changed now."

Mick watched the cold water run from the plastic bag down the drain. "Good-bye, Margaret." As he said it, he took note that the sound of those words had a wonderful ring to them.

Margaret walked out the door. The barrel of shame had emptied itself down the drain along with the water from Mick's stupid little plastic bag. What did he know?

———

The third door that had been closed the entire night before the big show was Margaret's. She had felt OK for a few precious hours after she'd left Mick's room. She'd even made it through a civil dinner with a table of excited exhibitors, but once she was back in her own room her head began to swim through the rough waters of a litany of unbearable facts. First, Stella had been clever enough to call Charlene on Margaret's cell phone which meant neither she, nor Charlene, had the evidence to prove it was, in fact, Stella who had set Charlene up to slap Mick. Secondly, Mick had refused to join her in her anger at Stella and it was possible, though a distant possibility, that Charlene might tell Mick that Margaret was the one who told her it was him who was responsible for Molly getting kicked out of the ring. Thirdly, Charlene had the phone records to prove Margaret had been in close communication with her after the meeting, shamefully enough. Fourthly, Charlene might give someone else this information and that someone else would tell Mick. Fifthly, there was the possibility that Stella would tell everybody she had spent the afternoon with Margaret and that it was Margaret who had set Charlene up to slap Mick and Charlene had the phone records to prove it. And if that weren't enough, that stupid Mexican girl could tell everyone Margaret had been smoking pot in her room!

Her head was swimming and her stomach had begun, once again, to sink and cramp, sink and cramp. She locked her door, slipped out of her dress, and lay down on her bed with her heating pad across her stomach. She never went anywhere without her heating pad.

She sighed and looked at the ceiling. She needed time to gather her thoughts and possibly even ... pray. Her stomach lurched. Such a thing had not occurred to her in years! The last time she had communicated with God, in any way, was when she prayed for her mother's death. Not long after this prayer, her mother's body was found in the bathtub.

Margaret felt an agonizing shudder of guilt and at the same time a rush of unspeakable power. She took in a long satisfying breath. There were a lot of bathtubs in this hotel and just knowing they could be filled with a prayer from her was enough! She didn't need to have it actually happen. There would be no show if it did. She turned the heating pad up and allowed the deep heat to soothe her into sleep.

At around 2 a.m., there was a knock on her door.

"Margaret, I have to talk to you!"

Margaret opened her eyes. *Where am I? Is that Molly's voice? Why is my stomach so hot?* She looked around and oriented herself. She had fallen asleep with the light on, lying on top of her bed, in her underwear, and had forgotten to put a towel between the heating pad and her stomach! "HOLD ON! GIVE ME A MINUTE. PLEASE!"

How dare someone knock on my door when I'm in this state! She removed the heating pad. Her stomach was bright pink, not burned, thank God.

She got up, turned the Weather Channel off, grabbed her robe from the hook on the bathroom door and threw it on. "ONE MORE SECOND!" She walked quickly into the bathroom, wrapped her hair up and stabbed it into place. She looked in the mirror and suddenly felt quite good. "OK, I'M COMING!" As she walked towards the door tying her robe snugly to her body, she prepared herself for the unexpected, though much needed, gift of an apology from Molly for her and Biff's behavior at the meeting, which would then be followed by a desperate plea to be put back in the ring. She smiled to herself as she imagined it. *Then I'll tell her I'm sorry, but my hands are tied.* She double checked the knot on her robe and patted it in place. She was more than happy to accept Molly's apology, but the rest was not up to her. She opened the door.

"Hello, Margaret!" Molly brushed past her, knocking into her as she did so.

Margaret turned. This was not a good sign.

Molly stopped at the table by the window and turned around. "I know it's late, but I don't really care because I'm here to tell you that you have no choice but to allow me in that ring tomorrow!"

Margaret loosened her robe slightly and sat down on the foot of her bed. As she did so, the idea of prayer popped back into her head.

Molly had only stayed in Margaret's room for ten minutes at the most, but those ten minutes were all it took to put Margaret flat on her back, once again. This time with the heating pad hugged tightly against her terrycloth covered breasts. What more could possibly happen? Biff had contacted his father, Albert Bradford, CEO of Bradford TV Cable and Satellite Company in Los Angeles, who then contacted one of his lawyers, who then had a conference call with Biff and Molly. What it all boiled down to was, since there didn't exist an official ABC rule about one not being allowed to have dinner with the judges during the week before a show, the ABC could be sued for denying Molly, a member in good standing, the right to show her dog for no reason at all other than they felt like it. On top of that, the club could and would be sued for denying them the right to exhibit their stud dog to potential puppy buyers and/or people in search of stud services. All in all, it would add up to a very large sum of money AND get them shut down or, at the very least, tie them up in a legal battle that would last a very long time—which would probably be the end of the club. Either way, it wasn't pretty.

And the way Molly exited the room was the final straw for Margaret—the one that pushed her back into bed. She had no doubt Molly had practiced that exit a thousand times—the way she lifted her chin, puffed out her chest, clenched her fists, and spun such a precise ninety degrees on her heels was flawless—but even still she found no solace in knowing that.

Within a half hour, Margaret grew tired of hugging the heating pad and called Frank. He was tired too, but glad she called. He listened to her saga, then told her the only thing in what Molly had said that didn't sound like "hogwash" was the part where they said they could tie up the club with legal wrangling. "Anybody can sue anybody for anything in this country, honey. The question is, if they actually have lawyers who are willing to take the time and energy to pursue such a ridiculous case, then are you and the club ready and willing to take that on?" He didn't wait for her answer. "I say let them show their damn dog and try not to get yourself into this kind of tangle again! Now, sweet pea,

I really need to go back to sleep. I have a full day at the new dealership tomorrow. Please don't make yourself crazy over this. Remember, it's only a dog show. Everything will be…"

Margaret hung up before he could finish. Frank always managed to put his foot in it. She made a note to herself never to call Frank when she was in trouble because it was bound to fall flat in the end. She picked up the phone again and dialed the first of the seven board member's rooms.

Within an hour the board held their second emergency meeting in two days, the outcome of which was to let Molly show Tank. Their reasoning was that they didn't have a leg to stand on. This was their first National Show and the full board of directors had only been in existence for nine months. In short, they had no 'official' rules in place, except those scribbled on notepads or sitting on seven different hard drives. What they were doing right now was flying by seat of their pants and/or finding guidance from other established breed clubs. This was not the time to take on any kind of legal battle—and each member, in the privacy of their own mind, was quite clear they would leave the club if such a thing were to happen. They just wanted people to get along and enjoy the experience of the first national Dogue de Bordeaux show, which marked the beginning of the American Bordeaux Club. It was that simple. Of course, now they were faced with the issue of what Stella might do with this turn of events, but they would just have to cross that bridge when they came to it.

Mick had not attended the meeting. When Margaret called and woke him at 3:30 a.m., he mumbled, quite gruffly, that it would take a herd of elephants to get him out of bed for what he referred to as a "ridiculous turn of events." He then added, in the same tone, that whatever they decided he would be in "joyous" agreement with. Then he hung up. It was the "joyous" that had stabbed into Margaret's left temple and forced her to take two aspirin.

18

Envy

Stella, Lisa-Lee, and Mabel were the first exhibitors to enter the dining room on Sunday morning. They were, in fact, the first guests to show up period. It was 7 a.m. The stainless steel hot bar was in its bare beginnings—a long line of steaming rectangular holes waiting to be filled with trays of hot food.

The sign that Stella strolled past read "Sunday Breakfast is served from 8:30–11." However, when the restaurant staff tried to stop her, she pled her case which included that she hadn't slept in three days and didn't know what she might do if she wasn't at least allowed to just sit and watch the steam coming off the hot bar. "I'm barely keepin' them ships in my port, if you know what I mean and watchin' that steam risin' from that bar, it'll calm my nerves. Do you know…?"

She stopped and looked at the young man's label. "Do you know, Jerome, that today is a big day for us Dogue de Bordeaux people and what you need to understand is this— in the next half-hour you're gonna have a line of people that only got one or two of them ships left in their ports, out of a whole damn fleet, some—four that I can think of, off the top of my head—don't have any ships left due to the stress of the situation which I know you have heard somethin' about by now. If I don't know anything else at all, I do know every place on this earth has a gossip column, or the equivalent, and the Holiday Inn ain't no exception."

She nudged him gently on the arm and leaned in towards him as if sharing a secret. "The bare bones truth is this is a crazy bunch of people which you will be refusin' entry to in about thirty minutes. My advice is to go on ahead and let 'em in, serve 'em coffee, and they won't bother you. Most of 'em ain't gonna be able to eat a thing 'cause their stomachs is so tied up in knots. Alls they got is an appetite for winnin' and stabbin' each other in the backs. We're talkin' the equivalent of the Super Bowl, and I know you know all about how crazy people get over that. So you wouldn't want to stand in the way of those people now would you? Besides, Lisa-Lee, over there, who has so rudely gone ahead and picked herself a table, is a good friend of Billy who's up at the front desk right now. He told us to come on in and sit down as long as we don't get in your way."

Jerome of the Service team had physically stepped aside long before Stella was done, but pure intrigue kept him standing there next to her—and Stella saw no reason not to finish her conversation with her new young friend before sitting down.

Lisa-Lee sat and watched Stella do her business with Jerome. She was feeling pretty tired out from keeping up her end of the business, in spades, Billy being one of the spades. Just the previous night she'd called on him, once again, for a favor. He was ecstatic before he'd even heard what it was. She'd asked him to ask the night team of employees to keep an eye out for anything unusual.

By morning, the front desk reported that the only thing they saw was that the stocky lady with the bun—the one who owned "that ugly green car with the Porsche engine"—had left the hotel at 3:20 a.m. and returned twenty minutes later with a barrel of Dunkin' Donuts' coffee and a large bag of Munchkins. Now, this wasn't very exciting from their perspective, but it was just the bit of news that Lisa-Lee knew Stella wanted to hear. She knew that because she'd heard Molly at Margaret's door at 2 a.m., shortly after Stella had gone to sleep, leaving her strict instructions to keep the door open a crack and stay up as long as possible, just in case.

Lisa-Lee had even put in the effort to go down the hall and put an ear to Margaret's door. She couldn't make out the content of the very one-sided conversation, but she could tell Molly was no longer the whining victim she'd been at the board meeting. Her voice was confident and strong.

Ten minutes later, she heard Molly leave Margaret's room, then waited about half an hour and went back to Margaret's door and listened. Margaret was either speaking to herself or she was on the phone—the latter was the more likely possibility. After that she felt she had earned her right to shut the door and get some sleep.

Then around 5:30 a.m., Stella shook her awake, demanding to know if she'd missed anything. As soon as Lisa-Lee had told her everything, they sat together and kept watch over the parking lot. Stella was sure from all Lisa-Lee had told her that Molly would be showing Tank and, if this were the fact, she knew "beyond a shadow of a doubt," that Biff and Molly would be seen loading up "a bunch of show shit" and rushing off to the showgrounds as early as possible.

Sure enough, at 6:20 a.m. they spotted Molly and Biff, and for the next forty-five minutes watched them load a ton of gear into their van. Stella had explained to her that, according to Margaret, these people had brought their own tent, video camera, TV monitor, banners, and T-shirts to hand out to any fans they might have, and several outfit changes for Molly. As Stella put it, "Molly is a first in the Bordeaux community, as in she's ground zero for bringing the Art of Handling into the Bordeaux ring. Mind you, this is a bunch of people who never put much thought into that part of showin' a dog, at least not when it just came right down to the Bordeaux only shows. That all belonged to the AKC Breeds, but now here she comes and that's exactly why she ain't liked all that much. It's like she's bringin' the Hollywood end of life into the old neighborhood and people ain't happy about it 'cause it means more money, as in hiring 'handlers,' or learning to do it yourself or else your dog ain't worth jack. Lookin' dignified when you show your dog is one thing, but this is gonna open up a whole 'nother ball of gum—you just watch over the next year or two and remember you heard it here first, honey."

As Lisa-Lee sat there and watched Stella work her magic on Jerome, she wondered if Stella had meant what she'd said about her staying with Stella for the next few years or more. She couldn't help but think that Greta person could be the reason that might not happen. She didn't want to, but she wondered if she needed to be thinking about moving on. Stella was very mysterious about who this Greta was, never answered any of her direct questions. What she did know was that as soon as Greta came back, Stella took Lisa-Lee from her job in the kennel and set her up with a job in town at a restaurant. Lisa-Lee didn't even get the time to pack her things. Bobby delivered them to her.

Stella told her it was only temporary and to just be patient. "Greta ain't gonna be here all that long, I can guarantee you that. She run off on me before and she'll do it again."

Another thing Lisa-Lee knew was that just before Stella went to sleep each night since they'd arrived at the hotel, she quietly read from some papers she'd brought with her. Lisa-Lee had never seen Stella read anything quietly to herself. She usually talked, even yelled, while she read. She'd asked Stella what she was reading. "It's ain't nothin', just some stuff written by Greta, who's real good at writin'—nothin' you'd find interestin'."

Lisa-Lee felt uneasy as she sat in the dining room of a hotel in a state she'd never been to. She thought back to Stella's words. Stella didn't even look up when she said them. Of course, she hadn't looked up a thousand times when she said things to her, but this felt different. Who was this Greta? And how did she get to be so important to Stella? So important that Stella would actually shut up for as long as half an hour and give undivided attention to her when she wasn't even there!

Lisa-Lee made up her mind that she would try to learn more about Greta AND bring up the possibility of a raise during their long drive home. She didn't expect a raise; she just wanted to talk about it. Stella was more than generous to her, for the most part. Some days it felt hard, but this was not a bad life at all. It had a lot more up sides than her previous life, there was no doubt about that. She just wanted to have a discussion, mostly because this Greta person made her nervous. It was hard waiting in the wings, doing restaurant work again, wondering when and if she would get back to taking care of the dogs. She missed it, and she missed being around Stella, despite the crap that really was nothing compared to the life she'd had with Aaron, who hit her for things as simple as sneezing at the wrong time.

Stella was the best thing that had happened to her, ever. She had more guts than any woman she'd ever met. No one would ever back Stella into a corner and beat the crap out of her. It was just not possible. She would never regret or forget the day Stella walked into that diner and offered her a way out.

———

"Well, that was a waste of my time," Stella mumbled into Mabel's wide-open ears as the two of them walked away from Jerome. She then nudged Lisa-Lee on the shoulder as they passed by her. Lisa-Lee was seated smack in the middle of the dining room and that was not where Stella wanted to sit. Normally, she would've picked that table, but not this morning. What she wanted was to sit in the very back corner of the room, at the smallest table they could find. She didn't want people pulling on her. She needed to concentrate. A lot had gone on in the past twenty-four hours and the next twenty-four would be critical to her overall plan, which remained in a state of constant change, something which only the likes of her could handle. It was bad enough that she'd already tripped over Mabel who'd been sitting up against the wall, asleep, just outside her door at 6:45 a.m.

———

"Mabel, what the hell are you doing sittin' here like some kinda homeless person? I coulda cracked my face on the damn floor trippin' over your leg like that!"

Mabel's eyes flew open as she pulled in the offending leg. She looked up at Stella who was standing over her with one hand on her hip, the other holding a cigarette. "I'm so sorry,

Stella. I didn't want to disturb you, but I also didn't want to miss going to breakfast with you."

"Well, Mabel, that's mighty thoughtful of you, but ain't you ever heard of a phone? Or waitin' in the lobby or the dinin' room?" Stella studied Mabel's face. It was about as pitiful a face as she had ever seen. All she could think while looking at her was how many more of her so-so dogs she would be able to send on up to her place. "How long you been out here?"

"Well, I've been up and walking around the hotel since about 3:00 a.m. Sometimes I wake up early when I'm in a new place, especially if things haven't been going that well. I'm still a little shaken about leaving Angel on the sidewalk. It's just not like me to do something like that." Mabel slowly got to her feet. This was not going to help her mission to make a good impression on Stella. First it was Angel, now her leg. And on top of that, there was Lisa-Lee, who had it all and was standing there looking down at her with a holier-than-thou expression. Lisa-Lee was pretty as a picture, smart enough to be on top of everything Stella wanted her to be on top of, AND she was all snug and cozy under Stella's wing. Mabel would give up a lot to be under that wing, but what could she offer Stella that Stella didn't already have? Lisa-Lee seemed to be the all around perfect girl.

Stella caught the glare Mabel flashed at Lisa-Lee. It was so fast that the normal eye would not have seen it, but she did and she filed it away under *Mabel wants to kill Lisa-Lee for no good reason 'cept she's jealous.* She then continued as Mabel inched up the wall to standing, "Well, if you was walkin' the halls then you musta seen Margaret rustlin' up the board members and havin' another meetin' shortly after Molly visited her in the middle of the night." Stella waited as she watched Mabel's face flush with confusion. She figured anyone stupid enough to leave her dog on the sidewalk when coming to a show, was probably too stupid to pay much attention to anything of any importance.

"Why no, I didn't see anyone."

Something about Mabel's wide eyes made Stella feel like 'knocking her lights out'—a phrase she couldn't wrap her mind around until that moment. The feeling passed as soon as she took a good suck on her cigarette. "Well, then you musta either been walkin' in another wing of this hotel or out in the parkin' lot, which ain't possible cause then you would've seen Margaret drivin' off to get donuts and coffee and then drivin' back." She shook her head. "You got a lot to learn, Mabel, and if you want me to teach you then you gotta keep a close ear on all I got to tell you." Stella started down the hall, fully expecting Mabel to gratefully step in beside herself and Lisa-Lee, which she did.

————

All things considered, this was a morning that Stella simply wanted to sit quietly at a table and watch the comings and goings. It was unusual for her to feel this way just prior to a show, but this particular show was the first of its kind, as in very big, and she'd already had to file away a bunch of new faces and a ton of new information—and all before the show had even begun. She just needed a little rest before hitting the superdome.

She looked over at Lisa-Lee who was staring into her coffee whistling softly to herself. Lisa-Lee was no trouble at all. She would mind her own business, probably get up and go find Billy before long—and Mabel? Well, she was perfect to have at her side at a time like this. It was like having a big old 'Stay Away' sign. Plus, she had purposely dressed down, with Mabel in mind, in order to keep attention off herself. Now all she had to do was concentrate on pulling in what she knew to be her 'hundred foot wing span'—something Bobby had told her she had—and scrunch herself all up in a wad, just like Mabel. She looked at Mabel who if she had the opportunity would sit so close she wouldn't be able to breath without having to suck in whatever that was she put in that frumpy brown hair—God only knows—and she thought how amazing it was that she might actually learn something from Mabel, as in how to make people look at her and all they see is "Don't pay me no mind, none at all."

————

Stella's plan to simply relax and observe was a failure. As the tables filled up, each one sent a scout to her table just to find out if she knew about Molly being able to show Tank. Stella was irked, but took it in stride. She calmly spit out a fairly consistent message to each of the inquiring minds. "Of course, I know. I knew all about it before you opened your eyes this mornin'. Hell, I knew it before the Biffers even knew it and it's fine with me. I never wanted that to happen in the first place. I just wanted to get a message to the club and all the members that schmoozin' with the judge ain't right and a rule should be set in place regardin' that. It wasn't me that kicked her out. I never expected the board to have a damn meetin' about kickin' somebody out regardin' a rule that ain't even there yet. Hell, if I was the Biffers I woulda cried foul too.

"Now, I ain't heard all the facts yet, but I got a suspicion the word 'lawsuit' came up in their little conversation with the board and that is exactly what I woulda done. I was just helpin' the club out regardin' the future is all. Fact is, I'm looking forward to seeing Molly in the ring after hearin' all the talk about her at all them peewee shows out west. Apparently it's an amazin' thing to see her in action, even when there ain't any competition. 'Course the sad fact now for Charlene is, if Molly wins, no one's gonna know if it was the dog or the girl that won. As a breeder I wouldn't want there to be any doubt in anybody's mind now, would you? If I was Charlene and I thought my dog was the best one here than I would have insisted to the Biffers that somebody else show him, without all them frills—case closed."

Charlene and the Biffers never did show up at breakfast and neither did any of the board members, including Mick and Margaret. Stella wasn't so sure they didn't feel a little embarrassed about how they had all behaved, every one of them.

————

Mick reached a decision by 6 a.m., within seconds after the excruciating ordeal of opening his eyes. He was grateful he could open them at all. And the moment he knew he could still see, it came to him without hesitation. He would be resigning as president of this rag tag group that called themselves a club. He just needed to figure out how and when. Margaret's middle of the night call for yet another meeting regarding what he now referred to as "The Meathead and Molly Folly" had been the clincher. Oh, he needed a meeting all right, but not that kind.

Not only did he resent that two unbelievably shallow, probably sexually frustrated people were allowed so much power as to actually cause the board to cower under the threat of a ludicrous lawsuit, but he also dreaded any further interaction with Margaret under any circumstances. She was, frankly, unbearable. To be with her was to choose to be in the presence of long nails scraping slowly and with great pressure down a chalkboard. And the image of her bent forward in her chair, straining, appearing to be torn between whether to take a shit or fall to her knees to ask his forgiveness and God knows what else, was imprinted in his mind, possibly forever. There would be no getting away from it. The same went for Charlene's poignant display in the parking lot, along with Meathead's attack, and Molly's weeping as though the world had come to an end upon hearing she couldn't show her dog. There was no turning back the clock. All he wanted was to get out before his little collection of the bizarre grew any fatter.

He turned in his bed and squinted across the room, grateful for his ability to see sunlight squeezing around the thick curtains. He then could make out the chair that not all that long ago was filled to the tipping point with a woman in agony. As crazy as it seemed, he now fully believed that what he was participating in was a club put together and engineered by that woman, not for dog lovers or the breed, but rather for the sole purpose of lifting her out of whatever nightmare she was trapped in—and he truly didn't want to know what that nightmare was.

He lifted his head, reached up, and flicked on the light over the bed. Yes, he would go to the show, get through it, hopefully without any more 'glitches'—and be done with it. He squinted under the glare of the light and dropped back onto the pillow. There was absolutely no one in his real life, besides Pete, who would believe, for a second, all that had unfolded here in this hotel. And what scared him the most was that Stella Gale was actually appearing to be somewhat sane. And the irony of it all was that she and he now shared a similar goal—a desire to expose everyone in the club for the "whackjobs" they were. Of course, the important difference between the two of them was that he wasn't one of them, she was. He suddenly shuddered. What if he was one of them? What if he was as deeply entrenched in denial as she was?

He struggled out of bed and walked over to the mirror for what was possibly the hundredth time in two days, and was once again startled by his hideous reflection. "Eight years in AA, Mick, and just look at you!"

19

The Woman in Red

The show site was crawling with exhibitors and their dogues by 10:30 a.m., an hour and a half later than was expected. It had taken that long for people to stop gossiping in the dining room and get over there. Margaret was furious. She'd had to apologetically leave the judges at the site with only a handful of people, most of them BOD members, drive back to the dining room and bang a rather large spoon on an almost empty pitcher of water.

"Excuse me people! It's 9:30! Those of you who are here to show your dogs need to get over to the show site now! This is no time to get lost in the rumor mill. You can do that on your own time. This is our big chance to show off our wonderful dogues to two terrific judges who have traveled all the way from Italy and the Netherlands to judge at our first National show. Let's at least show some them some respect and, more importantly, show the international community that we in the U.S. are deserving of a place on the map regarding this wonderful breed."

Stella had watched 9 a.m. come and go. She could've been the one to tell the people just what Margaret was telling them right now, but thought it would be far more interesting to let them be and see how it would all turn out. She tossed her hair back over her shoulder and responded to Margaret's call to action. "Well, we can rest assured that at least the Biffers are takin' real good care of them judges, now can't we?!"

Low laughter was heard around the room and the few regular hotel guests who were there, minding their own business, looked blankly from Margaret to Stella, and then to each other with curious concern.

Margaret rebutted confidently. She was in no mood for Stella. "The exhibitors who are already at the site are the responsible ones, Stella, and you of all people should know the importance of us making a good impression on the international community!" She felt a marvelous tingle run all through her body. Stella was no more than an annoying housefly in that moment—and she had the fly swatter.

Stella barely blinked. "Oh, I see, and all you 'responsible ones' who are out there right now just happen to be the ones who were doin' sit-ups and beatin' each other up durin' an official meetin' of the board, leavin' people lookin' like they ran into a brick wall—people cryin', secretary sneakin' out in the middle of the night for a big ole bucket of munchkins to snack on while she hopes and prays the B.O.D., with whom she won't share them munchkins, can make good on a stupid ass mistake they made. Yessiree, I'd say you are leavin' a hell of an impression." Stella hadn't felt a need to raise her voice. She knew when she spoke people would open their ears up real wide.

Margaret's wonderful tingle waned instantly. She believed she could handle anything out of the fly's mouth, and she could have—all of it—except for the "munchkins" part. How did Stella know about the munchkins? Why would anybody even remember a stupid thing like that? More importantly, why did a stupid thing like that take it all away from her? She looked at Stella who was as calm as Margaret was undone. Seeing that made her suddenly feel the same hatred she felt the night she prayed for her mother's demise. One more move like that and Stella would be in her prayers. She hugged the clipboard against her breasts and turned slightly away from Stella. "We have a show to put on, guys, so let's get going!"

The quiet room filled instantly with excited chatter, rustling chairs, and laughter. Then it was empty except for the handful of regular guests and Lisa-Lee who sat stirring her coffee and whistling, just as she had been when they first sat down. She had a feeling this was going to be quite a day, something she knew for certain Billy would enjoy. She decided to sit there for a bit, until he finished up at the front desk, then they would walk Oz together, go back to the room, maybe finally have a good screw, and then get to the show site in time for the main event. Stella wouldn't need her until then, thankfully. After all, Stella had Mabel who would happily do anything Stella's heart desired, which gave Lisa-Lee a much needed break.

———

By 11:30 a.m., Margaret was finally able to breathe and release her clipboard from her breast. It would probably take some time for the jabbing sensation in her right breast to finally go away, but it was nothing she couldn't handle. Her show had begun! The first puppy class was done and the six-to-nine month was underway. No amount of breast pain, not even a hundred heartless "munchkin" assaults from Stella, would keep her from bathing in the glory of this day. All her hard work would finally reap its well deserved fruit.

———

As Stella strolled around the show grounds with Mabel dutifully at her side, giving a wide berth to the Biffer Pavilion, a flash of crimson red caught her eye. She came to a halt so suddenly that Mabel stumbled into her. About a hundred yards away, moving across her field of vision was what she knew to be the Mercedes equivalent of a fine cardigan sweater, opened loosely over a million thread count light cotton blouse, garnished by a simple elegant pearl necklace and hands that displayed, what she couldn't quite confirm from where she was standing, but knew to be a ring that was probably more expensive than most people's cars. Those things, in combination with the stonewashed jeans and soft worn leather cowboy boots, alerted her to the fact of very big money with a capital V. "Mabel, you need to go find out for me who that lady in red over there is!!" She looked to her right, but Mabel was gone.

A voice sounded from below her. "Hold on, Stella! Sorry, I wasn't looking where I was going."

Stella turned to see Mabel pushing herself up from the ground. "Well, I wasn't lookin' where I was going either, so how is it I ain't lyin' on the ground? I swear you need to see a doctor seein' as you just might have a brain tumor, which would explain exactly everythin', all the way from leavin' your dog on the sidewalk to lyin' on the ground every chance you get, to them headaches! But never mind that right now. You need to find out for me who that lady in the red sweater is, 'cause I will tell you right now that sweater and them jewels ain't made in Puerto Rico, that's for damn sure. Hell, maybe you oughtta warn her that none of what she's wearin' is safe around this bunch—'course they're all too stupid to know the real thing when they see it, so maybe you oughtta tell her instead that she's wastin' her time if she's tryin' to impress anybody."

Stella looked at the woman more closely. This was not somebody who had a mind to impress anybody. This woman had been swimming in money her whole life, had everything she ever wanted and then some. Plus she was real tall, as in the tallest woman there and not the least bit awkward about it. She moved through the crowd with a confidence that both inspired and irked Stella's inner stallion. *Who is she and why is she here?*

Stella watched as Mabel walked towards the red sweater that suddenly turned and headed back towards the Biffer Pavilion, which was set up right next to the show ring. Mabel walked slowly, trying to look as if she weren't headed to anywhere in particular but, to Stella, she was about as obvious as a country hick walking down Park Avenue. No one else walks a couple steps, stops, looks all around—eyes so wide open you want to knock 'em to kingdom come—walks a couple more steps, stops and looks all around and so on. Stella was half tempted to stroll on past her and take care of the matter herself, but the other half decided to wait. It would be best to have a few clues before introducing herself.

The red sweater finally stopped moving, allowing Mabel to reach her.

Stella breathed a sigh of relief. If the lady hadn't stopped, she would have been standing there until well into the next week before Mabel caught up with her.

The woman in red stepped in beside another woman who was seated in a lawn chair. Mabel stopped about six feet from the two of them and listened. The woman in red spoke first.

"I will stake my very fine eye for a dog on the one Dogue de Bordeaux I haven't seen yet because I'm not seein' anything that particularly ruffles my feathers, at least not yet. Of course, I know very little about this breed—but from a lifetime experience with German Shepherd Dogs, I will tell you, most of these dogs don't do a lot with regards to the working end of life and better than half of them have their tails tucked up, which irks me to no end."

Her friend, who was more Mabel's height and far less intimidating looking, responded with a chuckle. "There you go, rushing to judgment just like you do every time we test new waters. If you had walked through your beloved MOMA yesterday at the pace you just walked around these grounds, we would've been out of there in half an hour. Why don't you just slow down and enjoy?"

"Well, I think you being a vet has warped you into tolerating a bunch of under conditioned shy dogs! I don't know how else to put it to you, Midge, but I think we're both wasting our time here!"

Mabel sidled in until she was next to them with her right foot on the blue tarp that was the floor to the Biffer Pavilion. "Hi, I couldn't help but overhear your conversation and I think you should know that some of the best dogs here today are still back at the hotel. I suggest you wait to see them because this truly is the most wonderful breed in the world. I have two of them myself. One is a rescue who was taken from a guy who had cut down her ears and filed her teeth to razor sharp. He probably gave her up because she wasn't good fighting material—she's very timid. I named her Honey." Mabel lit up as she spoke. Rescuing a dog always made the best impression. She continued, "My other dogue I got from the finest breeder in the country. You'll get a chance to see her sire this afternoon in the championship class."

Stella watched as the tall woman turned and twisted her head slightly as she looked down at Mabel. So far sending Mabel over there was looking to be one big fat mistake.

The woman in red responded, "Oh? And who might you be?"

Mabel cringed for a moment, and then managed to breathe more freely as she thought about why she was really here—for Stella. "I'm Mabel Dowd, friend and lover of the Dogue de Bordeaux." Mabel looked over to where she had last seen Stella. She was gone. She then braced herself and turned back to the woman in red. "By the way, I heard you mention something about the German Shepherd Dog. I bet you might want to know that our president is a nationally renowned Schutzhund trainer who used to breed German Shepherds with his father."

"Bill Clinton is a Schutzhund trainer? Now, I canNOT believe that little bit of information would have passed me by!" The woman in red chuckled as she looked past Mabel to what seemed to be a large shadow lurking behind the screen of the big blue tent behind her. She decided it was probably just her mind attempting to keep her from dying of boredom. She looked back at the face that had planted itself tediously before her. "I'm Sally Elliot and this is my boring, though long standing friend, Doc Midge Rainer."

Midge raised her hand from the chair without turning around.

Mabel let out a self-deprecating laugh. "Sorry, I wasn't very clear was I? I meant to say the president of the club, not of our country! Anyway, his name is Mick Saber and it's nice to meet you both."

Sally Elliot stepped back. Now Mabel had her attention. "No kidding? Mick Saber! I haven't been in German Shepherd dogs for quite some years, but I do try to keep up with my ABCs in the working dog world as best I can. I do know that name and I believe his father is Alan Saber—the breeder who left the breed for all the right reasons! American German Shepherd dogs are pretty much train wrecks at this point in time. The good ole German Stock is kaput." Sally realized that she was wasting her air on Mabel, who looked unable to take in anything more after she'd said the bit about her ABCs. "Maybe you would be willing to point him out for me. I would love to pick that man's brain." She looked past Mabel again, just in time to see that her mind had not been playing tricks on her. The shadow was no longer a shadow and it had a voice—a loud thick voice.

"I'll introduce you to Mick. I know him real up close—hahahaha—and I'll have you know that none of my dogs are shy. I raise them with my husband's Pits who are the finest in the country, Pits that would take down anything for any reason and never back down even if their life depended on it." Charlene emerged from under the Biffer Pavilion and stuck her hand out in front of Mabel. "I'm Charlene Peets, been in this breed forever."

That's when Stella dropped her cigarette to the ground and stomped on it. She had NOT seen this coming! She had stupidly avoided paying any attention to the Biffer Pavilion. Had she taken just one second to look through the tent screens, she would have seen the nightmare in spandex was standing right there.

As she made her way over to what was now looking to be a small crowd gathering around the red sweater, she filed her mistake under S, as in the Second stupid mistake she'd made in years, sending Mabel over there being her First.

Sally looked squarely into the face of her newest 'friend,' then at the hand. She reached into her small leather satchel and pulled out her pack of Marlboro Lights. "And you think taking down 'anything for any reason' is a good thing?" She pulled out a cigarette, ignoring the hand and barely willing to look at the face—even the artist in her was stumped to find a reason to look, which was highly unusual. She then thought of her friend, Anna, who had recently shared with her the idea of doing a series of paintings entitled "Abject Desires." Surely there was room somewhere in there for this face! But since Anna was not there, she just might be inspired to start her own series of paintings entitled "Portraits of women who have been ridden hard and put up wet." She let Charlene's hand remain suspended in mid-air.

That's when Stella made her entrance, pushing Charlene's hand aside. "Charlene, if there's one thing I know for sure, this lady ain't interested in dogs that are trained to rip each other apart. Nobody is—case closed—'cept you and your skinhead husband and friends."

She turned to the lady in red. "I believe Charlene here forgot to tell you the part about her husband's Pits being raised strictly for the fightin' ring and I wouldn't put it beyond the stretch of the imagination that he's probably doin' the same thing with some of them Bordeauxs she's got."

Stella then turned to Charlene. "And another thing I know is this woman isn't (she thought she'd avoid 'ain't' for the time being) interested in shakin' hands with the person who punched our club president in the face for no reason 'cept she was pissed off about her dog's handler bein' kicked out of the show ring for tryin' to bend the judges, over dinner, in the direction of pickin' her dog, which is YOUR dog. You bein' allowed to set foot on these grounds is just plain amazin' and I will be bringin' that up to the membership when this show is over and done with."

Stella pulled her gold lighter from her vest pocket and offered the lady in red a light. "Now, I don't know what else Charlene has been tellin' you, but if she's been standin' here long enough I'm sure she's given you more than a ear should have to listen to."

What was amazing to Stella was how Charlene was killing herself with no help at all. It was both perfect and puzzling. She had never seen Charlene behave as badly as she had over the past two days. *She just keeps shootin' her mouth off and shootin' herself in the foot, over and over.* There was not a glimmer of her being anything close to a respectable breeder. Why? Charlene wouldn't have gotten as far as she had without pulling a lot of wool over a lot of people's eyes. Stella had seen this first hand, but from what she could tell there wasn't any wool left at all, zero. Also, there didn't seem to be a sheep within a thousand miles of her. *Charlene is settin' a whole new benchmark for ugly and that's just fine with me!* She did make a note, however, to get to the bottom of what was going on with

Charlene. She had a sneaking suspicion that lying on that bottom was the means to being able put the nail on the funeral of Charlene Peet's career.

Sally accepted the light from Stella and as she inhaled she entertained the very real possibility that this might not turn out to be such a waste of a day. She was intrigued by this rather tastefully dressed woman, though not her style at all, whose blazing red hair was almost as captivating as the huge multi-colored plume of "joie de moi" that rose up all around her. She even played, briefly, with the idea of putting her to the canvas.

She also knew from the accent that this woman clearly had her origins further south than her beloved Virginia. Nor was she educated, in the formal sense of the word, but she was smart, very smart. The only thing she was hoping not to hear was the one word that sent her around the bend regarding not a few of her fellow southerners. The word was "fixin'." If this woman was "fixin'" to do anything, she just might have to pack her bags and move on.

She heard her own mama's voice in her head. "Sarah Elliot, I don't want to hear that word come out of your mouth, not one more time. Your daddy would just fall down and die, twice over, if he heard you were in any way, shape, or form actively participating in the ruination of the South that he loves so dearly." She was too young at the time to understand the whole of what her mama, otherwise known as "The Great Gabby," was saying, but she was truly a formidable woman and a force to reckon with when she chose that tone of voice. Her mama's reprimand stopped Sally dead in her tracks from ever again "fixin'" to do anything.

She also knew her daddy had absolutely nothing to do with what her mama had said that day. He had happily spent fifty years designing and renovating some of the most beautiful buildings in Virginia. The word "fixin'" coming out of his six-year-old daughter's mouth would have brought nothing but a chuckle from him. She did, however, decide to take up her mama's banner regarding "fixin'"—and passed it on to her now grown children, who would pass it on to their children.

She tried to imagine the aging Gabby and this woman in the same room together and felt quite tickled at the prospect, though she knew hell would freeze over before her mama would ever let that happen. "Sarah, how is it you manage to find every social climber in all of Virginia and drag them into my presence? I have told you a thousand times I have no interest in the effort of putting them into their rightful place." Yes, Sally was truly intrigued by this woman. She exhaled and a plume of smoke passed over Mabel's head. "And you are?"

Mabel burst in. "This is Stella, the breeder I was telling you about."

"Mabel, I got my own mouth, thank God, and can speak for myself, thank you very much." Stella closed her lighter and smiled. "I'm Stella Gale and I don't know what Mabel has told you about me, but I would take it with a grain of salt considerin' the sad fact of the source and the sad fact she barely knows me. Fact is, I am one of the first of the crazies in this country to get into breeding the Dogue de Bordeaux." She let out a soft chuckle and purposely didn't offer her hand. Instead she pulled her Pall Malls from her vest pocket and continued, "And let me tell you, if you ain't a little crazy or don't tolerate bein' around crazy, you need to leave right now. You heard it here, mark my words. Now—that doesn't mean nothin' about the breed being crazy—these here are fine workin' animals that, God forbid, should never end up in the hands of the likes of this here Charlene or her husband." She flicked her lighter, sucked in, and blew the smoke out towards Charlene's pink sweater that she knew was near to bursting open from all the pressure that was building up behind it.

The pink sweater ruptured under the strain. "You're nothing but a liar, Stella, and if Gabe were here you would be begging for your life right now. And I will take you on anywhere, anytime, you just name it, bitch!" Charlene spread her legs slightly and took on the stance of a wrestler right before dropping into a fight.

Stella turned to respond, but Sally stepped in ahead of her and shook her hand between the two of them, cigarette held solidly in place by her middle and index fingers—her hand had done this a thousand times. "Excuse me? What is this? Middle school? Now, I don't know a thing about what y'all have going on here and I certainly don't mind being around a fine argument, but this doesn't cut it." She rested her judgment squarely on Charlene. "And, I'll have you know, I can also smell a load of alcohol on your breath, which unfortunately has made it over to my air space and leads me to the startling conclusion that you are engaging in drinking on the showgrounds at a dog show. Rest assured I will be mentioning this to Mick if I do, by chance, have the pleasure of meeting him."

Charlene turned to face her new enemy, keeping the same stance, though she lowered her voice a little. "You don't scare me. Not you or your high falutin' jewelry. I got more money invested in land and horses than you could ever dream of. If you are dumb enough to want to hear anything this bitch has to say, then you are too dumb to hang with me!"

Much to Sally's astonishment, saliva burst out from between Charlene's lips as she turned and pushed the tent screening aside. She stomped back into the Biffer pavilion.

Stella looked on with great satisfaction. "Looks to me like the sow just got stabbed in the ass by the farmer with his pitchfork and is all tore up about it 'cause there ain't a damn thing she can do! The last thing she wants is to end up in the slaughterhouse—case closed."

Sally let out a quick grunt and turned to Midge, who sat calmly in her lawn chair, paying little attention to any of it. She tapped her on the shoulder. "Can you believe this?"

Midge spoke without looking at her. "I knew you'd get around to enjoying yourself."

Stella studied the ring as Sally spoke to her friend—it was a fine emerald sitting in black gold and kept company by a couple of kick-ass diamonds—definitely not made in Puerto Rico and most definitely ONE of a kind. "If you got any questions at all about this breed, Sally, any at all, I got some answers that I believe you might find quite interestin'. Now, this breed ain't for everyone, just like with the German Shepherds, but if you is one of the everyones that is thinkin' about gettin' one, I'll be more than happy to help you out. Now, I got some things I got to attend to, but feel free to give me a tap on my shoulder if you need anything at all. It was very nice to meet you." Stella turned and strolled off allowing no opportunity for Sally to respond.

Mabel stood silently. She had sunk deep into the black bog of Stella's last words concerning her, "...considerin' the sad fact of the source and the sad fact she barely knows me." She felt sick. And in an effort to crawl out, she opened her mouth as Sally sucked on her cigarette and watched Stella walk away. "Stella knows almost every single Bordeaux in the world and their pedigrees, all by heart, starting back in the forties, which is when they were nearly extinct."

Sally turned. "Really? Now, why would she have to do that? Isn't there a database of all the pedigrees? You know, a place you can look that information up?"

Sally felt compelled to say what she meant in at least two different ways for Mabel, whom she already felt she knew far too much about. She also knew if she shared this little bit of information with Midge, Midge would accuse her of making one of her many 'unfair judgments' based on nothing. That's when Midge would remind her how much like The Great Gabby she was. However, most of the time, what Midge failed to remember was that Sally and Gabby were usually right.

Sally knew she had her mama in her. What she hoped to God was that her granddaughters would inherit it, because it had skipped right over her daughter who was too soft for this world. That child came right off her husband's side of the family. There was nothing in her at all from the Gabby tree, which was a shame because what the Gabby tree had to offer was what most women lacked, which was why she didn't like most women. Her assumption was that most women were too whiny and, worst of all, passive aggressive, which absolutely undid her. And she had more than a suspicion that this Mabel was of that ilk. Any mama who would give her daughter a name like 'Mabel' was wholeheartedly passive aggressive, and any daughter who had to bear that name would become the same. It was an unfortunate truth.

"There is no database—at least not much of one, meaning no central registry, which means there is no place to look up the information. Stella is our only real resource for right now." Mabel had squeezed herself from the bog. With Stella out of the picture, she could possibly stay out for at least a moment or two.

"Well then, Stella sounds like she's quite the resource. How do you know she's correct in her information?" Sally knew she'd hit the nail on the head. "Has anybody ever held her feet to the fire on this one or do you all accept what she spoon feeds you?"

Mabel took a quick deep breath. "Stella has no reason to lie to anyone about what she knows. Would you? If you were the top breeder in the country would you openly lie? It would be contraindicated, don't you think?"

"Oh, it would be a big risk—but one that could be easily taken if she knew all y'all were too stupid to figure it out. That would be what one might call quite slick, now wouldn't it?" Sally dropped her Marlboro butt to the ground and stepped on it. "There are a lot of stupid people in the world just waiting on someone to 'pluck 'em dry'."

20

Mick's Plan

The president of the club was MIA for the entire first half of the show and not a few people were frustrated, even angry about it. Nobody, not even Margaret, knew of his whereabouts. Some reported having seen his Land Rover leaving the parking lot at around 7:30 a.m. The assumption was he was on his way to the show site. When he didn't appear, that's when the rumor mill flourished. Some reported Mick had abandoned the show because his injuries were far more serious than anyone knew and he'd gone to the hospital. Others said Mick was indulging in a "pity party" and had gone to a bar to drown his miseries. One person claimed to have seen him stumbling across the parking lot towards his Land Rover with a brown bag in his hand. Others said Mick was terrified of Charlene and went into hiding. Then there were those who felt badly and said the poor guy had probably fled home. "Wouldn't you if you had been attacked twice and looked like a train had slammed into your face?" Still others declared Mick to be an irresponsible and selfish man and Margaret a fool to have picked him to be president in the first place.

Margaret squirmed under the weight of that one and, as she stood in the ring beside the judges, writing down each of the judge's individual critiques of the puppy, youth and open classes, she contemplated sending out a death prayer to Mick for dragging her into the rumor mill with him. He had no right to cast such a light on her!

As she tried to concentrate on the job at hand, she could feel the accusations flying through the air and stabbing into her chest, around the same area of her breasts that was already tender from hugging the clipboard. Mick's absence was interfering with her right to bask in the glory of being the first official scribe at her first national. He was a selfish, selfish man and she would make damn sure his presidential ship was sunk ASAP!

―――――

The good news was that at least Mick knew where he was and what his plans for the day were. At 7 a.m., after his brief examination on the status of both his face and his self, which left him a little shaken, he joined the judges in their room for a brief meeting, alone. Then, by 8 a.m. he was seated at the back of the room in the basement of a nearby Unitarian church. What he needed, before he could do anything else, was a strong dose of honest emotion mixed with the raw and sometimes gut wrenching details of the day-to-day struggles of an addict, along with a half a dozen cups from the endless tank of warm coffee—industrial strength. By 9 a.m., he had shaken the hands of fifteen strangers whose candor and courage had put his weekend of folly into a healthy and manageable perspective.

By the time he arrived at the showgrounds and unloaded the technical equipment he had picked up, it was 1:00 p.m. and the two judges were taking their leave for lunch before beginning the championship class, and then the final showdown of all winners from all classes. They both looked his way as they were being escorted to the Gremlin. He waved. They waved back. Margaret turned towards him and released a sharp and jagged arrow of outrage.

Unfortunately for Margaret, her impeccable accuracy was no match for Mick's renewed sense of purpose. He simply smiled. His brief tête à tête with the judges at 7 a.m. had been fruitful. What he had discussed with them was his desire to have the final rounds of the show broadcasted right from the judges' mouths through a pair of loudspeakers, ringside. That way everyone could hear firsthand what the two judges had to say about each of the dogs. He'd explained to them that he believed this would take out the middleman, so to speak, and allow for a more open and honest dialogue both during and after the show.

The judges responded positively which suggested to Mick that they were very likely aboveboard individuals—not always the case with judges. He then asked them to keep it under their hats until the very last minute. Their cue would be when he announced the plan. He explained that such a change of plan would probably cause a bit of a stir and he just didn't want people to have time to turn the stir into "a scene." That's when he pointed to his face as an example of what was possible. Pedro and Claude chuckled knowingly. They were no fools! They may have been sequestered from the follies of the weekend, but they were a far cry from ignorant regarding the alarmingly stupid and underhanded behavior dog exhibitors and breeders were capable of. They said "nonsense activity" happened in Europe as well and they would be happy to assist Mick in his attempt to bring more "respect and honesty" into the show ring. Mick also told them he would take all the responsibility for this action if the BOD were to come down on them anyway, but he doubted they would because they would look mighty stupid now, wouldn't they? The three of them shared a second chuckle and Mick took his leave. His presidency was beginning to show hints of a dictatorship, but by the time all was said and done, he could live with that.

―――――

During the hour and a half lunch break, some people went back to their hotels to grab a bite and walk their dogs, some stayed on the grounds, picnicked, and walked their dogs, while others simply paced and/or engaged in anticipatory chatter while their dogs stayed tucked away in their crates.

Mick's setting up of the equipment was given little attention, which he was grateful for. He guessed the reason was that people were so stirred up they didn't have one erg of energy left to give to their beat-up president who had finally shown up.

"So, Mick, can I ask you something?"

Mick was putting the final wire into place. The equipment he'd managed to gather from the hotel was not cutting edge but it would do the trick. He looked up. Standing over him were Stella's young sidekick, Lisa-Lee, whom he knew by sight but had never talked to, and Billy, the young man who had been so enthusiastic in helping him dig up the equipment he needed. "Sure," he responded, "you can ask me anything—but be warned, all you'll get from me are honest answers." He smiled and stood up.

"Well, first off, Billy says he thinks you're pretty cool and you don't seem the least bit like the person Stella says you are, so I was wondering why Stella says those things." Lisa-Lee sat down cross-legged on the grass beside the speaker. Billy sat beside her.

Mick surrendered to the pull to join the young ones in their powwow and sat down beside them. "Well," he said, "I don't know what she's told you about me and I really don't care." He looked across at the two of them. He figured them to be at least twenty years his junior and that, along with their attentiveness and genuine curiosity, made him feel somewhat Uncle-like, in the best sense of the word. And just as Lisa-Lee was about to launch into the litany of Stella accusations, he held up his hand to shush her. "Before you fill my ears with things I'd rather not hear, why don't you let me ask you a couple questions?"

Lisa-Lee and Billy looked at each other and shrugged.

"OK," said Lisa-Lee.

Mick nodded. "So, is this the first time you have had any doubts about what Stella has told you about anyone?" He was wishing this could be a longer conversation than he had time for. In about fifteen to twenty minutes, or less, people would begin gathering again.

"Well..." Lisa-Lee hesitated. She wanted to be careful because she knew Stella didn't like Mick, but she also knew Stella had only met him once, and only in passing. What she did know was that Billy had been quite taken with him, which was what had motivated her to approach him. "Yes and no," she said, as she started pulling at the grass and tossing the blades to the side. "What I mean is, sometimes I believe some of what she tells me and toss the rest. I mean, I know she can go a little overboard, but that's just who she is." Lisa-Lee glanced up at Mick. He didn't seem drunk or the least bit perverted. "She saved my life, you know."

"Oh, really, how'd she do that?" Mick felt Lisa-Lee's need for him not to rip into Stella. In the first place, that wasn't his style, and in the second place, he knew it wouldn't be effective. It was that middleman thing again.

Lisa-Lee kept tugging at the grass. "She helped me get away from Ron and Jimmy—my Dad and my boyfriend. Nobody else would help me because it was a tiny town and everybody was scared of them, especially of my father. Or maybe nobody cared. I'll never know now, will I?"

She tossed a final fist full of grass on the ground in front of her and looked over at Mick. "Stella knew from the minute she saw me that I was, as she put it 'a victim of a livin' hell' and that's just what she said to me when I was waiting on her in the diner.

"She also told me that I was beautiful and being wasted in that diner and that there was a better life waiting for me. I didn't think anyone noticed or cared anymore and she came along and saw how beaten down I was and offered me a chance to get out. I didn't think I would ever do such a thing, but there was something about her that made me feel more different than I ever felt before. She's stronger than any woman I ever met."

Mick observed Lisa-Lee closely as she spoke. She was, indeed, beautiful and Stella, regardless of her reason, had done a good thing—so far. He wanted to be careful.

"Well," he said, "from everything I've heard Stella is about as tough as they get—I have no doubt about that. I'm glad she helped you get out. Is she also helping you find what you want to do with your life?" He had heard Lisa-Lee's story a hundred times in AA—young, beautiful, and trapped by a thousand malignant arms. He wondered if she would find her way out before she ended up in a church basement or much worse.

Lisa-Lee, though sitting down, was more than prepared to jump up and walk away. This man was nothing to her, nor was his opinion. She remembered what Billy had said to her: "Mick's different, you know. I mean, he doesn't seem crazy, like the rest of these people. You know, different like you say Stella is; only he doesn't go on and on the way she does. He's real straight about everything. I asked him why some people said he was a drunk. He told me he was a drunk, a long time ago, before he ever met any of these people and that staying sober was a day to day struggle that wasn't anybody's business but his own, and he said that maybe being around these people was just another one of his big fat mistakes." Lisa-Lee didn't say anything to Billy, but when Billy said this she felt a little scared, in much the same way that the existence of Greta made her feel scared. Then she got curious, against her own better judgment, and ended up sitting here talking to Mick.

As he spoke, Mick watched her grab onto another hunk of grass and rather than pull it, she held on tight. "I'm sorry, it's really none of my business, is it?"

Lisa-Lee let go of the grass and looked up at the battered and bruised face. He looked real ugly in that moment, except for his eyes. "Stella treats me good and she trusts me to take care of her dogs." She hesitated and looked back down, "I mean most of the time."

Billy put his arm across Lisa-Lee's shoulders. "Yeah, and she pays her good money too."

Mick looked at Billy. He liked Billy. His refreshing, bordering on angelic enthusiasm was nothing he'd felt at that age. By the time he was eighteen, life had become something to overcome, not to celebrate. He fought first by hitting the books, hard—and once that was done, and he was well on his way to success, he hit the bottle equally as hard. He wanted to tell Lisa-Lee that she would be better off right where she was, under Billy's enthusiastic arm, rather than caught in what he believed to be the predatory stranglehold of Stella Gale. But it was not his place to tell her that.

He put his hand over Lisa-Lee's, which had gone back to nervously shredding the grass. "You know, I'm glad Stella helped you get away from your dad and your boyfriend AND I have no doubt you have what it takes to find just what you need." He lifted his hand from hers. "And as far as the things Stella has said about me—well, maybe you could suggest to her that she talk to me directly about her concerns."

Lisa-Lee pulled her hand back and tucked it in close to her body. "OK, well, you know, me and Billy should go." She pushed Billy's arm off her shoulder and stood up. She glanced over at the speakers as she did so. "So what are they for?"

Mick shrugged. "I thought it would be very educational for people to have the opportunity to hear what the judges have to say about each of the dogs."

Lisa-Lee laughed. "I think that will go over like a load of mud!"

Mick laughed with her. "Yup, could be another of the big fat mistakes I seem to be so good at lately." He was relieved to see that she was not clueless about the nature of the world she was presently rubbing elbows with.

Billy looked at the two of them, a little puzzled by their laughter. "Well, I think it's a great idea," he said.

21

Way To Go, Mick!

Stella sat quietly in her truck sucking on a joint. Though she'd only left the showgrounds for a few minutes when they broke for lunch, she had intentionally left the impression she'd be gone the entire time. As she walked away from the ring and the chatter, she pulled in her wings, which was especially difficult seeing as it was show time. She then climbed into her truck, drove to the nearest Dunkin' Donuts, came back and parked beneath the shade of a large tree in the far corner of the parking lot. Of course, Bobby's outstanding job of making her truck stand out above the rest was of no help to her, so she countered it by perching low in the front seat, which considering her height was not difficult, even comfortable. That way the truck, should it be spotted, looked empty except for the barely noticeable stream of smoke that squeezed out through the slightly opened window.

As she settled in to keep watch over the big picture, she noted that the only people who never left the grounds were the Biffers. From where she sat, she could see Molly prancing around in circles behind the Biffer Pavilion with Tank at her side, over and over and over, round and round and round—about enough times, she figured, to make any normal person barf. And she could see Biff busying himself with getting the billion cameras and TV monitors squared away.

She chuckled to herself. *They is dead set on winnin' this thing and that'll be just fine with me.* She knew she could swoop down on them and put them where they belonged—which was nowhere in particular—about as easily as someone could take meat from one of them vegetarians, like Greta was when she first met her. The moment Greta popped into her mind, she thought back to when she and Bobby made a steak dinner the first night they had her. Greta told them it was real nice of them, but she didn't eat meat. Stella was unimpressed.

"I know all about you vegetable-only people and I think it's just about as dumb a thing as I ever heard. There are a bazillion people who would damn near sacrifice their firstborn to have a steak and here you are sayin' you don't want it 'cause you feel bad for the animals! Honey, animals kill and eat each other all the time—or ain't you noticed?"

That's when Greta explained to her all the horrible things people did to cows and chickens and pigs long before they slaughtered them and that's when Stella almost became a vegetarian herself. It damn near made her sick hearing about it, so she started having conversations with the supermarkets about the treatment of the animals. "It ain't right and if I'm gonna go back to eatin' meat I want to be damn sure they had a life worth livin' prior to them getting' their heads chopped off."

Not one supermarket would sign her paper guaranteeing her that, so for about a month she stopped eating meat. She made Bobby stop too, which was when Bobby considered taking up hunting. That's when she put her foot down. "Nobody in this house is going out into the woods and killin' anythin'. If I got to choose between animals that is already dead and the deers and the birds and the rabbits that are out there mindin' their own business till Bobby comes along with his big ole shotgun and blows a hole through their side, well, I'll take the already dead ones—case closed."

So they started eating meat again and somewhere around that time Greta started eating it as well, though it was never clear why. Stella figured it had something to do with her argument regarding them already being dead, but she wasn't sure. Greta could've just kept on eating corn and potatoes and beans, but with all her going to fancy restaurants with rich, lonely, and sex starved men, maybe it just didn't seem to have a place anymore in the big picture. Her little lecture regardin' the way animals were treated before the slaughter was not exactly something that would fly over a filet mignon at the Hilton. It would've lost them a ton of clients.

Stella took a long hit on her joint. Greta was a boatload of puzzling things back in those days and she still was. Her leaving like she did was just another one of those things that made no sense. But boatload of puzzle pieces or not, she had no choice but to take her back. It wasn't everyday..."

There was a sudden knock on the driver's window followed by a now familiar caw. "Stella!"

Stella cringed and tried to pull her wings ever tighter in hopes it would just go away.

The caw continued, "Look what I got!"

Stella sighed, took a long hit on her joint, and looked over at Mabel's face, which in another two seconds would have been pressed flat on the windowpane, a sight she didn't care to see. She turned the key and brought the window down. "What is it?! Can't you see I'm tryin' to grab me a moment of peace and seein' your face at my window ain't exactly conducive to my plan."

Mabel shrugged, then fell into a moment of silent shock when she realized she was growing accustomed to Stella's barbs. She held her new pair of binoculars in front of the window. "Look what I bought. And guess what? They're stronger than the ones Margaret has!"

Stella was incredulous. "Don't you know binocular season is over? There ain't no need for them anymore, that part is done and gone. The part that ain't done and gone is the part where I need to grab me a little peace and watch the eye pleasin' flow of the people comin' and goin' all full of wonderin' what's gonna happen next. There ain't no more to be done 'cept sit back and enjoy the ride."

Mabel was feeling feisty. "Well, did you see that Lisa-Lee and Billy had quite a long conversation with Mick? Pretty friendly I'd say. Mick even took Lisa-Lee's hand at one point. I watched the whole thing."

Stella wondered what had happened to Mabel since she left her standing with Red Sally. She thought to ask, but changed her mind, realizing nothing that came out of Mabel's mouth would have much meaning. "Here's a newsflash, Mabel, in case you ain't heard, Lisa-Lee can talk to whoever she wants to. I ain't her mama and, by the way, I ain't your mama either, so you got no business actin' all like you is rattin' on your sister to me. Hell, for all you know she was gatherin' more information. Did you even think of that? No, 'cause you got the brain of a person who left her show dog on the sidewalk a thousand miles from the show—that right there says you got no business spyin' on somebody who wouldn't have done that even if you paid her a hundred thousand dollars." She hesitated. "Well, maybe for a hundred thousand, but my point is, you can't hold a candle to Lisa-Lee's bright shinin' headlights—fact is, one of yours is broke plus you got no bright switch. Now, get your ass in here before you let the whole world know I'm here 'cause I ain't interested in talkin' to the whole world right now."

Stella watched in her side view mirror as Mabel crouched, pushed her butt towards the sky, and moved around the back of the truck. She snorted. Mabel looked about as stupid and suspicious as a person could look. She wouldn't be surprised if someone called 911 seeing her creeping around the truck like that. Then the next thing would be people and cops and flashing lights all around her truck and she would be forced, for the second time this weekend, to swallow a perfectly good joint. Mabel was a car wreck just waiting to happen—but, oh well—God had put her in front of her face for some reason or other. She just had to figure out what it was.

The passenger door opened and Mabel slid in onto the passenger seat. She was delighted to have Stella all to herself. "Who do you think is going to win, Stella? I mean, I know you want Oz to..."

"Honey, Oz ain't gonna win this show and I never intended for him to. I mean if he does it will be fine, I can handle it better than most, but you got to understand whoever wins this show—the first national show in the USA—well, it will be the same as paintin' a big ole sign on their back that says 'eat me alive.'

"I'm tellin' you, mark my words, the winner—which will be the Biffers—will wish they hadn't won, case closed. Now, I ain't gonna break my neck while showin' Oz. I'm just gonna be respectful and quiet and do nothing to draw attention to myself—'course, seein' as Oz is the best dog here, my doin' nothin' could win him the champion class and then Best of Breed—but that won't be due to anythin' I coulda done. The point being, the winnin' ain't in the winnin', if you know what I mean, which you don't 'cause you ain't been around me long enough."

She watched Mabel's face twist up in ways she didn't think were possible, then turned and looked out at the tree that held strong and steady next to her truck. "Just sit there and be quiet till the Championship class is called." She re-lit her joint and handed it over to Mabel. "Take some of this. It'll help you calm down."

Mabel ignored the offer and took up the binoculars with both hands. She would find something of interest to Stella if it killed her.

Stella sighed, "Suit yourself," then settled back in her seat. "I figure we got about ten minutes, so don't say another word unless there's an emergency, meanin' my truck's on fire or Charlene is on her way over here—outside of them two things, be quiet."

Stella crossed Mabel out of her mind and went back to watching the flow of people. As cars rolled back in and the lot filled up, she spotted the red sweater. She'd missed seeing which car she had gotten out of, but she was sure it wasn't like any other car there and if she took the time she could find it easy. Red Sally, or whatever the hell her name was, was a lady she would be talking with again, probably within the next hour or two, and by the time they were done talking, she would have Red's phone number and, more importantly, Red would have hers because Red would ask her for it. She figured the call would come within about two weeks.

Stella could tell Red Sally thought she was as smart as her, but she wasn't, nobody was. Red would just need a little more than what most of these dog people required— something she was actually excited about. It had been awhile since she'd been in this exact type of situation. Red wasn't interested in being Stella's friend or working for her or being seen with her, Stella could see that. What Red was,

was downright fascinated by the facts of being Stella Gale, meaning she was looking at something so fine she couldn't bear not to know everything about it, which to Red's way of thinking was the next best thing to owning it and adding it to her collection of fine things. And knowing the facts of being Stella was something she couldn't get anywhere but directly from the source. She figured the only reason a woman like Red was at this show was because she was deep down bored, like a lot of rich folks were, and what she liked to do was dip in and out of things that grabbed her attention to keep her from dying of that boredom. And the only reason Red could strut around the way she did was because of her money and her ability to suck the interesting off of people a billion times more interesting than she was, and when there wasn't any more interesting left, she walked on without looking back.

Stella took a last hit on her joint, then reached in her breast pocket for her cigarettes. Bored was something she would never be, thank God. What Red didn't understand, yet, was there was no end to the fascinating facts of being Stella, which meant in the end she would be done with Red, not the other way around. Being an object of desire for people who were very rich and bored was exactly what had once made her very rich and very not bored. If for nothing else, she sure could use a fix of those days about now and maybe even sell a few pups to Red for top dollar along the way.

She watched the red sweater disappear behind the Biffer Pavilion, which now had about a dozen yellow things hanging off the top of it, flapping in the wind.

"Mabel, give me them binoculars." Stella grabbed them before Mabel had a chance to think and looked through them. She chuckled. "I swear, them Biffers deserve an A, as in amazin'. They couldn't get anyone to wear their T-shirts, 'cept Charlene, so now they got 'em hangin' off their tent. I wouldn't be one bit surprised if Molly hangs herself from them ropes if she loses. Hell, maybe I oughta pull Oz from the whole show considerin' if he won I would be partly responsible for her body hangin' up there, flappin' in the breeze."

Stella then spotted Mick walking out into the middle of the ring with a microphone in his hand. She dropped the binoculars on to the seat beside her. "Looks like the show's about to begin. Let's go!" She smooshed her cigarette in the ashtray and stepped out of the truck.

———

Mick had taken off his army coat and replaced it with a brown suit coat, no tie. If not for the now extremely deep black and blue rings around his eyes, he might actually have felt a smidgeon of cool importance as he walked to the center of the ring. He looked out at all the eager faces. He was eager too, but only because he knew this would be the beginning of his last afternoon as president of the American Bordeaux Club.

He cleared his throat and tapped on the mike. "OK, folks, this is it. We are delighted to have gotten to this point in this, our first National show. It is a truly big moment for the Dogue de Bordeaux in this country." Mick paused as applause broke out and the speakers screeched back at him. "Sorry, about that, there seems to be a little bit of a feedback problem with the equipment. I'll take care of that momentarily, but first…"

The speakers screeched again and fell silent.

"But first, I want to announce that there has been a slight change of plan. As the proud president of the club, I have taken it upon myself to gather this sound equipment and set it up so that everyone will have the privilege of hearing everything these two fine judges have to say about each of the dogues that are about to enter the ring. I believe this will make this event all that much more extraordinary and I'm sure you feel the same."

He turned toward the judges who were standing ringside just under the club tent. "I want to thank the judges for being open to doing this. It is rare, indeed, that exhibitors get the chance to hear what the judges are thinking as they look at each dog. I am excited and look forward to this unique learning experience. Thank you."

Margaret had walked out into the ring as Mick started to speak and was standing at his side, glowing. She had been under the same impression as everybody else—the sound system was for the sole purpose of announcing the final event and then the winners. So, when Mick's change of plan hit the air waves, her smile instantly turned plastic.

Mick handed her the microphone, told her she was "up" and went to straighten out the feedback problem. He was so calm Margaret wanted to spit in his face, but she couldn't because her smile would crack if she did and who knows what she might do next? It was not a risk she could take.

She lifted the microphone to her mouth and, as she did so, watched people turn from her to each other. Their surprise was as great as hers. She then watched as the majority of the remaining exhibitors turned with their dogs and began the short walk back towards the parking lot shaking their heads. The Biffers, of course, were not among them. They were thrilled to see their competition walk away. And Stella—she just stood there, cool as a cucumber, with Oz at her side. Margaret knew in her heart of hearts that Stella was taking it all in and chewing on it with the satisfaction of a cow chewing its cud. She wished, in that moment, that Stella had choked on the joint she'd swallowed the previous day. She cleared her throat.

"Hello all, I don't know about you, but when Mick told me about this plan, a short while ago, I thought it was wonderful and I applaud him for his hard work in making this happen. What an opportunity it is for us to hear directly from these two wonderful judges, whose critiques I have noted throughout the day. I, for one, am very excited that you too will now get a chance to hear what they have to say about our wonderful breed and what each of our dogs has to offer. It would be so discouraging, if ANYONE thought for a moment that their dog was not up to being critiqued openly and publicly. I am proud of what we are producing in this country and I know you all are as well. So let's hear it for all of us!"

She clapped, followed by a handful of others and then almost everyone. That's when the exiting exhibitors, like a school of fish, turned instantly and headed back towards the ring. Several of them were nearly yanked over backwards as their dogs continued their joyous trot in the direction of their cars.

"WAY TO GO MICK!" Charlene's voice rose above the rest.

Mick looked across the ring at the painfully familiar spandex pants, topped by the same pink sweater that was now spilling out from beneath a tight yellow T-shirt that read, in red, "Go Molly, go Tank."

Charlene's left fist punched the air as she yelled.

Mick put his hand over his right cheek and turned away.

22

The Show

Mick settled into his navy blue lawn chair as the final four bitches entered the ring. These were bitches that had earned enough points in previous rare breed shows to be considered Champions of the breed. Chances were the winning dogue at this show, as in most, would come from either this, the female champion class, or the male champion class. However, it didn't always work out that way. On occasion there would be a dark horse from another class, usually Open Dog or Open Bitch. It was a rare occurrence, but always an exciting turn of events.

He studied the four bitches as they lined up in front of Pedro and Claude and felt a renewed sense of discouragement. Champions of any breed were supposed to be stellar examples of the breed, which meant they met the standard in almost every way from head to tail—meaning they were excellent specimens for the futurity of the breed. The bad news was that none of these Champions did that. The really bad news was he had yet to see any truly excellent dogues produced in the U.S., period. There were many factors involved in producing fine examples of any breed, among them ethical breeders motivated to responsibly breed according to the standard, a thorough and detailed knowledge of that standard, a firm grasp on the lines of their dogs, a keen understanding of the genetics involved, commitment to optimal health for their dogues, and trust that the kennel they originally got their breeding dogues from did the same. Pete had been one of those breeders and he not only had failed, but was run out of the breed for giving a damn.

Mick's original breed, the German Shepherd, had come into this country on a fairly good footing and was slowly destroyed over the years by those who felt a need to change the standard to the present one which, in his opinion, was god awful. From everything he knew and had observed thus far, the Bordeaux had come into this country on poor footing, meaning fairly poor quality and also in the hands of people who, for the most part, saw nothing other than an opportunity to make money. These people had no standards and no ethics, breeding or otherwise. Perhaps he was bitter after everything that had happened to Pete and had therefore lost all perspective—either way the writing was on the wall as far as Mick was concerned.

As he sat there, he realized that his decision to resign his presidency by midnight just might be the beginning of the end of his days as a Bordeaux breeder. It damn near killed him to think of this breed being left in the hands of the likes of Charlene and Stella, but their foothold was strong and their determination to blow up anything or anyone that got in their way seemed insurmountable—Stella being the more dangerous of the two because she was a whole lot smarter. They were setting the benchmark for both the character of the breeders and the standard of the breed, and as far as he could tell, the benchmark was six feet under the ground with no sign of hitting air anytime soon. He feared that in the years to come the Stellas and Charlenes would draw in more of the same and the Petes of the breed would be snuffed out in short order.

Mick sighed beneath his little cloud of doom and gloom— *"God grant me the serenity to accept the things I cannot change, the courage to change the things I can, and the wisdom to know the difference."*

He watched the judges move from one bitch to the next, occasionally broadcasting positives such as "sufficient wrinkle," "good angulation," "correct broad deep chest," and "typical movement." Not surprisingly, there was a noticeable lack of enthusiasm from outside the ring, though the exhibitors whose dog received any of these positive comments responded with a nod and a smile.

However, when the judges courageously, in Mick's opinion, broadcasted faults such as "lacking in angulation," "croup too low," "insufficient wrinkle," "insufficient chest," "too long in back," "poor condition," and "lacking in bone," audible grunts, snorts and chuckles were heard from both within and around the ring.

Mick briefly entertained the fantasy that the judges would step up to the plate and make it loud and clear that faults such as these should not exist in a class of Champions and that an audience of breeders that showed no genuine appreciation for the positive, and gained audible sustenance from the negative, should not be breeding dogs, but rather should go back into the dark alleys of greed, ego, stupidity, gossip, and lies from whence they sprang. But, no such luck! A bitch was chosen, followed by a quick round of applause, and then the judges moved on to the highly anticipated 'Champion Dog class' which included both Oz and Tank.

———

Molly took the lead and pranced into the ring with Tank trotting proudly beside her. The two of them covered the hundred or so feet quite quickly and then, in perfect sync, came to a sharp and sassy halt in front of the judges. As the judges took their first gander at Tank, she smiled broadly, pulled on Tank's leash to lift his head up and spoke to him in her most enthusiastic voice. "Look at Grandpa!" Pedro smiled politely, but Claude did not. Claude stepped back, tilted his head to one side and looked at Tank with a mixture of surprise and curiosity. And as the other four Champion dogs entered the ring, Claude did not take his eyes off Tank, not for one second. In fact, he moved in closer to him and began examining him in a way that not only caused Molly's smile to broaden but initiated the rather loud buzz throughout the crowd that Judge Montforte was completely taken with Tank. Charlene and Biff even began jumping up and down yelling, "Way to go Molly, way to go Tank!" at which point Mick took the initiative, walked out into the ring, and took the microphone from Pedro.

"Please! Folks, keep your comments to yourselves or leave the show site!"

Margaret's cheeks went hot as Mick walked back out of the ring. It was her job to have done that, but she'd been so caught up in the goings on that she had failed in the responsibility. She glanced around, but no one seemed to care, which sent yet another hot flush through her cheeks.

Judge Claude Montforte was oblivious to the stir he was causing. His inspection of Tank had taken precedence over all else. Even when the four other Champions were in line and ready for the judging to begin, he didn't stop. He looked to be a man obsessed. Mick had succeeded in shutting people up, but all eyes were on Claude as he knelt and ran his hands over Tank's head, ears, back, hips, legs and then leaned forward and inspected his chest so carefully he might as well have had a magnifying glass. Before long, he was on his hands and knees.

Stella was standing within two feet of Pedro who was watching his friend's unexpected and overly zealous examination of Tank. He wasn't saying a word. She looked around the ring at the hundred and fifty or so people who were riveted and spoke loudly enough that her voice was picked up by Pedro's microphone. "I'll have to remember them words 'look at Grandpa' the next time I show a dog. No need to learn a damn thing about the breed, just speak them words and you got yourself a winner—case closed." She laughed. She knew she was out of line, but this was one of those opportunities she just couldn't resist.

Claude suddenly jumped to his feet and grabbed the leash from the still smiling Molly. He turned to the crowd and spoke loudly and harshly into his microphone, "Je we hebben een groot probeem! Deze hond is een jaar terug gestolen van hans. Ik heb er geen twijfels over dat dit dezelfde hond is. Ik kan het zien aan de aftekening op zifjn borst, het wit op zijn linker achter poot en de scheur in zijn linder oor. Hans heft deze hond als vermist opgegeven teza men met deze beschrijving en fotos. Maar hij kreeg nooit enige reactie. Zijn hond is nooit terug gevonden!" He faced Molly again, his anger still mounting, "Maar dit is de hond, wat heeft je bezielt om deze hond te stelen en te showen het is een schande!!" He threw the microphone to the ground, turned from Molly, and marched toward the club tent with Tank held close to his side.

Molly stood frozen. Her smile had fallen to the ground, hard, along with the mike. What was happening?

Nobody moved, except for the dogues in the ring, who had grown suddenly restless in the face of Claude's behavior. When the microphone hit the ground, Oz had lurched forward, all four legs planted decisively, hair up. He then let out a singular roar as Claude took hold of Tank's leash and marched away.

Stella moved in next to Oz and patted his head until he settled down. She was taking it all in, every second of it. This was going to be good. She could feel it sure as the sun was still shining. She mulled over the words and selected the ones she understood "grut probleme, deze hond." She wasn't a language expert, but it wasn't hard to figure out from these words that there was a big problem with Tank, and oh, what she would have given for a video camera in that moment! She turned and searched the crowd for Lisa-Lee.

When she spotted her at the far end of the ring, she signaled for her to get the camera and start shooting. Billy was standing behind her. He lifted the camera victoriously in the air and nodded his head. That boy was good! He had gotten it all! Stella blew him a kiss and tossed her blazing red hair over her shoulder. Billy smiled back and ducked under the ropes with the camera.

Meanwhile, Biff had jumped the rope and was in the ring the moment Claude turned and yelled at Molly. He rushed towards Claude as he walked away, Tank in tow. When he got close enough, he took a long low dive for Claude's legs. He slid about five feet before making contact and when he did, Claude toppled forward, nearly landing on Tank who jumped out of the way, dragging Claude further forward along the ground with Biff holding on tight to his legs. The "Go Molly" on the front of Biff's T-shirt was covered with dirt and grass stains. The yellow had gone brown.

Mick didn't think. He was up and out of his navy blue lawn chair before wisdom or serenity had a hope. As Biff crawled up Claude's body to launch yet another attack on an unsuspecting face, Mick threw himself on top of the now stained yellow T-shirt and pulled Biff's arms from Claude's body. Claude crawled free as the two men engaged in their second match of the weekend.

Margaret watched in horror as the two men rolled across the ground exchanging punches. A voice sounded behind her.

"This is incredible!"

She turned to see the very same young man who had snapped her photo in front of the hotel three days earlier. His excitement drove into her like a dentist's drill. As he dropped to his knees, anxious to get it all from the best perspective possible, she leaned over and grabbed on to his camera. "You have gone too far this time! I don't know exactly what you think you're doing, but you need to leave the ring immediately!"

Billy pulled back as hard as he could on the camera but, rather than let go, Margaret hung on as if her life depended on it. She was no match for Billy's strength. The blue cotton dress, dark sweater and bun tumbled to the ground. As soon as she hit the ground Billy let go of the camera. He hadn't expected her to hang on like that, but it was too late. Margaret rolled across the ground, and as she did so, the bun came completely undone. He quickly picked up the barrette that had landed next to his right foot and handed it to her. She sat up, her brown hair falling down across her shoulders, and snapped the barrette from his hand. He felt terrible. "I'm sorry. I didn't think you would hold on like that."

"Well, I did, and now look at what you've done! This barrette is worthless without the pin. We have to find the pin. I never go out in public with my hair down—and don't you dare point that camera at me looking like this!" Margaret grabbed her hair and pulled it back off her face. She quickly scanned the crowd. No eyes were on her. It seemed no one had even seen her fall. The good news was she still had time to get her hair up before anyone noticed, but that was the only good news in this godforsaken mess. She crawled around looking for the pin.

Billy took up the camera and left her there.

Mick was straddling Biff's chest. He had Biff's wrists pinned to the ground. "It's over buddy, you need to calm down." He then noticed bloodstains on Biff's T-shirt and thought for a moment he had inflicted some horrible wound on the man—but he hadn't. It was his own blood, coming from his own nose! A familiar searing pain shot through his face and he burst out laughing. He laughed so hard he released Biff's wrists. Biff was so taken aback by the laughter that he simply squirmed out from under Mick and stood up shaking his head. That's when the black spandex and yellow T swirled out from beneath the Biffer Pavilion and tore across the ring, like the Tasmanian devil, towards the laughing president.

As the swirl of black and yellow moved across the ring, Stella unfurled her wings and grabbed the microphone from Pedro, who had yet to move, and handed him Oz's leash. "CHARLENE, GABE JUST CALLED AND HE NEEDS TO TALK TO YOU RIGHT NOW!"

As her voice roared over the airwaves, the Tasmanian devil came to a sudden halt.

Stella stepped in front of her, the microphone still at her mouth. "Now you hold up, Charlene. Gabe didn't really call, but we have us a GRUT PROBEEM—I heard it loud and clear, only we don't exactly know what it is now do we? Unless you know Dutch, which I doubt you do 'cause I ain't heard nothin' but twisted English come out of your mouth, then you are sittin' in the dark of night like the rest of us, which means you are attackin' without 'cause— Now I don't know Dutch either, but when I heard them words 'GRUT PROBEEM,' I knew exactly what that meant. It don't take a rocket scientist or a bilegal person. I mean 'GRUT' sounds pretty damned important, now don't it? And "probeem" speaks for itself. Now, I know our president is laughin' and that could be cause for concern, but you need to stop right here and wait until we know exactly what Judge Claude was yellin' about 'cause it ain't every day a judge goes crazy like that in the ring. Fact is, I ain't ever heard of such a thing in all of dog history, so I'm thinkin' he made history today and with good reason, and we need to hear what that reason is 'fore we get into what's lookin' to be World War Three!"

The crowd burst into a round of applause that caused Stella's wings to span the entire show site. Charlene released her fists and stood glaring at her.

Stella continued, "If you got somethin' to say, Charlene, here's your chance. I ain't gonna get in your way." She held the microphone up to Charlene's face. Charlene pushed the microphone with her hands and walked away. Stella flung one end of her crimson scarf around her neck and then the other. She continued, "OK, now I propose we get Judge Pedro here to turn on the light switch in this situation and tell us what all the noise was about." She walked over to Pedro, took Oz back, and handed Pedro the mike.

Pedro, though visibly shaken, drew in a deep breath and took the microphone. Before he spoke into it, he covered it with his hands and asked Stella if Tank was Charlene's or Molly's dog.

Stella told him that Charlene had bred Tank and sold him to Molly and Biff when he was about a year old. She watched as Pedro shot an angry glance in the direction of Charlene who was stomping towards the Pavilion. Stella was no fool, she knew this was going to be a bomb and the bomb was going to include Charlene—there was no doubt about that.

Pedro waited until Charlene stomped all the way back into the Biffer Pavilion and disappeared into the shadows. He then held the microphone to his mouth. "I am so sorry that such an incident has happened today and this is a very sad day for the Bordeaux and for everyone who loves this breed. My friend Claude has recognized this dog to be the dog bred by his friend Hans Hulbert. This dog disappeared from Hans at the age of one year old and he has searched for him for over a year with no results. His descriptions are exact and it is without doubt that this is the dog! I am very sorry to have to say this."

The crowd let out a singular gasp, then morphed into clots as people turned to each other to express their varying levels of shock and awe.

"OH NO, THAT CAN'T BE!" Molly who had remained frozen until that moment, her smile still lying flat on the ground, burst into tears.

Biff rushed out from the club tent and faced her, putting his arms across her trembling shoulders. She rested her head against his grass stained T-shirt and spoke softly to him. As she spoke, he looked toward his tent and the muscles throughout his arms and upper back slowly contracted. His already tight T-shirt grew tighter and tighter and the "Go Molly" logo grew very broad. He was fully prepared to do what was necessary to his newest enemy, woman or not!

The Biffer pavilion shook and his target emerged from its shadows.

Charlene tromped slowly and decisively towards Biff and Molly. She passed within three feet of Margaret, who was still on the ground, holding her hair with one hand and grasping her clipboard with the other.

Suddenly, there was a loud crunch beneath Charlene's heavy left foot and Margaret looked down. Her barrette pin had been found and crushed and snapped in two. She glared at Charlene as she tromped on, oblivious to her destruction of Margaret's last hope to regain her tidy public persona. Margaret struggled shamefully to her feet.

Charlene came to a halt and faced the distraught Molly and taut Biff. "He's a liar! Somebody paid him off and we all know who that was!" She looked decisively at Stella who was standing calmly with Oz who was now lying comfortably at her feet, content that she had the mayhem under control. Charlene continued, "That bitch will do anything to bring me down!

She turned to the crowd. "ALL OF YOU KNOW SHE'S BEEN AFTER ME FOR YEARS BECAUSE SHE'S JEALOUS!"

Oz lifted his head as he sensed the incoming fire.

Stella remained unaffected.

Biff looked from Charlene to Stella as Charlene continued her assault.

"I'M TELLING YOU, THIS WHOLE THING IS HER FAULT!"

Mick lifted his head. Charlene was about ready to blow. It was time to stop the madness. He took the wadded yellow

T-shirt off his nose. A fellow board member had pulled one of the T-shirts off the Biffer pavilion and given it to him to stop the bleeding. He got up from his chair and signaled to three board members who were standing near by. They followed him out into the ring. They surrounded Charlene. Mick spoke. "Charlene, you need to leave the ring right now! This is a very distressing turn of events and from what we have just heard you're the one with the big problem, not Stella or anyone else."

Charlene curled her hands into fists and growled, "Oh no, Mister Mush Face, you're the one with the big problem. You are holding my dog and I will sue you and your puny little club if you don't hand him over right now!"

The three board members who stood with Mick looked quickly around in hopes that an escape hatch would suddenly appear. Mick looked at them and felt incredulous for the thousandth time.

Biff turned abruptly from his tender moment with Molly, inadvertently pushing her to the side. She stumbled slightly, but caught herself. "Tank is my dog, you dumb broad. I paid you thirty five hundred dollars for him and if this is true that you stole him, I will sue you for every goddamn thing you own!!!"

Charlene's nostrils flared and the stiff strands of partially bleached hair shook, "Oh yeah, Mister Muscle? You won't get shit from me! I am done with your game! It's time to tell the truth, don't you think? You two are the biggest criminals of all! You paid me big bucks—Gabe will vouch for that—to go to Europe and steal a good dog. You told me the Europeans will never sell anything but shit to America and I agreed!"

She turned to the people. "NOTHING BUT SHIT, FOLKS, THAT'S ALL EUROPEANS WILL EVER SELL US! I WENT OVER THERE AND GOT THE FIRST GOOD DOG TO EVER HIT THIS COUNTRY—AND HERE'S THE FUNNY PART. I DIDN'T STEAL HIM. I BOUGHT HIM. HANS SOLD HIM TO ME BECAUSE HE SAID HE WANTED TO DO A GOOD THING FOR THE BREED OVER HERE. HE SAID HE KNEW WE WERE ALL GETTING SCREWED! AND HE TOLD ME TO GO AHEAD AND MAKE IT LOOK LIKE I BRED HIM AND NOW HE'S CRYING

ALL ABOUT HOW HIS DOG WENT MISSING JUST TO COVER HIS TRACKS."

While Charlene was screeching, Stella roused Oz and together they strolled over to Pedro who was still holding the microphone. She gently peeled his fingers from their tight grip and took it into her possession.

The screeching continued, "THE EUROPEANS ARE SELLING US CRAP AND SOMETHING NEEDS TO...."

Stella held the mike right next to her mouth and hissed into it low and loud, "CHARLENE!"

The screeching ceased.

Stella pulled the mike back a bit and continued in a more official tone, "You need to stop right now! You are diggin' a hole deeper than I ever saw. I mean I have heard of diggin' a hole clean through to China but I ain't never seen a hole that deep till now. It's amazin' how you hear about somethin' that don't seem possible and the next thing you know you are lookin' at it! And, aside from diggin' yourself the deepest hole in the history of the world, you are buildin' the tallest pile of bull crap I ever saw and that ain't includin' the part where you say I paid the judge. That right there deserves its own special place in the giant book of world record bull crap piles!"

There was an audible chuckle from the crowd.

Stella turned towards them. "I suggest we all chip in and buy Charlene here a ticket back to Europe so they can tell her exactly how they feel about her insultin' their good nature."

Mick recovered from his incredulity long enough to walk over and take the mike from Stella. "OK, thank you, Stella. I think we get the gist of your words of wisdom. What we need to do now, is get on with the show. This has been an unforeseen and unfortunate interruption that will be handled elsewhere, between the parties involved. There's no need for it to take up any more of our time. I suggest we all take a ten-minute break and then get back to the reason we're all here. Claude and I will be excusing ourselves for obvious reasons, but I will see you all at the dinner tonight. Meanwhile, Margaret and the rest of the Board of Directors will be available to handle any concerns you may have."

He dropped the microphone from his mouth and looked over at the gaggle of board members who yet again looked to be searching for a way out. He was disgusted by all of them, by the whole kit and caboodle. It was no accident that he immediately handed the microphone back to Stella. As he walked back to the club tent to collect his things, the irony of it made him chuckle, painful though it was.

Margaret had gotten up and whisked by him, her hair flying through the air like it hadn't done since her mother had pulled her from the swing at age eight. "Margaret, you look just like a little witch on a broomstick with your hair like that! Only little girls who are pretty can have long hair and let it down. That's not for you, Margaret. How many times do I have to tell you this! Don't ever take the rubber bands out again or we'll just have to cut it all off. You simply cannot afford to let anything come undone with what God gave you!"

Stella smiled as Mick handed her the microphone and walked away. The whole world saw it, clear as day. The president of the ABC had handed HER the microphone. He didn't hand it to any one of the board members who were standing nearby, but to her. It was one of those signs from God that she counted on, on occasion. She put one hand on her hip, loosely holding Oz's leash, and calmly lifted the microphone to her lips. "OK, now Pedro here is..."

That's when Margaret whisked up and grabbed the microphone—hair be damned!

Stella took a step back, not recognizing Margaret at first. She'd seen her with her hair down before, but only once and that was when Margaret was hunched over the bed in her hotel room, crying. She hadn't seen her with her hair down while standing upright and with a blaze in her eye like she'd never seen before.

She snapped at Margaret as the microphone left her hands. "What the hell is wrong with you?! Goddamn, you scared the shit outta me! You need to rethink what you're doin' here, Margaret—that is YOU, ain't it?—'cause you might just scare the crap outta all these folks. Now, I don't scare easily, but you just shook me clear through and out the other side. What do you think..."

"Stella, I'll be damned if you're going to take over MY show. Now you better back off and let me deal with this!" Margaret stepped briefly outside herself and took a look back. She was magnificent!

Stella remained stuck on the blaze in Margaret's eye. It was a temporary blaze, she knew that, but it was a blaze nonetheless, and not something to take lightly or forget about.

As Margaret lifted the microphone to her lips, Stella reached out and put her hand over it. She spoke in a low growl, "Go on ahead, whoever you are under all that hair. My mission is accomplished, as in I got nothin' more to do here. It's gonna take a hell of a lot longer for you to put this mess back together than to put that mess hangin' off your head back into that ball! I will make sure of that—we're talkin' years, honey." She took her hand off the microphone and spoke loud and clear. "And remember, it was me who was sharin' a joint with you back in YOUR room when you nearly got busted! I saved your ass, as usual."

"That joint was yours and you know it!" As Margaret's response boomed out from the loudspeakers, her momentum was shattered. She flushed and glanced out at the chuckling crowd. She quickly put her hand over the microphone and turned to give Stella a final word, something she didn't have yet, but hoped she would find. Stella was gone. She turned to see Stella striding out of the ring with Oz at her side, the long arms of her crimson scarf swaying gently back and forth across her back.

———

The show went on without Claude, without Mick, without Biff and Molly, without Tank, and without Stella and Oz. The Best of Breed award from the first ABC national show went to a bitch from Open Class named Maxine. Maxine had been bred by a couple no one had ever heard of, or met—Otis Washington and Cindy Gill from Trout Point, Michigan.

Lisa-Lee, who up to this point had simply stood and watched all of it, made it a point to gather all the necessary information from Maxine's owners to pass on to Stella who would add their names to her ongoing list of *Get to know asap*.

Of even more importance was what Billy had to offer. When he'd finally caught up with Lisa-Lee, he danced around her for a good five minutes waving his camera in the air. He then bragged, in a manner she was unused to from men, about how skillfully he had crawled around in the middle of all it. To Lisa-Lee it was as if Billy had found a shiny penny on the sidewalk and felt like the luckiest boy in the world.

In her old life, a man bragging was more often than not a blustery chest thumping followed within minutes or hours by a beating and/or a string of abusive language—"you dumb bitch," "worthless piece of shit," "only your asshole is worth fucking," "my cock in your mouth is the only time you're good because then you can't say a word and I don't have to listen, and when you swallow my cum like a good girl, you get the only thing you deserve!"

Lisa-Lee smiled as Billy danced around her, beside himself with glee. Once he calmed down, he announced to her that he was either going into the film industry or journalism.

"I am done with Hotel Management and will do whatever it takes to get to where I want to be." He handed her the camera and kissed her on the cheek. "And I want you to be with me Lisa-Lee. I'm crazy about you!"

And she was crazy about him.

Lisa-Lee felt the squeeze of an impending dilemma as he took her hand and they headed back to the hotel.

———

Mabel had watched the whole show from behind the Biffer pavilion. In her mind, Stella was no less than a superstar. She stood out above the rest, unflustered by any of it. It was as if she had planned everything that had unfolded. When Stella walked out of the ring, Mabel rushed to her side. "You were wonderful, Stella!"

Stella stopped and looked at her. "And where were you?"

She pulled her cigarettes from her vest pocket. "Never mind, I'm guessin' you were hidin' somewhere, which is exactly what you don't do 'cause these is the very situations where you make your mark, in this case MY mark."

She lit her cigarette and offered one to Mabel for the first time.

"No, thank you, I don't smoke."

Stella put the pack in her pocket as she blew smoke into Mabel's face and looked past her. "Suit yourself! Now, what I got to do is get back to my room before I get swarmed by people like you wantin' to have a little sip of what I got. Mind you, under normal circumstances, which these ain't, I would be more than happy to stick around—but the best thing in this here circumstance is to make myself disappear till the dinner tonight. Sometimes it's best to leave the people wonderin'. Besides, between you and me, I need time to gather all the information, some of which is on its way to my hotel room right now in the form of Lisa-Lee, so I can make a accurate assessment of what we was just lookin' at—one thing bein' the beginnin' of the end of Charlene, the end of that beginnin' bein' what I'm real interested in—that, and a whole lotta of other beginnin's of the end and beginnin's of the beginnin's."

Mabel stood for a moment as Stella and Oz walked away then hurried to catch up. Her decision to do so was twofold. First, Stella had just said "between you and me," which was a personal victory. Secondly, she couldn't bear the thought of Lisa-Lee alone with Stella, not while she was around. She'd do whatever she could to take some of the shine off of that little bitch. She squirmed as the word *bitch* flew through her and was gone like it had never been. She caught up with Stella and stepped in beside her.

Oz's eyebrows rose and fell.

23

We Can Bury Her When You're Ready

Bobby stopped the tractor for no apparent reason and looked around. He'd driven to the perfect spot without thinking about it. He'd assumed it would take him a while, considering he couldn't concentrate or breathe very well, but here he was. He'd stood on it so many times it had become a part of him, like his hand or his foot—and when was the last time he had to think about finding either one of them? He managed to squeeze out a soft chuckle, despite the cinch that was pulling across his chest as he got off the tractor.

He walked about ten yards and turned and faced the five separate running fields. It was from that very spot he'd seen the change in Gracey the previous day. He saw it in the way her front legs reached across the ground when she ran. It was as if her paws had grown slightly heavier than usual. And when she sat in the far corner of the fields watching all the other dogs, a thing she did many times in a day, she never once lifted her head real high like she always did. None of it was something he'd felt was worth jumping up and down about, particularly because she'd had herself a litter of pups. For all he knew, it could've been the six weeks of raising them that was causing what he saw, which was why he'd just left a note for Annie rather than take the time to seek her out. Little did he know that note would start something in Annie he'd never seen before and that Grace would be dead within a matter of hours.

As he walked back to the wagon, he recalled Annie standing in her T-shirt, her face twisted into someone he no longer recognized. "What have you done to me, you bastard?"

His chest tightened more. He took as deep a breath as he could, grabbed the sharp shovel from the wagon and started breaking into the earth beneath his feet. He went from one shovelful to the next, breathing, sweating, digging, lifting, heaving, digging, breathing, lifting, heaving, sweating, digging, and lifting.

As the earth piled up, his thoughts turned back to Gracey and how sometimes he saw things in a dog a long time before it ever came to be anything. Stella claimed he had a gift for seeing when a dog was in trouble. "Outta the clear blue sky, Bobby can tell exactly which dog may or may not be havin' a problem today, tomorrow, or next month—don't ask me how, it's just a gift he has, which is damn lucky for him 'cause I would have no use for him if all he did was build fences all day. That, right there, is worth keepin' him around for."

Bobby was fine with Stella thinking he came up with these things "out of the clear blue sky." There wasn't much else she bragged about regarding him anymore, so he let it be. He once tried to explain to her that he spent time every morning and in the late afternoon—when the dogs were in the fields—to sit and watch each and every one of them. She knew the truth of the situation, which was that it was his years of being around dogs and watching them that gave him the gift, not God. Ever since he'd had the companionship of Do-this and Do-that, back in the foster home, he'd taken it upon himself to keep an eye out for animals, dogs in particular—dogs on the street, dogs in parks, the dogs that belonged to the prison guards, and the dogs he and Stella had long before the kennel. He could see things in an animal that most people never took the time to see.

He had, on occasion, walked up to total strangers and told them their dog was in need of one thing or another. Sometimes they ignored him or got angry, sometimes they appreciated what he had to say. It didn't matter to him one way or the other how they felt—he was doing it for the dog. It was the least he could do to give back what Do-this and Do-that had given him.

He was now waist deep in the earth, and the piles of red dirt rose higher than his shoulders. He straightened up and took a moment to suck in on the cool damp that now engulfed him. As he did so, it loosened his chest a little, allowing him to breathe more freely.

His thoughts turned back to Do-this and Do-that and he wondered what happened to them after he left. He chose to leave. They never had that choice, so the life they had was not one he cared to know about. *Fact is, they probly never saw a field in their whole life—and they's dead now, like Gracey.* He started to dig again. Those days in that home of sleeping and watching TV with those two dogs were probably the only days they had with anyone who gave a damn.

He began to dig more furiously. Why didn't he take them with him when he left? He couldn't. It just never would have worked out for any one of the three of them. Do-this and Do-that would have ended up in the pound and he would have ended up in another foster home—either way they would have ended up in two different places.

He continued to suck on the cool damp that surrounded him, in and out, over and over, as he flung the earth higher and higher. It was the craziest thing, all of it—like one big damn circle. Here he was all these years later, choosing the company of dogs over the people he lived with, watching TV while not sleeping, and building things. The same three things that had made his life bearable in his foster home made his life bearable now. It was crazy, but it wasn't funny, not one bit.

He was now soaked with sweat, two kinds of sweat—the sweat of hard work and a cold sweat that he wasn't familiar with. The cinch in his chest began to pull so tight he almost lost his breath completely. He sucked in on the cool of the earth as hard as he could and began to dig again. The tension began to ease, but before long the dirt was tumbling back down on him and he had to stop. He'd dug so deep he could no longer throw it high enough.

He dropped the shovel as a spike of fear ripped through his gut. Much more than the red dirt of Georgia was falling in on him. He quickly pulled himself out of the hole and onto the piles of freshly heaved dirt. As he did this, his hands and legs trembled, not like when they were tired of doing what they were doing, but in an unfamiliar and unnerving way.

He rolled onto his back and allowed his body to be cradled in the cool piles of dirt, but the trembling continued. He burrowed deeper, throwing dirt across his legs and belly. Once covered, he lay as still as he could and frantically searched the sky. Even the familiar signs of the slow transition from night to day—the fading stars, the change of light from black and white to soft grey, and the emerging brown and green of the tree branches that reached towards him from the woods—none of it gave him a hint of comfort. The trembling would not cease. All Bobby Kansas could think about was beer and his new pal Jack Daniels, whom he'd taken up with since Stella had left him here with Annie. That was where he'd gone each evening until this last one, to the nearest bar to be with Jack—and that was where he wanted to be right now. Nothing else mattered. As for beer, this was the first time he hadn't had any in longer than he could remember. All day, every day, the steady slow trickle of the bottled brew had been a constant, ever since the day Annie left. The only period of time the trickle ever stopped was during the few hours he managed to sleep on the couch in the house or the cot in the cottage every night. Those few hours had now stretched out to at least eight.

He pushed himself to his feet and walked over to the wagon. He searched it, top to bottom, in hopes he'd left a beer or two somewhere, but there was none. It was all back at the kennel. Drenched in sweat and covered in dirt, he climbed onto the tractor and turned the key.

———

Annie stood on the front porch of the house and watched, with considerable annoyance, as Bobby approached the kennel. She'd been up for most of the time he was out there digging, fully aware that his plan had been for her to sleep through until morning in the front seat of his truck. "How is it you got the ability to sleep through anythin', Greta?"

Well, Bobby's little plan had failed because there WAS something she couldn't sleep through and he'd helped her find out what that something was—he'd left the truck windows tightly closed! The combination of the stagnant heat, mixed with the stink of dried blood and antiseptic solution, had overwhelmed her not long after he'd left her there. She'd woken up gagging at around 3:30 a.m.

Annie shook her head as she watched the tractor move along the dirt track. Even Annie Evans couldn't sleep through the stink of death! She wondered what exactly he had planned for when she woke up. Was it to keep hiding from her?

When Bobby's tractor disappeared behind the kennel, she looked out across the fields. The pre-dawn light could have transported her to anywhere, but it didn't. She looked back to where she'd last seen the tractor. When she'd climbed out of Bobby's hot stinking truck, she'd come up to the house to check on Bertha, who was not fine. She'd nearly knocked Annie over as she came through the front door, exuberant beyond her norm, then proceeded to do what she'd probably been doing the entire time Annie was gone, which was pacing back and forth between the bedroom, the study, and the front door. Bertha had clearly come undone by a night filled with so much that was out of the order of things, which included watching Annie crawling around the floor of Stella's study half out of her mind. It had taken this long to calm Bertha down.

Annie heard a short burst of barking from the kennel and then saw the lights come on. In that moment she knew, absolutely, it was time to have that talk—whatever it was—with Bobby.

Still dressed in her sweatshirt, jeans, and oversized T, she strode off the porch and headed to the kennel. As she approached it, the barking started up again. She opened the door and announced her presence, "It's OK everybody, it's just me—and, Bobby, wherever you are, we need to talk!"

The barking ceased.

Bobby was sitting up against the far wall next to Ivan's pen—the one dog she'd never gotten to know. He had a beer in his hand and another lying in wait by his thigh. Without looking up, he spoke.

"I dug the grave. We can bury her when you're ready."

Annie was taken aback. He looked small again, just as he had at the clinic when he was talking to Doc Burns. He was covered in dirt and looked more worn down than she'd ever seen him. Was this a boy or a man? Her anger was immediately suffocated by the possibility that whatever was going on, aside from Grace's death, was her fault and it just might be her job to make it right. She stopped short of acting on her impulse to drop down beside him and hold him. "Bobby..."

"Annie, I just want to have me a couple of beers and put Grace in the ground. There ain't nothin' more to be said." Bobby finished one beer and picked up another. The tremors were already easing, though his chest remained tight. "I got me a tightness in my chest that ain't quit since you started on me last night. And just so you know, I never did shit to you, so I got nothin' to say 'cept we need to bury that poor bitch 'fore sun up, which is real soon."

He gulped down half of the next beer, took a deep breath, and burped loudly.

Bobby's burp pushed Annie back into annoyance. "Bobby you've avoided me since I got back here unless, of course, Stella's around and then it's like a fucking time warp, as if I never left and nothing ever happened. Some days I feel as if I've done something terrible to you, but I know I haven't. However, Stella tells me differently. She claims I broke your heart when I left and she seems to think it's up to me to fix it." She sat down on one of the benches Bobby had built into the wall, about six feet across from where he sat. This was it, she was going to get this out and be done with it.

The dogs had all settled down, some watching patiently, some snoring. She looked at the ceiling, lifted her hands, and let them drop heavily onto her lap. "Have you thought at all about what it was like for me, after twelve years, to be chased from what I thought was my home by one of the two people I trusted?"

"No, I ain't thought about you all that much. In fact, I ain't thought about you at all, if you want to know the truth of the matter, and I got no idea why Stella told you that about how you broke my heart and all 'cause it ain't true." Bobby reached into his dirt caked shirt pocket and pulled out his cigarettes. "Goddamn, woman, my heart was broke long before I ever met you. You just ain't that special, darlin'." He shook the dirt from the pack and pulled out a cigarette.

Annie didn't speak. She was flabbergasted.

Bobby continued without looking up, "Why do you believe everythin' she tells you? Why would you runnin' off this property to save your ass break my heart?" He pulled his lighter out of his front pocket and snorted. "I gotta agree with Stella on one thing, for a smart woman, you are damn stupid." His heart felt cold as clay in that moment, but the trembling had stopped.

Ivan shifted in his pen. His grunts and sighs were too loud too ignore. He'd been lying flat on his side. He was now on his stomach with his massive head resting between his front paws. Bobby turned towards him. "See this dog here?" He put his hand on the pen and Ivan lifted his eyebrows. "Stella's scared of him. She tells everybody, includin' you, that he's just plain crazy and she don't know why. Do you know why she says that? 'Cause he goes nuts when she's around, which is most of the time, and I don't jus' mean here in the kennel. He's got antennae for her that reaches clear up to the front porch on the house. He ain't goin' nuts now, is he? Has he ever gone nuts on you, has he? I mean, when she ain't around?" Bobby looked at Annie for a split second—it was all he could manage. "Heck, this boy will roll on his back like a damn baby and let me rub his belly. I say he's got a good reason for the way he is and it all comes down to Stella. She done wore him out with her bullshit. He's so wore out that he just can't be bothered to be 'round the other dogs, 'cept Grace—she don't pull on him for nothin' and she got no bullshit, she just stops by to say hi."

He put the cigarette to his mouth and lit it. "Now, I know Stella's told you he can't run with the other dogs in them fields 'cause he'll tear 'em up, but that ain't true. He just wants to be left alone 'cause he's so wore out by her. He ain't no 'killer dog' like she's wantin' you to believe. She just don't like bein' the one he hates."

Bobby realized his chest was loosening a bit. He sucked in on his cigarette and exhaled. "Fact is, I think she's deep down scared of him 'cause he knows all about her."

Annie looked across at Ivan. Bobby was right in that she had never paid any attention to him because Stella had told her not to. She simply put food in his pen twice a day, and when she wanted to clean his pen, she just waited till he was out in his run and then shut him out until she was done.

As Ivan lifted his massive head and looked at her, his head cocked slightly.

"See, he's lookin' at you like he never seen you before. He ain't never taken the time to see you separate from her 'cause you ain't never given him the time."

Bobby drank down the other half of the beer and dropped what was left of his cigarette in it. "If you knew Stella had killed her own daughter and there was nothin' you could do about it, wouldn't you go nuts every time she came 'round?"

He felt completely relaxed, just like he imagined it would be to watch a ball game with a buddy he didn't have and their team was so far ahead, they had all the time in the world to talk about nothing in particular and drink beer.

Annie stopped looking at Ivan and turned to Bobby. "What did you say?"

Bobby just kept talking, low and neutral. "And I can't do nothin' about it 'cause she knows about my papa killin' my mama then shootin' hisself—blood was everywhere and I just stood there and did nothin'. Plus I got the history of violence. Ain't nobody would believe my word over hers."

"Bobby? Are you talking about Greta, her daughter who committed suicide?" Annie felt as though the bench Bobby had built was floating off the floor and out from the wall.

Bobby felt suddenly bored with the conversation they were having, but thought he'd push ahead since he didn't have anything better to do. "It wasn't no suicide. I was there. Stella, she came in the front door that night. Me and Greta was foolin' around in front of the TV, like we done a hundred times before—I was ticklin' her is all. Bam, Stella started screamin' holy hell—accusin' her daughter of bein' a slut. Greta, she burst into tears and ran out the house. Stella was madder 'n I ever seen her and I don't care to ever see her that mad again—she was even madder than when she ran after Annie that mornin', which is lucky as shit—a couple more notches up and Annie might jus' be lyin' in the ground with Greta and Grace."

Bobby reached into the fridge and pulled out another beer. He didn't even bother to look at his TV buddy. "See, Greta ran out the door and down to the barn. Stella runs out after her, still screamin' like a goddam' crazy woman. I sat there on the couch and did nothin' for a couple minutes. I guess I'm good at doin' nothin'. Then I got up and followed after them. I could hear Stella clear down in the barn, still screamin' on about what a whore Greta was and she weren't no good for nothin' and on and on. I walked real slow. I don't know why I walked so damn slow. I got to the barn door an' I opened it. Greta she was all curled up holdin' Stella's unregistered gun to her head—the one she took from her crazy bastard ex-boyfriend, and she was cryin' and Stella was still screamin'. "Pull the damn trigger, you little bitch, you ain't worth a damn to anybody! Hell, that gun ain't even loaded! How 'bout I get you exactly what you need, so you can do the job right and take your miserable self right outta my life!"

Bobby took a few gulps of beer and rested the bottle against his thigh. "To make a short story shorter, she climbed up, got them bullets outta my tool box, made Greta load 'em into that gun and next thing I knew the screamin' and cryin' got real loud. 'Mama, don't make me do it, I don' wanna do it, Mama!' Then the gun went off and the quiet that come after that was more quiet than any quiet I ever heard before, and Stella, her arms they stopped dead in the air—I couldn't see her mouth or nothin'—but I swear it musta still been open 'cause she wasn't finished with the garbage she was spillin' all over Greta."

He swallowed some more beer. "Greta was lyin' there with blood pourin' outta her head. That's when Stella's arms come down and I hear her say, 'bout as low and mean as a voice can get, 'Good riddance you little bitch.' Then she turned 'round and sees me standin' there doin' nothin'—just doin' nothin'."

Bobby's boredom had become extreme to the point where if he didn't do something he thought he might just fall asleep. He looked across the kennel to the far window. The gray light was turning pink. The game was over. Their team won by a landslide. He turned to his buddy. "We got to get to burying Grace, the sun's 'bout to come up."

Annie was not looking for this, none of it. This was not the reason she had crawled desperately and angrily around the floor of Stella's study in the middle of the night. She was looking for truth, yes, but not this. Almost the entire time Bobby spoke, she had silently screamed at him to SHUT UP, but she heard him—every word—and she thought to leave a dozen times, but she didn't. And now, she felt stuck in mid air on a bench that it seemed he had forgotten to nail down.

Bobby slowly got up and pulled a six-pack from the fridge. He figured he'd be out there digging for a couple hours. He looked over at Annie who was sitting so still he thought maybe she'd gone to sleep, except her eyes were open. "Annie, we got to get a move on. This ain't no time for you to sleep." He waited for a response, but didn't get one. "I'll go along and get Gracey. You come on out there when you're ready."

Annie looked up as Bobby turned away from her and tucked his six-pack up under his arm. He walked slowly across the kennel towards the main door. Every head in every pen turned as he passed by. When he reached the door, she thought to call him back and beg him to please nail the bench back down onto the concrete so she could get off, but she didn't. She really just wanted him gone.

He walked out without closing the door fully behind him, which allowed for a large swath of morning light to reach in across the floor. The sun was up. She glanced over at Ivan, who was now quietly watching her. She made a note to take him out to the fields to see for herself who he really was. She then looked down the entire line of pens, both sides. Some of the dogs were standing, some sitting, some lying down, but all eyes were on her. She sat and she sat and they watched. She was desperate for anger and doubt to rush in and tear every bit of what Bobby had told her to shreds, but they didn't. The only thing she was aware of was if those dogs weren't there watching her, she would be utterly without meaning. Finally, the bench settled and she stood up.

A symphony of paws shook the fronts of the pens. Their day had begun.

- 24 -

Ivan Runs Free

Once Bobby walked out of the kennel and into the morning light, it was the dogs that had kept Annie from sitting stone cold on that bench for eternity. As they pawed at their metal gates, she rose up, by no will of her own, and walked to the pile of bowls that were stacked beside the food bin. She filled the bowls and walked them, one by one, to each of the pens. She moved slowly and deliberately. When she was done putting down their food, she walked over and picked up the broom. As the dogs ate she swept, and as she swept, the mission of clearing away every speck of dirt from the kennel floor became paramount.

It wasn't until the clamor of empty bowls and demanding barks could have been heard from as far away as the Cranshaws' that her singular focus was broken. In a flash of rage, she turned and swiped the broom across the counter by the utility sink, knocking a pile of unused bowls to the floor. As they banged onto the cement and rolled, she shouted, "SHUT UP, WILL YOU PLEASE JUST SHUT UP!!"

The entire kennel fell silent.

"CAN'T YOU FUCKING SEE I'M BUSY? JUST LOOK AT THIS FLOOR!" She looked wildly around from one dog's face to the next. "LOOK AT THE GODDAMN MESS YOU'VE MADE!"

Some of the dogs appeared shocked, some curious, some duly impressed. Some stayed standing, some sat, some even laid down, but they all watched her carefully, all except Ivan who had turned and sat facing the back wall of his pen. He wasn't interested in any of it. She looked at him and remembered what Bobby had said. "Stella's scared of him. She tells everybody includin' you that he's just plain crazy and she don't know why. Do you know why she says that? 'Cause he goes nuts when she's around, which is most of the time…"

Annie dropped the broom and walked over to Ivan's gate and opened it. All eyes remained focused on her.

As she stepped into his pen, Ivan didn't turn to look at her, but rather flicked his ears back to catch the sounds of her entering. "Hey, Ivan, we've never talked—you and me. I'm sorry about that little outburst, but I'm tired, like Bobby says you are. You really trust him, don't you?" She shut the gate behind her and sat down with her back up against it. "Bobby says you're sweet and gentle."

Ivan stayed seated, his ears twitching as she spoke.

"Was Bobby telling the truth? Do you smell it in her?" Annie leaned her head back against the metal gate and sighed. "I don't know what I feel except that I just went nuts myself, didn't I?—just like you do every time she's around. I know, I know, she's not here now, but unlike you we humans can have somebody around even when they're not. I suppose if you could do that you'd be dead from exhaustion, eh? Well, I should be dead—sometimes I wish I was. I have people with me all the time, right in here." She lifted her head off the gate and pointed to it. "Mostly it's those people who make me feel lonely and nuts, and maybe I'm both."

She pulled her legs into her chest, wrapped her arms around them and rested her chin on her knees. "Stella could have made my wish come true, you know. She had the gun. Maybe if I knew she was serious, I wouldn't have run and you know why? Because I trusted her like a mother and if I knew my own mother really wanted to kill me… well… why go on living?" Her throat tightened and tears pressed up around her eyes. "I know how mean she can be, I'm not so stupid that I don't see that, but I never thought she meant her meanness. I thought her meanness was just, well, her awkwardness with…I don't know…I mean…"

"Annie, you broke your father's heart. You broke all of our hearts."

Annie's tears came, slowly and tentatively. She answered the voice in her head out loud. "But Mom, don't you believe me? What he did to me?"

"Annie, he's dead now. Isn't that enough? I believe you believe he did those things. I find it all very sad. I hope you find what you need."

Annie's tears stopped as she pushed her face onto her knees.

"He's dead. Isn't that enough?"

Her mother's voice receded as an image of Stella standing over young Greta spilled into her mind. *"Pull the damn trigger, you little bitch, you ain't worth a damn to nobody."* She started to tremble as she hung over a dark hole that was a thousand miles deep. She then heard Stella's voice, just as Bobby had described it, low and mean. *"Good riddance, you little bitch!"*

Whatever had been keeping her from falling into that hole let go. She didn't flail or cry or scream, she just froze and dropped like a stone. As she dropped, she felt a sudden warmth brush across the top of her head and thought this must be the way it was meant to be, she was supposed to give in to the inevitable and drop into nothing.

Then, suddenly, something grabbed hold of one of her feet and she lifted her head. Ivan's giant warm muzzle was right there, inches from her face.

He moved in closer as she looked at him. The hold on her foot grew tighter. She glanced down. He had inadvertently planted one of his front paws squarely on top of her boot. His whiskers tickled across her face as he sniffed her eyes, ears, nose, cheeks and chin, all the while warm air pumped rhythmically in and out of his nostrils. She tried to look into his amber eyes, but they were so close they were a blur. She waited.

When he was done, he slowly turned around and planted his hefty rear on top of both boots. He waited.

Without thinking, Annie reached out and stroked his massive back and the sides of his belly. When she stopped, he turned and looked at her as if to say, "Don't stop." She began stroking him again in earnest and he faced forward again, satisfied. She then leaned in, resting her chest against his back, her cheek against his neck, and reached her arms fully around him. She remembered Bobby's words, "Hell, this boy will roll on his back like a damn baby and let me rub his belly."

She stroked his chest then moved her hands to his belly and scratched, gently. He took a deep breath and his entire body vibrated as a contented sigh rolled out into the room. She followed suit and drew in her first deep breath in what seemed like days, years, perhaps since she was a little girl— and as she released it, she realized what Bobby had told her was the truth. It was not the truth she had desperately sought in the middle of the previous night, not a truth she had anticipated, but it was the truth nonetheless, and it was as immense as Ivan and as cold and hard as he was warm and gentle. She shuddered quietly.

The other dogs had grown restless once again. When they'd lost sight of Annie, they'd lost interest in anything but their own driving desire to be out in the fields where they belonged at this late hour.

When their barking and the clanging of empty bowls reached yet another ear shattering pitch, Annie responded dutifully. She pulled her feet out from under Ivan who was surprisingly unaffected by all the commotion. He simply lifted his rear as she reclaimed her feet and sauntered over to his bed, which was beside the door to his outside run. She turned and looked at him as he lay down. His eyebrows rose and fell. He was always the last to be let out and would simply wait his turn.

———

Annie released the dogs into the fields to run. She was in motion, but her heart was not. As she stood at the fence, she could see Bobby off in the distance filling the grave. The death of Amazing Grace was sad, she knew that, but she couldn't feel it. Her ability to feel anything had been diverted to her effort to digest the truth that Bobby had handed her. She didn't know what it meant regarding anything. It seemed her every move was now in question. And she had a lot of questions.

She turned and went back into the kennel. She grabbed one of the leashes that hung from the hook inside the door and walked over to Ivan's pen and opened it. He was still lying patiently on his bed. She called to him.

Ivan lifted his head and looked at her, quizzically. Normally, the door to his outdoor run would magically open from the outside once the other dogs were cleared from the kennel and he would trot out and get on with his day. Nobody would bother him.

She called to him again.

He dropped his head back down onto the bed. It was a trick and he wasn't going to fall for it.

Annie then walked in and clicked the leash onto his collar, "Come on, big boy, let's go visit your buddy." As she tugged on the leash, Ivan slowly got up and followed her, reluctantly, out of his pen and into the main room. She egged him on, across the concrete floor and out the door.

Once outside, Annie suddenly found herself skidding across the grass on her belly. She had to let go of the leash to save her arm. She then lay on the ground and watched as Ivan thundered down the dirt tractor path that ran alongside the five exercise fields. All of the other dogs stopped what they were doing and hurried to the fence line to watch Ivan the Terrible roar by. Each grouping ran with him for as long as their fence would allow, then stopped and cheered him on.

Bobby turned his attention from shoveling as soon as the dogs had started barking. "I'll be damned if that ain't Ivan."

Ivan was headed up the dirt track straight towards him. His massive head dropped lower and lower as he picked up steam. His shoulder muscles bulged as his front paws reached out and grabbed the earth, and his thigh muscles, rock solid from jumping up against his run fence, day in and day out, rippled as he pushed his massive body forward. His ears were down and back, flapping in the breeze. As he got closer, Bobby could see his jowls rise and fall with every lunge, his teeth appearing and disappearing.

Bobby dropped his shovel and sat down on the enormous pile of dirt that had yet to be tossed back into the grave.

Ivan began to slow as he approached the pile, but he hadn't begun soon enough.

Annie was sitting up by now, feeling about as foolish as a person could feel. Ivan hadn't been on a leash for most of his life and he'd never had the opportunity to be free. She was no match for the combination of his enormous mass and his desire. She wondered if he'd even felt the drag on his leash for the few seconds he'd pulled her across the grass. She watched as Ivan ran towards Bobby, who was now sitting on a pile of dirt. From where she was sitting, it looked as though Ivan barreled right into him. The two of them disappeared from sight.

Bobby rolled down the back of the soft pile as one of the giant paws pushed off his chest and continued on.

Ivan came to a halt about ten yards from the backside of the pile. He shook his head and turned back towards the little man who was sunken into the dirt.

Bobby burst out laughing as he spit dirt from his mouth and wiped his face. "Whoa there, buddy! We gotta teach you a little somethin' about how to control all that get up and go when you is free. I know all about that." He sat up and opened his arms as the gentle giant walked over and sniffed his face, tail wagging.

Annie saw the two of them reappear around the side of the pile. Bobby looked in her direction and waved. She smiled and got to her feet. If it had been anyone besides Bobby she might have been concerned. If it had been Stella, Stella might well be dead, which at this point Annie had no feelings about, one way or the other.

She started slowly down the dirt track. What would she and Bobby talk about when she reached him? Did he remember? And if he did remember, would he be willing to say more about it? The only thing that was certain to her, in that moment, was the dirt track under her feet and the green fields beside her.

————

Ivan had settled down beside the pile that was slowly shrinking as Bobby tossed the dirt, shovel load by shovel load, into the grave. His presence was an unexpected blessing in the midst of what was now looking to Bobby to be a whopping big mess. He had told Annie damn near everything, which was the whole reason he had avoided her in the first place. If it weren't for Gracey dying, it would all still be his private hell. *Well, it sure ain't private anymore, that's for damn sure, and no amount of shovelin' is gonna bury it now.*

As he threw each load of dirt into the grave, he kept an eye on the approaching Annie. Did he regret it? No, he didn't. He felt lighter than he had in years. But being lighter didn't mean he wasn't more scared than he'd ever been. In less than thirty-six hours Stella would be back and that would be when he just might wish he was heavier again. That might be when he wished he had stuck to building his fences, drinking his beers, minding his own business, and thinking only about what to build next. Maybe his project in the backfield should have been his only concern. Maybe he should've kept his eyes off the dogs and ignored his concern for Gracey—left her for Annie to find dead. That way he would've only had to take the body out, dig the grave and bury her. Then there would have been no need to spend time with Annie and there would have been no crazy desire scratching away at him, telling him to spill his guts out.

His attention to Annie walking towards him disappeared into the shovelfuls of dirt. Stella was coming home and all hell was going to break loose, he knew that as sure as he knew Amazing Grace was dead. It wasn't beyond his thinking that he would soon be a man with nothing at all, living in the same old black-and-white world he'd lived in before he met Stella.

"Bobby, we have to talk." Annie walked slowly up to the pile.

Ivan rose and greeted her enthusiastically. It was the woman who had set him free!

Bobby didn't look up. He continued to shovel as he spoke. "Now, them words is not real pleasant to my ears. I said my piece and now I'm thinkin' on how I should've kept my mouth shut and how you better not go blabbin' to Stella 'cause if you do, I will be in more trouble than you will ever come to understandin' and you will be out on your ass yesterday—or worse."

"Do you honestly think I'm that stupid?" Annie climbed up onto the pile, reached out, and started brushing the dirt off Bobby's backside as he continued to shovel.

Bobby put his shovel down and looked at her. "What the hell are you doin'?"

Annie hadn't been thinking about what she was doing. She stopped. "I was brushing the dirt off your back. Thanks to Ivan here, you look like Pig Pen." She let out a chuckle.

Bobby was not amused. "Like who? Pig Pen? Never you mind the dirt. It wasn't me that set him free now was it? If Stella was here, she'da given you all hell for lettin' him out like that."

Annie walked over to Ivan who had settled down again—utterly content with his newfound freedom and his newfound job, which was keeping watch over his people. She sat down beside him and began stroking his head. "Well, let's assume you're right about this boy, and I believe you are. If that's the case, then if Stella were here she'd be torn to pieces and the pieces would be lying in that grave with Grace. No, on second thought, she doesn't deserve to be buried with Grace. In fact, she doesn't deserve to be buried on the same continent. Hell, let's just throw what's left of her in the Ganges River and be done with it! Oh, no wait! We can't do that either, because that river is sacred. How about we throw what's left of Stella into the Amazon so the piranhas can devour her or maybe we should just chuck her into the Mississippi or..."

"What the hell is wrong with you, woman?" Bobby turned and sat in the dirt pile across from Annie.

Ivan rose up from his spot beside Annie and planted himself at Bobby's feet. Bobby patted the top of Ivan's head, then lowered his voice to normal. "This ain't no time to go on and on with all them words. Stella did nothin' to you, she done nothin' to me, she did a real bad thing to Greta, real bad, but it wasn't like it didn't have no history behind it. She didn't like that girl for reasons that you ain't never gonna understand and her not likin' her just got worse and worse as the years rolled on by till she exploded due to her thinkin' I was foolin' around with Greta in ways she got fooled around with before. It was a bad mess, I'll tell you that—but it's only gonna get a hundred times worse if she finds out you know all about it."

"What are you saying, Bobby? That killing her twelve year old daughter has good reason behind it?" Annie started picking up small stones from the ground around her and pitching them into the dirt pile beside Bobby.

"No, I'm sayin' you need to leave this well enough alone 'cause you got no idea!"

Bobby started picking up small stones as well, occasionally the same ones Annie had thrown, and tossing them back, hitting the ground beside her.

"Oh, I have an idea all right. Stella was her mother for Chrissake! Mothers are supposed to protect their children from harm, not kill them—or are you thinking I have that wrong?" She picked up a slightly larger stone and chucked it at Bobby's feet slightly scraping Ivan's rear. Ivan lifted his head and looked briefly at her, then settled his head back down between his paws, his ears twitching as the two of them spoke.

Bobby retorted, "No, you ain't got that wrong and while we're on the topic, fathers ain't s'pose to shoot their wives now are they? But they do, and fathers ain't s'pose to shoot themselves either, now are they? The part you got wrong is Stella wasn't in her right mind that night—she was crazy like I ain't never seen her, at least not till that day she ran out the house and blew that hole clean through your bedroom wall. Sometimes people just lose their minds long enough to do things they wish they never done and leave a mess that can't never be cleaned up, not in a million years and by nobody, no how. What's done is done. There ain't no point in bringin' it out in the light of day."

Annie picked up a fist sized rock. "And so, does that mean you think fathers who screw their little girls shouldn't be brought out into daylight and the mothers who know about it should be left to lounge around on the goddamn beach of denial? Why don't we just let the daughters bleed their whole goddamn lives, or better yet, let's just let the mothers shoot the daughters and be done with it, that'd be just perfect, out of sight out of mind, out of the way forever. Let the world get on with its business, whatever the fuck that is, and leave all of us stupid losers to rot! Bobby, you are so full of shit!" She launched the rock with the power of annoyance rather than fury. The rock did a pop fly over Ivan's head and bounced off Bobby's right shoulder before landing in the dirt beside him.

Bobby didn't flinch. He didn't feel a thing. All he could think on was the look on Stella's face when she smelled the stinking heap of trouble that had gone on while she was gone. He had seen the devil in her, butt naked, in the barn that night with young Greta. One thing he knew for sure was he wasn't ever going to be ready to see the devil butt naked again.

X Equivalent to P?

Once the rather large rock had bounced off Bobby's shoulder and hit the dirt, the conversation was over. Bobby stood up, shook the devil from his mind, and pulled his shovel from the dirt pile. "Why don't we just get to what we got to do right now and finish burying Gracey?"

Annie looked at the half filled grave and thought about Grace, then the poor pups that had more than likely inherited the same short life. "Shit, I forgot about the pups!"

Bobby started shoveling. "Don't you worry 'bout them. I took care of 'em before you came to the kennel this mornin'. I took 'em out, played with 'em, let 'em walk all over me and tug at my clothes like I was their mama. Alls I got to say is it's a good thing they is weaned 'cause I ain't got the titties, which is the part they would be cryin' about." He stopped for a moment and looked over at Annie, who was looking back at the kennel. "They don't miss her like we do. They got a understandin' 'bout death that you and me don't got and never will." He went back to shoveling. "When I left 'em, they was sleepin' just like that big ole rock you hit me with now is."

Annie walked over to the tractor and pulled the second shovel from the trailer. She couldn't shut her mind off the way Bobby apparently could, and was determined to keep talking.

"Bobby?"

"Yup, that would be me, darlin'!" Bobby's only remaining interest was in getting the load of dirt back to where it belonged. He filled the shovel with as much dirt as he could, the heavier it was the better it felt.

"She told me Greta was mentally ill. Now you're telling me she was raped by her father and Stella finally had to kill her to get rid of the ugly reminder."

Annie's tone was that of someone having a conversation over tea. "Do you have any idea how ridiculous that sounds?"

Bobby responded reluctantly, "She didn't hate her and she sure didn't think she was ugly. Like I told you, there ain't no explanation and you ain't never gonna find one, at least not one that makes x 'quivalent to p which is why you best leave it be." Sweat beaded up on his forehead as he heaved the red dirt into the grave. The best part would be when it started to drip off his nose and chin.

Annie watched as he rhythmically filled, lifted, and emptied the shovel. How was it that he could just keep going? She cleared her throat before she spoke in another attempt to throw a wrench in his rhythm. "How can I 'leave it be' or has it slipped your mind that my father did the same to me?" Annie didn't wait for an answer because she knew it wasn't coming. She took her place by the pile and started shoveling. She couldn't find a rhythm and her only alternative seemed to be to keep talking. "I was proud to take on that name when Stella gave it to me. It was pretty much the best birthday present I ever got. The puppy my father gave me when I was eight would have topped it, had it not been just another little something to keep my mouth shut and ease his conscience, not that I had any awareness of either at the time—so actually, to be fair, lonely as I was, which was his doing, by the way—anything he gave me was the best. I was crazy about him and, believe it or not, as screwed up as it sounds, I actually still am at times and I still can't believe he's dead. Dead like Grace, dead like Greta, dead as this pile of dirt!"

She stopped and looked over at Bobby. His rhythm was relentless. "Of course then there were those days when I wished I could kill him myself and, as we both know, Stella was a big help in me having that wish. She never stopped letting me know how bad he was. You heard it yourself, Bobby! So how is it she wished her own daughter dead for having been dealt the same hand as me?"

Bobby just kept digging, didn't even raise an eyebrow.

Annie continued, "That day Stella gave me Greta's name I was so damned depressed I couldn't get out of bed and then there she was, standing over me—offering me something that helped me get up and get on." She stabbed the soft earth with her shovel as she tried to reclaim the feeling she'd had when Stella had handed her the name—nothing. She stabbed at the earth again and again, shovelful after shovelful. She couldn't find it, but she would keep looking until she did.

Before long she got lost in the rhythm and all was quiet except for the occasional bark from the dogs in the distance, Ivan's panting, and the sound of metal to earth and earth falling from metal into earth.

Bobby didn't want any creature to be able to dig Grace's body up, or any storm to be able to unearth it, so he dug the hole a foot deeper than he was tall and wider than his arm span, which meant there was a lot of dirt to heave back into it. When they were finally done, he rolled two giant rocks across the soft earth and planted them squarely on top of the grave. They each sunk about a third into the softened earth. He signaled for Annie to have a seat on one.

She sat and the rock sank a touch more.

He then went to his tractor, pulled two beers from the trailer, walked back, and sat on the other rock. It, too, sank a touch more.

He handed Annie a beer.

She took it.

Bobby pulled his cigarettes from his sweat drenched shirt pocket, shook one free, and offered it to her.

She took it.

He shook another one free, pulled it out with his lips, then reached into the front of his jean's pocket and retrieved the gold lighter Stella had given him years earlier. He paused to look at it—he hadn't done that in years—then opened it and flicked the wheel. He placed his cigarette in front of the flame, sucked in, then offered it to Annie. When her cigarette was lit, he closed the lighter and looked at it again before putting it back into his pocket.

Ivan got to his feet and walked from the comfortable shade of his tree over to the edge of the large square of soft red earth. He sniffed it carefully before setting foot on it, then moved slowly out across it, and stopped between Bobby and Annie. He stood there for a few moments as the wafts of smoke blew past his head and across his back. He sighed, pulling his feet from the uncomfortable sinking grip of the dirt. He hadn't been on soft earth his whole life. He moved on to where the earth was firm again and settled back down. From his new vantage point, he could keep an eye on the other dogs, the fields, and the house without people, rocks, or smoke getting in the way.

Bobby sucked his cigarette clear down to the filter, like he always did, dropped the butt into the earth, and pulled out the pack again. He didn't offer another one to Annie. He hadn't seen her take more than one cigarette in one sitting, except on occasion, but as he was putting the pack back into his shirt pocket, her hand appeared. He shook the pack and held it out.

Her hand took the cigarette.

He pulled the lighter out of his jean's pocket and once again felt compelled to look at it for a moment. Then, as he put it back into his jeans, he spoke. "She gave you that name 'cause she missed her and when she found you, you was as screwed up and lost as her Greta was—it's 'bout as simple as that." Bobby stood up to get another beer from the trailer. "You want another one?"

Annie shook her head. She didn't want more beer, she wanted more answers. She spoke as Bobby walked across the grave to the trailer. "Bobby, a lot of girls Stella found were screwed up and lost—why me? I'm not saying you have the answer. I don't think you do, but it's a question worth asking, don't you think?"

Bobby opened the cooler, pulled out another beer, and walked back to his rock. "I hope you ain't thinkin' on askin' any of them questions to Stella." He twisted the cap off and let it drop to the ground. "I'm tellin' you now."

He sat down. "What you got to understand is there ain't answers to a lot of questions and there's a ton of answers you got no need to hear. I learned a long time ago to stop askin' all them questions—in actual truth, I never even started askin' 'em in the first place, ain't nothin' but trouble waitin' down that road."

He tipped the bottle and took a few swallows. "Ivan here, he don't ask questions. He never says to himself, 'Why ain't I free? Why do I have to put up with her? Why does everybody look at me like I'm crazy? Why don't Bobby just up and leave and take me with him? Where's my mama and my papa?' Hell, no—there ain't any point from his way of lookin' at things. Things just is the way they is. All that boy is thinkin' right now is nothin'. He's just lookin' at them fine fields and that blue sky and pantin' 'cause he's hot as shit since he left the shade of that tree. When it's too damn hot, he'll get his ass up and walk back over to that tree. He don't ask why is it too hot and why was I so damn dumb to lie out here in the sun? He just gets up and finds a better place to be."

Bobby stopped, took a few more swallows of beer, and put the bottle on the ground next to him.

Annie looked over at Ivan who had just about reached his limit as far as the heat was concerned. It occurred to her that just maybe Bobby SHOULD just take him and leave, why not?

Bobby continued, "Stella, now she went outta her way to find answers to questions I ain't never asked. Don't get me wrong, I had them answers thrown in my face a couple times by the authorities, but I never believed 'em, not for one damn second. I figured they were just fuckin' with me like they always did. Then here she comes along and gives me them same answers. Comin' from her, I didn't have no choice anymore, all them doors that I generally kept locked so tight nobody could open 'em, not even me if I wanted to— well, she just walked through 'em, like they was nothin', and told me just like it was, there weren't no tornado and there weren't no Kansas."

He looked down and kicked at the dirt. "'Course, I already knew that. I ain't stupid and I knew there weren't one single person who believed a word of it, but I never seen anybody do nothin' but smile when they hear me tell it and I got no interest in changin' that. And that right there is why there's no point to bringin' the fact of my daddy shootin' my mama and killin' hisself out into the light of day. All them smiles I'm use to seein' would change to somethin' I just plain ain't interested in."

He picked up his beer. "'Course it's been a while since I've told anybody anythin'. Hell, I ain't had a conversation with nobody outside of you and Stella for comin' up on two years now." He tipped the bottle against his lips and swallowed.

Annie slid down onto the soft earth. The rock made a better backrest than a seat. She picked up a fistful of dirt as she considered everything Bobby had said. The dirt was still slightly cool and damp, though drying quickly under the heat of the sun. She opened her hand and with the help of her thumb crumbled it up and let it fall through her fingers. As she did this, Ivan slowly got up, glanced briefly at her, and headed back to the shade of the tree on the other side of the grave. It seemed to her as if her shifting to a new position was a signal for him to do the same, or was it that they each reached maximum discomfort at the same time?

Bobby rested his bottle up against his rock and looked over at Annie. "Just so you know, Greta, she wasn't raped by her daddy, he was outta the picture—it was husband number three, the one before me. I mean, they wasn't officially married, but they was together for a couple years, and when she walked in on him doing shit no kinda man should be doin', she chased him out the house with his gun—even shot him in the leg I believe, though I'm ain't sure on that 'cause Stella ain't got a record regardin' it. Anyway, it was the very same gun that killed Greta that night. And that right there is one of them coincidences that makes them goose bumps rise up on your skin."

Annie dropped a final fistful of dirt and rubbed her hand on her jeans, "It's called tragic irony, Bobby." She suddenly felt flat and tired.

Bobby stood up. "Call it what you want, Annie, but it don't change the fact of it makin' goose bumps." He picked up the two shovels and walked back to the trailer. "And what's givin' me more of them bumps is the fact that Stella'll be drivin' down that driveway tomorrow and you got to think on what you're gonna do about that. I got no problem with continuin' just the way things have been around here, but knowin' you, you ain't gonna be able to do that."

Annie stayed put. She listened to the clink of the shovels as Bobby threw them in the trailer, then as she heard his footsteps approaching, her stomach tightened. When she spoke, she was barely aware of it. "You killed her too, Bobby. You erased her right along with Stella and went on living like nothing happened. Now you're asking me to do the same."

The footsteps stopped.

Bobby looked at Annie as she sunk her hands into the dirt. The lightness he had felt was completely gone—what took its place was the weight of an image of young Greta lying dead and buried alongside Grace. He turned and walked quickly back to his tractor.

Annie waited till the sound of the tractor was off in the distance before she breathed again. She looked around for Ivan. He was gone. She then looked down the tracks. There he was, trotting alongside the tractor as if he had done it a thousand times before. It would be a terrible blow to him when Stella came back and he was returned to life in his pen. Annie wondered if she might have done a terrible thing to let him see what it was like to be free.

- 26 -

The Glass at the Door

Margaret turned on the Weather Channel and collapsed onto her bed. One more inquiry about the details of what was now known as "Margaret's bust" and she would tear her hair out, all of it!

"I didn't know you smoked pot, Margaret!"

"Why were you smoking in your hotel room? That's seems awfully stupid."

"Does Frank know you smoke pot?"

"You're darn lucky Stella was there to help!"

"You got to hand it to Stella—she's an ace at handling sticky situations! I mean, did you see how she handled things in the ring? I can't think of anyone who could've done it better. She saved the day as far as I'm concerned."

"I heard you were so stoned you passed out and when Stella heard the feds knocking on the door she lit a match to your hair to cover the smell and ate a whole quarter ounce of your pot just so they would have no evidence. My God, how'd she manage to be so cool today after dealing with all that! What happens to somebody if they eat a quarter ounce of pot? I mean, wouldn't a normal person die?"

"I am shocked, Margaret! You do realize that occurrences like this will not help the club's image one bit!"

"I heard you had planned on getting your hands on some coke, but Stella convinced you otherwise. I'd say you were real lucky!"

Not one person had bothered to ask if any of it were true or not. They just assumed, assumed, assumed, all based on Stella's say-so. Margaret turned, squashed her face into the pillow, and bellowed as loud as she could, "I'm so tired of that bitch, I wish she would fall in a bathtub and die!!!"

She fell silent as her saliva seeped into the polyester/cotton blend, then lifted her head and looked over at the table. She would have been horrified, though not surprised, if Stella were sitting there smoking marijuana and having a good laugh at her expense. She turned back to the pillow and squashed her face ever deeper, her mouth open and fully engaged with the poly/cotton blend. Her show had been a disaster and her reputation was in the mud!

She bellowed for the second time, but the soggy poly/cotton blend had crept so far into her mouth that the burst of air from her lungs backfired and was forced back down her throat. She gagged and fell into a fit of coughing that shook the entire bed.

"Are you OK in there?"

Still unable to stop coughing, Margaret responded in spits and spats, "What do you care? Go away!"

A couple of minutes later, there was a knock on her door. Margaret's coughing had ceased leaving her voice thick and raw. "I thought I told you to go away!"

"Margaret, it's Mick. We need to talk."

"I can't talk, Mick. I have something stuck in my throat, and I have nothing to say about anything, not to you or anyone else!" She would be damned before she'd let Mick see her in this state. He'd already seen way too much.

Mick looked at the door and immediately flashed to Margaret buckled forward in his room bemoaning her part in his parking lot encounter with Charlene. Much to his chagrin, the image was as vivid as when it happened. His fear, in hearing a voice that sounded eerily like a death rattle, was that if he entered the room he would have yet another image of Margaret to add to the first one. He hesitated as he considered walking away, but his sense of do-the-right-thing got the best of him. "Margaret, this has been a bad day for all of us and unfortunately it's not over. We need to talk."

Margaret rolled onto her side and sat up, resting her bare feet on the dark green carpet. Her dress had crumpled up, exposing her legs almost completely. She looked down and for the first time noticed that her knees, both of them, had grass stains and dirt and gravel indentations.

She quickly pulled her dress down and stood up. "Hold on, Mick, I'll just be a minute." She rushed over to the mirror. The only positive thing she could think of when she looked at her reflection was that her mother was dead—if she weren't, there would've been no end to the scorn that would have flowed from her mouth to Margaret's ears. *"How could you be so stupid letting yourself be pulled to the ground and left to crawl around like, like, like, like a whimpering child who has been blessed with nothing? Imagine what people are thinking! I will never live this down! And your hair, Margaret! One more incident like this and we will march you to the hairdressers and have it cut off! If you can't keep it under control, we will have to put it under control."*

Margaret reached up and pulled the makeshift barrette from her hair. Somebody, she couldn't remember who, had given her a pencil to use in place of the broken piece. She had tried her pen, but it was too fat. She pulled the pencil from her bun and watched her hair fall down over her shoulders. She then pretended to have a mike in her hand. "And now I am very pleased to present the final chapter, in this our first ABC national..." It suddenly seemed important for her to see how she looked out there, in front of everybody in that final hour of the show.

"Margaret!" Mick was trying hard not to imagine what was taking her so long or why he heard mumbling. He was also fighting his impulse to leave, even skip town without ever being seen or heard from again.

He tried to look through the little peephole in the door. Whatever she was doing, he was sure it was important to her. He took a deep breath and whispered silently to himself, "God grant me the serenity." He then sighed and leaned patiently against the wall next to her door.

A loud voice sounded, followed by banging. "Stella and Lisa-Lee, if you're in there, I need to talk to you!"

Mick turned to see Billy standing in front of a door down the hall, his expression surprisingly devoid of its usual confident and bubbling enthusiasm. "Billy, what's up? Or should I say down? You look like hell."

Billy turned at the sound of Mick's voice and immediately walked towards him. "Hi, Mick, gosh, I'm glad to see you!"

As Billy approached, Mick thought back to a time in his life when he deeply resented all the Billys in the world, even cursed them as he drowned himself in work or drink. If he didn't wish them dead he would, at the very least, have gained a certain joy in seeing a Billy flounder. Instead, as he watched Billy, he felt a surge of genuine compassion along with a surprising wave of paternal feelings.

"Mick, I'm in love with Lisa-Lee and I think I blew it. I told her I wanted to spend my life with her and she told me I was nothing to her! The thing is, I thought she felt the same way about me, I really did. I mean I really do. I know she does." Billy couldn't contain the unfamiliar raw hurt that was consuming him. He'd sat in his car for a brief time after Lisa-Lee had left him, but just sitting there made no sense to him. He had to do something and the only thing he could think to do was talk to Stella. He didn't believe a word Lisa-Lee had said and he couldn't understand why she would have said such things. His hope was that with Stella's help he could maybe find some answers. After all, she was like a mother to Lisa-Lee, and if Stella was anything like his mother, she would be able to help.

Mick turned towards Margaret's hotel room door. "Margaret, I'll be back in a few minutes!"

He then put his hand on Billy's shoulder. "Look kiddo, you didn't blow anything. You told her how you feel and that's never blowing it. Blowing it would be if you didn't or couldn't tell her how you feel."

He dropped his hand from Billy's shoulder and smiled. "Really blowing it would be if you lied about how you felt, to yourself or to her—or if you couldn't feel at all." He backpedaled as the young face suddenly looked puzzled. "Never mind about that last part."

"Mick, I don't want to lose her. I ..."

A loud brash voice sounded from down the hall. "You ain't gonna lose her. She's just got scared is all!"

Mick and Billy looked up at the same time. Stella had appeared out of nowhere.

Stella stepped in front of Mick and put her hand on Billy's arm. "You need to be talkin' to Lisa-Lee who, I might add, is waitin' on you in my room."

Billy looked blankly at her.

"GO ON! Don't you worry—I know all about it and alls I got to say is welcome to the family." She snorted a laugh and playfully pushed him off towards her room.

"Thanks, Stella! You're the best!" Billy smiled broadly and nodded in Mick's direction. "Hey, thanks to you too, Mick." He turned and trotted down the hall.

Mick didn't have time to respond. As he watched Billy disappear into Stella's room, all he could do was let go. It could've been a fine moment for him, trying to save young Billy from God knows what, but it wasn't really about him, was it? *God grant me the...*

"As for you, Mister Mick, I'd say you are one smart man decidin' to leave while the leavin's good 'cause we both know there ain't no room for you AND me in this place or any other and I know you know what I'm talkin' about. You're smart, I'll give you that, but you ain't got what it takes. I mean, look at yourself, all swolled up. Hell, the only reason I know that's you behind that beat up face is 'cause of your voice and that damn army jacket!"

Stella put both hands on her hips and leaned in towards Mick, close enough that she could smell his breath and it wasn't all that bad, much to her surprise. "AND besides that, a little birdie told me about you makin' a dirty old man pass at Lisa-Lee today and I will let it slide so long as you make yourself gone, as in G O N E. I know all about your alcoholic perverted ways and it all stops here. You screw with what's mine and you will find yourself in so far you ain't comin' out!"

She leaned away from him and waited, confident that he would back away about as quick as a cat looking down a hose that was fixing to be turned on.

Mick settled his arms across his chest and smiled back at the steely green eyes. "This is all about you, isn't it Stella? Or should I say Madame Stella, master manipulator of the lost and confused. You certainly have found your niche with this bunch, haven't you? The transition from your old job could not have been all that hard—once again, a big fish in a mud puddle. You're right, I am leaving the puddle, but I'll still be in the world, much to your dismay!" He paused for effect and narrowed his eyes. "Mark my words. That IS how you would put it, isn't it?"

Margaret dropped the empty glass from against the door and quickly got up from her knees. She'd heard enough. Another minute or so and there would be yet another train wreck with possibly dozens of onlookers emerging from their rooms to partake in the spectacle. It would be a miracle if the Bordeaux community were ever allowed into another hotel anywhere in the country. Enough was enough!

She opened the door and stepped out into the hallway. "Haven't we had enough for one weekend?! Here I am in MY ROOM, trying to get some rest before the big dinner, much needed rest I might add, due to an unbelievably stressful few days through which you two have been no help at all. Now here you are in front of MY DOOR peddling your loud-mouthed personal agendas! Have you no decency, either of you?"

Stella looked squarely at Margaret, her expression unchanged. "Well, well, look what the cat dragged out." She looked past Margaret and spotted the empty glass on the floor. "I see you been on your knees again, as usual, and as usual, it looks to me like 'resting,' to your way of thinkin', is the 'quivalent to bawlin' your eyes out, which is understandable considerin' it surely is a thing to cry about when a woman ends up crawlin' around on her hands and knees in a situation where she shoulda been standin' tall—case closed."

Stella dropped her hands from her hips and turned and strolled down the hall towards her room, still talking as she moved, throwing glances at the now small audience of people who had stepped out of their rooms. "Now I got me better things to do than stand there with the president of the ABC, who I still can't recognize due to the beatin's he got from a couple of big fat peanut-heads, and the secretary of whatever, who can't seem to stay up on the two feet God gave her—apparently he forgot to give her the instruction manual on how to use 'em!"

She disappeared into her room.

Mick couldn't help himself. He crossed his arms more tightly to suppress the laughter, but it came anyway. "You've got to hand it to her—that woman is a breed all by herself—truly a rare breed!"

He glanced around at the small gathering crowd and dropped his arms to his sides. His laughter softened to a chuckle. "Show's over folks, you can all get back to whatever you were doing."

He looked at Margaret whose valiant attempt at righteous indignation had been smashed to smithereens and lay scattered on the green carpet beside her petite, though plump, bare feet. He applauded her attempt. However, Stella was not a person to attempt anything with, especially anything that had not yet passed the stage of a practice run. Margaret had tried to tackle Everest after only having climbed a flight of stairs. He felt sorry for her in that moment. "Margaret, don't let her get to you like that. She's not worth it."

Margaret shifted and pressed her dress downwards with both hands, needlessly worrying that her indented knees might be showing.

She glanced down towards Stella's room, and then back at Mick, who looked all smug in his macho army jacket. "We'll see how you fare when she decides to spread the word of your sexual perversities! What WILL you do when that is all the talk and nobody believes a word you say?" Now it was her turn to feel smug.

Mick put his hands in his jacket pockets and looked past her to the empty dry glass that lay on the floor by her door. It was hard to believe she'd actually done that little trick. How old was he the last time he tried that? Five? Six?

He looked into her indignant face and responded calmly, "My reputation as an active alcoholic and pervert has already been well documented by Stella or haven't you been listening? And guess what? I don't care about her little gossip column and neither should you!"

Margaret blushed and twisted one of her chubby bare feet over the other. She had forgotten who she was talking to. Mick was impervious to Stella's arrows, something that never ceased to amaze her. It was another of the reasons she'd asked him to be president—the primary one being that he had a big bone to pick with Stella over how she'd treated Pete Strate, a very big bone.

She managed a smile and turned and walked through the open door to her room. "What is it you wanted to talk to me about?"

Mick followed her, shutting the door behind him, taking great care not to step on the empty glass. "I wanted to let you know that I will be saying adios to my position as president of the club as of tonight."

"Why?" Margaret's fantasy of a knockdown-dragout between Stella and Mick, with Mick on top, ruptured in her head. She grabbed her bun with one hand, worried it had somehow shaken loose, but it hadn't, thank God!

"You know what, Margaret? I don't care enough about this club or any of the people in it. I'd just like to get back to breeding a few dogs and leave the rest. You couldn't have paid me enough to attend this show, and that's not including my having been slugged a few times."

He stopped in front of the muted TV and watched the smiling faces of the weather people as they faced the cameras and dished out the good and the bad news about how "your Sunday is turning out." Why was it they used the possessive when talking about days of the week, "your Monday, your Tuesday, and your Wednesday"?

He turned back to Margaret, who had taken a seat on one of the two chairs by the window. So far, she was sitting upright, but he wasn't hopeful.

Margaret picked up the binoculars from the windowsill. She then turned around and began tapping them on the table. "I have worked my butt off to make all of this happen and now you're just going to walk out?"

Mick looked at the binoculars, then at the empty glass on the floor. "That's right, Margaret, I'm done with this silliness that has come precariously close to causing a major slip in my sobriety."

He turned towards the door, realizing that his decision to make a final speech at the dinner was nothing more than a pipe dream. He was done, NOW! He grabbed the door handle and looked back at Margaret in her blue cotton dress, still tapping the binoculars on the table. "Good luck, Margaret!"

As he opened the door, he heard the patter of feet. He glanced down the hall. The door to Stella's room quickly closed. This bizarre chapter in his life was over.

27

Mark My Words

Once Bobby and Ivan were out of sight, Annie leaned back against the rock and sank her hands deep into the fresh dirt. The coolness was a soothing antidote to the hot sun. She rolled onto her knees and started to dig.

She is at the beach with her brothers. They decide to bury themselves in the cool, wet sand close to where the tide rolls in. Once buried, with only their heads showing, the tide rises and the waves begin to cross over them, each time more and more. Slowly the sand is pulled off their bodies. She delights in the feeling of the weight shifting. She closes her eyes and waits. She hears the waves slapping the shore and her brothers' laughter off in the distance. Then there is a startling silence.

Annie opened her eyes to blue sky and the sound of hammering in the distance. She lifted her head and realized where she was, buried in dirt with Grace's dead body lying somewhere beneath her.

She froze in the sudden terror that her own death was imminent and no one cared. The sky was bigger than she could take in and the sounds of the birds were too far away to reach. She closed her eyes and searched for her father who had left her trembling and unable to find comfort. He had held her and told her how wonderful, beautiful, and courageous she was. And now she felt more alone and more scared than she could grasp. Her body was lost in a sea of feelings she didn't understand. Where was his promise of eternal comfort? Where was his promise of a special life, more special than anyone else's, destined for greatness, and always to be without harm? Why did she hurt more than she could bear, more than tears could relieve?

She was hanging over that hole again, only this time it had a clear bottom and on it was Grace's cold body sketchily stitched-up to keep her insides from falling out.

Annie held her breath in anticipation that her own insides might just fall out.

She braces herself as her father pushes slowly into her and swells until she thinks she might burst. Initially, his voice is reassuring and gentle like it always is, but then it starts to shake. He is breathing strangely and making noises she's never heard before. What did he leave inside her? Why is he wiping her with that towel? Why is he crying? There is a smell all around her—it is bad, very bad.

Annie opened her eyes for the second time. The bright sunlight hit hard. Nausea swept over her and it felt as though a thousand nails were being driven into her forehead. The dirt she had so carefully and playfully packed over her legs and belly flew into the air as she lurched up onto her hands and knees. She retched over and over and over. He was dead and it wasn't over, it would never be over.

The retching stopped and as she knelt there, trembling and barely able to breath, she thought of young Greta with a gun to her head and uttered words she'd never been able to reach. "I hate you Dad. I hate you, I hate you, I hate you. You killed me, you son of a bitch!!! You killed me before I ever had a chance."

She gagged as she gathered more courage. "I will find a way, you bastard, I will find a way. Mark my words." Stella had marched in beside her as usual, but Annie pushed back this time. "That's mark MY words—mine, not Stella's! I will find a way."

Unable to hold on to her anger, she collapsed back onto the grave and let it seep into the earth, down and down to where Amazing Grace lay dead and gone. She had been robbed, utterly and completely, by the two people whom she thought had loved her.

The hammering in the distance continued and her thoughts landed on Bobby. He had his fences, his projects, the dogs, and his loyalty to Stella, who despite everything, according to him, had given him more than he had ever hoped for in his life. But what about her life? Where would she go from here? What would she do? How would she begin to find what she needed to pick herself up from this grave and put one foot in front of the other? She'd come back here to be with the only sense of family she'd ever known and now it was in tatters.

She looked at her boots, her jeans, her T-shirt, her hands, and her feet. Here she sat on a grave in the middle of Georgia, covered with dirt from head to toe. What and who was left? Stella's message that no one could be trusted had finally sunk in and she was utterly dumbfounded.

As she drew in a deep end-of-the-road breath, a tiny window burst open and in squeezed Big Bertha, Ivan, and Grace's six pups, one by one. As she exhaled, they surrounded her and helped her to her feet. She had eight good reasons to walk off that grave and carry on.

Bobby had just pulled another fence post from the now dwindling pile when he heard the engine to his truck kick on. He looked in the direction of the house. He couldn't see past the line of trees, but he figured it was Annie. An hour earlier, he'd heard the dogs out in the fields again, so he knew she'd finally picked herself up off Grace's grave and gotten back to work. He'd taken care of bringing the dogs in during the hottest part of the day, and while he fed and played with the puppies, he'd cursed her the whole time. He didn't mind taking care of the dogs, or the pups, but it just wasn't right that she sat out there on Grace's grave doing nothing except feeling sorry for herself. It was Grace who was dead, not Annie. If he sat down and thought about all the times in his life he could have quit, he would never have gotten up, and nothing would be any different except he wasn't moving anymore and the dogs wouldn't have a fine kennel, fine fields to run in, and Grace wouldn't have a grave to rest in. As far as he knew, Annie wasn't any different from anybody else. *She makes mistakes, same as everybody else.*

He dragged the post off the pile and along the ground towards the fresh hole he'd dug. He didn't see any point in thinking about things the way she did, which was too damn much. And now she had young Greta in her head due to his big mouth and it wasn't going do either one of them any good, especially when Stella got back because Stella would smell it on Annie the minute she drove down that driveway. In fact, he wouldn't be surprised if she smelled it already from wherever she was.

He placed the post upright in the hole and kicked some dirt in around it. If he could find a way to knock out everything that was running around in Annie's head right now, he would do it. But what was done was done. He just had to pray she would find a way, sooner than later, to get on with things like it never happened, something he had learned to do without even thinking about it, before Annie was even born.

He packed the dirt in tighter and tighter around the eight-foot post which was now only five feet tall. It was sunk in deep, thanks to his pole digger, which meant nothing outside of what Stella might refer to as "God's will" could bring it down, especially when he was done shoveling and pounding the earth so tight not even an ant could dig its way through.

On the one hand, his left, he hoped Annie was driving out the driveway forever because then all Stella would get stuck in was hating on her for running off and stealing his truck again, just like before, which would be a damn sight better than what Stella would get stuck in if Anne stayed around. On the other hand, his right—the more important one, as much as he didn't understand it, even considered it just plain nuts—he didn't want Annie to drive out that driveway forever. He couldn't think of one reason why he felt this way unless it was because he knew deep down, Annie being here or not, Stella would know what had gone on and Annie's being gone simiply meant it would be all the worse for him.

He took hold of the pole and shook it, kicked it, and pushed on it with everything he had. It didn't budge. He stepped back and rubbed his hands together, then rubbed his damp forehead with his shirtsleeve. *Nope, that ain't the reason. It's got nothin' to do with Stella, nothin' at all.*

He looked down at his shadow. It was longer than he was tall, which meant the daylight would be coming to an end in an hour or two. *And it's got everythin' to do with Stella, which means it's just plain crazy and ain't worth thinkin' on.*

He picked up the pole digger and paced out where the next post would go. It was going to be a thing of beauty, this project, and it would be around long after he and Stella and Annie were dead and gone, like Greta and Grace were. Annie had told him many times about all the famous things people had made hundreds or thousands of years ago. "There are buildings and statues and paintings, walls and even fences, Bobby, and each one tells a story about the people who were alive back then. Some of the stories are tragic and bleak, some hopeful, some mythical, some funny and joyful." It was clear as day to him that damn near anything that was built, famous or not, had a story to tell—even while the people were still alive.

28

Only the Animals is Innocent

Big Bertha lay on the carpet in front of the television, her head resting comfortably between her paws as she perused a sweeping landscape dotted with giraffe, gazelle, and elephants—all grazing beneath the hot sun, flicking flies from their flanks with their tails as busy birds plucked ticks from their backs. Her eyebrows rolled from side to side as the camera zoomed in and out. Her ears were set forward at full attention as the narrator's voice rose and fell, and the calls of birds and buzzing of flies faded in and out.

On occasion, her ears flicked back to keep track of Annie who was pacing back and forth behind her, from the kitchen window through the living room to the front door, peering anxiously out of each into the dark. More often than not, she brushed against Bertha's rear as she did this. The click and scuff of her leather boots as they moved from tile to carpet, carpet to tile, were an obvious intrusion on Bertha's concentration.

Suddenly, the camera sped across the broad green expanse and zoomed in on a phalanx of lionesses closing in on a herd of wildebeest. Bertha lifted her head as the narrator's voice lowered to a whisper.

The stealthy felines moved in, their massive shoulders bulging as they dropped their bodies and reached long and low through the tall grass.

Bertha couldn't bear it. She sprang to her feet and positioned herself within inches of the screen—the exact distance she and Annie had agreed upon as the appropriate one under these circumstances. She stood riveted. Her body quivered with excitement as her eyebrows moved at near frantic speed from side to side. She was determined to keep careful track of both the hunter and the hunted.

Just as the lionesses were preparing to spring into action, Bertha glanced over her shoulder at Annie, who was at the kitchen window, then back to the screen, then back to Annie, then the screen, then Annie, until Annie finally responded and joined her for the moment of triumph which was the lead lioness hurtling herself full force onto the back of one of the wildebeest.

Bertha breathed a quick sigh of relief as Annie dropped to the floor beside her, and then returned her full attention to the spectacular kill.

Annie spoke into her ear with the same whispered excitement as the narrator. "Look at that girl, holy smokes, it's incredible!"

This, of course, sent Bertha into complete and utter ecstasy.

And when the kill was over and swallowed up by a toothpaste commercial, Annie scratched the back of Bertha's head, got up and walked quickly back to the kitchen.

Bertha returned to her previous position, fully prepared to wait for as long as it took.

Annie leaned across the sink and peered out the window for the umpteenth time. She looked at her watch. It was 1 a.m. and the light was still on at the far end of the kennel—the puppy quarters. Bobby was still awake.

She looked out into the darkness that engulfed the fields where Amazing Grace was buried, then focused back in on the patch of driveway that was illuminated by the lights from the front porch of the house. It was as it had been for hours, stone cold quiet.

She wondered briefly if Bobby was also pacing and obsessively peering out his little window, contemplating her lights and wondering what she was doing, but she knew him too well. He was either building something or playing with the pups. Pacing endlessly while accomplishing nothing other than increased tension was not Bobby's way.

She smacked the counter with her palm as she pushed away from the window, unable to decide if she was madder at him for his astounding ability to carry on regardless of the circumstances, or madder at herself for her inability to do so, or maybe it was neither. Maybe she was just mad at the sad fact that she'd been unable to drive away that afternoon, for good, rather than run errands and return to this house where there was nothing left for her to do but pace.

She looked over at Big Bertha, and as she did so, her body relaxed and she enjoyed a brief respite.

———

Bertha had been the first dog Annie ever met that showed such an interest in television. In fact, Bertha's first day in the house was almost her last because of this. Everything had been rolling along just fine until the TV came on and animals appeared. That was when Bobby, who could react with the speed of light when necessary, rolled off the couch and tackled Bertha in one singular motion as she lunged towards the screen.

As the two of them laid on the floor, Bobby holding Bertha by the neck, Stella launched herself from the kitchen table and burst into a flurry of protestations. "I swear that bitch is gonna be the death of me. It ain't enough that she had to tear ass down to the Cranshaws to prove herself and cause all hell to break loose. Now, it's lookin' like she's bound and determined to kill my brand new thousand dollar TV, somethin' which I ain't gonna be so forgivin' of.

"Now, I ain't stuck on what she did at the Cranshaws, seein' as that was normal on the scale of dog behavior, but this shit ain't normal, meanin' I ain't never seen it and I ain't riskin' losin' my TV." She stood over Bobby as he sat up, keeping hold of Bertha by the collar.

Bobby burst out laughing. "Goddamn, I ain't never seen a dog so dead set on killin' a TV!"

Stella leaned down and picked up the ashtray that had been knocked off the coffee table. She laid her burning cigarette in it, put it on the arm of the couch, and rested her hands defiantly on her hips. "I don't know what you think is so damn funny seein' as I don't believe dog attack is listed on the warrantee we got with that TV, so unless you can teach that bitch somethin' I don't believe she's particularly interested in learnin', she ain't stayin' in this house—case closed."

That was when Annie had taken the time to do exactly that, and it wasn't so hard in the end. Bertha had never been paid the kind of close attention that Annie gave her over the next few days in front of the TV and that attention was all it took to tone her down and set her straight. Annie was no expert in dog training techniques, but as Stella put it, "You got a way with that bitch, I'll give you that. She's so stuck on you, it ain't normal, 'course there ain't nothin' normal 'bout you or her."

The end result was if Annie wasn't around, Bertha had to be in her crate when the TV was on.

———

Annie broke from her respite and walked past Bertha towards the front door. Stella would be here all too soon.

Just as she reached the door, Bertha rushed to her side and stood with her head cocked, ears fully forward. Annie looked across the driveway to the kennel. The light had gone out, which in her mind meant things had settled. However, according to Bertha, something was stirring in the stone cold quiet.

Annie watched and waited.

Bertha let out a roar as Bobby appeared in the patch of light on the driveway and slowly approached the house. All the dogs in the kennel responded in kind.

Annie did the only thing she could think to do, which was to dash to the couch and sit down.

Bertha stayed at the door as Bobby's work boots hit the porch steps. She roared again and then the screen door opened.

"Settle down, Alice." Bobby patted her head and looked over at Annie who hadn't bothered to look up. He spoke a little louder. "I mean settle down, Bertha!"

Bertha wagged her tail as Bobby walked past her.

Bobby continued talking as he approached the couch. "I swear, I can't keep the names straight anymore. We got Alice changin' to Bertha, Annie changin' to Greta then changin' back to Annie again. Nothin' stays the same far as I can tell and alls I got to say is things would be a damn sight easier if they did."

He stopped and stood between the flickering TV screen and Annie. He faced her and waited until she looked up at him. Nothing had gone well for him since he'd parked his tractor in the barn for the night. He had tried to sleep, played with the pups, thought about his next day's work, even planned on driving to the bar, but none of it stuck. Something kept yanking him off of whatever he tried to do and pushing him into something which made him real uncomfortable, as in he had no idea what he was going to do next, which was why he was standing here, for no reason he could think of, looking at Annie. "Are you plannin' on goin' somewhere? I mean, you're wearin' exactly what you was wearin' when you came back here."

He glanced at the TV screen, then looked back at her. "Well, I say, if you are plannin' on goin', go on ahead now 'fore Stella gets back."

Annie looked down at her brown leather jacket, white shirt, jeans, and boots. He was right. She hadn't worn this particular jacket since the day she'd driven down the driveway. "It's just the jacket, Bobby. Everything else I've worn plenty of times."

Bobby responded more quickly than usual, "Like I said you're dressed just how you was that day. So why don't you just go on ahead and get up and leave the same way you came."

Bertha paced a half dozen times between the two of them, then sat on Annie's feet facing Bobby.

"Bobby." She waited a moment for him to show some kind of response to his name.

He looked from her to the floor, then back to her.

Satisfied, she continued, "I can't. I don't have anywhere to go, just like you don't, and all I've been doing is pacing like a caged animal since six o'clock, waiting, waiting, fucking waiting for HER to come down that driveway!"

She pulled her feet out from under Bertha's rear and stood up. "Now, I know exactly how Ivan feels."

Bobby looked up as Annie turned from him and walked into the kitchen. "You ain't in a cage, Annie. The door is over there and you got the hands to open it. Ivan don't have a choice, he don't got the means or the hands. He's stuck here, just like me, because it's the way it's s'pose to be, and he's doin' the best he can with it. Hell, you weren't lookin' to be here in the first place. I found Stella and I wanted her like I never wanted anythin'—I still do, as in I'm s'pose to be here for one reason or another. She found you and brought you here, and that's about as different as it gets, meanin' you got into somethin' you was never lookin' for. You ain't s'pose to be here, Annie. You weren't never s'pose to be here."

Annie pushed back from the kitchen window and steadied herself against the counter. She looked over at Bobby. "I've lived here with you and Stella and the boys for twelve years. You were my family, or didn't you ever see it that way?"

Bobby walked to the couch and sat down. As he did this, Bertha got up and walked into the kitchen. He turned to the TV and studied the two men who were discussing the mating habits of whales. It was no wonder Bertha had gotten up. He picked up the remote and surfed through the channels again. He finally settled on a preacher giving a rousing sermon to a crowd of people "... and it was his call to JESUS that stopped that wave from crushing that tiny town! JESUS knew he was a man of the Lord and do you want to know why?"

Bobby looked back over at Annie as he switched the channel again. "I don't have any answers to all them questions you keep comin' up with. Alls I know is, there is somethin' better for you out there, Annie, and you best go find it."

Annie breathed and felt the ground again. She walked over to Bobby and took the remote from his hand. "You didn't come up here tonight to tell me I have a better life out there somewhere. You came up here because you're thinking just maybe you can make this all go away again and things can get back to normal, which is what? You building fences all day, drinking beer, and talking to nobody?"

She clicked the TV off without shifting her attention from Bobby's stubbled and unusually weary face. It occurred to her that maybe he HAD been thinking about all of this as much as she had. "You know, you and Ivan aren't all that similar. Ivan doesn't trust Stella one bit. He hates her and tries to tell everybody exactly that, every day, in whatever way he can. You yourself explained that to me, or don't you remember? He's not willing to give her a pass like you have for all these years." She put the remote onto the coffee table and walked to the front door.

Bobby watched as she peered into the night. "It ain't like that, Annie."

He picked up the remote and rolled it around in his hand. "I'll tell you one thing, you don't hate her either, which is why you ain't gone. Oh, I can see you is tryin' to build up a head of steam on her, but it ain't workin', and you ain't afraid of her either, like you is actin' like you are 'cause you got no reason to be. Like I already said, what happened to Greta was a one time huge-ass mistake that happened due to a bunch of situations crashin' into each other. What you is afraid of or pissed off at got nothin' to do with Stella, nothin' at all. I have sat here and watched you these past couple months wantin' her to be somethin' she ain't. As far as I can see, you are done here because how you gonna stay in a place where you are wantin' somethin' that ain't never gonna be?"

He turned to the TV and clicked through the channels, settling once again on the preacher "It's JESUS that stands beside you every minute of every day! He knows your every thought, every hope and desire. You are never alone…"

Bobby switched his attention away from Annie, suddenly thinking about how Stella and he used to sit and watch that preacher crap on nights when they couldn't sleep. Stella would always put in her two cents right along with the preacher and they would laugh their ass off. On occasion he would suggest maybe it wasn't right to laugh, seeing as these people were dead serious and all, but she said it was just fine. "'Cause, Bobby, the real God hates that shit, thinks it's nothin' but a insult to his real meanin', which has nothin' to do with some guy all dressed up thinkin' he is all that, gettin' people riled up or flat out depressed and 'bout ready to shoot themselves based on nothin' but his own human imagination which is exactly what the problem is. See, it's the human part that screws this world up. What these preachers need to do is put a dog or a moose or a damn camel—any damn one of God's creatures—up there not havin' to say a thing 'cause they got the word of God in 'em without havin' to say a word. Far as I know there ain't a man alive that can do that! Now that right there would be a REAL church!"

Bobby pushed the red 'off' button and dropped the remote onto the coffee table. He stared at the black screen as Stella kept right on talking to him—"The animals is God's creatures, Bobby. They got the right to be and we got to earn that right."

He heard a chair squeal along the tile floor behind him and turned to see Annie sit down at the kitchen table and light up a cigarette. That's when that particular 'something' pushed on him again and he opened his mouth. "Greta killed a whole litter of kittens once, little itty bitty things that Stella rescued from a cardboard box that was lyin' on side of the road. Now, you know how Stella don't tolerate messin' with the animals and Greta, being one of her own and all, well, it damn near broke her in two to know one of her own blood had gone and done that—hell, when she found them strangled kittens she knew it was Greta who done it and she cried like a damn baby. She'd told Greta a thousand times, in a thousand ways, why hurtin' animals was the worst thing a human bein' could do. See, Greta had committed a prior stranglin', meanin' she strangled a baby chick at her school—I wasn't around then—but when Stella told me about it she weren't her usual self. It was like she done the deed herself and wanted God to forgive her. Anyways, the school called her and she had to go pick Greta up in the middle of the day in front of all them people." He leaned forward, picked up the remote, and flicked the TV on again. "Stella loves the animals more than just about anything."

Annie looked past Bobby to the screen that was rapidly shifting from one channel to the next. The whole room started shifting and she couldn't keep track of her own thoughts. She propped her cigarette on the ashtray, pushed her chair back, and stood up. As she turned to walk to the kitchen sink, she stumbled over Bertha who had been lying faithfully at her feet.

Bertha lifted her head as Annie's foot smacked into her back, then dropped it again as Annie caught her balance and continued.

Annie turned on the cold tap, held her hand under the running water, and waited for it to reach its absolute coldest—nothing short of that would douse the flush of heat that had rushed into her head. As she cupped her hands and splashed the cold water onto her face, she heard Bobby's voice again, off in the distance.

"See, only the animals is innocent in this world, everybody else got to pay one way or another for the bad they done."

Annie then ducked her whole head under the running water. She had heard enough. She stayed there as long as possible and let the water rush down across her ears, forehead, and cheeks. When the cold had finally reached in and caused her head to ache, she stood up and let the water drip from her face down onto her shirt and jacket.

She then pulled a long strip of paper towels from the roll on the wall over the sink and wiped her face. When she was done, all she could see was the side and back of the couch. Bobby had lain down. He was done talking.

She walked back to her chair and sat down, crossing her arms on the tabletop. She leaned forward and rested her chin on the soft leather sleeves of her jacket. What she could see was the ashtray and the still burning cigarette, and all she could do was watch the steady flow of smoke rise in two, sometimes three, separate streams towards the ceiling. *"Only the animals is innocent."*

———

Annie was ten years old and with a girl, Patty, whom she barely remembered except in name. Patty was a faceless, shapeless girl who would do anything Annie wanted her to do, which was the only reason Annie spent any time with her at all.

On this particular summer day, they were at Patty's place, a big sprawling house, complete with a half basketball court, tennis court, and two large ponds. The only other people around at the time were Patty's big brother and a friend who were out playing tennis. Patty had wanted to read comic books or go out and cheer the boys on, but Annie had a better idea, which of course would be the way they would go. She suggested they set up a science experiment with frogs they could catch in the ponds. When Patty inquired about what the experiment would be, she said she would explain it to her once they had caught the frogs.

Annie had no memory of the two of them catching the frogs, but they did because there they stood side by side at Patty's kitchen table looking at the shoebox that sounded as though it was chock full of giant jumping beans. That's when Annie announced that they were going to find out: 1) if a frog could live after being cut down its belly and sewn back up; 2) what would happen if they cut open the belly, removed the liver and sewed the frog back up; 3) what would happen if they removed the liver, waited a few seconds, stuffed it back in and sewed it back up; 4) what would happen if they took out the intestines and sewed the frog back up; 5) if they opened the frog, took out its liver and intestines and sewed it back up, what would happen? If they had any frogs left, they could take other stuff out and do the same.

Patty was hesitant, if not horrified, but Annie assured her that it was a real experiment and that she, herself, would do the hard work of the surgeries. All Patty had to do was take notes, which Annie would dictate, regarding everything that happened. She then reiterated to Patty that it was a real important experiment and added it was something that had never been done anywhere in the world. Patty was ready and willing and Annie was rife with cool determination.

Annie gathered the necessary equipment from the kitchen drawers—the knife sharpener, along with a variety of knives as she was unsure of which size would work best. Patty gathered the notebook, pencil, and sewing kit.

The experiment began, and one by one each frog struggled, squirmed, bled, and then fell limp, though not dead, under Annie's well-sharpened knife. Then, one by one each frog was pillaged in its particular preordained-by-Annie-manner and sewn back up.

Each slit and sewn frog was then placed on the kitchen counter atop a sheet of paper towel with a number written neatly beside it. Some died before placement, some managed to crawl an inch or two away from their number before collapsing and dying, and several had strength enough to crawl to the edge of the counter and fall off, only to be picked up and placed back where they belonged. Annie felt optimistic about the chances of those particular ones remaining alive. However, one by one, even their wet satiny gullets fell still.

The page of lab notes was completed:

> Frog B: time of operation—liver taken out—time of death

> Frog C: time of operation—liver taken out—liver put back in—time of death

And so on, right down the line...

The frogs that had died the most quickly were those who'd had the most stuff removed and the most stuff removed and put back. Some were dead before the stitching-up had even begun.

> Conclusion: The more stuff that is removed from a frog, the faster it dies.

> Note: if the heart is included with the 'stuff'—the minute it is pulled out, the frog dies.

In the end, there was only one frog that remained alive and that was frog A, the one that had simply been slit and sewn back up.

Annie gently put frog A back in the shoebox and placed it just outside the back door. The experiment was complete and the Grand Conclusion of the entire experiment was that frogs could not live if stuff was taken out of them and they could not live if stuff was taken out and stuffed back in, but they could live if they were just cut open and sewed back up.

Annie then announced to the faceless girl who stood in her shadow that their next experiment would be to cut off the legs of the dead frogs and fry them in butter to see if they really did taste like chicken as she had heard people say. It seemed the perfect time to learn the truth about that.

The conclusion was that frogs did taste like chicken.

The smoke had stopped rising towards the ceiling and Annie reached out and pushed the burnt-out butt into the ashtray. *"Only the animals is innocent."*

When her father picked her up from Patty's house that evening, Annie got into the car with the shoebox under one arm, the lab notes under the other. She distracted him from any possible questions regarding the box by describing her day of hunting turtles and frogs with Patty at the pond. No, they hadn't caught any, but then all they had was their bare hands. It was fun anyway.

When she arrived home, she took the box to her bedroom and opened it. Frog 'A' was upright and very still except for an ever so slight pulsing of its sides. She poked it with her finger and it responded by moving one of its front feet. She shut the box and placed it gently under her bed. Later, after dinner, after the evening had come to an end and her bedroom door was closed for the night, she pulled the box out and opened it again. Frog A was crumpled forward, its front feet splayed out to the sides. She poked it a few times and watched and waited. There was no response.

She closed the box, shoved it under her bed, and took up the notebook that held the results of her experiment. She added, in bold hard pressed lead, at the bottom of the page, below the Grand Conclusion, that even when just cut open and sewn back up a frog would die.

———

Annie stared at the butt on the bottom of the ashtray and felt a sudden deep exhaustion. She got up and walked over to where Bobby was curled on his side, sound asleep.

Bertha followed close behind.

Annie grabbed the blanket that hung over the back of the couch just above Bobby's head and lay down on the carpet in front of him.

Bertha, satisfied her world was settled for the time being, stretched out at Annie's feet—and the television droned on.

29

Stella Returns

Annie didn't see the cloud of dust that rose above the trees, not until the distant hammering suddenly ceased and every dog in the fields around her came to an unexpected, perfectly synchronized halt and lifted their heads. She followed their line of vision and saw nothing at first. Then she looked up and spotted the massive cloud hovering over the trees.

She sucked in her breath and waited until the familiar sight of the Galestorm truck rounded the last curve in the driveway.

Stella was home.

The dogs didn't move, not until the horn blared and the blazing red hair emerged from the driver's side of the truck. They broke from the grip of anticipation and charged towards the house.

Ivan roared from within the kennel.

Annie looked the other way, towards the far treeline. The hammering had started up again and, like Bobby, she considered the option of ignoring the arrival herself. However, unlike Bobby, she was in full view of Stella and doing nothing, except standing in the middle of a field.

The horn blared again. Annie succumbed.

Stella took her hand off the horn as Annie started walking towards her. She mumbled gruffly, "God damn, what does it take to be heard around here? You woulda thought that girl was deaf from lookin' at her just standin' there."

Her cell phone rang. She reached in the open driver's door and grabbed it from the passenger seat. "Hello? What! No, you just passed it. Turn 'round and go left when you get to the big red mailbox. Now, why would I wait? I already told you it was the red mailbox. It don't take a rocket scientist. Bye."

She hung up, put the phone back on the seat and continued the conversation to herself. "It's the only mailbox for at least a damn mile, 'cept for the Cranshaws which ain't red and ain't even on the same side of the road!"

She grabbed the pack of Pall Malls off the dashboard. "I swear, some days it's just amazin' I keep goin' all things considered."

She lit a cigarette as she watched Annie finish crossing the fields and open the gate nearest to the kennel. "She sure as hell ain't happy to see me. Fact is, she's lookin' like she's walkin' through mud that's a foot deep, only there ain't any mud, just dry, hard as rock earth, somethin' all of Georgia is gettin' damn tired of dealin' with."

She looked up the track and caught sight of a mound of dirt that hadn't been there when she left. "Somebody's been diggin' out there for some reason or another." She then listened to Bobby's hammering. "And we know who that somebody is, which means it's another one of his big ideas."

She sucked on her cigarette and waited until Annie had passed the kennel and was headed to the driveway, which meant she was well within shouting distance.

"Don't hurt yourself rushin' to greet me!" Smoke billowed from her mouth as she raised her voice. "It's been damn near a week and I ain't called you once, which is because all hell broke loose at that show! But, bein' the smart business woman I am, I ended up benefittin' from all of it, which is why I'm back now, instead of six hours from now—but, oh well, go ahead and take your damn time 'cause we got all day for me to tell you how I got the people eatin' off the backs and fronts of my hands. Hell, some of 'em are even wantin' to lick in between my fingers!"

She laughed and coughed.

Annie stepped from the dirt path onto the gravel.

Stella spoke again, in her more normal tone of voice. "I swear, Greta, it was a thing of beauty." She watched as Annie looked everywhere but right at her, which was not a good sign. As impatient as she was to tell her everything that had happened at the show, her keen eye for potential trouble never slept. As far as she was concerned, a person would have to be missing their brain to not know all about THAT little sign—it was kindergarten material.

Annie crossed the remaining patch of gravel that lay between them. The cheerful greeting that had slowly, against all odds, worked its way to her lips had stumbled and fallen mute the moment Stella called her Greta. She focused on the spits and spats of gravel and dust that shot out from beneath each boot as she walked, and when Stella's legs came into view she looked up and past her, to the truck and beyond, desperate for a little more time. That's when she noticed the cloud of dust above the trees had disintegrated and a fresh cloud was forming. She seized the opportunity. "I think somebody's coming."

Annie's blues finally met Stella's greens.

Stella sucked in on her cigarette, long and hard, then spoke quickly, smoke spilling out with every word. "Never you mind about them 'cause I know some shit has gone on here and I want to know what it is, right now, 'fore they get here, which may be quite awhile seein' as theys probably gonna hit a tree considerin' they're a damn sight dumber than you and you managed to hit one despite the fact you been down my driveway a million times."

She paused and dropped what was left of her cigarette to the ground. "Now there ain't no point in hummin' and sawin' around any big ole bushes, 'cause this is ME you ain't been lookin' at till right now, so spit it out."

Annie turned away from the determined green eyes and looked out over the fields. The dogs were standing, sitting, and lying along the various fence lines watching the two of them with tremendous patience and curiosity. Ivan still roared from within the kennel—what that dog knew, she wished she didn't. She glanced up along the track, half hoping to see Bobby driving down it on his John Deere—not that he would be of any help—but at the very least he might offer her a chance to breathe and think. *Come on, Bobby.* He'd put a pillow under her head sometime during the night. Didn't that mean he would come stand with her?

The hammering ceased for a moment, then resumed, and her hope stumbled and fell.

"Hello! I'm waitin' on you and I ain't got all day!"

Stella lit another cigarette. She was rapidly coming to the conclusion this was a capital T situation because she couldn't remember more than a few times when Annie acted this way—all of them a real long time ago. One time in particular was not too long after she'd found her in that bar. Annie had spent a whole week humming and sawing her way through a thousand bushes. Everything she did regarding the business or anything else only got a quarter done and when she was done with her quarter of everything, she would creep off to the couch and go to sleep.

She didn't answer questions back then, just like she wasn't doing now, and she barely even spoke whole sentences. By the end of what came to seem like a year, after she was done humming and sawing through every single bush in Georgia, she curled up on that couch in a ball so tight even Bobby couldn't straighten her out, not without getting a good kick in the head which he didn't care to deal with. He claimed he didn't want any part of being kicked by a woman because in all likelihood he'd kick back and he just didn't want to do that.

Annie was on that couch for nearly three days. Nobody knew how she went to the bathroom, or if she did. Stella thought to call the ambulance, but didn't like the idea of strangers being a part of their business and she definitely didn't want Annie in the hands of the authorities who could, if Annie talked, do damage to her business. It was bad though. She and Bobby and the boys had about had it. Living with somebody who only did twenty-five percent of what they were supposed to do and took up most of the couch most of the time—particularly when they had a perfectly good bedroom—was just plain miserable on all the people involved.

That's when Stella finally put her foot down. She filled a bucket with cold water and ice cubes and poured it all over the "sleeping beauty." And that's all it took! She wished she'd thought of it sooner. Annie rolled onto the floor and burst into tears, which in Stella's mind was a beginning, as in a lot better than her lying there like a zombie. And as soon as she stopped crying, just for one second, Stella let her have it.

"I ain't gonna take any more of your shit! Goddamn, you ain't worth investin' in 'cause all you do around here is twenty-five percent of a hundred percent. That ain't no business I want to invest in! So you either get up and get on with the other seventy-five percent or you are outta here! Now, Bobby don't wanna get mean, but trust me, if I ask him to, he will, and when he does you will be runnin' clear back to where you come from—case closed. Now, the boys is at school and Bobby's out workin', just like you should be doin', so if you got somethin' you need to get off your chest so you can get that other seventy-five percent to cooperate, you need to do it right now. And don't think I don't know when a girl is bein' eaten up by somethin'. I seen it before and I know, before hearin' it, it ain't somethin' I would want my boys to hear about 'cause they is too young, meanin' they is as innocent as the animals. 'Course it ain't gonna stay that way 'cause it ain't in God's plan for us humans to be innocent, but I intend on keepin' it that way for as long as possible. I ain't gonna let you or anybody else poison their ears with stuff they got no part in."

That was when Annie burst out with the real reason she'd been sitting in that bar in New Orleans in the first place. Back then, she'd told Stella she was on a college break and didn't care if she went back or not, she was fed up. Stella, however, knew there was more to the story than that—it was a weekday, three weeks before Christmas. She didn't know a lot about college, but she did know this wasn't any kind of "college break." New Orleans during a college break was a whole different ball of gum. There was more to this story. She just had to be patient.

So while the ice cubes were melting and in between the tears, Annie told the truth, and in many more words than Stella cared to remember. Bottom line was, Annie had sat herself down at Thanksgiving dinner and told her family all about her daddy having sex with her while she was growing up. It didn't go over real well, so she left and drove as far away as she could. Stella was astounded then, and still was to this day. That girl had gotten the foolish notion in her head that they'd be glad to know about it and, on top of that, she'd told them right there in front of a whole roasted turkey that they hadn't even started eating yet!

The first thing she explained to Annie, while trying to pick up the melting ice cubes, was if she had to tell them something like that, it would've been better to wait until their stomachs were full. Then, at least, they could've had some pleasure before listening to the kind of stuff that makes a person not want to eat in the first place—and as for what her daddy did to her, she told Annie it was a damn shame and that God should've struck him dead, but he didn't because God doesn't mess with the messes people make. She then had to go on to explain that God just watches and hopes the people clean it up themselves which in most cases they don't, which then makes for the living hell most people end up being stuck in.

"Annie, if your father had wanted everybody to know they would've known—case closed. Hell, the whole neighborhood would've known! This was a simple case of you ratting on your father in a situation where nobody was interested, plain and simple! You don't rat on someone to people who could give a rat's ass about that someone because then you end up being the someone nobody wants around, especially not sitting at the table at Thanksgiving in front of a whole roasted turkey!

"Honey, all they were thinkin' on was eatin' and givin' thanks to God for everythin' they got. They sure wasn't in any kind of mood to hear about Daddy screwin' his daughter—end of story! Hell, the whole bunch of 'em are thankin' God that you ran off and they, sure as shit, are hopin' HE, meanin' God, makes sure you never come back! But don't you worry 'bout that—you got a home right here with me and Bobby and the boys—so long as you can be a full hundred percent with us!"

Stella stood there, next to her truck, and studied Annie. She considered the fact that there was a big difference between now and back then. What she was looking at, in the present moment, was a woman who was stuck on not talking about something that had gone on within the last five days, here at HER HOUSE while she was gone, not something that happened a hundred years ago.

Just as she was about to lay into Annie, no holds barred, a red Suburban pulled up behind the Galestorm truck and every dog that had been waiting patiently at the fence lines leapt to attention. Then a dog barked from within the Suburban and every dog on the property roared in response.

A tall blonde woman emerged from the passenger side. Stella turned to her and started yelling. "Tiffany, you and Danny need to take a walk back up the driveway you just came down and see if I got any mail 'cause I got a situation here with my Greta that I need to set straight!"

She turned back to Annie, still yelling at Tiffany. "And take your dog with you so's all my dogs will shut up and I can hear myself talk!"

Annie watched as the tall blonde, who was clearly at a loss for words, walked quickly around to the driver's side of the Suburban. A man of average height with a balding head emerged and together they pulled a dogue from the back of the truck and obediently headed back up the driveway on foot.

She looked back into the green eyes that bored into her and felt a relieving rush of annoyance. "That was real nice, Stella. I am continually astounded by your infinite charm. And, by the way, my name is Annie, A N N I E!"

"Well, you go on ahead and be 'astounded,' A N E, but that don't change a thing."

Stella turned and watched as the pair and their dogue rounded the first curve and disappeared from sight. Satisfied they were out of earshot, she continued, "For your information, them two are here to pick out a pup from Grace's litter. I owe it to 'em considerin' that dogue they got is outta my kennel and, as you probably didn't notice 'cause you don't know shit about this breed, that dogue turned out to be a piece of crap. I had to make 'em that offer to keep 'em from A) showin' the dog, B) tellin' anybody it was from my kennel."

She sucked on her cigarette, exhaled and continued, "So, I ain't only charmin' but I'm generous as shit!" She dropped her cigarette butt to the ground and stomped on it. "But never you mind about that, it ain't your business. What is your business is tellin' me what the hell has gone on here at MY house while I been gone!"

Annie's mind had come to a halt the moment Stella mentioned Grace. Amazing Grace was dead. The loss had suddenly surfaced and overwhelmed everything Stella was saying, along with everything she had been feeling. She looked down at the butt Stella had just stomped on and spoke, but only barely. "Grace is dead, Stella."

Stella hadn't considered this in her thinking. She wasn't sure what she'd considered, but Grace dying sure as hell wasn't it. Her hands flew to her hips. "Say what?!"

Annie peered out at Stella from the abyss of grief she had so suddenly been sucked into. The shocked and angry expression on Stella's face had no impact on her. There was no place for Stella anywhere near what she was feeling. She responded from even further away, "I said, Grace is dead."

Stella's hands remained firmly planted on her hips. "Why the hell are you whisperin'? What did you do to that dog?"

She dropped her hands and started pacing back and forth on the gravel in front of Annie. "You need to start talkin' real fast 'cause I am fast arrivin' at a conclusion that will land you flat on your ass or worse!"

She turned and faced the far tree line. "Does Bobby know about this?!"

She walked furiously to the edge of the gravel. "I knew that big fat silence was nothin' but trouble!"

She cupped her hands around her mouth. "BOBBY, GET YOUR ASS IN HERE!" Then turned back to Annie. "And you best start talkin' right now, as in as soon as I get close enough to hear that wimpy-ass little voice of yours!"

She moved in so close to Annie, she could breathe on her face. "And don't lie to me, 'cause you know I know lyin' from a million miles away."

Stella's mounting anger reached in and shook Annie, hard. Annie looked into the green eyes that were barely a foot away and saw a faceless young girl, cold as stone, lying next to Gracey at the bottom of that grave. She felt a breath away from real danger. She seized a lung full of air, some of it Stella's, and kicked back. "I didn't kill her, you did!"

Stella stepped back in amazement. She dropped her hands from her hips, looked around as if to say "did anybody else hear that?" and then pulled her Pall Malls from her vest pocket.

She studied Annie somewhat warily as she lit up a cigarette. "Well, well, I do believe A N E here got a blaze in her eye." She sucked in and exhaled. "Only thing is, it's what we call a blaze with a itty bitty bit of oxygen, as in it got no stayin' power. There ain't no way, no way..."

Annie breathed in and stayed steady. "Stella, she had bloat. We got her to the vet in time, but her heart gave out from the stress of it. Nothing could be done to save her."

She brushed her brown curls from her cheeks, only to have them fall back again. "Doc Burns said it was a miracle she'd survived whelping a litter of pups."

For a brief moment, the only sound was Bobby's tractor starting up off in the distance. Even Ivan had stopped barking. Then there came the sound of voices and the scrape and scuff of boots and shoes on gravel.

The barking started up again from all corners of the property.

Annie kicked at the gravel and scoffed, "Looks like the newest members of your fan club are back."

Stella looked defiantly at her. "It ain't my fault I got a ton a' people breathin' all up and down my back, wantin' whatever they can get."

She turned and faced the duo and their dog as they rounded the final curve. "We ain't done yet, so you need to take that little walk one more time."

Knowing they would do exactly as she said, she turned back to Annie. "And, as I was tryin' to say until you interrupted me, exactly where do I fit into this little story of yours? Seems to me I was a thousand miles away workin' my ass off, doin' my part. From all ways of lookin' at it, you and Bobby was the ones who was here at this end."

She glanced up the driveway to be sure the duo was far enough away. They were, but she dropped to a loud, harsh whisper anyway. "There ain't no way on God's earth you're gonna blame me for Gracey dyin'."

As Stella was talking, Annie watched the couple and their dogue disappear around the curve for the second time and felt the impulse to run up, grab each of them by the shoulders, and yell at them for their passive compliance. Instead, she turned her anger back to where it belonged. "I'll tell you how you fit in. You never should have bred her! She had a bad heart problem for Christ's sake! Oh, she would've died from it eventually, but the stress of having pups made it happen all the sooner. Bobby said he'd seen it in her and he warned you, but you didn't listen, so now, not only is she dead, but all or some of those pups..."

Stella couldn't and didn't hold back. "I don't need no lectures from you regardin' my dogs and I don't know 'bout what Bobby told you, but it's a damn lie, or else you is lyin' bout what he said. Hell, he ain't a vet and he don't have x-ray vision. And speakin' of vets, I will tell you right now, I'm gonna sue that lyin' bastard, Doc Burns. I swear as much money as I have given him, you'd think he'd have the audacity to be honest with me. He couldn't save her, so now he's got to blame it on some 'heart problem.' Gracey was a fine healthy bitch. I don't got heart problems in my lines, 'specially not Oz's kin—case closed."

She turned from Annie, stuck the cigarette between her lips, and looked out over her fields. When she caught sight of that mound again, she suddenly calmed. Everything was just as she had thought it was.

She inhaled and spoke with a new relaxed confidence. "Hell, I knew this had somethin' to do with one of the dogs from the beginnin'. I seen that mound first thing when I drove in here and I says to myself 'that looks like a damn grave.' I figured it wasn't either one of you buried out there!" Her coarse laugh skidded out from behind the smoke. "But, on the other hand, you just never know what a big fat silence can do to a couple of humans left on their own. 'Course I heard Bobby hammerin' away and I seen you standin' out there in them fields, as usual, like a damn sheepherder, only you ain't one, and I realized the only possibility left was it was a dog lyin' under that mound. I just hadn't figured on it bein' Grace.

"If I had to hear about a death of one of my dogs, I guess you could say Ivan was at the top of my list. That boy is a miserable bastard and a little dyin' on his part wouldn't be such a shock. Anyway, you know me—I don't miss a thing! I just didn't want to jump to no conclusions is all, so I let you tell me somethin' I mostly already knew."

She lifted the cigarette to her lips, and this time fell silent as she sucked in. The cigarette glowed and went dim.

She turned and blew the smoke in Annie's direction, looking past her to the truck. "I just thank God it wasn't Oz, which did cross my mind like a damn lightenin' bolt—till I remembered he was right here in the back of my truck."

She walked past Annie and opened the tailgate.

Oz looked out at her, hot, annoyed, and impatient.

She opened the door to his crate, and he dropped slowly down to the ground beside her, his ears still back, showing his continued annoyance. She patted his head. "God knows, him lyin' dead out there woulda tore my heart out."

Oz left her side and moseyed over to greet Annie.

Stella shut the tailgate. "I just wish God would give me one damn month without some kinda crisis." She looked over just as Annie dropped to her knees to greet Oz. As far as she was concerned this conversation wasn't over, not by a long shot. *There is no way Gracey dyin' is the cause for all of that hummin' and sawin'.*

Her mind jumped swiftly back—beyond Annie's only doing twenty-five percent and ending up on the couch for days, beyond even knowing Annie—to her father telling her about how her mama had walked out on them to find a better life. What she knew, in that moment, was she was facing a situation that was a one hundred percent threat to her well-being. She knew, for sure, Gracey's dying wasn't anywhere near the bottom of it.

She walked over to Annie as Annie kissed the top of Oz's head. "When you two are done kissin', get them other dogs out of the truck, and when we're done with givin' Tiffany and Danny one of those pups and sendin' them on their way, be ready to get an earful regardin' that show. I'm telling you, it was like nothin' I seen in the history of the dog world! Oz and me, we made a big mark, and I got it all on video!"

She glanced up the driveway. "And speakin' of them two, you need to keep quiet about Grace—it's none of their business."

Annie wasn't surprised by the rapid shift in Stella's demeanor and tone. She'd seen it over and over and over again. However, she didn't know, in this situation, whether Stella had figured out a way, as Bobby had put it, "to smell out the truth of it."

She stood up and brushed the dust from her jeans. It was over for now.

Bobby was hard at work on the fence for the exercise track when he heard the dogs bark and saw the cloud of dust over the trees. He had wanted to be further along than he was by the time Stella returned, but it wasn't looking as though it would be that way. With all that had happened in the past five days, he'd lost time. So, on this day he had been determined to catch up as much as possible and, now, seeing her back, he pushed even harder. As long as there was daylight, he would keep going, then maybe by nightfall he would have something to show her that would make her proud.

His thinking about what would go on between Stella and Annie was a waste of time. *Annie's gonna do what she's gonna do and there ain't a damn thing I can do about it.* Besides, from his way of looking at things, Stella would figure it out anyway—it was just a matter of time. All he could do was keep doing what he did best and work up a good sweat, like there was no tomorrow.

It wasn't as though he hadn't already been to hell and back with Stella. They were meant to be together, that was as clear to him as the sky that cloud of dust was rising up into. And he had no doubt there would be another hell waiting at the end of this day. What he didn't know was whether Annie had what it took to survive it. When he'd seen her curled up on the floor that morning, he felt badly for her despite her carrying on about how he gave Stella "a pass" and she wasn't going to participate and on and on. *Fact is, much as Annie thinks she knows Stella, and even havin' been chased off with a loaded shotgun, she ain't nowhere near ready to face what she's gonna face.*

When he'd put that pillow under her head before he left the house at 4 a.m., he'd hoped and prayed she would have a good long sleep and when she woke she'd have the clearness of thinking to drive away, just like she should've done the day before—but didn't. Now there was nothing he could do except what he was already doing.

Then he heard the second round of barking and saw the second cloud of dust. He knew this meant the inevitable would be put off for a while longer. Stella was not so stupid as to jump on what she smelled while outsiders were anywhere in the vicinity. He went back to digging and hammering. More time passed.

"BOBBY, GET YOUR ASS IN HERE!"

He heard her, loud and clear, but chose to ignore it, like he did on most occasions. He knew, from the sound of it, it wasn't to do with what she wasn't done smelling out. And if there was any chance she hadn't smelled it out yet, his dropping what he was doing to see what she wanted, would set her on the scent like stink on shit.

What he needed to do was get on with his day and leave the rest up to God, whoever that was, be it a moose or a camel or nobody at all.

30

Chicken Little

Stella and Oz headed up the porch steps. Annie stood in the driveway and watched the Suburban round the curve and disappear from sight. She hadn't been prepared to say good-bye to any of the pups, not yet. They were just shy of seven weeks old. She'd had it in her mind she would have at least another week with them.

———

"Stella, it's too soon to take them away from their mother."

Stella shot Annie a withering look. "The pups are weaned and though it ain't usual practice, it'll be just fine and besides it's better for bondin' purposes. See, some adults, includin' the younger adults like your Jake, ain't thrilled with the initial presence of a pup, but a pup being this young and havin' the smell that tells him so, he'd have to be a whack job, like Ivan over there, to attack him—and seein' as most dogs like Ivan don't live very long 'cause most people don't have the tolerance for dogs like him—well, he's more likely to accept the young pup to save his own ass."

Tiffany chortled and hugged the little pup Stella had helped her pick out.

Stella soaked it all in and continued, "See, this way you won't have to go to the trouble of havin' to keep a sharp eye out every damn second. Mind you, you're still gonna have to keep a eye out every minute, at least for the first couple weeks, there ain't no way around that."

She went on to explain to them that the mama to the pups was off for the day with Bobby and wouldn't be back till late that night, but she would send a photo to them if they wanted and, as for the paperwork, she would get it to them within the next couple of weeks.

―――――

As Annie stood there in the driveway, she thought about the piles of "paperwork" on Stella's desk, along with the bong that sat precariously on top of them. She then saw herself frantically crawling around Stella's study floor in her nightshirt. The next thing she knew she was laughing so hard she had to sit down, right there in the dirt and gravel!

Stella had just opened the front door when she heard the laughter. As she turned to see what was going on, Bertha burst past her, nearly knocking her over, and raced down the steps.

Oz left Stella's side and followed suit.

When the two dogs reached Annie, they surrounded her, wiggling and wagging, playfully butting their heads into her.

Annie kept right on laughing and laughing and laughing, her light brown curls swishing across her face, her sky blues squeezed shut with delight.

Stella reluctantly walked back down the steps. "That Alice—I mean, Bertha—is gonna be the death of me and everythin' I own."

She stood waving her hand in front of her face as a cloud of dust rose up towards her from beneath the threesome. "What the hell is so damn funny?"

Annie looked up at Stella, all the while pushing playfully at the wiggling beasts that surrounded her. "I don't know, it's the paperwork, Stella. That mess in your study!" She howled again before being able to continue. "Is that where the paperwork for that pup is going to come from?"

Stella watched as Annie fell into another fit of laughter. She was completely baffled, a feeling she didn't much like. "What the hell is the matter with you?" She looked at Bertha and Oz, who in their enthusiasm were nearly smothering Annie. "And just so you know, you're damn lucky these two know it's you, 'cause it wouldn't be playin' that'd be on their minds if they didn't."

Annie caught her breath and spoke again from within the wiggling beasts. "Just a couple nights ago, I was crawling around your study in my nightshirt, hell bent on finding the truth behind all that mayhem!" She fell into laughter again.

"All that 'mayhem'?" Stella paused for a moment, trying to find the sense in what Annie was telling her. "How the hell is it you come up with words like that? Can't you ever just speak plain English?" As far as she could tell, Annie had lost all her stuffing and there was no point in trying to find the sense in what she was saying. What she did feel, though, was a sudden hundred percent drop in the threat level she'd felt earlier. It was back down to its normal every day seventy-five percent which made her feel a whole lot better.

She waved her hand through the cloud of dust that was still being generated. "Right now I got no doubt in my mind that you're about as nuts as I ever seen." She lowered her voice, "'Course, I always knew you wasn't right in the head. This just plugs the penny in the slot now don't it?"

Annie responded without hesitation, "You got that right. I'm not normal!"

Bertha was on her back rolling and bumping into Annie's thigh, her paws in the air.

As Annie spoke, she grabbed at each paw and Bertha mouthed her hand in delighted protestation. "Why else would I keep finding myself crawling around on floors, scared to death and half out of my mind? First at the 'Bears' and now here!"

Oz pushed his head into Annie's shoulder, nearly rolling her onto Bertha.

Annie pushed back against the massive head, one hand braced on Bertha's writhing belly, 'The Bears'! Can you believe I call them that! I am certifiable, there is no doubt about it." She started to laugh again, then ceased because she had to. Her stomach hurt too much.

As she calmed, the beasts calmed as well and sat down, one on either side of her. She rested her arms across each of their shoulders and took a few deep breaths.

Stella watched the dust begin to settle. "Are you tellin' me you was crawlin' around on MY floor lookin' for somethin' I was supposedly hidin' under all them piles?"

That's when it was her turn to laugh. "Yessiree, it's official. You ain't normal but, like I said, you ain't been for years. Hell, I seen you sleep for three days on a couch without peein'. I seen you cry over shit that I ain't never seen no one cry about and laugh over shit that either ain't funny or don't make a damn bit a sense—and Bobby, bein' not normal hisself, laughs right along with you. Then you run into a tree at two miles an hour and get knocked unconscious, write a million letters to some six-year-old girl you met the 'quivalent of yesterday, spend a year with a homo sheepherder in a country a thousand miles away after takin' off from here—where you got everythin' and more—without a word regardin' your leavin'. Then you come back like nothin' happened."

She let out a long sigh of acceptance. "Goddamn, I seen you behave in ways no other human bein' could tolerate, but bein' the toleratin' person I am, here I am watchin' you yet once again, actin' all crazy. And now that you're done, why don't you tell me what it was exactly you was thinkin' that somethin' was that you were lookin' for in my study?"

Annie looked at the ground and shook her head, which was tiny compared to the two broad canine heads next to her. "To tell you the truth, I have no idea. All I can tell you is I had gotten it in my mind that it wasn't like you to be so sloppy in your record keeping—or sloppy period—so I figured you had some secret vault of information that was for your eyes only. Why the hell I even gave a damn I can't remember, because that was the same night Grace died. Bobby interrupted my search with the news she was sick, so we rushed off to the vet and that was the end of it."

Stella reached down into her vest pocket, past the Pall Malls, and pulled out a joint. "Honey," she lit the end of the joint, sucked in, held the sweet smoke in her lungs for as long as possible, and then blew it out over the three heads in front of her, "this ain't like our business back in the day. I don't got to dot every I and cross every P. I mean you just met two of the kind of folks I'm dealin' with in this business. Like I been tellin' you, these people are dumb as the day is long and, on top of that, there ain't no authorities waitin' on me to fuck up so they can rush in and arrest me. I got all the time in the world to do my paperwork and when I need to, I just do what I got to do to please the people who are gettin' my dogs. Sometimes, I don't feel like pleasin' 'em and they get nothin'!!"

She took another hit off the joint. "Hell, there must be a few dozen dogs out there with Oz's name on the paperwork, and he don't got jack-shit to do with 'em. EVERYBODY wants a dog outta Oz and I just ain't got enough of 'em to go around. It's called supply and demand, and the demand is only gonna go up."

She laughed. "Oh, I got the correct paperwork on MY dogs, meanin' the ones I got right here in my kennel that are stayin' here, and I have kept them X's and I's crossed—and that's the somethin' you was lookin' for that you didn't know you was lookin' for, which is why you couldn't find it in the first place."

The joint glowed and she sighed. "And if you'd asked me, I would've showed 'em to you. It ain't no deep dark secret. Goddamn, how long have we been together?—too long for me to be keepin' secrets."

She took another hit and stepped in closer to the threesome. The dust had completely settled. "It's all right there in the bottom drawer of my desk."

She leaned forward and offered Annie the joint. "You be careful now, 'cause if you read that stuff, you ain't never gonna be the same!" She snorted a laugh and shook her head. "How the hell did we hook up anyway? We couldn't be more different, you and me."

Bertha and Oz were still sitting up against Annie. They turned their heads away as Annie took the joint, sucked on it, and blew the smoke back out.

She took a couple more hits, then turned and looked in the same direction Bertha and Oz had—towards the fields.

All of the other dogs were lying, standing, and sitting along the fence lines keeping a close eye on the activity in the driveway.

She smiled and waved.

They all cocked their heads and waited for her next move.

That's when Ivan's barking caught her attention. It had been so constant she'd lost track of it, along with Stella's question "how the hell did we hook up anyway?"

She heard the crunch of boot heels on gravel and turned to see Stella walking over to the truck. She spoke, half assuming Stella probably wouldn't hear her, half expecting she would and not caring either way. "Stella, we didn't hook-up, you hooked me in, just like you hooked Lisa-Lee in, just like you're doing with that Tiffany woman and just like you've done to lots of others. The difference is you got something with me that you weren't expecting to get." Annie didn't really know what she meant—her thoughts were sailing along unfettered by prudence.

Stella opened the back door to her truck and lifted the video camera off the back seat. "You got that right. I got someone who has drove me half crazy for more than a decade!" She turned, camera in hand. "And now that we're done, doin' God knows what, I got somethin' here you need to see. So why don't the three of you get up off the ground and behave like normal people and come on in the house."

Annie watched Stella climb the steps and disappear into the house. She scratched Bertha and Oz behind the ears, then put one hand on each of their backs, and pushed herself to standing. The two beasts waited patiently, until Annie was upright and walking, and then fell in behind her.

———

Bobby glanced through the trees and noticed the dogs had, once again, arranged themselves along the fences. He pushed his shovel into the dirt and walked to the tree line where he could get a closer look. All he could make out was Annie on the ground laughing and wrestling with Bertha and Oz, creating a sizable cloud of dust while Stella stood by and watched. He mumbled out loud, "All hell ain't broke loose yet."

He walked back and hoisted the next post—the muscles on his bare back taut and wet with sweat. "It ain't broke loose yet, but it will." He pushed the end of the post down into the hole. "Them two is headed straight for it."

As soon as Annie and Stella walked into the house, Bertha settled in her crate and Oz stretched out on the cool black-and-white squares. And when the familiar, endless rush of words began to spill from Stella's mouth they began to snore.

Stella had gone directly to the coffee pot. "Speakin' of Lisa-Lee, that girl went and fell in love with a boy who I believe is gonna be a fine help to Bobby with all them projects."

She walked back to the table with a mug of black coffee. "He's the one who took this video for me. A fine young man, if I say so myself. His name's Billy and they'll be down here in a couple days."

She sat down across from Annie who was lighting up one of HER Pall Malls. "And while you're at it, why don't you light one of MY cigarettes for me." She took a gulp of coffee and sat back. "So, check this out, the president of the club, who you'll see on this video—he's the one with the swolled up face—well, he left before the dinner 'cause he just couldn't take it anymore.

"Fact is, Margaret told me he's done with the club forever, which gets one big fat load off my back seein' as he was one of those who coulda made a whole lotta trouble for me. And he wasn't the only one who didn't go to the dinner. Just about every one of the important people didn't bother to go, which is exactly why I left after two minutes. It was mostly Margaret and the stupid people going on and on about how wonderful everythin' was and how proud everybody was of everybody else."

She laughed a hardy laugh as she took the lighted cigarette from Annie. "Honey, after you watch that video, you tell me if they was talkin' about the same show I was at."

She then sucked on the cigarette and let out a smoke laden snort. "It's an amazin' thing when a whole buncha' people see things like they want it to be 'cause they don't got the presence of mind to see it like it is."

Annie picked up the camera, looked in the viewfinder, and pressed the playback button.

Stella continued, "And I met Mabel, the one I told you about who I sent that pup to six months ago. She ain't as pretty or nice as Tiffany, and speakin' of Tiffany, there ain't any more to that girl than what you see in the first two seconds you meet her."

Annie responded from behind the viewfinder as she watched Stella and Oz stroll into the ring. "The word you're looking for is shallow."

Stella snapped back, "For your information, I ain't lookin' for any words. I got all the words I need! Anyway, Tiffany got the personality of one them lanky dogs that prances around the ring, hair flowin', sayin' look at me and I am just dyin' to be pleasin' to everyone, especially Stella." She laughed. "That girl don't know it yet, but she's gonna be showin' my dogs and housin' a whole bunch that ain't been born yet. Hell, I might even give her a couple of my best here-and-now dogs to take care of and co-own with me—not on paper mind you, I ain't stupid. Of course, that don't include Oz here."

Oz opened his eyes briefly, while still snoring, and then closed them again.

Annie chuckled as she watched the judge get up off his hands and knees and throw the microphone to the ground.

Stella looked across the table at her. "And that's just the beginnin', honey. Before long you're gonna be back down on the ground with them two dogs laughin' your ass off."

She waited a moment as Annie chuckled some more and continued on. "Anyway, Mabel ain't so dumb as she acts—she's just messed up, as in she was so excited about meetin' me she drove a thousand miles not knowin' she left her dog, one she got from me, on the damn sidewalk in front of her house! And now she thinks she's gonna be my best friend, like a lotta people do, and I'm gonna go on ahead and let her think that 'cause there's a use for her, I just ain't figured it out yet.

"Anyway, when I got up from the table at the dinner and told her I was goin' home, she looked like that Chicken Little looked after the whole sky fell on his head."

Annie spoke up from behind the viewfinder. "The sky didn't fall on Chicken Little, he only thought it did. It was just an acorn." She put the camera down on the table and pushed the off button. "He was what we call an alarmist and I can't watch this thing with you going on and on."

Stella snorted. "My point bein' that the Chicken Little I'm talkin' about DID have the sky fall on his head and it weren't just alarmin' to him, it damn near killed him and the look on his face, after the sky finished crushin' him, was just like the look on Mabel's face last night at the dinner table."

She picked up her mug and gulped down a few more mouthfuls. "Just let me finish what I'm sayin' and we'll put the damn video in the VCR and watch it on the big screen. Hell, maybe we'll even wait till Bobby gets in, so he can watch it too."

She sucked on her cigarette and put it back in the ashtray. "Anyway, so listen, as much use as Mabel might be to me, I got to keep a close eye on her 'cause she ain't the sweet kinda person Tiffany is. She's one of them that wants to snuggle up real close. Then, the next thing you know, she's got them big ole cat claws out and sinks 'em deep in your back while you're lookin' the other way. What she ain't figured out is I ain't never gonna look the other way, which means she's gonna be frustrated even more than she already is 'cause what she wants, that I got, has given her a whole other level of frustration that she ain't had before, as in one day that bitch is gonna die from wantin' so hard. I'm tellin' you now..." Stella suddenly stopped, mid-sentence. It wasn't the sight of Annie putting her cigarette out and standing up that caused her to stop, but rather the excessively loud squeal of her chair on the floor as she did so.

Annie spoke as Stella's incomplete sentence still hung in the air. "I can't listen to this anymore, Stella. I have to get the dogs in and run a few errands."

Stella snapped back, "And I can't talk anymore 'cause I got a hundred phone calls to make!" She went to the sink and dumped the last few mouthfuls of now lukewarm coffee from her mug and turned on the faucet. "Plus I'm waitin' on a few calls, one bein' from this Sally Elliot woman who's a whole other ball of gum from Tiffany and Mabel. She's smart as shit, richer 'n God, and real interested in me." She rinsed the mug and turned back around. Annie was gone. She listened to the sound of boots going down the front steps, then the hammering in the distance.

Oz lifted his head up from the black-and-white squares.

As she stood there, empty mug in hand, she now knew for certain the conversation wasn't over, not in a million years. She walked defiantly to the screen door and opened it. Annie and Bertha had nearly reached the gravel. "Annie, answer me one question 'fore you do all them things you need to do for me."

Annie turned out of habit, not because she wanted to. The red blaze of hair that stuck out from behind the screen door seemed miles away, but the voice was smack in the middle of her head, vociferous and jarring.

"Seein' as you and Bobby are all buddy-buddy again, when did you last see him?"

Annie braced herself as the miles had suddenly become inches and she could see and feel the piercing green eyes. She then heard her own voice loud and clear. "I haven't seen him since Grace died." She stepped out onto the gravel with Big Bertha at her side. For the first time in all their years together she had just handed Stella a flat out lie and it wasn't all that hard.

Stella continued, "Well, where the hell has he been sleepin' every night?"

Annie kept on walking. Stella's voice was behind her now. "How should I know? Like I said, I haven't seen him since Grace died." This time the lie rolled off her tongue as though she'd done it a thousand times before and, for a precious few moments, as she heard the door slam shut and the sound of her own boot heels to gravel, she felt a thousandfold stronger and lighter.

———

As Bobby pulled another fence board from the trailer, he heard his truck start up. He paused and listened, prepared for the worst, but there was no sound of sudden acceleration accompanied by the harsh scrawl of frantic tires to gravel, nor was there the bellow of the devil on a rampage.

He took a deep breath and glanced down at his shadow, which had grown a damn sight longer since the last time he'd looked. He figured it to be somewhere around 4 or 5 p.m., well within the time period of when Annie generally ran her errands.

He hoisted the board onto his shoulder. All he could think about was the work he'd done, how much more there was to do, and how grateful he was to oblige.

31

The Red Door

As the red door closed behind her, Stella felt half inclined to turn around and put her big DO NOT DISTURB sign on it just in case anybody, particularly Bobby or Annie, got it in their head to drop in without giving a thought to the rules of the house. The most important rule being when that door was closed, it meant no interruptions, excluding the fact of one of them dropping dead, or nearly dropping dead, and needing her to know about it. Of course, considering the present situation, one of them dropping dead was still no reason to come in through that door. *Far as I'm concerned that girl can drop dead in the middle of the driveway and I would use her as a speed bump. I swear, in all my years of toleratin' her and givin' her everythin' she needed, this is a first. She just took me for a fool and flat out lied!*

Ivan's roar came in through the open windows.

Stella turned from the living room and walked through the kitchen, nearly tripping over Oz, who hadn't even bothered to lift his head from the cool of the black-and-white squares when he'd heard the red door slam shut.

She looked back at him once she'd stumbled her way around him. "What the hell is wrong with you? I coulda been some kinda intruder and what do you do?—nothin' at all, just lyin' there like a big ass lump."

She continued to where she was headed, which was the kitchen sink, but she couldn't remember why. "I ain't never again tellin' anybody you dogs will protect their ass from danger 'cause that would be lyin' now wouldn't it—somethin' that's lookin' to be real common around here these days."

Oz raised his eyebrows, lowered them, and let out a huge sigh. His large lips softly slapped the floor as the air blew out from beneath them.

Ivan roared again, reminding Stella of what she had been about to do. She leaned across the sink and yelled out the open window, "SHUT YOUR ASS UP! I'M WARNIN' YOU!" She shut the window. "I swear, he is livin' proof God screws up sometimes, 'cause that dog ain't so innocent as all the rest of his animals, not one bit, and if that boy don't watch his ass, his days is numbered. He ain't normal, just like A N E ain't normal."

She walked around Oz to the couch and looked at the all too familiar dent of Bobby having slept there. She shook her head as she bent over and smacked it out with both hands, just like she'd done a thousand times before. As she did this, she looked at the floor and saw the familiar tiny rectangles of dried dirt which had fallen straight from the deep rubber treads of Bobby's work boots, the very boots he continually failed to take off at the door. Then she took note of the little pillow lying right there, next to the couch, complete with a strand or two of dirty blonde curls. It was all a story waiting to be told and she was real interested in hearing it. *If Annie was smart, she woulda got rid of the evidence 'fore she lied.*

One thing Stella was always clear about with her sons and anyone else who was interested in her advice, including Annie, was "you don't lie unless you can back it up or make sure there ain't nothin' pointin' straight at it sayin' you're a lyin' SOB." Her boys, as young as they were, never figured they'd have to lie about anything, but she told them there would be plenty of times when they would have to in order to save themselves from one thing or another. She also told them she hoped they never lied to family the way she had to do to her mama on a regular basis and the way her mama did to her.

Of course, she explained to them that her situation was different because she was forced at twelve years old to live with a mother who'd left her high and dry when she was only eight. It was one of those situations that wasn't meant to work out, meaning lying would be a part of it from the get-go. Her mama had already done her more harm than any mama should ever do, "but," she had told them, "in most cases, meanin' right here in this house, it's unnatural to lie to family and if you do, it means hell is comin' down on everybody concerned. Families can't never be made on lies—case closed."

Her own mama was always looking for anything that would give her the opportunity to accuse her of lying so she could beat her or say whatever she needed to say to try to squish the life out of her—'try' being the operative word because her mama had not only failed herself by intending to be rich and famous and ending up trailer trash, she had also failed to squish her own daughter into that same trailer trash slot.

What her mama taught her, not on purpose of course, was how to lie like the devil, and even then it didn't always work, because even if she weren't lying her mama would say she was, if she was having a bad day, which was most days. And sometimes, after a good beating, her mama would lock her in her bedroom, even board up her windows, like she did in the end.

Her leaving that picture of her and Danny kissing under her mattress seemed like a big mistake when her mama first found it, but in the end it wasn't, because her climbing out her bedroom window, after Danny ripped those boards off, and running away with him, was the very thing that saved her from ending up in that trailer trash slot. *As smart as I was, a girl can only take so much from her own mama 'fore she has no stuffing left.*

Stella pulled the upright vacuum from the closet and uncoiled the long black cord. Back in those days, she'd kept her bedroom as spotless and tidy as possible, just like she kept her house now, if for no other reason than to have a full understanding of what might've gone on when she wasn't there.

She plugged in the cord, and then lit up a cigarette—smoking while vacuuming was really satisfying to her, particularly when she was mad. The way she saw it, she and the vacuum cleaner were a team, roaring and sucking through all those layers of dirt and lies until it all came clear. And, right now, the only thing that was clear was she didn't mind Annie not being normal—hell, she'd tolerated it for years—but when she acted not normal on top of her already not normal self, then had the audacity to lie on top of it—that was a sure sign that something real fascinating was going on, as in there was a big ass problem.

She'd never thought for a second Annie had it in her to lie straight to her face, but there it was in black-and-white, and all she could think was that whatever had driven her to do so had to be something that was more than worth her while to get to the bottom of, as in she'd rot in hell before she'd let it go.

Bobby stood up and looked down his new stretch of completed fence. It surely was a thing of beauty. And the shadow it now laid out across the ground was about as big as he figured that "great wall of China" Annie had told him about was.

He pulled a cotton rag from his back pocket, wiped his forehead, then walked over to the tractor and took his shirt from off the seat. What he had to figure out, now, was whether to keep going until he couldn't see the nails to pound anymore, or head in to the house to face the trouble that was waiting for him as sure as he knew the night was coming.

He walked over to the treeline, carrying his shirt under one arm, and looked across the fields to the house. There it was, as visible to the naked eye as a fire in the pitch black. The red door was shut tight. Any of the tiniest bits of hope he might've been holding in his other back pocket, the one with the hole in it, were dead and gone.

She'd had him put that extra thick door in shortly after he met her, and she wanted it painted red on the side that would show when it was closed and black on the other side for when it was open. She'd told him that seeing as most churches had big red doors, she should too.

"My house is as much God's house as them churches, Bobby. There ain't a drop of difference between the two, except I got to pay taxes and they don't, which don't seem fair considerin' I got a direct line to God, unlike most of them priests who never stop for two seconds to listen to the animals."

That door was only closed some nights and during the most miserable heat of summer when they needed the air conditioner on to stay alive, or during a cold spell in the winter. But when she was alone in the house and that door was closed and it wasn't the dead of summer, dead of winter, or the dead of night, it meant she wanted total privacy, as in she was stewing on something and needed the time and space to see clear through to the truth.

"When that door is closed and I'm on the inside and everybody else is on the outside, it means church is in session and the only other person allowed in here is God and any of his animals."

Bobby slowly put his shirt on as he walked through the tree line and over to Gracey's grave. He pulled his cigarettes out of the breast pocket and settled onto the same rock he'd settled on a couple days earlier, all the while considering the fact he would have to do some engraving on both of the rocks if they were to stay there, something which only seemed right.

He lit his cigarette and scanned the fields, each of which had a couple of trees to provide shade for the dogs. The dogs were lying in various formations within the long shadows of those trees. Each one of them had their head raised and were facing the house, a sure sign it was nearly five o'clock which was time for Annie to come back down that driveway and bring them in for dinner. He watched with them for a time and, as usual, tried to see things through their eyes. The fences, the trees, the kennel, the driveway—*hell, they probly don't see the driveway as anythin' but a blank space*— it all looked the same to them until something or someone moved that wasn't a part of that same, which then gave them cause to shift from neutral into paying close attention. And then there were the sounds that came out of that same, as in the same bird calls, the rustle of the wind, Ivan's roar, his tractor in the far field, the hammering—none of it gave cause to do anything other than a little bitty twitch of the ear, which only meant they were listening to something that they were used to hearing. If there happened to be a sound that signaled that something was different or about to be, that's when they paid attention and their ears would cock forward in full alert.

He listened and watched and didn't want any of it to change, and he knew that was the part of him that had nothing to do with being a dog. They didn't care, one way or the other, as to whether things changed or not. Wanting or not wanting wasn't how they thought about things—things were the way they were and when they changed, they were the way they were again, and so on.

One thing that always gave him comfort when he sat with the dogs like this, was knowing that Do-this and Do-that, whatever happened to them after he left, they never held it against him. They didn't spend time hoping and worrying about when he would come back—and if he'd ever gone back they would've gotten on with him as if he never left. There was great comfort in knowing that.

He sucked in on his cigarette and looked from the dogs to the cloudless sky. He then searched the horizon in all directions. *It'll be a damn good thing if a few of them storm clouds from the north they was talkin' about on the TV wander down this way. We sure can use the water.*

He looked back at the dogs, their ears twitching, eyes still on the house, and realized not one of them ever had a thought like that. They didn't wish for something that hadn't happened yet and didn't worry if it never did. They never thought about taking something back, like his telling Annie what he told her. Oh, they knew when something was going to happen, but they didn't hope or wish for it, not the way people do. It was different for them and someday, before he died, he was going learn how to see it exactly as they did.

He settled back into looking at what was right in front of him, the dogs, the trees, the fields, the kennel he'd built, and the fences he'd made.

That's when the dogs' heads shifted slightly and their ears suddenly pricked forward.

He shifted with them and saw the red door turn to black as Stella walked out onto the porch and down the front steps.

Ivan roared.

Stella looked towards the kennel, then out over the fields.

Bobby waved his cigarette in the air.

She stopped for a second, as if she might've seen him, but didn't respond—she just turned and climbed into the Galestorm truck, then drove away.

He figured she probably hadn't seen him because he was in the late afternoon shadows of the treeline, or he figured she had seen him—either way it wasn't worth thinking about. But what was worth thinking about was how calmly she moved and how that cloud of dust that rose up behind her as she drove away was just a normal sized one, not something that happened all that often.

He looked back at the dogs. Their ears were down again and back to twitching—except for Ivan who continued to roar till the sound of the truck was gone.

He pulled another cigarette from his pack and considered how much more he still had to learn from these dogs.

————

Forty-five minutes later, after Bobby had walked back to his tractor and returned to Gracey's grave with a couple of beers, the Galestorm truck came back down the driveway.

Bobby finished the rest of his second beer and watched closely. This time, aside from Ivan, the other dogs had no response. They didn't even bother to prick their ears forward because they knew who it was, and the fact that it wasn't Annie was all that mattered to them for the time being.

The truck pulled up to the same spot it had been in before and the engine ceased.

Stella emerged, still calm as most days before sun-up, and walked around to the passenger side. She pulled out an armful of grocery bags, kicked the passenger door closed, and headed back to the house. She didn't bother to look anywhere but where she was going. She hesitated for a moment, then pushed through the screen door and into the house. The red door remained black, which meant to Bobby that the stewing part was done and gone. She had moved on to the next phase. What that was he had no idea, but he knew he would find out soon enough.

He finished his beer and slowly stood up. His time with Gracey was over and so was the longest day he'd seen in years. He glanced back at the driveway and wondered where Annie was. Somebody had to get the dogs in and feed them and it wasn't looking like it would be her.

He slowly picked up every cigarette butt he had stomped into the dirt, apologized to Gracey as he did so, and dropped them one by one into the two empty beer cans. He then walked off the grave and back to his tractor. That's when every dog in the fields began barking and, without looking, he knew his truck was coming down the driveway.

He shook his head. Why Annie hadn't just taken his truck and gotten the hell out was beyond his way of thinking. He had no understanding of how that woman ticked, or what the hell she was thinking, or what she wanted from him—or Stella. It was time for her to mind her own business and move on, just as he'd already tried to tell her. *All she's doin' is the 'quivalent of shootin' her own foot off—and that ain't never a good thing to do.*

He walked slowly through the treeline listening to the dogs bark and watching his thick brown boots kick through the green-brown grass, one after the other. He figured Annie was out of the truck and almost to the first of the fence gates. As soon as she reached that point, the barking would stop and he just might be able to hear that slight crunch of the grass under his boots.

The first time he ever heard that sound was the day after Annie was run off the property. For a few hours after the shotgun blast he was deaf—couldn't hear a damn thing. Unfortunately, he wasn't still deaf that night, under the moon and all those stars, when Stella told him all about what his father did to his mother. He'd heard every word. It was that next morning, as he walked across the fields to his tractor, that he heard that crunch under his boots. At first, he didn't know what it was, and then he looked down. It wasn't like it was something that hadn't been there for a thousand days before, but for some reason that was the moment he heard it, and from then on, he paid particular attention to it whenever he had the chance. He figured there were probably a million other things he never noticed that were waiting for him. Hell, most of the reason he loved to spend his days the way he did, besides liking to build things, was because whether it was driving the tractor, watching the dogs, walking from one post to the next, or sitting under a tree having a smoke, there was always the chance he'd hear or see something new that had been around longer than he could imagine.

The fact that it was new to him and maybe not to most other people made him feel lonely at first, because they'd known about it since they were little and here he was forty-five years old. Then there were people, like Stella, who didn't care about any of it. They'd think he was just plain nuts if he tried to point it out to them, which is why he didn't. Of course, all his life, since Do-this and Do-that, a lot of people, including Stella, appreciated the things he noticed about dogs that they never did, but that wasn't the same as noticing the sound of the grass under their boots, probably because dogs weren't as simple as grass.

The truth of the matter was, as time went by, every time he noticed something new like the crunch of the grass, the smell of Georgia's red earth, the difference in the sound of the wind when it was coming straight into his face, hitting him from the side or coming from behind, or the fact of different birds making different sounds—each time he felt less lonely and cared less and less about whether people thought he was crazy or not.

As he approached the tractor, he still hadn't heard the crunch under his boots, not because it wasn't there, but because not only had the barking not stopped, it had become louder. He turned back towards the treeline. From what he could see through the spaces between the trees, the dogs were running away from the kennel towards Gracey's grave, all eyes on the dirt track.

He put the two empty beer cans on the tractor seat and walked back to the treeline. From there he could see Annie's slim figure striding down the track towards him, the dogs running as close to her as they could, tails a' wagging, bouncing along the fences.

He noticed she wasn't slouching or moving slowly as she usually did these days or like she did back when she'd first moved in with them. In fact, he hadn't seen her walk like this since the days when their business was booming and she was chock full of all that confidence Stella had given her.

He leaned up against one of the trees. He couldn't think of a thing that would make her walk like that except if Stella had done something regarding this situation that hadn't occurred to him, which didn't seem likely.

He waited.

32

Fifteen Pairs of Amber Eyes

Annie spoke to the dogs as she walked and strained to look beyond the trees. "You all have to wait, I'll feed you as soon as I can. I have to talk to Bobby first." She glanced over at them as they trotted along the fence lines keeping pace with her.

Something she hadn't yet considered was life without them, or life beyond any of this for that matter. She looked up the track towards Grace's grave. All she could do right now was find Bobby, tell him what had gone on and what she had decided to do. It was only right that he know.

Bobby stepped out from the trees as Annie approached the grave.

Annie stopped abruptly. "Jesus, Bobby, you scared me! I thought you were still in the back field."

Bobby put his hands in his jeans pockets as he spoke. "I WAS in the back field till I heard my truck come in, then heard them dogs gettin' closer to Gracey here," he flicked his chin towards the grave, "instead of further away. Then I come over to see you walkin' out here like I ain't seen you walk in a long time. I'm thinkin', shit, maybe I don't want to hear what that woman is itchin' to tell me, or maybe I do, you tell me—which is it?"

Annie looked at Bobby, and for the first time since she'd slapped Stella with the lie and left her standing on the front porch, she wavered from her newfound sense of conviction. She could tell from the tone of his question that he really only wanted her there if she had the right answer.

She looked down at the well-worn toes of her cowboy boots and kicked at the ground. "I know you'd rather I just walk away from here with my mouth shut and leave you and Stella to your life, but I can't do that. I have ..."

Bobby interrupted her. "Annie, I already heard your little speech 'bout how you knowin' about Greta and not sayin' anythin' is the 'quivalent to you pullin' the trigger right along with me and Stella—seein' as I kept my mouth shut." He pulled one of his hands from his jeans pocket and held up three fingers. "That makes three of us, so far, who killed that girl and there's no tellin' how many more 'fore all is said and done and that ain't includin' the fact Greta went and got the damn gun in the first place."

He put his hand back in his pocket. "That's how you look at it and you got a right to look at it however you want. The real fact of the matter is, it don't matter anymore. Stella will do whatever it is she's gonna do about it. Like I told you already, in the best way I know how, I just hope you ain't steppin' into a pile of shit that's deeper than you can get out of."

Annie folded her arms across her chest as the sleeves of her "Georgia Gal" T-shirt flapped with the first gust of a warm early evening breeze. She looked up at the sky, then back at Bobby who had also shifted his attention skyward. "Bobby, all she knows right now is that Grace is dead and I crawled around in her study, half out of my mind, in the middle of that same night." She glanced over at Grace's grave. "And when she asked, I told her I haven't seen you since we took Grace to the hospital."

Bobby scanned the horizon above Annie's head as she spoke. There were no clouds yet, but maybe rain was on its way—all he could do was hope. He laughed as her words sank in, like an after thought. "Oh, now that right there was your big mistake, especially if you wasn't intendin' on tellin' her nothin' more."

He turned and started walking back towards the trees, speaking as he went. "See, between you lyin' to her and walkin' out here like you just did, in plain sight—alls I got to say is, you go on ahead and do what you got to do, and I'm gonna do what I got to do, which is go pack up my tractor and head on in—but darlin', don't ever say I didn't warn you."

Annie watched Bobby walk into the trees and uncrossed her arms. A second gust of wind blew into her and, this time, she took note of how the sleeves of her T-shirt flapped against her arms. Back when she and Bobby built the kennel, she'd worn the very same T-shirt, on many a day. By the time they were mid-way through the project, her arms filled the sleeves to the point where no amount of wind could flap them. She'd hauled plank after plank of wood, pounded a million nails, hauled, mixed, and laid thousands of pounds of concrete and plaster, day after day, week after week, month after month.

Bobby had joked with her about it. "I'd say your days as a pricey call girl are over for real now, darlin'. Ain't none of those men gonna pay to have one of them arms hooked up around his—mind you, you're still as beautiful as the day is long, but lookin' like you could whoop a man's ass in a arm wrestlin' match? Well, it just don't go over so good with a man who's so deep down small he's willin' to pay a thousand bucks to have a woman make him feel big."

She watched him leave the trees and walk into the far field, moving at his usual slow and steady pace. Whether he was mad, sad, or glad, he rarely moved otherwise. When he disappeared from view, she was struck with the unexpected pang of what she'd felt the day he'd driven off in his truck, leaving her standing in the Atlanta police parking lot with the warning that she should never come back. He was the big brother she'd always wanted and it seemed to her, in that moment, that the hardest thing about what she was about to do was the likelihood she would lose him again, and this time for good.

Her own two brothers, whom she'd tried to reach out to during her first months in Georgia, at first refused to accept her phone calls. When they finally did speak to her, it was to reiterate, with razor sharp clarity, that she was selfish, always had been, and as far as they were concerned, after what she'd done, she was no longer a part of the family. She never told Stella or Bobby about those calls, but it was the sting of these rejections that had pushed her to finally tell them the truth of why she landed in that bar in New Orleans—that PLUS the bucket of ice water Stella dumped on her.

Annie turned and looked beyond the patiently waiting dogs to the house. The breeze lifted her light brown curls from her cheeks. Suddenly, she was standing on the ferry deck as it plowed through the night towards Greece, away from Stella—and she felt the cold stone in her belly. She sucked in on the warm air as it blew across her face, then started to walk slowly back down the track.

All the dogs turned and raced ahead to their respective gates by the kennel. They were certain she was finally going to feed them!

She looked again at the house half expecting, even hoping, to see Stella standing on the front porch watching her—but she wasn't. Her thoughts then trailed back to her mother sitting across from her at the table that Thanksgiving, staring blankly at her as her father implored her to talk about why she would accuse him of such things. He said he would do whatever it took to get her the help she needed. That's when her mother's vacant eyes narrowed and turned cold—a silent and chilling admonition to her daughter.

In that same moment, her oldest brother shoved his chair back from the table and stood up. He walked to their mother's side and turned to face Annie with one hand on the back of their mother's chair. His eyes had also gone cold. She braced herself as he spoke. "Annie, you've been selfish your whole life, but this, this is way over the top. What you need, that Dad doesn't seem to understand, is to get up and get out." He then turned to their father. "Dad, you never got it, did you? She's a spoilt and manipulative brat. You gave her everything she wanted, which was a hell of a lot more than I ever got, and now look what she does!"

Annie sucked in again in an effort to bring herself back, but the memory was more real than the Georgia breeze. Her brother's bite had gone deep. She looked frantically to her grandparents who were seated at the far end of the table. They were frozen in an astonished and horrified silence. Then it sank in. She'd made a huge mistake.

All she could think to do was get up from the table and leave—which she did. And as she walked towards the front door, she heard her mother get up and go into the kitchen, followed by her brother's now concerned voice, "Are you okay, Mom?"

The floor disappeared beneath her feet, but somehow she was able to reach the door, open it and walk out.

Annie struggled to feel the Georgia earth beneath her boots as she walked.

It was her father who followed her out on to the front walk. When he caught up with her, he grabbed her arm and spoke with quiet urgency. "Annie, I've always wanted the best for you. You know that, don't you?"

She firmly pulled her father's hand from her arm and turned to demand an explanation for his having abandoned her so utterly and completely, but the agony in his face silenced her. Instead, she placed her hand gently on his shoulder and heard another voice speak from very far away. "It's OK, Dad, really, it's just time for me to go."

Annie squinted through the pain and watched the dirt track move slowly beneath her feet. She kicked at rocks and clumps of dried dirt that had fallen from Bobby's tractor tires over the past hours and days. Suddenly, there was only grass, and then gravel. She stopped and looked up just as Big Bertha stuck her head out of Bobby's truck. She was standing in the driveway.

That's when the screen door up at the house opened and all the dogs that had been patiently waiting by their respective gates, let loose with a frantic round of barking. Annie looked over at the house as the blaze of red hair strode out to the edge of the porch. Stella had been waiting. When she spoke, her voice was loud and firm.

"When you're done feedin' them dogs who, by the way, have been waitin' on you for a thousand hours, then you need to go get Bobby who you ain't talked to since Gracey died and come on in here. We got a dinner to eat and a show to watch."

Stella glanced over at Bertha whose head was still sticking out of the truck window. "And I swear that bitch ain't took her eyes off you the whole time you was out there blabbin' with him."

The dogs had fallen silent the moment Stella opened her mouth, except for Ivan who continued to roar wildly from within the kennel.

Stella snorted and spun back around to face the screen door. With the flare of a conductor in the final moments of a crescendo, she raised her hand high above her head. "And give that dog a message for me, while you're at it, which is his days is numbered if he don't shut the hell up." She dropped her arm and disappeared back into the house.

Annie stared at the empty porch, then breathed a sigh of relief. Stella was in fine form! That night with her family, her final words to her father, all of it had just been knocked to kingdom come, gone like it'd never been.

She walked to the truck and, as she let Bertha out, felt a rush of gratitude. She'd felt this time and time again, the first time being when Stella walked into that bar, placed her Herculean hand on her young shoulder and told those two men, in her own indomitable way, to back off. It was the reason she was here, the reason she'd come back and the reason she now found herself rapidly re-considering Bobby's warning to "leave well enough alone." Stella had just made it clear she knew she'd been lied to, but was unconcerned, even humored by it. Nothing had to change unless Annie wanted it to, and what would be the point?

As she rounded the back corner of the kennel, with Big Bertha at her side, she was blithely on the brink of allowing her waning convictions to also be knocked to kingdom come, but it didn't happen. Instead, when she rounded that corner she ran smack into fifteen pairs of amber eyes staring out at her from behind closed gates. She halted in her path, and they continued to stare. Every one of these dogs had been right there as Bobby sat limply against the wall of the kennel drinking beer and recounting the details of Greta's death. None of them would ever let her forget, hungry or not, and there was Ivan. He would..."

"I will tell you right now her wings is spread 'bout far as the eye can see."

Annie broke from the dogs and looked at Bobby who was approaching from the barn. She hadn't heard his tractor since she'd left Gracey's grave.

Bobby spoke again. "Oh, I saw her out there on the porch and heard most of what she said, and I will tell you right now that you best do what you think you gotta do 'fore she wraps them wings around you and makes you forget all about it, meanin' you'll be right back at the beginnin', stuck here just like me—which you ain't meant to be."

Annie struggled to get over the fact of not having heard his tractor enter the barn, something which had always been so audible to her, and she was confused by his words. "Are you saying now that you want me to tell her?"

"What I'm sayin' is you don't got a choice."

Bobby opened five of the runs that came off the back of the kennel and then walked to the gate opposite Annie. "Now, I ain't gonna clap while you do what you gotta do, and don't be expectin' me to pay you any mind once you're done 'cause I'll be busy mindin' my own battle with the devil in her."

He opened the gate and each of the first group of five dogs ran through it and into their respective runs. He patted the last dog on the rear as it ran by him. "I been through it before and I ain't dead yet, which means what I gotta do right now is go take care of them pups, take a shower, and put on my wrestlin' with the devil outfit."

He walked past her, then chuckled softly. "It's a hell of a sight that outfit, I'll tell you that."

Annie watched him walk away almost as unexpectedly as he'd appeared. His shoulders slowly slumped forward just as they had when he stood with Doc Burns in the doorway of the hospital. Then he was gone.

She turned and walked slowly along the back of the kennel, opening up the rest of the runs as she did so. She searched for any remnants of the strength she'd felt earlier, but all she could come up with was deep down dread.

33

God's Business

Annie hugged several bags of goods as she pushed through the screen door into the house. Her dread had subsided once she'd fed the dogs and spent a little private time with Ivan who'd happily rolled onto his back and offered up his belly for a good scratch. She'd considered it both a sign of his support and a reminder she wasn't doing this just for Greta. She was doing this for him and anyone else who was held hostage by what they knew and couldn't speak. It had been a righteous moment.

However, as soon as she'd left the kennel and heard the scuff of her boot heels on the gravel, she felt as bewildered as she had been the morning Bobby told her about Greta. Her legs went weak but, rather than collapse right there where she'd sat and laughed with Oz and Bertha only hours earlier, she somehow managed to get across the driveway to Bobby's truck. As she leaned into it to gather the bags, she steadied her legs with the knowledge she could do this in her own time—there was no rush. In the end, who was Bobby to tell her she didn't have a choice?

And so, as she pushed through the screen door, all that was left for her to do was to get her armload of goods onto the kitchen table.

That's when Big Bertha, who had been following behind her, caught the smell of roasting chicken and burst past her, knocking against her legs, causing her to drop one of the bags.

Annie exploded as she watched its contents spill out across the living room floor. "SHIT!! SHIT! SHIT!"

As soon as Stella heard the thud, followed by the yelling and the rapid stiff clicks of Bertha's nails on her kitchen floor, she knew exactly who was there and what had happened. Of course, she'd seen Annie from her kitchen window, which had given her a heads-up as to the "who" of the situation, which was a good thing because the yelling alone wouldn't have done it. She couldn't think of a time when Annie had yelled so loud she couldn't recognize the voice. Plus that yelling, added to her stumbling across the driveway, added to her not stumbling at all once she had those bags in her arms, added to her lying, added to her racing out to talk to Bobby, leaving all those groceries in the truck, then dragging herself back looking like her life was over—nothing about any of it made sense, at least not yet, and all because of five days, two days less than God took to make the earth, and the earth made more sense than this situation.

Without turning from her work at the stove, Stella responded to what she'd heard. "A N E, it's time you get out the nail cutter 'fore that bitch splits her nails and ends up at the vet, addin' on to what I'm thinkin' is already a mighty big bill from Gracey's dyin'. That is, unless I figure out a way to sue their ass for malpractice. And I will add, it's a good thing I ain't got them expensive wood floors in my house 'cause there'd be nothin' left of 'em by now, due to your neglectin' to keep that bitch's nails down."

Bertha skidded past Stella and banged into the cabinets beside her. She then shook her head and walked to Stella's side where she sat with her rump leaning up against Stella's leg.

Stella put the potato masher down on the counter and patted the top of Bertha's head. "I know just how you feel, girl. Yellin' like that is enough to make any livin' creature haul ass from the situation, and this situation is not lookin' good, now is it? Hell, it seems like there ain't a person around here who thinks about anybody but their own selves. Dogs are left to starvin', some of them driven to bangin' into walls they's so hungry, while the people they is dependin' on spends all their time blabbin' about God knows what while standin' on a grave, givin' no peace to poor Grace. Then when they is done, they go about their business 'bout as slow as a turtle in a bowl of mash potatoes, just like this bowl sittin' right here. And one person—the only one who is thinkin' on somethin' besides their own selves—is cookin' up a storm for them two—and only God knows why, 'cause I ain't asked him yet."

She scooped out two large spoonfuls of mashed potatoes onto a plate and set it down on the floor. She shook her head as she watched Bertha gulp down the warm white pile, complete with butter and milk, gave her another scoop, then walked through to the living room to have a good gander at Annie, who she figured was on her hands and knees, right where she belonged, picking up all the spilt goods.

Annie put the last of the items, three cans of baked beans, back into the partially torn bag. She had no idea why she'd yelled like that, and even questioned whether it was her own voice. She'd heard it from some far away place, and then it was gone. The next thing she knew she was on the floor picking up Morton salt, cheese that had softened from sitting so long in the truck, bread, a carton of now warm milk, and beans, all the while taking in every word of Stella's stirring little monologue, embedded with the same litany of grievances she'd already heard earlier in the day, and then some. However, unlike Stella's porch performance, this time she didn't feel any relief. She took a deep breath and heeded Bobby's warning—"Her wings is spread about as far as the eye can see."

That's when she heard Stella cross the kitchen floor and stop several feet from her. She straightened up and sat back on her heels. Then her blues met the greens and she sighed. "Look, you've made it clear that you know I lied to you and, frankly, it was a stupid thing for me to do."

"You got that right." Stella wiped the large potato spoon on her red lettered 'Don't Mess with the Cook' yellow apron, then tapped the arm of the couch with it. "And I know for a fact that Bobby slept right here last night."

She then pointed the spoon in the direction of the spot where she'd picked up the pillow with the brown curls. "PLUS I know for a fact you slept right there on the floor on top of all that dirt he dragged in on those damn boots of his."

She turned and walked back into the kitchen, satisfied she'd gotten what she wanted, which was for Annie to come clean about her lying. There was no point in her lying because she would know. Of course, the actual truth of the present situation remained to be seen.

She reached into the boiling potato pot with the metal tongs. "I spent all day cleanin' up after the two of you, not countin' the time I spent talkin' to Margaret, who has talked to damn near everybody and it's lookin' like she's finally seein' the light regardin' me, meanin' that show would have been all over if it weren't for me—you'll see what I mean when you watch the video."

One by one she pulled out a few more potatoes and added them to the bowl of the already mashed, to make up for what Bertha had eaten. She then picked up the masher. "Bottom line is I sure as hell don't appreciate havin' to come home, after workin' my ass off, to one of my own lyin' straight to my face."

Annie got up off the floor and hoisted the bags, one by one, back into her arms. "Well, the bottom line is that I lied because I was mad at you for leaving me with fifteen dogs, some of them pregnant, and expecting me to be able to handle anything that might come up."

She hugged the bags and walked past Stella to the kitchen table. "I'm still mad about it."

She dropped the bags onto the table with a deliberately loud thud in hopes that Stella would buy her own performance. "How could you do that to me? And on top of that, leave me here with the ridiculous idea that I broke Bobby's heart by leaving, when you know full well it was YOU who ran me out of here with a loaded shotgun? Or don't you remember that?"

She looked at the back of Stella's head, the red hair bobbing up and down as she mashed the potatoes. She felt her stomach grow tight with every bob.

Stella pushed the masher into the potatoes and left it there as she turned to face Annie who wasn't looking to be as angry as she sounded. She snorted to herself. *Two can play this game, and there ain't anybody who can do it better than me.*

"Oh, I remember clear enough and I remember clear enough that you was like one of them little birdies whose mama had to shove them outta the nest to make them see they got the wings to go on and fly. It was heartbreakin' to do what I had to do, but there weren't no other way, and it was heartbreakin' to Bobby 'cause he never heard a word after you left. There you was, flyin' halfway 'round the world whoopin' it up with some sheepherder and his sheep, livin' high off money from OUR business, which I ain't never asked you for, and not sendin' a word to Bobby. Now, I didn't need to hear nothin' from you 'cause I knew you would be comin' back—which means you really ain't like one of them little birdies 'cause they don't got the need to come back— but Bobby, no matter what I said and I got damn tired of sayin' it, he was sure as the day is long that you was never comin' back. Now here you are and thanks to my leavin' for five days you two are back talkin' like you used to."

She turned back to mashing the potatoes. "It just ain't all that complicated."

As Annie stood there and watched the red hair bob, she recalled the shock of the shotgun blast, followed by the screeching, "YOU'RE NOTHIN' BUT A CONTAMINATED WHORE!"

She placed her hands on the table to steady herself, and the next thing she knew she was near shouting. "You're damn right Bobby and I are talking again—we have talked and talked and talked. And the truth is, it was damned stupid of you to leave us here together, damn fucking stupid." She fell unexpectedly silent, poised just short of the point of no return.

The head continued to bob.

Oz, who had been pro-active and retreated to the far end of the living room early on, merely raised his eyebrows.

However, Big Bertha, who had settled in her crate to digest the mashed potatoes, emerged the moment she heard Annie's voice change to something she was unfamiliar with. She rushed over to her, took a sniff, then began to pace between her and the front door as if to say, "Let's go, let's go, let's go." And the click, click, click each time she hit the kitchen floor was the reason the head stopped bobbing.

Stella turned around as Bertha crossed the black-and-white squares for the fifth time. "Alice, you need to stop that. It's gonna drive me just plain nuts. Goddamn, what does a woman have to do around here to get some peace!"

She looked over at Annie who was standing on the opposite side of the kitchen table staring across at her. "And speakin' of peace, I ain't gonna get none standin' next to that blaze comin' off you—and for no damn reason that I can see."

She grabbed Bertha by the collar as she clicked across the kitchen floor for the eighth time and put her in her crate. "And as for you bein' pissed at me for leavin' you with fifteen dogs?" She shut the crate door. "That's just plain dumb, honey, 'cause you weren't alone, not for one second, not regardin' them dogs. Bobby was here and we both know for a fact he watches them more careful than you or me and from a hell of a longer ways away. I wasn't worried, not one bit, meanin' you're wastin' your time bein' mad about that. Now I ain't heard the whole story of what happened to Grace, but I'm guessin' it was Bobby who saw somethin' that weren't right long before it weren't, which is exactly why I didn't have no concern about leavin' you here not knowin' squat—end of story."

She picked up the long fork from the counter and opened the oven door. "As for you two talkin' and talkin' and talkin', probly from sundown till sun-up, knowin' how you two used to talk, well..." She pulled the oven rack out and poked one of the two roasting chickens. "You're damn right I was countin' on that comin' to be while I was gone 'cause I was sick to death of the two of you actin' like you was from two different planets, unless I was sittin' right there—and I can't be no babysitter."

She pushed the rack back into the oven and closed the door. "Maybe now things will be back to normal."

She snorted a laugh and dropped the fork in the sink. "Normal being a far stretch from the normal most people is used to, but normal enough so when Billy gets down here, he won't run the first chance he gets."

Annie struggled to break the silence that had engulfed her, but as she watched Stella move about the room, the indomitable redhead suddenly appeared to her to be frantic, small and scared, as if she were hanging by a thread over her own thousand-foot hole. She'd seen Stella vulnerable before, but this was more than that. This was a woman who was desperate for her to keep her mouth shut. And when she heard Stella say "maybe now things will get back to normal around here," what she heard was Stella admitting she'd done a terrible thing—she was asking for forgiveness and wanted Annie to let it go so they could get on with their lives.

Annie pulled the chair out from the kitchen table and sat down. She couldn't be the monster.

Stella turned when she heard the chair squeal across the floor and felt nothing but disgust at the sight of Annie dropping down onto it. She wasn't worried about getting to the truth. She had that little problem locked up. What she was, was sick to death of cowardly people. She'd just spent five days with a whole bunch of them and now here was one, right in her kitchen, probably a few seconds away from crying her eyes out, not a sight she was interested in seeing.

"A N E, you're nothin' but ambers and you ain't never gonna be nothin' but ambers. Hell, all these years of me teachin' you everythin' I know and you still can't hold onto a blaze for more than two seconds. Oh, I know you thought you was somethin' lyin' like that to me and all struttin', like you did, out to tell Bobby all about it—and you mighta been if you coulda backed it up with a little more spine than what I'm lookin' at."

She walked over to the table, placed both hands on it and leaned in towards Annie who was no longer looking at her. Her voice dropped to low and mean. "Now, since you is choosin' the little girl's way out, how 'bout we back up to the part where you said I was 'damn fucking stupid' to leave you here with Bobby. You and me both know I ain't stupid, so you best explain to me why you said I was somethin' I ain't. And you best understand this ain't no game anymore."

A strong and steady voice suddenly came from across the room. "Because, darlin', it ain't Annie's place to tell you somethin' that wasn't never her business to begin with."

Like a lioness abruptly distracted from her prey, Stella turned. Bobby was standing a few feet from the arm of the couch, his dirty work boots flirting with the edge of the black-and-white squares.

"Where the hell did you come from? I didn't hear no door, no nothing!" Stella looked from Bobby over to Bertha who was standing up in her crate looking suspiciously at HER rather than him.

She straightened up and walked across the kitchen, past Bobby, to check on Oz, who was sound asleep on the living room rug. She then walked back to Bobby and stood on the black-and-whites, two feet in front of him. "Neither one of them two seems to give a damn about the fact of you showin' up outta nowhere, but I do, meanin' me and Annie are havin' a private conversation, and private means excludin' you."

Bobby looked at Stella. He knew she wasn't half as mad as she was going to be, and mad wouldn't even come close to describing what he'd seen, butt naked, only once before. He was only as ready as a man could be, which wasn't all that ready, but it was better than him standing out in the driveway, like a coward, waiting for all hell to break loose and more than willing to let it all come down on Annie.

It was when he heard Annie shout at Stella about how stupid Stella was to leave them together, then go dead quiet before saying what she was about to say, that's when he knew Annie was scared out of her mind, and no matter how scared he was, there was no way it made it right for him to leave her like that. The next thing he knew he was standing there looking at the two of them. He couldn't remember a thing about walking up the porch steps and walking through that front door. He figured that was partly God's doing. And now with Stella staring him dead in the eye, he didn't have the time to think about it.

He pulled one of his hands out of the pocket of his overalls and ran it slowly through his hair as he spoke. "I can see you two are havin' a conversation, but it sure as hell ain't private seein' as I could hear every word of it clear out in the driveway and, from what I been hearin', this particular conversation don't exclude me one bit."

He tucked his hand back in his pocket, letting God keep his eyes and voice steady. He figured if that's who got him up them steps, then that's who was going to help him through this. "See, what you're tryin' to squish outta Annie here, ain't her business to say and wasn't never her business to know."

He stepped out onto the black-and-white and walked around Stella towards the counter.

Annie had tried to signal to him by putting her finger to her lips as he passed by the table, but he didn't look at her, not even for a second. She'd had no choice but to speak. "Bobby, don't. It's not necessary."

Stella walked rapidly past him and grabbed the bowl of mashed potatoes from off the counter. "A) you can't have any of these potatoes till I say so, so keep your fingers out, B) I spent all day cleanin' up the dirt from those damn boots of yours, so you need to go take them off at the door, and C) don't think for one second I don't got a clue about what's been goin' on around here. Who the hell do you think you're dealin' with?"

Bobby stopped at the sink and turned the cold tap on. "I know exactly who I'm dealin' with."

He pulled a clean glass from the cupboard and held it under the running water.

"Oh, so now you're mister super hero come to rescue the little princess, is that it? Only she ain't no princess, now is she? We both know that. And she don't need no rescuin' from nobody I know."

Stella looked back and forth from Bobby's back to Annie's pale face. "If I didn't know the truth 'bout the two of you, I'd be the dumb bitch who would swear you was havin' sex behind her back, but I ain't that dumb 'cause I know it ain't possible. Besides the fact of you two dependin' on me for damn near everythin', which I am damn tired of, Bobby ain't been able to get it up since I told him about how his daddy killed his mama and then shot hisself. All he can get up these days is fence posts—case closed!"

She then turned to Annie, who looked to her about as pitiful and weak as a girl could look. "And you, you don't have sex period, at least not normal sex. Don't think for a minute I didn't talk in private to every man you were with all them years. I got it all in black and white. You never let any of them screw you, or touch you, period!"

She walked over and leaned across the table for the second time, her face not two feet from Annie's.

Annie looked down at the table as Stella continued, "And who do you think saved your ass from gettin' raped, or worse, a hundred times? There ain't nobody ever gonna be up in there but your daddy, is there? And that ain't never gonna happen again seein' as he dropped dead due to his heart givin' out on account of you and your big mouth. The sad fact bein' that you is doomed to live like one of them nuns—the only difference bein' the father you is stuck on ain't the same father they is stuck on, as in they got the 'our father who is in heaven', meanin' God—and you got the 'my father who ain't in heaven' cause he screwed his little girl."

She turned and looked at Bobby's back. "—'course then YOU got the father who shoots his own wife and then his own self right in front of his own son!"

She pushed away from the table, walked across the black-and-white squares and into the living room. "I got me a couple of real losers livin' under my roof and God only knows what I did to deserve this!" She dropped onto the couch.

As Stella talked, Bobby stood and watched the water spill endlessly over the top of the glass he was filling. When she was done, at least for the time being, he reached over and turned the faucet off, then glanced out the window onto the dimly lit gravel and listened to Ivan who was roaring from within the kennel. He wondered how it was Ivan knew what he knew and the others didn't. And he felt sorry for him because there was nothing he could do except roar, day in and day out.

He lifted the glass to his lips and emptied it.

Big Bertha had turned nervously in her crate at least a dozen times.

Oz was up and sitting at Stella's feet panting slightly.

Annie's chair squealed for the second time as she stood up and pulled a white paper bag from one of the bags that had yet to be unpacked. She then walked deliberately across the kitchen to her bedroom door and opened it.

Stella spoke from the couch without turning. "Where the hell do you think you're goin'? We ain't done here." As she spoke, she turned on the TV and then the video machine.

Annie stopped, one hand on the doorknob, and looked at the back of Stella's head. She spoke from her belly, firm and steady. "I'm going to take a shower, thanks to you, and then I'm going to put on some clean clothes. I'll let you know what I feel like doing after that."

Stella pushed the 'pause' button right as she and Oz were strolling into the ring. She felt no need to turn from the screen. "Well, I ain't done, so maybe you want to hold off on that shower—'course it ain't easy bein' the filthy little girl you are, is it? And while you're at it, you need to tell me exactly what it was you took from that bag."

Annie pulled a box of tampons from the white bag she was holding, then crumpled the bag and threw it on the floor. "Since you seem to think you know everything about me, including the life of my vagina, I'm surprised you don't know I got my period this morning." She waited for Stella to turn around, but she didn't, so she continued, "What I have here is a box of tampons, forty to be exact."

She walked to the couch, held the box in front of Stella's face, and then walked back to her bedroom door. She looked over at the head that hadn't moved. "I came back here despite everything, despite what you yelled at me that day, which by the way won't work this time, because you already dragged me down that road. Looks like you're going to have to find something else to beat me with."

Stella's head remained stock-still. Cigarette smoke rose up around it.

Annie turned the door knob and continued, "I came back here because A) I'm a fool and, B) I didn't know the whole truth of who you are, not until this past week, maybe even not until right this moment. And, yes, I depended on you, something I can only chalk up to stupidity and loneliness. And to think I felt compassion for you just ten minutes ago."

Annie walked into her bedroom and shut the door behind her.

Stella got up from the couch and walked calmly to Annie's closed bedroom door and stood facing it. Her voice blew right through it. "Honey, there ain't no 'seem' about it. I DO know everythin' about you. Fact is, I know more about you than you know about you, which is exactly why you came back here. See, like I told you already, you don't got the wings to fly and you ain't never gonna have 'em. The difference between you and me is I grew myself some big ass wings a long time ago, as in before I could talk 'cause I knew I'd be needin' 'em and nobody had to teach me how to use 'em. See, I don't need nobody, period, never did. You ain't but a whole lotta nothin' without me, so you can take that compassion you had to give me and shove it right up there with one of them tampons. I got all the compassion I need, which is none!"

She turned to Bobby who had put his glass down and was leaning back against the counter facing her. "You got some fast talkin' to do, buddy, 'cause that girl is fast approachin' the end of my line. And don't even think about sayin' what we're lookin' at is that PMS shit!"

Bobby pulled his cigarettes from his shirt pocket. Watching them go at it had slowed his mind down to where all he could think about was having a smoke.

Stella walked over to him. "How 'bout you give me one of them things 'fore I have a damn stroke."

She reached out her hand. "I have seen it all now. We give years and years of our life to that girl, take her in like she's one of our own, and this is the thanks we get."

Bobby shook a cigarette from the pack and held it out to her, then took the lighter from his pocket. As he watched her, he wondered how many times he'd done this for her—a hundred thousand, two hundred thousand—and she always made the same face when she put that cigarette in the flame, whether she was fuming mad, or just woke up, or was in the middle of running around from one thing to the next. It just looked older now was all—that, and the fact of her letting out a bunch of coughs after her first lungful of smoke, something that never used to happen.

He put a cigarette in his own mouth and lit it.

Stella coughed and walked over to the stove. "Ain't you got nothin' to say?"

She sucked in on her cigarette and opened the oven door. "At least our dinner ain't been ruined."

Bobby watched her pull the chickens out and put them on a plate and finally spoke. "You never talked to all them men Annie was with about what they did in private, and there ain't a one of 'em was ever gonna rape her."

Stella started pulling dishes out of the cupboard and setting the table. "Bobby, you don't know jack about what I did and didn't do. The fact is, you'd a killed anybody who messed with her, meanin' the point I was makin' was how we looked out for her like she was our own."

She set the plates down on the table and glanced at Bertha who turned again in her crate. She walked over and opened it. "Alright, alright, you can come out. I'm not gonna be responsible for you fallin' over from bein' dizzy with turnin' round and round like that."

Bertha rushed out and stood in front of Annie's bedroom door, looking from Stella to the doorknob.

Stella walked over, opened the door, and gave Bertha's rear a shove with her cigarette free hand. "Go ahead in there, maybe you can talk some sense into that girl, but I doubt it 'cause you ain't got any more sense than her."

Bobby sucked on his cigarette, blew the smoke out into the room, and the words followed as if everything was just like it always was, no different than Stella's face when she sucked in on that flame. "I told her 'bout what happened to Greta that night."

Stella pulled the silverware from the drawer. "So did I, TEN YEARS AGO, meanin' that ain't exactly breakin' news." She rested her cigarette in the ashtray on the table and placed the spoons and forks and knives, one by one, and waited for Bobby to deliver the rest to her.

"I mean, I told her everythin'. I told her how you got them bullets and put 'em in that gun, and how you called her names and hollered at her to go on ahead and kill herself, and how she was cryin' and you just got madder and madder, and how I didn't do nothin' but stand there and watch."

Stella put the last piece of silverware down and picked up her cigarette. She sucked in deep and looked at him as he looked at the floor. She exhaled and shook her head as the plume of smoke made Bobby appear hazy. "You are one sorry-ass motherfucker, you know that?"

She put the cigarette back in the ashtray and walked over to the cupboard that was just behind Bobby's head. "Are you tellin' me that's the cause of all the lyin' and blabbin' and sneakin' around behind my back?" She pulled three glasses and a pitcher from the cupboard brushing against Bobby's hair each time she reached past it.

Bobby didn't answer. All he could think on were the black-and-white squares and how maybe it was time to replace them with something else. They'd been there since he'd put them in all those years ago, a year before Greta died. He used to tell her that one day soon he'd make some wooden checker pieces, just like the real ones, only real big, so they could play checkers on that floor. And he told her if there weren't enough squares on the floor he'd make the kitchen bigger so there would be. She was crazy about that idea, only he never got around to it due to there always being something more important to do, which now that he thought about it was just plain stupid. If he'd gotten around to it, they might've been playing checkers when Stella came home that night and none of what happened would've happened and Greta would still be alive.

Stella put the glasses on the table and pulled a frozen lemonade canister from the freezer. "Her knowin' that is the same thing as her knowin' about you killin' somebody in prison over a peanut butter sandwich." She ran the canister under hot water, opened it, and plopped it into the pitcher.

Bobby shifted and crossed one foot over the other. "That was self defense and much as you keep blabbin' to everyone 'bout it bein' over a peanut butter sandwich, you know damn well that ain't the truth—and due to your blabbin', it ain't no secret either."

He listened as she filled the pitcher with water, then put it on the table. He felt a thump, thump, thump in his chest, squashed his cigarette out and pulled out a fresh one.

Stella laid out the mashed potatoes and roasted chickens on the table, then went to the bathroom door. "I'm guessin' you gotta be squeaky clean about now, so how 'bout you get on out here and have some dinner."

She turned back to Bobby, who was looking small enough to stomp on, as was usual these days. "You killin' that guy from bein' stabbed and almost raped ain't gonna have the same meanin' on people, now is it?"

Annie turned from the bathroom mirror. The half empty Tampax box sat on the top of the toilet, a roll of adhesive tape next to it. Despite her conviction that afternoon, when she'd bought the supplies and stuffed them in amongst the tampons, throwing most of them out to make the space— she never really believed she'd be able go through with it. But now here she was taping the tiny recorder to her chest, under her bra, and running the wire out her arm. "Never go anywhere without a gun and a tape recorder cause', honey, them two things just might save your life someday."

She turned towards the door and responded to Stella's dinner call. "I'll be out in a minute."

She assumed, from the tone of Stella's voice, Bobby had failed to say anything, or else had made something up because he just couldn't do it. Stella crept into her head again. "It don't matter what anybody tells you, you're on your own in this world from the beginnin' to the end." However, those words had no impact this time, because regardless of what Bobby had or hadn't been able to say, when Annie had heard him speak on her behalf and saw him standing there at the edge of the kitchen, she knew she wasn't on her own. And the feel of that was what helped her begin the shift from the fear that had overwhelmed her when Stella growled into her face to what she felt now, which was cold hard resolve. Her life here was over, but she wasn't going to leave with nothing.

Stella returned to the living room and flicked off the VCR. They would get to viewing the show later. Right now, there was dinner and some business that needed taking care of.

The phone rang.

Bobby jumped at the chance to stop the thump, thump that had crawled into his throat from his chest and started towards the study.

Stella rushed past him. "I'll get it. We know it ain't for you, so why don't you just settle down and roll me a couple joints while I talk to whoever it is."

She shut the study door behind her and picked up the receiver.

Annie took one final look in the mirror. The worn sage green three-quarter sleeve T was perfect; there was no sign of the recorder, the mike, or the wire. She just hoped Stella wouldn't see what she saw as she looked in the mirror—a cool, calculated woman. She wondered, briefly, if young Greta had lived this long would she have become the same. If so, the apple would not have fallen far from the tree.

She took a deep breath and stepped over Bertha, who immediately rose to her feet and followed her out into the kitchen.

Bobby was seated at the table with a pack of rolling papers and baggie full of pot. The thumping in his chest had calmed due to his hands being busy at something he had done a million times before.

He looked up as Annie and Bertha re-entered the room. He'd half expected she might've climbed out the bathroom window and be well on her way out of the state, because looking at it from her perspective, he saw no reason she would stick around. "Why ain't you gone yet? Just like I said, this ain't your business, never was."

Annie sat down kitty-cornered from him. "Because, I'm not done here." She could hear Stella behind the closed door, loudly immersed in a phone conversation. "Look, I know you couldn't say anything and I understand why, but I'm going to do it, Bobby, if for no one else, for Greta."

Bobby held the white paper in a v-shape, sprinkled the pot into it, and rolled it skillfully with one hand. The other hand pushed his pack of cigarettes towards her. "Oh, I told her alright, like I said I would, and while she's in there blabbin' on the phone actin' like it wasn't nothin', it's rollin' around inside her figurin' a way to come back out and set you and me straight, meanin' I'm sorry you ain't in your van and on your way out of Georgia." He licked the paper then ran the whole joint lightly in and out of his mouth and laid it on the plate in front of him.

Annie was taken aback hearing he'd told Stella. Almost immediately her newfound persona softened, something she hadn't prepared for. She picked up the pack of cigarettes and took one. "I don't suppose you want to go with me, do you?" She looked at the closed study door, "We have plenty of time. Heck, we could be halfway to Mexico by the time she gets off the phone."

The laughter that broke from her was unexpected.

Then Bobby joined in.

And when their laughter seeped under the study door and into Stella's ears, she hung up the phone, mid-sentence, and marched into the kitchen.

She looked at the two of them, smug as shit and laughing like she was supposed to know what the hell was so funny. "There's nothin' funny about interruptin' me while I'm tryin' to talk business, as in talkin' to a very rich woman who I met at the show while you two was back here talkin' about somethin' that's ancient history, as in over and done with, and all actin' like that Chicken Little Annie knows, the one who thought the sky was all fallin' down on his head, when it was nothin' but a pine cone."

Much to her liking, the two of them stopped laughing and were paying her the attention she expected.

She reached down and grabbed the fresh joint off Bobby's plate. "Let me tell you a little somethin' about that ancient history you is so dead set on bringin' into my house in the present day."

She walked into the living room and picked her lighter up from the coffee table. "Now, I'm only gonna tell you this the once, so you listen to me real good and then we're gonna bury it just like Grace out there and let it be God's business, as in case-closed and AMEN."

She lit the joint, words still pushing out as she sucked in. "First, I'm gonna put Oz here out on the porch." She exhaled.

"And one of you two need to put Bertha in Annie's bedroom 'cause neither one of them need to hear what I got to say. No point to it."

She took Oz by the collar and pushed him out onto the porch.

Oz settled down with a loud sigh, his rear up against the closed red door.

Annie glanced at Bobby, who was busy sprinkling pot into a third paper. She figured at the rate he was going, he'd fill the plate with joints inside of ten minutes. She got up and led Bertha into her bedroom. When she came back out, Stella was seated where she'd been sitting, her purse on the plate in front of her, so she pulled out the chair opposite Bobby.

As Annie sat down, Stella reached into her purse and pulled out her wallet. "What I got in here, tucked behind one of my pictures of Oz, is a picture of me and my Greta when she was five years old. Now, I keep it where I keep it 'cause, as you know, I show a ton of people these pictures—the dogs, the kennel, my sons, Bobby, things that get the people interested. Bobby's seen all of 'em. Annie, you ain't seen all of 'em 'cause a bunch of 'em are from since you left."

She opened the wallet to a random photo and held it up. "See, here's one of Bobby with Ivan. Now, we know Bobby's the only one who can sit next to that dog with his arm around him like that—anybody else he'd tear their throat out—but he's kick-ass good lookin', just the dog I want people to see, right along with Oz, and Grace who's dead and gone, no thanks to Doc Burns—and look at Bobby, he ain't so bad lookin' hisself." She laughed. "Alls I can say is it's a good thing you can't see crazy in a photograph."

She started flicking through the rest of the photos. "Now, the ones that ain't nobody's business, as in I don't want to answer any questions regardin' them 'cause it makes for me havin' to explain things that I don't feel like explainin'— those are the ones I keep tucked in behind the other ones."

She looked up at Annie. "I got that one Bobby took of you walkin' tall out to your MG from one of them days when you was dressed to the nines and everyone, and I mean men-women-cats-dogs you name it, damn near passed out when you walked by—just like they did with me back in the day, and just like they woulda done with my Greta if things had worked out different."

She took another hit off the joint and continued to flick through the photos. "That particular picture is back behind one of these, I can't remember which one. 'Course when we were runnin' our 'escort service' I kept it front and center as you well know. Anyway, I keep them 'special' photos out of sight 'cause they got a special meanin' to me and they ain't nobody else's business. 'Course, right now I'm fixin' to take A N E right on outta here cause I don't got a clue, right now, about what the meanin' of her bein' in here is."

She sucked in on the joint again and flicked to the first photo of the bunch, a photo of Oz at the world show. "Nobody, not even Bobby has seen this particular picture of Greta and me. I got a big one plus the negative in my secret files, the ones A N E was lookin' for the other night."

She laughed and dug in behind the photo of Oz. "'Course, I've had this picture of me and Greta a hell of a lot longer than I've had Oz, meanin' it's been tucked behind a ton of other photos in a ton of other wallets and the only person that's seen this photo is Greta and man number three."

She looked over at Annie as she pulled the photo out. "I'm assumin', of course, in all that blabbin' you all did regardin' Greta, that Bobby told you 'bout what happened to her in the first place, which was the main reason for what happened in the barn all them years later, and how I shot that bastard in the leg for doin' what he did to her—or maybe he skipped that part. There's no tellin' what parts of a story Bobby chooses to tell—and if it's a long one, like this one, chances are he left a few big fat holes in it—and the thing of it is, Bobby don't even got the whole story."

Bobby dropped another joint on the plate and picked up another paper. He spoke without looking up. "Yup, I told her all that, and I told her there weren't no record regardin' you shootin' him, and I told her the gun in the barn was the same one, which was his gun before it was your gun. Now, I know you wanted to shoot the bastard. Hell, I would've done it myself, I just didn't know if you wantin' to do it got mixed up with you maybe not havin' the means to do it at the time." Bobby didn't look up, just kept his focus on his job at hand.

Stella put the photo out on the table. "Bobby! I already explained to you exactly why there weren't no record—you just can't seem to keep things straight when it comes to me shootin' a gun and actually hittin' somebody. It's like you got some kinda brick in your head that don't allow you to know I got what it takes."

She looked at Annie. "After I ran you off with my shotgun and didn't hit you 'cause I wasn't intendin' to, Bobby freaked out and wandered off to build fences till long after dark. He even told me later he went deaf for most of that day. I believe it's a man thing, as in men just seem to have trouble, even go deaf, when tryin' to wrap their mind around the idea of a woman usin' a gun if the need arises."

She grabbed another joint off Bobby's plate. "It ain't about balls, Bobby. It's called doin' what's necessary. And as for there bein' no record of it, that's somethin' I have explained to you a thousand times."

She put the joint in her mouth and turned to Annie. "Do you know, after I told him this part of the story, he insisted if it was true—me shootin' him—the police would have a record of it. What I told him then and what I'm tellin' you now is if you raped a little girl and her mama shot you in the leg because of it, would you run to the authorities and tell 'em the mama shot you in the leg?—'course, all of that is beside the point 'cause he didn't run off anywhere, which is the part I didn't tell Bobby, but I will tell you now. And, no, it weren't HIS gun, it was mine."

"But why the hell DIDN'T you call the police? He raped your daughter for Christsake!" Annie's face flushed. "How do you know he didn't go on and rape more girls after that?"

Stella picked up Bobby's lighter and looked impatiently at Annie. "Now, you need to settle down if you want to hear this whole story 'cause I ain't gonna tolerate you jumpin' in every two seconds, neither one of you."

She lit the joint, glanced over at Bobby, then back at Annie, and then exhaled. "Now, the only reason I'm gonna answer them two questions is because I was gettin' to that part anyway. You're jumpin' ahead just like you usually do.

"So, as I was about to tell you, there he was lyin' on the living room floor, holdin' his leg and cryin' like a baby. I told him to shut up and be glad it was just his leg. I then called two men friends of mine, who I knew would do anything for me. I had a lotta men like that in my life, as you well know."

She took another hit and exhaled. "Anyway, they came right over and took care of the nearest neighbors, who was standin' out in their front yard. They told 'em Christopher had shot hisself in the leg by mistake and it was no big deal. They said they were takin' him to the doctors. It wasn't any kinda neighborhood where anybody gave a shit unless their own life was on the line. Anyway, my friends came in and I told 'em what happened. They said they'd be happy to beat the crap outta him and throw him in a river somewhere, but I said that wasn't worth doin' seein' as we'd all probably end up in prison if them detectives was as good as they are on the TV."

Stella offered the joint to Annie who shook her head. She snorted and took another hit. "Meanwhile, my little Jonathan, who was two at the time, was wailin' from in his crib. I'm tellin' you, all hell was broke loose, and that's when I heard my daddy speakin' to me, 'No matter how bad a situation is, there's always a way to get some good from it.'

"He told me his daddy told him that. He also told me that takin' care of your own is number one over everythin', meanin' in this situation there was no way any police or prison was gonna take over what was mine to do, which was to make him pay for what he done. I told them two friends of mine, Daryl and Jack, to check Christopher's wound to make sure it was nothin', like I thought it was, and give him a towel to stop the bleedin' while I went into my bedroom and got me some paper and a pen."

Stella paused and studied the ceiling for a moment. "Before I go to that part, I need to explain somethin' about Christopher which I already told Bobby, but Annie ain't heard it and, besides that, I just gotta say it again and don't ask me why 'cause I don't got the answer.

"Anyway, I met Christopher at the supermarket, if you can believe that, and to make a long story real short, I was desperate, as in I needed somebody to look after my kids while I worked at night. He seemed like a good man. He was good lookin', loved kids, and meetin' in a supermarket seemed like a decent beginnin'. I know, I was only about twenty-one and still had a lotta learnin' to do—'course I knew more than most people did by that age."

She sighed. "You know that curve they talk about regardin' learnin'?—mine wasn't no curve, it went damn near straight on up from that point till after I met Bobby and got the business underway. Then it settled down to a level that was head and shoulders over everybody else and stayed that way."

She took another hit and blew the sweet smoke across the table. "I never would've staked him to be a child rapist, not in a million years. 'Course his insistin' on bein' called Christopher instead of just plain Chris mighta been a sign, I don't know."

She put the joint in the ashtray and settled back in her chair. "I liked him well enough. There just wasn't no fireworks between us or anything, at least not for me, but it seemed like one of them relationships that had workin' possibilities. He'd just lost a job with some company, was lookin' for another and needed a home to come to at night, and I needed my kids looked after. I know, it was damn stupid of me, but like I said, I was desperate. Hell, I had two kids and I wasn't gettin' anywhere makin' money and spendin' it all on baby sitters, most of 'em not givin' a damn 'bout anything but watchin' TV and gettin' paid. Christopher was my ticket out. When he moved in, I picked up a ton of extra hours workin' the bar, making connections for the future—as in rubbin' elbows with the rich—and rakin' in the tips. Some nights I didn't come home till 5 or 6 a.m. due to followin' through with connections and all—you know what I mean.

"Anyway, things seemed to be workin' out real good, till I got real sick one night at the bar and went home early, around midnight. That's when I walked in on Christopher and Greta, right there on the couch in the livin' room. I told him to put his pants on and to wait right there. He looked scared as shit and was yellin' after me while I ran into my bedroom and got my gun. He was tryin' to tell me that what I was seein' wasn't what I was seein'.

"I came back in and shot him in his leg, then told Greta to go to her room. My little girl was stark naked and had blood drippin' down her leg. I swear it took God's hand to stop me from blowin' his brains out 'cause that was what I was wantin' to do.

"See, Greta didn't move, she just stood there and started cryin' and God knows I wasn't gonna blow his brains out in front of her. So, while Christopher was layin' on the couch holdin' his leg and squealin', I got a towel and wrapped it around my little girl and sat her down on the rocker on the other side of the room—same rocker we got right here in our living room.

"And that's when I called Jack and Daryl. So, when I came back into that room with the paper and pen, I told Jack to write out a confession for Christopher to sign, but first I had to get him to tell me exactly what I needed to put on that confession.

"I walked over to that couch and put my gun to Christopher's head and I told him, 'So help me God, if I think you're lyin' for one second, I will blow your brains out!

"He knew I was dead serious. He was scared as shit and shakin' so hard the couch jumped, I swear to God. So, I asked him how long my little girl had been his little sex toy. He wouldn't answer and I knew it was 'cause he was so damn scared his mouth wouldn't work, so I said, 'A year?' He nodded. I said, 'More than a year?' He nodded, then, bless his bastard heart, he found his tongue and said he just used his finger most times and jerked off.

"Well, soon as he said that my own finger trembled on that trigger. There wasn't nothin' I wanted to do more than kill him right then and there. Musta been God who told me to put the gun down 'cause I did, which is when I grabbed his dick and his balls and twisted till I felt somethin' pop and he almost passed out. I'm thinkin' I probly neutered him for the rest of his life!"

Bobby put a half rolled joint onto the plate—he was stuck on little Greta with blood dripping down her leg. His voice remained slow and steady. "There ain't no reason on God's earth for you to be tellin' us them details. If you got a place you're goin' to, then get to it 'cause I got no reason to listen to this."

Stella snapped back, "Bobby, if you're gonna get to that place then you gotta hear the details 'cause they is just like them toes on your feet, without 'em you ain't gonna get there! And just remember, it ain't me that started this."

Annie couldn't speak or move. Her cigarette had burned down to her fingers, and the burn she felt was the only thing that gave her a reprieve from the ocean of sick that had washed through her. She held on to the burning Pall Mall until it got too small for her burning fingers to hold, then dropped it to the floor.

Stella looked over at her. "Since when is my floor an ashtray?" She got up, stomped on what was left of the butt and sat back down. She then continued, without missing a beat, "Anyway, I had only been livin' with Christopher for a year and half, so he musta started in on Greta pretty quick and lookin' back on it, it all came to light as to why Greta had started actin' different, as in cryin' a lot, havin' fits—some nights she refused to say good-bye to me—and a couple times she hauled off and hit me in the stomach. I thought it was just the blaze showin' itself and she just needed some help with how to use it was all, and I figured she was mad at me for leavin' her every night, which is somethin' I hadn't done for none of them years leadin' up to when that was taken." She pointed to the photo that lay in the middle of the table.

"See, the one you know as husband number two, Jonathan's daddy, the one before Christopher—well, his name was Derek. He met us in a diner and, to make a long story one sentence, we moved in with the whole family on one big ass farm in the middle of Missouri. That family took us in like we was their own. Me and Greta helped with the livestock, cows, chickens, pigs, and a couple of horses. We loved bein' with them animals. My Greta's face lit right up, just like in that picture, every single day when we was on that farm. It's the main reason I bought this house and this land with the help of Mister richer-than-God. I thought it would bring that shinin' light back into her face. The sad fact is, that picture was just about the last time she had it."

Stella pulled a Pall Mall out of the pack on the table. "That girl was my heart and soul. I used to tell her there wasn't nothin' gonna tear us apart, that we was gonna reach for them stars together, which is why we eventually left that farm. I knew them stars wasn't there. I didn't know where they was, but I was gonna find 'em. I never told Derek I was pregnant because it woulda been harder on him after I snuck off in the middle of the night."

She lit her cigarette and exhaled. "They was kind people, but they wasn't like me. They wasn't hungry like I was."

She looked back and forth from Bobby to Annie. "See, as Bobby already knows, when Greta was born, I was sixteen and livin' with her father, Danny, who, as you both know, saved my ass from my mama. And, like you both already know, we ran off to California where he stole cars and anything else he could get his hands on for our livin' and wouldn't let me do shit 'cause I was pregnant—the pregnant part bein' the part Annie don't know 'cause I never talked about Greta after she died, except the day I gave Annie her name."

She looked at Annie. "And what I told you then was only 'bout as much as would fit in a peanut shell and as small as that was, only twenty-five percent of it was true. The twenty-five percent bein' that she was dead and she had the blaze, just like her mama."

Stella stopped looking at either of them. "Anyway, Danny, he said seein' as I was the girl I was s'pose to be home in our piece-of-shit trailer, doin' whatever it was women was s'pose to do, which wasn't my cup of tea. See, here I was sixteen years old and it was beginnin' to look like I was gonna end up like my mama—trailer trash and mean as shit. My mama bein' the very same mama who gave me the hunger I got for findin' them stars back when I was young like Greta in that photo."

She glanced down at the wallet-sized photograph on the table. "And just like my mama left my daddy and took off to find that somethin' better, I took off from Danny in one of his stolen cars with a chunk of his stash of cash, a month shy of Greta's first birthday—only I took my little girl with me 'cause I wasn't gonna be the mama who left her little girl, turned into a hundred percent failure, and then took her back after her daddy died, then tried to beat the life outta her. Some days I wish she'd let me be with my uncle and my brother and left me thinkin' on how she was out in Hollywood and one day I was gonna see her on the movie screen. That's exactly what I wish woulda happened."

Stella sat in sudden silence and sucked on her cigarette. She thought about how, if her mama had become rich and famous, she wouldn't be sitting at this table and never would've had Greta, or met Christopher. She would've been living in a whole different world, not this one.

Annie suddenly felt more than the burn on her fingertips and what followed were words. "You're right, you didn't leave Greta like your mama did you. You killed her!"

Stella looked up at the ceiling, then down at the floor to where she had stomped on Annie's cigarette butt. "That girl was already dead and she knew it—all that was left in that little body was the excrutiatin' pain of the evil that was growin' inside of her on account of Christopher puttin' it there."

She looked over at Annie, leaned towards her, and waited for her to lift her eyes to where she could see them straight on. "Have you ever seen a animal hit by a car, then flop around in the middle of road not dead, with no hope of livin'? I have, and I ain't like them people who drive on, or walk right on by, like it's nothin'. I don't leave it floppin' there. I finish the job 'cause it just ain't right to let that sufferin' go on. That girl was dead long before we were in that barn. What I did that night was help her do somethin' she wanted and woulda done all by herself in time."

She sat back as soon as Annie started looking anywhere but at her. She couldn't figure if Annie was scared or about to cry, or both. "Bobby told you somethin' that wasn't none of your business, just like he said, and you coulda just let it be, but you couldn't do that, now could you?"

Silence fell over the smoke filled room.

Annie settled on looking at the window over the sink. She wished she'd gone out through the bathroom window when she'd the chance, she wished she'd gone out through the bathroom window, she wished she'd gone out through the bathroom window—this wish repeated itself over and over in her head.

Bobby broke the silence. "That weren't no mercy killin'."

He had just rolled the last joint. The bag was empty, his plate was pretty much full and he had heard a whole lot more than he cared to. He was tired of all her talk. "Oh, I seen you do mercy killin's just like you say you have, but I ain't never seen you standin' over one of them animals while it's floppin', yellin' at it, and then when you killed it, growlin' in the meanest voice I ever heard, 'Good riddance, bitch!'"

He got up from the table.

Stella turned. "Where the hell you goin'?"

She watched his back as he walked to the fridge and opened it. "Bobby, none of them animals had the bad in 'em. Not a one of 'em ever strangled a whole litter of kittens for no damn reason, or killed a baby chicken at school that she was s'pose to be takin' care of, or God only knows what else. It makes my skin curdle just thinkin' on it, somethin' I ain't done in years, but now you two just had to bring it up in my face, not considerin' for one second the pain it causes me. You got no idea the hell of watchin' your own kin slowly dyin' away and seein' the bad slip in and take her place, all in the same body. There weren't nothin' in them animals that needed stompin' out, they was just innocent creatures who needed help gettin' to dyin' quicker than they was. That girl—and I ain't callin' her Greta unless I'm thinkin' on the girl in that photo—she had the bad put in her, and it had hold of ninety-five percent of her by the time she was in that barn. The other five percent was all that was left of Greta, which I never saw 'cause it was damn near smothered to death under all that bad. Soon, it woulda been gone, like Greta never was, and we woulda had a big problem on our hands, a hundred percent problem."

She glanced at Annie, who looked to her like she was sittin' there, but had got up and left at the same time. "Annie here, we been watchin' her flop around for years—and from the looks of her right this minute, I'd say she's floppin' right now, but she ain't never crossed that line into killin' innocent animals and makin' my skin curdle in a bunch of other ways, so she got the chance that my Greta never had."

She looked back at Bobby, who was on his way back to the table with a beer. "How many girls did we see come and go in our business early on? 'Cept for Annie, we picked a bunch of 'em who was already dead as in they was livin' in the same hell and didn't give a rat's ass about whether they lived or died. Every one of them girls, I can guarantee you didn't make it past twenty-five percent. They either killed theirselves or we-don't-know-and-we-ain't-never-gonna-know-and-we-don't-wanna-know. They was whores who didn't have a drop of decency left in 'em, not one drop—and I did everything I could to give 'em a chance."

She watched Bobby sit back down, not expecting him to respond. "See, once that bad has taken over more than seventy-five percent, there ain't no chance."

She looked over at Annie, who wasn't looking at her. "Annie here, was the one who kept me thinkin' we could run a decent business without all that bad. If we, meanin' me, hadn't been arrested, we'd be richer than God right now 'cause we were finally, after all them years, gettin' only the cream of the crop to work for us. We woulda had everythin' we dreamed of, and Annie never woulda had to be shoved outta the nest, and there woulda been no big fat silence that busted open while I was gone, and I wouldn't be sittin' here talkin' about ancient history with you two actin' like it's the end of the damn world when it ain't. The only thing I see that's real wrong, right now, is a bunch of food I spent all day cookin', goin' cold."

Stella's chair squealed as she stood up abruptly and went into her study.

Bobby tipped the bottle to his mouth, then put it down on the table.

He looked over at Annie, who was looking nowhere in particular. He noticed there were tiny sweat drops on her face, but not enough heat to cause them. He then picked up the photo and studied it. Little Greta was leaning back against Stella who was leaning back against a black railing and beyond that was some kind of mist—it was hard to tell what it was because the photo was so small. Stella had her hand resting across Greta's chest and they were both smiling, not the kind of smiles that people do just because they are having their picture taken, but genuine smiles— and the two of them were spitting images of each other, just like a baby elephant and its mama.

When he heard Stella walk back into the room, he spoke without bothering to look up from the photo. "That's a whole lotta talk you just did, that don't make any sense. Greta wasn't no ninety-five percent bad, you just stopped seein' the good is all and I got no explanation for why you did that. Hell, the way I see it, I could cross out the good in damn near anybody and see nothin' but bad, or I can cross out the bad and see nothin' but good, and if I was to look at you right now and think on which you are, I'd say you was reachin' the ninety-five percent bad, only I got the sense to know there are other times when I see the ninety-five percent good—but in thinkin' on it now, maybe there won't be any more of those times."

Stella picked her purse up off her plate and dropped it on the floor. In its place she dropped a folder and sat down and opened it. "Bobby, I don't know what the hell you're talkin' about! As usual you just gotta make everythin' way more complicated than it is, so I ain't gonna pay it any attention and just go on and finish what you started."

She pulled a single piece of paper from the folder and put it on the table where the photo had been. "What I got right here is Christopher's confession."

She reached back into the folder and pulled out a driver's license. "I also confiscated his driver's license and told him he'd just have to go get hisself another one assumin' he could walk again, which I knew he could 'cause it was nothin' but a thirty-eight. Fact is, I found the bullet under the couch the next day, half buried in the floor, so it couldn't have done more than scrape his leg. Anyway, I been meanin' to burn this stuff 'cause it ain't no use to me anymore. In thinkin' on it, maybe God made me wait till right now to do the burnin'—maybe tellin' the whole story, like I'm havin' to do, was what needed doin' before the burnin'."

Bobby put the photo on top of all the joints he'd rolled and looked at Stella. "I ain't interested in readin' that, but I am interested in knowin' why you lied to me all them years. Here I was thinkin' you had it all takin' care of, as in that bastard got hisself killed—at least that's how you made it seem. Now, I believe what you're tellin' me is that son of a bitch is still alive. What I want to know is where the hell that bastard is 'cause if you didn't have the guts to do what shoulda been done, I sure as hell do!"

Annie didn't know why, but she picked up the sheet of paper and read it:

> My name is Christopher Bradley Norman and I molested and raped Greta Gaille over a period of more than a year without her mama knowing about it. I touched her private parts. I made her play with my dick. I jerked off in front of her and I screwed her too. I told her if she told anybody she would be real sorry and a whole lot of hurt would come to her and her mama and her brother. I promise from this day till I die I will pay for this in whatever way Stella Gaille wants me to and if I don't, god help me. The first way being, that I will send Greta Gaille five hundred dollars a month forever, in a money order payable to Stella Gaille, so Greta doesn't have to go through the hell of hearing from me.
> Signed,
> Christopher Bradley Norman

Stella ignored Bobby for the moment and watched Annie read the confession. She spoke as soon as Annie was done. "Jack wrote them words from what Christopher told us, and that's his for real signature at the bottom. Now, I made it real clear to him that I was not who he thought I was, as in just a single mom workin' in some bar, and that Jack and Daryl would verify that sure as I was standin' there. I explained to him that I had connections far as the eye could see, and some of them connections was not somethin' he ever wanted to mess with, so he better not even think about tryin' to run and hide—and if I was to hear he ever so much as looked at a little girl again, he would wish he was dead, which he is."

She looked over at Bobby. "Did you hear that, Bobby? He's dead, so you need to calm your ass down."

Annie stared at the page.

Stella snatched it from her as soon as she saw the tears coming. "Ain't no point in gettin' your tears all over it. When we burn this I want it to be as is, meanin' no tears 'cause he don't deserve one drop."

Bobby picked up the driver's license and looked at the tiny photo. His head started spinning even more than it already was. "That ain't Christopher, that right there is Kevin or else he's Kevin's twin brother, but he didn't have no twin brother, so what the hell are you tryin' to pull?"

Stella put the confession on Bobby's plate. "You need to settle down, Bobby, 'cause I ain't done tellin' you what you asked for. I was gettin' to that part."

She pointed to the paper on his plate. "What you gotta do before I go on is read that, so you got a full understandin' of the whole picture."

Bobby dropped the license on top of the confession. "I don't need to read that. I got a full understandin' of what the son of a bitch did and I don't need one ounce more of it. What I don't got a understandin' of is what Kevin is doin' on this license."

Stella picked the confession up off his plate. "You got no need to read this 'cause your readin' skills are a damn sight worse than mine, which ain't all that good, so how 'bout I read it for you. "My name is Christopher Bradley Norman and…""

In one singular swift movement, Bobby jumped to his feet, picked up his chair, and threw it across the room where it smashed against Annie's bedroom door and fell into pieces on the black-and-white squares. His voice was stretched tight. "I ain't gonna say this again. I got no need to hear no confession by that son of a bitch. What I got the need to hear is why Kevin's picture is on his driver's license."

34

God's Business Continued...

Stella smacked the confession down on her plate and stood up. She looked rapidly, back and forth, between Bobby and the pieces of the yellow wooden chair that lay on the floor and, as she did so, her red hair swung from one shoulder to the other. When she finally settled her attention on Bobby, her cigarette-free hand flew onto her hip. "Bobby, what the hell is wrong with you?"

She shook her cigarette at him so hard it fell from her fingers to the floor. "You got us into this and now you is gonna sit your ass down and hear it through."

She looked down at the cigarette and stomped on it. "You havin' a tantrum ain't gonna make it stop, darlin', 'cause what I got to say has been sittin' way back in my mind behind a big ass door that I ain't cared to open for a thousand years, and now, due to you and A N E, it's charged right through that door and is right up here." She tapped the front of her head with the tips of her fingers. "And it's poundin' so hard to come on out I'm surprised Alice ain't broke A N E's bedroom door down tryin' to get in here and see what the hell all that bangin' is. 'Course, every one of them dogs 'cept Ivan seem to have the good sense to shut the hell up and listen 'cause they know there ain't no point in interruptin' me. It's called survivin' and stayin' that way. Goddamn, that crashin' sound you just made wreckin' that chair ain't nothin' next to that bangin' in my head, so you need to sit your ass in that one empty chair that we got left at the table and hear me out!"

She sat back down, satisfied she'd made her point and he would obey.

Bobby pulled the fourth chair out from the table and sat across from Stella, now kitty corner to Annie, who was so quiet it seemed as if she wasn't there. He'd considered walking out—going to the barn to start building another chair, to replace the one he just broke, but knew it wouldn't make any difference. Whatever Stella had to say was going to make it into his ears, one way or another, and besides that, he could build a hundred chairs and there'd still be no peace for him because Kevin being on that license would bug him to no end. Maybe hearing what she had to say wouldn't give him peace either, but the way he saw it he had no choice.

Stella looked at Annie. "Now, just so we know you is still alive, like them chickens on the table ain't, and to avoid you havin' a tantrum like Bobby just did, or more than likely havin' you fall asleep on that couch for a hundred years, why don't you go on ahead and say what you got to say." She waited.

Annie sat looking at the sheet of paper on Stella's plate. For a moment she'd imagined her own mother standing over her father with a gun to his head. He was reading. His voice was soft, almost a whisper. *My name is Grantwood Evans and I molested and raped my daughter Annie Evans over a period of more than six years. I took from her more than any amount of money could ever buy back.* And when Bobby flung the chair across the room she'd imagined her brother doing the same as he yelled. *You son of a bitch, Dad! How could you do that to her?*

She slowly looked up. "You killed him, didn't you?"

The greens narrowed. "Killed who?"

"Christopher." Annie already knew the answer. It was right there in the green eyes.

Stella lit another cigarette and looked across the table at Bobby. "Now to get to your question regardin' that license and what Kevin's doin' on it. There weren't never a Kevin. I mean, there was as far as you was concerned, but he was always Christopher to me.

"See, besides the money he sent me every month—which he did, right on time—he knew I just might want more from him, which I did after my little girl died. Oh, I thought to blow his brains out that very next day, considerin' he was the whole reason for her dyin'—but I didn't. For one thing, as you well know, the death of that girl was all I was willin' to deal with for a lotta months. Plus we had the boys to think on—though bottom line is they was afraid of their sister by the end—and I believe they breathed a little easier once she was gone. What I'm sayin' is we needed all the help we could get."

She inhaled, then added more smoke to the thick haze that had settled in the room.

Bobby was resigned to remaining steady and having God help him. He saw no point to busting up another chair. He looked down at the license that lay on the table. "So, what you're tellin' me is that I was associatin' with the bastard who raped my little girl and I didn't know it."

Stella watched him carefully. "That's exactly what I'm tellin' you and, before you go off and wreck somethin' else, you need to think on a couple things A) She wasn't your little girl, B) If I was to tell you back then who he was you never woulda associated with him and we never woulda gotten squat done 'cause you know, as well as I do, you wasn't even half interested in gettin' the business goin' in the first place, let alone goin' out and helpin' find the girls we needed and who we wanted to help. No, you didn't see no point in tryin' to help them girls, you were just as happy as a goose in the spring, out buildin' houses. You didn't have a damn clue about my miserable self."

She let out a long smokeless sigh. "After that girl died I came to a full understandin' of how tired I was of livin' the way I was livin', which was doin' less than a hungry person like me can bear. Once she was dead there weren't any more pain-in-my-ass emergencies and misbehavin's or animal killin's. The boys were normal and off at school durin' the days. Everything was normal, and borin' as hell, I might add. I had been out of my world for three whole years busy bein' somethin' I wasn't cut out to be—just like with Derek, only at least back then I had my Greta, which made the achin' to leave our life on that farm not so pressin'. In fact, some days I wonder if I shoulda stayed there and disrespected the hunger my mama gave me."

She took a few silent drags from her cigarette before speaking again. "The good news is I had the good sense to keep up with all them connections I had made durin' them years 'fore I met you, particularly them high class ones that I made after I met Mister-richer-than-God. He got me into circles that a lotta people only dream about. That man woulda done anythin' for me and he did. He helped me get this house, which I wanted for Greta's sake. 'Course, it didn't do a damn bit a good in the end, now did it? I tried, though. God knows I tried. And seein' as this is all about you two wantin' so bad to know the real truth on things, and seein' as the bangin' in my head ain't lettin' up one bit," she tapped her forehead again, "I'll have you know Mister-richer-than-God is Darren's daddy. I know I told you I didn't know who the daddy was, but that weren't the truth. See, I promised him I would keep it secret forever, but since you don't know his identity then I ain't really breakin' that secret, now am I? And truth be told, I think he was as generous as he was 'cause of that more than anythin' else.

"I wasn't stupid you know. I knew from the get go, no matter how much he said he loved me, there wasn't nothin' gonna make him more generous than me havin' his baby. Oh, he wanted to marry me, but I knew that wasn't ever gonna happen 'cause, Bobby, the bottom line is he wasn't you, meanin' he didn't like kids and he didn't love the animals. Kids, to him, was things you put away in places where rich folks who don't like kids put 'em, and animals, all they was, was things you eat."

She paused and studied Bobby as he looked from her, to Annie, to the kitchen window, and then down at his dirty boots. He was settled down nicely. In point of fact, he was actually looking like the Bobby she'd seen every day before he started building all the fences, even maybe back so far as the Bobby she knew before that girl died in the barn.

She sucked in on her cigarette and continued, "Now, I never regretted leavin' that life to settle here with you, but with that girl dyin', things changed, as in I knew there had to be a way I could make a livin', as in be real successful and help girls like her at the same time. 'Course, like I already said, almost none of them girls Christopher helped us find, 'cept Annie here, was worth it in the end."

She glanced over at Annie to be sure she was listening carefully, not off thinking about something else like she did sometimes. Satisfied, she continued, "Now, if I knew that little fact from the beginnin' I woulda taken my chances with somebody else, but we didn't know that, did we? From my way of lookin' at it, which was not knowin' that fact, we needed Christopher 'cause there weren't a soul on this earth we coulda trusted to do what he did without the possibility of him turnin' on us, screwin' us, or screwin' them girls. Christopher wasn't in no position to do any one of them things. Now, I know I told you he was a distant cousin of mine which was why we could trust him, but the fact is, I don't got a distant cousin that I know of, so he was the next best thing."

She sucked in and decided to blow a few smoke rings while the two of them took it in.

Bobby had stopped looking at Stella. He was watching Annie, who had gone from being the color of the moon on a hazy night, to the color of the red door that was presently shut tight, despite the fact of it not being too cold or too hot outside, and he knew exactly why. This wasn't something he'd ever wanted her to know about.

He spoke softly to her. "Annie, first thing you got to understand is I didn't know Kevin was Christopher, and the next thing you got to understand is I wasn't a part of findin' you and if I knew who you was, like I know now, I never woulda let it happen like it did. I wasn't even in New Orleans when it happened. I was back here takin' care of the boys and...." He stopped. He knew no amount of explaining would make the fact of what happened go away.

Stella looked at Annie. "Looks to me like she's floppin', Bobby, and you know exactly why. So when she asks, which she's gonna do in about ten seconds, unless she chooses to wind up on the floor again, then you're gonna answer her question 'cause I need a break from bein' the one who has to lay out the whole truth of the situation."

Annie looked back and forth between Stella and Bobby. When the rush of confusion settled, she looked down at her empty plate. All she could feel was the cold stone in her belly. "From the beginnin' to the end you are alone in this world."

Bobby watched Annie's face go even paler than the moon. Not since he'd sat with Do-this and Do-that and told them he was leaving, had he felt the ache he felt in his heart right in that moment.

Stella sat up. "Seein' as Bobby don't got the nuts to tell you what you need to know, let me explain it to you in one sentence."

She put out her cigarette and pulled out a fresh one. "Kevin, who you now know was Christopher, was the one who saw you, called me, then followed you into that bar. He was one of them two men I told to get lost. I got no idea who the other man was except Christopher, smart as he could be, had got him to join him in approachin' you, which he was more than happy to do—end of story."

She picked up Bobby's gold lighter from the table and sat back. "The ironical part of that story bein'—as you would say—it was YOU who was the main reason I figured I'd had enough of Christopher and it was time to set him free and, when I say free, I don't mean free like a eagle in the sky which is where my Greta is, I mean free to rot in hell with the part of hisself that had took over what was left of Greta on this earth."

She flicked the lighter and stuck a fresh cigarette in it.

That's when Annie felt a small jolt on her sternum. She took a sudden deep breath and put her hands across her chest. The tape-recorder had clicked off.

Stella looked at Annie. "Honey, don't act all like you're shocked. God damn, couldn't of been but five minutes ago you told me I killed him—'course, you put a question mark somewhere in there, but I knew you knew I did, and you knew that 'cause I've told you a thousand times that's exactly what your daddy deserved, a bullet to the head on some lonely back road where he thought he was about to get a dose of my generous and forgivin' heart."

Stella lifted her cigarette free hand and gestured as if she were on the phone. "Christopher, I been thinkin' on it and with my daughter dead and gone, and through all my grievin' and hard work this past year and a half, I have been comin' to know that what she woulda wanted more than anythin' is for me to forgive you and set you free. So I got some money, which you have earned. It's not a whole lot, but some, and seein' as I ain't never given you any, it's a Godsend."

She looked at Annie. "I used that particular terminology on purpose 'cause you had just used it that very day—and then I told him I got his license and that paper he signed and I wanted him to meet me in the usual place so we could settle this once and for all."

She held her hand back up to her face again, as if it were a phone. "I got me a life to get on with and don't need you hangin' around anymore. You got to go on and find yourself a pitiful life to live somewhere else."

She put her hand down. "Mind you, I weren't no fool. I had to end it like that 'cause he woulda got suspicious if I was too different from my usual self. Plus, I had called him from a pay phone not far from the meetin' place, which is far outside of our county so as not to bring any suspicion down our way. You, Bobby, and the boys had gone into Atlanta to see some movie and, if I think on it long enough, I'll remember the exact one. A woman don't forget the details of the night she blew the brains outta the man who raped her daughter and killed her—it just don't work that way. He was about as pathetic as I expected he would be…"

Annie stood up, desperate to get the recorder out from between her breasts. She couldn't think. *What the hell am I doing sitting here taping this?*

Stella looked at her. "A N E, sit down. I'm thinkin' you need to hear the details, seein' as it's exactly what your daddy deserved and seein' as it was YOU who was the very reason I did what I did when I did.

"See, you wasn't dead yet, like most of them girls he found, and the ones that weren't dead, they didn't have enough ambers in 'em to make a for-real blaze, like my Greta woulda done. Oh, they woulda lived past twenty-five, but their lives would have got to no more than zero. You had the ambers—I saw that from the beginnin' and that's exactly why I took you into my house and eventually gave you my Greta's name—and I'm thinkin' you might just want to hang on to it 'cause Annie ain't any kinda name, not to my way of thinkin' anyway."

She watched as Annie dropped her arms to her side and continued. "And just so you know, before I blew Christopher's brains out I said to him, and I swear on all the innocent animals on the earth I said this, I said, 'I got Annie now, and I have you to thank for that 'cause she ain't like all them others you sniffed out and I don't want there to be a chance in hell—hell bein' the place you're goin' to in about five seconds—I don't want there to be a chance in hell you ever lay eyes on her again, amen.'"

Annie sat down. She didn't know what to do.

Bobby sat back and hooked his thumbs under his overall straps. He liked overalls for the very reason they gave him a few things more he could do with his hands in situations like this, including fiddling with the extra pockets if needed. God, or whatever had got him up those front steps in the first place, was holding him steady. If it weren't for that, there wouldn't be a scrap of furniture left in one piece.

"Well," he said, feeling God's steady help, "you just done in all the innocent animals on earth 'cause I think you're lyin'. How the hell do you expect her, or me, to believe you said that? There ain't no way in hell you was thinkin' on Annie when you shot that bastard! Right now, I don't see no reason to be believin' anythin' that comes outta your mouth after you bringin' the likes of Christopher into my life without me knowin' it. Here I sit thinkin' on how I drank beers with him, took him in like a friend, and now I come to find out..."

Stella squashed her half smoked cigarette in the ashtray. "Bobby, what I'm tellin' you is that even if it weren't what I actually said in those last few seconds, which was 'go to hell you dumb piece of shit bastard,' it woulda been, but seein' as I was about to kill a man in cold blood from the law's way of lookin' at it, I had to keep my mind on the business at hand which was to blow his brains out and get the hell outta there. There was no way I was goin' back to knittin' scarves and I mean a million of 'em, not just two hundred and seven, not on account of his sorry ass. 'Course, like

Annie explained to us once, about them laws in France, if I was livin' there I woulda been set free on account of it bein' a 'crime of passion,' meanin' it was justifiable accordin' to the rules of my heart which he broke in a thousand pieces all them years ago, along with killin' my Greta.

"Now, what I'm tellin' you regardin' what I was thinkin' on in that present moment—which, by the way, you got no right to say squat about—is just like what Annie told us about, which is where you take a actual fact and add to it accordin' to what you woulda thought or done if you knew at the time what you know when you're tellin' it, as in right now. People write whole books based on that kinda after the fact thinkin,' and I got a right to do that as much as anybody. The truth is that's exactly what I woulda said to that bastard, along with a thousand other things if I had the time, like I do sittin' here, which I didn't back then—case closed—and that's the damn truth."

Annie got up again and this time didn't hesitate. She looked at Stella. "Please don't ask where I'm going because I think that'll be pretty obvious in about one second, and when I'm done in there, I'm going to walk into my bedroom and check on Bertha."

She turned and walked to the bathroom door, put her hand on the knob and paused. "What you're doing right now is saying anything that you think will pull me away from seeing the stone cold truth of who you are—a manipulative selfish woman who has duped me for all these years."

The moment she closed the door behind her she rushed over, turned on the faucet full blast, then dropped to her knees holding her head over the toilet. She heaved and heaved, but nothing came up, she was empty. She turned and pulled off her T-shirt. The wire was still in place and the recorder sat tidily between her breasts. She pulled it out and looked at it as it sat in the palm of her hand. *God almighty what've I done?*

That's when there came the familiar bang on the door.

"You got it all dead wrong, honey, and you throwin' up in there ain't gonna make it any different. You ain't no sorry ass little victim, no sir. There's no way in hell you didn't already know all about how I got you seein' as it was you who helped me set it all up different so we could get the better girls to work for us. Most of them years, you were right in there with me, up to your neck, and you loved every minute of it and weren't never lackin' in anythin'—end of story. Any part of them years when you was miserable weren't on account of me and you know I am one hundred percent correct about that. You didn't know about Christopher, I'll give you that, but God damn, if you didn't know 'bout the rest it was 'cause you didn't want to know, which is none of my business, meanin' it ain't gonna give me any sleepless nights, so don't you even try to hang that poor-me-I-been-had bullshit on my head. Now, you got about ten seconds to stop throwin' up or whatever the hell you're doin' and come back out here and face the facts you was so dead set on hearin' all about since I came back. We ain't done yet."

Annie looked up and saw that she hadn't latched the door. She quickly ripped the wire from her chest and arm and put it, along with the tiny recorder, into the wastebasket. She knew if Stella walked in through that door it wouldn't take her more than an instant to figure out what she'd done—the signs were all over her bare chest and arms in the form of raw, red tape marks. She grabbed the wadded up T-shirt from the floor and slipped it back on.

Stella turned the doorknob and pushed the door open.

Annie was sitting with her back up against the toilet.

She stepped in about two feet and stopped. She shook her head as she spoke. "Goddamn, you look about as nasty as I ever seen you. Bobby, you need to see this. She ain't Annie or A N E or Greta or anybody I know of, but I do know she's gonna hear me out, irregardless of the fact of her lookin' like she's ..."

Bobby had gotten up from his chair the moment Stella put her hand on the doorknob. There was no telling what would happen next. He walked up behind her as she stepped into the bathroom, grabbed each of her arms before she had a chance to know what was happening and pulled her back through the door into the kitchen. Her cigarette flew from her hand and spun out across the floor. He held her arms firmly at the elbows and pushed her up against the wall, face first, just beside the open bathroom door and leaned into her hard enough so she couldn't move.

"Now, I ain't gonna hurt you, darlin', but you need to stop stompin' on her. She's in there right now tryin' to make sense of a whole lotta stuff that don't have any sense and I'm doin' the same out here."

As soon as Stella was pulled out into the kitchen, Annie got up, shut the door, and latched it.

Stella struggled to free herself, but couldn't. Bobby had never crossed this line.

She growled into the wall. "If you don't take your hands off me right this second, I am callin' nine-one-one and won't they be interested to know you got your daddy in you. You will find your ass back in prison so fast you won't know what hit you."

Bobby held on, but his head felt as if it was going to bust open. He squeezed his eyes shut to try to ease the pressure that was building behind them. It hadn't been one bit hard to grab hold of her and stop her dead in her tracks. The fact of that raced down to his hands and began to suck the strength out of them. He squeezed his eyes tighter, till he couldn't hold on anymore, then let her go and stepped back.

Stella turned around. "And don't think for one second I wouldn't call 'em."

She shook her arms and steadied herself as she studied him. "Look at you with them itty bitty tears on your face. I'll tell you one thing, it ain't a man I'm lookin' at right now!"

She scanned the floor and spotted the still burning cigarette at the edge of the kitchen. "A few more feet and you coulda set the couch on fire."

She walked over, picked up the cigarette, and put it to her lips. "Goddamn, I feel like I'm livin' with a couple of crazy motherfuckers. What the hell is the matter with the two of you?!"

Bobby looked at her. There was nothing left to say. It was all laid out clear as day. He was as guilty of killing Greta as she was. Annie had gotten that right, only not the way she thought.

He walked past Stella, into the living room, and sat down on the couch. He felt as if he'd just dug a million postholes, pounded in a million posts, and put in a thousand miles worth of boards between them. His bones had crumbled and his muscles were spent.

Stella stood and looked at the back of Bobby's head for a moment, then walked to the table. "When A N E gets back out here, we're gonna eat this dinner, cold as it may be, and then we're gonna burn this thousand year old shit and be done with it, once and for all."

She picked up the confession, the license, and the photograph, shoved them back in the folder, and put it on the counter by the sink. "And just so you know, I never cashed one of them money orders, not a one. They're all right here, just like they was when I got 'em, carbon copy and all. The way I saw it, usin' that money for anythin' other than me likin' the fact of his losin' it every month woulda been just plain wrong."

35

The Ashes

Annie heard a long low sigh as a warm gust of air swept across her face. She opened her eyes, which then unleashed the triumphant thud-thud-thud of Bertha's tail smacking the wall. She smiled, but the smile flinched and vanished. Something horrible had happened. She glanced around the room. The light that was slipping in around the window shades told her it was early morning. *Her father will wake her for breakfast any minute now, as he always does the morning after—never any other morning—and he will be smiling and he'll hug her as he always does, and she will feel better and climb out of bed. She waits, but he doesn't come. He's not coming. Something is terribly wrong. What happened was really bad. Her father even cried. Where is he? She needs him. What if she can't get up?*

Bertha pushed her head against Annie's arm, insistent.

Annie patted her distractedly as she scanned her own body. She ached. Something must be broken inside. *The door opens and her mother leans in to tell her it's time to get up because she can't be late for school.*

Bertha pushed into her arm again and Annie turned abruptly, a hairsbreadth from shouting at Bertha to go away and leave her alone. Bertha's tail smacked the wall again—thud-thud-thud. Annie took a deep breath and reached over to scratch the broad furrow between Bertha's eyes. Bertha grunted her approval and waited for Annie to sidle over on the bed and pat the mattress. She then leapt up and rolled onto the covers beside her.

The moment Annie rested her arm across Bertha's withers, the whole of the previous night broke through, all of it, right up to where she'd laid down on her bed and wished it away.

She reached under her pillow, into the pillowcase, in hopes she wouldn't find what she was looking for, but there it was. She grasped the tape recorder, then released it as if to avoid a sting to her finger tips which were already raw from the cigarette that had burned them.

Bertha squirmed, impatient for Annie to resettle her arm.

Annie dropped onto the pillow and put her burnt fingertips to her lips. What had she done? What had Stella done? What the hell was she going to do now?

She quickly turned her attention back to Bertha and gently stroked her. However, the soft coat and deep sighs faded quickly from her awareness. She was not safe here. She was never safe here. She was right back to where she was before Stella's hand had landed on her shoulder in that bar—she was nowhere. No, it was even worse than that, much worse. She strained to see the faces of the two men, one of whom she now knew was Christopher. She couldn't see them. Stella was all that came in, loud and clear. "Honey, did you see how all them folks couldn't take their eyes off of you and me? It's like we was meant to meet. I swear, on days like today I know there's a God—not the God that lives in them churches—but the for real one that nobody but me seems to pay attention to 'cause they're all too busy payin' attention to the wrong one. Anyways, some days I think the for-real God knows exactly what he's doin', like he did just now, puttin' you in this bar and havin' me walk in."

Annie continued to stroke Bertha, still deaf to the loud satisfied snorts and sighs.

She'd spent those next two nights with Stella in a suite at the New Orleans Hilton. Stella knew nearly everyone in that hotel, including many of the guests. This only served to increase her trust tenfold, plus she felt that familiar long lost glow of being somebody very special.

As she and Stella walked through the lobby, the halls, or sat in the bar, it was as if she was with the Queen and the Queen had chosen her, not anyone else.

She then saw herself in the hotel suite, sitting across from Stella who was stretched out on the maroon couch, blowing smoke rings at the ceiling, all the while telling the story of her father's death, her subsequent horrific life with her mother, and how she'd run away from it all when she was seventeen. That was when Annie cried for the first time since she'd walked out of her home on Thanksgiving.

"Honey, it's alright, no need to say a thing. I see it clear as day when someone has to run from their circumstances—it's like a damn neon sign—and I don't need for you to tell me a damn thing. You just go on and cry. We all got pain we carry around and some of us got pain so bad, like my Bobby, who I hope you get a chance to meet. Bobby, he had such a load of pain when he was just a kid that he clean forgot about it. He doesn't remember a thing before age ten. Now, the reason I know it's pain, is 'cause there ain't a person on this earth that forgets ten years if it was a whole lotta pleasure—unless they got a brain injury, which he don't.

"So, just like Bobby clean forgot his pain, some people don't talk about it 'cause it's how they keep goin' day in and day out. Me? Now, I talk about mine 'cause it clears my head. But I know from knowin' Bobby and a ton of other people, that we each got to do whatever it takes to keep it from runnin' over our hearts like a damn Mack truck, and leavin' it squashed to nothin' in the middle of the highway—case closed."

All Annie had told her that night, and for months after, was that she'd left her home because she had to. Stella didn't intrude. She accepted her as she was, and her use of "honey" had gone deep. By the time she'd heard it a thousand times, from a thousand strangers, it was too late.

That next day Stella took her around New Orleans, showed her the sights, and continued to talk about herself, her family, her boys, Bobby, and life in general. She had swallowed the bait, hook, line, and sinker. She was in awe of Stella.

Annie picked up the tape recorder as her mind sped through fourteen years. A thousand images, and words exchanged—the bucket of ice water, her nineteenth birthday, Stella's constant refusal to leave her in the clutches of the dark depression that was forever just over her shoulder, Stella's rage at her father, Stella's ability to make her laugh when she would otherwise have cried for days, the fights that ended in peace, the business...

She dropped the tape recorder, unable to hold onto any of it in light of what she now knew. She then thought about Bobby and flew back to the beginning again. During that first forty-eight hours in New Orleans, Stella had called him several times, with Annie standing or sitting right there. "She's real quiet, Bobby, kinda like you, and drop dead gorgeous—not like you—and smart as shit, which ain't like you either (she snorted a laugh and glanced at Annie) and, Bobby, she could use a helpin' hand right about now." She told him what they were doing and how she hoped Annie would want to travel back with her to their house, even if only for enough time to get her head straight.

Annie stared at the ceiling through the morning light. Bobby said he'd had nothing to do with any of it and she believed him. She felt sick. In all likelihood it had been Christopher on the other end of that line. And all those people in the hotel, how many of them knew she was just another girl who was now caught? How many were paid to say or do certain things? How could she let all this time go by and not know? Stella was right when she said if she'd wanted to know she would have. How could she have been so stupid! From the first day she'd moved in with Stella and Bobby, she never thought for a second she was walking in the same shoes as the others who were shacked up in that for-shit hotel.

She cringed as she corrected herself. No, she wasn't in their same shoes, because every single one of them knew what they had gotten into, and every one of them had gotten out, whether on their own or by Stella's cruel hand. Not one of them had been sucked in as deeply as her. Here she still was, the last one standing, and there was nothing special about it—nothing special about her.

She sat up abruptly, much to Bertha's annoyance. She had to get out before Stella woke. Or maybe Stella was already up and sitting in the kitchen waiting for her.

———

With Bertha at her heels, Annie slowly opened the bedroom door. She immediately saw and smelled fresh smoke mixed in with the rank, stale haze left over from the previous night. She noted that some of the fresh smoke held the acrid scent of burnt plastic. She glanced around. Stella and Bobby were nowhere to be seen, though clearly one or both had been there within the hour.

The table was still set and the chickens, the mashed potatoes, and the peas, were as they had been when she'd left the room to throw up—cold and untouched.

She walked closer and saw that Stella's plate had Christopher's half burnt license on it, along with the ashes and crumpled remains of what she assumed was the confession. And the floor beneath and around Stella's chair was black with ashes and partially burnt papers and carbons. The ashes were so thick that she could see blackened footprints leading out from them, clear across the kitchen into the living room. She bent down and picked up a fairly large remnant of paper—"make payable to Stella Gai..."—was all she could read. She picked up another remnant—"... ount of 500.00."

Bertha stepped around Annie and stuck her nose to the floor. The ashes scattered as she swished and snorted through them, leaving behind her own partial paw prints.

Annie followed the Stella-sized ashen footprints to the living room carpet, then stopped and looked over the back of the couch. Bobby was curled up, still in his overalls, asleep. So soundly asleep that even Bertha's nudging had no effect.

She called to Bertha, not wanting her to wake him, which she would have, even if it meant jumping on top of him.

She looked again at the footprints. They shrank to tiny smudges of black as they crossed the carpet and went up the stairs by the front door. Stella had gone to bed.

She glanced at her watch that, like her clothes, she hadn't taken off before she'd gone to sleep. It was 5:30 a.m. She looked back at Bobby. She hadn't seen him asleep at this hour since she'd arrived back from her failed escape to Greece. She spit Greece from her mind and went back to her bedroom, pulling Bertha along by the collar to keep her from trying to rouse Bobby again.

She re-checked the bathroom to make sure she'd done a thorough job of gathering all the evidence, which had included retrieving the bits of tape and the empty Tampax box from the wastebasket. Despite her state of confusion and sickness the previous night, she'd done a good job. All the evidence had been cleared and was now at the bottom of the duffle bag she'd shoved under her bed. She pulled it out, dropped the tape recorder in, and gathered only the clothes she'd come back from Greece with. The remaining items, the sultry sexy dresses, silk blouses, scarves, and high heels, she left behind. They were from a life that was no longer hers. She was done here. She froze. *I'm done here, I'm done here, I'm done here.* What was next? She reached through her confusion, zipped up the duffle bag, then spoke softly to Bertha. "Let's go, girl."

She took a final look around the bedroom. She was done.

Bertha followed her through the kitchen, the living room, and out the front door.

Once in the barn, Annie tucked the duffle at the back of her van, under the sleeping bag, and hurried out to the kennel. As she approached, she spotted Oz lying in front of the door to the puppy cottage.

Oz raised his head when he saw her.

"Hi buddy, have you been here all night?"

He wagged his tail and slowly got to his feet.

Annie patted his head as the pups and all the rest of the dogs burst into their morning round of barking. She was surprised the pups had remained quiet for as long as they had. Then she realized that probably Oz's presence outside their door had provided them with comfort through the night. In all likelihood, he'd heard the pups' cries and wandered over to give them, and himself, some peace. What was most astonishing was that Stella had forgotten to let him back into the house, something that never happened— that, along with the fact that Stella left her alone after

Bobby had pulled her out of the bathroom. She had no idea what happened between them after that. She didn't care at the time, and she didn't care now.

She watched Oz walk slowly out across the gravel, back towards the house, then opened the door to the nursery. The pups needed to be fed and let out to do their business. If Stella woke during the time it took her to this—well, she would just deal with it.

————

"So, I guess you'll finally be leavin' now like I been tellin' you to do."

Annie was seated on the ramp watching the pups at play. She turned, startled, as Bobby sat down beside her. If she didn't know it was early morning she would have guessed from watching him move that it was the end of a very long day of hard work, except that his overalls and white T-shirt were still clean. She hesitated to answer him. She didn't want him there and now wished she hadn't taken the extra time with the pups.

Bobby looked down at his overalls as she scanned him. "This was the outfit I was tellin' you about—my wrestlin' with the devil outfit." His smile was hard for him to get to because he was more tired than he could remember ever being. If it hadn't been for the roar of the dogs, he'd still be on that couch sleeping. Any other loud noise, even a bomb, wouldn't have done the job—only the sound of the dogs could have dragged him off that couch. And it'd been a long time since he had slept so deeply he forgot where he was when he opened his eyes. All he knew was he was somewhere where there were dogs around, which meant it couldn't be anywhere that was all that bad, the main thing being he wasn't in prison—thank God.

Annie laughed despite her wishing him away. "You've worn a thousand white tees and I've see you in overalls plenty of times."

Bobby picked up one of the pups as it ran up and tried to grab hold of his boot strings. "The point bein', you never know when the devil just might turn up. It's always good to be ready." He tussled with the pup in his arms, and then put it back down.

Annie turned and looked in the direction of the house. She couldn't see it from around the corner of the nursery, but she knew it was still there.

"Don't worry about her, she ain't gonna be wakin' anytime soon. She smoked most of them joints I rolled PLUS she took a bunch of them little yellow pills just a couple hours ago, when she was done burnin' what she had a need to burn. Last thing I remember was her tellin' me to go on to sleep and leave her all by herself, just like you did."

He shook his head and tried to chuckle, but it came out as more of a groan. "She was mad you went off to bed 'fore she did the burnin'."

"Well," Annie felt annoyed, "she's had no trouble barging into my room and waking me up in the past. I'm surprised she didn't this time, though I have to say, I'm glad she didn't."

Bobby dropped down from the ramp and sat cross-legged on the ground. He spoke as the pups rolled joyfully in and out of his lap and tugged at his overall bib and boot strings. "Oh, she did try to wake you, but there weren't much noise behind it. She knocked on your door, said a few things, but she never did touch that knob. Now, I don't know if that's on account of me pullin' her out of the bathroom or not. Only thing is, I can't think on why that would be considerin' she threatened to call the police on me for pullin' on her. See, she knew damn well I knew she could make up a hell of a case against me considerin' my history and all—and I sure as shit didn't want to end up back in prison."

He rolled one of the pups onto its back and tickled it. "So, I don't really know why she didn't go in there after you, 'cept she didn't seem all that interested in you bein' there or not, once you was gone. It was like you was never there to begin with.

"She talked on and on about Christopher, Derek, Danny, the rich guy, how much she missed Greta—mostly the same stuff you already heard. She said it all over and over and over. Hell, by the time she got around to burnin' that stuff,

I believe she said damn near everythin' she's ever said in her whole life."

As Bobby tickled the one pup, two others began tugging at his pant legs, another at his bib. "And when she was done with the burnin', she said, 'It's over and done with,' and got up and went up to bed without another word. I guess she's plannin' on gettin' up sometime today and startin' over, meanin' minus a bunch of them words she used up last night. I wouldn't be a damn bit surprised if God doesn't go on ahead and take some of them words right out of the human vocabulary on account of her usin' 'em so damn much she killed 'em."

Annie was paying far more attention to what Bobby was doing than what he was saying. She watched the pups bounce in and out of his reach, tug on his overalls, jump in and out of his lap, roll beneath his hands—and he, without a thought, was managing the perfect balance between gentleness and commanding respect, much like Grace did when she was alive.

When she spoke, it was in response to what she saw. "Bobby, why don't you come with me?" As the question rolled out she realized just how agonizing it was going to be for her to do what she had to do—alone.

Bobby rolled onto his back and grunted as the several hefty young pups bounded on and off his belly. "Darlin', like I told you before, this is where I'm meant to be. Now, I know you keep wantin' me to explain it in a way you understand it, but I can't. It's as clear to me as that grave out there."

He sat up to give his stomach a break. "Grace was born here and she died here. Well, I was born here too, meanin' I was nothin' before I met Stella—and I'm gonna die here, just like Grace. It's that simple and when I do die, I hope you'll know about it somehow and be here to help bury me, just like you helped bury her."

Annie could barely see him through the quiet tears that were building in her eyes. She took a deep breath and wiped them with the back of her hand. "Bobby, you're lying to yourself because you're scared. Stella didn't give you what you have. Those things were there long before you met her.

Don't you want to find that out? You keep telling me you're stuck here and I'm not. You don't think I'm terrified to leave here? You don't think despite everything, including what I heard last night, that there's a part of me that wants to hunker down and stay until I'm out there next to Grace? What the hell am I going to do from here, you tell me? I have nobody but you and Stella, sick as she makes me feel right now—and you keep telling me I have a life waiting for me out there! What the hell does that mean and why don't you think that about yourself? You and I could help each other find something else."

Bobby reached out and grabbed the smallest of the litter by the scruff of its neck as it ran by. The pup struggled, making it hard for him to get a good hold. "These pups sure are gettin' big." The pup calmed and he put it in his lap. "See this one here? She's been beat up, pushed over, stomped on by all them other pups, but she ain't one bit unhappy about it. She just goes on livin' and seein' just what's in front of her. That's the difference between you and me. You're unhappy about the stompin' you been handed from your daddy, your kin, from Stella. You have a heck of a time thinkin' on what's right in front of you. I seen it in your eyes every day since you got here, way back when you was just seventeen—always thinkin' on somethin' else or some place else 'cept where you are. Now maybe it's because I ain't read all them books you have or seen anythin' of the world, maybe that's why I ain't hungerin' for somewhere else to be—maybe I'm just too damn tired, but the reason don't matter, now does it?"

He put the pup on the ground and stood up. He looked at Annie. "I'll bet you're thinkin' on ten different things right now and just barely hearin' what I got to say, ain't that right? Now, what you got to do is go on and find somewhere where you ain't got to do all that thinkin'. I'm here and I ain't goin' anywhere 'cept back to prison if Stella ever gets it in her mind to make that happen, which she will if you ever tell the law or anybody about Greta, 'cause Annie, I'm the one with the history of violence and if it come down to me or her, the law would believe her."

Annie looked straight into Bobby's blues. They were a different shade of blue than hers, but blue nonetheless. "Bobby, I heard every word you just said and I don't believe most of it." She was sick of his lies, and hers. "Don't worry, I would never tell anyone anything that would land you back in prison, I promise. But the truth is, you're already in prison and sitting here listening to your screwed up logic about how you're content being here is making me feel all the better about getting out."

Bobby walked over to the gate of the puppy play area, all the pups trotting at his heels. He talked as he walked. "You ain't never been in prison, Annie, so you don't know what you're sayin'. Now I'm goin' into town for a couple hours and I suggest, while I'm gone, you gather Bertha and whichever one of them pups you want and get on your way. This is the only chance you're gonna get to get out of here without havin' to deal with her again. You don't wanna be stuck here in 'prison' with me."

"Bobby!" Annie called out to him as he opened the gate and gently pushed the puppies back with his foot.

He shut the gate, leaving the pups on the inside, and looked over at her. "Yup?"

Annie's voice was barely audible. "Good-bye."

Bobby smiled another hard smile. The pups stood at the fence and barked frantically as he turned from the gate and walked up onto the gravel. When they stopped barking, he knew they'd stopped thinking about him and had turned to thinking about what was right in front of them. And when Annie left they would do the same.

He listened to gravel crunch beneath his work boots and watched the dust rise around them. Summer was well on its way and it was going to be a hot dry one, unless they got some rain real soon. He glanced up at the clear blue sky. As much as he hoped those clouds from the north were coming this way, the wind had long settled, and it seemed more than likely they were headed somewhere else.

———

Annie waited until she heard the truck leave, then walked over to the gate. The puppies bounded back and forth in front and behind her, just as they had with Bobby. She looked up at the house and noticed the red door was closed again. Bobby must have done that. As she stared at it, it occurred to her that if Stella were to walk out that door, right then, she would have nothing to say to her. There was nothing left to say. How was that possible?

She turned from what she couldn't grasp and herded the pups across the yard and back up the ramp. She glanced at her watch; it was 7:30 a.m. She couldn't risk taking the time needed to feed the other dogs. Bobby would tend to that when he returned. She settled the pups into their room, kissed each one on the muzzle, then picked up the little girl Bobby had grabbed by the scruff of the neck and tucked her firmly under her arm, "You, little Grace, are coming with me."

Bertha, who was sitting patiently in front of the nursery, exactly where Oz had been, jumped to her feet the moment she heard the doorknob click.

Annie stepped out, "Come on, girl, it's time for the three of us to go." She turned and walked quickly back towards the barn.

Bertha fell in beside her at a trot, all the while sniffing at Little Grace's rump.

Once in the barn, Annie took a small crate from the stack that was piled up against the back wall and put it in her van, on the mattress just behind the driver's seat. She gently pushed little Grace into it, then stepped back and signaled to Bertha who was already in motion.

Bertha leapt onto the mattress, then scooted up between the two front seats and settled onto the passenger seat.

Annie climbed into the driver's seat and turned the key.

As she drove slowly out of the barn and up onto the gravel, she took one last look around at what was once her home. It may not have been what she'd wanted it to be, but it was what it was, as Bobby would say.

She drove slowly by the front walk, looked up at the red door, rounded the first turn, past the very tree she'd run into months earlier, and then suddenly hit the brakes.

Bertha, who had been anxiously waiting for the window to magically open, as it always did, barely managed to keep herself from falling off the edge of the seat. She looked over at Annie as the van backed down the driveway and stopped.

"Wait here, girl!" Annie hopped out of the van and trotted down to the kennel door. She'd forgotten to leave the note.

Stella, I'm done here.

Annie

She stuck it under the same tack Bobby had used for his note concerning "gracey" and started back up to the van.

She stopped.

There was another rather huge something she had forgotten. She pulled out her pen and walked back to the note.

P.S. Ivan is finally free.

She then opened the kennel door and walked in.

When she next emerged she had Ivan at her side.

Ivan immediately looked down the dirt track. His afternoon at the grave had been the only freedom he'd known and he was more than happy to go for it again.

Annie gave his leash a quick tug and spoke firmly. "Come on, Ivan, this way! Let's go."

Ivan turned. The woman who had set him free was going in a direction he'd never been before and that was OK too. He trotted beside her, wagging his tail with great vigor.

Annie opened the back of the van. "Up we go, boy!"

Ivan hopped up and settled onto the mattress next to Little Grace in her crate.

Annie smiled and closed the door.

Bertha turned from the window and leaned over the back of the seat. She took a good sniff of the only part of Ivan she could reach, which was his right ear.

Ivan was oblivious to both Bertha and her scrutiny. He raised his massive head and looked past her, out through the front window. He was eager to see what would happen next.

- 36 -

The Cabin

Once she was out of Georgia, Annie kept on driving—right through Tennessee, Kentucky, Missouri, and Illinois, without much thought given to where she was going. She stopped only for gas, food, walks, and occasional necessary naps in rest areas.

The question as to whether Stella had called the police, reported her dogs stolen, and given Annie's license plate number, stirred both fear and hope—one no stronger than the other—not unlike when she'd taken off to Greece. The difference was that now her fear was not of Stella's wrath and her hope was not for Stella's concern or desire to find her and take her back.

This time her fear was that the police would find her and she'd have to play the tape in order to defend herself AND her hope was that the police would find her and she'd have to play the tape in order to relieve herself of the very dilemma that spurred her foot to the gas pedal. Bobby had made peace with all he knew, but she was headed straight into that bottomless hole she was so terrified of. "You have a heck of a time thinkin' on what's right in front of you. You got to go on and find somewhere where you ain't got to do all that thinkin'."

It wasn't until she pulled into a rest area just outside of Peoria, Illinois, that she took a long hard look at the map—where she'd been, where she was, and where she might be going.

She breathed her first full breath. *I'm headed to Wisconsin.* The instant she thought it, young Emily burst into her mind, smiling, soothing the sharp edges of her fear. She hadn't thought about Emily since Stella's discovery of the unsent letters all those months ago.

She looked up as a Mack truck squealed off the highway and pulled in front of her. As she took in the truck's plates, 'America's Dairyland,' she remembered that Wisconsin was where Emily had been born.

'The Bears' had told her many wonderful things about their life there, the best part having been their summer treks to the far north with its clear lakes, vast forests, and the luxury of so much space and so few people.

As she sat there, Bertha panted impatiently over her shoulder, Ivan sat calmly looking out the front window, and little Grace was fast asleep.

She broke from her thoughts. "We're going to northern Wisconsin!"

Bertha shook her head and let out an anxious yawn. She was delighted action would soon begin. Ivan flicked one ear and kept his gaze steady. Little Grace didn't wake.

She shoved the map into the glove compartment and turned the key. Once she reached her destination, she would search until she found what she was looking for, and she had no idea what that was. One thing she knew, for certain, was she wanted to be as far away from people as possible without severing the cord completely. She trusted no one and yet wanted people within distant reach, even if they were people she would never talk to except in passing—perhaps while picking up supplies in the nearest town—supplies which would now include a pair of overalls and several plain white T-shirts.

———

Three weeks and many towns, forests, and lakes later, Annie found herself standing in the parking lot of the Stretch Out Motel just outside of the tiny town of Maverick, talking with a stocky, broad faced, bearded man named Pete Strate. The common thread had been the dogs. Her realtor, Bernie Cavanaugh, the only realtor in town, had only ever seen a Dogue de Bordeaux at Pete's house. He'd been unable to keep the news of the arrival of three more of them to himself.

Pete had been standing next to his blue pickup watching her as she returned from a morning walk with Little Grace. Her first impulse upon seeing a person who was entirely too interested in her, had been to turn and walk back into the forest she'd just walked out of. However, as if he'd sensed her uneasiness, the bearded man walked quickly towards her, smiling broadly, and looking down at Little Grace.

His voice was not as deep as his looks might have predicted.

"I'll be damned!" he said. "It IS a Dogue de Bordeaux! I didn't believe Bernie. I thought to myself, what are the chances?" He kept his attention on Little Grace until he was right in front of Annie, then looked up and reached out his hand.

Annie looked deliberately at the hand and then at the bearded face. "And you are?"

The hand retracted. "I'm Pete, Pete Strate, ex-Bordeaux breeder turned boat builder." He looked down at Little Grace. "Bernie tells me you have three of these guys, one of the other two I assume to be the source of the barking behind that door."

He laughed as he looked in the direction of her motel room. "I guess the third one must be the alpha of the crew— quiet and steady unless and until the need arises, which it won't up here."

He looked back at her. "So, Bernie tells me you've fallen for this place and are looking to settle in for a little while?"

Annie didn't know if she had actually stepped back a few feet, or just imagined it. Either way the bearded face was suddenly further away than it had been. She hadn't anticipated meeting anyone who knew the breed, let alone a former breeder—not here in the middle of nowhere! The possibility that this man knew Stella, or at least had heard of her, was all too real.

She braced herself, reluctant to go any further with the conversation. "That's true," she retorted, "it's a beautiful area and what I'm looking forward to most is spending time in it, sans people."

She leaned over and picked up Little Grace, thinking she just might have to move on to another town or even another state.

Pete reached out and patted the top of Grace's head as she stretched happily from Annie's arms towards him. "Well, you picked the right place. I know all about 'sans people.' It was a good month or so before I had more than a one sentence conversation with anybody when I first arrived here. I was sick to death of people."

He dropped his hand to his side. "I think you'll be pleasantly surprised by how many around here respect that. They'll be curious just like I'm being right now, but they won't push it. Most of them, like me, have been there. I think the name of the town must be part of the draw."

He chuckled and continued, "They'll just make up some great stories to fill in the blanks until you start talking, or not. It'll all be up to you. I don't talk much about my pre-Maverick life anymore, just the gist of it—which is that it was bad and I'm glad to be free of it. "

He laughed. "I never would've guessed, a couple years ago, that I'd be the one on this side of this conversation."

Annie searched his face. He seemed genuine, but what did she know?

She looked down at Grace and spoke with no feeling at all. "Well, it was nice meeting you but now I have two other dogs I need to walk before Bernie gets here." She turned and started towards her motel room.

"Can I at least have a look before I go?"

Annie turned and looked blankly at him. "Excuse me?"

"The other two dogs, can I see them? I'm more than happy to just stand right here or sit in my truck and look when you bring them out. It's been over two years since I've seen another Bordeaux besides the occasional one my friend Mick brings with him when he visits."

Annie suddenly felt completely undone, so much so that her thoughts spilled from her mouth. "God, there's another one? For Chrissake, of all the places I have to pick, I have to pick this one? Small fucking world! But then there's no getting away from it is there! No getting away from any of it. It's just going to be right there day in and day out, no matter where …"

She stopped when she realized she was actually speaking out loud. She refocused on the bearded face. *Where's Bobby? Where the hell am I?* The bearded face appeared concerned, but what did she know? When he next spoke, his voice had lost its exuberance.

"Look, I can see you're upset and I'm sorry I intruded, out of the blue, like this. I don't know what I was thinking." He hesitated. "Well, actually I do know. It was the dogs. I once lived and breathed this breed, wanted nothing but the best for them and it didn't work out. Please don't let my intruding like this put you off giving Maverick a try. It's a good town, it really is."

Pete looked down at Little Grace who was slapping her paw at a large ant who had foolishly zigzagged within reach. "I'd be happy to meet the others another time."

He reached into his rear pocket, pulled out his wallet, and opened it. "Here's one of my cards. It's got my address and phone number on it. Call any time. You'll either get my fiancé or me—it'll be the second marriage for both of us. Her name's Margo."

He placed the card in her hand. "I think you'd like her."

He turned and walked slowly over to his truck. As he climbed in, he stopped, one foot on the ground, the other in the truck. "I think we may have more in common than owning the same breed of dog."

He drew his leg in, pulled the door shut, and continued talking through the open window. "You know, two years ago I would've reacted the same way as you, if I were in your shoes."

He started the truck and backed away from the motel.

Annie listened as the blue pickup crunched across the dirt parking lot. When the crunching ceased and the sound of the engine moved off into the distance, she looked down at the card he'd handed her, Benchmark Kayaks and Canoes—Peter Strate and Margo Cunningham. She didn't bother to read the rest, just tucked it in her pocket, then pulled little Grace from her hunt for fast moving six legged critters.

It would be three months before she saw Pete Strate again.

————

Within a week, Annie negotiated on a lease with the option to buy up to three hundred acres of land, complete with a small cabin that needed some work, but nothing major. And incredibly, as remote as it was, the cabin had electricity, a solid back up generator, good plumbing, and a deep clear well—even a phone line if she wanted to have a phone, which she didn't.

Bernie told her the previous owner had built the place. "He sunk more money into it than most out here would have." His intentions had been to use it as a year-round retreat from a busy life in Chicago. As it turned out, the man couldn't get away as much as he'd planned. He gave it up after two years for a price Bernie couldn't refuse. Bernie then used it for himself and his hunting buddies, which included Pete Strate and Pete's good friend Mick Saber, who was from Philadelphia.

He'd said he occasionally rented it out to "big city folks" who wanted what they thought the cabin had to offer—"Life without all the hassles." He'd laughed. "Not one of those people ever came back for a second time." He'd made it perfectly clear to her, over the course of their conversations, without saying it directly, that he liked her, but also knew, once reality set in, she'd give up and move on.

This unspoken assumption peeved Annie more than a little, but she'd let it pass without challenge. She was well aware she stood on shaky ground when it came to declaring who she was and what she wanted. She simply signed the rental agreement and turned her attention away from what Bernie and the townspeople might or might not think and put it on the job at hand.

Had she known what would unfold once she had settled into her 'home away from it all,' she might never have considered it in the first place. However, her determination to make it possible was unshakable.

————

She spent her first week driving the ten miles, two of it dirt road, back and forth from town, stocking up on everything she would need to fix the cabin, along with enough food for her and the three dogs for at least two months, most of it in the form of canned and dried goods.

She spoke as little as possible to anyone, which only stirred more interest in her rather than less. And, unlike what Pete Strate had told her, the uninvited questions did start coming, though she was quite adept at handling them with as few words and as little information as possible.

Then, for the next four weeks she worked twelve hours a day sweeping, scrubbing, painting and, thanks to Bobby and the kennel project, sheet rocking, building shelves, a table, a small desk, a new bed, and a new kitchen counter. None of it was as good as Bobby would've done, but functional nonetheless. She took a few breaks each day to spend time with the dogs and to eat.

By day's end, she was so exhausted she barely remembered getting into bed. "You need to go on and find somewhere you ain't got to do all that thinkin'."

On the afternoon of July 2, when all was as she wanted it, and her belongings were finally in their place, she washed her hands in her new kitchen sink, wiped them on her now not so new overalls, and walked victoriously out onto her front porch.

Little Grace and Ivan were fast asleep on the mattress she'd placed by the door.

She looked around for Bertha, who suddenly appeared and rushed up the three porch steps to greet her.

As she patted Bertha's head, she looked up at the blue cloudless sky. It was perfect. She took a deep breath and fully expected to feel the same relief and exuberance the three dogs had shown over the past month as they ran together in their new field, explored their forest, and splashed around in their very own lake.

However, as she stood there on the porch and felt the clear air fill her lungs, what happened instead was a sudden stab of terror, and everything for as far as she could see—the sky, the distant dark hills, the trees, the grass, the green tractor, the pink, blue, and yellow patches of wild flowers, all turned dull and sickly. As she released her breath, what followed, from deep within her belly, was the high-pitched keening of a child who has lost everything.

Little Grace, who had remained comfortably asleep until the moment the sound hit her ears, leapt up and bolted across the mattress towards Ivan who had opened his eyes and raised his eyebrows. As she barreled into him, Ivan's concern mounted and he raised his head. Grace then settled up against him.

Big Bertha began to pace anxiously between the two of them and Annie.

After what felt like an eternity, when the grief-stricken cry had fully emptied from Annie's lungs and belly, she slumped down onto the front steps and dropped her head into her arms. Her exhaustion was desolate and utterly without sound, except for Bertha's panting, along with the click, click of her nails on the cedar boards of the porch.

And when Bertha stopped and sat down beside her, she heard a hundred doors closing, each one shutting her deeper and deeper into the dark—the door to the guestroom, the door to her bedroom, the door to her dorm room, the door to every hotel room she'd ever been in, door after door. And when the final door closed, she could barely breathe. She then saw the big red door and reached to open it, only to find herself on the cold linoleum floor of the bathroom frantically trying to pull the tape-recorder from her chest.

As Annie's hands began to flail, Little Grace left the safety of Ivan's side and attempted to push her way onto her lap.

Inadvertently, one of Annie's hands smacked her hard and sent her tumbling down the steps onto the grass.

That's when Ivan rose up from the mattress and walked over to the top of the stairs. He looked down over Annie's shoulder, watched Grace right herself, and then stuck his head between Annie's chest and flailing hands.

Annie reached for the final piece of adhesive tape and Ivan cried out, bashing his muzzle against her chin, as she grabbed onto his ear and yanked. Startled, she opened her eyes. Ivan's massive face was just inches from hers, her hand still gripping his ear. She released her grip as he leaned in and sniffed over her entire face, as if in search of something. When he was done, he looked directly into her blues and she looked back.

Little Grace climbed up the three steps she had tumbled down. She was finally able to stick her head successfully onto Annie's lap.

When Mick Meets Annie

Mick Saber downshifted as he turned his Land Rover onto the narrow dirt road. He'd initially been miffed when he heard somebody had leased, with the option to buy, the cabin he'd become quite fond of. Bernie Cavanaugh, his friend and Maverick's town realtor, had assured him it would always be there when he wanted it. "It's not going anywhere," he'd said with a chuckle. "That place is, shall we say, doomed to be here for you and me and a small handful of folks who appreciate a little time with the fish, the moose, and the deer." Granted he and Bernie never had the 'but what if?' discussion, but then why would they have? Bernie had never given a hint of a suggestion that selling the cabin was a possibility. So, how was it—knowing how much Mick loved the place—that Bernie hadn't thought to pick up the phone and give him a heads-up?

What had been even more aggravating to Mick was that Pete hadn't given him a heads-up either. His best friend for Chrissake! When Pete called with news regarding a woman who had bought the cabin, he was taken aback by Mick's abrupt anger. It had never occurred to him that Mick would want to buy it.

"Look, Mick, I know you love the place, but you live over a thousand miles away from here! Good Christ man, you've only stayed in it five times tops since I moved out here. Why would I think you'd want to buy a place you would visit maybe two or three times a year?"

It hadn't been so much Pete's words, but rather his tone that helped Mick get a grip and realize he was hanging a ton of old baggage on this deal. He'd been in AA too long to allow that little drama to play itself out, which was his father's having denied him two weeks away at his favorite camp solely because he'd realized just how much his son loved it. Well, that wasn't Pete or Bernie's burden to bear and the pity-pot was not where he wanted to be.

Mick sighed and settled into the slow, bumpy drive up the dirt road. It never ceased to amaze him how so much of his present life could still be dictated by the subtle, and not so subtle, hand of what had already been. Yes, he probably would have bought the place if he'd been given a heads-up, and then what? It would have been an impulsive buy, carrying a burden of impossible expectations. Anyone but Pete would have hung up on him during his childish tantrum. Pete simply waited patiently for him to see the light, bring the tantrum to an abrupt end, and apologize. Then they laughed.

When the laughter ended, Pete got back around to telling him about the woman who had leased his beloved cabin. He said her name was Annie Evans and he'd met her in the parking lot of the Stretch Out Motel two days after she'd arrived in Maverick. She'd contacted Bernie, who then contacted him, due to the fact she owned three Bordeaux, two adults and a pup. Pete said he was curious, of course, and drove over to the motel the next morning.

"Walt told me she was out walking one of her dogs. He apologized for not calling me the day she arrived—said as manager he didn't feel it was right to intrude on her privacy. Pretty funny, eh? Walter Boots is in love. I reminded him I'm almost married, so I was no threat to his not-so-secret crush."

Pete chuckled, but there was an edge to it, which kept Mick from enjoying something that was truly funny. It had been a long time since Mick had heard that edge.

"Anyway," Pete continued, "she appeared about ten minutes later with the pup on a leash and the first thing she did when I stepped out of my truck to greet her was start to turn away. But she stopped herself, with great effort—I could see that. Actually, I think she wanted to run. I know what scared her was my excitement over seeing a Bordeaux at the end of her leash. It was the first thing out of my mouth because, frankly, I didn't believe Bernie when he told me. You know how Bernie is—for all I knew she had three Boxers or Pits or Danes. I mean, what were the chances they were Bordeaux?

"Our conversation was brief with very little eye contact from her end. She wasn't interested in chatting, which isn't unusual considering I was a total stranger. But there were a couple things that struck me. First, when I welcomed her and suggested she'd like Maverick, she said she thought it was a beautiful area and was looking forward to spending time here 'sans people.'

"Well, for some reason I ignored her little suggestion that I go away."

Pete laughed. Mick didn't.

"I don't know what it was. Well, actually I do. I felt like I was talking to the me that arrived here two years ago. Granted she's a woman, a damned beautiful one at that— Walter's got good taste—but I could feel the similarity. And the thing that set it in stone was when I asked if I could see her other two dogues before I got on my way. I told her I used to breed them and hadn't seen any for a long time except the occasional one or two that my friend brings out. Well, that was it. All that tension I picked up from her popped right out. 'For Chrissake,' she said, 'there's another one?! Of all the places I have to pick, I pick this one!' Then she dropped to a nervous mumble and said, 'There's no getting away from it, is there? It's just going to be right there, day in and day out...' Then she stopped herself. I could tell she didn't know she'd been talking out loud.

"I'm telling you, Mick, she was freaked."

Pete's quiet groan was loaded which was when Mick knew Pete had called him for more than just to tell him about this woman.

Pete continued, "She is beautiful, though, Good Christ! I mean BEAUTIFUL—no frills beautiful. If I weren't already engaged and in love?—whew, I don't know. On the other hand, she's only a thread or two away from where I once was. Not somebody I want to spend time with. I'm not like you, Mick."

Pete managed to laugh when he said that. "Anyway, I told Bernie he needed to remember how I was when I arrived here and give her as much space as she needed. I know I will."

The coincidence was damned intriguing to Mick. Just a week prior to that phone call, he'd received a call from Margaret Appleman, aka gossip central. She wanted to inform him of the latest Dogue de Bordeaux news, which was that Stella Gale had put the word out that someone had stolen her dogs. She wouldn't give a name, but she quoted Stella as saying, "That ungrateful bitch stole three of my best dogs" and "I gave that bitch everythin' but the clothes off my back!" Mick got a kick out of both Margaret's poor imitation of Stella's voice and the notion that Stella would give anything to anybody. He told Margaret he felt more than a lick of joy at the thought that somebody had the balls to take three of Stella's dogs and he knew full well that was precisely what she expected to hear from him. Margaret despised Stella, albeit for all the wrong reasons—jealousy being at the top of that list—but still she despised Stella as much as he did.

Margaret then claimed she'd made the call to him because he'd so recently been the president of the club and she knew how much he cared about the breed. "I'm sure you can sympathize with how distressing it would be to have some of your dogues stolen. Stella just wants people to keep an eye out for her dogues."

Mick responded by telling her he found it amusing that Stella hadn't just gone to the police and had an APB put out. And he said he wondered why Stella had given no name to this supposed thief.

Margaret was predictably indignant. "Mick, Stella has no interest in dealing with the police. Surely you know that! I am simply putting the word out. It's not my job to make judgment calls about what someone should or shouldn't do. Besides, Stella said the woman is crazy, not someone who would hang on to the dogs for more than the time it would take to dump them somewhere, or even kill them!"

He laughed and told her if this person existed at all, they couldn't be any crazier than Stella was. He knew Margaret was counting on him to express what she couldn't, which would then free her to go on ahead and make a hundred more calls adding his reaction to the mix. He was happy to be of service.

So, when he heard from Pete about this Annie who'd showed up in Maverick with three dogues and was to be the new owner of his beloved cabin, he was hard put to not look into it. And he was concerned about Pete. He purposely didn't tell him about Margaret's call because he knew that would have been just the thing to push Pete over whatever edge he was on. He'd told Pete he'd get out there as soon as he could.

"That's great! It'll be good to see you. Who knows, if Walter doesn't get her attention first, you just might have a shot."

Mick had been relieved to hear Pete's hardy laugh.

Mick glanced over at his four month old canine passenger. "How're you doing, little buddy? You think we can go down this road and not end up in a ditch?"

He chuckled at his clever little metaphor as Maestro turned calmly from the window and looked at him. "Pete was a fool to turn you down, but his loss is my gain. So I now officially dub you my partner in this mission."

Mick had disregarded Pete's declaration that he never wanted another Bordeaux and brought Maestro along thinking he would be unable to resist what was possibly the best pup he'd ever bred. He was proved wrong. Pete was truly done with the breed.

He reached over and scratched the top of Maestro's head, then put his attention back to the task at hand. It had been four weeks before he could put the time aside to drive to Wisconsin and explore the Annie situation. During that time, no one except Jacob, who ran the general store in town, had interacted with her since she'd moved in to her cabin. Apparently, she'd stuck to her guns regarding her "sans people" philosophy.

A number of folks had seen her in town the afternoon of her interaction with Jacob. They each declared, later on, to eager ears, "She looked angry," "She looked tired," "She's a knock-out, even in dirty overalls," "She looked sad," "That woman is tough as nails," "She's a mess from what I could see." Mick found it amusing—yet another astounding aspect of being human, the eye of the beholder!

The interaction between Jacob and Annie, which had happened just a week shy of Mick's arrival in Maverick, had been the catalyst to Annie suddenly becoming the 'talk of the town.' Up until then she'd been pretty much off the radar. It was a brief interaction, but clearly a significant one. Jacob had reported that she'd purchased a bunch of dried goods, just as she had during her first week there.

"Only this time it was enough to feed an army. Plus she bought a couple of rifles, a pile of plywood, some fence posts, and asked me if I'd be willing to order her a bugle, a flag pole, a small TV, a video player, some wildlife videos, and a bunch of books. I can't remember the titles of the books at the moment, but they were nothing I'd heard of. Most of them were in Spanish, German, or Greek."

Jacob added that she looked completely different from when she'd first arrived. "I'm telling you, that woman has grown some muscles on her skinny arms and she didn't seem the least bit shy. When she asked me if I'd be willing to order those things, she looked me right in the eye rather than glancing around the store like she did during that first week. I told her I could order the flagpole, but she'd have to go to the city to pick it up. The bugle and everything else I could get, but I'm telling you, something's going on out there that might be worth looking into."

The town police, Jim and Allen, had listened to Jacob's concern and checked in with Bernie, who had already checked out much of Annie's record before he gave her the lease to the cabin. It was clean. Jim and Allen ran their own check and, like Bernie, found her record clean, except for one little item that Bernie had not found—a stolen car charge by Stella Gale almost two years earlier, which was then dropped a year and a half later, which was just six months ago.

This information, of course, sent the cops directly to Pete who then intervened on Annie's behalf and told them to back off and let Mick look into the situation when he got there. He said Annie had broken no laws. "So leave her alone for now."

The reason Jim and Allen had gone to Pete in the first place was because back when Pete had finally started to open up about the tough times that had brought him to Maverick, he made it loud and clear, within the walls of all four of the town bars, that Stella Gale had been the force behind those tough times. His bitter tales of her destruction of his life and reputation had riveted more than a few of the town's people, including Jim and Allen. He told them about Stella being an ex-madam who'd become a Bordeaux breeder after she'd been busted and sent to prison for a year. Jim and Allen couldn't verify she'd been a 'Madam,' but they could verify she'd been arrested and imprisoned for money laundering, which was enough for them, along with the entire town, to stand with Pete and feel his anger.

Pete was now a beloved citizen of Maverick. He'd picked himself up, built a respectable boat building business, a business which was already renowned throughout Wisconsin and would no doubt make its way onto the national scene—and he was about to marry Margo, a rugged and respected woman whose family had been here for generations. He'd all but forgotten Stella Gale.

However, Stella would never fade from the town's memory and she would never fade from Mick's memory either. Mick was just glad that when Jim and Allen had told Pete about the Stella connection, Pete could tell them Mick was coming and would deal with it.

Mick downshifted, abruptly—then moved his hand quickly to Maestro's chest to steady him on the passenger seat as he applied the brakes and came to a near halt.

"Hold on, buddy, sign up ahead." He read the bold red letters—'Big Dogs Run Free.' Then fifty yards beyond that was another sign—'Walk softly and leave your stick behind.' And beyond that—'Teach your children well—case closed.' That's when Mick's smile slipped into a chuckle, and then a grimace—it was a mixed bag. Then there was another—'Home of Annie, Ivan, Big Bertha, and Grace.' And the final sign read—'If the red door is closed and it ain't winter, come back later.'

He looked up at the cabin as he slowly approached it. Fortunately, he saw no red door. Not that he would have heeded the warning, but he was grateful he didn't have to consider it. He then caught sight of a flag that fluttered atop a makeshift flagpole. "Don't Tread On Me" was printed around a tightly coiled snake. He recognized it immediately. Jacob had been right about this woman being deserving of attention, but not the kind he had implied.

He pulled in at the bottom of the grassy slope and shut off the engine. He heard a single bark and turned to see three Dogues appear from behind a wood shack that was off to his right, one huge male and two females, one still a pup. They stopped in perfect synchronicity and looked over at his Land Rover—he surely did appreciate that magnificent moment a Bordeaux takes to assess a situation. The two bitches then launched into roaring out a warning. The big boy simply watched.

———

Annie was in her woodshed when she heard Bertha, then Grace, launch into a fury of barking. She chose to ignore it because she'd never chopped wood before and her determination to get it right stood before all else. It was the abrupt silence that broke her concentration. The dogs had ceased barking as suddenly as they'd started.

She dropped the axe and walked over to the door of the shed. There was a Landrover parked between where she was and the cabin. Her dogs were neatly gathered around the passenger door staring up at the window, ears cocked forward. They turned when she called to them, but rather than run to her, they simply went back to their business of staring at the window.

Annie quickly glanced at the license plate on the Landrover. It was a PA plate, which was the only reason she didn't pick up her rifle. The possibility that young Emily and her parents had come to visit was both astonishing and disarming. She trotted towards the vehicle, smiling with anticipation. The glaring fact of her having not been in touch with Emily or her parents since she'd gone back to live with Stella had not discouraged her from thinking they knew exactly where she was.

The driver's door opened and a clean-shaven man, donning a disheveled head of brown hair and an old Army jacket emerged.

At the sound of the door opening, the dogs broke from their positions at the passenger side and rushed around the Land Rover.

The man received the incoming three hundred and fifty plus pounds of dogs with great confidence and calm. He squatted down and spoke quietly. The dogs nearly bumped into each other as they came to a skidding halt a few feet in front of him.

Annie froze as her excitement at the prospect of seeing Emily tumbled to a mix of fear and anger. When she finally managed to speak, she was defiant. "Who the hell are you?" She tried to call the dogs to her, but the only response she got, once again, was a glance from each of them. She thought to run back for her rifle, but it was too late. She stood there for quite some time.

The man didn't seem to hear her or even take note of her until he was done with his rather long canine conversation. When he did finally look up, he smiled. "I'm Mick Saber and my buddy there is Mister Maestro." He gestured to his Land Rover.

Against her will, Annie looked back at the Land Rover. The wrinkled mug of a Bordeaux pup was pressed up against the rear window. The pup was looking back and forth from her to her dogs that were now surrounding the aggravatingly confident man named "Mick." She glared at her dogs. They were as calm as if they'd known him forever. Tails were wagging and Ivan had actually begun to roll onto his back for a tummy rub! She was speechless.

Mick patted the big male's tummy and stood up. "Look, I'll cut to the chase. My best friend, Pete Strate, and his fiancée Margo live in town here. Pete informed me of your presence here a few weeks ago—he said he'd met you briefly in the parking lot of the motel when you'd first arrived.

Bernie had told him you had Bordeaux etcetera, etcetera. Well, when he called to tell me about you and the dogs, I was intrigued because just a few days before that a woman named Margaret Appleman had called to tell me that a certain Stella Gale had fallen victim to the crime of 'three of her best dogs' being stolen from her." Mick watched as Annie's shoulders tightened even more. "I will add, as an aside, that I know Stella Gale is never a victim to anything. So, I put two and two together and now I'm here to meet the woman who had the balls to commit such a 'heinous' act." He laughed and approached her with an outstretched hand. This wasn't going to be easy, he could see that.

Annie tucked her clenched fists deep into her overall pockets and stepped back as he approached. "Look, I don't know what you want or why you think I'm that particular woman because I'm not—and another thing that I'm not is someone wanting to meet anybody—case closed." She wished she could've taken those final two words back as soon as they slipped from her mouth. She looked at him and knew from his expression that he knew exactly what she'd just revealed.

Mick stopped a few yards from her and dropped his outstretched hand to his side. The woman who stood before him was wearing paint splattered overalls and a pale green T-shirt with a hint of blue letters peeking out from beneath the bib. Much of her dirty blonde hair was tied back into pigtails, at least three that he could see. He honestly didn't know if there was such a thing as three or more pigtails. All he'd ever seen were two. Maybe when there were more than two they were called something else, he had no idea. The rest of her hair, which had either fallen from the grasp of the rubber bands or couldn't reach them, hung in random curly strands over her ears and finely sculpted cheeks. He might very well have taken her for a ten year old, albeit a tall one, if he hadn't looked into her eyes—they'd seen a lot more than ten years—and if he didn't already known from Bernie that she was thirty-two years old. He quickly flipped back through the various assessments he'd heard from those who had glimpsed her ten days earlier, "gorgeous," "sad," "angry," "a mess," "fearless," "she's got muscle she didn't have before." From what he saw in that moment, they were all correct—and taking into account what she'd just said along with the signs she'd posted along the road, as well as the flag and yet to be seen bugle, he would throw *wry* into the mix along with something he couldn't quite put his finger on. As he met the intensely blue eyes, he heard that little voice in his head. *Mick, this one will rock you.* The tone of the voice was completely neutral, which took him off guard considering that little voice had always been anything but neutral.

He looked at the three dogs before he spoke again. They had lost interest in him and were gathering under the rear window of his Land Rover peering up at his pup. "Well, can they at least meet Maestro?—and while I'm here, would you like some help with the wood chopping?—it didn't sound like it was going all that well and I could use the exercise seeing as I just spent two full days driving."

Annie barely heard him as her fists fell open in her pockets. Seeing the dogs respond to Mick in the way they did had sunk in, and it was painful. She missed Bobby. She missed him terribly.

Mick turned and walked back towards the Land Rover. He could see he had overstepped his bounds and felt badly. "It's alright. Maybe another time. I can see you have a lot on your mind. I was told I shouldn't just show up, but I did and I'm sorry."

Annie peered through the smoke of pain and watched Bobby walk up the driveway. She heard his voice. *"You best go on and find somewhere where you don't got to do all that thinkin'."* She watched him climb into his truck. "Wait!" She ran to the door of his pickup and kicked it as it closed. "I can't do this alone! Can't you see that? I can't do this! I fucking need you to help me!" She kicked at the door again and again. Bertha began to bark. Grace paced back and forth behind Annie, and Ivan sat, patiently, as close as he could to Annie without getting in the way of her frantic feet.

"Whoa! Hold on there. Okay, Okay, twist my arm. I'll help you with the chopping. Good God! Life is just full of surprises." Mick kept his voice steady, but Annie didn't stop. He had to force open the door against her kicking feet, grab her by the shoulders and push her to the ground, but not before taking a couple of direct punches in the face.

The next thing Annie knew, she was on her couch with Ivan lying on the floor beside her. The front door was open. She could hear Bertha barking in the distance, and the sound of wood being chopped—steady and rhythmic. Bobby came to her mind again, then disappeared as soon as she remembered she was in Wisconsin, a thousand miles away, at least. It was the man in the army jacket who was chopping the wood. A tinge of righteous anger ran through her. How was she supposed to know how to chop and stack wood? She wasn't from around here! She'd never had a wood stove. She got up and walked out to the shed, Ivan at her side.

Mick paused for a millisecond as Annie's shadow spilled across the floor of the shed. He then dropped his arms, splitting the log laid out in front of him. He spoke as he placed the fresh cut pieces onto his fairly large pile of already split logs and leaned the axe up against the rough pine wall. "Okay, time for you to take over. I'm getting tired."

Annie stood in the doorway and stared at the man who had walked into her life, barely skipping a beat.

Mick looked at her. This one will rock you. He bent forward and wiped the sweat from his face with the front of his T-shirt. "Come on, I'll show you how to do this, the right way, not the 'hit and miss style' that I heard you doing earlier." He chuckled. "I did it that way when I split my first logs, which happened to be a very long time ago, at a summer camp I loved."

Annie walked over to him, and her blue eyes narrowed as she met his browns. "Well, I've never had a wood stove. I went to a few camps as a kid—however it was always the boys who did the chopping. I never had that option."

Mick picked up the axe. "Well, now you have a wood stove, a long winter in front of you, and a MAN who's willing to turn over the axe to you." He laughed.

Annie hadn't wanted any help with anything anymore, not from anyone, but his point about the long winter ahead pushed her to accept his offer. The good news was she was a highly motivated student. Before long she was chopping away without him.

Mick had settled on the floor just inside the doorway with Ivan sitting beside him. He was impressed with how fast she'd caught on and how easily he slipped into being contented with no words spoken between them. She hadn't needed him after about ten minutes and that was just fine with him.

Annie let the agony of the lesson slip from her mind, confident she would've eventually succeeded on her own had Mick not shown up. The rhythm of what she was doing brought Bobby back loud and clear. *"You got to go on and find somewhere where you ain't got to do all that thinkin'."* She would have kept going until her arms fell off except that Big Bertha's relentless barking finally succeeded in breaking her concentration.

"BERTHA!" She felt annoyed with the intrusion, put down the axe, and walked briskly by Mick and Ivan, glancing at the two of them as she did so. "If you two hadn't noticed, Bertha's been barking the entire time we've been in here." She was annoyed that the two of them had simply sat there while Bertha barked so frantically. "It's way past time for our walk to the lake—plus she's missed target practice." She stood out in the grass and called to Bertha again.

The barking stopped and Bertha appeared from behind the cabin. Upon seeing Annie she bolted towards her. Once she reached her, she nudged her head urgently against the leg of Annie's overalls. *Let's go, let's go.*

Mick stepped in beside Annie. "My guess is this bitch is not hard to upset. She's, shall we say, high-strung?"

Annie looked at the man in the army jacket and her eyes narrowed slightly. "You've been an annoying interruption to her routine." She turned from him to check on Grace and Maestro who were racing and tumbling across the huge field in front of the cabin, reveling in each other's company, pup to pup. Bertha had left her side and was already up on the porch of the cabin waiting for Annie's next move.

Mick was unruffled by Annie's annoyance, and he was curious. "So, do you do target practice every day?"

Annie patted the top of Ivan's head as he strolled up and settled between her and Mick. "I do, every day after lunch, and the dogs love it! Well, at first they didn't, but it didn't take long. Now they focus right along with me and when I hit a can, or box, or whatever I've lined up—which is a lot more often now than when I started—Bertha, she barks and races in to give the fallen item her two cents, which is to push it along the ground with her muzzle while Grace rushes in and pounces on it. Ivan sits and watches, somewhat bemused, I think." She patted Ivan's head again.

"And you do this because?"

Annie looked into the curious brown eyes. "I do it because it's fun and it keeps me thinking only on what's in front of me—like most of what I do out here does." She looked at the pups that had made their way down to the far end of the field. She lifted her fingers to her lips and belted out a sharp whistle. The gyrating distant brown dots halted abruptly, but only for a moment. She then belted out another whistle and dropped her fingers as the dots bounded towards her.

She started walking towards the cabin. Mick and Ivan followed suit. She continued, "And if my mind strays—and tries to run me ragged—I have the dogs to pull me back."

When they reached the front porch, she hesitated. Her own candor surprised her. She looked over at the man standing beside her and her renewed search for Bobby was dashed instantly. He looked nothing like Bobby. His complexion was inherently dark, rather than white like Bobby's if-not-for-endless-hours-in-the-sun, his hair was deep brown, rather than the thick waves of blonde mixed with white, and his sharp brown eyes and brow were quick and responsive, rather than Bobby's slow and steady sea blues. They did seem close in age, though she guessed Bobby to be a few years older. The only thing they seemed to have in common was Ivan's trust.

She glanced down at Ivan as she spoke. "So, Mick," she said his name emphatically to remind herself he wasn't who she wished he was, "if you'd like to join us for our walk. I'll run in and get a couple towels in case we want to swim."

"I'd like that." Mick was genuinely enjoying himself. He watched her trot up the porch steps and turned to look at the flag that now fluttered over his head, then back at the cabin. He then remembered her written warning regarding the 'red door.' All he saw was the open wood door he was already familiar with from his stays here, which either meant she had painted it red on one side or hadn't gotten around to painting it yet, or she was simply alluding to something he had no knowledge of. He looked down at Ivan who was perfectly contented to sit right there with him. "I bet you know all about that 'red door,' don't you big guy?"

That's when the near breathless pups barreled past Mick and Ivan, Grace in the lead, and up the front steps. Grace stopped abruptly in front of the screen door, Maestro skidded into it, shook himself and then looked in through the mesh right along with Grace, as if he'd done so many times before.

Mick didn't bring up the subject of Stella again; it had sunk to the bottom of his bag of things he wanted to know the moment Annie had made it clear that's where it belonged. He asked her only about what was right in front of him— her cabin and the work she'd done on it, the dogs—how old and what was special about each one, what she needed to get done before winter, could she hunt? Did she want to learn? He shared a bit about his own life as an architect and Shutzhund trainer—but not a lot. He didn't ask her about the flag, the red door, or her kicking and punching frenzy followed by a total black out. He left those things for another time, hoping there would be one. By the end of the afternoon, his face had swelled and the skin around his eyes was showing signs that it might turn black and blue. When Annie pointed it out and apologized, he laughed and said the last time he'd taken a beating like that was at the first national Bordeaux show a few months earlier. He'd told her he'd quit his position as the first American Bordeaux Club president during that show in part because of the 'beating,' but mostly because he was fed up with all of it and all of them. He confessed that his years of sobriety had been sorely tested that weekend and he was unwilling to put that on the line for anything or anybody.

That was when Annie brought up Stella.

Mick had put Maestro in the Land Rover and was just getting in himself. She put her hand on his shoulder and as he turned to face her, she spoke. "You said you came here because you thought I was the woman who'd 'stolen' Stella's dogs." She hesitated and glanced at Maestro who was peering over at her. "Who is she to you?"

Mick climbed into the driver's seat and shut the door. He looked back at her through the open window. "She's the woman who once brought Pete—who happens to be my best friend—to his knees, which is why he moved out here and started over. That's who she is to me, and if you stole her dogs, my hat's off to you." He started the Land Rover and buckled his seatbelt. "Look, I came here thinking you might have information about her that would help me in my little project to exact revenge. Pete has let it all go, because he's had to. I haven't. Now all that aside, I had fun today and would like to spend more time with you. No need to ever mention her name again. I will get revenge, eventually. I am a patient man with a life to live in the meantime."

To be continued in Book II